RAW MISTAKES

A heart-wrenching story of love, loss, and forgiveness.

GWEN COURTMAN

Raw Mistakes
A heart-wrenching story of love, loss & forgiveness

Copyright © Gwen Courtman, Italy, 2023

Cover by Exceller Books using resources from Pixabay.com

All rights reserved. No portion of the book may or should be reproduced, stored in any retrieval system (including but not limited to computers, disks, external drives, electronic or digital devices, e-readers, websites), or transmitted in any form or by any means (mechanical, recording, electronic, digital version, photocopying, or otherwise) without the prior, written permission of the publisher, nor be otherwise circulated in any form of binding or cover other than that in which it is published and without a similar condition being imposed on the subsequent purchaser.

The book has been published with all reasonable efforts taken to make the material error-free after the consent of the author. Any resemblance to actual events, locales, organizations, or persons, living or dead, is entirely coincidental. The views and opinions expressed in this book are the author's own and the facts are as reported by her. The author, publisher or editor shall not be liable whatsoever for any errors, omissions, whether such errors or omissions result from negligence, accident or any other cause or claims for loss or damage of any kind, including without limitation damage arising out of use, reliability, accuracy, sufficiency of the information contained in this book.

ISBN: 9798883619235

Dedication

To my girls,

Thank you for making sure I never ran out of wine and tissues when things were tough. I thank you even more for the Prosecco and softer tissues when things were going great and we needed to dry our tears of laughter.

I would like to thank Beba, Bethan, Ada, Gillian, Amelie, and Helen for their constant support and for never complaining (to me, at least) about my constantly changing storylines and ideas over the last year.

To my readers,

Why not join our community on my author blog? You'll have the opportunity to ask questions, get previews of upcoming books, and explore photos and videos of the locations that inspired my stories.

Join us at: www.gwencourtmanauthor.com

1 | Bree

Bree Morgan hadn't always been in love with life. For years, it felt as though life merely tolerated her, handing her just enough to keep moving forward but never enough to thrive. She started her adult journey bright-eyed and brimming with dreams—romance, a family, and a career that would make her parents proud. Raised in a household where money was treated as sacred, Bree learnt early that worth was measured in earnings, savings, and a stable relationship. She envisioned a life much like her parents': steady, predictable, and tied neatly to tradition. Yet somewhere along the way, her meticulously laid plans unraveled, leaving her to wonder where it had all gone wrong.

Her first taste of independence was as harsh as the cold, rain-soaked English mornings that accompanied it. At fourteen, she delivered newspapers, her hands stiff with the bite of early frost as she navigated sleepy streets. At fifteen, she traded her bicycle for a job in a vegetable shop, sorting bruised produce from fresh, discarding scraps unfit for sale. The sharp chill of the storeroom clung to her long after her shifts ended, embedding itself in her bones. Bree hated the monotonous work but clung to it fiercely, hoarding every pound she earned as though it might one day shield her from some unseen calamity. Even then, she understood that survival demanded sacrifice.

In those early years, Bree found comfort in her sister. Together, they quietly rebelled against their parents' rigid religious expectations, sneaking out of church services to wander the streets and laugh at the absurdity of it all. Their bond was a lifeline, a whispered pact to protect one another from being crushed under the weight of their family's traditions and beliefs..

For all her pragmatism, Bree never let go of the hope that love might one day find her. That hope dimmed when she was seventeen and still living in her small hometown on the outskirts of Manchester. It was there that she met Murray—a tall, charismatic man with tousled brown hair and a smile that hinted at mischief. His confidence made her heart skip in ways she hadn't known it could. Murray was the kind of man who made you feel as if the world paused when he looked your way, and when he finally noticed Bree, it felt as though the universe had shifted.

Murray's attention was intoxicating, his flirtations deliberate and unhurried. After weeks of playful exchanges at the office where Bree worked part-time, he finally asked her out on a double date. It was Bree's first-ever date, and her excitement was laced with an undercurrent of dread. Her wardrobe, a collection of practical hand-me-downs and uninspired basics, felt wholly inadequate. She spent hours scouring local shops, finally settling on a fitted navy knit top that toed the line between alluring and modest. Paired with low-waisted trousers, it was the closest she'd ever come to feeling confident in her own skin.

The night of the date, Bree's aging red-and-white Mini coughed and sputtered as she pulled into the restaurant's car park. Her palms were slick against the steering wheel, and she fidgeted with her top in the rearview mirror before stepping out. She waited at the bar, scanning the crowd nervously for Murray. Relief swept over her when Anita and her partner—a cheerful couple from the office—arrived hand-in-hand. Bree managed a smile, trying to ignore the growing pit in her stomach.

"Bree. You look incredible," Anita gushed, her surprise softening into warmth. "That top suits you so well, and your hair—it's gorgeous."

"Thanks," Bree murmured, her cheeks flushing with both pride and discomfort. Compliments were unfamiliar territory, and she wasn't sure how to navigate them without stumbling.

Minutes stretched into hours, and still, there was no sign of Murray. Bree's initial nervous energy gave way to a hollow ache of disappointment. Anita and her partner did their best to buoy her spirits, their kind words and light-hearted jokes about Murray's poor manners filling the silence he had left behind. But even their laughter couldn't mask the sting of rejection.

Each forkful of scampi Bree forced herself to eat felt like a lump of resignation, its buttery richness failing to mask the bitter taste of the evening. She wanted nothing more than to retreat to the safety of her small room, wrap herself in her duvet, and erase the night from memory. As the evening wore on, Anita, her tone gentle but insistent, said, "Listen, Bree, someone as sweet and genuine as you deserves better. Murray? He's not worth a second thought."

Bree nodded, but Anita's words barely touched her. She wasn't mourning Murray—she barely knew him. What she mourned was the idea of him, the possibility he represented. For a fleeting moment, she had glimpsed a version of herself that felt beautiful, wanted, and deserving of something more than bruised vegetables and cold, damp mornings. And now, that version felt farther away than ever.

By the time she returned home, the quiet she once craved felt heavier than ever. She lay in the dark, staring at the ceiling, replaying the night in her mind. Murray had been a lesson, not a loss, she decided. The world had a way of teaching hard truths when you least expected them. And Bree Morgan? She was just beginning to learn.

The next morning was deceptively bright, sunlight streaming through the windows, mocking Bree's cloudy mood. She sat stiffly at her desk, her mind looping through the awkwardness of the previous evening. She tried to focus on her work, but every tick of the clock only heightened her anticipation—and dread—for Murray's arrival. Her stomach churned when she finally spotted him strolling through the door, his disheveled appearance a stark contrast to his usual polished charm.

"Bree, I'm sorry," he said, his voice low and gravelly, his eyes rimmed red. "You have no idea what happened."

Relief and confusion washed over her in equal measure. She managed a weak smile and mumbled, "Okay." But her calm exterior masked the cyclone of emotions brewing beneath the surface.

"You know my friend Ian?" Murray asked, his face shadowed with something that looked like guilt. Bree nodded cautiously, her throat too tight to speak. "He was in a crash last night," Murray continued, his words deliberate. "He didn't make it. Died in the ambulance on the way to the hospital."

Bree's eyes widened in shock. She stood abruptly, nearly knocking over her chair. "Oh my God. I'm so sorry, Murray. I don't know what to say." Her hand hovered over his, a hesitant attempt at comfort.

She forced herself to suppress the awkward flicker of relief she felt. He hadn't stood her up on purpose; he was grieving a friend. It was wrong to feel anything but sympathy, and yet... something about his delivery didn't sit right. Still, the tragic news cast a heavy pall over the office, and any mention of rescheduling their date disappeared.

By the following Friday, Bree had managed to tuck the incident away into the corners of her mind. She focused on her duties, waiting for her lunch break. At precisely twelve-thirty, the office's heavy entrance door swung open with a creak. A gust of wind followed, rattling the blinds and momentarily blinding her as sunlight spilled into the room.

"Hiya, Bree." a loud, confident voice rang out, slicing through the buzz of the office.

She blinked, the sunlight streaming in from behind the figure momentarily blinding her. As her vision adjusted, her breath hitched. Ian stood there—alive, grinning, and utterly oblivious to the storm he'd just unleashed in her mind.

"Err... hello," she stammered, her pulse racing.

Ian rested casually against the counter, his expression softening. "Look, I'm so sorry about last week," he said, his tone almost apologetic. "I know you were supposed to be going out with Murray. That's on me. We got carried away after winning the match—too much to drink. I'm really sorry."

Bree stared at him, her mind racing. Her heart pumped rapidly as she reached over to the switchboard and buzzed Murray. "He'll be right with you," she said, her voice trembling.

Murray appeared moments later, his posture stiff as he greeted Ian with a curt nod. Without so much as a glance in Bree's direction, he ushered Ian out of the building and into the car park. When Murray returned, his expression was unreadable.

"What's wrong, Bree?" he asked, his voice almost too calm.

"I thought Ian was... dead," she replied, her voice barely above a whisper.

Murray's lips twitched into a fleeting smirk. "Oh, not him. Another Ian," he said dismissively, his tone sharp. Bree blinked in disbelief.

"But Ian said he was with you that night," she pressed, her palms growing clammy.

"Yeah, we were all together," Murray replied quickly, his tone flat and unconvincing. Before she could ask anything further, he walked away, leaving her questions unanswered. Bree slumped back in her chair, confusion pressing down on her chest.

At lunch, she recounted the bizarre encounter to Anita, her voice shaky as she tried to make sense of it. Anita listened intently, her frown deepening with every word. "Bree," she said finally, her tone sharp with certainty, "he's lying. This whole thing stinks of deceit. You've got to get away from him. Trust me—he's trouble."

Bree pushed her salad around the bowl, appetite gone. She nodded weakly but couldn't shake the gnawing doubt twisting in her gut.

Later that afternoon, the switchboard buzzed incessantly, dragging her back into the flow of work. She welcomed the distraction until a call came through that stopped her cold.

"Hello, could you connect me to Murray in sales?" a bright, confident female voice asked.

"Of course," Bree replied automatically, her voice steady despite her inner turmoil. "May I ask who's calling?"

"I'm his girlfriend," the woman said proudly.

The words hit Bree like a slap. She froze, her fingers trembling over the switchboard. Somehow, she managed to transfer the call, but she couldn't stop the flood of emotions that followed. Rage, disbelief, humiliation—it all swirled together, leaving her lightheaded.

She sank back in her chair, staring blankly at the office walls as questions swarmed her mind. Who was this woman? What game was Murray playing? Her chest heaved as she let out a long, shaky sigh, her frustration spilling out in a stream of whispered curses.

2 | Bree

Exhausted from the emotional turbulence of the day, Bree arrived at her second job as an evening waitress, her professional smile firmly in place. After spending a few cathartic hours venting to her sister, Amber, she pulled on her uniform, steadied her composure, and pushed open the heavy restaurant door.

Meanwhile, Kay, an Englishwoman residing in Italy, had returned to Manchester to visit her family. Eager for a taste of home, she and a friend ventured out for dinner, armed with a two-for-one voucher her mother had given her. As they shrugged off their coats and handed the vouchers to the hostess, they were met with an apologetic smile.

"I'm afraid you're in the wrong restaurant," Bree explained kindly. "The one you're looking for is about four miles up the road."

The friends exchanged a look, shrugged, and opted to stay. "That's fine," Kay said. "We'll grab a drink at the bar first, if that's all right, and then eat here."

A refreshing pint of cider later, they moved to their table, where Bree greeted them once again. Despite her earlier rollercoaster of emotions, Bree's charm and warmth left a lasting impression on the pair.

At the end of the evening, Kay looked at Bree with newfound enthusiasm. "You're just what I'm looking for at my restaurant in Italy. Have you ever thought about working abroad?" she asked, her short red hair bouncing as she stood.

Bree blinked, surprised. "Wow, that's such a lovely offer," she replied, her smile polite but hesitant. "I have a good life here, but thank you."

Kay extended a crisp white business card. "If you change your mind, the position starts in a month. Just give me a call."

Later that night, Bree returned to the family home she'd shared with her parents and older sister since birth. Her weary legs begged for rest, but her parents were waiting, brimming with excitement.

"We've found a job in Scotland—running a campsite," her dad announced, his voice bright with joy.

"That's amazing news," Bree said, her enthusiasm genuine.

Her mum chimed in, "We've been waiting for you and Amber to be settled. Now that your sister's married and you've got two jobs, it feels like the right time."

"You both deserve to be happy," Bree agreed warmly.

Her dad's expression softened. "Thank you, love. We're telling Amber tomorrow. There's just one thing... the house. We can't afford to maintain it and move to Scotland. You'll need to find somewhere to live when we go."

Bree's joy evaporated. "So I'm homeless?" she asked, incredulity creeping into her tone.

"Of course not," her dad reassured her. "You can come with us to Scotland."

Bree shook her head, already retreating to the stairs. "Thanks, but I'll pass."

In her room, Bree emptied her pockets, her fingers lingering on Kay's business card. She turned it over thoughtfully before reaching for her phone.

The dial tone buzzed twice before a cheerful voice answered. "Hello?"

"Hi, Kay," Bree said, her voice shaking slightly. "This is Bree—the waitress you spoke to earlier. I've been thinking about your offer... is it still available?"

"Absolutely," Kay's excitement was palpable. "The job's yours if you want it."

"I think I do," Bree replied, her words carrying a resolve and uncertainty.

"Brilliant. You won't regret it—it'll be the adventure of a lifetime," Kay promised.

After the call ended, Bree sat on the edge of her bed, staring at her reflection in the dark window. Her parents' sudden announcement replayed in her mind, mingling with Kay's invitation.

The following days were a blur of preparation. Between shifts at the restaurant, Bree scoured every resource she could find about Italy, packed her belongings into a single suitcase, and unearthed her long-neglected passport.

3 | Bree

A few weeks later, at just eighteen and brimming with nervous excitement, Bree left behind her home, friends, and two jobs. Her parents had been unwaveringly supportive, though their sadness at her departure was plastered on their faces. On the morning of her flight, her mum hugged her tightly. "We're so proud of you, Bree," she said, her voice thick with emotion. "You're braver than you realise."

Clutching two suitcases filled with her most cherished belongings and a well-worn Teach Yourself Italian handbook, she wrapped her sister in a tight hug.

"I'm going to miss you so much," Amber said, tears shimmering in her eyes.

"Me too," Bree replied, her voice catching. "I don't think we've ever been apart for more than a week."

Amber smiled through her tears, trying to be brave. "Make me proud out there, Bree. Look after yourself, text me all often, and send photos."

"Of course. And you have to visit me. It'll be a proper girly holiday."

The sisters laughed softly, hugging once more before Bree turned toward security at Manchester Airport. Dragging her trolley behind her, she glanced back one last time, her heart torn between excitement and dread.

As Bree boarded the plane, exhilaration surged through her. The roar of the engines was deafening as they ascended. She gripped her bag tightly, silently praying Kay would be waiting for her at Venice Airport as planned.

Kay's bright smile and welcoming hug at the arrivals gate immediately put her at ease. On the drive to her new home, Bree gazed out of the car window at the rolling Italian countryside.

The restaurant, nestled in the heart of a cobblestone piazza, was alive with energy when they arrived. The chatter of guests mingled with the clinking of glasses and the mouthwatering scent of garlic and freshly baked bread. The staff greeted Bree warmly, their friendliness easing some of her nerves, before she was thrown straight into the frenzy of dinner service.

Instinct took over as Bree balanced trays, took orders, and charmed guests with her easy smile. The hours flew by in a blur of activity, leaving her exhilarated and exhausted in equal measure.

Later that night, Bree collapsed onto the bed in her tiny yet cosy apartment above the restaurant. As she stared at the ceiling, listening to the sounds of life outside her window, she felt an unfamiliar but welcome sense of satisfaction.

4 | Bree

Each morning, Bree awoke to the surprise of the summer sun streaming through her window. She strolled to work with a spring in her step, almost pinching herself at the thought that this was now her life. The warmth and vibrancy of Italy seemed to embrace her, and she adapted effortlessly to the heat.

The job was exhilarating. Despite being the youngest on the team by far, Bree quickly found her place within Kay's established circle of friends. Her enthusiasm bridged the gap of experience, making her feel part of something bigger than herself.

Determined to immerse herself fully, Bree dedicated each morning to studying Italian. The basics came easily, and on her days off, she borrowed Kay's bike to explore the flatlands of Lido di Jesolo. The warm morning breeze against her tanned skin made her feel more alive and free than she ever had before.

Yet, one aspect of her new life left her flustered: the unabashed openness of her flatmates when it came to their relationships. Inexperienced in love and intimacy—her only date having been a lacklustre outing with Murray—she found the constant parade of male visitors overwhelming.

Most evenings, she retreated to her room, pressing a pillow to her ears in a futile attempt to block out the sounds of passion echoing through the thin walls. The apartment offered no sanctuary from her embarrassment.

A few days after settling in, Bree's eyes widened in surprise as she spotted a printed note stuck to her door—and to the doors of her three flatmates.

'Rules for Passion.'
Bed heads must be kept 50 cm from the wall.
Moans and screams must be kept to a minimum.
If you use a condom from the bowl, please replace it the following morning.
Orgies are not permitted unless flatmates are invited.
Visiting men must use a towel while walking around the house, with no hanging willies in view.

Bree felt utterly embarrassed, wondering what sort of life she had been introduced to. Keeping her head down, she threw herself into her work with a passion she had never experienced before. She arrived at work early and stayed late each night, avoiding the naked men who, seemingly, couldn't read the rules plastered on the doors.

"You have to go home sometimes, Bree," Kay said, trying to get Bree to finish her shift.

"I'm here to do a job; I don't feel at home in that house. I'd rather be here," Bree replied.

"Ah, yes. Living with Susie and her endless stream of men can't be easy," Kay remarked, with a knowing smile.

"Exactly, and they've put these rules up on the doors. I think they believe I'm doing all that stuff too; otherwise, why would they put them up?" Bree explained, feeling frustrated.

"I've heard about it from Roisin. Don't worry, those rules are purely for Susie. Roisin put them up because she's fed up with the noise. She loves you and knows it's not you."

Feeling a wave of relief, Bree smiled and returned to work, greeting a familiar face—Micky, who was always in the bar. He came in every day, always managing to time his arrival just before Bree started her shift. He helped set up the tables and followed her around with a dustpan as she cleaned. His dark brown eyes, radiant smile, and military uniform won her over instantly.

Their romance blossomed quickly, and they became inseparable for several months. Together, they savoured every moment, knowing that Micky could be shipped out with his military division at any time. As expected, the dreaded long-distance posting arrived. With a heavy heart and tearful eyes, Bree waved Micky off at the station. The months apart were difficult for both. They exchanged letters, sent messages at all hours, and had phone calls that were often stilted and awkward, in both Italian and English.

They dreamed of a life together: lazy summer days and hot nights in the Italian countryside, running a quaint bed and breakfast in Puglia. Bree was certain that love would conquer all, and she waited eagerly for the quick trips to Micky's hometown in southern Italy during her days off. Their romantic weekends—those few precious, unforgettable days every month—gave Bree the strength to survive the weeks apart, with only phone calls and messages to sustain them.

They stayed in a little guesthouse by the beach, just like the one they dreamed of owning one day. Micky treated her to quiet dinners on the rocks and long drives through the countryside in his old Fiat 500. Those humid summer days and sticky nights, spent in a dream-like, loved-up haze, were everything Bree had ever imagined for her future.

Two months after an overseas posting, Micky returned to Italy. Bree was ecstatic as she prepared to visit their little corner of paradise. This was going to be her last quick trip to see him—after this, she planned to stay for the winter, perhaps forever. In the final days before her trip, she carefully packed the gifts she had collected during their time apart. She chose her outfits carefully, ready for anything—from mountain walks to evening picnics.

Her freshly cut blonde hair danced in the light breeze, and her perfume was packed at the top of her bag, ready for a quick refresh after the eight-hour train journey. The trip down was always an adventure. Italian families, noticing her slender figure, took pity on the lone traveller, insisting on fattening her up by sharing freshly prepared, homemade delicacies.

Just before dawn, Bree placed her bags to the side as she approached the ticket station. Picking up the phone, she chatted excitedly with Micky.

"I'm in Venice. I'm just walking to my train now; it's on time," Bree said, her voice full of excitement. She couldn't contain the joy bubbling up inside her. She'd imagined this moment so many times: seeing Micky again, feeling his arms around her, tasting the reunion she had longed for. She pictured him standing at the end of the platform, his dark eyes lighting up when he saw her, and she could almost hear the beat of her heart quicken.

"Bree," Micky's voice came through, soft but unmistakably serious.

A chill ran through her. "What's wrong?"

"Don't get on the train." His words were heavy, slow, as though he was choosing them carefully, trying to soften what he had to say.

"Why? Micky, what's happening?" Bree said, confused, her heart still soaring despite the shift in his tone.

He was silent for a moment. She could hear him breathing, maybe steeling himself. "I've got some bad news. You can't come here." His voice cracked slightly, and it felt like a door had slammed shut in her chest. "I can't let you come."

The words hit her like a punch to the gut. Bree froze, her mind scrambling to catch up with the confusion and hurt twisting inside her. "I... I don't understand," she whispered, her voice barely audible, trembling. The distance between them suddenly felt like a vast, uncrossable ocean. "What are you saying?"

Micky's next words were soft but cruel. "I'm getting married next month," he said, his tone hollow. "My girlfriend—my other girlfriend, the one from home... she's pregnant." There was a long pause, as if he was hoping she might interrupt, but he pressed on. "It's all arranged. My parents... they've set everything up."

Bree's knees went weak. She grabbed onto the nearest railing, the phone slipping from her hand momentarily as she tried to hold herself together. She couldn't breathe. The world around her felt like it was spinning, everything blurring together. "Micky, no..." Her voice broke on his name, the disbelief clawing at her throat. "You... you're not serious, are you?"

But she could hear it in his voice—the finality. "I'm sorry, Bree. I love you... but this is happening."

The words scraped across her chest, leaving raw, jagged scars in their wake. She pressed the back of her hand to her mouth, trying to hold back the scream that threatened to break free. "But why?" she gasped, desperate. "Why didn't you tell me? Why did you need to have two girlfriends?"

Micky didn't answer right away. She could hear him shifting, his voice thick with regret, but it didn't change anything. It didn't undo the damage.

She closed her eyes, trying to find some stability, but all she could feel was the loss crashing down on her. "Please," she whispered, the tears finally breaking free, streaking down her face. "Tell me you're joking. Tell me this is some kind of sick joke. You can't... you can't do this to me."

"I'm sorry," Micky said again, but it was empty, hollow. His apology wasn't enough to fix the wound he had just carved into her heart. "I'm sorry, Bree."

The sound of his voice, so apologetic, so distant, only made the pain worse. She felt it in her chest, sharp and suffocating, spreading like a dark cloud.

The phone in her hand felt heavy, as though it was dragging her down. Her fingers were numb, trembling as she gripped it. "I can't... I can't hear this," she said, her voice barely a whisper. "I thought we had something... I thought it was real."

"I never meant to hurt you," Micky said, his words strained. But they felt like empty echoes in her mind.

Bree couldn't listen anymore. She slammed the phone down with a force that shocked her. She stood there, breathless, a hollow ache gnawing at her insides. The future she had imagined with Micky—the warm afternoons in the sun, the quiet nights in the countryside—vanished in an instant. It wasn't real. None of it was real.

She grabbed her bags, feeling like she was moving through water, slow and heavy, her limbs uncooperative. She didn't look back as she walked down the platform toward the bus stop. The tears continued to fall, but there was no comfort, no release. The life she had dreamed of, the love she had fought for, was now an empty shell, crushed by his betrayal.

5 | Bree

Kay used her connections to find Bree a job at a friend's hotel in the Italian Alps for the winter season. Excited about her fresh start, Bree couldn't wait to leave Micky behind once and for all.

He'd called her relentlessly at her last job, but now, he had no idea where she was. Finally, she could be free of the memories that had haunted her. He'd tried to explain his actions—his family had accepted his 'other' girlfriend, and the families were friends, so that was just how it was. "If you like, you can be my lover once I'm married," he'd suggested.

"You're kidding me, right? Why would I want that?" she had replied, her eighteen-year-old self knowing she deserved more. She hadn't heard from Micky since, not in the six months since that conversation.

The hotel where Bree worked was an Italian-run, old-fashioned ski lodge catering to English tourists. The furnishings were dated, with worn brown sofas and chipped tables that contributed to an overall feeling of neglect. Bree had originally been hired to tend the bar, but within days, they moved her to the office. She quickly proved herself, efficiently liaising with tour operators and managing the office's demands.

On her nineteenth birthday, snow blew off the tall, white trees as Bree and her new friends trudged through the snow to a small mountain hut for a quiet evening of ice cream and pizza. No big, drunken celebrations—just large, colourful bowls of ice cream in a wooden chalet. The dim lighting, dark wooden benches, and blazing fire stood in stark contrast to her previous life. In her knee-high snow boots and jeans, Bree realised how much her world had changed.

Weeks passed, and Bree had settled into her new routine at the reception desk. She felt a sickness stir in her stomach when she saw Micky walking toward her, a confident smile plastered across his face.

"Hey, sweetie," he greeted her, the same tone he used when they'd been together.

"What are you doing here?" Bree stepped back, instinctively distancing herself.

"I found you. I miss you. I need to talk to you," he said.

With a straight face, Bree replied, "No, not here. I finish at two; meet me outside."

Micky nodded as she turned back to her work, trying to distract herself from the thoughts of him.

At two o'clock, Bree's hands trembled as she locked the office door and stepped outside. Micky was pacing, waiting. He reached for her hand, but she quickly pulled away.

"What do you want?" she asked.

"You. I want you back," he said, twiddling the wedding ring on his finger.

"Did you get married?" Bree asked, sitting back with a mixture of disbelief and disgust.

"Yes, but the pregnancy was a lie to trap me. It wasn't true," Micky explained, shaking his head. "She told me after the wedding that she wasn't pregnant—it was a false positive test."

Bree laughed in disbelief. "So, that's supposed to make it all okay then?"

"Well, I don't love her. So, I don't see why you and I can't be together," Micky said, his eyes locking on hers.

Bree glared at him, the anger rising inside her. "You're still married. I can't forget that."

"Bree, the universe brings people together; we have to let the universe guide us," he said, nodding solemnly.

"You've lost the plot. Don't you realise how crazy this is?" Bree replied, unable to hold back her frustration.

"You can be my lover. We can be happy. It's normal for an Italian man to have a wife and a lover; there's nothing wrong with it. Everyone does it."

The rage inside Bree burned as he reached for her hand again. "No. Hell no. Never," she said, rising to her feet.

Micky grabbed her arm, pulling her back down, but Bree's defiance only grew. "You have to accept the consequences of your decisions. You left me for another woman. You married her. What do you expect from me?"

Micky refused to listen, his expression undeterred. With a sad sigh, he slid a small jewellery box across the table to her.

"Our photos are in there," he said.

Bree stared at the silver heart pendant inside, then slammed the box shut, her frustration boiling over. "You are not me. You don't know what I want. I know I don't want you. I don't want to be your lover."

"I knew I'd face some resistance, but not this much," Micky said. "Bree, please, think about it; I love you."

"I've thought about it. The answer is no." She pushed the box back towards him and stood once more. For a brief moment, she thought she saw awe and respect in his eyes.

"I've got nowhere to stay. Can I stay with you?" he asked, desperation creeping into his voice.

Furious, Bree grabbed the phone and dialled for a taxi. "A taxi will be here in ten minutes to take you wherever you need to go, anywhere but here. Goodbye, Micky." She turned her back and walked away, her head held high.

Through the window, she watched as Micky climbed into the taxi, her heart pounding with a sense of closure. As the car sped away, she felt free, untethered for the first time in a long while.

At the end of the season, Bree and Kay decided to travel across Italy. Ten years older than Bree, Kay became like a sister to her—a wise, older sister who kept Bree grounded while showing her the unspoiled beauty of Italy. They travelled by train, bus, and even hitchhiked, exploring the hidden gems of the country.

Arriving in Rome, Bree's heart skipped a beat. This was where she was meant to be. As Kay met up with friends, Bree wandered the streets, taking in the sights, sounds, and smells. She admired the charming Italian men from a distance, still healing from Micky's betrayal, and not yet ready to re-enter the world of dating.

But Bree, feeling more alive than ever, was ready for her next adventure.

6 | Petra

Petra had spent years trying to soften her strong Yorkshire accent, the sound of it like tying her to a past she desperately wanted to escape. It clung to her like a stain she couldn't wash away. As the eldest of five siblings, she often felt like an afterthought in her own family. Babysitting her younger siblings wasn't just an expectation—it was the role she had been cast into, the identity that was thrust upon her without her consent. The older she got, the more it felt like she was fading into the background of her own life. With each passing year, the gap between her and her siblings grew wider, leaving Petra drifting, adrift in a sea of resentment and unspoken pain.

Money was tight in their respectable, hard-working household, and love came at a cost Petra could never quite afford. Her father rarely spoke to her unless it was to bark out an order or deliver a scolding. Still, she clung to the hope of winning his approval, like a starving animal desperate for scraps. She studied her mother's every move, tried to mirror the little rituals that seemed to keep her father content—the slippers by the door, the warm meal waiting for him, and that relentless, hollow smile that never faltered, even when it felt like the world was falling apart.

"Persistence and a good, old-fashioned showering of love will make any man love you," her mother would say with an air of finality, as though the formula was foolproof.

The words carved themselves into Petra's mind, a mantra she repeated in her head, each time the void between her and her father grew larger. She tried, she really did—she threw herself into pleasing her family, hoping for a flicker of warmth, a word of approval, but her efforts were met with the same indifference. Nothing ever changed. It never would.

Petra's identity was an anomaly within her family. Her mother's strong Chinese features and her father's striking Indian looks seemed to bypass her entirely. Apart from her jet-black hair, Petra felt like an imposter in her own skin. She avoided mirrors, unwilling to confront the reflection staring back at her—sunken cheeks, eyes heavy with the too many unspoken things. She was a ghost in her own life, caught between two worlds but belonging to neither. The sight of her face only deepened her sense of alienation.

Her youngest sister, Hannah, embodied everything Petra wasn't. Hannah's life glittered with achievements—pageants, awards, auditions. The hallway walls, plastered with Hannah's glossy portraits, became a daily reminder of Petra's own perceived insignificance. Each step past those walls felt like a silent reprimand, a reminder that no matter what she did, she'd never measure up.

Birthdays were no different. Petra leafed through old photo albums, tracing her fingers over the faded pages, and the disparity hit her like a punch to the stomach. Her birthdays had always been simple affairs—quiet family gatherings, a white cake, maybe a few candles, nothing special. But her siblings' birthdays? They were grand, filled with costumes, balloons, laughter—everything she had never been given. The sharp contrast left a scar on her heart, one that never healed.

On her fifteenth birthday, Petra woke before the sun, her heart thumping in her chest with nervous excitement. This year would be different, she thought, clinging to that fragile hope. This year, they'd remember. She rushed downstairs, a wave of excitement rushing through her, only to find... nothing.

No balloons. No gifts. No cards. Just the mutter and mumble of her family's voices around the breakfast table, discussing Hannah's latest audition as though Petra didn't even exist.

The disappointment hit her like a physical blow, knocking the wind out of her. She stood frozen in the doorway, her chest tight with a mixture of anger, humiliation, and hurt. The toast popped out of the toaster, its crunch the only sound that broke the suffocating silence in her mind.

Without thinking, she grabbed a plate, her fingers trembling with fury, and hurled it to the floor. The sharp crack of ceramic against tile sounded like a gunshot, the noise ringing in the hollow space of the room.

Her family turned to her, their expressions a blend of irritation and confusion, as though she were the one who had done something wrong.

"What's gotten into you, Petra?" her mother snapped, already bending down to clean the shards with the same practised indifference she used when wiping away her own tears.

"It's my birthday," Petra said, her voice thick with unshed tears, barely above a whisper, but it felt like she'd screamed it to the heavens.

Her mother glanced up, and for a brief, fleeting moment, there was a flicker of realization in her eyes—something resembling guilt. But it was gone in a heartbeat, replaced by the same dismissal. "Don't be dramatic, Petra. We've got more important things to think about today."

Her stomach churned, bile rising in her throat as she grabbed another plate and threw it onto the floor, letting it shatter, fragments of broken china mixing with the carpet beneath her feet. She turned away from the scene, the anger still hot in her veins, and stormed out of the house, the cold wind biting her cheeks as she ran to school, as though distance could erase the ache in her chest.

That afternoon, she returned home, her anger dulling to a simmer, replaced by quiet resignation. She tossed her bag onto a chair, the sound of it hitting the wood too sharp, too final. She reached for a biscuit, her stomach gnawing with hunger, but before she could take a bite, her mother slapped her hand away with an unexpected force.

"Don't touch that. You clean up the mess first," her mother said, her voice low, her expression stern.

Petra stood there, her hand still hovering over the plate, the broken china at her feet. There was something in the shards that called to her, something broken and sharp, like the pieces of herself she couldn't fit together. She crouched down, running her fingers over the jagged edges, a strange, unbidden sense of calm washing over her. The broken pieces mirrored her own reflection—fractured, overlooked, and yet still there, still holding on.

Peering through the family room door, Petra watched her mother's arm snake around Hannah and one of her brothers, pulling them close, wrapping them in the warmth of a love she could never seem to reach. The TV flickered with images of Hannah on a pageant stage, strutting in a glittering red dress and matching heels. The applause from the speakers echoed through the room, but all Petra could hear was the pounding of her own pulse, drowning out the rest of the world.

She clenched the doorframe until her knuckles turned white, the anger and bitterness rising like a storm inside her. But instead of shouting, instead of saying what she longed to say, she turned and retreated to the kitchen, her jaw tight with unspoken words, the ache of being invisible to them—no matter how loudly she screamed in her own mind—settling in her bones.

She pulled the heavy curtains shut with a deliberate tug, blocking out the sunlight. A grim smile spread across her face as her eyes fixed on Hannah's pink bicycle, hanging neatly on the garage wall. In one swift motion, she yanked it down, the metallic clang reverberating through the empty space. Petra stared at the bike for a moment, her chest tightening, then stomped down hard, slamming her foot into the wheels and frame with a force that made her heart race. By the time she was done, the once-sturdy bike was nothing more than a mangled heap of warped metal. A strange, twisted sense of triumph washed over her as she grabbed a bag of crisps and retreated to her room, locking the door behind her.

That evening, the house buzzed with accusations. Her brothers loudly defended themselves, each pointing fingers at the other. Gordon, closest in age but a stranger in spirit, was particularly vocal. His shouts echoed down the hallway before he stormed into Petra's room, slamming the door behind him.

Before Petra could react, he grabbed her wrist and shoved her against the wall. His voice dropped to a dangerous growl. "You think you're clever, don't you? Smashing her bike like that?"

"I don't know what you're talking about," Petra said, trying to sound defiant, but her voice cracked under the intensity of his gaze.

"You'll regret this." Gordon's grip tightened before he shoved her away. She stumbled back, her body crashing into the bed as he stormed out, slamming the door so hard it rattled the frame.

Petra was left trembling, the anger from breaking the bike now morphing into a hollow emptiness. She glanced at the mirror on her dresser, her reflection blurred by a streak of dust. She couldn't meet her own eyes. The rage she had let loose on the bike only deepened the chasm within her.

From that day on, Petra withdrew even further. At family meals, she picked at her food in silence, her brothers' laughter and her mother's scolding fading into background noise. The walls of the house seemed to close in, suffocating her with expectations she couldn't meet, and a family that barely saw her.

When she finally left for university, Petra saw it as her escape from the invisible shackles that bound her to her family. Medicine, law—both fields promised prestige and independence, the things she craved most. But each time, her unchecked anger and the loneliness that followed derailed her plans. The friendships she tried to form were fleeting, tainted by misunderstandings and her tendency to lash out.

By the time Petra returned home, defeated, she carried the toll of her failures like a stone strapped to her chest. She dreaded the disappointment in her parents' eyes, but couldn't seem to pull herself out of the spiral she had fallen into.

One morning, the smell of coffee wafted downstairs, where her parents sat at the table, their faces etched with frustration. Her mother's sharp tone shattered the silence. "Petra, we've had enough. You need to figure out your life."

"I'm trying," Petra protested, her voice faltering. "I just need time."

"You've had time," her mother snapped. "All you do is sit around, angry at the world, angry at us. We can't keep supporting you."

Petra's father sat in silence, his eyes fixed on the crossword in front of him, but Petra felt his judgment in every furrow of his brow.

"Where do you expect me to go?" Petra asked, her voice rising in desperation.

"Anywhere but here," her mother replied. "You have two weeks to figure it out."

Petra stared at them, fury and fear rising in her chest. She wanted to scream, to shout that this was their fault as much as hers, that they had failed her as much as she had failed herself. But instead, she turned and walked away, the sound of her slippers scuffing against the floor the only indication she had left the room.

When she returned later, her father's eyes followed her every step. He didn't speak, but the intensity of his scrutiny was unbearable. Petra felt as if her entire life was a series of closed doors—each one locked, with no key in sight.

As she lay in bed that night, Petra made a vow: she wouldn't let them push her out without a fight. If the world wanted her to sink, she would rise. But how? The question lingered in the dark like a challenge, daring her to find an answer.

7 | Petra

The next morning, Petra smoothed down her simple summer dress, its soft fabric a small comfort against the whirlwind of emotions that had taken over her life. Her mother had given her the ultimatum to leave, and with no other option, she wandered aimlessly through Leeds city centre, letting the busy streets and sun-warmed cobblestones numb her thoughts. The chaotic energy around her only emphasised her own sense of displacement, like a threadbare rug she was desperately trying to shake off.

A brightly lit travel agency caught her eye. The 'Wanted' ad in the window seemed almost too good to be true. Without thinking, Petra stepped inside, her heart racing in a way that was both thrilling and terrifying. "I'd like to speak to the manager," she said, voice steadier than she felt.

An hour later, her pulse still racing from the conversation, she stood shaking the manager's hand, the warm summer sun greeting her like a long-lost friend. The job didn't require qualifications—just an outgoing personality—and that, Petra thought bitterly, she could fake well enough. She had faked enough for her whole life, hadn't she?

The first month on the job was a whirlwind of self-discovery. Every evening, as the city quieted, Petra found herself hunched over travel brochures in her small first-floor flat, absorbing the names of countries like they were sacred texts. She learned the jargon, the allure of faraway places, and how to sell them with an easy smile that masked her inner turmoil. She became good at it—effortlessly anticipating what her customers wanted before they knew themselves.

Helen, her colleague and friend, was a quiet anchor in the whirlwind of her life. Her calm nature was a balm for Petra's raw, ragged edges, and Helen never once judged her outbursts, her anger, her broken pieces. It was a comfort Petra had learned not to take for granted.

One summer morning, Petra asked Helen for help. "Will you come with me to pick up my stuff from the house?" Her voice cracked, the words too heavy for her to carry alone. "I can't go back there by myself."

Helen nodded without hesitation, and they drove through streets Petra had once walked with a sense of belonging, a sense of being rooted. Now, they felt foreign—like a past she was determined to outgrow.

As they approached the house, students in their fresh new clothes streamed past. Fear gripped Petra's chest, cold and suffocating. She felt small again, like the girl who used to shrink under the power of her mother's cold stare. "Let's just get this over with," she said, her tone sharp with control. "In, grab my stuff, and out."

Helen, ever steady, simply said, "Okay."

When Petra's mother opened the door, there was no warmth in her greeting, just the usual icy stare. Petra awkwardly reached for a hug, but her mother stepped back, the space between them palpable. A cold, unspoken tension filled the room as Petra moved silently through the motions of packing, her hands shaking with every item she shoved into her bags, trying not to remember the house that used to be home.

Helen watched silently, her presence a quiet reassurance. "Let's go," Petra whispered once everything was packed.

As the car pulled away, Petra gazed out of the window, watching the house fade into the distance. "My little sister will move into my room within minutes," she said, her voice tight with emotion. "She'll fill the shelves with her pageant trophies, and I'll be forgotten."

Helen's voice softened. "Your mum didn't have much to say, did she?"

"Oh, she had a lot to say," Petra replied bitterly, a dry laugh escaping her lips. "That silence... that awkward, suffocating silence? That said it all. After twenty-four years, we don't even know what to say to each other anymore. How sad is that?"

Helen reached over, her hand a comforting weight on Petra's shoulder. "It's their loss, you know? You'll show them how wrong they are."

Petra managed a small smile, her chest heavy with the bittersweet relief and sorrow. She wasn't sure she'd ever let go of the ache that came with her mother's indifference, but for the first time in a long time, it felt like the right decision. She was free.

Back at her flat, Petra poured all her emotions into her work. She hadn't returned for a single family birthday since she left, and the thought of going back—of facing their cold indifference—felt impossible. But every day, she immersed herself more deeply into the job, using the void left by her family to fuel her ambition.

The manager, noticing her drive, congratulated her as she quickly became the top salesperson in the office—not just in Leeds, but across the company. She had found something she was good at, something that didn't require her to be the Petra of her past. It was exhilarating, like a breath of fresh air filling her lungs.

One afternoon, her manager called her into his office. A flutter of dread washed over her, and as she sank into the worn armchair, she tried to mask her nerves by focusing on the framed brochures on the walls.

"Petra," he began, adjusting his glasses, "I have an opportunity for you. We want you to move to London. There's a promotion for you—a team leader position in our head office, with a pay raise." He paused, watching her closely, as if gauging her reaction. "You've done an excellent job. You really understand what our customers want."

Her heart skipped. "Me, in London?" she asked, her voice barely a whisper. For a moment, she didn't dare hope.

He pulled a shiny brochure from his briefcase and slid it across the desk.

"You'll head up a new sales team. There's a company car, a housing allowance. You've earned it."

"Thank you," Petra replied, her fingers trembling as she gripped the edge of the brochure, her mind spinning with the possibility of something more than she had ever dreamed.

"There will be a lot of travel, too," he added, his tone almost conspiratorial. "We're launching a new brand for elite travellers, 'Deluxe Dream Travel.' It's for those who want a holiday tailored to their every whim—a life of luxury and indulgence."

Without thinking, Petra's answer was out before she could stop herself. "Yes."

That night, as she sat alone in her flat, the city lights sparkling outside, Petra allowed herself a rare moment of wonder. London—her new start. The possibility of becoming someone else, someone bigger than the girl who had walked away from her family with nothing but a suitcase and a dream. This was her chance. And she was ready.

8 | Petra

Unwrapping his arms from the desk, Petra's manager sank back in his reclining black leather armchair, the soft creak of the leather squeaking as he did so. He stretched, his arms sweeping over his bald, reddened head, a man who wore the power of corporate ambition like a second skin.

"These people want to be pampered," he said, his voice almost theatrical, "They expect private jets, limousines, the whole shebang." He reached into a drawer, pulling out glossy printouts with images of white sand beaches and crystal-clear waters, and pushed them towards her. "They won't be satisfied with crowded excursions; these travellers demand private yachts, boats, helicopters—hell, even private chefs."

Petra's brow scrunched her mind racing to picture such a lavish world, one that seemed both foreign and impossibly close. She had never once flown first-class or set foot on a private yacht—how could she sell a dream she barely understood?

"When do I start?" she asked, the curiosity in her voice almost too eager to mask her nervousness.

"Just under three weeks, on the first of November, if that works for you," he said, his fingers tapping ally on the desk as he studied her with calculating eyes.

Petra had never left the UK, never even travelled outside Yorkshire. She had grown up dreaming of escape but never quite knowing how. So, with only a handful of vacation brochures and the vague knowledge of package holidays she had gathered from her brief time in the agency, Petra booked herself on two short breaks. She needed to understand it—what people expected, what they craved. What was normal for them? And how could she possibly offer something better, something that felt extraordinary, if she had no clue what "ordinary" even looked like?

Those three weeks passed in a blur of planning and shopping. The blue skies, the warm breeze, the glittering hotels and indulgent buffets—everything was new to her, as though she had stepped into someone else's life. It was a world of perfection she couldn't quite grasp, like watching a dream unfold and not knowing how to enter it.

On the plane back to Manchester, Petra slumped low in her seat, her eyes light with the novelty of it all. She opened her notebook, the pages filled with scribbled notes, some half-formed, others unfinished. She drew a giant question mark on a blank page and wrote beneath it: How to improve on perfection? It felt both absurd and necessary—how could she improve on something so flawless, when all she knew was the grey normality of her own life?

Several days later, Petra felt the first true sense of freedom as she watched the British countryside flash past her window, the rolling hills and fields of green blurring into one. The crisp, fresh air that filtered through the train window felt like a cleansing breeze, and for the first time in a long time, she felt lighter. Leeds was behind her, and she could almost taste the promise of something new in London.

When she walked into her new office, it was an entirely different world. The polished floors, the sleek glass desks, the people in smart suits who moved with purpose—Petra's heart raced as she shook hands with her new manager. He greeted her with a smile, but there was something calculating in the way he sized her up. "I'll introduce you to your team in a bit," he said, drumming his fingers on the armrest of his chair. "But first, let me give you the rundown."

He flipped through papers on his desk, the rustling of them sounding like an orchestra of opportunity and expectation. "We've had a few false starts with this programme," he continued, his voice casual but edged with the pressure of his own ambitions. "Your job will be to get it running smoothly, to make it thrive, and, most importantly, to promote the hell out of it."

Petra nodded nervously, her mind still reeling from the rapid shift in her reality. She smiled, hoping it would mask the vulnerability she felt. As he spoke, she tried to focus on his words but found herself distracted by the moment. She was no longer the small-town girl hiding in the shadows—she was here, in London, and everything felt both exhilarating and terrifying.

Fiddling with a paperclip, her manager flicked it toward the trash can, missing by a mile. He grabbed a pen and began flicking it between his fingers, a nervous habit that mirrored the energy in the room. "You're going to be our guinea pig," he said with a grin, as though he were letting her in on some grand secret. "We'll pay for you to travel to all the destinations we've set up. You'll come back, promote them, and give us feedback on how we can improve. You'll write a blog, take photos and videos, and present your findings to the team."

Petra's heart skipped at the idea. The thought of actually experiencing these places, not just selling them to others but living them, felt like a dream come true. She scribbled notes furiously, muttering sounds of agreement as she absorbed the vastness of the opportunity in front of her.

"Your first trip is on Friday, so you've got time to get yourself an elegant travelling wardrobe and, of course, to do some research." His words were almost an afterthought, and Petra's eyes widened at the idea of preparing for something so lavish, so unlike her old life.

"Yes, of course," she said, eager to prove herself, to show him that she was capable of handling this. She wanted his approval more than anything, wanted to be the kind of woman who could step into this world without hesitation.

"And your first journey is to the Bahamas," he continued, the words hanging in the air like an impossible promise. "Private jet. After that, it's all first-class travel." His voice cracked slightly, as though he almost pitied her, imagining her life would somehow fall short of the opulence he was describing. But Petra was already lost in the allure of it—her mind racing with excitement and a tinge of disbelief.

He stood up, grinning, and introduced her to the team waiting outside. Petra's eyes scanned the travel books lining the shelves, the titles all seeming to promise a life of luxury and wonder. As her manager clicked his pen, she felt a rush of nervous energy course through her veins. This was it—her chance to step into a new life.

In the first year, Petra travelled to Dubai, the Seychelles, Jamaica, Italy, Andalucía, Croatia, Ireland, Finland, Las Vegas, and Jordan. She stayed in five-star hotels with private chefs, explored exclusive villas with staff on hand to cater to her every need.

Her manager welcomed her back each time with a warm smile, presenting her with printouts of glowing sales figures. After the first year, he arranged a special welcome back to the office. Champagne corks popped as Petra entered, the sound of celebration in the air. Her colleagues clapped, and the excitement in the room was palpable.

"Petra," her manager said, a broad grin on his face, "You did it. You got the programme up and running. This is now the most profitable branch of the company." He handed her a sealed envelope, and Petra's hands shook slightly as she tore it open. Inside was a cheque—a reward for all her hard work, all the places she had been, and all the new lives she had touched. "Thank you," she whispered, her voice tight with emotion as she shook his hand.

This was her life now. And she had made it

9 | Petra

During her time in Ireland, Petra met an Irishman named Liam. She'd been instantly attracted to his rugby-playing physique; his shaggy brown hair, contagious laugh, and charm sent her into turmoil. Their relationship had grown quickly after a chance meeting in a cinema queue.

Blinded by his good looks, Petra had brushed aside his lame excuses and last-minute cancelled plans. Petra had willingly agreed when Liam invited her back to his small village for a few days together.

Arriving early in the morning, a warm spring breeze caressed her face. She'd chosen her most flattering summer dress, tied back her hair, and smiled at the hotel receptionist as she waited for Liam to collect her. Petra felt a flutter of excitement—since Liam had said he needed to speak to her, she'd thought about the possibilities. Perhaps, she dared to dream, he would say those three words she longed to hear—those three words that would make her life feel perfect.

Liam blasted his horn and stuck his hand out of the open window.

Petra jumped into his waiting car, her heart racing as the engine started with a gentle chug. He drove slowly, his brow tense and his silence palpable. The car felt too small, the air too thick, and Petra's excitement quickly shifted to unease. With a deep breath, Liam finally spoke. "I wanted to talk to you about something."

Petra looked lovingly into his eyes, trying to ignore the knot of dread forming in her stomach. "I'm all ears," she replied, her voice steady but her mind already second-guessing the mood in the car.

"Being with you has made me realise how much I love my wife," Liam said in a low voice, barely above a whisper.

Petra's heart stopped. Her mind whirled, each word feeling like a blow. "What?" Her mouth dropped open, her breath catching in her throat. She blinked rapidly, trying to process what he'd just said. The words bounced around in her head, refusing to settle.

Liam sighed, his eyes shifting away from her, as though unable to meet her gaze. "I'm sorry, Petra," he said, his voice faltering. "I just needed to tell you."

Petra stared at him, her lips trembling. "So, you're getting back with her?" she asked, her voice trembling despite her efforts to stay calm. It was a question she never thought she would need to ask, but now it felt like the only one that mattered.

"Well, we're going to give it another go. She's moved back into the house,"

Liam said, his voice flat, as though the decision had already been made and there was nothing left to discuss.

"So, that's it? We're over?" Petra asked, her throat tightening. She felt the sting of tears threatening, but she managed to swallow them back. It wasn't about him anymore. It was about her. She needed to be strong.

Liam glanced at her, his expression unreadable. "Yes, I have to end this," he said, as though it were an inevitability, as though there was no other choice. "My wife doesn't know about you, so I'd rather keep it that way."

Petra's eyes welled up, her heart breaking. "No, please don't do this," she begged, her voice shaky but firm, as though pleading might somehow change the direction he'd already chosen.

"I think it's best if we don't go for lunch. I'll take you back to your hotel," Liam said, pulling into a car park to make a turn. He sighed deeply, his face a mask of reluctance that held no hint of emotion.

"But I've booked for a week," Petra said, her voice quiet but full of disbelief. "I've taken a week off work to be here."

Liam said nothing, his face a blank canvas. Without another word, he dropped her off at her hotel, offering only a polite nod. "Bye, Petra," he said coldly, his gaze drifting away from her and toward the hotel, as though she were no more than a fleeting moment in his life.

Petra sat there, frozen for a moment, the stress of the situation settling heavily in her chest. She had imagined so many different endings, but none of them had been like this. Her hands shook as she grabbed her bag from the back seat, her fingers numb with the effort to hold it together.

She stepped out of the car, her legs unsteady on the gravel as she forced herself to stand tall. Liam didn't even look back. He slammed the door shut, and his car sped off without another word. The sound of the engine faded into the distance, but Petra stood still, the finality of it all settling in.

Her body felt heavy, her chest tight, but she didn't allow herself to collapse. She had wanted this life, this adventure, and now it was all gone. The dream of it was already slipping away, and all that was left was the cold, empty space he had left behind.

10 | Petra

Petra walked to her room, grabbed a chair, and placed it on the balcony. She lit a cigarette, her eyes fixed on the white wooden church with its little spire. Just hours ago, she had imagined it as the setting for her wedding to Liam. Now, it felt like a cruel reminder of what she'd lost, and the anger bubbling up inside her was almost overwhelming.

She stubbed out the cigarette in the ashtray. With bare feet against the warm wooden floors, she paced the room, trying to shake the tension in her body. Throwing herself face-down onto the four-poster bed, she buried her face into the soft pillow, muffling the screams of desperation that shook her.

After what felt like an eternity, Petra bolted upright. She grabbed her computer, her fingers moving quickly as she opened a browser and typed "Orla Cleary" into Facebook. A dark smile tugged at her lips when she easily found a picture of Liam's wife.

Orla had short blonde hair, soft features, and an almost vulnerable appeal. Petra scrolled through her profile, pausing on pictures of Orla smiling with friends, walking a collie, and enjoying various activities. She clicked through to find images of Orla and Liam together.

Petra snapped photos of the screen, her eyes burning with anger. She sat back on the bed, her stomach tight as she studied the images and notes, piecing things together. Each click of the mouse felt like a step deeper into her carefully constructed plan.

The next morning, Petra slipped into her yoga shorts and left the hotel. She ran five miles, stopping only when she reached the outskirts of the village. There, in the shade of a stone wall, she waited, her breath shallow and controlled. She had memorised Orla's routine from Facebook—every morning, she tagged herself near the local pub at exactly 7:45 a.m.

Petra glanced at her watch. A slim figure appeared in the distance, moving briskly. Squinting, Petra saw her—Orla, older without the flattering filters of social media. Her complexion was duller, her blue eyes still striking but now edged with the kind of weariness that only time could bring. Her hair was neatly cut, her posture confident. Petra took a deep breath, then moved to the side of the road as Orla approached.

"Morning," Petra called out, waving as she sprinted past.

"Morning," Orla replied, nodding politely at the passing runner.

Petra waited until Orla was out of sight, then quickly assessed the road ahead. She faked a stumble, clutching her ankle as she dropped to the ground in mock agony.

Orla's head snapped around at the sound. Her eyes widened in shock as she rushed towards Petra, her voice full of concern. "Oh, my God. What happened?"

"It's just my ankle. I'll be fine," Petra whimpered, squirming slightly to sell the act, her voice trembling with feigned pain.

"Let me help you," Orla said, looking around for someone to assist. She pulled out her phone, already dialing. "I'll call my husband. He'll help and take you to the hospital."

Petra nodded gratefully, clutching her ankle even tighter. "Thank you."

Within minutes, Liam arrived, his car pulling up with a screech of tyres. He glanced at Petra with a look of detached curiosity before shifting his focus to his wife.

"This is Petra. She tripped and twisted her ankle," Orla explained, her voice soft with concern.

"Sorry," Petra said, managing a grateful smile for Liam as he looked her over with little interest.

"Can you take her to the hospital? I've got to get to work," Orla added, glancing at her watch. She grabbed her bag, brushing a kiss against Liam's cheek. "Thanks, sweetie."

"Take care, Petra," Orla said, handing her a business card. Petra slipped it into her pocket, suppressing the urge to smile.

Liam waved at his wife as she disappeared down the road, then turned to Petra, his expression flat. "Are you really hurt?" he asked, his voice lacking even the faintest trace of concern—just annoyance.

Petra smirked, leaning forward and running her fingers down his neck as he drove. "I'm fine. I faked it," she admitted with a hint of amusement. "I wanted to see your wife."

Liam slammed on the brakes and whipped the door open, his face contorted in anger. "Get out. Stay away from us," he shouted, his voice sharp with fury.

Petra calmly pushed her legs out of the car, planting her feet firmly on the ground. She hunched forward, wrapping her arms around the headrest as she looked him dead in the eye. "You don't love her. You love me. You'll come running soon enough. And I'll be waiting." She blew him a kiss, her heart racing with the thrill of the moment as she stepped out of the car and walked away.

Once she was out of sight, Petra turned the corner toward the shops. She slipped a few notes from her bra and went into Boots to buy an ankle brace. As she sipped her coffee, she passed the office where Orla worked. Sitting at the bus stop, she saw Orla round the corner, her eyes widening when she spotted Petra.

"Petra. Wow, are you feeling better?" Orla asked, her face full of concern.

"Hi, Orla. What a surprise." Petra tried to stand but winced, clutching her "injured" foot and sitting back down on the bench. "Just waiting for the next bus," she said casually, trying to seem relaxed.

"Did Liam take care of you?" Orla asked, sitting down beside her.

"Oh yes, thank you. He was great. Thanks for helping me this morning," Petra replied with a smile. "What about you? What are you doing here?"

"I've just finished work. I'm going to the gym before heading home," Orla said with a small smile, her eyes still full of concern for Petra.

"Oh, I love the gym. But I guess this ankle is going to keep me down for a while," Petra said with a scoff, making a note to herself. "Where do you go?"

Orla gave her gym details, and Petra memorised every word. "Well, enjoy," Petra said with a smile as she stood up, clutching her foot in mock discomfort.

She hobbled to the bus, waved to Orla, and boarded. Once settled, she pulled out her notebook and jotted down everything she'd just learned. As the bus pulled into her stop, Petra jumped off and meandered back to her hotel. In her room, she opened her notebook, studying the new details with meticulous care. Every detail mattered now, and she wasn't going to let anything slip.

11| Bree

Bree had picked up the Italian language easily, a skill that made it easier for her to land a job as a holiday rep. She used her connections in Italy to apply, hoping it would lead to the perfect opportunity for adventure and new experiences.

Sitting in the interview room, her shiny new boots gleaming on the floor, Bree glanced nervously around at the older, more experienced applicants. In the sea of polished professionals, she felt invisible and out of place, a sense of doubt creeping into her mind. Yet, almost inexplicably, she was offered the job and told to prepare to move to Italy in a few weeks.

But Bree's excitement soon began to fizzle when she opened the job acceptance envelope. "Welcome to Regent Travel. Please complete and sign the acceptance slip for your summer season in Crete." Her eyes narrowed in confusion. Geography wasn't her strongest subject, but even she knew that Crete wasn't in Italy. She had been hired for her Italian skills, but there was no mention of Italy in this new opportunity.

Despite her confusion, Bree's longing for adventure took over. Shrugging off the mix-up, she accepted the role, packed her belongings into two large, heavy bags, and boarded a flight to Crete, determined to make the best of the situation.

The first few days were a blur of intense training. By the end of the five-day course, her boss handed her a key to an apartment, offering little more than a quick, "Enjoy, see you next airport day." Bree's excitement about the new role quickly evaporated as she realised the extent of her isolation. They had talked endlessly about teamwork during the training, but here she was, left to manage on her own with no team to rely on.

The only thing she had to guide her was a list of arrivals, destinations, and the name of a local agent, Anna, who was supposed to help with everything once she settled in. But the specifics of her role were still unclear.

Her new apartment was bright, the sunlight streaming in through large windows and casting warm, almost blinding light across the room. It was too much—she was used to the quiet shadows of the mountains, the calmness that had surrounded her life before this whirlwind change. The walls of her apartment were decorated with pictures of ancient Greek ruins and serene ocean views, a reminder of the world she was now a part of, a world she was still trying to understand.

She fumbled with her company phone, frustrated to find it barely worked.

The signal was spotty, and she couldn't figure out why the SIM card wasn't working as it should. She picked up her holiday brochure, trying to familiarise herself with the hotels where her guests would stay. As she read through the pages, trying to make sense of everything, her mind drifted to what she should be doing. What had she gotten herself into?

Three days before her first group of holidaymakers was set to arrive, Bree was curled up on the couch, reading through her notes, when a loud knock at the door startled her. Her heart skipped a beat as she jumped to her feet, nerves on edge. Cautiously, she peeked through the peephole.

Standing on the other side was a man with short black hair and dark, smiling eyes. "Hello, I'm Nik. I work for Anna, your agent," he said, his voice warm and easy, almost as if he knew exactly how out of place she felt.

Bree let out a breath she didn't realise she'd been holding. "Hey, I'm Bree," she said, extending a hand. They shook hands briefly, and she stepped aside, inviting him into the apartment.

Nik glanced around, a playful grin on his face. "I must get back to my office; Anna's worried she hasn't seen you yet. Can I take you there now?" His eyes flicked to his watch as he waited for Bree to gather her things.

"Sure," Bree said, quickly grabbing a few essentials. She glanced around the apartment at the papers scattered on the floor, the washing draped over the backs of chairs, and felt a pang of embarrassment. "Sorry about the mess."

Nik smiled knowingly. "It's okay, at least I can tell you're living here. Don't you use your phone?" he asked, raising an eyebrow.

Bree's face flushed slightly. "I can't get it to work. The SIM card they gave me isn't doing anything," she replied, a bit sheepish.

Nik reached for her phone and, with a small smirk, said, "I'll sort it out. Let's get you to Anna." Bree followed him out, the heat of the sun instantly hitting her skin, and realised in that moment that she had forgotten her sunglasses. She touched her nose absently, but it was too late to ask him to go back.

"We were all just concerned why you hadn't been to the office yet," Nik said casually as they walked towards his car.

Bree felt a slight panic rise in her chest. "I didn't know where to go. They didn't tell me," she explained, hoping to reassure him that she wasn't entirely useless. "I was planning to call the head office today."

When they arrived at the office, Nik took her phone, giving her a teasing look. "I'll fix this for you. You need to see Anna." He gave her a small, reassuring smile before disappearing into the back office.

Inside the office, Bree was greeted by Anna, a middle-aged woman with glasses and strong shoulders, her short black hair shot through with grey. As Anna puffed on a cigarette and placed it in the ashtray, she stood to greet Bree with a direct, unbothered air. "Bree, is that your name? Like the cheese?" she asked, her voice smoky and dry as the cloud of smoke drifted between them.

Bree, caught off guard, smiled awkwardly. "Yes, like the cheese, just spelled differently."

Anna's expression remained skeptical. "Why not Cheddar or Feta? Why this French rubbish?" she asked bluntly, causing Bree to blink in surprise.

Bree hesitated, her cheeks flushing slightly. "It's because my dad is Brian, and my mum is Eve. They just... combined the names," she explained, trying to sound matter-of-fact.

Anna gave a small, understanding nod, her attention flicking back to her work with a quiet nod of acknowledgment.

As Bree turned to leave, she caught Nik's eyes from across the room. His expression one of amusement. Bree, on the other hand, was still left with a hollow sense of uncertainty and the sinking feeling that maybe this wasn't the adventure she had imagined.

12 | Bree

Bree quickly grasped her role in the office: overseeing the daily operations of the resort and managing the weekly tasks. Her desk, tucked in the corner of the office shared with the other reps, became her little corner of order in the total frenzy around her.

Nik handed her the phone with a small, reassuring smile. "I've fixed it. You've got a message from head office with all the details of the office and a note to call Anna." His eyes lingered on her for a moment, softening as if seeing something more. "I told Anna why you didn't come to see us. I've put my number in there, too."

Bree nodded, her heart fluttering slightly at the sudden warmth in his gaze, but she quickly shoved the feeling aside.

Anna quickly assumed the role of Bree's Greek mother, and the other reps became her new family. They worked hard but played harder, each day blending into the next with laughter, camaraderie, and the promise of adventures to come. They sold the most exciting tours and excursions so they could experience them firsthand. On their days off, they hired cars and drove aimlessly across the island, reveling in the freedom.

Bree loved her job, but more than that, she loved the life she was building here. The rep family made every moment count, and the social life was busy, fun, and unexpectedly thrilling. The work was tough, and the hours long, but they always ended the day together on the roof with a bottle of Ouzo, sharing stories of their guests and their travels.

Nik occasionally joined in with the reps. A palpable buzz followed him as he cheerfully engaged with everyone, smiling at the wide-eyed girls who tried to catch his attention. At twenty-three, he was fluent in English and often arranged and guided tours from the office. There was an effortless charm about him, and Bree could see how easily people were drawn to him.

"Bree, can't you see? He spends more time with you than with us. He likes you," Elka, her friend, teased one evening, her voice light but pointed. "He glows when you walk into the room."

Bree scoffed, shaking her head. "Don't be silly. He's just friendly with everyone. Have you seen the guy? Women practically fall at his feet. There's no way he'd be interested in someone like me."

Elka's eyes widened. "Yeah, but have you seen the Greek ladies? They can't keep their eyes off him. Everywhere he goes, it's like he's drunk some kind of elixir."

Bree laughed, but it lacked conviction. "Exactly. He's nice—I mean, really nice—but I've seen him turn down so many women. I don't intend to be one of those girls."

"But he's always so polite when he turns them down," Elka giggled, spotting Nik nearby, his attention on Bree as she spoke.

Bree, completely unaware of the way her tanned skin, now-wavy hair, and infectious laugh affected the men around her—especially Nik—felt a small tug at her heart. The heavy perfume of the women who greeted him as they passed by made her pause for a moment, but she quickly shoved the thought away.

The next morning, at the break of dawn, Bree and a few other new reps were sent on an excursion to experience the sixteen-kilometre Samarian Gorge walk. The idea was for them to hike the difficult path firsthand so they could sell it to their guests. Bree woke up with a sense of dread, her body sluggish from too little sleep. She wiped the sleep from her eyes, showered, and threw on some clothes in a hurry before stepping out into the cool, starry night. It was 3 a.m.; she'd had only four hours of sleep. Her body, already exhausted, slumped against the wall as she waited for the lights of the coach to appear.

She dragged herself onto the bus, scanning the faces of the other reps, who were also half-asleep and quiet. A smile didn't come easy, not even for Nik, who would be guiding them that day. She regretted not brushing her hair, having cursed at it in the mirror earlier, and now it lay unkempt on her head.

When Nik's gaze met hers, it softened, a look of silent understanding crossing his face. He saw her tiredness, the way her body slumped from running for the bus, and something in his expression warmed her—comforting, but fleeting.

Bree pulled her jumper over her face and closed her eyes, managing to catch an hour of sleep as the bus rumbled along the winding road.

The day before, Anna had been insistent: "You must wear sturdy shoes. If you don't have any, let me know, and I'll find a pair for you." Panic rushed over her as the bus neared the starting point. She could picture them by the door; she'd tripped over them as she hurried outside.

She hoped the lack of proper footwear would be her ticket out of the grueling, eight-hour hike through the heat, something her exhausted body was desperate to avoid.

As she approached Nik, she threw him a look of perfectly faked dismay, pointing down at her feet—bare except for her Havaiana flip-flops.

Nik said nothing. Turning to the coach, he pulled a pair of walking shoes and socks from his bag and handed them to Bree. "They might be a bit big, but they're better than those flip-flops." He smirked, the warmth in his eyes softening the teasing tone. "I'll walk with you; we can't have you falling and blaming my shoes, can we?"

As promised, Nik stayed by Bree's side the entire hike. They talked and laughed, their easy banter drawing them closer with every step. Occasionally, they caught up with the others, who swiftly walked ahead, leaving the pair alone.

Despite her exhaustion, Bree found herself laughing as the hike slowly came to an end. All she could think about now was a hot shower and collapsing into her bed; her body was aching in every way imaginable.

"Fancy dinner later?" Nik asked as they finished, his tone hopeful.

Bree's eyes widened at the suggestion. She shook her head with a soft laugh. "I'd love to, but can we take a rain check for another day? I'm too tired to sit at a table and make conversation."

Instead of dropping her off first, Nik surprised her by changing the plan and making sure they were alone at the end of the trip. "If I can't take you to dinner, at least let me buy you something to eat," he said, pulling over to a small takeaway sandwich shop.

"Thanks for a great day, Bree," he said, handing her the tightly wrapped sandwich. He gently took her arm as she trudged towards her front door, her small rucksack weighing heavily on her shoulders.

"Great? It was a nightmare," she joked, her smile betraying her words. "Seriously though, thanks for the shoes, the company, and the food. You really saved me today." With a playful wave of the sandwich in the air, she wrapped her arms around him in a spontaneous embrace.

Nik's watched her as she hobbled down the path toward her home, his mind already imagining the stiffness she would feel in two days. The thought made him smile. He knew her well enough to know she'd play it off with that trademark warmth of hers—her smile always made everything feel easier.

Suddenly, Bree turned back, catching his gaze. "Hey, Nik, do you want to eat your sandwich with me?" Her voice was softer now, more tender.

"Yeah, why not? Give me ten minutes to park the bus and grab my car."

Bree moved quickly. She showered, the kettle went on while she scrambled to tidy her small flat, tossing clothes and stray objects into the laundry basket.

Nik's knock at the door pulled her out of her thoughts. She called out for him to come in, and with an awkward, rushed movement, she poured him a cup of tea, spilling most of it onto the saucer. They sat together on the couch, the blanket draped over them despite the warmth of the room. Bree savoured the soft warmth of his breath on her hair, the quiet closeness between them feeling completely natural.

She relaxed into the moment, feeling an unusual peace as her body unwound. Her eyelids fluttered shut, and she was drifting in that hazy space between sleep and wakefulness. When she woke, she was lying flat on the couch, a pillow from her bed carefully placed under her head. Sitting up, she saw the note: "I didn't want to wake you. Good night, and thank you, Nik."

Bree dragged her aching body to bed, clutching the blanket and the note with her. There was something about Nik, something magnetic and unspoken, that lingered in her thoughts long after the night had ended.

Two days later, Bree walked into the office, her steps slowing as she took in the empty desk where Nik's chair used to be. His seat was vacant, his desk cleared. A blue hoodie was forgotten on the back of his chair, the small detail making her heart tighten with an unexpected pang.

13 | Petra

Petra looked at the birthday card she had bought for Liam, a smile growing on her lips as she slipped it into the white envelope. She had planned this day for weeks, determined to shower him with love on his birthday. Nothing—and no one—was going to get in the way of her seeing him. Running her hand over the blue and green gift-wrapped box, she set it down by the bed and began mentally rehearsing her plan for the morning.

Waking early, Petra carefully placed the gift into her rucksack and hired a pushbike from the hotel. She cycled the entire way to Liam's farm, the wind in her hair, each turn of the pedals adding to the thrill that was growing inside her. When she arrived, she parked the bike by a tree and glanced around, looking for a spot where she wouldn't be seen. She caught sight of his silver Mercedes driving past and, with a determined push of her feet, began pedalling faster, pulling up alongside his car.

Grabbing the box from her rucksack, she knocked on the window. Liam's eyes widened in surprise as he rolled it down. "Hello," he said coldly.

"I bought this for you for your birthday," Petra said, stretching out her hand toward him, the box in her grip.

"I can't accept it," Liam replied, pushing the box away.

Petra thrust the parcel toward him again. "But I bought it for you. Please take it—I'm not going to carry it home on the plane again."

Liam shot her an annoyed look, but reluctantly accepted the gift, placing it on his lap.

"Open it," Petra urged, her voice almost pleading. She tossed her bike on the ground, then jumped into the passenger seat and slammed the door behind her.

"Petra, you need to go. My wife may see you," Liam said urgently, glancing outside at the sound of another car approaching. He exhaled in relief as a farmhand parked nearby.

"Orla's at work. I saw her leave." Petra placed her hand on his knee, fingers gently rubbing his thigh. Liam froze, his breath catching. She didn't let up, reaching for the gift and unwrapping it for him. "Look, it's some new gloves for your tractor, and a voucher for a romantic weekend in Paris."

"Petra, I can't take these," Liam said firmly.

"Please, I bought them for you. The trip to Paris is for us." Petra gazed at him through her long lashes, her voice low, almost coaxing.

Liam remained still, shaking his head slowly. "No, Petra. No." He pushed the parcel back onto her lap. "You keep it."

RAW MISTAKES

Desperation flickered in Petra's eyes as she shifted forward, grabbing his hands and pulling him toward her. "I love you. I know you love me too." Her eyes were wild with longing, and she kissed him, her lips pressing against his with a raw, unrestrained intensity.

"No. Petra. Stop it." His voice boomed as he pushed her away with all his strength. He flung open the car door and jumped out. Straightening his tweed jacket, he glared at her. "I'm sorry. I should have told you before you came. I know, but it wasn't until I saw you that I was sure of my decision," he said calmly, though there was a note of regret in his voice.

Petra's face crumpled, disappointment crashing over her like a wave. She swallowed the burning sensation rising in her chest and wrapped her she let her fingers run down his shirt, trembling as they grazed the fabric.

"Petra, don't," Liam said softly, pushing her away again.

"I need closure. You can't do this to me," Petra whimpered, her voice barely a whisper as she looked down, her eyes searching his for any trace of emotion.

Liam glanced at her, his expression conflicted. After a moment, he sighed. "Let's go inside and talk," he suggested, turning toward the house.

Petra followed him into the kitchen, where Liam filled the kettle. She sat in a rickety wooden chair, her eyes glinting with hope and mischief as she waited for him to speak.

"Petra, what do you want me to tell you?" Liam asked, his tone weary as the water splashed around the cups.

"That you made a mistake. That you love me," she replied, walking in a slow circle around the chair, her eyes lingering on the brightly lit car park outside.

"Petra, I'm sorry. I didn't meet you thinking I'd get back with my wife. It just happened," he explained, his voice steady but filled with regret.

"Okay, that makes more sense." Petra nodded, her face unreadable. She took a step closer to him, but Liam instinctively moved away, his body tense. She ignored the distance and stepped toward him, gently placing a hand on his chest. "Oh, baby, please. Just look at me," she begged, her voice soft.

Liam hesitated, his glance shifting from her eyes to the floor and back again. After a long moment, he surprised even himself when his hand instinctively reached behind her neck, pulling her closer. The kiss was sudden and unthinking, more a release of everything he'd been holding back than any conscious decision. It wasn't full of longing but rather a reckless impulse, an uncontrollable act driven by the sheer intensity of the moment.

"Not here," Liam muttered suddenly, pulling back. He turned quickly, striding down the dusty corridor and flinging open a bedroom door. Petra followed him inside, glancing around at the neat, tidy room. The bed was made, the curtains tightly drawn, the atmosphere heavy with tension.

Liam pushed her toward the bed, and Petra quickly undressed. He folded his work clothes and placed them on a chair before joining her on the bed. His hands roamed over her body with a rough passion, pressing himself against her, his mouth capturing hers with a hungry urgency.

An hour later, Petra, content but with a hollow ache in her chest, glanced over at Liam. He was sitting in an old armchair, his expression unreadable.

"What are you doing there?" she asked sleepily. "Come back to bed."

"Petra, you've had your closure," he replied coldly, his voice hurried and distant. Before she could protest, he slammed the door behind him as he left the room.

Petra sat on the bed, her hands trembling as she pulled on her clothes. Numbness crept over her as she rushed down the corridor. She reached the kitchen and spotted her shoes by the door. Panic flared inside her as she grabbed them, her gaze darting around, searching for Liam.

The eyes of the farmworkers lingered on her, making her feel exposed in her torn shirt. She forced the fabric closed, offering a weak half-smile before looking at the car. The key dangled from the ignition. Without thinking, Petra slid into the driver's seat, turned the key, and sped off, her tyres kicking up a cloud of gravel dust as she left Liam's farm behind.

14 | Petra

Parking the car at the hotel, Petra grabbed her phone from her tiny bag and stared at a message from Liam."You stole my car. I want it back."

She quickly typed a reply: "I didn't steal it; I borrowed it to get home. My shirt was ripped, and I couldn't cycle home like that."

His reply was swift: "Okay, sorry, I understand."

"Thanks for today; it was nice," she typed, hesitating before adding a kissing emoji. The conversation quickly escalated as she promised to return the car later and collect her bike. "I'm having a birthday dinner later at home, so please bring it before five," Liam insisted. "I don't want to have to explain where my car is to my wife."

Petra read the message multiple times, her fingers tightening around her phone. She snorted at his concern over his wife and not her, and ignored the beeping phone as she jumped into the shower, then spent a lazy afternoon basking in the sun on her balcony.

At eight o'clock, Petra parked Liam's car on a suburban street near his house. The driveway was lined with cars, and music spilled out from inside. She knocked on the door, which opened easily, and stepped into the bustling house. Vases of flowers lined the tables, and laughter echoed from the kitchen. Petra grabbed a drink from a nearby table and sipped the chilled champagne. Her eyes scanned the room, landing on Liam. As soon as he saw her, his face darkened.

His blood pressure spiked as he approached her, grabbing her arm and pulling her aside. "What are you doing here?" he scowled, his eyebrows gathered, waiting for an answer.

"I've returned your car," Petra said, holding up the keys. She shook them in front of him, but Liam snatched them away, placing them on a nearby shelf. Two guests slowed as they passed, casting curious glances at the pair. Liam forced a smile and tried to regain his composure.

Petra, ignoring the tension, slipped further into the house, following a lady in a tan coat. She grabbed a few prawns off a platter and popped them onto her plate, but Liam caught her arm again, spinning her around. His voice was low, almost a growl. "You need to leave. Now."

Petra shot him a sharp look, wrenched her arm free, and then—on a sudden impulse—picked up a tall glass vase and turned it upside down, spilling water onto the rich, dark carpet. Liam's hand shot out to grab the vase, but his focus fell to the now-crushed white roses scattered on the floor. Petra's eyes locked with his as she pushed past him, grabbed the keys from the shelf, and held them up.

"Give me a lift, or I'll take the car," she hissed.

Liam opened the door, his face pale with frustration. Petra stood her ground, fury building.

"Get a taxi," he spat, his voice cold. He pulled twenty euros from his pocket and shoved it into her hand.

"No. Give me a lift, or I'll take the car," she retorted, her voice dripping with venom. "You have no idea what I can do. I've been studying your wife. I know her every move—it's my new obsession."

Liam's eyes darted around the room, and for a moment, he looked defeated. He seized Petra by the arms, shoving her toward the door. "You're crazy. Leave us alone," he muttered, his voice heavy with finality. He stood so close she could barely breathe.

Liam slammed the door behind her, but Petra didn't leave. She lingered on the doorstep, eyes blazing. Moments later, Orla appeared in the doorway, bending down to gather the scattered flowers.

"What happened here?" she asked, gently picking up the petals.

"Oh, I knocked it over," Liam muttered, crouching to help her. "I was about to clean it up."

"Please be more careful," Orla said with a smile, bending to kiss him on the cheek.

An hour passed. Liam glanced at the clock before noticing Petra's tall figure lurking at the edge of the driveway, hidden partially by the weeping willow trees. He saw her approach the window and heard the soft tap on the glass. He quickly drew the curtains, then stepped outside, arms folded tightly across his chest.

From the corner of his eye, he saw Petra climb into a taxi. She didn't break eye contact, her gaze intense. She pushed her head out the window and mouthed, "See you soon."

15 | Nina

Nina's idyllic childhood shattered into pieces on a foggy, drizzly day, when she was fourteen. What should have been a normal walk home from school with her cousin in Monza, an industrial town in the north of Italy, was anything but routine. It was a walk Nina had taken a hundred times before, always with the comforting rhythm of familiarity. Every day after school, she'd walk Julia to her house first, then race the last few hundred metres home alone, feeling the pulse of the world moving around her.

Fabio, Nina's older brother, had long ago found endless excuses to avoid walking them home, dismissing them as "annoying children." The dry orange leaves crunched beneath their feet as Nina pulled up the collar on her raincoat, feeling the damp air bite at her skin. She linked arms with Julia, their usual routine, as they crossed the stretch of rural road, the cold air biting into their skin as the weak sun dipped below the horizon.

"Hey, girls, you look cold," a husky voice called out from a dirty station wagon. The words hung in the air like a sinister cloud. Nina's stomach lurched, and her instincts screamed at her to be wary. She turned quickly, her eyes darting around as she searched for the source of the voice, feeling a ripple of unease spread through her. She didn't know why, but something about that voice felt wrong, thick with a strange, unsettling undertone.

A man stuck his hand out of the window, his fingers beckoning them in a way that made Nina's skin crawl. "Over here," he called, his voice unnervingly deep and rough. He was a bulky, tanned man with a white, stubbly beard and greasy hair, combed over too far from one side. His eyes were dark, deep-set and piercing. He stared at them with a look that felt too calculating, too predatory. Nina's heart hammered in her chest as she froze, caught between instinct and the fear of escalating the situation.

She turned to Julia, her voice barely a whisper. "Ignore him. Let's go." Her voice trembled despite her best efforts to stay composed. She tugged at Julia's jacket, urging her to hurry along, her pulse quickening with every step they took. But the sound of the car followed them, growing closer. The engine roared to life, revving ominously, sending a shiver down Nina's spine. It was as though the world had narrowed down to that single moment, the air heavy with dread.

"Put your head down and run," Nina whispered urgently, her grip tightening on Julia's arm as they broke into a frantic sprint. But the car wasn't giving up, its engine still chasing them, the sound of tyres skidding closer. Each second felt like a lifetime as they raced down the road, the trees lining their path thick and menacing, offering no escape.

And then, the sharp, blood-curdling scream. "Nina, help!" Julia's voice sliced through the air, raw and filled with panic. Nina's blood ran cold as she whipped around, horror seizing her heart. She saw the man, now out of the car, his hands wrapped around Julia's waist with terrifying ease. He yanked her away from Nina, his strength inhuman. The car door slammed open, and he shoved Julia inside like a rag doll, her body limp against his assault.

Everything inside Nina froze, her thoughts scattered, her body paralyzed with fear. She couldn't breathe, couldn't think—just an overwhelming rush of adrenaline coursing through her. Instinctively, she ran towards the car, her fists pounding against the door, begging, pleading for it to open, her voice cracking as she screamed. But before she could make any impact, a strong hand grabbed her from behind, pulling her back with unnatural force. Panic exploded in her chest as another pair of hands shoved her into the car. She hit the cold floor with a sickening thud, her breath knocked from her lungs.

For a moment, everything was dark, her chest heaving as she tried to orient herself. She reached out with trembling fingers, desperately searching the shadows until she felt Julia's small, trembling hand brush against hers. Their fingers intertwined in the dark, and Nina squeezed so hard her knuckles burned. She didn't let go—not even when the car lurched forward, throwing her body against the unyielding floor.

A damp, scratchy material was shoved over her head, and her heart pounded faster, the air suddenly too thick, too suffocating. She fought to stay calm, listening for anything that could guide her. The muffled purr of the engine was the only sound as it faded in and out, the smell of stale smoke and the car's musty interior filling her nose. She counted the turns, feeling each shift of the vehicle's tyres beneath her, the grinding of gravel, the slowing of speed as they approached some unknown destination.

The car came to an abrupt stop, its engine falling silent. The door opened with an unsettling creak, and Nina was yanked out by her legs, scraping her skin painfully on the rough ground. The stone beneath her back was sharp, cold—grating against her raw skin as she was dragged across the rough surface. Her head hit the ground with a sickening thud, sending a jolt of pain through her skull. Her vision blurred, and for a moment, she could taste the coppery tang of blood in her mouth. She couldn't think, could barely process the sheer brutality of the situation.

Her screams were muffled, swallowed by the shock and pain as she was pulled into an unlit, unfamiliar building. The door slammed shut behind them, the click of the deadbolt ringing in her ears like a death knell. Silence pressed in from all sides, thick and suffocating, her heartbeat thudding loudly in her chest as she struggled to push herself up.

"Julia," she called, her voice trembling with fear, weak from the shock and pain.

A harsh slap across her face sent her reeling, knocking her back against the stone wall. Her hand flew instinctively to her cheek, the sting sharp and burning. "Julia," she cried again, her voice cracking with desperation.

Then, the door opened again, and Julia was thrown inside the room, her body sliding painfully across the floor toward Nina. Every inch of Nina's body screamed to reach her, to hold her, to shield her from whatever horrors they were about to face. She scrambled toward her cousin, tearing the bag off her head, her fingers frantic as she tried to uncover the girl's face.

Julia's eyes were wide with terror, her breath ragged. But when she saw Nina, it was like the air in the room shifted. Julia lunged into her arms, her body trembling violently as she clung to Nina with a desperation that mirrored her own.

Nina held Julia tightly, pressing her cheek to her cousin's trembling face. She could feel Julia's shallow breath against her skin, the strain of their fear pressing down on them both. The door slammed shut behind them, followed by the unmistakable sound of the lock turning. The finality of the click sent a chilling wave down Nina's spine. She held Julia tighter, as though by sheer force of will she could shield them from whatever horror awaited.

The room was suffocating, an oppressive darkness that seemed to swallow any glimmer of hope. The stone floor beneath them sent icy fingers of cold through Nina's bones, her muscles aching from the tension that coiled tighter with every passing second. She pulled Julia toward the couch, its frame battered and broken, a grim, hollow place to rest. They sank onto it, a faint moonbeam slipping through the high, small window above, but it barely offered any comfort—only the cruel reminder of how far out of reach the light was.

A voice broke through the silence, low and guttural, coming from the other side of the door. "Girls, be quiet. Otherwise, we'll kill you."

The words cut through Nina like a blade. Her blood ran cold, and her heart dropped into her stomach. She clutched Julia even tighter, her fingers digging into her cousin's fragile frame, afraid that even the smallest sound might tip them over the edge into the unthinkable. She held her breath, not daring to move. The sound of heavy boots retreating echoed down the corridor, and Nina exhaled shakily as the key turned in the lock again, leaving them once more in unbearable silence.

Julia trembled in Nina's arms, her body stiff and trembling with fear. Nina stroked her hair gently, whispering in a voice that shook almost as much as her hands, "Shh, it'll be okay. Just stay quiet. We'll be okay."

Julia's tear-streaked face turned towards her, her silent nod breaking Nina's heart even more. There was no comfort in this place, no safety. The darkness pressed in from all sides, suffocating them both.

Hours passed like years, each minute stretching into eternity. Nina's eyelids grew heavy, but she fought the pull of exhaustion, knowing that even a moment's lapse in vigilance could mean the end. The stillness was unnerving, broken only by the distant sound of boots crunching on the stone floor. The door creaked open, and a pair of hands shoved a bottle of water and stale bread through the crack.

The door slammed shut again with a sickening thud.

Nina's hands trembled as she reached for the bottle, instinctively checking the seal before handing it to Julia. She pressed the cold plastic into her cousin's hands. "Drink," she whispered, her voice hoarse from the tension that had built up in her chest. But when her eyes fell on the bread, her stomach twisted in revulsion. The bread was old, the edges dry and cracked. She pushed it away, her throat tight as she whispered, "No, I don't trust it."

The two girls huddled together on the couch, trying to preserve whatever warmth they could, but exhaustion clung to them both. Their limbs were heavy, their eyes fluttering shut for a moment, but the silence was shattered when a voice, gruff and demanding, called from the door.

Nina leapt to her feet, her body instinctively shielding Julia. Her heart hammered in her chest, and the blood drained from her face as she stared at the man standing in the doorway. His presence loomed large and menacing, and she felt as though the room itself had grown smaller, suffocating her.

"How old are you?" he asked, his voice thick with something dark, his gaze roaming over her like a predator sizing up its prey.

"Fourteen," Nina replied, forcing the words out, even as her voice cracked with fear, trying to sound defiant, but failing miserably.

"And her?" he sneered, turning his face to Julia.

"Eleven," Nina whispered, her chest tightening as she looked down at her cousin. Every word she spoke felt like a betrayal to Julia. It was as if she were offering her up on a silver platter.

The man turned to his partner, muttering something in a harsh language Nina couldn't understand. Then he turned back to her, his eyes narrowing with calculation, as if weighing her worth, considering what to do with her.

"You're too old," he said, his words cold and dismissive. "We don't need you. Your friend... we want her."

Nina's stomach lurched violently, a sick feeling spreading through her. The world spun around her, and she fought to keep her voice steady as she spoke, the desperation in her words unmistakable. "Take me," she urged, her voice a desperate plea. "Please, take me. Don't hurt her. Let her go. I'll do whatever you want. Just don't touch her."

The men exchanged a glance, their eyes flickering between Nina and Julia. The older man grinned, a slow, predatory smile that sent a wave of panic crashing through Nina's body. Without another word, he reached for Julia, grabbing her roughly by the arms, dragging her toward the door with frightening ease.

Nina's world collapsed. Her body screamed at her to act, to do something, anything, to stop this nightmare from happening. She lunged forward, her hands gripping at the man's arms, pulling desperately, her voice breaking as she screamed, "No. Let her go. Please. Let her go."

The other man yanked Julia away with a strength that knocked Nina back, and she could do nothing but watch as they dragged her cousin out of the room. Julia's terrified, panicked cries rang in Nina's ears, but her hands were useless, her body useless. She slammed her fists against the door, her sobs raw, her throat burning as she screamed until her voice gave out.

But it was no use. The door slammed shut, sealing Julia's fate, and Nina crumpled against it, her chest heaving with sobs. Tears streamed down her face, dripping onto the stone floor, mixing with the dirt, as she sobbed, the sound of her own despair echoing in the empty, cruel silence that surrounded them.

16 | Nina

The days blurred together, one indistinguishable from the next. Nina realised that if she remained silent, she would receive something that vaguely resembled food and water. But if she made a sound, she would be left alone in the suffocating darkness of the room with nothing. The window had been boarded up the morning after they arrived, and now, darkness was her only company. The distant sound of revving engines and voices—laughter, shouting—drifted in from outside.

Her mind kept circling back to Julia, who hadn't been seen since they dragged her away. She tried to reach out mentally, hoping to sense her cousin's energy, but there was nothing—just the hollow stillness of the room. Occasionally, a door would creak open, and people would enter her space, glance at her, then leave without a word. When they were gone, Nina would slump back onto the sofa, hugging her knees to her chest, rocking herself as if the motion could quiet her thoughts.

Her fingers traced her face, where the freckled softness of her youthful cheeks had faded, leaving sharp cheekbones that had grown more pronounced. Her long, mousy brown hair was hacked off crudely by one of her captors, the uneven edges a reminder of the brutality that had stolen her identity. She barely recognised the reflection in her mind anymore.

Nina had learned the routine of the two men who held her captive. Each night, as the light filtering through the slats of the boarded-up window began to fade, the men would leave together, laughing and joking. Hours later, she would hear the soft sound of car engines and the voices of women, followed by the gradual hush of the house. It had been two weeks, maybe more. Nina woke each morning, grateful to be alive, yet dreading the continuation of this unrelenting captivity. The men never seemed interested in her, just parading her in front of their friends with smug grins.

"Too old," one man had said as he inspected her. "No use to me," another muttered in English, scowling before walking away. Panic flooded Nina's chest at his words. Julia was only eleven. The thought of what might be happening to her cousin was unbearable.

One evening, the men didn't leave. Instead, a procession of cars pulled up outside, the sound of music filling the room beneath the crack of the door. The pungent smell of rubber and exhaust fumes crept in through the vents. Nina's mouth went dry, her body tensing in the cramped corner where she stood. She dreaded what new visitors might want, and whether they'd find her young enough for whatever twisted desires they had.

Then, the soft laughter of female voices floated through the crack under the door, followed by the loud cackle of one woman. Nina's heart sank as the door opened, and a woman in a leopard-print dress stepped inside, red lipstick smudged at the corners of her mouth. Her wild hair and revealing outfit made Nina's skin crawl. The men dragged Nina out of her corner, forcing her to stand in front of the sofa as the woman eyed her up and down.

"She's pretty," the woman said, glancing at Nina. She turned to the men, her voice dripping with curiosity. "How much?"

"We'll talk outside," one man replied, his smile widening, making Nina's stomach twist with fear. The woman looked back at her for a second, then followed the men out, leaving Nina standing still, frozen in fear.

After a long moment, Nina returned to the sofa, shifting nervously, hoping sleep would take over, even though her heart refused to slow.

The next morning, she woke to the sound of heels clicking in the hallway. "Nina Ruggero?" a voice called, and Nina's head jerked up. She replied cautiously, unsure of what would happen if she confirmed or denied her identity.

"Yes," she murmured, her voice barely above a whisper.

A tray was set down in front of her, the woman with the heels tapping the spoon against the plate. "Here's your food," she said confidently, her eyes scanning Nina's face. "Eat."

Nina's hand trembled as she reached for the steaming plate of goulash, the rich smell making her mouth water. She stepped back to the sofa and hungrily scooped up a spoonful. It tasted better than she expected, comforting in a way that almost made her forget where she was.

The woman lingered for a moment, her eyes darting nervously. "I'll help you escape," she whispered, glancing at the door as though someone might hear. "I'll leave the door unlocked later, but after that, it's up to you." Her voice dropped to a conspiratorial tone. "When I open the door, you need to run. Run as fast and as far as you can."

Nina's heart leaped. She could hardly breathe as she looked up at the woman, eyes wide with hope. All she could manage was a shaky "okay," offering a grateful nod.

The woman turned and left, locking the door behind her. Nina didn't return to the couch this time. She sat up against the cold metal door, straining to hear any sounds that might signal her escape. The minutes stretched into eternity.

She finished every last bite of the goulash, the hunger pangs that had plagued her for so long finally easing. As the night deepened, the house grew silent—no more cars, no more laughter. Nina felt her hope slip away, replaced by a cold anguish of uncertainty. Her eyes stung with the threat of tears, but she blinked them away, determined not to show weakness.

Suddenly, the door rattled. Nina's heart leaped into her throat as the key turned slowly in the lock. This was different—softer, unsure. It wasn't the usual quick twist; this was tentative, like a heartbeat in the dark.

Her breath quickened, every muscle tensed. As the door creaked open, a shadow moved past the gap. Nina's body shot to its feet. This was it. Time to act.

17 | Carla

Carla was just eighteen when she decided to hit the road, leaving her dysfunctional family behind. She had no doubt that they loved her—maybe a little too much. Their love was like a blanket—suffocating, knitted with expectations. They were obsessed with her education, her acceptance into the best universities, and the life she would lead. They had her whole future mapped out: she'd follow in her father's footsteps, become a doctor, marry, have kids, get two dogs, and holiday in the Bahamas and Italy, just like the family had done when she was little.

Their house was larger than the others on the street, the kind of house where the front lawn looked like it belonged on a gardening show. Her father spent every spare moment landscaping—probably because it was the only thing he could control. The weekend patio parties were the neighbourhood's social event, complete with cucumber sandwiches and lawn games. The maze in their garden was the envy of Carla's childhood friends. They'd race through it, shrieking and laughing, trying to beat each other out of the tall hedges like characters in a bizarre episode of Survivor. But now, those same gardens felt more like a gilded cage. From her bay window, Carla would stare beyond them, her eyes fixated on the distant lights of the city. The future? It was anywhere but here.

Carla had always felt like a disappointing project to her parents—a work in progress that wasn't quite measuring up. Their unrealistic expectations pushed her further away, and by the time she was a teenager, the nagging and complaints about her grades turned her into a rebellious caricature in their eyes. They never understood that she wasn't trying to ruin their plans. She just didn't want to be their little project.

Her brother, Charlie, was the golden child. His dark curly hair, pale skin, and squashed face—like a bulldog—made him impossible to criticise. He excelled at school, and no doubt, he'd do everything they ever dreamed of. As twins, they should've shared a special bond, but that bond was more like an unspoken competition. They didn't exactly play the part of the cute, inseparable siblings you see in movies. In fact, they treated each other with the kind of disdain usually reserved for distant cousins at family reunions. And they couldn't have looked less alike. Carla, tall and full of energy, with her curvy figure and black curls, looked like she belonged on a beach in the Mediterranean. Charlie, on the other hand, looked like a frog—if frogs had dark curly hair and pale skin, that is.

The day after her eighteenth birthday, Carla started her first job. She was so sick of hearing, "While you live under our roof, you follow our rules," she could've recited it in her sleep. She quickly found herself at the local pub, The Vernon Arms, slinging drinks and washing glasses. It wasn't glamorous, but it paid the bills.

Within two months, Carla had saved enough for a place to rent with three other girls. The house wasn't much—a tiny, damp place with walls as thin as paper and carpets that looked like they'd seen better days in a previous century. The fake marble kitchen countertops were so stained they looked like they'd been in a crime scene. But to Carla, it was perfect. The washing-up rota was completely ignored, and the Hoover had more dust on it than the floor, but she didn't care. The room she claimed as her own was her sanctuary. The shelves were neatly stacked, the books arranged by size and her clothes—pressed and perfectly stored away—looked like they belonged in a catalogue. She was saving up to move out again. This place was temporary—just like her parents' plans for her life.

One day, she stepped over a half-packed suitcase in the lounge and realised one of her housemates had returned from somewhere—or perhaps was about to leave. Either way, she didn't care. The smell of unemptied bins hit her like a brick wall. She held her breath- she'd be out of there soon.

A few months later, Carla felt an overwhelming thrill as she handed her hard-earned cash to a used car dealer. She drove away in a blue, rusted Austin Metro—her Austin Metro, despite the fact it looked like it had survived a minor hurricane. The red key fob felt like a treasure in her hand. She glanced at the dealer in the rearview mirror, then, once she was out of sight, gripped the steering wheel and kissed it like it was a long-lost love.

"Hello, Austy," she murmured, stroking the dashboard like it was the most precious thing she'd ever held. "Nice to meet you. I'm going to take good care of you."

18 | Carla

A year after driving away in her beloved Austy, Carla scraped ice from the windshield with a credit card. She pulled an extra pair of gloves over her already cold hands and shoved a hat over her ears. She couldn't help but be surprised that the engine still roared to life when she turned the key. She adjusted the cushion under her behind, trying to tame the protruding spring in the driver's seat, then set off to work, her breath fogging the air like a miniature cloud.

Blowing on her gloves, hoping to somehow heat them through the thick fabric, Carla jolted as the car lurched forward with a loud bang. She squinted through the foggy windshield, cursing under her breath as a slow stream of smoke seeped out from under the bonnet. As the traffic lights turned green, she slid out of the seat with an exaggerated sigh and ran her fingers through her black curls, muttering a few choice words for the drivers who honked and shouted at her.

"Yeah, keep honking, I'm sure you'll get to your meeting with a smile on your face," she mumbled sarcastically as the traffic backed up behind her, a symphony of frustrated beeps ringing in her ears.

As she pried open the door—praying the rusty hinges wouldn't betray her—she heard a voice.

"Carla, need some help?" The voice was recognisable, but it was just distant enough that she had to squint to make out the figure approaching her car.

She groaned, rolling her eyes. Of course it's him.

Johnny. The barman from her work with the opposite of a self-love problem. He cracked the window just enough to let out a cloud of smoke.

"You reckon?" Carla shot back, her arms flung out in a dramatic gesture that screamed 'please, leave me alone.'

To her surprise, Johnny didn't just wave and drive off like most people would. No, he got out with all the swagger of a man who'd recently taken a selfie with a mirror and liked it. He pulled a woollen hat over his thick hair and popped the bonnet of her car like it was some kind of challenging puzzle to solve.

Carla rested against the frame of the car, arms crossed, watching as Johnny fiddled with the engine. His confidence was the kind you'd expect from someone who considered himself the king of the world, especially at The Vernon Arms. Maybe he thinks he's saving the damsel in distress, she thought with a smirk.

"I wanted to call my dad," Carla admitted, kicking the front tyre with frustration, "but he'll just give me a lecture about how I never should've bought this thing. He never wanted me to get a car that wasn't... new.. or whatever."

Johnny glanced at her, his eyes flashing with that self-assuredness, though it was something like real concern. "Look," he said, "if you call work and let them know we're going to be late, I'll sort this out." He moved quickly, heading for the boot of his massive black Ford GT, a car that looked like it could eat her Austin Metro for breakfast.

Carla watched him tie a tow rope to her car's undercarriage. "Ready? Get in the car, put your hazard lights on, and don't forget to make engine noises—really helps with the vibe," he laughed, his voice dripping with the smugness of a man who thought his charm could fix anything, including her broken-down car.

Johnny towed her to the nearest garage. Carla watched from the sidelines as Johnny talked to the mechanic, gesturing with wild enthusiasm toward Rusty, her beloved car. She rubbed her hands together, trying to keep warm as Johnny's charisma took centre stage.

The mechanic came back, wiping grease off his face and through his slicked-back hair. He pulled out a scribbled notebook and started droning on about the state of the car.

Carla listened, barely holding back a sigh.

The mechanic finally broke the silence. "This car's heading to the junkyard, lady," he said, crossing his arms. "It'll cost you more to fix it than it's worth."

Carla stared at him, blinking in disbelief. She turned to Johnny, as though he were some kind of miracle worker who could sort this out. "What now?" she asked, feeling a bit more defeated than she'd like to admit.

Johnny, however, didn't even flinch. "Get us a quote," he told the mechanic with a casual wave of his hand, "and we'll decide." He wasn't phased, though Carla felt the panic start to rise in her chest.

The mechanic sighed dramatically, clearly uninterested in negotiating. "I've told you. This car's done for. Anything more and you're wasting your money. That's my quote." He stood up, dismissing them with a flick of his wrist.

"We'll be back tomorrow with our decision," Johnny said, leading Carla out of the garage.

Carla, feeling completely out of sorts, threw the trash—empty sandwich boxes, cigarette packets, and bottles—into the back seat of Johnny's car. She swished her hand over the seat fabric, silently cursing herself for ever getting attached to Austy.

Sinking into the seat, she glanced out the window, her thoughts spiralling. The stale smell of smoke lingered in the air, and the quiet purr of Johnny's engine only reminded her of how little she had in her bank account. She couldn't afford a new car, not even another wreck like Austy. Panic hit her like a cold wave, and she slumped deeper into the seat, staring blankly ahead.

Up until that morning, she had nothing but contempt for Johnny who spent most of his time flirting with anyone who could still hear him over his own ego. He was a walking cliche—a man who could bat his eyelashes at anyone within a five-foot radius, regardless of age. The pub staff had made him the running joke. Carla had seen him work his charm on every new barmaid that walked in. *He probably thinks his eyebrows have magical powers*, she thought, rolling her eyes.

But here he was, helping her. And oddly enough, for all his swagger, she was grateful for him. She hated it, but she couldn't deny it.

She thought back to her conversation a few days earlier when Johnny had said, "Hey, Carla, babe, loving those curls. How about whipping them all over my naked chest tonight?"

"I'll save you the trimmings next time I go to the hairdresser, then you can do whatever you like with it," she'd retorted, spinning on her heel and strutting away, her black curls bouncing over her shoulders.

Johnny had always been a drain on her energy, and she'd learned to walk away, shaking her head in disbelief at his audacity.

But now, sitting in the car, she realised Johnny the barman was just an act—a persona he put on for the world. There was nothing showy or insincere about the man beside her now. He sat calm, competent, and unguarded, his usual arrogance replaced with quiet authority.

After a moment, he spoke, his voice soft but somehow more commanding. "Carla, don't worry. I've moved out of the pub. I'm on your estate now. I can give you a lift to work every day until you sort this out, if you want."

"You'd do that?" she asked, her smile wide with a surprise and something else she couldn't quite place.

"That's the smile I like to see," he said, grinning, clearly pleased. "It's just a car, a little bump in the road. You'll sort it."

For the next few weeks, Johnny did exactly that. When their shifts didn't line up, he left his car for her. "I'll borrow my dad's, don't worry," he'd say, tossing his keys into her bag like it was nothing.

"And have him tell you, 'I told you so'?" Johnny laughed.

"Good point. Thanks, I'll take you up on that offer," Carla replied.

On these drives, their conversations shifted. Johnny stopped flirting, stopped being the cocky barman with endless cheesy pick-up lines. Instead, he became... well, not just a nice guy, but someone she could talk to without rolling her eyes.

Carla couldn't deny it—he'd cleaned up his act, and she found herself looking forward to their drives. It wasn't just the convenience; it was his newly sharp jawline and the warm, inviting smile he seemed to wear more often these days.

His mission now was clear: get Carla a car. "I've found you one. It's a steal," he said one misty morning, practically bouncing with excitement as he pulled up.

Her eyes lit up. "Really? How much?" she asked, already knowing she didn't have the cash for anything, even if it was a "steal."

"A thousand pounds, but trust me, it's worth it," Johnny said with enthusiasm. "It's a friend of my mum's. She's losing her sight, can't drive anymore. You know how it is. She wants it to go to a good home, and I've told her about you. It's worth about five grand."

"Thanks, Johnny, but I can't afford even that," Carla said, a little embarrassed. "I'll have to start taking the bus. I can't keep asking you for lifts. You've been more than kind."

Johnny's voice cut through her thoughts. "How much can you afford?" he asked, pulling up outside her house. He glanced at the peeling paint and the overgrown garden but said nothing. Just waiting.

"About six hundred quid," she muttered, a little defeated.

Johnny cleared his throat, his eyes narrowing slightly as he processed her words. "Okay. You pay five hundred, and I'll lend you the rest. You can pay me back a little at a time. How does that sound?"

Carla hesitated, her hand already halfway to the door handle. "Well, I guess I should see it first," she said, her voice softening. "But if I like it, yeah, that could work." She reached over and touched his arm, staring at him for a moment. "See, you're not so bad when you're not being a creep." The words hit her before she could stop them, and immediately, guilt stung her.

Johnny raised an eyebrow. "Come on, surely you know I have to hide how magnificent I am." He chuckled, pulling up his leather jacket collar like a rockstar.

Carla had to laugh as she shook her head. This guy had more self-confidence than anyone she'd ever met. She swung her legs out of the car, wrapping her jumper tighter around her shoulders. "Thanks, Johnny. I'll owe you big time if this works out." Her eyebrows lifted in genuine surprise as she shut the door.

Carla stood on the driveway, waiting for Johnny to pull up with the new car. As he arrived, his arm waved out of the window, a proud grin plastered across his face. The curtains on a nearby window twitched, and a voice from inside shouted, "I'll put the kettle on, my dears."

"This is it," Johnny said with all the pride of a man presenting a prize. He stroked the roof of the freshly polished car, watching Carla's hands fly up to cover her growing smile. "Told you, a bargain."

The winter sun glinted off the silver roof, and Carla inhaled deeply, relishing the un scent of a brand-new car. She absentmindedly tugged at the plastic still covering the Ford logo, her fingers brushing against it as if she could already feel the vehicle's history unfolding beneath her touch. Johnny circled the car, running his fingers over its smooth surface with exaggerated care.

"No rust at all," he declared, his voice filled with mock seriousness as Carla slid into the driver's seat, her hand gliding over the dashboard in gentle appreciation.

"Don't forget the engine noises," he teased, laughing heartily.

Carla's eyes wandered beyond the car, drawn to the landscaped gardens of the house. A frail woman stood by the door, tightening a black wrap around her shoulders, her curious gaze fixed on them. The gardens, with their carefully trimmed bushes, tall pine trees, and perfectly mowed lawns, reminded Carla of her childhood—of the secret spots where she'd hidden as a teenager, trying to smoke a cigarette without getting caught.

"I'll take it," Carla called out, her voice carrying around the corner. The elderly woman, her grey hair matching the colour of the car, smiled warmly and patted her hair. She waved them inside for a hot drink, her gratitude for the company clear.

After handing over the cash the following day and stepping back outside,

Carla felt the weight in her shoulders ease, her body relaxing in a way it hadn't in a long time. She threw Johnny a grateful glance, her smile soft but genuine.

Two days later, insurance documents in hand, Johnny dropped her off to pick up the car. As she gathered her things, he turned to her, his tone quieter than usual. "Okay, Carla, since I'm not driving you to work anymore, how about I take you out for dinner instead?" He scanned her face, a hint of vulnerability in his eyes, and his usual bravado seemed to slip away for a moment. "I'm really going to miss our chats."

Carla raised an eyebrow, a smile tugging at the corners of her mouth. "Sure, but if I'm paying, it's going to be fish and chips. After all, I just bought a new car, you know?" she teased.

Johnny's face lit up with delight, a laugh escaping him as he relaxed into the moment. "Exactly. I'll pay. You pick when, and I'll book the table," he said with a saucy glimmer in his eyes.

Carla watched him lean back, a calm satisfaction in his posture that was un but not unwelcome. Her eyes narrowed slightly, her confusion momentarily winning out. She couldn't quite place it—the kindness, the attention—it was all new, and she wasn't sure how to react.

19 | Carla

Carla opened the car door and hung an air freshener around the mirror. Inhaling the vanilla scent, she slid into her seat, giving the interior a critical once-over. She pulled the chair into position, adjusted her mirrors, and gave a dramatic sigh as she introduced herself to the car.

"I'm Carla, and I'll think of a name for you soon. We're going to have a long and happy life together. I'll look after you as best I can... until you break down on me, that is." She turned the key, admiring the soft purring of the engine, and couldn't help but miss the sickly-sweet sound of the Austy, recently sent to the bashers.

Johnny arranged to take her to Manchester City Centre for their first date. A sly grin crossed his face when she opened the door to greet him.

Carla's curly hair had been straightened—though not quite straightened enough, it seemed, to hide the defiant flick at the ends—and it gently caressed the middle of her back. Her makeup was subtle, her jewellery practically non-existent, and her jeans, with a heel, made her legs look suspiciously longer. The yellow shirt peeking from under her denim jacket said, "I'm casual, but I still have standards."

"Don't say anything; I don't want to hear your creepy comments," she warned, flashing him a cold, almost professional stare.

"No, just that you look... hot—sorry, I mean, really nice," he said, glancing elsewhere for a second.

He felt the biting cold on his face, realising it was probably time to grow up and invest in a coat that didn't scream 'midlife crisis'. Johnny threw his jacket over him, took Carla's arm, and walked her up the steps, praying he wouldn't freeze to death.

The soft scent of lemongrass welcomed them into the Thai restaurant. The space was sleek and modern, and the menus looked as foreign as the food. Johnny glanced at her, perplexed, as he asked, "Do you think we should ask for some help ordering? I have no idea what any of this stuff is."

"Definitely," she said, not missing a beat.

Johnny fiddled with his drink, looking nervously at the diners around him who were happily devouring food without nearly as much as a second thought. Only one red-faced man was wafting the menu in front of his face, gulping iced water and loosening his tie.

"Oh yes, I love spicy food; the hotter, the better," Johnny replied confidently to the waitress, who asked how spicy they wanted their food.

"Not for me; I want mild, please," Carla chirped in.

"Are you sure?" the waitress asked. "Really spicy? We use flaming hot chilies."

Johnny nodded confidently and muttered, "Yes."

The waitress quickly disappeared through a white door, wafting curry smells behind her as if she knew exactly what was coming.

Ten minutes later, Johnny stared greedily at his food, trying to act tough.

"Spicy Khua Kling," said the waitress, a hint of laughter in her eye. "Please, enjoy."

"I will, rest assured," Johnny replied, studying the dry, pasty curry topped with lemongrass, spur chili, and kaffir lime leaves. He smiled at his dish like it was his personal conquest, fishing around with his spoon. He eyed the dish before picking up his fork and mixing the striking greens with the rice.

The strong scent wafted around his face, and he quickly shoved the first mouthful into his mouth, swallowing it down. His eyes opened wide as he flapped his hands in front of his mouth, his face glowing red.

"Are you okay? Are you choking?" Carla asked with a deadpan expression, her lips twitching with the tiniest hint of enjoyment.

He shook his head, managing only two words: "Too spicy." He reached for the water, splashing droplets on the crisp tablecloth before gulping it down.

"Shall I ask the chef to make the next course less spicy?" Still unable to speak, Johnny nodded desperately. "This should help," she said, pointing at the bread and dip with a cheeky gleam.

Carla hurriedly filled his glass of water, spilling most of it on the table in her attempt to hide her laughter.

As he shifted in his chair, the light fell on his painfully red face. He tapped his shoes rapidly on the floor, now thoroughly regretting his bravado. Several minutes passed before he could speak again.

"Well, that told me. It's my fault for being cocky, I suppose." His words were breathy from laughter, though it sounded more like he was struggling to breathe at all.

"Did you see that waitress?" Carla chuckled, taking a bite of bread and dipping it into her lime and kaffir sauce. "She was watching you like you were a spectacle. If you were a cartoon, you'd have steam coming out of your ears by now."

The overflowing, steaming hot dishes arrived mild, yet as promised, the flavours—spicy, sweet, and sour—simultaneously made their mouths pop in delight.

Johnny walked her to her door at the end of the evening, resting his hand softly on the curve of her back. The night was lit only by the two streetlamps outside. He looked at her nervously before awkwardly leaning in to kiss her lightly on the lips. As he pulled back, he watched her blush, and for a moment, he was unsure whether he should be proud or terrified.

He hesitated, then mumbled, "Goodnight," before turning back to his car. Over his shoulder, he shouted, "Thanks for a great evening." hoping she hadn't noticed his still red face.

20 | Bree

Bree was finally starting to regain a semblance of normality in her stiffened muscles, after waddling like a duck for two days post-gorge walk. She missed Nik's smile and his cheeky comments, his usual presence hovering around her desk as he urged her to hurry up with the excursion sales list that morning.

Today, Anna was the one staring at her expectantly, tapping her fingers on the desk, waiting for the list. Bree had sold triple the number of excursions compared to the others, meaning it would take her three times as long to log the sales. But Anna didn't have the patience for that—she flicked cigarette ash into Bree's bin, her eyes narrowing in silent judgment.

When Nik had asked for a transfer—for two, maybe three weeks—Anna had been blindsided. He'd been with her for three years, never asking for anything, always working even on his days off. She'd pushed him for a reason.

"I'm a mess. I need time to sort my head out," he'd said, his voice soft and his face colder than usual.

"Are you okay, my dear?" she'd asked, her voice laced with genuine concern, though she couldn't shake the feeling that there was more to it than he was letting on.

"Don't worry, I'll be fine. Just problems with a girl to sort out," he'd said, tapping his chest with a resigned, almost defeated look.

"Okay, my dear, you take care, get better, and come back when you're ready." Anna had been caught off guard; she'd never known Nik had a girlfriend, let alone that they were having problems. He never discussed his love life, and with the number of women falling for him, Anna had never considered the possibility that he could be hurting.

She'd arranged for him to go to Corfu for a couple of weeks—always short-staffed there, and the agency boss was the stuff of nightmares, scaring off anyone who dared step out of line with her cruel outbursts.

As the days passed, Bree forced a smile, but deep inside, she was unravelling. She missed him more than she was willing to admit, running her fingers over his neatly folded sweater, forgotten on the back of a chair.

She occasionally mentioned him in passing to Anna, hoping for any hint about when he might return, but Anna just shrugged, lost in a cloud of cigarette smoke, clearly uninterested.

Bree's wide, forced smile became a shield, hiding the turmoil she refused to acknowledge, even to herself. She slowly accepted that she might never see Nik again, going through the motions, pretending he wasn't the first thought in the morning and the last before sleep.

Two weeks later, another long day of airport duties awaited her. The airport supervisor handed her the list of arrivals. Bree's eyes quickly scanned it, her heart skipping a beat as she searched for any special needs or requirements for her guests.

Bree's finger paused on the list, her heart pounding. She studied the words, feeling a rush of emotions she wasn't ready for: "The first coach available should collect Nik Daskalakis and drop him off at the Rethymnon office. Staff returning from Corfu."

She walked briskly to the coaches outside, trying to keep her mind off Nik. Her customers began filtering through, and she held up her board, hoping the flood of emotions wouldn't make her crack.

Then, she felt a hand on her arm.

"Miss me?" Nik's voice, soft and teasing, made her freeze. Bree turned to find him, relaxed and tanned, in his crisp white shirt, his eyes sparkling with mischief.

Bree's face flushed with a rush of emotions she couldn't hide. Her heart raced as she ticked his name off the list with a trembling hand. "You can move my bag if you like; sit up front," she said, her voice betraying her nerves. A quick, nervous laugh escaped her throat. The relief was palpable as she felt her face return to its natural colour, her hands steadying with each breath.

Bree quickly touched each row of seats, counting the passengers, before instructing the driver to leave. She pulled down her folded seat next to the him, picked up the microphone, and started her usual speech. But in the rearview mirror, she saw Nik, his eyes closed and a soft smile playing on his lips, looking far more relaxed than she felt.

For a moment, she forgot the usual spiel, flustered and distracted. She breathed a sigh of relief when they dropped off all the passengers at their hotels. Only the two of them were left.

"Bree," Nik's voice interrupted her thoughts, "Can I take you to dinner, just you and me?" His tone was bold but hopeful as he caught her gaze in the rearview mirror.

Bree's expression shifted. Her smile softened, and her eyes lit up, betraying her inner joy. Slowly, she rose from her seat, turning around to face him. "Of course, I'd love that."

"When?" he asked, his grin widening.

"Not tonight," she replied, her voice betraying the exhaustion she had been trying to suppress. "I've been up since five. Tomorrow?"

"Cool, I'll pick you up at seven. Your house?" Nik asked.

Bree quickly agreed, jumping off the coach with a smile that made Nik's heart race with happiness.

21 | Bree

Feeling amused and delighted by the sudden shift in her day, Bree excitedly packed away her airport uniform, smoothed out her crumpled bed sheets, and took a long, refreshing shower. She waited for sleep to wash over her, her mind still lingering on the surprise that awaited her in the evening.

The next morning, as Bree passed by the office, she noticed Nik sitting at his desk, looking unusually calm. The reps were flitting around, preparing for what they hoped would be a successful sales day with the new arrivals. Anna, unusually relaxed, sipped her coffee, her shoulders no longer tense. The scowl that had once marred her face was gone. Bree flinched, briefly recalling the angry faces of guests dissatisfied with their hotels—the lack of hot water, the ongoing construction noise—but she quickly pushed the thoughts aside. Her mind kept flickering back to tonight's date.

Grabbing her bag, Bree stepped out into the warm morning air. It kissed her face as she left the cool confines of the office. Nik appeared by her side, his voice soft as he whispered, "You haven't changed your mind, have you?" His eyes twinkled with playful teasing.

Bree smiled at him, her nerves fluttering. "No, I haven't changed my mind. See you at seven," she replied, flipping her long blonde hair over her shoulder before striding towards her moped.

Several hours later, Bree stood in front of her mirror, nervously adjusting her red sundress. The soft fabric clung to her curves and pinched at the waist, perfectly accentuating her figure. She smoothed down her freshly curled hair and checked the time. The door opened, and she caught sight of Nik standing by her gate, his posture tense as he watched her walk towards him.

She giggled as the wind caught her dress, making it flutter around her legs. Nik's expression softened, and a small, relieved smile spread across his face. "Ready?" he asked, turning the key in the ignition of the car.

The conversation was stilted at first, with Nik feeling like a bumbling idiot and Bree shyly looking out of the window, turning away whenever she caught his glance. For a few minutes, they drove in silence, each lost in their own nervous excitement.

"A hotel?" Bree asked as Nik pulled up outside a luxurious stone building. She raised an eyebrow. "You think this date's going to go well, then?" Her voice was light, teasing, relieved to finally find her playful tone again.

Nik's eyes widened in disbelief. "No, Bree, oh God, no. Please, believe me." He shook his head, his expression warm and reassuring. "Come with me. You'll see." Without waiting for her response, he grabbed her hand gently and led her through the hotel's lush green gardens, down a winding sandy path that led straight to the beach.

Bree's body warmed at the feel of his hand in hers. As they walked, Nik glanced at his watch. They were perfectly on time. When they reached the beach, Bree stopped, squinting at the stunning view. Her breath caught in her throat as she took in the sight: a blanket was spread on the sand, candles flickered softly in the evening breeze, and drinks waited for them. She hadn't realised this was for them until Nik guided her to the blanket.

"The hotel owner owed me a favour," Nik said, a touch of pride in his voice. "So, he lent me the private beach for the evening."

Nik opened the wine, carefully pouring two glasses before handing one to Bree. He clinked her glass. "To us. To this evening. And to the meatballs being properly cooked, and us not getting food poisoning."

Bree laughed, the sound light and carefree. "Cheers to all of that."

Nik spent the next while telling her stories of his life. "I'm from a small village in the north of Greece, Aígio Haídēs, near the Turkish border. I grew up planning my escape. I never saw myself as a farmer, working the fields all my life."

Bree giggled. "No, I can't picture you as a farmer."

"My parents expected me to stay there, marry a local girl, and live out my days in the village. They didn't take kindly to me leaving as soon as I could," he explained.

After finishing their meal, they lay back on the blankets, staring up at the stars. Nik loosened his skinny black tie, glancing at Bree as he did. "Bree, look, I don't want to scare you off or mess this up, but not saying what I feel has never done me any favours."

Bree turned to him, confused. "Okay," she replied softly, wondering where this conversation was heading.

"I noticed you the day you arrived, lugging around all that unnecessary luggage," Nik continued, his grin wide and affectionate. "The reps are always in uniform, so I wondered why you always had so much stuff with you."

Bree smirked. "Very observant."

"I noticed you. You looked so confident, even though you had no idea where you were supposed to go. I liked you as soon as I laid eyes on you."

Bree listened, her heart fluttering at his honesty. She felt herself blush deeply. "And?"

"When I saw you that day, when I came to find you—remember?" Nik's eyes softened as he watched her nod. "I couldn't believe my luck that it was you. That you were here, on this side of the island." He paused, topping up her drink before continuing. "I thought maybe I could get to know you, but every time I tried, you just blanked me."

Bree's eyes widened. "I didn't mean to blank you," she said, her hand instinctively going to her cheek, embarrassed. "I just didn't think you were interested in me that way. You're always so nice to everyone. I didn't realise you were flirting. Were you flirting?"

"Well, yes, but I'm not very good at it," he admitted, looking embarrassed for a moment as he struggled to find the right words. "In my mind, you aren't just

Bree. I have a nickname for you—Breezy."

Bree's eyes softened, and she smiled. "I like that name, Breezy. You can use it if you like; it sounds nice the way you say it." She touched his arm gently, wanting him to know she appreciated his honesty.

Nik smiled, visibly relieved. "Then, on the gorge walk—that was my chance to spend time with you. It was the best day of the whole summer for me, until yesterday, when you said you'd come out with me."

Bree shifted slightly on the blanket, her smile fading as she thought back. "It was hell for me," she confessed, her voice low. "I hated every single moment of it." She hesitated, then added, her voice softening, "Apart from spending time with you." She blushed, looking away slightly.

Nik's expression softened, his gaze thoughtful. "I wanted to ask you out a while ago, but I overheard you talking about your boyfriend, Micky. Then, after the gorge walk, I saw that photo of you and a man at your flat. Was that him?"

Bree shook her head, feeling a rush of warmth in her chest. "Oh, him? No, we split last year," she reassured him. "That photo's of me with a friend I worked with back in Italy. I think I look great in it, so I kept it. I should probably just cut him out of it," she added with a cheeky smile.

Nik chuckled, his eyes lightening. "Okay, well, I wish I'd just asked you instead of guessing."

There was a pause, then Bree's curiosity got the better of her. "Why did you leave? Why Corfu?" she asked, her voice gentle but insistent. She needed to understand.

Nik hesitated, his eyes darkening for a brief moment. He winced before speaking, as if the memory pained him. "Because I knew I'd fallen for you," he said, his voice quieter now. "But I knew it wasn't the same for you. I needed to clear my head. Seeing you every day was killing me, so I decided to leave and try to forget you."

Bree fought to keep a straight face, but the words escaped her before she could stop them. She burst out laughing, the sound bubbling up unexpectedly. She watched as his face froze in mortification, and she couldn't help herself.

"How's that going for you?" she giggled, her eyes sparkling with amusement. "Asking me out wasn't exactly the best way to forget me."

Nik's face slowly relaxed, a sheepish grin spreading across his lips. "When I saw you at the airport, I figured I might as well give it a shot and see what you said. And here we are."

Bree smiled, her heart light. "Yes, here we are." She shuffled back on the cushion, the evening air cool against her skin. "You know, I went crazy when you left. I felt sick thinking you weren't coming back. I would've asked you out, but..." She paused, thinking, then blurted, "Actually, no, I wouldn't have. I've seen you turn down so many girls. I thought maybe you weren't into girls."

Nik raised an eyebrow, his smile widening. "Bree, rest assured, I like girls. Especially you." As the orange sky turned to dusk, Nik wrapped a blanket around her shoulders and moved closer.

"I don't bite," he whispered, his voice low, teasing. "You can sit on this blanket with me, if you like."

Bree's smile deepened, her eyes gleaming in the fading light.

Nik grinned, his eyes twinkling with mischief as he shuffled over to pour her a glass of ouzo. "I noticed that you like this."

"Yes, I call it my magic juice." Bree took the glass, inhaling the scent before sipping it slowly. It warmed her throat as it slid down. "Mmm, welcome back, my friend," she said to the glass, the words playful. She quickly turned her eyes away from him, but as she did, his shadow fell across her face. He tilted forward and kissed her gently on the lips.

Bree looked up at him, her smile spreading across her face. "Mmm, you taste like ouzo, my favourite," she said, her voice a soft murmur.

Nik reached forward for another kiss, pulling her gently closer. His kisses were warm, different from Micky's—more certain, more tender. The touch of his lips left a lingering warmth on her skin.

As the last of the candles flickered and blew out, Bree felt a shiver of cold run through her. She slowly withdrew from his arms, standing up quickly. "Swim?" she asked, tossing the blanket off her shoulders and heading toward the water's edge.

She dipped her toes into the cool waves, turned around, and flashed him a grin before unbuttoning her dress and tossing it onto the sand. She walked confidently into the ocean. "It's warm; come on," she urged, glancing back at him.

Nik rolled his eyes but quickened his pace, running to catch up with her. "Bree, you lied. It's freezing," he complained, rubbing his arms as he took her hand and eased her out of the gentle waves.

After packing up the remains of their picnic and driving her home, Nik's eyes sparkled in the dim light as he dropped her off at her gate.

"Bree," he said softly, his voice dropping low, "we can't tell anyone we're dating. Trust me, no one can know about this."

Bree stepped back, squinting at him in confusion. "Why?" she asked, her voice quiet, wondering what he had to hide.

22 | Carla

Carla lay on her bed, wrapped tightly in her duvet, staring at the ceiling. She gently touched her lips with her finger and smiled. Her mind wandered back to the image of Johnny: his face flushed, sweat dripping from his forehead, and she laughed softly again.

She'd admired how he handled himself. He'd laughed it off and blamed only himself. It surprised her how much she hoped he'd ask her out again.

The following day, the gravel crunched beneath her feet as she unlocked her new car, and the smell of vanilla hit her as she sat down. There was a note on her windscreen: "I hope we can do it again soon, and next time you choose my food, though." It wasn't signed, but she knew exactly who it was from.

They started dating, and much to the surprise of all their work friends, their relationship blossomed into something more than anyone could have imagined. His flirting with customers didn't bother her; she knew it was just part of his charm and the way he earned better tips. Johnny had big dreams—he planned to travel the world and open a restaurant, and the tips were his way of getting there faster.

Two years passed, and they saved money to move in together. There were no more flatmates, no more shared kitchens or bathrooms. Johnny was promoted to pub manager, and Carla returned to her studies, focusing on business and languages. She also filled in for extra shifts at the pub whenever she could to help out and save money.

As part of her international business course, Carla travelled to Italy. She spent a year at Milan University, where she fell in love with the culture and the people. She and Johnny had agreed to date other people while she was away. Carla tried to, even having a brief fling with a guy whose name she quickly forgot. Maybe it was the Italians she met, but they had nothing on Johnny. He wasn't gorgeous like the men she'd encountered in Italy, but that didn't matter. She liked Johnny's assertiveness—how he exuded arrogance and superiority at work, but at home, he was as soft and loving as a puppy.

Johnny, too, had dated a few times while she was away but hadn't found anyone who intrigued him as much as Carla. The other girls seemed shallow, too made-up, with nothing behind their smiles. He liked that Carla was complex, intelligent, and a little bit messed up because of her family. Her obsession with cleanliness had been her only annoying trait—until he was left to clean up after himself. After a few months, Johnny flew to Italy to see her, and they both agreed that dating other people had been a stupid idea. They made long-distance work for the rest of her time there.

Carla knew she had gotten lucky with him, now a boyish-looking twenty-six-year-old. His uneven but kind-looking face always made her feel safe. Everyone, including her family, had told her it wouldn't work between them—they were too young, with no real life experience. Carla didn't mind; everyone was entitled to their opinion.

Their wedding was simple, a no-frills affair. The thrifty Johnny insisted on getting married at a registry office, with the reception in the pub garden. He invited only a few friends, colleagues, his parents, and siblings. The only thing he that he cared about was getting the finest imported soft cheese and Italian truffle oil—a childhood memory from his holidays in Sicily with his grandparents.

They weren't interested in having children, at least not immediately, or perhaps ever.

Carla laughed and said, "Kids? Oh, no, they'd just ruin the tidy, perfection of my house. Can you imagine? Sticky little fingers on my furniture? No, thank you."

Johnny smirked, playing along with her eccentricities. "Oh, absolutely. I can't even begin to imagine how they'd manage to make a mess of that spotless kitchen... that I've never once been allowed to help clean." He was well aware that him even picking up any cleaning products in the house was utterly impossible; Carla would never let him. "Besides, who needs kids when we've got a perfectly clean house and endless peace and quiet?"

"Exactly," Carla agreed with mock seriousness, "It's a full-time job, really. Kids would just be... unnecessary. And loud. And messy. Definitely messy."

Four years had passed since they'd moved in together. It hadn't been easy; it was a passionate, turbulent marriage. The fights were loud, fiery, and often long-lasting.

On two occasions, the police were called after neighbours complained. But when they made up, they were the perfect couple, unable to stand being apart for more than a few hours. Their friends couldn't fathom it—how could you love someone so intensely one moment, and in the next, be at each other's throats or completely ignoring one another?

Crawling into bed, Carla glanced at the new socks and white work shirt she'd bought him, now discarded on the chair beside his bed. She sighed, praying the simple gesture wouldn't ignite another fight. At that moment, she saw his silhouette against the streetlamps as he entered. He stopped at the chair, snatched up the clothes, and flicked on the light.

"What the hell is this?" Johnny demanded, holding the socks and shirt like they were the source of all evil.

"Socks," Carla replied flatly, her voice thick with irritation, "You know, to wear on your feet." She checked her phone—it was already 1 a.m. "Can we do this tomorrow?" she asked, her tone quiet, already bracing for the inevitable eruption. "I'm tired, Johnny. You know how this goes."

"Why are you wasting money on this crap?" he snapped, his voice rising in fury, his eyes blazing. "This is our future you're flushing down the toilet."

Carla sat up in bed, feeling a simmering anger. "You need socks. I threw the others out, and that shirt? It's greyer than you are. You want to look like a manager or a homeless guy?"

Johnny's face flushed crimson, his hands already starting to flail wildly. "You should've just fucking darned them. Why the hell are you throwing them away? I worked hard for those socks."

Carla rolled her eyes and hunched forward. "I worked hard too. And that shirt? You're not going to get promoted looking like you've been dragged through a hedge. It's not about socks or shirts. It's about respect."

"Oh, so now I'm old and grey, huh?" Johnny spat, his arms waving dramatically. "Is that it? You wanna just trade me in for a younger, better version? Is that what this is about?"

Carla fought to suppress a smirk. "Oh please. No, I just want you to dress like someone who didn't just crawl out of a dumpster. That's it." She raised her eyebrows sarcastically. "Is that too much to ask for?"

"Fine." he roared, his fists slamming against the wall. "I'll buy my own shirts when I damn well please. Don't buy me anything anymore."

"Well, if you're so bloody capable, maybe you can also darn your own damn socks," Carla shot back, unfazed. "I'm not living in the Stone Age. The socks were two pounds. The shirt was twelve. It's hardly a fortune."

"It's fifteen pounds to many." Johnny replied as he slammed the door as he stormed out.

"Learn to count, Johnny." Carla yelled after him, unable to help herself. "Two and twelve make fourteen, not fifteen." She switched off the lights, flopping back onto the bed, pulling the sheets over her with a satisfied sigh.

Early the next morning, the rain lashed against the windows, and Carla glanced over to find the other side of the bed cold and empty. She got up, padded silently around the house, and heard him snoring in the spare room.

Carla knew the drill. Three days of cold silence, clanging plates, and doors slamming. By day four, Johnny would give in. She'd make sure to cook his favourite food—just enough for herself—walk past him with the scent of it filling the air, and then eat alone at the table with her earphones in, enjoying every second of the petty torture.

On day four, Johnny always broke. He'd flash those wide, soulful eyes at her, wrap his arms around her, and kiss her passionately. And when that happened, the screams from the bedroom weren't out of anger, but out of a desire that could never quite be quenched.

23 | Petra

Petra checked her phone with sleepy eyes, her thumb scrolling mindlessly through Facebook. She stopped when she saw the photos on Orla's page—Orla, Liam, and their friends grinning, carefree and happy. Petra's stomach churned, and her fingers tightened around the phone. The smile on Orla's face was a slap to her chest. She forced herself to take a deep breath, closed Facebook, and switched to her contacts. Her heart hammered in her chest as she picked up the phone and dialled his number.

Liam hesitated before answering. The sound of sheets rustling and the soft creak of the bed made Petra's pulse spike. He swung his legs off the bed, grabbed the phone, and snuck out of the room.

"Hello?" His voice was groggy, reluctant, like he'd been dragged out of sleep.

"Morning, baby," Petra replied, trying to sound casual, though her heart was pounding in her throat.

"What do you want?" Liam's tone was sharp, abrupt, like he hadn't fully woken up. "I was asleep."

"I just wanted to see what you wanted to do today," Petra asked, carefully masking the desperation in her voice.

"I'm working today. And then I'll be home tonight," Liam answered curtly, the irritation already seeping into his words.

"Okay," Petra said, forcing the optimism into her voice, "I'll come see you at the farm then."

Liam let out a long sigh, heavy and defeated. "No. You can't. Don't you understand? This thing between us is over."

"I know what you said on Monday, but you can't deny what happened yesterday," Petra said softly, but the insistence in her voice was clear. "We can't just pretend that didn't happen."

There was a long pause. "Yesterday was closure," Liam's voice dropped, solid and unyielding. "It was a way of saying goodbye."

"Don't say that," Petra whispered. "Yesterday was amazing. I could feel how much you wanted me. You can't deny that."

The silence stretched. She could almost hear his breath on the other end of the line.

"We have something special, Liam. Please," she continued, her voice barely more than a plea. "You have to see it."

Liam exhaled, his breath sounding more like a defeated sigh than anything else. "Petra, it was lovely. But I'm back with Orla. You need to stop calling me. Stop contacting me."

Petra let out a short, bitter laugh. "Don't be ridiculous."

"Goodbye, Petra," Liam said, his voice sharp now, cutting through the line with finality before hanging up.

Petra stared at the phone, her hand shaking as she placed it on the bed. The tears came without warning—hot and urgent, soaking her pillow. She let out a jagged scream into it, muffling the pain that was twisting inside her. The force of of his words, the finality in them, crushed her.

She wiped her nose and struggled to regain her composure, taking a deep breath. She glanced at the time on her watch, grabbed her jeans and a pastel shirt, and left the hotel.

As she walked towards the farm, her eyes landed on the bike lying on the floor. She picked it up and propped it against the wall, her chest tightening with each step.

Liam was watching her from the back gate, his eyes following her every move as she took in the farm.

"Liam? Are you here?" Her voice wavered, despite the calmness she tried to project. She checked her reflection, quickly dabbing at the tear tracks on her cheeks, then walked toward the entrance.

Liam, hidden from view, pressed his back against the stone wall. He inhaled deeply, bracing himself. He heard her footsteps—each one felt like a hammer to his chest. His pulse quickened.

Petra crossed the walled courtyard, the gravel crunching beneath her boots. When she saw him, a small, sad smile played at her lips. "There you are, baby." She took a step forward for a kiss. He stood frozen, his eyes wide, unable to pull away, but not willing to stop her either.

"I just came to say 'hi' and pick up my bike," Petra murmured, pulling back slightly.

Liam was silent, his eyes darting to her face, noting the redness around her eyes, the telltale sign of crying. He fought to suppress his own feelings, unsure how to proceed. "Petra... well, glad you got it," he said, his voice flat, and stepped aside as he turned away.

"Tonight?" Petra asked, her tone laced with a mixture of hope and expectation. "Come to the hotel. Pick me up."

Liam stared at her, disbelief twisting his features. "Petra, I've made my feelings clear."

She stared at him, reading the frustration in his eyes, but she wasn't ready to give up. "I'm here until Sunday. Come whenever you like. I'll be waiting for you in room 217."

His voice faltered as he tried to find words. "Ehhm..." He let out a low, uncertain sound, unsure whether he was still speaking to Petra or just trying to convince himself.

Petra paused, then stood still for a moment, her face softening as she finally asked the question that had been gnawing at her for days. "Were you with Orla... while we were together? Were you sleeping with both of us?"

The question hung in the air, heavy and suffocating. His face turned serious, the lines on his forehead deepening. "No, Petra," he replied, his voice firm but tired. "I wasn't. We got back together after you left last month."

Petra nodded, the impact of his answer washing over her, but she wasn't entirely convinced. Her fingers brushed the side of his cheek, and with a soft kiss to his skin, she murmured, "See you around then."

She turned to leave, the sharp, painful sting of his rejection echoing in her chest. As she walked to her bike, the thought lingered in her mind: if she played her cards right, maybe—just maybe—she could win him back. After all, he'd only been back with Orla for less than a month.

Cycling through the dusty, dry lanes, Petra hesitated briefly at the corner, before pushing ahead. She turned left towards her hotel, then rode past it, heart racing as she approached Liam's house. When she reached the gate, she parked her bike by the garage, offering a small, almost innocent smile, just in case any prying neighbours happened to be watching.

Sliding her hand beneath rocks and potted plants, she muttered a curse under her breath. She paused, her eyes scanning the landscape, until she spotted the misplaced, blue garden gnome, standing out like a sore thumb amid the otherwise neat and orderly plants. Smirking, Petra lifted it, her pulse quickening when she uncovered the key buried beneath. She gripped it tightly in her hand and, without hesitation, walked over to the lock, twisting the key until it clicked open with a satisfying sound.

The door creaked as Petra stepped inside, rubbing her hands together as though to warm them, though the chill that crept down her spine had nothing to do with the temperature. She glanced at the table—unopened post, a symbol of the life Liam had built, the one she wasn't part of.

She walked through the house, her fingers grazing the cold, smooth marble of the kitchen counters, tracing the edge of a wooden knife block. She selected the longest knife, dragging it across the countertop like a whisper of danger. Her eyes flicked to the spice rack, and she spun it, the sound almost mockingly loud in the silence of the house.

At the fridge, she yanked open the door, her fingers itching to take something—anything. She grabbed a bottle of water, cracked it open, drinking deeply, and then, as if on impulse, dipped her fingers into a dish of lasagna. She scooped some up to her mouth, wiping the remnants on her jeans as she savoured the absurdity of it all.

She meandered up the stairs, pausing at a photo of Liam and Orla—happy, glowing, a perfect couple. The sight made her chest ache, a knot tightening in her stomach. Petra's fingers clenched into fists, and without warning, she yanked the picture off the wall. It hit the floor with a sharp crack, the glass splintering across the carpet, each shard like a symbol of the fractured reality she now faced.

The bedroom door was slightly ajar, and Petra pushed it open, stepping inside. She sat on the edge of the unmade bed, her fingers brushing over the sheets, still warm with Liam's scent. She slipped her feet into a pair of pink slippers that felt too small, too innocent. The wardrobe doors creaked open, and she ran her fingers over Orla's dresses, each one a reminder of the life Petra was now trying to erase. She held them up to her own slim frame, her reflection staring back at her like a stranger.

Petra's eyes shifted to the underwear drawer, and with a flick of her wrist, she rifled through it until she found what she wanted. A pair of silky black panties, delicate and fragile. She stretched the elastic, feeling the resistance before it snapped with a satisfying sound, the fabric falling away like everything else in her life that had been torn apart.

She grabbed a silk scarf, running it over her face like a lover's touch, before grabbing the knife and making slits in it. The fabric parted easily, and she tossed it carelessly behind her, the act as cold as the way Liam had left her.

Then, as though the house itself were mocking her, Petra moved to Liam's wardrobe, inhaling the faint scent of his cologne that lingered on his clothes. Her fingers brushed over the shirt he'd worn on their first date. The memory of that night, so full of promise and possibility, made her stomach flip. She pulled it from the hanger, clutching it to her chest like a treasure, then dropped it into her bag—her final act of possession.

She stepped into the bathroom, her fingers trailing over the iron legs of the free-standing marble bath. She perched herself on the edge, looking into the mirror for a moment as if searching for the woman she used to be. Then, with a deliberate motion, she turned on the taps, the water flowing slowly at first, then filling the tub with a warm, soft hiss. Petra peeled off her clothes, kicking them aside carelessly, before pouring in a generous amount of pink-scented lotion that filled the room with a sweet fragrance.

As she sank into the hot water, the bubbles soft against her skin, Petra closed her eyes. She felt alone, but there was a strange comfort in the solitude. In the quiet. In the illusion of control.

The silence stretched on until it was broken by a hand tapping her shoulder. Petra's eyes snapped open, her body tensing. She looked up, her heart skipping a beat as she saw Liam standing there, his face pale and his glasses fogging up in shock.

"What the hell are you doing here?" His voice shook, panic rising in his tone. He stood frozen, his body trembling, as if he couldn't quite process the scene in front of him.

Petra, however, wasn't shaken. She broke the silence with a soft, almost sleepy voice, her smile bright and unfazed. "Hey, baby," she said, her words dripping with something darkly seductive. "Are you going to join me?"

24 | Bree

Two weeks passed, and the summer sun remained a brilliant, blinding yellow. Looking for a calm and relaxing retreat, Bree sank into Nik's ocean-facing grey sofa. The ocean breeze slid through the gaps in the wooden window frame, providing light relief from the oppressive heat. Bree rested on Nik's chest, lazily turning the pages of a book. His tired eyes closed as the stomp of footsteps neared the corridor.

Suddenly, a heavy hand thundered on the front door, followed by a screeching female voice that pierced the silence.

Nik swung his legs off the bed, rubbing his eyes, his body still heavy with sleep. He muttered a curse under his breath, gently pushing Bree off his chest. "Not again," he groaned, running a hand over his face. He threw his head in his hands for a moment before saying, "I'll get rid of her." He scrambled from under Bree's arms and rushed out of the room.

The shouting became louder, making Bree wince as she sat up, her heart racing. She heard the front door open and then slam shut with a force that made the walls shake. Footsteps began pacing around the next room, the angry words flowing indistinctly, but she caught enough to know the argument was escalating.

Bree's skin crawled as the term 'whore' floated through the air. Her body tensed, and her stomach churned with dread. She sat nervously on the large sofa, glancing at the door, waiting for the confrontation to reach her.

Then the door swung open, and in stormed the woman, red in the face, her arms flailing with each furious word.

"Whore!" The woman's voice rang out, now in English, her finger stabbing the air as she pointed at Bree. "He's my man, not yours. You're a slut; stay away from my man," she screamed, her voice shrill and high-pitched.

Bree's eyes widened, a wave of discomfort rushing over her as the woman's eyes locked onto hers. The lady's large chest bounced as she furiously waved her arms around, the anger radiating from her like a storm.

Nik appeared from the other room, his face flushed with rage. Without a word, he grabbed the woman's arm, yanking her towards the door. "Get out," he barked, his grip tightening as he dragged her out of the room.

His eyes flashed with an emotion Bree couldn't decipher, but his glance at her told her everything. He was furious.

"Don't you ever come back here," he shouted as he pushed the door open. The woman shot Bree one last disgusted look before Nik slammed the door behind them.

Bree could still hear their raised voices, but now muffled and distant. The pictures on the wall vibrated from the sound of the door crashing shut, and then—an eerie, unsettling silence filled the house.

A wave of nausea hit her, and her skin felt clammy. She hurriedly gathered her belongings from around the room, slipping on her shoes, her mind racing. She needed to get out. She couldn't stay here, not with whatever was going on in the other room.

Her stomach twisted as she slipped through the garden door, each step feeling heavier than the last. She didn't know where to go or what to do, but she knew she needed to escape.

Her mind replayed the events as she made her way to the beach. She sank down to the sandy ground, her back pressed against the wall, and closed her eyes as her legs gave way beneath her. Her breath caught in her throat as the tears she'd been holding back began to sting her eyes.

Nik's voice echoed in the distance, but it sounded distant, like it was coming from a place far away. "Bree. Please wait." His voice cracked with worry, but Bree didn't move. The sound of a car door slamming in the distance cut through the air, followed by the unmistakable roar of the engine. Tyres screeched as the car peeled away, leaving her alone in the fading light.

Her breath hitched, her chest tightening. She felt like she was suffocating. She grabbed her shoes, her hands trembling as she searched through her bag for her phone. It was still on the kitchen table, she realised with a sharp pang of frustration.

Her feet were unsteady as she found an isolated spot between the dunes. She collapsed to the sand, her phone nowhere in sight. The silence was almost deafening. She couldn't make sense of what had just happened.

Bree thought about the Greek woman. If it weren't for her screaming, she might have been beautiful. Her fiery brown eyes and tight, dark curls framed her long face, giving her an exotic allure. The figure-hugging short dress she wore left little to the imagination, and while Bree would never wear the large gold earrings that swayed with every movement, there was no doubt the woman would turn heads wherever she went.

Quickly, Bree realised she needed to move. If Nik came back, he would surely find her. With a sigh, she strutted back up the sandy path, past the house she had just fled so abruptly, and began heading towards her flat. But before she reached it, she stopped in her tracks, hesitated, and changed direction. The now-dark and overcast sky would help her remain unseen. She was more worried about running into the bitter Greek woman in the dark than encountering wild dogs or dangerous men.

Deciding instead to head for the shared flat of the Finnish reps she was friendly with, Bree kept to the shadows, ducking beneath trees and hiding behind bushes, as car headlights illuminated her path.

When she finally reached the door, she exhaled in relief. Quietly, she rang the bell, catching her breath after the brisk uphill walk.

Elka opened the door, smiling in surprise. "Hey, what a surprise. Come on in. What are you doing at this end of town?"

Bree scrambled for an answer but immediately regretted coming here. The rush of voices and questions made her head spin. Elka ushered her inside, where the bright kitchen lights revealed Bree's red, tired eyes and her tanned but somehow pale complexion.

"Sit down," Elka insisted kindly, leading Bree to a chair. "You look like you've been through the wringer. Juice?"

Bree nodded numbly, her mind still reeling. As Elka poured the drink, she asked softly, "What happened to you?"

"I'm stupid," Bree muttered, wiping the tears that had started to fall. "I'm just so bloody stupid. I thought he liked me..." She buried her face in her hands, sobbing into Elka's shoulder.

Elka frowned, brushing Bree's hair from her face. "Who are you talking about?"

Bree hesitated, her hands trembling. "It's... it's just someone," she finally said, her voice shaky. "Someone I've been seeing for a while. He—" She paused, swallowing the lump in her throat. "He's got someone else. I didn't know. Not until tonight."

Elka's brows puckered, her expression one of confusion and sympathy. "Are you serious? What did he say?"

"It wasn't what he said—it was the way he acted. It all clicked, you know? Plus, she's beautiful." Bree shook her head, biting her lip to stop it from trembling. "And the worst part is, this isn't the first time. It's like I have a radar for men who are already taken."

"Hey, come on now," Elka said gently, placing a hand on Bree's arm. "This isn't your fault. You can't blame yourself for other people being dickheads."

Bree gave a bitter laugh. "Can't I? It's not just him. There were others—Murray, Micky. Same story, different names." She stared at her juice, her voice lowering to a whisper. "Maybe it is me."

Elka reached across the table and squeezed her hand. "Bree, stop. You deserve better than this, and you know it. You've just had bad luck—that's all. He's the one who should feel stupid, not you."

"Well, it's not that easy," Bree muttered.

Elka gave her a sympathetic look but didn't hesitate with her advice. "So, I hear everything you've said, but you need to talk to this guy. Can you call him?"

Bree shook her head, her face falling. "I left my phone at his house when I rushed out."

"Okay, I'm guessing you don't want to go back there." Elka raised an eyebrow. "You'll need to sleep on it tonight. Tomorrow, you can go see him at work."

Bree winced at the thought of going to the office. "Ugh... I can't," she muttered, her stomach churning at the idea.

Elka nodded, understanding. "I take it you don't have transport home?" she asked gently. "Do you want me to drive you, or would you rather stay here?"

Bree hesitated. "I'm worried he'll find me at home. I can't face him yet." She accepted Elka's offer for the spare bed with a sigh. "I'm sorry to be such a pain."

Elka gave her a warm hug. "Don't apologise. You're not a pain."

Just then, the door opened, and Alenka, the other flatmate, arrived, dripping with sweat after her run. She kicked off her running shoes and headed for the shower.

"Bree, here you are." Alenka greeted her, glancing at Elka. "You'd better call Nik. He has your phone. I just saw him on the beach, and he told me to call him if I saw you."

Elka's expression shifted to one of surprise. Her mouth hung open, her eyes wide. "Nik?" she gasped. "That changes everything."

Bree nodded, feeling the weight of the situation. "Yep," was all she could say. "Sorry I didn't tell you. I'm just too embarrassed."

"We should call him. He must be worried if he's asking people to call him."

"Nope. Not going to happen," Bree said sharply.

Elka's phone rang just then, cutting through the tension. The name "Nik" flashed on the screen. She looked at Bree, who immediately covered her eyes with her hands, mortified.

With a light-hearted tone, Elka answered the call, "Hey, Nik," she said, watching Bree frantically wave her hands around in a gesture of denial.

After a few moments, Elka spoke again. "Okay, well, if I see her, I'll tell her. But we're at home, and we're on the other side of town, so I can't see her coming here."

Bree heard a faint "Thanks" as Elka ended the call.

Bree's blood ran cold. "Thanks for covering," she added, pulling her knees up to her chest, the tension in her body slowly mounting again.

The kitchen air grew thick with the smell of body lotion as Alenka returned, now dressed in a long grey shirt. "One question: Why does Nik have your phone, and why is he going out of his mind looking for you?"

Bree sighed deeply, letting her legs relax and leaning back on the sofa. She repeated the story she had told Elka, this time not omitting Nik's name.

"So, honestly, I'm not surprised you're together," Elka said, grinning. "I've seen the way he looks at you when you walk into the office, that wolfish twinkle. And the notes he leaves when he thinks no one's watching." Bree blushed, embarrassed to have been caught out so easily.

"We were together," Bree clarified quickly. "Not anymore."

Bree asked if she could go to bed. It wasn't late, but her body was drained, and her mind was too tired to stay awake any longer. She tossed and turned for what felt like hours, staring at the ventilator fan spinning endlessly above her. She could hear Elka and Alenka's voices in the kitchen, and though they were probably just chatting, Bree couldn't shake the feeling that they were laughing at her. But she didn't care. She just wanted to lie alone, to let the hurt fill her body while her mind tried to escape the reality of the mess she was in.

25 | Bree

Bree pulled back the rumpled sheets and winced as the sound of her friends moving dishes in the kitchen reached her ears. She sat up slowly, staring at the reflection in the mirror across the room. Dark rings under her eyes framed the remnants of streaked mascara—a cruel reminder of the night's tears.

"Morning, Bree. How are you feeling? Did you manage any sleep?" Alenka's voice was soft but filled with concern as she peeked into the room.

"Not much," Bree admitted, forcing a weak smile. "I dozed off for maybe an hour this morning. Thanks for letting me crash here. I really appreciate it."

"Anytime. You know that," Alenka replied with a reassuring smile. She hesitated before adding, "What's the plan for today?"

Bree sighed, pulling herself to her feet. "Can you let Anna know I won't be in the office? I'll still handle the hotel visits but there is no way I'm going anywhere near the office. Dealing with complaining clients might actually distract me for a few hours." Her voice carried a sharp edge of bitterness.

"You'll have to face him at some point," Alenka said carefully, casting Bree a sideways glance. "You can't avoid him forever."

Bree's jaw tightened. "He's probably already forgotten all about me. Spent the night with her, no doubt." She said the words with forced detachment, though the bitterness in her tone betrayed her hurt.

"I wouldn't be so sure," Alenka replied softly. "He seemed pretty shaken last night. Worried, even."

"Yeah, well, I'll buy a new phone before I let him find me," Bree muttered, grabbing her bag and digging through it. Her hands shook slightly as she searched instinctively searched for her phone despite knowing it wasn't there.

Alenka frowned. "You know he'll come looking for you. He has the keys to the reps' accommodation."

Bree's lips twitched into a sardonic smile. "I thought about that last night. I'm glad I didn't go home. I doubt he'd bother coming in—he has better things to do."

The thought of facing him sent a jolt of anxiety through Bree, but she forced it aside. Her stomach twisted too much to eat, the sight of her friends savouring their eggs Benedict only intensifying her unease. She picked half-heartedly at her fruit and yoghurt, barely tasting the soft strawberries. The once comforting buzz of conversation now felt distant, a reminder of the warmth she struggled to embrace.

By the time the others were gathering their things for work, Bree had steeled herself to leave. "Could I catch a ride home with you?" she asked, her voice quieter than she intended.

They agreed happily, and soon, Bree found herself in the passenger seat, watching the world blur by through the window. The chatter in the car washed over her, providing a small reprieve from the storm in her mind.

As the door of her flat clicked shut behind her, she exhaled a shaky breath. The surroundings offered little joy, but she needed the space to reclaim some sense of normality. She dropped her bag on the sofa and made a beeline for the shower. The rush of hot water was a small mercy, grounding her in the moment. She scrubbed her skin with almost frantic energy, as if the heat could erase the remnants of the past two days.

Emerging from the bathroom, her hair wrapped in a towel, Bree brushed it with unnecessary vigour, as though shaking off more than just tangles. Her reflection in the mirror stared back—a pale shadow of her usual self, but at least she looked awake. She pulled on her uniform, determined to lose herself in the distraction of work.

As she turned toward the door, something caught her eye on the dining table. A handwritten note lay there, its edges slightly curled, sitting beside her phone. She froze, her heart skipping a beat. Nik had been here.

Her breath hitched as she approached the table. The sight of the note sent a surge of conflicting emotions through her. Her lips twitched into the faintest of smiles. At least he cared enough to come here, to leave something behind. But the idea of reading it—letting his words into her fragile resolve—made her chest tighten.

She picked up her phone instead, unlocking it to a flood of notifications. Bree scrolled past most of them without a second glance, but her eyes lingered on the glaring Forty-three unread messages from Nik on WhatsApp. Not now. She slipped the phone into her bag with a sharp, decisive motion, as if to bury the thought.

Her focus drifted back to the note. With trembling hands, she picked it up, the paper cool and fragile between her fingers. For a moment, she stood there, paralysed by the possibilities of what it might say. Then, with a quick, almost desperate motion, she crushed it into a ball and tossed it toward the bin. It landed just short of the rim, a fitting metaphor for the day so far.

The rest of the morning passed in a blur of hotel visits. Customers peppered her with questions about excursions, pick-up times, and local recommendations. For lunch, she avoided Giro's, opting for a small takeaway shop Alenka had mentioned.

Alenka was already waiting on a nearby bench, unwrapping her lunch. "I figured you'd be here," she said with a knowing smile as Bree approached. They exchanged a quick hug before Bree went inside to grab a slice of spinach and feta pie. Returning to the bench, she joined Alenka.

"Any updates?" Alenka asked between bites of her wrap.

Bree shrugged, picking at her pie. "I've gotten good at dodging him. Now I just need to figure out tonight. I was thinking of driving into the hills. Maybe finding some quiet taverna where he won't think to look."

Alenka chuckled. "Good luck with that. I saw him this morning. He looked awful—like a kicked puppy. You know how he's always so put together? Not today. Anna thought he was ill and tried to send him home, but he refused. He just sat there, glaring at the door like it had personally offended him. It was... unsettling."

Bree's lips pressed into a thin line. "He should have thought about that before causing this mess," she said, her tone cutting. But her voice wavered slightly, betraying the lingering hurt.

"Has he stopped texting?"

"No. Still sending messages. I haven't read them. I don't want him to know I've been home or that I've got my phone. I even called Anna from a hotel landline this morning."

"Give me your phone," Alenka said, holding out her hand. "I'll tweak your settings so he can't see when you've read his messages or when you're online."

Alenka worked quickly, returning the phone with a smug smile. "All sorted. Are you going to read them now?"

Bree shook her head firmly. "Not yet. I probably won't."

26 | Bree

Later that evening, the women gathered for dinner, joined by another colleague, Jeanie. Over glasses of wine, the four of them laughed and swapped stories about the day's most absurd client complaints.

Jeanie, a warm but no-nonsense Dane, usually avoided the younger reps, finding their energy more tiring than invigorating. Tonight, though, her curiosity got the better of her.

"What on earth was wrong with our office hunk this morning?" she asked, her sharp eyes sparkling with intrigue.

Bree stayed quiet, keeping her expression neutral, though her ears perked up at the mention of Nik.

"I've never seen him like that," Jeanie continued with a chuckle. "He was a nightmare. I asked for a new ticket book, and he looked at me as if I'd asked him to carry me to Athens on his back. The only one he didn't snap at was Anna. Bree, didn't you notice?"

"I wasn't in today," Bree replied carefully. "Overslept. Went straight to the hotels afterward."

Jeanie's eyes glinted with the buzz of scandal or gossip. "He's usually so professional. You wouldn't think he'd ever lose his cool. Although, there was that girl last year who made his lose his shit."

Alenka smirked. "Ah, yes. I'd forgotten about that Greek girl last summer—short skirts, big curls. Crazy, from what I've heard. What was her name?"

"Alexis or Alexia," Jeanie supplied, laughing. "She was a piece of work. She showed up at the office once, called us all bitches, and told us to stay away from her man."

Bree's eyebrows shot up. "Seriously?"

"Yeah. They split because she wouldn't leave him alone. She followed him everywhere. One night, she stood outside his flat screaming until he threatened to call the police." Jeanie explained enthusiastically.

"Didn't he say he came to Corfu to get away from a girl?" Alenka asked.

Jeanie nodded. "Not Alexis, though. She was a stalker, not a girlfriend. He said it was someone he wanted but couldn't have. Never said who. Honestly, can you imagine anyone not wanting to give that Nik good old, well, you know what I mean."

The table dissolved into laughter, though Bree remained quiet, her mind racing. She forced a smile when prompted by a funny comment but kept glancing at Jeanie, willing her to finish her wine and call it a night. Jeanie's casual remarks about Nik and Alexis had only scratched the surface, leaving Bree desperate to dig deeper into the story, but not in front of her Danish colleague, whose sharp observations might catch on too quickly.

Bree fidgeted with her napkin, her fingers twisting it into a small, frayed spiral. Each second felt agonisingly slow as Jeanie poured herself another half-glass of wine. A knot of frustration built in Bree's chest as Jeanie chuckled at Alenka's latest quip, clearly in no rush to leave.

Finally, Jeanie set down her glass with a satisfied sigh. "Well, ladies, this has been fun, but I'd better head back before I turn into a pumpkin. Early morning tomorrow." She grabbed her bag and stood, her chair scraping the floor with an exaggerated screech.

Bree nearly sighed with relief but kept her face neutral, nodding politely as Jeanie adjusted her scarf. "Goodnight, Jeanie," Bree said, her voice even, betraying none of her eagerness to see her go.

"Goodnight, all," Jeanie replied, throwing a casual wave over her shoulder as she left the restaurant. The sound her car pulling away was like a release valve for the tension coiled within Bree.

As soon as Jeanie was out of sight, Bree turned to the girls, her voice barely above a whisper but brimming with urgency as she said, "Tell me all you know about this Alexa-Alexis woman,"

After Jeanie left, Alenka turned to Bree. "You have to call Nik. He's worried sick. He keeps texting me."

Bree shook her head. "No. If it's not what Jeanie said, I'll just end up humiliated."

"At least let me text him," Alenka insisted. "I'll tell him you're safe, but I won't say where you are."

After a pause, Bree nodded reluctantly. Alenka typed a quick message and set the phone down. It vibrated almost immediately, messages pouring in. Bree stared at the screen, her heart pounding.

Hearing the story from Jeanie unexpectedly lightened Bree's mood. For the first time in days, the weight on her chest began to lift. She finally felt ready to hear what Nik had to say.

Alenka read the messages aloud, her face softening into a smile. Occasionally, a quiet "aww" slipped out. Bree tapped the table, impatient for her to finish.

"Sixty-eight messages and nearly as many missed calls," Alenka grinned. "Do you want the highlights or the whole lot?"

"Start with the highlights," Bree replied.

"Most of them are, 'Call me,' or, 'Where are you?' Then they get angrier—'Why won't you call me?' There's a few, 'It's not what it seems; I can explain.' Around lunchtime, he wrote a long one explaining his ex, Alexis—how she was a stalker he couldn't shake off."

A flush of hope warmed Bree's cheeks. She felt foolish for jumping to conclusions.

"You haven't heard the best ones yet," Alenka teased. "Later, the messages get desperate. Here's my favourite: 'Hell, Bree, where are you? Forgive me; I should've told you. I miss you. I love you.'"

Bree nearly spat out her wine. "He's never said that before."

RAW MISTAKES

Alenka scrolled further. "'I mean it, I love you. Dammit, Bree, answer me.' Then, at seven: 'I'm at your house. You threw my letter away; did you read it? Where are you? I'm worried.'" She paused then read the last one. "'Thank you for letting me know you're okay, Alenka. I understand if you hate me, but we need to talk.'"

Bree's lips curved into a guilty smile. "I'm such a bitch," she murmured.

"You're not a bitch; you're in love," Alenka said softly, refilling their glasses.

When the phone vibrated again, Alenka read aloud: "'I'm starting my own stalking now, Breezy. Where are you and that little grey scooter?'"

"Give me the phone," Bree said, snatching it. She quickly typed, I'm in hiding ☺, and hit send.

Moments later, the phone vibrated again. Startled, Bree tossed it like a grenade. Alenka caught it, accidentally answering the call.

Alenka ended the call with a firm, "Goodbye," setting the phone down and offering Bree a reassuring smile. "There," she said softly. "He knows you're okay. Now you can breathe."

Bree let out a shaky laugh, the tension in her chest easing just slightly as she sipped the last of her wine. Finally, she felt a glimmer of calm. Alenka's firm handling of the situation had defused the emotional storm in her head, if only temporarily.

As the evening wound down, the three women left the restaurant together, their steps light against the cobbled street.

At her flat, Bree wasted no time. She brushed her teeth, slipped into her softest pyjamas, and crawled into bed. Uncertainty didn't press down on her chest as she sank into the mattress. Instead of staring at the ceiling, her mind racing, she felt a sense of peace, however small. The sound of the fan spinning above her faded into the background as sleep claimed her almost instantly.

The next morning, Bree woke to the sound of her alarm, the sunlight flickering through her curtains. She blinked at the clock and smiled faintly feeling refreshed. After a quick breakfast of toast and tea, she dressed smartly for work, tying her hair back neatly and donning her usual work smile.

She hadn't been in the office long by the time Nik's footsteps approached. He reached into the drawer, pulled out the note, and placed it on her desk. Bree stared at it for a moment before wordlessly pushing it into the bin. Without lifting her head, she resumed typing.

Ten minutes later, Nik grabbed his bag and left the office. Bree quickly retrieved the note, read it, and laughed softly. She straightened in her chair, grabbed her accounts, and headed toward Anna.

An hour later, Nik held the door open for her as she left the office. Bree flashed him a bright smile, and his eyes lit up. He knew instantly—she'd read it.

27 | Carla

Carla jumped out of bed, pushing the duvet away in a surge of excitement. It was their wedding anniversary, and her heart raced with a excitement.

"So, have you got something exciting planned? Remember, we are on a budget," Johnny had teased the night before.

Carla bit her tongue, resisting the urge to make a sarcastic comment about their constant budgeting. "Yeah, it's cheap and fun; I can't wait," she said instead, snuggling up to him on the pillow. She had to admit, despite her frustrations with his penny pinching, she loved these quiet moments.

This year, it was Carla's turn to plan their anniversary, and the tradition required the date to be something they'd never done together. For their first anniversary, Johnny had taken her to a fairground. They rode the teacup rides and bumper cars, ate candy floss that stuck to their fingers, and laughed at the children clinging to their mothers' legs in terror. It had only reinforced their mutual decision not to have kids.

For this year, Carla had planned an ice skating date, followed by dinner at Johnny's mum's favourite Indian restaurant. Simple, cheap, and guaranteed to be fun. They didn't do gifts—just cards. Every pound saved was tucked away for their future.

"Romance is a con; we don't need it," Johnny had once declared, sparking a four-day argument. Carla had almost thrown her mug at him, but over time, they'd settled into their own version of romance—quirky and practical.

They hadn't fought in weeks, but Carla knew another one was brewing; it was just their rhythm. Still, she had no intention of letting it ruin their anniversary. That morning, she left a card on her pillow, knowing Johnny would find it the moment he woke up. The front depicted two ugly frogs kissing. Inside, she'd written, "Happy Anniversary, Johnny. I love you. See you at Carton Gables parking at seven; bring gloves."

Johnny smiled when he read it, immediately guessing they were going ice skating. He rested back into the pillow, relishing a rare quiet lie-in. He'd already left her card the night before, tucked under her car's windscreen wiper.

Carla found his card as she headed to work, brushing away the morning frost from the car. The card featured the same two ugly frogs. Inside, Johnny had written, "Happy second anniversary, Babe—second of many more. I love you to the moon and back." She chuckled, touched by his predictable sweetness.

Later, Carla nipped home to change, giving Johnny a quick kiss as she left. "See you in a while; don't be late."

"Of course," he said. "Just got to hand over petty cash to the next shift, and I'll be there."

RAW MISTAKES

But waiting outside the ice rink, Carla scowled at her phone, her breath visible in the icy night air. Her fingers, stiff from the cold, hovered over the screen.

Johnny's message flashed back at her: "Ten minutes late. Staffing hassles." She slipped off her gloves, rubbed her hands together, and shoved them into her coat pockets, pacing the near-empty car park.

Each minute dragged. When Johnny stopped answering her calls, unease prickled her skin. She checked the time again. Forty minutes. A hollow ache settled in her chest as dread crept in, its icy tendrils tightening with each unanswered ring.

Flanked by long brick buildings, supermarkets, and clothing stores, Carla paced the car park, checking her watch. Each time she returned to her car, she switched on the engine, warming her hands over the heater. The cold seeped through her coat, and the night felt darker and emptier with every passing minute.

When the police car pulled up, its headlights briefly cutting through the gloom, Carla barely registered it at first. It wasn't until the officers approached, their deliberate strides and sombre expressions piercing the cold night, that she felt her stomach knot.

"Are you Carla Carpenter?" one asked, his voice gentle yet unyielding. The tension in their faces told her this wasn't a prank.

She nodded, her smile uncertain. "Yes. Am I in trouble?" She half-laughed, thinking Johnny might've set up a prank.

"Please sit down," the officer said, gesturing to a bench. His tone and the gravity in his eyes froze her smile.

"What happened? Is Johnny alright?" Her voice cracked, each word trembling in the brittle air. The officer's pause—measured and suffocating—felt like an eternity before he spoke again.

"There's been an accident," he said, his voice careful, deliberate. "It involves your husband, Mr. Johnny Carpenter." He glanced at his notepad, his words measured.

Carla's breath hitched. "What happened? Is he alright?"

The pause that followed was suffocating.

"It happened on Park Lane," the officer continued, his tone hesitant. "A truck lost control and struck your husband's vehicle. Regrettably, when we arrived... he was already gone. The paramedics couldn't save him."

The world tilted. Carla gasped, her hand flying to her mouth as the words shattered the fragile bubble of her reality. The sounds of the bustling car park faded into silence as her chest tightened. Tears blurred her vision, and the officer's voice became a distant murmur. She clung to the bench, her body trembling under the importance of the news.

Johnny was gone. Just like that, their anniversary, their plans, their future—all of it—was gone.

28 | Petra

Petra pushed herself up in the bathtub, flashing Liam a flirtatious smile as she said, "Waiting for you to come home." She pulled herself out of the water, the bubbles clinging to her bare skin. As she neared Liam, she placed a hand on the back of his neck, letting her wet body lean against his.

Suddenly, he froze, his voice low. "We can't do this." He nodded as if trying to convince himself.

Petra rose onto her tiptoes, took his hand, and placed it around her waist. She caught the flash of interest in his eyes behind the spectacles and saw the hunger stirring beneath the tenderness. She brought her lips close to his, inhaling his quick, shallow breaths before kissing him. Surprising both of them, he pushed open the bedroom door and pulled her inside by the hand.

Loosening his grip, he threw her onto the bed. His shirt came off in a rush, and he slipped out of his trousers, his arms wrapping around her naked body.

Orla smiled when she spotted Liam's car parked in the driveway. Her eyes lingered for a moment on the sight before drifting to the bike leaning carelessly against the garage door. With a small shake of her head, she headed inside.

Dropping her bag onto the kitchen stool, she scanned the room. Everything seemed in its usual place, yet something felt...off. A strange stillness hung in the air. Frowning, she made her way upstairs.

Halfway up, her steps faltered. A sharp crunch underfoot drew her eyes downward. Shattered glass. Her pulse quickened as she carefully stepped over the fragments, her unease mounting with every creak of the stairs.

At the top, she froze. The bedroom door was ajar, revealing glimpses of the room beyond. Holding her breath, she pushed the door open wider.

And there they were.

Two naked bodies tangled in the bed. The sight sent a jolt through her, like a slap she hadn't seen coming. Her stare locked on the woman whose arm rested possessively around Liam's waist.

"Petra?" The name slipped out as a whisper, barely audible over the pounding of her heart.

For a moment, she couldn't move, couldn't think. But then anger surged, a tidal wave drowning out the initial shock. She turned and paced the hallway, her movements sharp and restless. Every few steps, her eyes flicked back to the bed as if trying to convince herself it wasn't real. But it was.

On her next pass, she stopped, breathing hard. This time, she stepped back into the room, her movements purposeful. She loomed over Liam, her hand trembling as she reached out and gripped his shoulder. "Liam," she said, her voice low and tight with rage. "Wake up."

Liam jolted awake, his eyes darting between Orla and Petra. He read the raw anger and pain etched into Orla's expression. "I can explain," he stammered, scrambling out of bed and hastily pulling on his boxers.

Orla didn't respond. She wiped her tears and moved to Petra's side of the bed. Without hesitation, she yanked at Petra's hair until the woman stirred.

Petra woke groggily, a smile forming on her lips—until she saw Orla. Her smile vanished, replaced by a look of shock and dread. She froze, barely breathing.

"Downstairs. Now," Orla ordered, her voice low and icy.

Petra glanced at Liam, who nodded reluctantly. The two followed her downstairs in silence, the tension suffocating. Liam reached the kitchen first, watching as Orla poured herself a vodka with trembling hands. She slammed the bottle down and sat at the counter, her expression unreadable.

When Petra entered, she hovered near the door, clutching her bag.

"You both disgust me," Orla hissed, her voice suddenly sharp. With a burst of fury, she hurled the glass across the room, shattering it against the wall. She pointed at Petra. "I'm not sure where you fit into this mess, but you—" she turned to Liam, her voice rising—"you did everything to win me back, and this is what you do? You cheat on me?"

"Please, Orla," Liam pleaded, his voice cracking. "Let me explain."

Orla stepped back, taking a measured sip of her drink, her expression stone-cold. "Oh, I can't wait to hear this. Explain how this woman ended up in your bed, in our bed, and why I'm supposed to listen to your lies."

"I think I should leave," Petra whispered, edging toward the door, her face pale and streaked with tears.

Orla snapped her head toward her. "Oh no, you don't. You wanted him so badly? Stay. Hear his excuses."

Petra froze, glancing at Liam, who rubbed the back of his neck, avoiding eye contact. "Fine," Petra murmured, stepping back hesitantly.

Liam sighed heavily, his shoulders slumping. "She... she seduced me," he said finally, pointing at Petra.

Petra's jaw dropped, her wide eyes brimming with fresh tears. "What?" she whispered, her voice shaking.

"Is that true?" Orla demanded, her fury laser-focused on Petra now.

"Not exactly," Petra began, swallowing hard. "He—he seduced me. At first."

"At first? When?" Orla barked.

Petra hesitated. "Five months ago. In Dublin."

Orla staggered back a step, her breath hitching as her mind reeled. Her voice was a whisper now, raw and broken. "So, you knew each other before Monday?"

Liam looked down, unable to meet her gaze.

"You lying bastard," Orla spat. She spun towards Petra, her eyes blazing. "And you—I don't know whether to pity you or hate you."

"I didn't know he was married." Petra protested, her voice thin and desperate. "Not until this week."

"But you knew today. And yet you still slept with him. In my bed," Orla hissed.

The room fell silent except for Orla's laboured breathing. With a sudden burst of movement, she swung open the patio doors, letting the cold air rush in. She turned back to them, her voice deadly calm. "Out. Both of you. Now."

Liam started to protest. "But I live here."

"Not anymore, you don't," Orla snapped. "Last time, I left this house. This time, you do." She turned her glare to Petra. "Take him with you. Get out before I use this bottle for something worse."

Petra didn't wait to be told twice. She grabbed her bag and headed for the door. "Coming?" she asked Liam, her voice flat.

"Out." Orla shouted, pointing at him.

Liam hesitated, his face pale and drawn.

Petra shot him a cold, hollow look before slipping outside. She grabbed her bike and pedalled furiously down the street, her heart raging with every turn of the wheels.

Inside, Orla watched as Liam finally slouched towards his car. His shoulders sagged under the pressure of his mistakes. He hesitated, looking back at the house, but Orla didn't flinch. With a screech of tyres, Liam reversed out of the driveway.

29 | Petra

The rage hadn't faded when Petra arrived, breathless, at the hotel car park. She ran past the receptionist and up to her room, slamming the door behind her. She threw herself onto the bed, burying her face in the pillow. But then, she heard pounding on the door. Sitting up, she wiped her tears away. Peering through the peephole, she saw Liam standing there.

"Can I stay here with you, baby?" he asked, his voice low as he pushed past her, throwing his coat onto the bed. He walked to the window, staring out at the darkening sky, lost in thought.

Petra felt a strange sense of invincibility in that moment—like she could take on the world. "So, what now?" she asked, her grin forcing its way through her unease.

"Well, I'll stay here tonight with you since I don't have my keys to the farm. Then I'll move in there until I find a new place," Liam said, his voice flat.

"Well, you can stay with me until I leave, if you want," Petra said with a smile, imagining a future together.

Liam sat on the bed, untying the laces of his shoes. "Thanks. I guess I need to start over though. I can't stay hidden in here like a fugitive with you," he said, the words falling from his lips like a weight.

Petra narrowed her eyes, suspicion creeping into her mind. Moments ago, she had convinced herself everything would be fine. But now, doubt gnawed at her. Her face twisted in pain, and hot tears sprang to her eyes. "But I've got a few more days here. We can spend them together," she said, her voice barely above a whisper.

Liam ignored her, picking up the remote and flicking through the channels. He turned the volume up as high as it would go.

As the morning light rested on his eyes, Liam abruptly yanked the duvet off the bed and paced restlessly, a wild look in his eyes. Petra stirred, pulling herself out of bed to see him standing at the window.

"So, I'm off then," Liam said, his face hard as stone. He picked up his coat, giving her a small, stiff wave. "I'll see you."

Overwhelmed, Petra felt a twist in her stomach. She stood frozen, listening to his footsteps as he walked down the corridor. She watched from the window as he climbed into his car and slammed it into gear, the tyres screeching as he drove away.

After showering and dressing, Petra grabbed her bike and stopped for coffee and breakfast along the way. She sped up as she passed the office where Orla worked, glancing at her silhouette through the window, trying to avoid being noticed.

Once at the farm, Petra rested her bike against the wall and draped her coat over a fence post. She swung open the kitchen door and stepped inside. Her eyes drifted to the uneaten cake on the counter. Setting the coffee she'd brought beside it, she wandered through the farmhouse, her voice breaking the stillness.

"Liam? Where are you?"

"Over here," came his muffled reply.

Petra turned towards the sound, and soon, Liam emerged, wiping his hands on his mud-streaked overalls. As she stepped closer to kiss him, he pulled back sharply.

"Not here. Someone might see us," he muttered, glancing around nervously.

"We're the only ones here," Petra shot back, irritation creeping into her voice. "Why did you rush off this morning?" Without waiting for a response, she added, "I've left some coffee in the kitchen for you. Oh, and I brought a few of my things over so I don't have to keep going back to the hotel."

Liam frowned, his confusion mingling with frustration. "Why would you do that?"

"So we can be together, silly," she replied with a teasing smile, reaching for his hand. But he pulled away, his retreat stinging her confidence.

Picking up a bucket, he started walking again. Petra followed. "Are you seriously following me now?" he asked, not bothering to glance back.

"Liam," she snapped, her voice faltering slightly. "I'm running out of patience. Why are you acting like this?"

He kept walking, silent until they reached the pig pen. Then, finally, he stopped and turned to face her, his expression guarded. "Petra, you need to stop. I've told you before—we're over. I need you to leave me alone." His tone was firm, though his eyes betrayed hesitation, as if he doubted his own words.

Petra stepped in front of him, desperation flickering on her face. "I don't understand," she said, her voice soft but insistent. "You're free now. Your wife kicked you out. There's nothing standing in our way anymore. We can be together."

Liam's jaw tightened. "It's not that simple. This is a small town, Petra. If you move in here, people will talk. I can't risk that."

He brushed past her and set the bucket down outside the pen with a frustrated grunt.

Petra stood there for a moment, her mind racing. Then, forcing a smile, she turned to him with forced cheerfulness.

"Fine. I get it. I'll just stay out of sight, then. I'll keep to the house so no one sees me," she said, her voice light yet trembling with restrained emotion.

She ran a finger down his chest, the gesture lingering with unspoken longing, before turning on her heel and heading back toward the farmhouse.

From the kitchen window, Petra watched Liam intently, her eyes tracking his every movement. She wiped a cloth over the greasy hob, trying to restore some semblance of order to the chaotic kitchen. Satisfied with her small accomplishment, she swung open the door and called out towards the courtyard, where the farmhands had gathered.

"Boys, lunch is ready," she shouted before returning inside to set out plates of sandwiches and crisps on the table.

"You can make us lunch anytime you like, Miss. This is brilliant," one of the younger workers said, grinning as he reached for another sandwich.

Liam, washing his hands under the hot tap, hurried over to the table and switched on the TV. The farmhands joined him, chatting and laughing as they wolfed down the food Petra had prepared.

Petra's lips twitched into a subtle smile as the workers thanked her and retreated into the sunshine. But Liam twisted in his seat, fixing her with a glare.

"Have you lost your mind?" he snapped, his voice raised. "You're supposed to be lying low, not cooking lunch and playing the perfect hostess."

"So, I was the perfect hostess?" Petra countered, arching an eyebrow. "Thanks. Tomorrow, I'll just leave the food and hide in the bedroom, shall I?" She dipped the dirty plates into the soapy water, her tone dripping with sarcasm.

Liam's expression hardened. "I think you should go now. We're finishing early today. I've got stuff to do, and I'm stressed." He opened the door, forcing a strained smile as his hand gripped the handle tightly.

"That's okay," Petra said softly, her eyes flashing with a mischievous determination. "I'll help you relax, baby." She nudged the door shut behind him and slowly unzipped her red woollen top, revealing a lacy bra. With deliberate movements, she lifted his shirt and placed her soapy hand on his bare skin.

"Baby, come to bed," she murmured, standing on tiptoe to nuzzle the nape of his neck.

"Petra. No." Liam stepped back abruptly, his frown deepening. "It's bad timing, okay? You need to leave." His voice was firm as he turned towards the door again.

"I leave in three days. For now, I'm all yours," she whispered, wrapping her arms around his waist from behind. She kissed his back, her fingers tracing along his skin as she lifted his shirt.

Despite himself, Liam couldn't resist. Weakness overtook him. He spun around, kissed her with urgency, and roughly led her towards the bedroom.

For the next three days, Petra stayed at the farmhouse, playing the part of the doting housewife. She teased Liam with her body every time he resisted her advances until he inevitably gave in. Satisfaction swelled in her chest whenever he called her name, surrendering to her completely.

"Bye, baby. I'll see you next time. I'll be back in a couple of weeks," she said, zipping her bag and preparing to leave.

"Sure, whatever," Liam muttered, his tone indifferent. He sat upright, his impatience obvious. "Your taxi's here."

Petra clung to him as he briefly hugged her. Stepping out into the warm late afternoon, she turned and called from the taxi window, "I love you so much." She kept her attention on him until he disappeared into the distance, a slumped figure on the horizon.

Back in London, Petra collapsed onto her sofa, gazing at the bright, airy kitchen as she poured herself a glass of white wine. With a heavy sigh, she grabbed her phone and dialled Liam's number. Minutes later, she tried again, but the line stayed silent. Her messages remained undelivered.

"You blocked me?" she whispered. A guttural scream tore from her throat as she hurled the wine glass at the wall, watching it shatter into fragments. She threw herself onto the bed, desperation clawing at her chest. Grabbing her phone, she scrolled through her calendar. Upcoming trips to Italy and Jordan stared back at her, unimportant distractions.

In three weeks, she'd be back to see Liam. She would get him back.

30 | Carla

Carla's hand moved instinctively to her chest. Her breath quickened, and her body went limp as the blood drained from her face. "This can't be happening. Not Johnny."

The police officer's voice continued, but his words seemed distant, floating in the air without meaning. Carla barely registered them.

"It can't be him; he's at work. It's our wedding anniversary." The words tumbled out, sounding absurd even to her. Under her breath, she muttered, "Of course, it's him. He's an hour late and not answering his phone."

"We found a card in his car that says, 'See you at 7 p.m., here,'" the officer said gently. "Is there someone we can call for you? We'll drive you home and arrange for someone to collect your car."

Carla nodded numbly and gave him her brother's name. She followed the officer's instructions mechanically, climbing into the car as though moving through a thick fog. Her head spun, her breath catching in her throat as if the air had grown heavier.

"We'll need you to come to the station tomorrow," the officer said softly as they pulled up outside her house. "We'll wait with you until your brother arrives."

He took the keys from her trembling hand, her knuckles pale from gripping them too tightly. Unlocking the door, he guided her into the lounge, steering her towards the tall black and grey armchair.

"No, not there," she murmured weakly. Her gaze fell on Johnny's coffee cup, still sitting on the table without a coaster. The sight stirred a flicker of irritation—so small, so meaningless, yet somehow unbearable. She stumbled towards the sofa instead and sank into it, pulling a blanket around her. Staring out of the window, she watched the flicker of headlights passing by, the room dipping in and out of shadow. "Curtains, please," she whispered, her voice barely audible.

The officers complied, drawing the heavy curtains before turning on the overhead lights. A sharp ring of the doorbell shattered the silence, followed by a gust of cold air as the door opened and closed. Carla's brother and his boyfriend arrived, kneeling on the floor beside her, holding her hands. For a moment, she almost smiled.

Johnny had always joked about them, calling them "the two frogs." Her brother had found a partner with a squashed nose and beady eyes that mirrored his own.

The officers spoke briefly with them before leaving, offering no condolences—just polite nods as they disappeared, their expressions unreadable.

The days that followed were a blur. Her friends and family were predictably supportive, but their efforts felt robotic: feeding her, washing her, helping her survive the endless hours. The frogs moved into the spare room, and her mother visited every morning, staying for a few hours. Carla tried to muster a smile now and then but couldn't help thinking Johnny would be laughing at the absurdity of it all.

After the funeral, Carla withdrew entirely, retreating into silence. Grief swallowed her whole, leaving her hollow. Tears welled in her eyes as she sat alone in the darkened house, the curtains drawn. The days melted into each other as she binge-watched Netflix, clinging to horrors and thrillers—anything that didn't remind her of love, of Johnny.

She pushed the food her friends brought around her plate, unable to eat. The curtains stayed closed, creating an illusion of absence. The constant knocking on the door filled her with dread, and she sat frozen in the corner, waiting for the visitors to leave.

With each passing day, Carla withdrew further, becoming good at online shopping. She had her groceries delivered and left outside, and weaved elaborate stories about her whereabouts to anyone who asked her. Her most convincing lie was that she was visiting Johnny's family regularly. It worked; her own family stopped coming by.

Her routine became achingly hollow: eating, sleeping, and the occasional shower. She resigned from her job—there was no reason to face the world anymore.

Even cleaning, once her greatest pleasure, held no appeal. Johnny's belongings remained untouched, each item a reminder of the life they had shared and the life she had lost.

31 | Carla

Financially, Carla was struggling. Waiting for Johnny's insurance payout after the accident, she was forced to dip into her savings. Memories of their countless arguments about money and saving resurfaced, sharp and painful. She'd fought him on it so often, resenting his insistence on putting something aside. Now, she was grudgingly grateful. At least his foresight meant she could survive for a while—just until the insurance came through.

But her mind refused to focus. All she wanted was to curl up into a ball, block everything out, and never wake up again.

The table was buried under unopened envelopes, a mountain of dread she could no longer ignore. She picked them up one by one, flipping through the ominous pile before tossing them back down in frustration. Her hand trembled as she reached for her phone, her breath uneven. Dialling her brother's number, she whispered, "Please, I need you."

Even as the words left her mouth, doubt crept in. Could she trust him to help without taking over, without unravelling the fragile thread of control she clung to in Johnny's absence?

An hour later, Charles arrived, immaculate as ever in a crisp blue shirt and tie. His reaction to the state of her home was impossible to miss. The moment he stepped inside, he shrugged off his raincoat and grimaced as the stale, sour smell of neglect hit him. Without a word, he opened the windows, letting in a sharp gust of fresh air.

His eyes swept over the dirty dishes stacked around the sink and the overflowing bins. Taking a deep breath, he approached Carla, who sat slumped on the sofa. Moving some of the envelopes from the chair, he sat down beside her.

Carla turned away, brushing a tear from her cheek. She gestured feebly at the pile of paperwork. "I can't deal with it. Bills, I suppose, maybe something from the insurance. I don't know. I need you to help me sort it out."

"Of course," Charles replied, his tone gentle yet businesslike. "Why don't you take a shower and freshen up while I go through these?"

His suggestion hovered in the air, more of a veiled criticism than a genuine offer. Carla hesitated before shaking her head. "No, let's get it done now," she said, surprising herself with how much lighter the room felt just from his presence, clumsy affection and all.

Charles got to work, opening envelopes and jotting down notes. As he fired off questions about household bills, insurance, and bank accounts, Carla's inability to answer made her feel like a child. Exhausted, she curled up in the armchair, her body aching from the strain of simply being present.

"Right," Charles said finally, glancing at her with a hint of exasperation. "If you give me Johnny's death certificate, I'll take care of everything for now. But you can't keep burying your head in the sand, Carla. Sooner or later, you'll have to deal with this."

"I'll do my best,"

"You need to promise me you'll start taking care of yourself. And clean this place up—it's disgusting."

Carla gave a weak nod, wrapping the blanket around her shoulders. "I will. I promise," she said, her voice barely audible.

Charles began tidying up, loading the dishwasher with as many dishes and glasses as he could find. The sight of him bustling about, a flurry of efficiency, filled Carla with frustration.

"I've just had the flu," she mumbled, offering a weak excuse. "That's why everything's such a mess. I'll clean up tomorrow."

Charles paused, holding up a bulging rubbish bag. "Empty the bins once in a while, Carla. You'll have mice at this rate." His tone was light, almost joking, but his words stung.

Carla forced a tight smile and waved him off, though her lips trembled as she struggled to hold back tears. As the door clicked shut behind him, she exhaled in relief, sagging against the sofa.

In the quiet, her eyes drifted to the kitchen counter, where bottles of sleeping pills stood in neat rows. For months, she'd ordered more than she needed, buying from multiple shops to ensure a steady supply.

She had a plan. Wait until she had enough. Take them all at once. Wash them down with Johnny's whisky.

End the pain. End the grief.

And never wake up.

When Carla opened the cupboard, her hand hovered over the whisky. It was the one thing she couldn't bring herself to touch. She found more comfort in food now than drink, in the dull numbness of overeating rather than the sharp sting of alcohol. Sleeping on the sofa, wrapped in a single duvet, was her small, fragile refuge. The sheets on her bed—tangled and creased from her frequent nightmares—irritated her too much to lie in it.

Johnny's shoes still sat by the door, untouched. His faded grey shirt, the one they'd argued over, hung limply on the back of the armchair. His phone charger remained plugged in by the bedside table, its empty cord an aching reminder of his absence. And the pillow, faintly carrying his scent, still bore the creases from his last night in bed.

This plan—this one, terrible plan—was the only thing keeping her going. It gave her a perverse sense of purpose, a marker to tick off the endless days that passed. She didn't call it living. No, this was enduring, waiting—nothing more than a grim game of patience until she could finally escape the hell she found herself in.

Opening the fridge, she let out a frustrated sigh. It was nearly empty. She needed milk; how could she make coffee without it? Checking the crumpled shopping bags strewn on the counter, she confirmed what she already knew—there wasn't a drop in the house. She rushed to her computer to place an online order, but the earliest delivery slot was for the next day.

The realisation hit her with a weight she hadn't felt in months: she would have to leave the safety of her home.

She stared out of the window, unsure of the date or even the month, but she knew the days were growing longer. The trees in her garden were budding, their branches scratching against the windows with the morning breeze. The sound grated on her nerves, a taunting reminder of life outside her closed walls.

Unable to summon the energy to dress properly, Carla pulled on baggy joggers and an oversized fleece, shoving her feet into the nearest pair of shoes, pressing down the backs as she slid them on. She found her darkest sunglasses—not for the sun, but to shield her from the world—and grabbed her credit card before stepping out.

The fresh air hit her like a slap. The brightness of the spring day felt alien, almost hostile. She blinked against the sunlight, her ears catching the sounds of children laughing, the rhythmic thud of a football, and the chatter of girls stretching on the grass in leggings and joggers. Carla paused, her breath catching in her chest as an overwhelming wave of anxiety swept over her. Her legs felt weak, and she had to steady herself with a deep breath.

Ahead, the supermarket's car park glimmered in the sun, and she quickened her pace, desperate to finish the errand and retreat to her cocoon.

Inside, she grabbed a trolley and moved aimlessly through the aisles. Milk, chocolate, ice cream. It all felt oddly comforting, almost like normality. For a fleeting moment, she felt as though she was simply living—just another woman on a mundane shopping trip.

But as she approached the exit, her path was blocked. A large, unkempt woman stood directly in front of her, dressed in ill-fitting clothes and an unflattering scarf. Carla hesitated, her heart racing.

She stepped aside to let the woman pass, but the woman mirrored her movement. Frustrated, Carla shifted the other way, only for the woman to do the same. As the door slid open, Carla braced herself for an awkward collision, but when she looked up, the woman was gone.

Confused, she glanced around the shop, her eyes darting from aisle to aisle. There was no sign of her. A strange sensation rippled through Carla, as though the woman had vanished into thin air.

Then, she saw her again—outside, standing on the other side of the sliding glass door. The woman was now wearing a scarf identical to Carla's.

Carla froze. The woman's appearance was dishevelled: her untied shoes scuffed and her wild curls tumbling in all directions. Instinctively, Carla touched her own hair, feeling its unruly texture beneath her fingers. The woman did the same.

It wasn't another person. It was her reflection.

For a moment, Carla stood paralysed, staring at the stranger in the glass. The truth hit her like a cold wave. She was the messy, unkempt woman blocking her way.

RAW MISTAKES

Her hands trembled as she ran them through her hair, and the woman in the glass did the same. She turned away sharply, staring at the ground as she hurried out of the store. Her pace quickened as the edges of her vision blurred, her heart pounding with each step.

Halfway home, she paused to catch her breath, clutching her shopping bags. Her chest felt tight, but she forced herself to keep going. Step by step, she stumbled back to the safety of her walls, retreating from the brightness of a world she no longer recognised.

32 | Nina

Taking a deep breath, Nina slid her hand down the door and pulled the handle. As her head emerged into the dim corridor, she saw a woman standing at the far end of the hall. The woman's eyes met Nina's, but she didn't speak. She simply nodded once and disappeared up the stairs without another glance.

Nina's heart raced. Her hand trembled as she closed the door behind her, taking a long, shaky breath. Music blared from somewhere in the house, its pounding beat like a constant reminder of the nightmare she had been trapped in for the past two weeks. Pushing forward, she stepped out into the cool night air, each step making her feel more alive than she had in days. But there was no turning back now.

The moment her bare feet hit the grass, she glanced around, eyes darting nervously. The house behind her looked like a rotting shell, a memory of something once whole. She didn't know what she was expecting, but hadn't been in the woods. She stopped for a moment, disorientated. The forest stretched in every direction—dark, impenetrable, and unfamiliar. The house was already far behind her, swallowed by the trees.

Her breath caught in her throat as she noticed the path ahead—rugged and overgrown. She forced herself to move, stumbling through brambles and thorns. Her feet burned, but she couldn't stop. Not now. She scrambled up a steep hill, slipping on the slick earth. With a loud thud, she crashed to the ground, pain shooting up her legs. For a moment, she lay there, gasping for air, the sting of tears mingling with the cold dirt on her skin.

But there was no time for pity. She pushed herself up, gritting her teeth as she scanned the dark landscape. A flash of movement in the corner of her eye made her freeze. She couldn't afford to stop.

Taking a deep breath, she resumed her run, heart hammering in her chest. Each step felt heavier, each breath more laboured, but she couldn't stop. She couldn't look back. The woods seemed endless, the rain now a steady drizzle, slicking her hair and clothes. She pushed forward, the cold biting at her skin.

Through the dense trees, she saw it again: the yellow light, now much closer. The steady glow seemed like a beacon of hope, but Nina wasn't sure if it was real. She didn't trust anything anymore. With every step, the light grew brighter, and before long, she realised it was coming from a house—a small, weathered farmhouse, isolated in the heart of the forest.

She approached the door, her stomach twisting with anxiety. Her hands were icy and stiff from the rain, her breath shallow as she knocked on the door, praying someone would answer. Her body trembled with exhaustion, but the need for help drove her forward.

The light flickered inside, and a voice called from above. "It's 3 a.m.; leave me alone."

"Please." Nina cried out, desperation bleeding into her voice. "I've been kidnapped—I need help. Please."

A long pause followed, then the man's voice, this time tinged with suspicion. "Is this some kind of joke?"

Nina's stomach churned, and she choked on a sob. "I'm not joking. Please, my name is Nina Ruggero. I've was kidnapped. I need to call my family—or the police. Anyone, please, help me."

The man grumbled in disbelief, widening the gap in the window to see her more clearly. He growled in frustration, a deep, guttural sound, before muttering under his breath. "Nina Ruggero?" He disappeared from the window as Nina wasn't sure whether to wait or run.

Her chest tightened as she heard his foot steps draw closer. The door trembled as the man turned the key in the lock, and then, to her relief, it creaked open. He grabbed her arm firmly, his grip surprisingly strong for someone so old, and led her inside.

Inside, the house was dimly lit, dusty, and forgotten. Furniture was covered in faded sheets, as though no one had lived here for years. The man paused at the door, looking around as if searching for something—or someone—before gesturing for Nina to sit. He pulled out a wooden chair and shoved it toward her, his movements slow and deliberate.

He rummaged through a pile of faded newspapers, his fingers picking through the pages as though searching for something specific. His eyes narrowed when he found what he was looking for. A small flyer, hastily pushed through his door, showed Nina's face under the bold headline: "Missing."

He slid the flyer across the table, his finger tracing her face. "So, it's really you," he said, his voice quieter now, almost reverent. "Nina Ruggero."

Nina froze, the wonder in his words sinking in. Her heart skipped a beat, but she didn't know whether to feel relief or fear. He was staring at her, his eyes hard and somehow scary.

She wanted to ask him for a phone—needed to—so she could call her parents, but her voice caught in her throat.

"What do kids drink nowadays?" he asked, his voice unbothered as he shuffled toward the stove. "I've got hot chocolate, water, or coffee."

"I don't want anything," Nina said, her voice barely above a whisper. "I need to call my mum and dad. Can I use your phone?" She could feel her stomach twisting as the words escaped her mouth.

The man paused and shook his head. "I don't have a phone." He motioned vaguely around the dim room. "I live off the grid. You know what that means?"

Nina shook her head.

He poured her a glass of water and placed it in front of her, his eyes narrowing as he watched her. "I don't like people much," he muttered, "so I stay away from them."

Nina's heart sank. She wanted to run, to leave, but her body felt like lead. What if he was just another part of her nightmare?

The man lit the gas hob with a spark, the flame flickering to life. He turned back to her, grinning as he set a kettle on to boil.

Nina shivered, the uncertainty thick in the air, as she realised that whatever happened next, she was no longer in control.

"Do you have a family?" Nina asked, her voice curious as she searched for signs of life if the house..

The man's expression hardened for a moment, and he looked away. "I did," he said quietly. "My wife died two years ago." He nodded toward a framed picture on a wooden cabinet in the corner of the room. "My son left when she died. He's in South Africa now."

"I'm sorry," Nina said, her voice soft with sympathy.

"Cancer," he muttered, his tone distant as he took the water off the hob, pouring the steaming water into a cup. He added too much chocolate powder, stirring it carelessly before sliding the cup toward Nina. "You need to keep warm."

Nina wrapped her cold hands around the cup, the warmth of it a small comfort in the otherwise cold room. "Thank you."

He glanced toward the door. "Stay here. I'll see if I can find you some dry clothes."

Nina listened to the floorboards creak beneath his weight as he left the room. She hugged the cup tighter, trying to calm her racing thoughts. Moments later, he returned with a pair of jeans and an oversized jumper, holding them out to her. "These are my son's," he said. "He left them behind. I don't think he'll be needing them anymore."

Nina took the clothes and held them against her chest, the gesture feeling strangely intimate. "Thank you," she mumbled, her voice barely a whisper.

"You can change in here. I'm going to light a fire." he said, pointing to the sitting room.

Nina nodded, her hands shaking as she peeled her damp clothes off, throwing them into the sink with a soft thud. The fabric of the oversized grey jumper felt comforting against her skin as she slipped it on, and she struggled with the baggy jeans, pulling them up her legs.

"You'll need socks too," he said, his expression softening as he eyed the cuts on her feet, now caked with dried blood. "But I think we should look at those first."

Nina winced, but she didn't pull her feet away. "It'll be fine," she said quickly, though her voice cracked. "My mum will take care of me as soon as I get home." She bit her bottom lip before asking, "You will let me go home, won't you?"

The man didn't answer right away, his eyes flickering to the fire he was setting. For a long moment, Nina felt as though the room had grown colder. Her throat tightened with fear, the uncertainty gnawing at her. Would he let her go? Or had she just traded one cage for another?

33 | Carla

Turning the key in the door, Carla dumped her shopping bags on the floor. She gasped, quickly covering her mouth and nose with her scarf to block out the pungent odour. She reeled in astonishment, leaving the front door open to let in some air. Taking a deep breath and rolling her shoulders back, she pushed all the windows open in the lounge and dining room before finally reaching the bedroom. She stopped in front of the tall, mirrored wardrobe, gently touching her bloated face. Her hands moved slowly down to her belly as she turned to the side.

Rolling up her sleeves, she squished her untoned arms, frowning and flapping the loose skin. "What have you done to yourself, Carla?" she muttered. "Johnny wouldn't want to see you like this."

She ran her fingers through her hair, only getting an inch before a nest of knots stopped her. She thought about the last time she washed it but couldn't remember—maybe weeks ago. Shaking her head, she wiped the hair off her face. She couldn't deny it: she'd been staring at her own reflection earlier that day.

"Right, girl. You've got to get your act together. You need to look good for Johnny. He'll send you back down to this life if he sees you like this," she muttered to herself, sucking in her cheeks as she struggled to find her familiar, face in the mirror.

Carla stomped downstairs and carefully placed the newly purchased food in the fridge, but the foul smell was even worse here. She wrinkled her nose and flung open the kitchen windows, tying back the curtains to allow the light to finally fill the dusty room. As she walked through the house, she felt increasingly disturbed, picking clothes off the floor and taking coffee-stained mugs to the dishwasher. The crunching of chocolate wrappers beneath her feet no longer went unnoticed, and she scooped them up, one by one, tossing them into the bin. The scattered clothes were washed load by load, each one hung carefully in the garden to air out. She emptied the bins throughout the house, placing them outside for the next rubbish collection.

As Carla cleaned, she felt more alive than she had in months. It was as if she had reclaimed some control over something, anything. She sprayed oven cleaner inside the oven and left it to work its magic as she went upstairs for a long-overdue shower. The water rushed over her like rain on a hot day—a welcome relief to her heavy, exhausted body. She found her razor and gently removed the hair that had claimed her legs.

Rubbing conditioner into her hair, she massaged her face with the Clinique cleanser—a birthday gift from Johnny. The cool cream sank into her pale, tired skin, while the scent of Argan oil in her hair lingered in the steamy bathroom. After a few minutes, she let the water rinse away the freshly scrubbed skin, swirling it down the drain along with the residue of creams and the unwanted hair. Stepping onto the damp carpet, she wiped the steam from the mirror and glared at herself with rapidly blinking eyes until she couldn't look any more.

On her knees, she tugged yellow rubber gloves onto her hands. The sound of scrubbing filled the room, and the scent of cleaning products made her cough sharply. The Hoover clunked and jerked as it sucked up papers and dirt. Her stomach rumbled, and her eyes flicked to the clock on the wall.

It was already eight o'clock, and the darkness outside was creeping in, filling her with a deep weariness. Flicking on the light, a smile crept across her face. The plumped-up pillows on the impractical white sofa stood tall, and streaks from the soft movements of the Hoover remained on the carpet.

After dragging the Hoover and cleaning supplies upstairs, Carla shivered at her reflection once again, quickly turning her face away in disgust. Her skin was blotchy, her hair—though clean—was dry and frizzy, and she couldn't even bear to look at her body. She blinked several times, trying to clear the redness from her eyes. For the first time since the police had told her about Johnny's accident, she felt better—though not good, not happy, and certainly not whole. But it was a start. She pulled out the scales with a sigh of resignation.

Dashing downstairs, she grabbed the framed photo of her younger, more vibrant self, pulled it out of its frame, and stuck it on the fridge. While waiting for her computer to boot up, she ordered a fresh delivery of fruit, fish, and vegetables for the next day. She stared blankly at the pantry. Finding some lentils, potatoes, and spices, she hurriedly cobbled together something for dinner with the few ingredients she had. Then, for the first time in a while, she took her usual seat at the table—no longer on the sofa.

34 | Bree

Nik's steps carried a spring that had been absent for weeks. His mood was buoyant, and the weight that had hung over him had finally lifted. Glancing around cautiously, he slipped a note into Bree's drawer: "7 pm; I'll pick you up from your house."

By seven, he was perched nervously on the low brick wall outside Bree's house. His hands fidgeted with the keys in his pocket as he glanced at his watch, uncertain if she'd even turn up. He tugged at his fitted white polo shirt and straightened his denim shorts, wishing he'd picked something more impressive. Then he saw her.

Bree stepped lightly down the path towards him, her figure framed by the golden light spilling from her front door. She wore a low-cut white top and frayed denim shorts that accentuated her long, sun-kissed legs. Nik's throat tightened, and his eyes stung with emotion at the sight of her smiling so freely.

"Breezy, babe, you look stunning," he breathed, his voice trembling slightly as he held out his hand. "Thanks for coming."

She grinned, brushing a strand of hair from her face. "Nik, we're practically matching," she said, gesturing to her shorts. "It's nice to see you waiting outside for a change—not sneaking in like a burglar."

His face coloured as he stammered, "I—I'm sorry, Bree. I wasn't thinking straight. I swear it won't happen again."

She raised an eyebrow, her tone playful but firm. "If you know I'm home, you can use the key. But if I'm not—no sneaky business, all right?"

His eyes widened in surprise. "So, I can come around if you're there?"

She tilted her head, a small smile pulling at her lips. "We still need to sort out the madness with that Greek woman, but yes, I think I'd like you to come around more."

Before he could respond, she slipped her arms around his neck, pulling him into an embrace. He clung to her tightly, his voice breaking. "Don't ever do that to me again, Breezy. Those were the longest two days of my life."

Her expression softened, though a hint of mischief lingered in her eyes. "That depends on you... and the crazed Greek monster," she teased, slipping out of his hold. She took his hand and led him to the car. "Now, where are we going? Please don't tell me back to your house."

They arrived at a quaint restaurant nestled beneath a grove of olive trees. The dim lighting and rustic wooden tables gave it an intimate charm, though the chairs creaked ominously under their weight.

Nik cleared his throat, his nerves suddenly sharp. "Bree... I need to tell you everything," he began.

As he spoke, Bree's face shifted between concern and understanding. Alexa, the woman who had haunted his life for over a year, had started as sweet and unassuming. But her behaviour had spiralled into obsession.

"She seemed fine at first," Nik said, running a hand through his hair. "I told her straight away that I wasn't looking for anything serious. She said she understood, but... she didn't. She'd show up at my flat every night, banging and screaming. It got so bad the neighbours threatened to call the police. I had to."

Bree processed his words. "And that's why you didn't tell anyone about me?"

He nodded, his voice dropping. "I couldn't risk her coming after you. She's calmed down a bit lately, but I'm scared she's still watching. I don't know what to do, Bree. I... I don't want to lose you."

Her hand reached across the table, steady and reassuring. "Now that I know, we'll figure it out—together."

Nik exhaled, a visible weight lifting. "This is new, I know, but I want to make it work—with you." He paused, his voice catching. "I love you, Breezy."

For a moment, she didn't move. Her heart swelled, and her lips curved into a tender smile. "I love you too. Apart from the last forty-eight hours, you've made me happier than I've ever been." Her hands cupped his face as he pressed a kiss to his nose. "We'll sort this. Whatever it takes."

Over the next few weeks, their lives became a dance of secrecy and thrill. Nik found himself embraced by Bree's circle of friends. The girls flocked to him, unabashedly flirting, but his eyes always darted back to Bree, silently apologising before gently dismissing the others.

One evening, as they sat on her balcony, the laughter from their dinner party still echoing in the background, Nik turned to her. "How'd you feel if I told everyone I'm gay? That'd stop the vultures."

Bree snorted with laughter. "Don't be daft. You'd just have queues of blokes after you instead."

"You know you've got your own share of admirers, don't you?" Nik said, a teasing grin spreading across his face. "But you scare them off with that look—the one you used on me."

Bree raised an eyebrow and flashed the infamous look.

"That's the one." he laughed, shaking his head. "You can use it on anyone you like—just not me, alright?"

Her laughter faded, replaced by a more serious expression. "I want to come clean, Nik. I feel awful lying to everyone. We don't have to share all the details, but I want them to know we're together. Properly."

Nik's smile faltered. "I know. But what about the monster? And Anna?"

Bree sighed, reaching for his hand. "If we deal with the monster, I can start coming round to yours again. And we can reconnect the doorbell at mine." Her voice softened, but there was determination in her eyes. "Ignoring her isn't working, Nik. We need to face her. She needs to see we're serious."

RAW MISTAKES

On a sultry June evening, Nik parked his car outside Alexa's house. The streetlights barely peeked through the thick trees lining the road. Bree tightened her grip on his arm as they approached. A light shone faintly in an upstairs window, but as they rang the doorbell, it flickered off.

They waited, the oppressive heat adding to their unease. Curtains twitched, but the door remained shut. Pacing up and down the driveway, they called up at the window.

"Alexa. We just want to talk." Nik's voice echoed into the night.

The only response came from a neighbouring building, where a gruff male voice bellowed, "Shut up."

They returned the next evening, determined. Again, the curtains twitched. Again, the door stayed closed. This time, a disgruntled neighbour hurled a bucket of water over them.

Bree shrieked, startled, while Nik wiped his face, laughing. "Cheers."he called out. "Thanks for cooling us down."

On the third attempt, the door finally creaked open. Alexa stood there, framed by the dim porch light. Her feet were planted firmly apart, her arms crossed like a barrier. Her brown eyes burned with a volatile fury and hurt as she glared at them.

"You want this pale skinned, blonde Barbie? Fine. You can have her," she spat, her voice venomous. Her furious glare bore into Nik, almost pleading, even as her tone seethed with anger. "When you get bored of her, I'll still be here. She's not one of us, Nik. She's an outsider."

Bree's breath caught at the insult, but she held her ground, squeezing Nik's hand for strength.

Nik's eyes darkened, his voice low and sharp. "Maybe I'll get bored of her; maybe I won't. But if you keep this up, Alexa, I'll marry her just to make sure you never have a chance."

His words hit like a slap. Alexa's expression twisted, her anger giving way to something raw and unspoken.

35 | Bree

The Monster's face dropped, and a curse burst from her lips. Unfolding her arms, she spun around sharply and walked back inside, slamming the door behind her.

Nik took Bree's shaking hand and walked her quickly down the path. He opened the windows, letting out the hot, stuffy air in the car and said, "You know I didn't mean a word of that, don't you? It just popped into my head as I was talking."

Bree stared at him open-mouthed, taken aback by his words and startled by his anger towards this cruel and broken lady.

Two weeks had passed since that evening, and they'd heard nothing from the monster. There were no more nighttime visits, no more notes on his car, and no more scratches on her moped.

They felt free to enjoy this evening; they were going to come clean to the others. It was their mid-season party, a night meant to build enthusiasm for busy and exhausted reps before the hard work of the summer months ahead.

Nik and Bree didn't want to make a big deal of it; Elka and Alenka were the only two to know so far. The two girls had kept them up to date with the office gossip. Some thought Bree and Nik were just good friends; others couldn't care less. Bree felt the chill and resentment from Nik's admirers and was ready for it to be over. She hoped that evening would stop the endless stream of flirtatious messages from girls at all hours.

The event, the talk of the travel world for weeks, was finally upon them. Conversations about outfits and the perfect dress for the occasion were discussed every morning, and pictures of colourful gowns and heels were shared in groups.

It was the event of the season, to be held on a British ship docked in the harbour of Chania. The owner of the agency had somehow managed to hold the party on board. As Bree and Nik approached the ship, they heard the upbeat Nineteen Eighties' music and admired the fairy lights hanging over the deck.

Bree and Nik arrived fashionably late, though it wasn't by design. His obsession with perfecting every strand of hair and inspecting his reflection from every angle had pushed them well past the agreed time. Bree, only half-joking, muttered complaints under her breath as she waited by the door, tapping her red-heeled foot impatiently.

As they finally stepped out of the car, Nik smoothed down his sharp black jacket, adjusted the skinny tie, and turned to Bree with a mischievous grin.

"If you ditched those flip-flops, you could pass for a red-carpet star," Bree teased, her eyes narrowing playfully.

"Right back at you," Nik shot back with a soft laugh, his gaze lingering on her.

Her figure-hugging black gown, offset by scarlet heels and a matching belt, gave her an air of effortless sophistication. He reached for her hand, his fingers brushing against the topaz necklace he'd given her, which hung perfectly against her collarbone. Gently, he pushed back the soft blonde curls framing her jawline, taking a moment to drink in her beauty.

"You ready for this?" he asked, pressing a tender kiss to her forehead.

"As I'll ever be," she replied with a hint of nervousness in her voice, though her smile betrayed her excitement.

They stepped into the grand venue, accepting glasses of chilled champagne from waiters at the entrance. The lively conversation and music drew them further inside, where a crowd of travel industry professionals mingled beneath glittering chandeliers.

At the top of the steps, they paused, surveying the sea of faces. It only took seconds for the room to notice them. Conversations faltered, and a collective gasp rippled through the crowd. All eyes were on them—and more specifically, on their intertwined hands.

"Well, it's about bloody time, you two." Alenka's delighted voice broke the stunned silence as she raised her glass high.

"Finally." Elka chimed in, her grin wide and infectious.

Even those who hadn't noticed the clasped hands now turned, curious. Loving a touch of drama, Nik seized the moment. He leant down, capturing Bree's lips in a kiss that was as bold as it was heartfelt. A murmur of approval and light applause swept through the room. Bree, caught somewhere between embarrassment and exhilaration, felt her cheeks flush crimson.

"Show-off," she whispered, trying to keep her composure as he pulled away.

He chuckled softly, his grip on her hand tightening as they made their way down the steps. They stopped first by Alenka and Elka, exchanging a bit of banter, before Nik led her confidently through the throng of onlookers.

As they approached the bar, Bree's smile faltered. Standing near the end, clutching her own champagne glass with a sour expression, was Anna. Her piercing stare fixed on them, or rather, on her.

Nik noticed too. Without breaking stride, he gave Bree's hand a reassuring squeeze.

"So, you like the cheese?" Anna asked, looking flummoxed and stroking the red cocktail glass in her hand. When she managed to refocus, Anna continued, "No PDA in the office, though, okay? Do you hear me? Do what you like, just not in the office." She clinked their champagne glasses and laughed again, turning away to get the barman's attention.

Relieved they no longer had to hide, Bree slipped off her heels and made her way to the dance floor, her bare feet brushing against the cool tiles. She wrapped her arms around Nik as they swayed to the rhythm. It wasn't long before she winced as his foot collided with hers.

"Right, so dancing's officially not our thing," Nik said sheepishly, guiding her off the floor with an apologetic grin.

"Perfect excuse to avoid it forever," Bree replied, her smile softening the teasing edge in her voice. She sank into a black plastic chair, massaging her sore feet with exaggerated theatrics.

They left the party early, exhilarated but exhausted. Closing the door behind them, he gently pressed Bree against it, his hands framing her face as he kissed her—a kiss full of pride and gratitude.

Their fears that the passion would fade now that their relationship was out in the open proved unfounded. The thrill of secrecy—the stolen glances and fleeting touches—was gone, but what replaced it was deeper, richer: a sense of unity, a belonging they hadn't realised they craved.

Nik found his happiness amplified with Bree by his side. Their home quickly became the heart of the community—roof parties that stretched into the early hours, tables laden with Nik's culinary creations, and laughter that spilled over into the streets below. The invitations to those nights became coveted, eagerly awaited by friends and acquaintances alike.

But Mondays were sacred. Their shared day off was reserved solely for them. Sometimes they vanished, driving along winding island roads or hopping ferries to explore neighbouring isles. Other times, they stayed close—lounging on the balcony, toes buried in the warm sand, or simply losing themselves in quiet conversation by the beach.

Yet even in this paradise, shadows occasionally crossed Nik's face. The thought of his family back home, and the worsening health of his father, weighed heavily on his mind. He tried to keep the sadness at bay, but Bree saw through the cracks.

"They just don't get it," he confided one evening, his voice thick with frustration. "My need to see the world, to live outside their expectations."

His parents, steeped in tradition, expected him to fulfil the path they had set out for him: to return home, marry, and settle into the role of the dutiful son. They had envisioned him back at twenty-five. At twenty-six, he felt their disappointment pressing against his every choice.

Whenever he visited, the same script played out. His father would lecture him on his responsibilities, reminding him of his duty to the family name. His mother silently pleaded for him to conform.

Each visit made leaving harder. Returning to the island brought relief but also guilt—a constant, gnawing tug at the edges of his happiness. Bree tried to ease his burden, but she knew some struggles were his alone to bear.

For now, they had their Mondays. And for Nik, those stolen hours with Bree—whether driving through sunlit landscapes or lying side by side beneath the stars—were enough to keep him smiling.

36 | Bree

Several months later, Bree took Nik to Scotland to meet her family. It was a journey filled with laughter and shared discovery, blending her world with his. They extended their travels to New York and California before returning to Greece, where Bree made the bold step of moving into Nik's house—a decision that felt totally natural.

Not long after, Nik left to visit his own family, leaving Bree behind. He had spoken often about his family's deeply rooted beliefs and their struggle to accept her. Upon his return, he always brought with him a collection of photographs, each one brimming with stories. As he described every inch of his homeland—the olive groves stretching endlessly, the small, sun-soaked village, and the home he grew up in—his eyes shone with love and pride.

For Bree, it was bittersweet. She saw how much he ached to share this world with her, yet the barriers imposed by his family's expectations and their unwillingness to embrace her were impossible to ignore. Their differing nationalities and upbringings seemed an insurmountable obstacle in his family's eyes. Bree felt the intensity of it, not just for herself but for Nik, who bore the pain of being caught between two worlds.

As he spoke, she could picture herself walking alongside him through the olive groves, their hands brushing against the low-hanging branches. She imagined them weaving through the village streets, pausing to greet neighbours and sharing laughter in the quiet corners of his childhood home. She longed to make that vision a reality, to bridge the gap between his family and the life they had built together.

But for now, she waited. She stayed behind in the home they shared, counting down the days until his return. Around them, their friends whispered predictions of a fairytale future: marriage, a life rooted in Greece, children, and travels that spanned the globe. To those who knew them, Bree and Nik embodied the ideal—two people who had found "it." The elusive, profound connection that others spent a lifetime searching for. For Nik and Bree, it felt as if the universe had conspired to bring them together, gifting them a love that others could only dream of.

The seasons turned, carrying them along in the gentle rhythm of life. Their second summer together mirrored the first, full of love and laughter, punctuated by moments of quiet understanding.

They slipped into a routine of blissful domesticity, one that neither had anticipated but both cherished. Their days off became sacred adventures: hopping between sunlit islands, indulging in the flavours of local cuisine, or simply losing themselves in the serenity of each other's company. With each passing day, their love deepened, becoming a constant in an ever-changing world.

Nik thought only of his future, placing his family pressures behind him until a phone call woke him early one morning.

"Your father is ill; he's had a heart attack," his aunt explained. "You have to come home." Staring at the phone, he sat back in disbelief. He would have to leave his job, but worse than that, he would have to leave Bree.

37 | Nina

The old man rubbed his wrinkled face with hands speckled with age spots and said, "Come, sit by the fire." Nina stood frozen, still cautious of him, as he tossed a cushion towards the hearth. "The chairs are too heavy to move close; you're young, so sit there." The warm light from the fire bathed his face, revealing laugh lines and crow's feet that spoke of a life filled with joy and kindness.

"Thanks," Nina murmured, her voice barely audible over the crackle of the flames.

"Of course, I'll let you go home," he said, glancing at the window, "but there's a big storm brewing out there. It's not safe on these muddy roads, especially for an old man like me driving in the dark."

Nina silently exhaled, the tension in her chest easing. She edged nearer to the fire, soaking in his reassuring words.

"Don't let this place fool you," he continued, gesturing around the modest room. "I'm a father, a grandfather—just an unfortunate and lonely one. I had a house like yours once, I imagine, until my wife passed away."

Nina thought she saw his eyes glisten, and without thinking, she reached out, placing her hand lightly on his. "I don't know your name," she said.

"You can call me Jack," he replied with a smile. "Like Jack and the Beanstalk."

"Thank you, for... everything," she said, glancing down at her borrowed clothes and finishing the last sip of her hot chocolate.

His pale face flushed slightly. "It'll be light in a few hours," he said, pushing himself up from the chair. "Then I'll take you to the police station or your home, whichever is nearer."

"Okay." Nina said, "Early, right. I just want to get home."

"You can sleep here, on the sofa, by the fire," he added, motioning for her to add more wood to the fireplace.

"Thank you," she replied, her voice warm with gratitude.

"Go to the kitchen," he instructed, "take the water off the gas, and fill it nearly to the top with cool tap water."

Nina rose slowly, her aching body protesting with every step. Following his instructions, she returned with the tin pan. Jack took it from her and placed it on the floor near the fire. From a small bottle, he poured a clear liquid into the water. "Disinfectant," he explained. "Put your feet in it."

She sat on the sofa and dipped her feet gingerly into the water, wincing as the tingling warmth spread through her sore skin. Jack rummaged through a box of plasters and ointments, setting aside what he needed.

"Where are we?" Nina asked, eager for distraction.

"About an hour north of Bologna," Jack answered. "Twenty kilometres, maybe, but the dirt roads make it slow going."

"I went to Bologna once, on a school trip. I'm from Monza," she said, a flicker of nostalgia in her voice.

Jack nodded, tossing her a towel. "That's all I've got, I'm afraid."

"It's perfect," she said sincerely, drying her feet and applying the plasters he'd offered.

Jack settled back into his chair. "How did you end up here, at my house?" he asked, his weary face softening with curiosity.

"I ran," Nina said, her voice quivering. "I saw your porch light and headed this way."

Jack looked at her with a tender expression as he caught the shimmer of tears in her eyes. "I'm glad you did," he said simply. "Now, get some sleep. We can talk more in the morning."

With that, he shuffled to his room, closing the door quietly behind him. Nina curled up on the sofa, pulling a dust sheet over herself like a blanket. The warmth of the fire lulled her into a deep sleep.

Nina woke abruptly to the clatter of pans in the kitchen. Jumping to her feet, she hurried towards the sound. "Morning, Jack," she greeted, taking in his dishevelled appearance—shirt tails untucked and mismatched slippers.

"Morning, Nina. Did you sleep well?" he asked, hobbling about the kitchen.

She nodded. "Can I help you?" she offered.

"Can you scramble eggs?" he asked, sheepishly. "My wife always made them. I can't get it right."

"Of course," she said, pulling eggs, milk, and butter from the fridge. She worked quickly, while Jack heated toast in a pan.

Murmuring with delight as he tasted her creation, he grinned. "These are the best eggs I've ever had. Can you teach me how to make them?"

"Now?" Nina asked, puzzled.

"Why not? They're too good not to learn how to make them." he chuckled, his tone lighthearted.

Relieved he wasn't asking her to stay another day, Nina smiled. "Alright, Jack. Let's get started."

Jack, eager to learn, watched her as he scribbled notes. "I collected those eggs this morning from my henhouse. If you wash up, I'll get the car ready," Jack said as he headed outside the farmhouse.

Nina peered out of the window, eyeing his crops; it seemed he was friendly with anything that grew in soil: tomatoes, herbs, onions, broccoli, and lettuce. She heard the rattling of the beat-up old van as the engine roared. Jack called out, "Nina, come on, let's go."

Throwing down the dishtowel, she grabbed a pair of shoes Jack had left for her and ran to the waiting car. She left the trainers unlaced, jumped into the passenger seat, and watched Jack lock up his house, shaking the door to confirm it was locked, before she joined him.

"Put this on," he instructed, handing her a woollen hat. "The guys you escaped from will probably be looking for you by now."

She felt her stomach churn as her thoughts threw her back momentarily to the house she had fled from just hours earlier. Nina looked back at the stream of black smoke coming from the farmhouse, worried there was no one tending the quickly diminishing fire.

Jack swerved as the van bumped down the streets, avoiding the muddy puddles left behind by the rain. They sat silently until they reached the tarmac.

"So, the police station is about twenty minutes from here; I'll leave you there." Nina was surprised to see a look of sadness in his eyes. She sank into her seat as they passed cars; his slow speed would not make a good getaway if they were spotted. Nina stared out of the windscreen, wiping away smudges with the sleeves of her jumper as they reached a small town. The streets were crowded with children heading to school; Nina scanned the faces of people walking on the street, hoping to recognise someone.

"Here you go," Jack said as he pulled up outside a red building with tall iron gates; the blue and white sign read, 'Carabinieri.'

"Thank you, but please, will you stay with me? Don't leave me outside," she asked as she grabbed his arm, her eyes wild with fear.

"Okay, just till you're safe," he said, releasing a reluctant sigh.

Nina swung her car door open, placing her feet on the tarmac, waiting as Jack buzzed the intercom on the police station gate.

"Hello," a voice answered.

"It's about Nina Ruggero, the missing girl," Jack said and paused. The gate clicked open as he held his hand out for Nina to join him. Nina's legs gave way to fear or maybe relief, as she took Jack's arm; his face was pale, his eyes watering.

Jack led her up three small steps to a stern-faced police officer holding a door open. He looked at them suspiciously and ushered them into a brightly lit room. Three plastic chairs lined the wall, and he gestured for them to sit. "You have news on the Ruggero girl?" he asked.

Jack pulled off Nina's woolly hat and looked at her, then said to the policeman, "This is Nina Ruggero."

The policeman stepped back sharply, his eyes narrowing in suspicion. "What kind of joke is this?" he snapped, before shouting over his shoulder, "Captain."

A short man with a receding hairline marched over, irritation etched on his face. "What is it now?" he barked, glancing around the room until his eyes landed on Nina.

"My name is Nina Ruggero," she said firmly, sensing for the first time that her name carried some weight.

The captain's eyes flicked between her and Jack, his scepticism evident. "Who's this man? Did he hurt you?" he demanded, eyeing Jack suspiciously.

"No, he saved me," Nina replied, her tone firm as she reached for Jack's hand. "This is Jack; he brought me here."

The captain hesitated, then gave a brusque nod. "Come on through."

He led them to a larger room cluttered with neatly stacked files, their handwritten labels barely visible through layers of dust. Pictures of grinning policemen hung crookedly on the walls, and filing cabinets with peeling stickers loomed on either side of the door.

"What's your date of birth?" he asked abruptly, his tone clipped.

"Can I just call my parents?" Nina pleaded, exasperation creeping into her voice. "That's all I want."

"We need to verify who you are first," he replied curtly, motioning to the other policeman, now idling by the window. "Ring the number on the missing flyers," he instructed.

"Surely my parents can tell you who I am?" Nina shot back, her voice dripping with sarcasm.

The men exchanged glances and left the room without a word, leaving Nina and Jack alone.

"That wasn't quite the welcome I was expecting," Jack muttered, attempting a small smile.

"Thank you for staying with me," Nina said softly. "I think I'd have run away again if you weren't here."

Having found their smiles, the two policemen returned to the room, along with two fresh, warm croissants, two glasses of juice, and a coffee for Jack.

Nina squinted as a light flashed on her face. "It's a photo for your parents," the captain said as he looked at the image on the screen and began fiddling with his phone.

"Are you hungry?" Jack asked Nina, who shook her head.

"To go," he said, carefully wrapping up the croissants and tucking them into his pocket.

"What about my cousin, Julia?" Nina's expression turned serious. "Have you found her?"

"We're not at liberty to discuss the case," the policeman replied as Nina caught the faint sound of a text being sent.

When he turned away, she muttered some choice curse words under her breath.

A shrill ringtone startled Nina. The policeman answered, put the call on speaker, and then handed the phone to her. Nina's heart raced as she snatched it up. "Hello," Nina said quietly.

"Nina, is that you?" Her father's voice crackled through the phone, shaky but unmistakably familiar. The sound of his voice, after all the uncertainty, was a lifeline.

Nina closed her eyes and let out a shaky breath, feeling the tightness in her chest loosen just a little. "Dad. Come and get me," she begged, her voice breaking.

"Are you okay?" he asked immediately, his tone laden with panic.

Nina could hear the raw fear in his voice, and it made her chest tighten again—only this time with something closer to hope. "I'm fine; Jack is looking after me," she said, squeezing Jack's hand in a gesture of gratitude. "But please, hurry. I want to go home."

RAW MISTAKES

Before her father could respond, the policeman interjected. "We'll be taking her to the hospital for a check-up. Jack tells us her feet are badly infected."

"Okay," her dad replied quickly, his voice tight with urgency, "but can I speak to Jack?"

Nina and Jack exchanged a glance as the phone was handed over. Nina could see the concern in Jack's eyes, but she felt a sense of calm now that her father was on his way.

"This is Jack," he said, his voice a little uncertain but trying to steady himself.

"I don't know who you are," her dad said, the words rushed, "but thank you for looking after Nina. Please stay with her until we get there."

"Of course, no problem," Jack replied, his voice steady now, a hint of reassurance.

"Dad, what about Julia?" Nina asked, leaning forward in her seat, the trembling in her voice betraying her hope.

"She's at home with her parents," he answered calmly, though Nina could hear the faintest edge of sadness.

Nina let out a shaky breath and covered her face with her hands. Her body trembled, her emotions breaking through as everything hit her. Tears spilled down her face, relief and frustration mingling.

The call ended, and she stood slowly, feeling as though the ground beneath her had been pulled away.

The police escorted her into the back of the car. As they drove off, Nina stared out of the window, her eyes fixed on Jack, who was standing alone by the entrance, his brows pinched in quiet concern.

Later, Nina lay wide awake in a hospital bed, her mind racing despite the exhaustion. Her mother, father, and brother burst into the room, their faces streaked with tears. Her mother's mascara had smudged into dark streaks on her cheeks, and her father's eyes were swollen, red from crying.

The sight of them brought a sense of finality, of something healing in Nina's chest. It was overwhelming and comforting all at once.

In the corridor, Jack lingered for a moment before stepping away. He strolled out of the hospital, a small, contented smile on his lips. He reached into his pocket for the croissant he had saved and took a bite, the normality of the gesture a quiet contrast to the chaos of the last hours. Climbing into his car, he started the engine and began the drive home, his mind clear for the first time in a while.

38 | Carla

Carla groaned as she threw the covers off her bed; the freshly washed sheets seemed not to want her to let her go. With tight muscles, she thought longingly of the time of her life when she'd started each morning with a salute to the sun. Now, a simple house clean left her with an aching body. Quickly, she washed her hair, drawing it back from her forehead. Grabbing her trainers, she headed out into the cool, crisp morning. She used to run with Johnny, but now walking only a five-mile route left her weary.

Returning, her body slumped onto her sofa, her legs unable to carry her further; the many months of sitting on the couch had taken a toll on her legs and feet. She rubbed her feet, gently touching the newly formed blisters, before laying them comfortably on a soft pillow.

As the following morning welcomed a well-rested Carla, she pulled the heavy garage door up and eyed Johnny's bike. She wiped the dust from the seat and pulled it from the damp-smelling garage. Rolling it down the road, she greeted the cheery shopkeeper with a smile, asking him in a soft, gentle voice to give it a once-over.
Her voice surprised her; she welcomed the reply from the only other person she had spoken to, apart from her brother, in over six months with a smile.
With freshly pumped-up tyres, the shopkeeper wiped freshly sprayed oil from the spokes and handed the bike to Carla. "He loved this bike, you know; I'm glad to see you using it," he said, squeezing the brakes and avoiding eye contact. She didn't want to think about the questions she might be asked: should she, in reply, offer more than a simple nod and thank you.
Carla thanked him, waiting to be around the corner before she tried to mount the painful-looking seat. She didn't remember the bike being white and grey; she wasn't sure how much attention she had ever paid to Johnny's most loved treasure stored carefully in the cluttered garage.

As the days passed, she increased her cycling; her butt hurt; everything hurt. She could hardly lift her body due to the throbbing pain. She ran her hands over the unflattering padded cycle trousers she'd bought online, which seemed not to help. Despite the aches and pains, her mood improved each day. The fresh air and the sense of achievement were what she needed to get up and put herself through it again.

RAW MISTAKES

By midday, the sun shone onto the glass panelling of the pub where Johhny had worked. Carla stared in through the windows from a distance; she'd managed to cycle that far but couldn't find the courage to step inside. The slamming door she'd nagged Johnny to fix had ceased its banging, and the rusted iron railing around the bins had been painted.

She was too conscious of her body to enter the pub, instead, she rested on a freshly polished wooden bench, wincing at flashbacks of Johnny scurrying around the tables, smiling at the happy diners. Her stomach flipped as she recognised the outline of a man wearing Johnny's uniform. She placed a foot on the pedal and moved onto the road.

Carla arrived flustered and sweaty at her parents' house; she cycled up the winding road through the manicured gardens. Leaning her bike on the red brick garage, she stared at the door, unsure whether to knock or walk in; she opted for the first. Carla stared up at the imposing black door. She ran her fingers through her hair, pulled down her Lycra t-shirt; she placed a firm smile on her face and banged her knuckles on the door.

"Carla, darling. What a nice surprise, " her father said, tapping her on the shoulder and shutting the door behind them. Carla pulled off her shoes and walked into the kitchen. "Coffee?" he asked, filling the kettle.

"Sure, why not?" Carla replied, her tone dripping with indifference. She heard the heeled footsteps of her mother entering the kitchen behind her.

"Carla, what are you doing here?" her mother asked, standing by the door, confusion written all over her face.

Carla turned slowly to face her with a smile that barely reached her eyes. "Hi, Mum."

"Oh god, darling, what happened to you?" Her eyes quickly scanned Carla's plus-sized figure and her round, bloated face, lingering far too long on her body.

"My husband died, remember?" Carla replied, her voice laced with sarcasm.

Her mother scoffed, rolling her eyes. "Oh, but that was almost a year ago; surely you're over that by now." She poured the boiling water into the cups, clearly unfazed by Carla's sharpness. "You were both so young; it would never have lasted anyway." Despite her words, her mother couldn't look at her for more than a second. "What about money? Are you working?"

"No, I'm too busy figuring out my life," Carla said, a sardonic grin playing on her lips. "I might even go to Italy for a while." The words surprised her as they left her mouth; she hadn't actually considered Italy until then.

"So, you're here for money then," her mother said, casting a knowing glance at her father, who didn't seem to be paying attention.

Carla shook her head, stifling the urge to snap back.

"Charles told us you're living in a slum and that your house is a disgrace," her mother remarked, pulling cakes from a box and placing them on a plate. Carla reached for the plate, but her mother slapped her hand away. "None for you," she sneered, her eyes flicking over Carla's body, "Look at you, you don't need to be eating any more than you already have."

Carla's face tightened, but she kept quiet, choosing instead to make small talk about the family dogs, trying to steer the conversation away from the usual digs. She took her coffee, shaking her head in disbelief at how utterly pointless this visit was.

The conversation remained shallow and hollow; Carla lied about her social activities, pretending to be out more, seeing friends, living a life.

"Are you dating anyone, darling?" her mother asked, her eyes narrowing as they burned into Carla.

"Of course not," Carla snapped, her patience beginning to fray. "Johnny just died, Mum, please." She could feel the anger bubbling inside her, but she bit her tongue, not wanting to lose control.

Carla stood up, her coffee still steaming on the kitchen bench, unfinished. She turned sharply, her tears threatening to spill as she headed for the door. Without a word to her mother, she kissed her father on the cheek, a quick and detached gesture, then stormed out, cycling home in silence.

Over the next few weeks, Carla started to feel herself again; she was now cycling most mornings for, usually, four hours and walking in the afternoon for a few hours. Six months after she'd started her new routine, she weighed herself, and a wide grin passed over her face. She studied herself in the mirror, touching her quickly shrinking belly, waist, and legs. She reached for her phone and began to call friends. For the first time in over a year she felt the need for human contact.

39 | Bree

As the summer season came to a close, Bree arrived first at the beach bar, eagerly waving as her supervisor approached. She found a spot under the sun umbrella, and together they ordered drinks.

"Bree, I have some news about next season," her supervisor said, cutting straight to the point. "You need to go back to Italy."

Bree blinked, her mind trying to process the words. "What? Why me?" she asked, her voice laced with confusion.

"Next year, the company's expanding the programme here. We're bringing in more hotels, more guests—basically, it's going to be a team of reps, not just you anymore," she explained. "But they've got a perfect spot for you in Italy."

Bree's stomach dropped, and she stared at her supervisor, struggling to keep her voice steady. "No. I don't want to go. Please don't do this to me. I can stay here and work with other reps—I don't care—I just want to stay here."

"Bree, please," her supervisor urged, her tone soft but firm.

Bree's face flushed with frustration as she tried to make sense of it all. "I don't understand," she said, her voice rising. "What have I done wrong?"

Her supervisor watched her carefully, a satisfied grin spreading across her face. "You don't get it, do you?" she said, her voice almost smug. "You haven't done anything wrong. It's just—you're one of a kind. It's impossible for me, or the head office, to find a rep who can work alone for nine months at a time without a single issue. You're a star."

Bree's shoulders stiffened, and instead of accepting the compliment, she shook her head, her expression one of defiance. "I'm not going," she muttered, almost like a petulant child.

Her supervisor sighed, leaning back in her chair. "You'd be wasted in a team, Bree. You're a born solo rep. We need you where you're most effective, and that's Italy. You speak Italian after all. Think it over. There's no rush—you've got a couple of weeks before the season's over. You finish here, then you've got a ski season in the Dolomites, followed by a summer season in the Italian Lakes. It's a perfect fit for you."

Bree's jaw tightened as she shot back, her tone sharp and defensive. "I'll just stay here and get a job with another company. It won't be a problem." The arrogance in her voice was hard to miss, but it hid the vulnerability she wasn't ready to admit.

Heading home, Bree yearned for the comfort of Nik's arms, a place where she felt truly safe. But he was away with his family for a long weekend. Lying on her bed, she mulled over the conversation about her possible return to Italy, searching for the right words to tell him. Deciding it was a discussion best had in person, waited for his return. In the meantime, she browsed online for jobs with other travel companies.

When Nik finally came back a few nights later, he seemed distant and heavy with thought. His saddened face and damp eyes were impossible to ignore. He hugged his arms close to his body, then let them drop as he began rummaging through the bottles on the stand, avoiding her gaze.

As he played with his glass, watching the ice swirl, Bree's worry deepened. "Please, Nik, tell me what's wrong," Bree pleaded, her voice trembling.

He sat at the wooden table, drained his drink in a gulp, and poured another. Pressing his hands to his face, he hesitated before reaching out to her hand, gripping it tightly. His beautiful face, usually so full of life, now bore lines of strain, his dark eyes brimming with unshed tears.

"Breezy," he began, his voice cracking. "I don't know how to say this."

Bree felt the colour drain from her face as fear rooted her to the spot.

"I have to leave you," he said at last. "My father had a heart attack, and my mother's stroke has left her paralysed on one side. They're alone, Bree. They can't work, and there's no one else to help them. Just me." His eyes darkened as he tried to gauge her reaction. "I've decided to give notice tomorrow. I'll finish in two weeks and then fly home—for good."

Bree squeezed his hand, trying to steady them both. "Nik, slow down," she urged softly.

"I'll have to manage the land, the animals, the olive trees... They can't do it anymore." His tone was resigned, a man stepping into an unavoidable storm.

Words escaped Bree as she watched him tremble. Pouring another gin for both of them, she tried to hold herself together. Halfway through her second glass, she wiped her tears with the sleeve of her jumper, her mind racing but offering no solution.

"Bree, please, say something," he begged, his eyes finally meeting hers, desperate for a response.

She shook her head, rising unsteadily to her feet, only to sink back down again. On her second attempt, she managed to stand, clutching the table for balance. Slowly, she made her way to the door. Nik, sensing her distress, unlocked it without protest. Bree stepped outside, walking until the soft sand of the beach muffled her hurried steps.

The warm ocean breeze brushed against her tear-streaked face as she sank to the ground, hugging her knees tightly. When her tears finally ceased, she stood and walked to the water's edge, letting the gentle tide lap at her toes.

Returning to the house, she found Nik slumped on the sofa, clutching a cherished photo of them from the night their secret had been revealed. Bree carefully pried the picture from his hands, setting it aside before sitting beside him. She took his hands in hers, squeezing them tightly.

"Look at me, Nik," she whispered, gently tilting his face toward hers. She wiped his damp eyes with her fingers and kissed his nose, their gazes finally meeting.

Her voice wavered, but her resolve was clear. "Nik, family is important. One day, maybe we'll have our own, but for now, you have to take care of your parents. You wouldn't be the man I love if you turned your back on them."

Nik stared at her, his fingers brushing her cheek. "You're my life, Bree. This is only temporary, I promise. Once they're better, I'll come back. We'll get married—you know that's what I want more than anything, don't you?"

She nodded. "I know. It's just a short time apart; we'll get through it."

As exhaustion overtook him, Nik drifted to sleep. Bree lay beside him for a while, listening to his steady breathing, her thoughts tangled. Rising quietly, she moved to the sofa and poured herself another gin. Staring out at the sunrise over the ocean, she made a decision.

If she stayed in Rethymnon, Nik's divided loyalties would weigh him down. He would try to manage both worlds, breaking himself in the process. For his sake—and for the love they shared—she knew she had to let him go.

As dawn broke, Nik stirred, his eyes adjusting to the light filtering through the curtains. The rain had ceased, leaving the air fresh and cool, and he instinctively reached out for Bree. Shielding his eyes from the light with one hand, his other found its way to her thigh.

"Morning, Breezy," he murmured, his voice still husky with sleep. Rolling toward her, he pressed a tender kiss to her stomach.

Bree inhaled deeply, steadying herself. It was now or never. "Nik," she began softly, "I'm going back to Italy."

Nik's brow gathered in concern as her words sunk in.

She continued before he could respond. "You need to be with your family—they need you. And I... I can't stay here without you. My heart would break every day, every night, surrounded by the memories of us in this place."

Nik's eyes widened, concern etching deep lines into his face. He pushed himself up against the pillows, pulling the sheet over his bare shoulders as if bracing against an unseen chill. "What are you saying?"

Bree explained everything—the conversation with her manager, the unexpected offer, and how she had initially dismissed it. But now, with the reality of his departure, she saw no reason to stay.

They held each other tightly, as if trying to imprint the moment into their souls. Nik's mind raced, picturing an impossible future where Bree joined him in his hometown. Shaking his head, he knew it was a dream that could never come true—not now, not with the burden of his family's needs pressing down on him.

"I can't see any other way," he said finally, his voice breaking with resignation. "I have to care for them. My aunt has made it clear what's expected of me. I don't have a choice."

The room fell silent save for the distant song of birds outside. They both knew this wasn't what either of them wanted. But love, as much as it bound them together, also demanded sacrifices they never anticipated.

40 | Bree

As the next two weeks passed, Nik barely left Bree's side. Every waking moment was spent together, their bond growing even stronger in the shadow of his impending departure. The lively parties he once loved to host ceased entirely; he no longer wanted to share Bree with anyone.

Anna, ever perceptive, turned a blind eye to their constant touching and lingering kisses in the kitchen. She had watched their relationship blossom and knew how deeply they were suffering. Nik, who had been the happiest she'd ever seen since meeting Bree, now carried an undeniable sadness.

As the final day approached, Bree felt as though her heart might shatter under her grief. Nik, too, was consumed by guilt—torn between leaving her and the aching regret of not being with his family.

At the airport, they clung to each other, trying desperately to hold on. They had promised themselves they wouldn't cry, determined to preserve some dignity, as Nik had managed while saying goodbye to their friends the day before. But that resolve quickly crumbled; Bree's mind fogged with despair, her tears spilling over at the slightest touch or glance. Slowly, she pulled herself from his arms, her legs trembling beneath her.

As Nik walked away, disappearing into the depths of the airport, Bree's knees buckled. She felt faint, barely able to stand until Elka's gentle hands steadied her and guided her back to the waiting car.

The drive from the airport blurred past her in a haze of numbness. The scenery outside the window seemed distant and irrelevant. Unable to face their home and the memories of Nik that lingered in every corner, she directed the driver to the office. Bree waited for a moment before stepping inside, taking a deep, steadying breath. Ignoring the pitying glances of her colleagues, she walked to her desk, her eyes firmly on the floor.

Out of habit, she pulled open a drawer, half-hoping to find one of Nik's cheeky notes tucked away. Instead, her fingers brushed against an envelope with "Breezy" written in his handwriting. Her heart skipped a beat as she quickly opened it, revealing a simple yet powerful message: "I love you," accompanied by a flight ticket.

Her face lit up for the first time in weeks. Holding the ticket above her head, she declared to the room, "I'm going to Nik's hometown. I'll see him soon."

The next few days dragged by. She clung to his morning and evening calls, savouring their long chats before falling asleep. Bree busied herself with preparations: closing up their house, packing his belongings, and stroking the fabric of his clothes as if they could bring him closer. She slept with his jumper by her side, his t-shirt against her skin, trying to hold on to his presence.

Each day, Nik shared updates about his parents' struggles and his efforts to help them. Bree worried about him overworking himself; his voice always sounded strained with exhaustion. She wondered if her trip would add to his burden—dividing his attention further between his family, work, and her.

A week after Nik's departure, Bree lay in bed, ashamed of having devoured three croissants for dinner the night before. She stared at her phone, willing a message to appear on the screen. Checking the time, she scowled and pulled the sheets over her head, shutting out the brilliant sunlight streaming through the blinds.

It was her first day off without Nik, and she couldn't bring herself to face the world. Offers from friends to join them on various outings were met with polite refusals. Silence and solitude felt easier than the pressure of conversation. She ached to touch him, to feel his presence beside her.

As she turned away from the window and closed her eyes, a sound jolted her—a key turning in the lock, followed by footsteps.

"Breezy, babe, are you here?" Nik's voice filled the house.

Her heart leapt. She shot out of bed as though struck by lightning, hastily running her fingers through her hair and kicking aside a pile of unwashed clothes. Flinging open the bedroom door, she raced toward him and threw herself into his arms.

Melting into his warm embrace, Bree's tears spilled over as Nik kissed her—first gently, then with the passion of six long days apart.

Her wide, dancing eyes met his. "How? Why? How long are you here for?" she asked breathlessly.

Nik smiled, letting her go as he moved toward the coffee machine. Pulling out cups, coffee, and sugar, he began to explain. "One question at a time," he teased. "How? My mum is staying with her sister for a few days, and my dad is in the hospital, so they're both well looked after."

Bree nodded, relief washing over her. "That's good."

"Why?" He turned to her, his face softening. "Because I missed you too much. You've been in my thoughts and dreams every second."

He placed two steaming cups of coffee on the table, grabbing the nearly empty biscuit tin.

"And how long?" He grinned. "I'll stay until you leave. Then we'll fly to my hometown together—if that's all right with you."

Bree squealed with delight, snatching the biscuit from his hand. For the first time in weeks, she felt truly hungry.

"I need a shower," Nik said, pulling off his top, his toned chest making Bree's cheeks flush. "Join me?" he asked with a cheeky grin.

Bree hesitated for only a second before pulling off the t-shirt she'd been sleeping in and slipping out of her pants. Taking his hand, she led him to the shower.

Hours later, they finally pulled themselves out of bed, both laughing at their reluctance to face the day. Nik grinned as they climbed onto Bree's moped, the sensation of the ride bringing him comfort. He held her waist as the breeze tossed her hair.

"Anna's going to kill me if I don't pass by," he said as Bree steered the moped towards the office and parked outside.

Bree felt lighter than she had in days as she floated through the doors. Anna noticed her first, her eyes lighting up.

"Finally, you're smiling. I've missed that smile," Anna said warmly before spotting Nik. "Ah, the cheese lover is back. I knew you couldn't stay away for long," she teased, pulling him into a fond hug.

As Anna and Nik chatted in Greek, Bree wandered away, spinning around in the swivel chair by the entrance and flashing smiles at everyone who passed.

Nik wasted no time in planning his grand return. "Biggest party yet," he announced later that day, brimming with enthusiasm.

Though Bree preferred quieter nights in with small groups, Nik's excitement was contagious. She threw herself into helping him prepare, decorating the roof terrace with twinkling lights, selecting music, and ferrying plates and bottles wherever he needed.

Bree didn't feel ready when the guests began arriving one by one, greeting Nik with hugs and warm welcomes. Many commented on Bree's recently forlorn expression, making her blush. Nik, ever protective, pulled her close with a grin.

More than fifty people spread out across the house and terrace. The air buzzed with lively conversation and laughter, while Bree lingered near the fridge, watching the scene unfold.

As night fell, Nik let out a sharp whistle, gathering everyone's attention. The chatter subsided as he raised his voice.

"Everyone, I've missed you all this past week," he began, his tone playful. "But as much as I love you all," he paused, turning to Bree with a loving smile, "this stunning woman is the one I missed the most."

He stroked her back as he spoke, his eyes sparkling with affection. "I mean, look at her," he said with a laugh.

Bree's heart melted, though she rolled her eyes in mock exasperation. But before she could respond, a collective gasp rippled through the crowd. Cheers and whistles erupted around her.

Confused, Bree turned to see what had caused the commotion. Her jaw dropped, and her eyes widened.

Nik knelt before her on one knee, a small blue box in his outstretched hand. Nestled inside was a diamond ring that shimmered under the lights.

With a cheeky grin, he looked up at her and began to speak, his voice steady and filled with emotion. "Breezy, I love you more than anything. You're my love, my life. I know we can't be together right now, but I can't leave here without knowing that soon you'll be my wife."

He paused, drawing a deep breath, and the room fell silent. Even the laughter and whispers of the crowd faded away.

"Will you marry me?" he asked, his words slow and deliberate.

For a moment, the world seemed to stand still. Bree stared at him in stunned disbelief, her face unreadable. A nervous chuckle escaped from one of the guests, breaking the silence.

Nik's smile faltered, and a flicker of panic crossed his face as he searched her expression for an answer.

41 | Carla

Carla dressed carefully before heading to her parent's home for a family dinner that had inexplicably become a weekly event. Finding the most flattering outfit, she pouted her face in the mirror. A pair of simple black trousers with a loose-fitting, layered black top would have to suffice.

Every week since her trip to see her parents, she'd been forced to make a decision between two very unsavoury options. She had to find an excuse not to go to the weekly family dinner and suffer a week of insulting, angry phone calls from her mother, or sit through three hours of mundane conversation and criticism. She weighed up the risks and decided she would attend the dinner that week. Feeling stage fright, her body stiffened as she rang the doorbell of the family home.

Her mother opened the door; her pearl necklace sat low around her neck on her red and black woollen top. She looked Carla up and down and said, "Oh, Carla, I thought I asked you to make an effort on Friday evenings. You know how important it is to dress for dinner."

Carla mumbled an embarrassed apology as she stepped into the house. As she entered the immaculate sitting room, her father glanced up from his newspaper, nodding in Carla's direction as he continued to read. Carla soothed down her trousers and sat in the armchair.

"No, not there tonight; sit on the sofa," her mother said.

Carla moved to the sofa, fiddling nervously with her necklace. Her dad looked up for a second; he winked, folded the newspaper up, and placed it on the table.

"No, darling, not there," her mum said as she whisked the newspaper away from his sight.

Carla saw her father looking disturbed; he offered her a subtle nod reached for his newspaper and asked, "What are you drinking?" Without listening to her reply, he walked towards the wooden drinks cabinet and pulled out a bottle of red wine. Handing Carla a glass, he stopped to admire her and said, "You look very nice tonight. Oh, also, I'm sorry."

Carla replied with a confused shake of her head as a car pulled up on the gravel drive. She heaved a sigh of relief; as much as Charles frustrated her, his arrival always took the pressure off her. The frogs fitted in easily into this environment, and she felt the expectations to be perfect slip away.

As Charles entered the door, followed by his boyfriend, she heard a quiet muttering, making out a few words; she heard him ask his mother, "Has he arrived yet?"

Carla jumped to her feet and asked, "Has who arrived yet?"

RAW MISTAKES

"Carla, darling, we've invited a guest, a male guest, for dinner this evening. He's about your age; he's single, and I'm friends with his mother."

Filled with dread, Carla needed clarification. She shot her mother an exasperated look and asked, "A setup? You have arranged a setup here, at your house, for me."

"If you want to call it a setup, then yes." Her mother hovered at the door and said, "Let's face it, no men are pressing for your company, and you have no visible means of income."

Charles joined in, "Carla, come on; you can't stay locked up in that house forever; you look so much better now; you're in your prime; it's time you give Mum and Dad some grandchildren."

Carla, exasperated, felg ganged up on. She interrupted with a snort, rose to her feet, looked at her family and hissed, "So this is all about you, not me. I expected better than this; I'm not interested in being set up with one of your stuffy friends."

Carla bit her lip as they threw accusations her way. She stormed out of the room, picked up her coat and bag, and headed to the front door. She had to do whatever it took to pull the plug on this stupid project. Carla stood with her hand hovering on the front door handle as she prepared to leave. She heard her name and stopped and looked over her shoulder.

"Carla, please, for me," her dad pleaded across the room.

She saw lights brighten the door from outside, then the windows turned dark. Carla let out a long eye roll and stepped back from the door.

"Oh, great, he's here," her mother said joyfully. With no time to think of another solution, Carla sighed as she opened the door.

A smartly dressed man stretched out his hand and said, "Hello, I'm Kevin; Thanks for inviting me."

Carla turned in embarrassment and forced herself to smile. Her eyes met his, and for a second, she was sheepish. "It's nice to meet you too; I'm Carla. Please come in; give me your coat." Remembering her manners, she spotted her mother smiling in the dining room, walking over to greet him.

Carla looked at him. He wore a sharp white blazer; she could see he was heavy in the midsection, and his thick beard and glasses hid a large proportion of his face. Carla heard giggles from behind the corner; she shot the frogs an annoyed glance.

Kevin handed some flowers to Carla's mother, a box of Cuban cigars to her father, and a box of chocolates to Carla before joining her on the sofa.

Carla took the box of chocolates, set them aside, and crossed her arms across her body. Shooting her mum a look of rage, she turned her body away from Kevin and towards Charles and asked him about his day.

Charles watched her eyebrows raise. He could see she was disgusted by Kevin. They shared suspicious glances as Carla shot Charles a warning look. Charles mouthed 'Sorry' to her as he turned his attention to Kevin and said, "So, Kevin, please tell us about yourself."

Kevin pinched his trousers at his knees and sat on the front of the sofa, turning his body towards Carla. "Well, I work in investment banking, as you all know. I work in the city, London City, of course; where else is there?" He took a sip of water, loosened his tie, reached for his drink, and swirled it around in the glass. "I work at Goldman Sachs in the advisory department." He nodded as he talked, there was a pause, and his tone changed, entering into detail about his biggest account.

Carla rolled her eyes at her brother, realising he was just getting started. Unable to listen to the drones of an investment banker, she excused herself and crept upstairs, over the squeaky floorboards, to her childhood room. Perched on the edge of the bed, she looked around her and thought about Kevin. It took her a second to realise who he was. He was an exact copy of everyone she had gone to school with—an older version of her male classmates. Feeling miserable, she looked down from the bedroom window and shook her head. It was too far to jump for freedom.

"Carla, come downstairs now. Don't be rude to your guest," her mother called from the doorway.

As soon as Carla heard her name, she frowned. "Mother, he's your guest, not mine. I didn't invite him; you did."

With an irritated scowl, Carla's mother motioned at her to keep her voice down. Carla crossed her arms in anger and said, "Downstairs, now."

"You know I'm not a teenager anymore, don't you? I don't live here. I don't have to abide by your rules," Carla said, suddenly feeling playful. Using her mother's own words against her, she smiled.

Her mother's smile faltered as she repeated herself, "Downstairs, now."

Carla entered the sitting room and looked over at Kevin, who still seemed to be droning on about his job. Charles, bored stiff, yawned and slumped back into the pillows.

Carla poured herself another drink and scowled at Kevin. A yawn escaped her lips; she took a deep breath, pulled up a heavy chair, and sat by the frogs.

Noticing Carla's yawn, apologies started pouring out of Kevin's mouth: "Sorry, I just am so passionate about my job."

Carla's dad offered him another drink; Kevin inspected his Rolex. "Well, I don't see why not," he smiled.

Carla realised her parents had underestimated her. "I'll have another one, too, please," Carla said.

"Haven't you already had one? We haven't even had dinner yet, darling. Shouldn't you be worrying about your figure?" she said in a condescending tone.

"Oh, Mum, I'm just getting started," Carla said. Her thick, dark hair cascaded down her back as she flipped her head back. They all stared at her. She raised her glass, grinned and took a long gulp of her drink.

Kevin whistled nervously as he sat. He seemed terrified of letting his mother down. She'd arranged that date for him; he'd remembered Carla from school and had found her to be different from the other girls. Regretting coming, he could tell she didn't want him there.

As they ate dinner, Carla filled up her wine frequently. Her mother rose wordlessly from her seat and removed the bottle of wine from Carla's reach. Carla slid her hand over to Charles' glass and pulled it towards her, taking a long gulp. Her mother, appalled, stared at her. Carla sat across from Kevin, her heart pounding with frustration.

"So, Kevin, what are your plans for your future?" Charles asked, seeking a distraction, wishing to take the attention away from Carla.

Kevin barely took a second to consider the question, "I'd like to marry within two years and have two children within two years of marriage. I can see myself living in the city at first and then moving out to the country and commuting."

Carla stopped listening. As Kevin droned on, a sudden realisation hit her like a lightning bolt: she knew this man. Determined to put an end to his smugness, she cut him off with a dramatic, exaggerated cough. Turning towards him with a sharp stare, she bent forward slightly, her tone biting.

"Kevin Orme," she began with mock surprise, "Of course. I remember you from school. You were quite the overachiever, weren't you? You excelled at stealing Jason Holmes's lunch money, hiding his books, and copying his homework. Really, top marks all around." Her words dripped with sarcasm as she gave him a pointed look.

Kevin's face darkened. "No, Carla, I think you've got the wrong person. I don't recall going to school with you," he said, his voice low and defensive, though his eyes betrayed a flicker of hostility.

"Oh, come on, Kevin. Surely you don't think I'd forget the school bully. The boy who made tripping people in the corridor look like a sport."

Charles, who had been quietly sipping his wine, suddenly stood. "She's right, you know," he chimed in, his tone light but laced with mock indignation. "You tried to bully me too, though I guess I wasn't worth your full attention like Jason. Still, you had your moments." He crossed his arms and dipped back in his seat, smirking.

Their mother, who had been watching the exchange with a growing frown, finally spoke. "This really isn't helping create the perfect evening I'd imagined," she muttered under her breath, glaring at Carla and Charles.

Kevin cursed quietly, his face reddening. "I think you've mistaken me for someone else. Kevin Orme is a common name," he said, his voice strained as he checked his watch for the third time in a minute. Standing abruptly, he tossed his napkin onto the plate and muttered, "I think I should be going."

"Oh, but you can't leave without your jacket." Carla said, her voice dripping with fake concern as she leapt to her feet. Fetching his white blazer with theatrical flair, she held it out like she was presenting a royal robe.

Kevin snatched the jacket without a word. He hesitated at the door, glancing back at Carla and then Charles, before storming out. The soft purr of his Porsche retreating down the street was the only sound that followed.

Their mother rounded on them. "You two have humiliated me," she snapped, her voice trembling with indignation. "What am I supposed to tell Mrs. Orme now?"

Charles didn't miss a beat. "Tell her that her son, who terrorised half the high school, is as dull as he is insufferable." He collapsed onto the sofa with a dramatic sigh.

Their mother let out an exasperated gasp, threw her napkin onto the table, and stormed out of the room without another word.

Carla snorted, unable to hold back a laugh. "Cake, anyone?" she called out, disappearing into the kitchen. Moments later, she returned with a massive chocolate cake and three oversized slices. "More for us, then," she said with a sly grin, biting into hers.

Later, as Carla and Charles said their goodbyes, she felt his hand slip into hers.

"You were brilliant back there," he said, grinning as he helped her out of his car. "I'm proud of you."

Carla smirked. "See ya, Bro. That was actually... fun." For the first time in twenty-eight years, she felt like she and Charles were on the same wavelength.

42 | Nina

Nina's heavily bandaged feet rested on the wheelchair as her father pushed her out of the hospital later that day. Nina shielded her eyes from the bright sunlight. Journalists formed a ring around her as the police escorted Nina and her family away to the safety of their car.

Sitting in the back seat, her brother squeezed her hand tightly. A concerned, awkward silence filled the air as they drove slowly past the journalists. "You're famous; do you know that?" Fabio laughed at her and said, "You're the hottest story in the news right now."

Nina shook her head. "I don't want to be famous. I want to see Julia. It's all my fault," she sobbed as the car sped towards the motorway. Nina rested her head on his lap, welcoming his protective touch.

"Your fault? No, Nina," Fabio whispered. "None of this is your fault; I should have walked you home; it's all my fault."

"This is the fault of those who did this; nobody else is to blame." Nina's dad piped up in frustration. "Now, rest; we'll talk when we get home."

As they neared the family home, Nina focused on the 'missing' flyers stapled to trees; her smiling face loomed large on the bright pink papers. Nina's dad honked his horn loudly as he drove through the waiting journalists, who had formed a barrier on the driveway. Once Gianni had ushered Nina through the garage into the kitchen, he approached the sea of microphones.

"Thank you for your interest in our family; our daughter is now home, and we ask you to respect our privacy."

"Did they hurt your daughter? Have the police caught the kidnappers?" The voices shouted out as Nina's dad turned away and closed the heavy garage door behind him.

Over the following days, two heavy-set men stood guard outside the house day and night. Nina, exhausted and preferring the sounds of her family to the silence of her room, stared out of the window at the hovering, curious press.

Fabio took to sleeping in his sister's spare bed, guarding the room against intruders. Three years older than Nina, he dropped his social life to stay with her. Refusing to eat or talk to anyone apart from Fabio about her experience, Nina became the shadow of her former self.

A week passed before she was allowed to see Julia, who had closed herself off to the world, refusing to speak to anyone. As she approached, her glazed eyes fixated on Nina; she wrapped her arms around her waist and cried.

Fortunately, they kept Julia in the house for a few more days, cleaned her up, and paraded her around unknown buyers before selling her to a policeman infiltrating the trafficking ring. The world had kept her identity and location a secret until Nina's safe return.

Nina insisted on returning to school, and her parents, although reluctant, agreed. The school allowed Fabio to leave his classes early and walk Nina to the next lesson. No longer permitting her to walk outdoors alone, her dad arranged a schedule of family members to drive her.

Nina dreamt and longed for a sense of normality without all this protection. Her bond with Fabio was like none other; she felt physically and emotionally safe with him around. She confided only in him about her experience, and although her parents insisted on her talking to a therapist, she refused.

On her first day of school, she was met by a sea of journalists. Ducking her head down, Fabio placed a protective arm around her and pushed her through the crowd. She felt the eyes of every pupil in the school watching her walk to her locker; people who had never spoken to her were now desperate to be noticed by her.

"Welcome back, Nina; we missed you," students called out as Nina politely nodded and smiled. Resting her hand firmly on her locker, she inserted the tiny key in the padlock; envelopes and letters fell lightly to the floor. She removed the ones still stuck in the grates and handed them to her brother with a disinterested shrug.

Her three best friends greeted her with hugs, linked her arms, and whisked her off to her first class. "We've got your back; you aren't alone, you know that," Linda shouted, proud to be seen with her friend, whose face was still all over the news every day.

Nina took her usual seat in the classroom; she grabbed Linda's arm, pulling her in close and said, "Talk to me; I need to look at you; everyone is staring at me."

Silence fell over the room as the teacher entered, with the headmaster standing next to her desk. The teacher wiped the blackboard clean as the headmaster cleared his throat.

"All of you, please join me in welcoming Nina back to our classroom," he said loudly.

A round of applause rippled through the room, growing louder as Nina stared down at the floor. She sank into her seat, trying to steady her breath, but the sudden burst of attention only unsettled her more. Before she realised what she was doing, she stood again, her voice cutting through the noise.

"Look, everyone, I want to go back to normal," she began, her tone firm despite the quiver in her chest. "I don't need all this fuss. If you didn't speak to me before, don't feel like you have to now. If you were my friend before, you know who you are. Just... keep being my friend."

She met the eyes of her close friends, drawing strength from their silent support, before continuing, "I know you all want to know what happened. Maybe it's time to get the truth out there."

Nina walked to the front of the room, her steps deliberate, her face steady.

"Call her brother, now," the headmaster murmured urgently to the teacher. "He should be in the hall."

Moments later, Fabio burst into the room. Placing a reassuring hand on her back, he asked, "What's going on? What happened?"

"Nothing," Nina replied curtly, brushing him off. "I just can't stand everyone staring at me like I'm some kind of idiot." She drew a deep breath, squaring her shoulders. Turning back to her classmates, she addressed the room, her voice clear.

"I wasn't harmed, raped, or beaten," she declared, letting the truth settle over the group. "I was locked in a room with no food and barely any water. That's it."

Pointing to her bandaged feet, she added, "These aren't from torture; they're from running through the woods to escape. I got out on my own." Her eyes scanned the room. "Does anyone have any questions?"

The class fell into an uneasy silence until one brave student finally spoke up. "Is it true that a crazy hermit rescued you and then held you hostage, too?"

Gasps rippled across the room, and Nina let out a frustrated sigh. "No," she said sharply. "I escaped and ran to a house in the woods. The man who helped me wasn't crazy. He didn't have a phone, so I stayed until the storm passed and it was daylight. That's all."

She glanced around, her irritation rising. "Any other questions?"

No one responded this time.

The headmaster, sensing her fraying patience, stepped forward. "Alright," he said with quiet authority. "Let's get back to class."

Fabio gently took her hand and led her into the hallway. "That was brave of you, Nina," he said softly.

She shrugged, brushing a strand of hair from her face. "I didn't know what else to do. At least it's done now."

Fabio nodded thoughtfully. "If you want to get rid of the journalists, you might want to tell them the same thing. It could shut them up for good."

That night, however, Nina's courage gave way to her fears. The faces of her captors haunted her dreams, their leering expressions jolting her awake in a veil of sweat. She would scream herself awake, her heart racing, the echoes of her nightmares reverberating through the dark.

The police found the house where she had been held, but it was too late. It had been abandoned, stripped bare, and torched. The rain had extinguished most of the fire, but faint traces of her presence remained in the scorched room.

The two men responsible had vanished. Their names remained unknown, but their faces were now plastered across Italy's most-wanted list. For Nina, they lived in her memory, vivid and unwelcome. Every scent, every shadow, seemed to conjure their images, her mind unable to let go of what it could not fully comprehend.

43 | Petra

As Petra lay in bed at night, she imagined her dream life: a loving husband and an adorable child splashing in the gentle waves of a white-sand beach. Her two years of travel had blurred into one long stretch; the countries, luxurious hotels, and villas all felt too similar to distinguish. Now, sitting in the first-class lounge with a scowl, she flicked through photos of the villa she was heading to while waiting for her flight to Italy to board.

The villa lay nestled in the heart of the Italian vineyards, surrounded by rolling green hills and winding gravel paths. Petra could picture the stuffy owner she had yet to meet, the crisp white sheets, and the plump cushions awaiting her. But she had resented this trip from the start. She'd scrambled for excuses not to go, preferring to visit Ireland and check on Liam. Her manager, however, had been unapologetic, insisting she stick to the itinerary.

Arriving at the estate, she barely noticed its beauty. Instead, she mulled over how to describe its 'enchanting panoramic views, Mediterranean gardens, pure perfection, and vintage charm' without ever leaving her room. Perched cross-legged on the bed, she flicked through a brochure until her eyes lit up at the mention of a self-guided cycle tour of the vineyards. Suddenly slightly more excited, she booked it online and soon set off on a sparkling blue mountain bike.

The bike's frame was too small, and her feet clipped the tyres when she turned, but the fresh air lightened her mood. As she pedalled along, she daydreamed about Liam cycling beside her, the towering cypress trees and sprawling vineyards providing the perfect backdrop. When the gravel road became steep and winding, she pushed herself hard, legs burning as she climbed. Out of breath, she eventually dismounted, prodding the tyre in frustration.

Certain it had a puncture, she searched fruitlessly for a repair kit. Nothing. The afternoon sun warmed her pale complexion as she trudged alongside the bike, the gravel crunching underfoot.

Turning a bend, she stepped aside as a tractor rumbled past. It stopped suddenly, and a tall man with jet-black hair climbed down, his expression intrigued. Petra couldn't help but smile at the sight of him.

"Hello. Are you Petra Bennett?" he asked, his rich, lilting accent arresting her attention. Taking the bike from her hands, he added, "We were worried when you didn't arrive for the wine tasting."

Petra pointed mutely to the tyre, struggling to form a coherent sentence. "Yes, I'm Petra," she managed, sounding flustered.

"Ah, a puncture. No problem. Let's get the bike on the tractor and get you up the hill," he said, flashing a smile that made her heart skip.

"Thanks," she murmured, regaining a measure of composure. "That would be great."

He introduced himself as Rico, and Petra marvelled at how effortlessly he carried himself. His casual work clothes—a checked shirt, blue shorts, and a straw hat—had an air of elegance that would have made anyone else look like a simple farmer. As they ascended the hill, their conversation was light but pleasant.

When they arrived at the main house, an imposing structure perched atop the steep incline, Rico unloaded the bike with ease and offered her a chilled drink. The wine cellars were shaded by a dense pine forest stretching beyond the estate's boundaries. Inside, the air was cool and heavy with the scent of ageing wine.

Adjusting to the dim light, Petra listened intently as Rico guided her through the cellar, explaining the vineyard's history and its blend of old and new winemaking techniques. He gestured towards rows of barrels, describing the process of cultivating and processing the grapes. By the end of the tour, he handed her a bottle of wine with a warm smile.

"I'll give you a lift back to the villa," he said.

"Yes, please," she replied, her smile mirroring his. "Thank you so much."

As they reached the villa, Rico paused beside a line of trees and pointed to where his initials had been carved into the bark. "One day, my children's initials will be here too," he said with a wistful grin.

Petra ran her fingers over the carvings, a flicker of hope sparking in her chest.

"Do you have plans for tomorrow?" Rico asked, leaning casually against the tractor with his hands in his pockets. "I'm heading into the city—if you'd like, I can show you around."

Petra felt her pulse quicken under his intense gaze. Barely able to contain her excitement, she murmured a timid, "Yes."

The following morning, she rummaged through her suitcase, deliberating over what to wear. Finally, she settled on a flowery, knee-length sundress paired with white strappy sandals—perfect for what she hoped would be a memorable day.

Petra's heart skipped a beat as Rico wrapped his hand around hers and led her into an elegant restaurant. She marvelled at the imposing high ceiling and gilded pillars, the quiet squeak of the polished floorboards accompanying their steps. The arched walls sectioned off smaller, distinct spaces, each fitted with its own unique décor and palette of colours.

Though Petra felt sure Rico's kindness was simply an attempt to impress her into promoting his luxurious—and ridiculously expensive—villa, she couldn't deny her enjoyment. The flavours of the grilled cheese, tender and marinated in ginger and garlic, delighted her palate. Her glass of full-bodied wine sat untouched as their conversation flowed easily, like two old friends catching up after years apart.

"How long have you worked at the vineyard?" Petra asked, eager to learn more about the enigmatic man before her.

Rico laughed, a warm and genuine sound. "Since I was four, but I don't just work there—I own it," he replied with a playful grin. "It's my family's vineyard. I'm the only one of my siblings who wanted to stay involved. The rest are happy to just collect the money. But for me, there's nothing else I'd rather do. I love it; it's the best job ever. This restaurant is mine too, but it's just a little hobby—nothing serious."

Petra raised an eyebrow, sensing an edge of arrogance in his humility, but she offered a polite smile. "That's very impressive," she said, keeping her tone light.

Rico dabbed his upper lip with a napkin, lifting his glass in a toast. "I've got some errands to run—boring stuff. I'll leave you to explore for a bit, and I'll pick you up in a couple of hours, alright?"

Agreeing, Petra placed her napkin neatly on the table and pushed back her chair. As she wandered the streets of Verona alone, her thoughts drifted ahead to the possibilities with this charming man. She found a shady spot beneath a statue and watched the bustle of people coming and going near the arena, her mind a pleasant haze of romantic hope.

Later, Rico approached with a broad smile, waving two tickets in the air. "We've got tickets for tonight. There's a concert in the arena. Have you ever heard of Eros Ramazzotti?"

Petra shook her head. "No, I don't think so."

"It doesn't matter. By tonight, you'll love him," Rico assured her, grinning as he opened the car door for her.

Back at the villa, Petra rummaged through her suitcase, holding up different outfits before discarding them with a huff. Finally, she settled on a flattering maxi skirt and a blouse, smoothing down the fabric with her hands. She tied her hair back with a ribbon, applied a touch of makeup, and frowned at her reflection before mustering a determined smile.

When she descended the steps to meet Rico, he kissed her on both cheeks, his greeting warm and appreciative. "You look stunning," he said, adjusting his tie and smoothing his jacket. Smiling, he offered his hand, which she took gladly as they headed to his car.

The concert in the Arena di Verona was a spectacle Petra would never forget. As they entered the ancient Roman amphitheatre, the sheer scale of it took her breath away. The massive stone arches towered overhead, bathed in the warmth of stage lights, and the ancient walls seemed to hum with the echoes of centuries of history.

The venue was alive with sound, the crisp, clear notes of Eros Ramazzotti's voice resonating throughout the open-air arena. Petra could feel the vibration of the music in her chest as it reverberated against the ancient stones, a harmony of modern and timeless. The crowd around them was a sea of faces, some swaying to the music, others waving their hands in the air, fully immersed in the experience.

Despite the overwhelming energy of the concert, Petra felt a sense of intimacy with Rico, as if the noise and the crowds had faded away, leaving just the two of them in their own world. She found herself swept up in the music, her senses alive with the beauty of the performance, the rich melodies filling her with a sense of joy.

As the concert reached its climax, the crowd erupted in applause, a roar of appreciation that echoed into the night sky. Petra joined in, clapping along with the others, her heart racing from the sheer exhilaration of it all. When the final notes faded away and the lights came back on, the magic of the night lingered, leaving her with a sense of awe and wonder.

Under the moonlit sky outside the villa, Rico tilted forward for another kiss, his lips soft and unhurried. Petra felt herself purr softly as he pulled back. Embarrassed, she looked away, muttering, "Sorry."

He paused, his voice low and steady. "Sorry about what? I kissed you." He shifted forward again, his hand gently brushing her cheek before he wished her goodnight and closed the door softly behind her.

Petra stood frozen in the moment, a smile tugging at her lips as her attention wandered to the portrait of Rico's grandfather, hung high above the door. With a fluttering heart, she stepped into the hallway and made her way to her room.

44 | Nina

"I want to go back there, to the house," Nina announced quietly on a grey, wintry evening, the family gathered around the dinner table.

Her father looked up at her in shock, his fork pausing halfway to his mouth. "Why? What good will it do?"

Nina's gaze remained steady on her father, her voice soft. "I just need to do it. I need to see it with you. Maybe... maybe seeing it will make the nightmares stop."

Her father's expression softened, but the concern in his eyes didn't fade. He knew how hard Nina had been since her return, how every little thing seemed to set her off, like a pressure cooker on the edge of exploding.

He sighed, exhaling slowly. "Okay, Saturday then. I'll speak to the police and let them know."

Nina nodded, her fingers playing absentmindedly with the edge of her plate. "And... I want to see Jack too. He just disappeared, and I never even thanked him properly." She looked up, meeting her father's confused smile. "I need to give him his son's clothes back."

Her father paused for a moment, digesting the request. "Alright. I'll arrange it. We'll go on Saturday morning. Who else do you want to come with us?"

Nina paused, looking down at her lap before glancing back up. "I know Mum wants to pretend it didn't happen, but it did. So... you, Mum, and Fabio, please."

As he walked away, Nina's voice called after him. "Dad, can I place an order on Amazon for Jack? He needs a few things... bits and bobs."

Her father stuck his head back through the door, raising an eyebrow with a small smile. "That man can have anything he wants. He saved you, Nina. I want to meet him, thank him personally."

Saturday morning arrived. As Nina peered out of the window, she saw light snow lying on the trees. Nina had always considered snow magical, and this covering of delicate flakes changed her frame of mind about the visit to the house. Fabio packed the car full of boxes, the Amazon arrows stacked on each other until the car boot was filled to the brim.

The car ride was silent, the heavy fear pressing down on Nina's chest. As they approached the house, her stomach twisted in knots.

When the car stopped, she opened the door with a trembling hand, the crunch of snow beneath her feet the only sound that reached her ears.

She rubbed her brow, fighting the flood of flashbacks that began to assault her mind—the sharp, violent tug as she'd been dragged from the car, the taste of cold metal against her cheek as her body slammed into the ground. The images felt as raw and real as the day they'd happened.

As she stepped out, her legs shook with unease, each step a battle against the dread rising in her chest. "I think I banged my head here when they dragged me out of the car," she said, her voice distant, barely more than a whisper, as though the words could somehow make the memories less painful.

Her father and Fabio followed behind her, their presence a quiet comfort, but it didn't ease the heaviness in her heart. She moved slowly toward the house, her feet dragging in the snow as she neared the door to her old room. She stood there for a long moment, hovering at the threshold, hand resting on the cold metal of the lock. She turned it slowly, letting the sound of the deadbolt echo through the stillness. Her breath caught in her throat as she slid the bolt back and forth, the clink of it sending a shiver down her spine.

Finally, she stepped inside. The air felt thick with memories, but the room itself had changed. The sofa she'd once sunk into, seeking comfort from the nightmare outside, was gone, replaced with the emptiness of the room. The scent of gasoline lingered, sharp and cold, cutting through the musty remnants of body odour and sweat. It felt like the house was breathing with her, exhaling a history she couldn't escape.

"This was my room," she muttered, her voice small, as though speaking it aloud might make it all real. She dragged her fingers along the walls, as though searching for something—anything—that would ground her.

She wandered through the house, her eyes scanning every corner, trying to place the sounds that had once kept her awake at night. The kitchen—now nothing but a blackened ruin, the charred remains of what had been. She kicked at a pile of empty beer bottles, their broken glass crunching beneath her boot, a sound that seemed to reverberate too loudly in the silence.

Snowflakes continued to fall softly outside, their quiet descent at odds with the storm of emotions inside her.

Nina paused at the door, looking out towards the hill in the distance. The snow crunched beneath her boots as she walked out into the yard, her breath misting in the cold air.

"That's where I ran when I escaped," she said softly, her expression distant as she stared at the hill where so much had happened. "There wasn't as much snow then, just... leaves underfoot. It was dark. It's all a bit of a blur now, though."

Her father, his voice strained, tried to offer some semblance of comfort. "You must have been terrified," he said, his eyes glistening with unshed tears. "But, Nina... I'm so proud of you. For getting out. For surviving."

Nina swallowed hard, her eyes closing briefly. "It was that woman," she whispered, almost to herself. "She opened the door for me. I wonder if we'll ever find out who she is."

She turned, taking one last, lingering look at the house, the place that had once been her prison. "It doesn't scare me anymore," she said, her voice steadier now, stronger. "I needed to see it again. To face it."

Nina moved away from the house, her family following closely behind, the crunch of snow beneath their feet blending with the silence that surrounded them.

The drive to Jack's house felt like another lifetime.

"Do you recognise any of it?" her father asked.

Nina searched the landscape, her eyes scanning for any hint of familiarity. "No, not really," she replied when her father asked if she recognised anything. "We were going the other way when we went to the police station, and I was hiding most of the time."

They drove for what felt like hours, until Nina's sharp eyes caught sight of the dilapidated house in the distance. "There," she cried out, excitement rising in her chest. "That's it." This time, the fear that had once gripped her heart was replaced with something different—something she hadn't expected. Relief. Gratitude. She was returning to the place that had given her a sense of safety when she had nothing else.

The air was crisp, the snow now falling in delicate flakes, and the sound of the wind through the trees was like a soft whisper of welcome. As they made their way to the door, her heart thudded in her chest. She knocked softly, then called out, "Jack, are you here?"

Her voice echoed through the stillness, only to be met by a distant voice. "Leave me alone. I have nothing to say."

"Jack," Nina called again, her voice filled with determination. "It's me. Nina."

Moments later, the sound of footsteps grew louder, and Jack emerged from behind a wooden fence. His blue, ripped raincoat was dusted with snow, and when he saw her standing there, his face broke into a smile.

He opened his arms wide, and without a second thought, Nina ran into them, her heart swelling with gratitude. She had come back to the place that had saved her, to the man who had given her hope when she had none.

Nina's father wiped a tear from his eye as he neared Jack, his hands still trembling from the emotions of the day. "My name is Gianni," he said, his voice thick with gratitude. "I'm Nina's father. These are her mother and brother." He stretched out his hand towards Jack, the gesture one of warmth and acknowledgment.

Jack waved his hand in front of him, smiling with an easy, unburdened grin. "It's too cold to take the mittens off," he said, his voice rich with a kind of self-deprecating humour. "Come in. It's warmer inside."

Nina entered first, her feet crunching softly in the snow as she stepped inside the warmth of the house, followed by her family. The smell of freshly brewed coffee mingled with the earthy scent of the wood-burning stove. The room had transformed since she'd last been here. The floor, once cluttered with discarded newspapers, was now clear and tidy. The kitchen counters, once laden with dirty cups and neglected dishes, were now immaculate and inviting.

"Jack, this looks great; you've really tidied up," Nina said with a smile, her voice full of both surprise and appreciation. There was something about the simple neatness of the space that felt like a reflection of Jack's own sense of order amidst the mayhem of their lives.

"Well, the day I left you at the hospital, I walked back into the house, and I saw it through your eyes," Jack said, his tone reflective. "I was shocked you stayed even a moment. You must have been petrified when I walked you down that dark corridor."

"Not really," Nina replied, her lips curling into a faint smile. "It was dark; I only saw it once I'd figured out you weren't scary." Her eyes softened as she wrapped her arms around his waist, holding him in a quiet embrace.

"I want to thank you for what you did, Jack," Gianni said warmly, his voice filled with gratitude. "And so does my family."

Jack shrugged, his expression humble. "Anyone would have done the same. I'm just sorry I didn't have a phone at the time." He glanced at his new black cell phone, holding it up proudly. "But now I have one. Just in case any other strangers show up on my doorstep in the middle of the night."

Nina laughed lightly, shaking her head. "Nice. Much better."

They walked into the lounge, and Nina took in the changes that had been made. "You got rid of those dust sheets. The table looks nice. I slept here." She gestured to the sofa, where she had spent hours in silence, staring at the ceiling, wondering when she would wake up from this nightmare.

"A television?" she asked, spotting the new addition.

"Yes," Jack replied with a smile. "I bought it so I could watch the news and see what happened to you." He gestured to the table. "Take a seat, everyone. Coffee? Juice?"

"I'll do it," Nina said, heading to the kitchen. "Unless, of course, you've moved everything around."

"Food and drink are all in the same place," Jack said, settling into his armchair.

Fabio returned from the car with some boxes. "Jack," he said with a grin, "Nina bought you some gifts." His expression softened with understanding, now that he knew the significance of Nina's thoughtfulness.

Jack placed his hand over his heart, a genuine gesture of appreciation. "Well, that is just too kind of Nina. I'll wait until she finishes with the drinks before I open them."

Nina returned to the lounge after making two trips to the kitchen, carefully balancing mugs and glasses. She sat down on a cushion by the fire, handing Jack one of the boxes. "I don't know what's in each one, sorry," she said with a sheepish grin, "but who cares? It's the thought that counts."

Jack opened the first box with a chuckle. "Slippers. You noticed my others are a mismatch." He placed them to the side with a bright smile.

"This is an egg poacher," Nina continued, her voice soft. "I know you like scrambled eggs, but you said you had too many eggs you couldn't cook."

Jack pulled out a woolly hat, thick ski gloves, and four new cups. "To replace these chipped ones," Nina explained, pointing to her father's chipped cup. "And some new towels—remember I got blood on your other ones, you know from when you cleaned my feet."

Jack pulled out a fireplace set, complete with pokers, shovels, and a silicone glove so he could move wood without burning his hands. His eyes lit up with laughter. "Nina," he said, "this is incredible. You've really thought of everything." He stroked the tools gently, a wistful smile crossing his face as he placed them carefully next to the fire.

The last box contained simple kitchen essentials—cutlery, silicone spoons, and spatulas. "You can't cook healthy food with just one wooden spoon," Nina said with a laugh. "Next time I visit, I'll bring you some new pans. You can't cook with rusty ones."

Jack shook his head, his smile genuine but a little sad. "Nina, you didn't need to bring me anything, but thank you anyway."

"I'll never be able to thank you enough," she replied softly.

"No," Jack said gently, his voice full of emotion. "Nina, you helped me more than you know. You were in that house for nine hours, and in that time, I felt more joy than I'd felt since my wife died."

"Me?" Nina said, her brow furrowing in confusion. "I didn't do anything except use your stuff and teach you how to scramble eggs."

Jack's face softened. "For me, it was more than that. When I got back from the hospital, I wrote to my son, and he wrote back. Well, I'm going there in the New Year, to South Africa. I haven't seen him since the funeral."

Nina's heart swelled with emotion, and before she knew it, she was up and hugging him tightly. "Jack, that's amazing. And of course, at Christmas, you're coming to our house, right?"

Gianni smiled, his voice full of warmth. "Yes, you must come. We'll come and collect you. You can stay with us."

Jack's eyes misted over, and he nodded enthusiastically. "Yes," he said, his voice breaking with emotion. "I'd like that. Very much." As they drove away, Jack pulled the collar of his overcoat higher.

Later that night, Nina lay in the soft warmth of her bed, the sheets cocooning her like a protective embrace. For the first time in two months, she slept soundly, the nightmares kept at bay by the day's healing moments. The memories she had buried seemed to settle into a peaceful corner of her mind, leaving her with a quiet sense of hope, one she hadn't known she still had.

45 | Nina

Six months after the kidnapping, with a renewed media presence after the capture of the two kidnappers, Nina suffered a nervous breakdown. Jack sat by her side for three days in the hospital as she refused to see her parents or talk to anyone but Jack and Fabio.

The last year had been tougher on her parents than it had been on Nina. Her mother's refusal to talk to Nina or accept what had happened, and her father's need to discuss it, had caused too much strain on the marriage. Listening to the arguing night after night, she dreamt, while lying in bed, of leaving and staying at her grandparents' house in the beautiful lakeside village of Rocca Pinta, where virtually no one knew her.

"Come on; it's the safest place in the world; we have been going there every year since we were kids, please." Fabio begged his father, "It will do Nina a world of good to get away; you know people are still strange around her here. They treat her like she has a disease."

Her father agreed, to the annoyance of her mother, and packed the two kids off to Rocca Pinta, a small, lakeside town where people live their own lives, uninterested in the events of the outside world; they seemed to have missed the news of the kidnapping or at least forgotten it.

For the first time in months, Nina felt alive; she met with friends from her childhood holidays and spent time at the beach. Fabio, now a young man, with his skin cleared from acne, and his hair cut short, turned heads with Nina's friends, who all fought for his attention.

Visiting Rocca Pinta on the weekend, Nina's father surprised the kids by announcing, "We're moving here, into the house my parents bought me, that one day will belong to you two, so it's time we use it," he said with a smile.

"What does Mum think about this?" Fabio asked.

"Your mum will stay in Monza for a while, and then we'll see," he said.

"Oh," replied Nina, guessing this meant a divorce and a life without fighting for both of them.

"I'll find a job here easily, and your mum wants to stay at her job, so we will just have to play it by ear," her dad continued, "We'll get you enrolled in school here, and Fabio, you still have to decide."

"Well, here, I don't need to protect Nina; she'll be fine, so I guess I could look at university."

"You said you didn't want to go to university," Nina said, glaring at him.

"Well, I do, but I didn't want to leave you alone, but here, it's different; I don't have to worry about you here." He tried to keep the grin from his face as he finally envisioned a life away from his family.

"Yeah, I agree, and can Jack come and stay?" Nina asked, concerned that they were moving further away from him. Fabio and Gianni had painted Jack's home recently, repairing the damaged exterior and installing a new fireplace to provide hot water.

"Of course, but there's a spare room, too; you can all stay," Gianni announced. He sat back in relief. He had gotten the message about the separation without any confrontation from his kids.

46 | Bree

Bree realised she hadn't yet said anything; feeling paralysed with shock, she nodded and smiled, watching Nik's face relax slightly, finally, she managed some words. "Nik. Yes, yes, yes, of course," she whispered.

Nik stood up, placed the ring on her finger, and slipped a hand around her waist. He pulled her close, kissing her passionately. The group of friends cheered loudly with an outburst of applause. He grabbed her hand and raised it like a triumphant boxer in a fight, and said, "She said yes." The pair took in their friends' faces and smiled, listening to the murmurs and cheers of approval.

Four days later, with bags packed and the house closed, they arrived at Nik's family home. He showed her around the land and introduced her to the workers; they were friendly, not as cold as she'd imagined they'd be towards her. Remembering his warnings, she'd prepared for the worst.

"They aren't local; they don't even know me. To them, I'm the owner's son; I'm not their boss yet; they are workers from Romania," Nik explained.

Bree stared at the house, an old tumbledown wreck sitting at the end of an unpaved road; a wire fence surrounded the property, and a wooden gate hung from its post, squeaking in the breeze. The bushes and brambles growing against the walls scraped the already peeling paint from the window frames. Inhaling the smell of the damp grass, she was shocked at how different his life was there: simple—no rooftop parties, beach picnics, or long lunches. He'd have to be in the fields from morning to night and run the business on Sundays. Bree looked around her, trying to imagine herself there; it wasn't as bad as he'd described; it would be a culture shock, but it could work. She was excited to suggest it to him before she left for Italy.

The following morning, Bree stirred, her face pressed into the pillow. She reached for Nik, but the space beside her was already cold. With a deep sigh, she pulled herself out of bed, her bare feet meeting the cool floor.

Her eyes drifted to his shirt hanging on the back of a chair. She grabbed it quickly, slipping it on without thinking, the fabric too large for her shoulders. The buttons hung undone, and she felt a flush of heat creep up her neck, aware that the shirt barely covered her. As she pulled open the bedroom door, she heard footsteps in the kitchen.

"Nik, are you there?" she called softly, her voice a little too loud in the still, cold air of the house.

Instead of Nik, a woman sat at the kitchen table, dressed in black, her face weary and lined. She set a small bag down with a jingle of keys, then glanced up at Bree with a look that could only be described as fatigue. In the dim light, Bree could make out the faded pattern of a rug in the adjoining room, its corners sagging, and a leaky tap dripping steadily, like the steady ticking of a time bomb in her chest.

"Who are you?" The voice was sharp, with an edge that made Bree's skin prickle.

Bree instinctively tugged the shirt tighter around her, the flush of embarrassment deepening as she realised just how little it covered her. She clutched at it, self-consciously trying to cover the exposed skin at the top of her thighs.

"Excuse me," she said, striving for composure, though her cheeks burned. With as much dignity as she could muster, she turned, retreating back toward the bedroom, trying to keep her body hidden from view. "Shit," she muttered under her breath. Her heart pounded at speed, her mind racing with the humiliation of being caught so vulnerably. She hastily grabbed some clothes, threw them on, and tried to fix her hair into a ponytail, doing her best to look presentable.

She returned to the kitchen, this time with a quicker, more awkward step. The two women hadn't moved. They sat still, staring at her, their expressions unreadable. Bree walked over to them, her face still flushed, and reached out her hand.

"Sorry about that," she said, her voice faltering slightly. "My name is Bree."

The woman who sat in the chair, older, with tired eyes and rough skin, ignored her extended hand and instead studied Bree with cold detachment. "We know who you are," she said, her voice flat. "You're the English one." The words fell like stones, each one heavy with meaning.

Bree's stomach twisted as she quickly deduced that this was Nik's mother and the other woman, her aunt. They were both similar, with their short, dark hair, but Nik's mother bore the added strain of age, grey strands threading through the dark. They both looked at her with stern, unblinking eyes, their faces set in hard lines.

Nik's mother, murmured something in Greek, her tone bitter and strained. The aunt translated, her brow as she spoke. "You're not welcome here. You don't belong with my son. You must leave."

Bree's heart stuttered in her chest, the words sinking deep into her like blades. She took a breath, trying to steady herself, but her hands trembled. "I love your son very much," she said, her voice tight. "I just want him to be happy."

The mother repeated her words slowly, as if savoring the power she held. "He will not be happy with you. We will never accept you. He will never marry you. You don't belong here." She pointed at Bree's hand, the ring there now feeling like a foreign object, something she didn't deserve. "Leave my house."

Bree tried to keep her composure, but the words stung, the dismissive tone cutting deep. Her eyes filled with tears, but she blinked them back, swallowing the lump in her throat. She glanced down at the piece of paper thrust into her hand, the coldness of the gesture matching the ice in their eyes.

"I'm sorry," Bree whispered, her voice barely audible as she turned away, desperate to flee from the suffocating impact of their disapproval.

She left the kitchen, walked through the house, and burst out into the open air, her breaths coming fast, her heart racing.

The sun hit her face as she ran, the heat of the day only adding to the burn inside her. She didn't stop until she found herself beneath the shade of an old olive tree, the gnarled roots like twisted hands reaching up to hold her steady.

Bree sat on the large, twisted roots under the shade of an olive tree and kicked off her dusty shoes. Picking off the crunched-up leaves from the soles, lost in her thoughts, she fumbled around in her pocket for her phone. She pictured it clearly on the bedside cabinet; her face dropped in the realisation that she couldn't warn Nik before he returned. Bree unfolded the note that had been thrust into her hand minutes earlier and started to read. "Breezy, I've gone to see my dad; I should be back about ten. Feel free to take your beautiful naked body back to bed so I can drive you crazy when I get back. Love you."

A wild, bitter laugh bubbled up from deep within her. She shook her head, the tears now spilling over despite her best efforts to hold them back.

She wandered aimlessly around the fields, the wind brushing against her face, as the sounds of an approaching car eventually reached her ears. She stood up and wiped her eyes, trying to pull herself together. When she spotted the blue station wagon, she forced a smile, her heart still heavy.

Nik spotted her, slowed the car, and wounded the window rolled down. Beside him, an unfamiliar figure sat, his features solemn and aged.

"Nik," Bree said, her voice strained but steady.

Nik smiled awkwardly, though his father remained stoic. "This is my father. The hospital sent him home a day early."

Bree smiled at the older man, but he only grunted in response, removing his glasses to rub his tired eyes.

"Your mother and aunt are in there, too," she said, motioning toward the house, her voice now steady, though the knot in her chest had yet to loosen.

Babbling to his father, Nik stepped out of the car, and moved uncomfortably by her side.

"It didn't go well. You'll find me out here, and of course, I left my phone in the room," Bree whispered as she rubbed her temples.

"I'll be back as soon as I drop him off. Wait here," he said, brushing her off as he shrunk away from her back into the car.

Bree watched the dust trail settle to the ground and ducked out of view of the house. She shifted further along the wall; she felt sweat dripping slowly down her back as Nik scuttled towards her on foot. He sat on the wall and pulled her into him, placing her between her legs. He kissed her with a painful intensity in his eyes. She turned to look at him as his feet thundered across the stones, and his gloomy face struggled to smile.

"Bree, I'm sorry about the note. It seems they read it, and then you came out naked. Things have gone from bad to worse, I'm afraid," Nik said.

"I wasn't naked; I was almost naked." She paused for a moment and pictured the scene in her mind. "They were so cruel to me; what a terrible first impression. They must hate me." Her face managed a forced smile, and she let out a small giggle to hide her tension.

"The first impression didn't help, but it isn't you; it's the idea of you. It's exactly as I thought it would be; they hate anyone who will take me away from them and this land." He looked around him at the fields and said, "They expect me to return now, stay here, and grow old here. They don't care if I'm happy; they don't think like that around here. Let's go for a walk; give them time to cool off, then I'll introduce them to you properly," Nik said.

With her mind racing, she slipped on her shoes as he gently clasped his hand around hers and led her away from the house. They strolled aimlessly around the village, followed by the knowing stares of the people passing by.

Bree slowed down, hearing loud discussions as they neared the house. Filling her lungs with a deep breath of air, she glanced at Nik and said, "I can't do this."

"We'll do it together." He shifted closer, resting his stubbled jaw on her forehead. Holding her hand tightly, they walked past the thick steel gates into the overgrown, neglected garden. "I'm pretty sure you can win them over."

The aunt sneered at Bree as she hung out the bedsheets. "Sex sheets," she hissed as a frown crossed her weather-beaten face. Walking too close for comfort, she followed Bree and Nik back indoors.

Nik's eyes twitched nervously as they entered the cold, draughty kitchen. A thick layer of dust covered the chipped wooden table. With a look of disgust on his lined and leathery skin, Nik's father stood, his hooded eyes piercing into Bree's face. His shirt hung from his thin frame as he managed to say a few words in English. His voice cut through the uncomfortable silence.

"Now you have clothes on, good," he said as he sighed and rubbed his tired eyes. Bree and Nik stood with their hands knitted together. The enraged voices surrounded her as the family screamed in loud, anguished tones.

The noise level rose, and Bree observed a chaotic mess of grunting and waving arms. Mouths opened and closed with unwanted opinions and screams until Bree could no longer stand it. Letting go of Nik's hand, she retreated swiftly to the bedroom. She stumbled over a case and kicked it angrily. Hurriedly, she packed her clothes into a bag, dragged them to the car, and stepped back to the kitchen, standing in the shadows, hoping it would soon be over.

Nik, whose face was red in anger, shouted in a desperate voice; he saw her return and put his arm around her. Her heart rate slowed down when she heard his voice switching to English.

"This is the woman I love; I will marry her, with or without your permission. Aunty, please translate this," Nik said, his face red and flustered.

More frustrated Greek words flew around the room. Suddenly, the aunt glared at Bree and then at Nik as she loudly slapped his cheek. He glared at her and wiped the corners of his mouth.

"Nik, you must choose her or your family; you will not be welcome here again if you say you're with her."

His eyes burned with rage as he paced in circles, scowling. Once again, the table fell silent; all eyes were on Bree.

Nik cleared his throat, said nothing more to them, and turned to Bree. "We're leaving," he growled, massaging his brow in frustration and yanking Bree out of the doorway.

"My bags are in the car," she murmured, feeling deflated.

He ushered her out, returning to throw a few things in his bag for himself, and dashed for the car.

Outside, Bree breathed in the fresh air. They quickened their pace, walking quickly away from the house.

He drove his battered car as fast as he could to leave the village. "I never want to go back there again," she said, rubbing her teary eyes. Relief washed over Bree as the house grew smaller on the horizon, but unlike Nik, she knew she never had to return.

.

47 | Bree

The journey passed in silence; a rage burned inside Nik, easing momentarily as he felt Bree's soft hands stroking the back of his head. The implications of his actions and decision to leave with her immediately appeared on his face. He didn't look at her for the rest of the journey.

They pulled over at a car park. He killed the engine and grabbed his phone to make some calls. "Okay, we have a hotel for tonight," he said, pulling back onto the road. Bree had seen him like this once before, after he heard the news of his father's heart attack. "I cope in silence," was how he explained it.

She had so much to say, but his blank stare held her back, pushing her words down her throat. When he started to talk, she'd have her moment to say what she thought. She rested her face on the warm glass of the car window and watched the scenery blur past her. The further they distanced themselves from the angry voices, the calmer Bree felt. How could Nik be so friendly, so perfect, living in that house all his life?

They pulled up into a car park, staring through the windscreen at the hotel. Nik finally spoke: "Before we go up, I have one thing to ask you."

"Okay," she said, clearly worried.

"How naked were you?"

Bree laughed at his cheeky grin. "I was wearing your white shirt, the one you were wearing yesterday; it was open at the front; they saw everything," she said, giggling quietly.

"I have it in my bag; I look forward to seeing it on you later, then taking it off again," he said with a mischevious smirk.

"We need to talk, though; we can't ignore it," she said, gently touching his arm.

"I know, just not yet, okay? I'm still too angry," he said as he massaged his eyebrows in frustration.

"I'm sorry," she said lovingly.

"I'm not angry at you or at them; they knew about you; I told them I'd asked you to marry me; I knew they weren't happy, but they said we would talk about it once I was back." Nik shook his head, his eyes narrowing into an angry slit.

The evening sun reflected off the television screen as they entered the room. Squinting, Nik quickly closed the curtains. He sat on the bed and looked at her. "So, how about showing me the shirt?"

Unable to suppress the urge for mischief, she unfolded his shirt, took it into the bathroom, undressed, and placed it on, ensuring the unbuttoned shirt was open, and strutted around the large bedroom.

"Slutty enough for your parents?" she giggled.

All he could manage was a mutter; he was already pulling off his shirt. "Plenty slutty enough for me; come here," he said, pulling her towards him.

The night had cooled as they left the hotel to find an Italian restaurant appropriate for their last dinner. "I'm never going back there again, Bree; I can't. They humiliated you; they told me to choose. I choose you."

"Nik, you can't choose me. They are your family. You may hate your life there, but you love them; they raised you, and you can't turn your back on them now." Her smile faded as she spoke. "They need you; the land needs you. You can live without me; they can't live without you," she paused while the waiter took their order.

Nik shook his head. He looked at her as he pushed a strand of blonde hair from her face and said, "No. Never."

She took his hand across the table, squeezing it tightly, and said, "Yes, Nik, this has happened, and we can't change it. I will, one day, laugh at what they said to me, but these people are your family; you can't leave them." She paused, looking to see if the words were registering and said, "You'll find another woman to love; maybe you'll marry; maybe you'll have children. You'll forget me; you'll move on, and so will I." Her eyes teared up, but her voice was still solid and determined.

Nik said nothing; he sipped the wine from his glass. Bree saw a slight nod, his eyes fixated on the tablecloth. His thoughts consumed him as they dined in silence. How could he choose between his family and the girl he wanted to marry? He couldn't imagine his life without her, but he remembered her words: he had to do this; he couldn't leave them now. An idea started to formulate in his mind. He watched as Bree picked silently at her food. The waiter hovered, frequently replenishing their glasses.

"Bree, I'll tell them it's over. I'll tell them I'll stay there, but we will stay together; secretly, we'll write, we'll call, and one day, we'll be together again." His voice was sharp as he finally pushed a fork full of pasta into his mouth. "It won't be now, but one day, I promise you, I'll find an excuse to leave, maybe to visit a client. Instead, I'll come to Italy."

"We can try, yes; why not?" Bree flashed him an unconvincing smile and said, "I can't call you at home. You won't be able to sneak away. You will have to make them believe it's over. Can you do that?" she asked, not as convinced by the idea as he was.

"Yes, I have to; we'll find a way."

They clung to each other through the night, their breaths mingling as if to ward off the dawn. Bree awoke to the comforting smell of fresh coffee, but the sight of Nik's sombre face sent a ripple of panic through her chest. He set the coffee on the bedside table, then crouched before her, resting his head gently on her lap. His hands wandered across her body, as though memorising every curve one last time.

Reluctantly, they separated, their movements slow and heavy, like they were breaking apart a shared cocoon. At the airport, Nik pulled her close, his breath warm against her ear. "See you soon," he murmured. "I love you."

Bree's wide green eyes shimmered with unshed tears, framed by her dark lashes. She managed a small nod, her voice lost in the moment. Turning away, she walked through the sliding glass doors, her shoulders slumped and her steps dragging as if each one carried the impact of her leaving. This was it—leaving Greece, leaving him, leaving a piece of herself behind.

Seated in the cramped aeroplane seat, Bree slid her sunglasses over tear-streaked eyes. Her fingers lingered on her phone's lock screen, tracing the edges of the photo of her and Nik. A single tear fell onto the screen, distorting the image for a moment before it disappeared.

48 | Bree

Bree's arrival in Italy was marked by a palpable sense of animosity. Italy was the enemy in her eyes—a land that had stolen her away from Greece and, more importantly, from Nik. She stepped into her new life with a broken heart and a battered spirit, determined to avoid entanglements with men or anything that might deepen the ache she carried. Bree dreamt of the day she'd feel nothing again, free from the pain that paralysed her heart and twisted her stomach into knots. She felt adrift, as though she belonged nowhere—not in the UK, not in Italy, and not even in the warm embrace of Greece.

After a whirlwind five-day training seminar, Bree found herself on the road to Calenda Alto, a lesser-known ski resort nestled in the Italian Alps. Her new area manager, Debby, was a tall and stocky woman whose broad smile could quickly turn intimidating. With her hair slicked back into a severe bun and large-rimmed glasses perched on her nose, she reminded Bree of a schoolteacher she'd once feared back home.

Bree had pictured a charming, snow-covered village when she accepted the job. Instead, Calenda Alto greeted her with stark grey tower blocks rising against a backdrop of treeless mountains. The air, sharp and icy, stung her cheeks as she stepped out into the cold. She shivered, taking in the disappointing sight of the mountains. Where she'd imagined fluffy white slopes, she saw strips of artificial snow carved into a patchwork of brown and green terrain, evidence of the snow cannons' relentless work. It was a far cry from the romanticised alpine paradise she'd envisioned.

She was a ski rep in a ski resort, yet she couldn't ski. She was adept at donning the gear and looking the part, but her true skill lay in watching others gracefully—or not so gracefully—navigate the slopes. The days at the airport, where she greeted incoming guests, were long, and the weeks seemed to stretch endlessly. Winter in the Italian Alps felt like an eternity compared to the dreamy, sun-soaked days she'd spent in Greece.

Nik was never far from her thoughts, no matter how hard she tried to push him away. They spoke frequently, their conversations filled with longing and updates about their separate lives. Nik shared his plans and dreams for their future, and Bree tried to believe in them, but realism tugged at her, whispering that they might never reunite. Every goodbye over the phone felt like a fresh wound, the ache spreading through her entire body.

As Christmas approached, Calenda Alto transformed. Snow finally arrived two days before the holiday rush, blanketing the mountains in pure white. Colourfully clad skiers descended upon the slopes, bringing life and vibrancy to the resort. The beauty of the mountains was undeniable, though the roads became treacherous with ice, and slush seeped through her shoes, leaving her perpetually cold and damp.

Bree's life in the resort settled into a rhythm. She met other holiday reps, both from her company and others, forming a motley crew of camaraderie and competition. They spent their days learning to ski—her progress slow but determined—and their evenings immersed in the lively world of après-ski. Nights blurred into a haze of music, laughter, and occasionally translating in the hospital for injured tourists who had collided with the slopes, either drunk or overconfident.

Despite her attempts to adapt, Bree often felt like an observer, watching life unfold around her without fully participating. The laughter of her colleagues, the thrill of skiers carving their way down the mountains, and even the festive energy of the season seemed to exist on the other side of an invisible barrier. Yet, amidst the noise and activity, there were fleeting moments when she allowed herself to imagine a different life—one where Greece and Nik weren't just memories, but part of her present.

Towards the end of the ski season, Debby, Bree's supervisor, contacted her for the usual end-of-season chat. Bree was feeling smug; she was confident she'd be heading to Lake Valdo for the summer season—it had been pre-arranged ages ago.

Debby intercepted her as she clomped off the slopes, her ski boots leaving a trail of wet snow behind. "Fancy a drink?" she asked.

Bree raised a brow, smirking. "Do you even need to ask? I never say no to a drink," she replied, adjusting her goggles dramatically for effect as they trudged through the swirling snow.

Once inside the bar, the warmth hit them like a blissful slap in the face. They shook off their jackets, sending tiny snowflakes scattering onto the scraped wooden floors. The place was buzzing: the clink of glasses, the stomp of ski boots, and the endless chatter skiers reliving their wipe-outs. It was the same every evening, and somehow, it never got old.

They ordered steaming mugs of mulled wine and parked themselves by the crackling fire. Bree stretched out, feeling every bit the exhausted yet victorious ski rep she pretended to be.

Debby sipped her drink, her expression shifting as she got to the point of their meeting. "Bree, you've been amazing this season. Honestly, we've never had such a quiet season on the complaints front. You've run this resort like an expert."

"What can I say? Some people are just naturals."

Debby chuckled but quickly grew serious again. "We're giving you a choice for next season. We'd like to keep you in Italy, but..." She paused for effect, the drama queen. "a mutual friend mentioned your time in Greece—and your boyfriend. If you want, I can recommend a transfer back there."

Bree froze, her drink halfway to her lips. She set it down carefully, narrowing her eyes. "Are you serious? You dragged me out of Greece, tore me away from my life there—forced me to come to Italy—and now you're suggesting I go back? What's the game here, Debby? Are you trying to see how far you can push me?"

Debby raised her hands in mock surrender. "Relax, Bree. I'm just giving you options. You don't have to decide now."

Bree let out a sharp laugh, though it lacked any humour. "Right. I just can't believe it. I need time to think." She shook her head and took a long sip of her drink, her jaw tight with frustration.

The conversation meandered from there, the wine loosening tongues as it always did. Bree eventually asked, "What about you? Where are you off to next?"

"I'm heading to Crete," Debby said, her voice full of excitement. "We'd love to have you there too. You'd be brilliant as a resort manager. It's between Rethymnon and Chania—your job would be to make sure the reps toe the line. You'd love it."

Bree frowned, but before she could respond, the flash of blue ambulance lights outside the window caught her attention. She jumped up, already slipping into her coat. "Probably one of my guests. I'd better check."

With a quick goodbye, Bree darted out into the freezing night, her mind swirling. As she finally crawled into bed later, excitement tingled at the edges of her exhaustion. Pulling out her phone, she called Nik.

"Nik," she began. "I've got a chance to transfer to Crete. If I'm near Rethymnon, do you think you could visit me? Even just for a little while? It's better than nothing."

Silence. Too much silence. Then Nik's voice came, soft and hesitant. "Breezy, there's something you need to know."

Her stomach clenched. Nothing good ever started with that tone.

"My parents... They've found someone for me. A girl from my village. They're worried about how sad I've been, and they think... they think I should marry her."

Bree blinked, trying to process the words. "What?"

"I've met her a few times. She's sweet, kind. I don't love her, but life would be simple with her," he continued, as if simplicity was somehow a selling point.

Bree felt her body turn numb. "No. No, Nik. You can't mean this."

His voice cracked, pleading. "You're the love of my life, Breezy. I'll always love you. Please understand."

But Bree didn't understand. She couldn't. His words hit her like blows to the stomach, leaving her breathless and reeling. She ended the call, her mind blank, her heart shattered once again. Just like with Micky, she was the second choice.

49 | Bree

The next morning, still wrapped in her bed sheets, Bree lay with her eyes open. Her life with Nik flashed before her, doubts coming to her mind about everything he had ever said, their dreams and promises. His empty words reverberated in her head. If he'd moved on so quickly, that meant that his words meant nothing; it was all a game, a show, and a lie.

She twirled the engagement ring on her finger, eased it off, placed it in the box, and slid it into her bag. She grabbed an envelope and quickly, scribbling Nik's address, called for a courier to collect it. She wrote, 'I guess you'll need this again,' on a post-it, and nothing else—no kisses, no message, no 'I love you.' She brushed the snow off her coat and held back the tears as she handed the ring over to the courier.

Bree promised herself that she would never again think of him and their time together with fond memories and smiles; instead, she would try to forget about him completely. She placed all of his notes and letters in a box, removed all his photos, and deleted them from her phone; she blocked his number and then deleted his contact information. She wanted no reminders of him in her life.

The day he signed for the ring delivery, she received a text from the courier; a chill froze her to the spot. Bree felt a knot in her stomach, and her eyes filled with tears.

Later that day, she stepped out into the soft, falling snow to meet Debby. "I'm staying in Italy. Tell me where to go and I'll be there." Bree announced to Debbie with a shrug.

A month later, Bree found herself standing in the room that had been her home for the past few months, her suitcases packed and ready.

Relief coursed through her veins as she looked around. She was finally leaving this cold, dark mountain prison—a place where her dreams had not just faltered but been utterly shattered.

She let out a heavy sigh and glanced at the cardboard box on the floor, marked with hurried black ink: Summer Clothes. Inside were not just her breezy dresses and sandals, but also a collection of unopened letters from Nik.

The sight of them made her chest tighten, a mix of anger, sorrow, and something she refused to name. Each envelope, with its slanted handwriting, was a painful reminder of the life she had tried to leave behind—and the man who had betrayed her heart.

RAW MISTAKES

Since that dreadful phone call, Nik had kept writing, pouring his soul into words she refused to read. She had shoved each letter into the box without a second thought, letting them pile up like a collection of broken promises. Now they sat among items that no longer had a place in her life—flimsy dresses unsuited to the mountains, old souvenirs from her time in Greece, and a pair of sunglasses she hadn't worn since that tear-streaked flight to Italy.

Bree crouched down, her hand hovering over the box. For a brief moment, she considered tearing open one of the envelopes, just to see what he had written, to feel the raw emotion she knew would spill from the pages. But then she clenched her fist and pulled back. No. Those letters were part of a past she needed to leave behind. They belonged to another version of her—a version who still believed in impossible love stories.

She taped the box shut. It was just a box now, Bree stood, brushing her hands on her jeans, and glanced at the suitcases lined up by the door.

With one last look around, she zipped up her coat, grabbed her bags, and stepped into the crisp mountain air. The village, with its grey tower blocks and dirty snow, seemed to sag under her resentment. She hadn't just survived this place—she'd endured it, and now she was done. Done with the mountains, done with the cold, and done with the person she'd been when she arrived.

As she walked towards the waiting car, her boots crunching against the icy ground, Bree felt the first flicker of something unfamiliar: hope. It wasn't much, just a tiny spark buried beneath layers of pain and anger, but it was there, warming her as she moved closer to a future free of broken dreams and unopened letters.

50 | Bree

Bree's new home for the summer season was Riva del Valdo, on Lake Valdo. The imposing mountains blocked the beautiful sun that Bree loved. In contrast to her previous seasons, many of her fellow reps during the summer season in the Italian lakes had been there for years; some were married to Italians and had families and lives outside the job.

In her house which sat at the end of a long, muddy drive surrounded by tall Cyprus trees, Bree settled in for the season. Rushing around from hotel to hotel on a rusty old moped, she was doubtful whether she would even finish the season. She could find nothing she liked about the area, but she had nowhere else to go. Her only choice was to cooperate with good grace for the next few months before she asked for a transfer to somewhere else, anywhere but Italy or Greece.

Within a couple of weeks, Bree met with the other reps from other countries and companies. She accepted invitations to go out; anything was better than staring at the four walls of her house. Slowly, she settled into her life and even started to enjoy it along with her new friends.

Bree forged a strong friendship with Erin, a dazzling girl from London who had also found herself in Riva del Valdo. Erin's striking cheekbones and large, expressive eyes seemed to betray every thought that crossed her mind, from mischief to melancholy. She shared a flat with her inattentive boyfriend, an Italian shopkeeper more absorbed in his store than in her. Their dynamic left Bree quietly grateful for her own single status, even if she still carried scars from her relationship with Nik.

As the days melted into weeks, Bree began to fall in love with Italy once again, though she hardly noticed it happening. Her anger towards relationships, however, remained firmly in place.

Slowly but surely, Bree stopped feeling like a temporary visitor and started becoming one of those reps who truly lived in Italy—crafting a life that wasn't just about work but about belonging.

Eventually, Erin dumped her neglectful boyfriend, and she and Bree decided to rent an apartment together. The space was small but charming, with faded terracotta tiles and a tiny balcony that overlooked a bustling shopping street.

By the time the second season in Riva del Valdo began, Bree had bought herself a little car—a battered Fiat that rattled on uneven roads but felt like freedom. She found herself looking forward to the summer, to lazy afternoons by the lake and evenings sipping Aperol Spritz with Erin and other new friends.

Erin insisted on dragging Bree along for a double date one evening. She'd had taken a shine to a guy she'd met at a shop, and the idea of a friend tagging along with his friend was too convenient to pass up.

Bree resisted at first, but Erin's relentless enthusiasm wore her down.

"I swear, you don't even have to talk to him," Erin promised. "Just sit there, look fabulous, and I'll owe you one."

Reluctantly, Bree agreed, though she had no interest in meeting another man. The evening, however, was a spectacular failure. As the group sat on the restaurant's terrace, surrounded by the distant purr of Vespas, Bree and Erin exchanged increasingly exasperated glances.

"Oh my God," Bree muttered under her breath. "How boring can one person be?"

"And his friend?" Erin snorted, tilting her head towards Bree's supposed date. "What a miserable git. Honestly, he looked like someone dragged him here against his will. You—blonde, leggy, and sexy—and he looked at you like you were, I don't know, a cartoon."

"Trust me, the feeling's mutual," Bree replied with a smirk. "If tonight is a sample of what's out there, I'm officially out of the dating game. Forever."

They shared a laugh as they waved goodbye to their dates, neither of whom seemed particularly disappointed by the lack of sparks. Walking back to their apartment under faint light of the streetlights, Bree realised how much she'd changed. She no longer needed romance to feel complete. Italy had started to work its magic on her—not through a man, but through its beauty, its chaos, and the unexpected joy of sharing life with a friend like Erin.

One hot summer morning, walking into the hotel for her early morning visit, Bree tied her hair back, twisting the hair bobble twice around her ponytail. She was shocked to see the miserable guy from the date the previous week working as a waiter in the breakfast room.

It amused her to see he wasn't just sad on dates but at work, too. He made rude comments to the customers, whom he considered nothing more than an inconvenience.

Bree noticed his name on his battered name tag, Luca. He held out his hand, indicating she could help herself to the breakfast buffet. Bree dug into the steaming hot sausages, bacon, and eggs and waited for customers to come and see her.

After enjoying the breakfast selection, she revisited it the following week. Tying her hair up as she walked through the door, she smoothed down her skirt and looked around the empty room.

The buffet display was empty, and the shelves covered with tablecloths were bare. She checked her watch; she was only fifteen minutes earlier than last time, and customers would be arriving soon. She waited, searching for some staff to pour her a coffee.

She heard shouting and cursing from the kitchen; she popped her head curiously around the corner.

"Hello, breakfast will be late today; the waiter hasn't turned up," the chef told her.

Bree acted decisively, feeling like she had no choice. "Okay, my customers are going to Venice in forty minutes, and they need breakfast. Tell me what I need to do."

"All that needs to go out, go on the table," the chef said, pointing to the large selection of freshly cut bread. "Those need to be poured into the containers," another said, pointing at the cereals and muesli.

Bree took a deep breath and lifted the heavy brown tray. "Got it," she said. She threw her bag on the floor behind the two mock marble columns and started to place the items on display. They thrust something else in her hand each time she returned to the kitchen: "Milk, yoghurt, butter, they go in the cool display."

Managing to remain calm, she rushed out again to work out where each item belonged. The customers arrived as Bree still stacked the buffet. As they eat, she replenished. Back and forth until they all had everything they needed for the morning.

Luca finally arrived as Bree was stocking up the displays for the next hungry guests due to arrive soon.

"Everything is in the wrong place," he scowled as he marched over to her.

"You were in the wrong place," she hissed in reply as a group of chatty diners entered the room.

Bree heard screaming in the kitchen again, with Luca adding to the commotion. She raised her voice over the chaos. "Guys, the restaurant is full of guests; keep it down," she said. The voices stopped instantly.

Once Luca had put things where they belonged, Bree grabbed some muffins and shoved them in her bag. Luca didn't thank her, but she was sure she spotted an appreciative nod.

51 | Petra

Petra woke with a jolt of excitement, her senses heightened as if seeing her room for the first time. Her eyes wandered over the neatly arranged paperbacks on the bookcase and the gilded frames of family portraits hanging above. A fleeting frown creased her brow as she pictured the relentless drizzle of London. But the thought quickly evaporated as she opened her suitcase, the crisp click of its locks reminding her that she was leaving it all behind.

Once dressed, she hurried downstairs to breakfast. As she reached her table, her breath hitched—a bouquet of twelve red roses stood proudly in the centre, a crisp envelope nestled among them. She snatched it up and tore it open, her heart pounding. Inside, the note read: Fancy a trip to Lake Valdo this morning?

Her fingers trembled as she reread the words, scanning the room nervously as though someone might steal her moment.

Rico entered the dining room with his signature air of effortless elegance, a smug smile playing on his lips. "Ready?" he asked, his deep voice smoothing over her nerves.

"Yes, I'll just grab my bags," she replied, trying to sound calm despite the racing of her heart.

"Don't worry about that," he said with a casual wave of his hand. "If they're packed, I'll have my driver bring them to the airport."

Outside, Rico held the door of his sleek sports car open for her. They cruised through the Veneto countryside, the wind teasing her hair as they passed rolling vineyards and cypress-lined roads. Rico finally parked in the grounds of a faded yellow villa, hidden amidst ancient trees on Via Catullo.

"That's the villa of Maria Callas," he said, gesturing towards the building. Petra turned, her focus lingering on its weathered beauty, hoping she looked suitably impressed.

They strolled along the beach, the sun warm against their shoulders. From there, they ambled up to the Roman ruins of the Catullo Villa, pausing to admire the panoramic view. The sulphurous tang of the nearby thermal baths filled the air as they wandered past the steamy pools, their surfaces rippling gently in the breeze.

"When you're back, I'll take you there," Rico offered. His words hung in the air, heavy with unspoken possibilities. Petra fought to keep her excitement in check, masking her eagerness with a careful smile.

The narrow streets of Sirmione bustled with tourists, the air alive with chatter and the clink of glasses. They passed restaurant after restaurant, their outdoor terraces stretching towards the lake, menus enticingly displayed on wrought-iron stands. Rico finally chose one with an over-water terrace, where the occasional splash of cool lake water seeped through the wooden slats, brushing against Petra's legs like a secret.

As the afternoon faded, Rico drove her to the airport. His goodbye—a quick hug and a kiss that barely brushed her lips—left her yearning for more. "I hope to see you again soon," he said, his words warm yet curiously distant.

"That would be nice; I'm sure we can arrange that," she replied, forcing a smile as she walked away. Turning back at the entrance, she found him already gone. She rubbed her brow, confused by the contradiction in his actions and words.

A few days later, her heart soared as an email landed in her inbox. The subject line was simple but potent: Miss you. Attached was a plane ticket to Verona. Two weeks later, as Petra settled into her first-class seat aboard a British Airways flight, enthusiasm bubbled within her. She clutched the ticket as reading over and over again the Miss you message.

Rico was waiting at the airport, his sports car ready to whisk her through winding, tree-lined roads to his villa.

Dressed in a new camel cardigan that flowed elegantly to her knees and matching ankle boots, Petra felt a subtle but welcome transformation in herself. She'd shopped carefully for this trip, packing clothes that suited the polished lifestyle Rico seemed to embody. Her excitement dimmed slightly when he led her to the airy guest room he'd prepared for her. Standing by the window, she gazed out at endless rows of sunlit vineyards, her reflection faint against the glass. The warmth of the sun seeped through, but it didn't touch the creeping sense of disappointment that stirred within her.

"Tonight, we're going out with my friends," Rico announced, stepping into the room. "I want to show you off. Wear your nicest dress."

Swallowing her desire for time alone with him, Petra forced a smile and began unpacking. She selected a simple but elegant black dress, pulling her hair back and slipping on her favourite black heels. Admiring herself in the mirror, she let her hands glide over the fabric before heading downstairs.

Rico's disapproving scowl stopped her in her tracks. His eyes swept over her before he remarked coldly, "I'll buy you a new dress next time."

The sting of his words froze her momentarily. Without another glance, Rico turned, opened the car door, and drove them towards the restaurant in tense silence.

Petra felt the buzz of excitement as they entered the dining room, her arm tightly linked with Rico's. But the thrill quickly gave way to a rising wave of panic. The room filled with an assembly of elegant women, their flowing dresses sweeping gracefully across the marble floors. Jewels glimmered under the opulent chandeliers. These women looked like they'd stepped out of a film—stunning, poised, and untouchable.

A sense of inadequacy settled over her like a heavy shawl. Petra longed to fade into the walls, to vanish entirely. Her black dress, bought in a rush, now seemed painfully plain. The costume earrings dangling from her ears and the modest clutch in her hand felt like glaring symbols of her unworthiness. Her pale skin peeked through the soft black fabric, emphasising her unease.

She forced a smile, her lips tight and unnatural, as the air around her filled with the melodic sounds of Italian—a language she didn't yet understand. The initial excitement of the evening was rapidly dissolving.

Rico let go of her arm, disappearing into a dense haze of cigarette smoke as he greeted the crowd of men with confident handshakes and easy laughter.

One woman, a vision of perfection with her glossy hair styled into an impeccable chignon, paused to speak with Petra. Her English was stilted, but her tone was unmistakably condescending. Fingering an ornate necklace, she said slowly, "This is from Jerusalem. It cost half a million dollars. A man gave it to me." She giggled, a sound sharp enough to cut glass. "I couldn't bear to wear fake diamonds."

As the woman glided away, her perfume trailing behind her like a final insult, Petra instinctively touched her earrings. She'd paid twenty five pounds for them—more than she'd usually spend—and now they felt like a glaring mark of her inferiority.

She glanced at Rico, surrounded by these glamorous, polished women, and wondered why he wasn't with one of them instead. The men accompanying the women, most of whom were significantly older, exuded wealth and power. Petra assumed it was the same here as it was at home—older men doting on younger women, perhaps auditioning them for the role of a second wife.

Feeling increasingly like an intruder in a world she didn't belong to, Petra slipped towards the shadows by the door. She edged her way up a carved wooden stairwell, her heels clicking softly on the polished steps. From the bannister, she watched the scene below: people chatting, laughing, and dancing with an effortless grace that only deepened her sense of alienation.

Her attention sharpened as she noticed cash discreetly changing hands—paying for drinks, dinners, drivers, and tips. Money seemed to flow freely, yet it was something Petra hadn't had to think about recently. Rico had taken care of everything. Still, the sight unsettled her. She watched as he introduced the women to various men, one by one, and they disappeared into the night. When his eyes met hers across the room, his expression flickered with something she couldn't quite name—contempt, perhaps? Whatever it was, it made her stomach twist.

Needing an escape, Petra retreated to the small bar by the entrance. She perched on a tall stool, crossing her ankles and ordering a whisky. She swirled the ice in the amber liquid before downing it in one gulp, savouring the burn as it slid down her throat. She ordered another, leaning on the bar and watching couples drift past her, wrapped in their own effortless worlds.

Finally, Rico appeared, his head peeking around the door before he made his way over to her. "Are you all right? I couldn't find you in the room," he said, his tone casual but probing.

"I was here," Petra replied, trying to keep her voice steady. "I felt... out of place. Underdressed. And I don't speak Italian." She took a moment, not wanting to sound pathetic but needing him to understand. "What was all that about? Those girls—are they your friends?" she added, the bitterness of jealousy creeping into her voice despite her best efforts.

Rico chuckled, the sound dismissive. "That? Oh, it was a singles' night for the rich," he said, as if it were the most natural thing in the world. Taking her drink, he downed it in one gulp before continuing, "Don't worry, my dear. The next two days are just for us. Venice tomorrow."

He pulled a handful of notes from his bag and handed them to the barman with practised ease. Then, without another word, he led Petra out into the cool night air. The streets were silent except for the soft echo of their footsteps, but Petra's mind was loud with questions she couldn't yet bring herself to ask.

52 | Petra

The evening faded from Petra's mind as they set off for Venice the next morning. The life she was experiencing with Rico made the luxurious villas she'd visited around the world feel like nothing more than quaint farmhouses or humble stables by comparison.

"Venice by night, darling," he said with a twinkle of excitement, pushing open the door of a small boutique. "I want to buy you a stunning dress for the occasion."

He tipped the shopkeeper generously, then edged closer and whispered, "Find her something I can be proud of; we're going to the casino."

Petra nodded as the shopkeeper gently guided her away into a wide room lined with dresses. The woman didn't speak, merely holding each garment against Petra's frame, nodding to herself as she murmured softly in Italian.

Unconvinced, Petra stared at her reflection in the mirror. The dress she had been handed felt too ornate for her taste, but as she spun slowly, she couldn't deny it looked flattering.

The silver silk clung to her form in all the right places, catching the light with every movement. The heels were impossibly high, and she could barely balance in them, but they accentuated the intricate crystal embroidery that lined the hem of the dress. For a brief moment, she felt like she could belong in this world. If she dressed like this, she might blend in with the women who had made her feel so out of place the other evening.

The soft click of a camera phone broke her thoughts. The shopkeeper smiled and said, "Your man approves." She helped Petra undress, then cast a disapproving look at Petra's simple black lingerie. "I don't sell this kind of thing here," she muttered dismissively. "But you really need to get that sorted."

A flush crept up Petra's neck, and a rush of anger stirred in her stomach. She offered a strained smile, choosing to sit on the nearby bench and look out of the window as the frustration simmered.

Rico returned shortly, taking the bag containing the dress from the shopkeeper and handing her a thick bundle of folded notes. The woman nodded gratefully, and with a smile, closed the door behind them.

The gleaming white water taxi pulled up to the casino, its polished wood gleaming in the fading light. Petra followed Rico inside, her nerves tightening with each step. They were greeted by the staff, who seemed to know him well. A hostess, tall and graceful in a long black dress, escorted them to the casino's main restaurant. The expansive glass walls offered a breathtaking view of the gaming tables, where well-dressed patrons congregated, laughter and the clink of chips filling the air.

Rico seemed to command the room effortlessly, a man in control, the pulse of this world that Petra was only just beginning to understand.

They were quickly swept into conversation with a group of loud people, their accents a mixture of American and British.

Petra felt Rico's approving gaze on her as she joined in, her initial unease giving way to a confident, slightly performative version of herself. The dress felt like a costume, but one that allowed her to step into a world she'd only dreamed of—gracious, chatty, and effortlessly entertaining.

Rico proudly kept her by his side for the first few minutes, holding her hand as they mingled. The men and women around them moved with the confidence of those who were comfortable in their wealth.

Petra tried to keep up, her thoughts spinning as they discussed large sums of money, and the others revealed their winnings, each with a display of bravado.

As the night wore on, the group moved toward the roulette tables. The women, dressed in glittering gowns, linked arms with their partners, leaving Petra and Rico to play alone. She felt like an outsider again, watching as Rico confidently placed his bets, his movements assured. He won thousands of euros, then lost them, only to win it all back. He was clearly an expert, always tipping generously after each big win. He shrugged out of his jacket with ease, wiping the sweat from his brow, the thrill of the game evident on his face.

"Why don't you go play over there?" he suggested, nodding toward the buzzing slot machines. He handed her a few hundred euros before turning his back to her, absorbed in the game.

Petra sat at the machines for a while, her attention drifting as she glanced around the room. She couldn't spot him anymore, the sea of faces blurring into one. Her patience began to wear thin. She couldn't quite understand what was happening, and the flashing lights from the machines only made her feel more restless. After what felt like an eternity, he returned, his eyes glassy, and his expression distant.

"Let's go," he said curtly, grabbing his jacket and placing a hand on her shoulder. His impatience was palpable as he ushered her toward the door, flinging it open with an abruptness that made her feel small.

"Where did you go?" Petra asked, her voice betraying her unease. A tightening in her chest made her nerves flare. She hadn't expected this from him, and as he glared at her, a sinking feeling began to rise in her stomach.

Rico shrugged, his expression turning colder. "There's more than one room, and why do you care? Aren't those clothes enough for you?" His words were clumsy, and his discomfort was evident.

"I missed you, that's all," Petra replied, her fists clenched in growing frustration. She didn't understand why he was acting this way—what had she done wrong?

"I can't talk to you when you're like this," he snapped. "You're always so emotional. Get a grip." He grabbed her arm with a force that made her wince, pulling her out into the moonlit night. His frustration was clear as he cast her a last, contemptuous look.

Petra stood frozen, horrified disbelief settling over her like a heavy fog. She fought back the urge to cry, her eyes flashing with disapproval before she looked away, letting out a long, deep sigh.

The drive home was silent, thick with tension. Petra couldn't shake the sense of distance that had crept between them. She noticed a subtle hesitation in Rico's movements as he approached the bed, his eyes avoiding hers. He hugged his pillow tightly, turning his back to her, and the usual warmth of their closeness seemed to evaporate into the cold air around them.

When she awoke, the room was still dark, the silence oppressive. Slowly, her surroundings came into focus, and she saw him hovering above her, his smile detached. She forced a polite nod in his direction, the coldness of his presence stinging her.

"I'm sorry about last night," he said, his voice sounding distant. "I don't know what came over me." He dipped down and kissed her, but the gesture lacked warmth. "It's time to go. We have a long drive to the airport."

Petra responded with only a brief nod. She threw on some clothes quickly, grabbed her bags, and followed him downstairs. Her mind wandered to the coffee she had yet to drink and the breakfast her stomach longed for, but the coldness of the morning matched the chill in the air. She slid into the car, tied her hair back, and let the wind from the open window sharpen her senses as they sped along the motorway.

At Verona airport, Rico barely spared her a glance. His attention was already fixed on the departure doors ahead as he bent to kiss her, a quick and impersonal touch to her lips. Then, without a word, he turned and walked away.

The lack of a warm goodbye left her feeling empty, her heart tight with a mixture of confusion and loss. She bit her lip to hold back the flood of emotions rising inside her, then turned to leave, her steps heavy with dread.

As she sat in her seat on the plane, her thoughts raced. She closed her eyes, trying to block out the noise of the engine and the bustle around her. She could still see his smile, quickly followed by the flash of his anger. The memory of his coldness sent a chill through her. What had happened? Why had he become so distant?

One thing was certain: if she saw him again, she wouldn't ask any questions.

53| Bree

After that morning in the breakfast room, Luca occasionally smiled in Bree's direction. Sometimes, he attempted to be friendly, prioritising her customers over others when they were in a rush to jump on an excursion.

Over the next few weeks, they inexplicably became friends, and eventually, he asked her out on a date, and surprising even herself, she accepted.

Luca seemed different; he'd taken his time to ask her out. Behind his stern face, kind brown eyes, and low cheekbones, she felt he was a man to be trusted.

Bree, uninterested in having her heart broken again, took things slowly. The more Bree pulled away, the more he pushed.

At the close of the summer season, Luca took Bree to his family home in the south of Italy. She was fascinated as she watched his mother tend to the vegetables, chase chickens around the yard, string peppers together, and let them dry in the sun. Bree accompanied her to the local washing station, where women scrubbed clothes with water from a mountain spring. She welcomed the warmth and attention from his parents, who showered her with hugs, gifts, and platters of local specialities.

After a year of dating, Luca sat Bree down by the sea. Below them, waves crashed against the rocks as he handed her a small white box.

"Bree, will you marry me?" he asked, his voice calm, almost matter-of-fact.

"What?" Bree stared at him, her mind reeling, her focus fixed on the waves as she tried to make sense of what he had just said.

"Will you marry me?" he repeated, his voice shaking slightly.

Bree's heart thudded painfully in her chest. She hadn't seen this coming. She blinked, then looked away, her eyes wandering over the vast expanse of sea before returning to his eager face. She felt Luca's needy smile and the expectation hanging in the air like a heavy, unwanted fog.

"Eh, oh, I wasn't expecting this," she muttered, her fingers playing with her ponytail, her nerves making her fidget. Her lips quivered, caught in a strange side-to-side movement.

"Well?" His tone turned slightly impatient, urging her response.

Bree flinched as the words caught in her throat. Everything inside her screamed to take a step back, to say something—anything—that would give her time to think. But then he smiled at her, that warm, reassuring smile she had come to know so well, the smile that made her feel safe, yet trapped at the same time. She felt her resistance crumble beneath it.

"Er, yeah, okay," she finally said, her voice barely above a whisper. She held out her ring finger, forcing a smile she didn't feel. She was suffocating beneath his smile, the pressure of his proposal weighing heavily on her, making it impossible to refuse.

Later, as she waited for Luca to visit his sister, Bree signalled a server for a coffee and sank into her seat in a local bar. She grabbed her phone and dialled Erin's number, fanning herself with the menu as she listened to her friend's horrified screech on the other end of the line.

"What did you say?" Erin asked, her voice high with shock.

"Well, I think it's harder to say no than yes, so I said yes," Bree replied, her laughter thin, betraying her unease.

"You're kidding. You can't marry him, you don't love him." Erin scolded, her concern evident.

"Yeah, I know, it was a bad move. I'll let him down gently," Bree said, though the words felt hollow in her mouth. She paused, hearing Erin fall silent. "Mind you, I think marrying him might be the safe option, and I guess it's expected. You and I are the only two single ones left, after all."

"Oh, Bree, think about it carefully," Erin insisted before they swiftly changed the subject.

"Too late for that," Bree said as she ended the call.

That evening, Bree sat alone on the sofa, her mind drifting back to the night when Nik had proposed on the rooftop with their friends. A pang of sorrow tightened in her chest as painful memories resurfaced.

With a sigh, she opened Facebook on her phone and searched for Nik Daskalakis. Her heart skipped as his profile picture appeared: his dark eyes smiling into the camera, his perfectly styled hair, and his sharp dark suit and tie. He stood beside a woman in a wedding dress, his arm around her back as they posed together in a weed-choked courtyard—his family's home. Bree's heart lurched, and without thinking, she dropped the phone onto her lap. She stared at it for a moment, gathering herself before she picked it up again. She zoomed in on the photo.

Making a steeple with her fingers, she rested the phone on a cup and stared at the image, her attention fixating on the engagement ring. It wasn't hers—the one she had returned. At least that was something. She quickly navigated to the block option, shutting him and that hurtful image out of her life. She never wanted to see him, or that picture, again.

Tears slowly began to fall down her cheeks as she grabbed a cushion and hugged it close to her chest, the strain of everything pressing down on her.

54 | Bree

From that moment on, Bree changed her attitude toward her wedding. It was as if the decision had already been made for her, and there was no room for second-guessing. She threw herself into the planning with a new sense of purpose, almost as if to convince herself that this was the right choice. The wedding had to be perfect. Every detail needed to be flawless.

She poured herself into every aspect of the event—the venue was transformed into a floral wonderland, the musicians flown in from London, and her friends and family gathered from home to celebrate. It felt like everything had to be grand to make up for the knot in her stomach, the growing sense of unease she couldn't shake.

The only thing understated about the entire event was her dress. Bree had chosen a simple Charleston-style gown—white, full-length, and elegant in its simplicity.

As Bree stood at the altar, the moment felt surreal. The church was beautifully decorated, every corner filled with the scent of fresh flowers. Luca stood before her, his face radiant with excitement, but something inside Bree felt off. She held back for a few moments, her heart pounding in her chest as she knew she was making a huge mistake.

Her family was sitting in the front row, her mother's proud smile almost too much to bear. Her sister gave her a reassuring nod, but Bree could barely focus. It was as if time had slowed down, the eyes of everyone around her feeling heavier with each passing second. She had dreamt of this moment for years, but now that it was here, it felt suffocating.

She looked at Luca, his handsome face beaming with joy, and for a fleeting moment, she imagined saying no. The word formed in her mind, ready to escape her lips, but then her attention flickered to her parents and sister, their faces full of joy. The pressure to make them proud, to uphold the expectations of the day, overwhelmed her. And before she could stop herself, the word 'yes' slipped off her tongue.

A wave of regret washed over her, but it was too late. The moment was passed, and there was no turning back.

The honeymoon was supposed to be an idyllic escape. But instead, it became a nightmare. Bree had imagined Zanzibar to be the perfect paradise, a place where they could relax on golden sands and bask in the warmth of the sun. But reality was far from it. The room smelled damp from the moment they arrived, and the air in their hotel had a heavy, musty quality that stuck to her skin.

Her blonde hair, always smooth and straight, turned frizzy and wiry. She spent hours in front of the mirror, trying to tame it, but the humidity had other plans. It felt like everything she had taken pride in was being undone.

But it was the stomach cramps that really got to her. It started innocently enough, a bit of discomfort after a seafood meal, but it didn't let up. Every day, she would be running to the bathroom, feeling the sharp pangs of nausea and stomach cramps, followed by an overwhelming wave of diarrhoea.

"Are you going to spend our entire honeymoon in the bathroom?" Luca asked impatiently as he rested against the door, his arms crossed.

Bree could feel the frustration radiating from him. She had tried to push through it, tried to appear normal, but her body wouldn't cooperate. "I can't help it," she mumbled, her voice barely above a whisper. "It's not like I planned this."

She wanted to shout back, to tell him how miserable she was, how trapped she felt in this sweaty hotel room, with the constant pressure of being near him and constantly running to the bathroom. But instead, she kept silent, feeling her self-esteem crumbling with every passing moment.

To make matters worse, the beach boys, young local men hired to promote excursions, were always around. They would hover outside their door, trying to persuade them to join their tours or buy souveniers
. Bree had hoped for some quiet time, but instead, she felt trapped in the hotel, constantly being pestered by them, the constant reminder of how out of place she felt.

"You should get out more, Bree," Luca would chide her, his tone condescending. "It's a beautiful place, and you're just wasting the time away in here."

Bree felt a wave of guilt wash over her, but she knew she couldn't risk another bout of illness. Every time she tried to venture outside, the heat and humidity hit her like a wall, and her stomach would protest, forcing her back inside.

Luca's criticisms didn't stop. "This is ridiculous," he muttered as he checked his watch one afternoon. "You're ruining our honeymoon with your illness. I don't even know who you are anymore."

Bree wanted to cry, but the tears wouldn't come. She felt numb, like her entire being was drained by his words and her constant physical discomfort.

It wasn't long before their time in Zanzibar ended. The honeymoon that should have been the beginning of their happily ever after felt more like a trial run for a life she wasn't sure she wanted. They returned to Lake Valdo, but things didn't improve. Luca's attitude had shifted, and it was as if the man who had once been so easygoing had disappeared, replaced by someone demanding and critical.

Luca had begun expecting more from her—things she hadn't signed up for. He was no longer attracted to the Bree who didn't care about traditional roles. He wanted a wife who cooked, cleaned, and obeyed.

"Why aren't you preparing breakfast and dinner?" Luca would demand, shaking her awake at six in the morning, his words harsh in the cold morning air.

RAW MISTAKES

Bree had never been a fan of the housewife routine. She had always been independent, happy to let someone else take care of the cleaning and cooking. But now, it felt like that was all Luca wanted from her. The fights were long and loud, every one a reminder that their marriage was already starting to fray at the edges.

"I don't get it," Bree would say, confused and exhausted. "Why is everything so important now? We didn't live like this before."

But Luca's response was always the same: "You're my wife now. You're supposed to do these things. It's what's expected."

Slowly, Bree began to shrink. Every criticism, every sharp word, took its toll on her. She tried to keep the house immaculate, tried to please him in every way, but no matter how hard she worked, it was never enough. His insults became a daily routine. "You've gained weight," he'd say, or, "You look tired. Old."

She felt like she was drowning in his expectations, and nothing she did seemed to make a difference.

Eventually, Bree found an escape. She started a wedding planning website on a whim, just as a hobby. But over time, it grew. The more she threw herself into it, the less time she had to spend with Luca, and that, at least, was a relief. She poured herself into planning other people's weddings, creating something beautiful when everything in her own life seemed broken.

She'd quit her job at the tour operator—where she made bookings for Russian tourists, a job that she hated more than anything—and used her newfound time to focus on her wedding business. It wasn't just a hobby anymore; it was her lifeline. It allowed her to escape, to be her own person, even if only for a few hours each day.

At home, Luca's criticisms didn't stop. He loomed over her as she worked, throwing his judgment on every part of her life. "You've become lazy. You're always on that damn computer. Can't you do something useful for once?"

Bree started to avoid him. She'd tiptoe around the house, staying out of his way, but it wasn't enough. He still found ways to criticise her, still found ways to belittle her. And each time, she felt smaller and smaller.

Her friends stopped coming around. They could no longer bear to see the way Luca treated her. They didn't want to be around someone who was constantly belittled and humiliated.

And as she stared at the computer screen, booking weddings and planning events for other women, Bree felt like she was planning her own escape. One day, she told herself, she would be free. She would leave Luca and this life behind. She didn't know when, but she knew it was the only way forward. She had to get out.

55 | Bree

The wedding company became Bree's safe zone, her happy place. As the weddings increased, Bree set up an office in Rocca Pinta, employing an ex-colleague to help her with the weddings so Bree could try her hand at wedding photography.

Bree spent more and more time in Rocca Pinta, sneaking out of the house early morning and returning late at night, setting up a sofa bed in the back room in the office for her to stay over when she couldn't face going home. Luca didn't seem to care where she spent her nights. As time passed, unbeknownst to Luca, Bree managed to buy a house in Rocca Pinta, decorating it in white and pastels, the opposite of the darkness of her marital home.

With large glass patio doors, the sun streamed into the lounge all day, and the view of the lake just metres away filled her heart with joy. Bree started to move things out of the house—clothes, books, photo albums, skis—all the things she knew he wouldn't notice, and within a month, it felt like home.

With her confidence at an all-time low, Bree knew the time had come to leave Luca. She had suspected him of cheating once, maybe twice, but each time he denied it. However, her latest discovery—that there was a new woman in his life—had been the final straw.

On a weary Monday evening, disillusioned by her marriage, Bree returned home early, her mind made up. She waited in the silence of their living room, tension building as she anticipated the perfect moment to confront him. As Luca walked in, hanging his coat behind the door, his usual aloofness settled over him. He didn't even look at her as he busied himself in the kitchen, his back turned.

Bree could feel the anger bubbling up inside her. She wasn't sure how much longer she could hold it in. Finally, she broke the silence. "Are you seeing someone else?" she asked, her voice shaking only slightly as she fought to remain calm.

Luca turned, his scowl deepening. "You're pathetic. You think I'm cheating? Well, look at you. I'm not cheating, but if you don't get your act together, I will," he snapped, his words sharp, designed to wound.

Bree's chest tightened. "You disgust me," she muttered, her voice thick with disdain.

"I only married you because I felt sorry for you," Luca's voice followed her, loud and venomous through the open door. "You make me sick. You and your bloody weddings—get a real job."

His words struck her with a force she hadn't expected. A sickening wave of realisation hit her, but the fury it ignited was stronger. She turned to face him again, the words rising, more vicious now than they had ever been.

"My money pays for us to travel. It pays for all of this." Bree screamed, her hands shaking as she lunged toward him, pushing his phone from his grasp. "You don't seem to complain about that, do you?"

Luca, unfazed by her outburst, sneered. "Well, at least you're good for something. You should be grateful to have a man like me taking care of you," he shot back, his voice dripping with contempt.

Bree's face reddened, a rush of emotion flooding her chest. "Well, I'm not feeling so thrilled right now, Luca. You didn't help me. You left me to fight the system on my own, and you were a total waste of space. Setting up the business was a nightmare, and you didn't lift a finger." The words she had kept buried for two long years finally came pouring out, each one a bitter reminder of the suffocating hold he had on her.

He stared at her for a moment, his face contorting in frustration. Then, without warning, he stepped towards her, his body tense with rage. He raised his fist, hovering it in the air as if contemplating his next move. In a swift motion, he shoved her toward a steaming radiator, pinning her to it with painful force.

Bree cried out in shock and pain as the metal burned against her skin. The suffocating impact of his aggression pressed down on her, but just as quickly as it had happened, he released her, pushing her away with a look of disgust. She stumbled back, her breath ragged, her chest tight with fury.

Trembling, Bree turned away from him, retreating into the guest room. She slammed the door behind her and collapsed onto the bed, gasping for air as though the very act of breathing was a rebellion. The sound of Luca's footsteps faded as he went about his usual routine, indifferent to the devastation he had caused.

The following morning, as the door slammed shut behind him on his way to work, Bree wasted no time. She grabbed her bag and stuffed her remaining belongings into it with frantic energy. The importance of the moment didn't settle on her until she was in her car, heading down the winding mountain road, a sense of freedom filling her chest with each passing turn.

As she drove, the first smile in what felt like forever broke across her face. For the first time in two years, she felt like herself again. The future ahead was brighter, freer, and filled with the promise of something better. No more fear, no more guilt. Just freedom.

Finally, she was free—truly free. This time, the thought of being alone no longer terrified her; it sparked hope. Hope for the first time in years. As she drove down the winding roads to her new life, the uncertainty ahead felt exciting rather than daunting. She knew what she wanted: to build her thriving wedding planning company, and to immerse herself in her newfound passion for wedding photography. These were her dreams now, her future, and nothing would hold her back.

A few days later, she reluctantly agreed to meet Luca for coffee. She wasn't sure why—perhaps for closure, perhaps for one final glimpse of the man she had married.

As she sat at the table, fiddling nervously with her keys, she caught sight of him walking in. His arrogance and entitlement were as present as ever. He barked his order at the waiter, demanding a double espresso, and then slid into the chair across from her with a heavy sigh.

"Why did you leave me?" he asked, his voice unnervingly soft, almost pleading. The vulnerability in his tone caught her off guard, but only for a second.

Bree stared at him for a long moment, disbelief flooding her. "What? You don't know? Come on, you're a smart guy," she replied, her voice laced with irony. She couldn't believe he was still pretending not to understand.

He shifted uncomfortably, looking down at his coffee. "You didn't leave a note; you just... left me." His voice faltered, and Bree saw a tear slip from the corner of his eye. It made her stomach churn, but she forced herself to stay composed.

Her eyes remained fixed on the juice in front of her, unable to make eye contact. She ordered a muffin, more out of habit than hunger, and stayed silent.

Finally, Luca spoke again, his voice low, almost desperate. "Bree, come home. I love you. Everything will be normal if you come back, I promise. We can fix this."

She almost laughed, the absurdity of his words hitting her like a slap in the face. "Normal?" Bree repeated, her voice overflowing with disbelief. "Everything in that house is far from normal. You especially."

Her words hit their mark. She watched as his face shifted—his soft expression hardening into one of pure rage. A flash of anger flared in his eyes, but it wasn't enough to intimidate her anymore.

Luca pushed the muffin away from her, his lip curling in disgust. "That's why you're so fat," he sneered, his words meant to wound.

Bree stared at him for a long moment, her heart pounding in her chest, but there was no hesitation this time. No fear. "That's it. I'll send you the divorce papers," she said, her voice steady. "And I expect you to sign them."

Without another word, she stood up, walking briskly towards the door. The cold spring air hit her as she stepped outside, and for the first time in what felt like forever, she took a deep breath. She knew—no matter what came next—this was her fresh start.

56 | Carla

Waking suddenly, adrenaline burst through Carla's veins; she unwrapped her legs from her body and reached for her phone. The day after the dinner with Kevin Orme, flipping through channels with a coffee in hand in frustration, she scoffed out loud. Frustrated with her family and knowing she wouldn't be welcome home again for a long time, she decided it was time to finally do something to gain a purpose in her life once more.

Carla knew it was time to start living again; she was in a quandary about what to do next. She reached for her laptop, wiped the sleep from her eyes, and briefly massaged her chin. Putting her coffee aside, she dusted off the laptop and opened it up, staring blankly at the Google home page.

'Jobs,' she typed quickly. She then scrolled through pages of job announcements. She closed the page without clicking any further and snapped the computer shut. She lay alone in bed, thinking of a thousand different careers.

Realising that this was her chance to start afresh anywhere she liked. Nothing was keeping her here now. "Italy," she said out loud. "I'm going to Italy." She texted a friend from her studying days and arranged to rent a room in her flat in Milan.

Snapped out of her daydream by the ringing of her phone, Carla reached over and answered. "Hey," she said, recognising Charles' voice immediately.

"How's the hangover?" he asked, his tone light but with a hint of concern.

"Fine, actually," Carla replied, a spark of excitement rising within her. "But I've made a decision. I'm going to Italy. I'm going to find a job and see where life takes me."

"Wow. Okay, that's unexpected," Charles said, the surprise evident in his voice.

Carla could practically hear his brow furrow. She sighed softly, gathering her thoughts before responding. "Look, after last night, I realised something. The folks aren't going to leave me alone. They don't get me. They honestly thought that prick was good for me," she added, a bitter laugh escaping her lips as she grabbed a yogurt from the fridge.

"Yeah, well... even if he wasn't a bully and a downright bore, he's pompous. All you ever wanted was to get away from that," Charles replied with a laugh.

"Exactly," Carla said, the words rolling off her tongue with an easy confidence. "I've had enough. I'm getting away. I'm booking flights now."

Carla heard a long sigh from Charles before he spoke again. "Well, I'll miss you at Friday night dinners. Guess they'll have to turn to me for someone to pull to pieces."

Carla laughed lightly. "Do not suggest Friday night video calls, okay?"

There was a pause before Charles let out a chuckle, but she could hear affection in his voice. "Alright, I'll let it slide. But seriously, take care of yourself."

"Don't worry, I will." Carla smiled.

Less than half an hour later, Carla sank into Johnny's old armchair, giddy and wide-eyed as she clutched the printed itinerary for her flight to Italy. There was something about the impact of the paper in her hands that made everything feel real. Three weeks in the UK before she left to tie up loose ends. It felt like the end of one chapter, the beginning of another. The thought of Italy wasn't just about escaping; it was about building something for herself, something she had craved for so long.

Carla had made her decision: she wouldn't sell the house. Instead, she planned to leave it empty, a place to come back to if Italy didn't live up to her hopes. If it didn't work out, maybe the frogs could rent it out for her.

As she began to pack up her things, she stumbled across a pile of sleeping pills tucked away in a drawer. The sight of them sent a brief pang of unease through her chest. For months after Johnny's death, they'd been her crutch, her escape when everything felt too much. But now, with the future ahead of her, she didn't need them anymore. Not now. Not ever again.

She lined the pills up, staring at them for a long, silent moment. Then, with a deep breath, Carla scooped them up in her hand and walked toward the bathroom. She held the pills over the toilet, smiling softly to herself as she dropped them in. With a simple twist of her wrist, she flushed them down, watching as they disappeared. The old temptation, the crutch, was gone. The thought of them had gotten her through those first few unbearable months after Johnny's death, but now... now she had something to look forward to. Something real.

Carla was determined to make Johnny proud. She promised to be the best version of herself and to never look back with sadness, just with the happiness that she'd shared those years with him. He'd helped her become the strong, courageous person she was now.

The day of her flight, her palms were sweaty as she popped her knuckles. She looked and fiddled with her hand luggage every few minutes for no reason at all. Her mind was elsewhere as she turned her head to look at the clock every few seconds and peered out of the window, looking for her brother's car. She knew this moment would change everything; suddenly, she picked up her keys and rushed out of her house to his car.

As Carla sat on the train from Milan Linate towards the city, the roads were unfamiliar; buildings now stood where before there had been a wasteland. She stepped outside the station into bright sunshine, and raised her hands to her eyes, almost tripping on the uneven pavement.

Carla spent the first few days catching up with friends, walking the streets of Milan, gazing into windows at clothes she couldn't afford, fascinated by people who seemed to be strangers talking and gesticulating enthusiastically. The people seemed exuberant, happy, and busy, rushing from corner to door to bus.

She knew she didn't want to live in the city, a fast-paced metropolis where money talked. She was more of a simple girl; she fitted in well at university there with all the students, but the city had changed in her eyes, now full of pretentious strutting and self-important people. Among these well-dressed professionals, she felt out of place.

Carla found a job waitressing at a restaurant; it wasn't her dream job, but it helped out with the bills at her friend's house; at least she could contribute something. Underneath the dust and the hurried life, there was a soul in the city; it just took her a while to find it.

57 | Petra

Chatting with her friend Helen, Petra replayed the weekend in her head. "I don't know what happened; it was all going so well, and then it changed because I asked him a question."

"How much do you know about him? Have you met his family?" Helen asked with a look of concern, "I know you're a seasoned traveller, but I think there is something strange about all this gambling and the money too."

"It's just some fun; it's his hobby." Petra defended him, regretting even bringing it up in conversation.

"Keep your feet firmly on the ground; don't get swept up in it all," Helen said. "I know you; I know you're already planning a wedding, kids, and a happy-ever-after romance." She took Petra's phone from her hands and said, "Please, stop with the obsession with the phone, and don't force a relationship that isn't for you."

Petra felt irritated as she internally cursed and flashed Helen a cold stare.

A few days later, Petra felt her heart jump with joy when Rico surprised her by telling her he was coming to London to see her. He'd never asked her anything about her life or job; he knew nothing about her circumstances. As she looked around her house, she frowned; this was nothing like his villa. Not small compared to many of her friends' homes, spacious and luxurious almost, but compared to his villa, it was a shed. If he wanted to get to know her, he would have to see the house, her life, and all that came with it.

"Can you sort out a night in the casino in London?" he asked two days before his arrival.

"I'll do some research and see what I can find," she replied, annoyed that she'd have to change the plans she had in place.

Excitedly, Petra prepared for him to arrive; she tried on new outfits, pulling an assortment of clothes from the thick paper shopping bags and tossing the shoe boxes to the side. She matched outfits together and hung them at the front of her wardrobe. She tested the size of her designer clutch bag with her lipstick, keys, and phone before emptying the contents on the cold stone floor once more.

Rico glanced around the house, the large windows overlooking the docklands of her fashionable London flat. "Cute," he said, "like you." He wrapped her up in his arms. He guided her to the bedroom, expertly removing her carefully chosen new underwear and throwing his maroon collarless buttonless shirt to the ground. She felt drawn into the unaccustomed arms of a man. Humbly, she watched his beautiful body sleep beside her, feeling reborn by his side.

He wrapped his hand around hers as they entered the casino, and with ease, he merged into one with the environment. He walked smoothly, drinking in his surroundings, quickly changing his money for chips.

Petra struggled to hide a yawn as he handed her some cash and said, "Take this, have some fun, and try your hand at the machines." It seemed more like an order than a suggestion; she found the electronic tables, worked out how to top up her slot card, and sat down with a glass of wine to try her luck. Occasionally, she looked over to see if Rico had a smile or not; he had a poker face, but most of the time, it was hard to tell how it was going for him.

Petra was fascinated by the small electronic roulette machines; a rush of adrenaline washed over her as she pressed the numbers on the screen and waited for the wheel to spin. She had been so overly engrossed in the devices that she overlooked when Rico moved.

Petra was frustrated; she didn't spot him on her trip to the bathroom, despite taking the longest route around the entire space.

A noisy crowd emerged from an almost secret door; it was the same colour as the panelling, seemingly hidden. A group of men hung by the door, shaking hands and nodding.

Petra spotted Rico in the group; he blended in easily among the sea of suits. She wanted to head over, but something in the air told her to stand back. A group of beautiful women glided over to the men, linking arms with them; the group split off to the gambling tables. She was relieved to see Rico didn't have a beautiful female escort on his arm, and as soon as the group left, she saw him pick up his phone and text her. "Sorry, I met some people; where are you?"

Petra stepped to the side to avoid being spotted and texted him a reply: "In the bathroom; I'll meet you at the bar. "

"On my way, " he replied.

She watched as he swiftly moved into the bar. Unfamiliar faces approached him, shaking his hand and smiling like long-lost friends.

He took Petra's arm and led her to the restaurant, effortlessly charming her once more with his smile, and easy banter.

The following morning, choosing her morning bagel from the counter, they discussed their plans.

"What are we doing for lunch?" Rico asked. "I want to go to Hyde Park this afternoon, if that's okay with you."

Petra nodded and made a few restaurant suggestions. He left the choice up to her, settling on a Japanese and Chinese fusion restaurant. Leaving the warmth behind and heading out into the cool afternoon air, she felt Rico's excitement at being in the city. Hyde Park was shrouded in a misty haze; soft drizzle fell around them. The soft tunes of Canon in D and Paccabel filled her ears.

Petra turned her head with curiosity to find the source of the music, and she gasped, pulling her hand over her mouth and stared in amazement.

Rico knelt on one knee, holding out a stunning white gold ring, a halo of round-cut diamonds gleaming atop it. His smile was nervous, his breath soft and regular as he gazed into her eyes. The damp grass beneath him didn't seem to bother him as he waited for her answer. "Petra, will you marry me?" he asked, his voice barely more than a whisper.

Petra's breath caught in her throat, almost causing her to drop her phone in shock. Her hands flew to her cheeks, her heart racing as a cold shiver ran through her body. She was overwhelmed—by the ring, the moment, the unexpectedness of it all. Ignoring the damp soil that clung to his knees, she looked at him, wide-eyed.

"Petra?" he asked softly, sensing her silence.

"Yes, of course... oh my god, this is... oh god, I'm speechless. Yes. Yes." Petra stammered, her voice shaky with disbelief. Despite the chilly spring weather, she felt beads of nervous sweat form on her skin. Her mind whirled, and she couldn't quite believe what was happening.

Petra dipped down to kiss him, her lips trembling as she tried to steady herself. She helped him up, feeling his hands shake as he brushed the damp grass from his trousers, scowling at the large wet patch on his knee. "Oh god, is this really happening? Are we getting married?" She bounced into his arms, joy seeping out of her.

Rico laughed softly at the shock in her voice, feeling her tremble in his arms. Relieved that his surprise proposal had worked, he couldn't help but feel smug. Petra would fit perfectly into his life, he thought. Of course, he would have to refine her a bit—get her some new clothes, teach her how to blend into his social circle—but he was confident she would be an asset. An English woman would always be an excellent introduction to any social event; they were seen as more reliable than the average Italian, and there was something about their quiet dignity that made them stand out.

Rico was certain that Petra was naïve enough not to question the shady individuals he rubbed shoulders with in his business dealings. He'd told her that the people he worked with at the Venice casino and his friends in Verona were simply contacts for his wine business—a convenient story he could easily expand upon to make it sound more plausible. She would never pry too deeply. Petra was eager to travel, to explore the world with him. The idea of being a married couple, moving through social circles together, was far more discreet than him travelling alone.

In his mind, she was a useful tool—someone to present at events, a companion who would fit into his polished world. He didn't care that she wasn't as glamorous as the escorts he was often around; that wasn't the point. They were part of his business, a fleeting diversion he could indulge in when necessary. Petra, however, was different—she was meant to be his wife, a steady presence. He didn't need her to be stunning or perfect, just pliable enough to fit into the role he had scripted for her. She was convenient, a companion who would allow him to maintain a façade of normality, while he continued with his unsavory dealings behind the scenes. The thought of marrying one of his escorts never crossed his mind; they were just work. He didn't need them for anything permanent—he needed Petra for that.

Feeling triumphant, with hurried footsteps, they raced against the uncertain weather; he led her to the shelter of the waiting car.

Petra had booked tickets to a London show, Jersey Boys. Rico looked so relaxed in the dark theatre; he held her hand tightly, applauding loudly as the curtain fell. Her heart was full of love for this complex man, who held her tight all night, breathing gently into her ear. At the first glimmer of daylight, she smiled at the faint chirp of the birds. Unfolding herself from his tanned arms, she wrapped a soft towel around her, letting the steam of the hot shower carry away any doubts she had before this weekend with a new lease for life in Italy.

58 | Petra

As an engagement present, Rico booked flights to Barcelona for a long weekend for the two of them. Petra hoped this would finally be a chance for them to discuss the wedding and their future. Where would they live? What about a job for her? Could she help in the vineyard or villa instead? She had so many unanswered questions swarming around in her mind, but he had been too busy in London even to have time to talk about them.

Rico flew from Italy to Barcelona the day before Petra. She hid her disappointment as a driver greeted her and looked around for Rico. Petra was met by a limousine filled with red and white roses. Pushing the flowers to one side to make room to sit, she took an envelope from the driver's outstretched hand. Ripping it open impatiently, she ran her fingers over the one-hundred-euro notes. Pulling out a message, she read, 'Buy yourself something special to wear tonight; look sexy.' A rush of joy filled her heart—a warm, tingly sensation in her skin as she blushed at his words.

"I'll wait here for you," the driver said as he dropped her off at the hotel. "Then we'll go shopping."

Petra quickly changed into a light sundress; never before had she gone away for the weekend with so many cases with her. The driver pulled up outside a row of shops on Passeig de Gràcia. Looking at him as if he had a solution to offer, he pointed her towards Loewe.

Offering a shy smile, she asked the assistant for help, "A little sexy dress that is sophisticated, too." When people saw her, they assumed she was Spanish, with her long dark hair and golden tan; they were always shocked when she spoke such perfect English. The assistant, a petite, mousy brown-haired lady with breasts too big for her slight figure, sat her down on the soft leather sofas and wheeled out a selection of dresses to look through on a silver rack. They were all beautiful, without price tags; she was pretty sure they were less than eight thousand euros each, the amount in the envelope.

The third dress Petra tried on was the one; it was a long, black, and gold mermaid-style dress, strapless on top. Taking the assistant's advice, she selected shoes and a bag. Daring to ask the price, the assistant confidently said seven thousand, two hundred euros. Petra flipped through her envelope full of money and pulled out the cash, giving the girl a three-hundred-euro tip. Petra smiled as she looked at her reflection. Walking confidently, she waved the bags in the air at the driver, who whisked her off once more.

"Your next appointment, madam." He walked around to the back door and offered her his hand as he escorted her to the front door and a waiting hostess.

Petra looked up at the sign over the entrance, deciding it must be a beauty salon. Without saying a word, the hostess escorted her to a peaceful-looking relaxing area, decorated all in white with large white sofas, floor-to-ceiling mirrors, and ice buckets filled with a selection of drinks for her to choose from.

A lady in a blue uniform approached her and said, "Hello, my name is Carmen; I'm your carer today. We have booked you in for a manicure, pedicure, full-body massage, body workover, hair styling, and makeup. Is that okay for you? Would you like some lunch before we start? Or a drink?" She had a pleasant, playful voice, smiling and whispering; she exuded a confidence Petra could only dream of.

"Of course," replied Petra, her face open and expectant as a food menu was placed in front of her. She wasn't sure what a body workout actually was, but she was sure she would find out soon.

"No rush, madam; we will prepare for your manicure and pedicure while you choose." Petra was tempted by an avocado and melon salad that she liked the sound of. She didn't even wince at the price of sixty-four euros alongside it; she ordered a glass of water, and looking at her watch, she declined the champagne.

Petra relaxed into the white, soft, cushioned lounger, selected the music of her choice, and closed her eyes into deep relaxation. To her dismay, the workover, involving scrubbing, plucking, spraying, and shaving, forced her out of her state of relaxation. A few hours later, she looked at herself in the mirror, staring at herself in disbelief. The lady in the mirror was stunning. They had sprayed a tan on her, plucked her eyebrows to perfection, and applied the makeup with a gentle hand. The silky hair extensions reached her lower back and flicked around her as she twisted and turned in front of the mirror. She looked like one of Rico's beautiful lady friends.

"My driver?" she asked.

"He's here; we've called him."

Petra tried to pull out some money discreetly to give the girls a tip and said, "This is for you."

"No, your boyfriend has already taken care of this," she said, nearly bowing.

As she left the salon, Petra took a deep breath and entered the limousine. On the short drive to the hotel, she rummaged around her purse for a tip for the driver.

"No, madam, it has been paid already; I will see you here in thirty minutes," he said, pushing her hand filled with notes away from his with a subtle nod.

Running upstairs, Petra changed into the dress quickly. She carefully avoided messing up her hair, every strand perfectly in place as she slipped on her shoes. Tossing a few essentials into her bag, she felt a flutter of excitement, though the source of it remained unclear. Whatever Rico had planned for tonight, she would be ready.

The sharp pop of the champagne cork echoed through the room, and she lifted the glass to her lips, letting the chilled drink soothe her nerves. She waited for thirty minutes, the minutes stretching on like a slow, anticipated moment. Sitting on the edge of the bed, she faced the mirror and caught her own reflection. The sight of herself took her by surprise; the woman looking back at her was someone she hardly recognised.

She touched her face, her fingers grazing her skin as if she were seeing it for the first time—soft, glowing. For the first time in her life, she didn't just see herself; she felt beautiful. And not just beautiful, but admired. The realization made her heart race, her breath quickening as she lingered in the moment.

59 | Petra

The wait to see Rico was agonising; with an excited beat of her heart, Petra grinned as Rico pulled his hands out of his pockets as the limousine parked up. He extended his arm to help her out of the car. "You have never been so beautiful, my dear," he said, kissing her on the cheek as she felt herself blush. "May I?" he asked, linking her arm and escorting her up the steps to the restaurant.

Petra took a deep breath as they entered a round, glass hall. She turned to look at him; he was beaming with a wicked sparkle in his eye. Unconsciously, she touched her hair as her eyes scanned the room.

"For us," he said as a waiter appeared with two crystal champagne glasses. Petra took in the room around her, the glass walls and roof, and thousands of fairy lights hanging from the ceiling, twisting their way amongst hanging glass vases filled with flowers. There were over a hundred people, including friends and family, all looking at them. "Welcome to your engagement party; well, our engagement party, my dear," he said as he grabbed her hand and pulled her forward. A loud burst of applause filled the room as they walked towards their table.

"You did all of this for us?" Petra asked.

"Go and see your family," he said, watching her as she moved across the room. Petra observed the awe in her mother's eyes; the awkward teenager had vanished, replaced by this beauty. The girl they had thought would never amount to anything stood before them, gleaming with happiness. Her parents hugged her joyfully. She received an icy reception, accompanied by a look of pure envy from her younger sister, Hannah.

"My god, Petra, he's wonderful. He paid for everything—our hotels, flights, and even parking—and look at this," her mother said, opening her arms wide, taking in the splendour of the dining room.

Petra spotted Helen racing towards her. "Okay, I take back everything I said; go for it; he's amazing," she said, embracing Petra warmly.

The couple danced the evening away with their friends and family in between courses; he was always by her side, his arm around her waist, holding her hand, showing his support, nibbling her neck from behind, and turning her face crimson at his touch.

Rico whisked her off to the waiting limousine as people started to leave. She glanaced across the room and the rows of empty bottles and glasses on the tables and said, "I haven't said my goodbyes to anyone; I have to go back." Petra whispered in dismay.

"Don't worry; you'll see them all again soon," Rico said softly. The limo purred quietly as it pulled away, arriving at Barcelona Casino after a minute or two. As they entered the casino, Petra could see most of her guests were waiting amongst excited chatter. They were greeted with glasses of champagne; Petra felt the colour drain from her face as they walked into a private room filled with gambling tables.

"Do you mind if I have some fun?" he asked her.

"Of course not; it's your evening, too," she replied, hoping that, for once, a line of glamorous young ladies wouldn't suddenly appear to steal her spotlight.

Occasionally, Petra popped over to his table to say hi. Although polite, he brushed her off with a flip of his wrist and a shrug of his shoulder.

Shortly afterwards, Petra noticed he was gone. As hot, dry wind blew as her tired but exhilarated guests were taken away by drivers, the tables were wiped down and the glasses were carried away. Petra remained alone in the hall, desperately scanning the building for Rico; she kicked a chair with frustration. After waiting an hour, frustrated, she strutted to the exit in search of her limousine.

She heard chatter in the distance; the faces of beautiful young women swarmed before her eyes, exiting an outbuilding. Even under the dark, starry sky, she recognised the lady whose necklace cost half a million dollars, linking arms with one of the guests she'd seen earlier. Rico appeared behind them, comfortably linking with a tall, voluptuous blonde lady. Petra stood in the shadows and watched as he shook hands with all the men and smiled at the ladies. The atmosphere was jovial, exciting, and mysterious. Observing the loud group as they went their separate ways, Rico rushed up the stairs. Petra hid behind a door, fumbling with the remaining few coats hanging in the cloakroom.

With very little energy or enthusiasm left, Petra paced around the cloakroom, listening for his heavy footsteps on the marble floor. She tried to look nonchalant as she appeared from behind the coats.

"Hey, I've been looking for you everywhere," Rico said, with his eyes trained on her. He stood straight with his shoulders tightly back as he strutted towards her, offering no explanation for his disappearance for almost three hours.

Petra knew better than to pester him with nervous questions and said, "I was just checking that no one left anything behind." She slipped her jacket over her shoulders, keeping her eyes down for fear of showing her dismay. "Can we go now? I'm exhausted?"

"Of course. Did you have fun?" Rico asked her as they sank back into the soft seats of the limousine.

Petra nodded tiredly; he looked out of the window, pensive and silent.

60 | Nina

Nina shook the snow off her jacket and warmed her hands at the garden heater. Looking around her, she spotted her three friends walking heavily in their ski boots in her direction.

"Going to the bathroom is not easy when you're dressed like this." Linda laughed.

Picking up the skis they'd left by Nina's feet, the four women trudged through the thick, well-trodden snow towards the ski slopes. Chatting excitedly, they slid onto the ski lift and amused themselves with selfies on the way up the mountain. They had decided to get away for Linda's birthday weekend, driving up to Madonna di Campiglio for two days; they were relying on Nina's experience of the mountain and ski slopes.

"This way, ladies," Nina shouted, pushing herself on her skis away from the crowds hovering around the lift. Checking over her shoulder that the girls were following, she led them through the tree-lined pistes. It was the second day of their trip, and the four were exhausted. Having skied the whole day before, they planned to spend most of the day today in a mountain hut, drinking hot chocolate and eating stodgy food.

Sticking to the easier runs for her friends, Nina dropped them at the bar. "I'm just going to go and do a harder run; I'll be back in about half an hour," she said. The girls nodded and waved, watching Nina expertly ski away in the direction of a black run she'd talked about since the previous day.

Entering the run, she watched a group of men dressed identically in a red and green ski club uniform; they appeared from off-piste, navigating the moguls at high speed, thrusting snow around them as they turned.

Surrounded by snow-capped mountains, the group's laughter and shouts of joy echoed through the hills. She watched in admiration as they vanished at speed past the trees and out of sight. Nina's legs ached from the previous day so she set off slowly down the run, taking her time and turning carefully. She felt a surge of adrenaline rush through her as she reached the end. Checking her watch, she decided to do the run once more. Heading up the ski lift, she spotted the four men higher up on the mountain, skiing a slalom of moguls. She skied off the lift, looked around her, and set off. Spotting three of the men ski past her at high speed, she waited for the fourth to pass; with no sign of him, she entered the piste. Suddenly, from behind her, a voice shrieked.

Nina heard a male voice scream from behind her, "Attenzione." She froze in panic, feeling an almighty thud. Her ski snapped off, pushing her body to the floor with great force. She felt the weight of another person on top of her. She tried to turn, but unable to move easily, she shouted to the man. He didn't reply.

Lying face down in the snow, Nina scrambled free. Pain ripped through her as she pushed her body through the powdery snow. Staring at the man, she wondered if he was unconscious or dead.

A crowd of people gathered around her, watching her, seemingly unperturbed by the accident they'd witnessed. Her eyes were watery behind her thick-framed goggles. She wiped her nose and looked around her. "Can somebody help us?" she asked as one of the group snapped into action, releasing a ski from Nina's other boot.

"I'll ski down and get help," one of the onlookers said, taking his family with him.

Nina nodded and knelt in front of the man, who lay still before her. More skiers appeared, gathering around. Looking out at the sea of worried faces, Nina felt her hand shaking, and a bead of sweat formed on her brow.

A man, covered from head to toe in black, apart from his mouth and nose, skied over to her. "Keep him still, keep him warm," he said as he took off his jacket and placed it over him.

"Thank you," Nina whispered to him.

"It happened to me a few years back; that's all I remember, to be still and warm."

"Oh, okay," Nina replied, unsure of what to do next. The injured skier moved his head slightly and let out a loud, painful scream. Nina almost jumped in shock, her mind swirling in relief. She steadied herself and grabbed his hand.

"My name is Nina; I'll stay with you until help arrives," she said.

The pain seemed to have made him delirious; he spoke sentences that Nina didn't understand, although clearly in her native tongue. He chuckled as she wiped her hand with her glove, and her breathing steadied. She smiled casually, trying to hide her troubled look; his screams made her uneasy.

She wiped his face from the sprinkling of snow as he closed his eyes. "No, you need to stay awake; look at me." Nina heard a commotion behind her; mountain rescue appeared from down the mountain, speeding towards them on a snowmobile.

"Move aside, everyone, please; let's give him some air," they said in an annoyed tone. Sliding him slowly onto a stretcher, they checked his vitals, turned to Nina and asked, "Are you with him?"

"Erh, yes," she replied, her voice shaky.

"Okay, we are going to take him down the mountain slowly; please follow us, not too close. Can you ski this run alone?" they asked.

Nina nodded in reply as she clicked the skis back on. She watched as they wrapped him up in a blanket, tied his skis to the snowmobile, and handed the jacket back to the kind skier, who shivered as he watched.

Arriving at the bottom of the mountain, Nina locked her skis up and climbed into the ambulance with him. As the door clicked shut, sensing her friends' panic, she called to update them as the ambulance stopped a short distance away. Looking up at the entrance, 'Private Medical Clinic,' she took off her hat and gloves and entered.

Nina watched as the man was wheeled off on a stretcher. Left to pace aimlessly through the short white corridor, hit with a feeling of dread, the ugly reality set in that this man could die, and it was her fault.

A nurse approached her, handing her an incident report to be completed. Nina rose from her metal chair, grateful for distractions, took the pen, and filled out as much as she could.

Two hours passed before a nurse gestured that she could enter his room. She tentatively pushed the door open, fearing she would see a man fighting for his life.

"You've got a hard head," the man said.

"I think the morphine is making you delirious; my head is soft, like a pillow." Nina laughed.

He looked at her, took a deep breath and said, "I'm sorry, I was skiing way too fast."

Nina nodded as she took in the full view of the accident. He had a leg in plaster and a large dressing across his nose. Nina watched him wince in pain as he tried to move. "I've broken a couple of ribs too."

She turned to him, a small tear forming in her eyes. "I'm sorry; I should have seen you; I knew there were four of you; I only saw three pass," Nina said as she struggled to suppress a sigh.

He shook his head, insisting it was all on him and refusing to entertain the idea. "This is no longer up for debate. I was in the wrong." There was a pause as he struggled to take a deep breath. "I'm Manuel Genta. I would shake your hand, but I have a feeling it will hurt way too much."

"I'm Nina." She paused before saying her surname. Then, taking a quick breath, she finally said, "Ruggero."

She watched as he searched his mind, wondering where he'd heard that name before. Desperate to change the subject, she interrupted his thoughts: "Shall I call your friends? Do you have a phone?"

Manuel pointed to his jacket hanging on the chair by the bed. Nina took it out of her pocket; he told her the code and who to call.

"See, this is getting serious; you already know my phone code," he chuckled.

Nina felt herself blush as she took in his square jaw and thick brown hair.

She noticed the look of recognition on his face and looked down; she knew what was coming next: "Nina Ruggero, the girl that was kidnapped years ago?"

"Yep, the one and only," she said. She reigned in her annoyance, forcing a half-smile.

Manuel took a moment to gather his thoughts. He could see she looked bothered and uneasy. "Well, by all appearances, you're doing fine now—more than fine, I would say."

Nina picked up a magazine and flipped through the pages as he spoke to his friends.

"They went to the hospital, not the clinic. They're coming now," Manuel replied.

Suddenly, the door flung open, and the room erupted with noise. Nina eyed the newcomers suspiciously. Nina stepped back out of the room, listening to the muffled sound of laughter as she pulled her hat firmly down over her ears.

Wobbling on the ice, she quickly caught her balance and began making her way across the street to her skis and her friends.

Later that evening, while caressing a mug of steaming mulled wine with her friends, the anxiety of the morning melted away. Nina picked at her meal as she told the girls of her adventure. Rubbing her aching shoulder from the fall, she heard loud male voices enter the quiet bar.

"Oh, could that be him?" Linda asked, pointing over Nina's shoulder to a man on crutches.

Nina glanced around, her cheeks burned as Manuel winked at her.

"Guys, this is Nina, the girl I skied into, and who, god knows why, stayed with me," he said to his friends, gesturing for them to come over.

"How are you feeling?" Nina asked.

"Re-energised," he said, laughing. His friends pulled up chairs and joined the girls at the table. "The next round is on me," he said as he hobbled closer to Nina, putting his crutches down by his side as he sat.

Nina was enthralled by their ski antics around Italy and France as they told stories in a way that had everyone in fits of laughter.

As they said goodbye, Manuel put his number in Nina's phone.

"Call me," he said confidently. "I pass by Monza quite a lot."

"Okay, but I don't live there anymore. I live the at the north of Lake Valdo."

"Even better, so do I, at the south, though."

Nina watched as he limped and hobbled towards the slippery, icy exit. He turned over his shoulder and, with a wide smile, said, "This ice is even more dangerous than you."

Nina felt redden as a smile split across her face, and he disappeared through the door.

61 | Bree

Over the few weeks since Bree had left her husband, Luca regularly turned up at Bree's new house unannounced, knocking on the door and bringing her home-cooked meals and gifts. One morning she awoke to an unusual sound outside her bedroom window; she threw on her dressing gown and looked outside. The sight of Luca trimming her hedges with a chainsaw made her blood boil. She felt compelled to do something about it and instructed the security guys not to let him through under any circumstances. He left gifts at the gate; she only opened one, a large knife with a pink handle. Bree dropped it to the floor and decided not to open any more gifts from him.

Feeling a prickle of discomfort at the sensation of being watched, Bree rounded the corner in the supermarket and collided with Luca. he stood there, his posture casual, as if nothing had happened between them.
"There you are. Doing a bit of shopping?" His voice was too smooth, too calm.
"A girl's got to eat," Bree replied with an edge of bitterness.
Luca didn't seem fazed. "Do you want me to come round and cook for you?" he offered.
Bree stiffened, her gaze flicking away as she tried to keep her distance. "No, thanks. I've got Erin coming over tonight," she lied, her words a little too quick.
He didn't miss a beat. "Oh, that's a shame. I just bought some fresh fish. I thought I could roast it with potatoes... for us." He shifted forward slightly, trying to close the gap she was creating.
Bree's skin crawled. She stepped back, the air between them suddenly suffocating. "Well, thanks, but I can't."
Before she could escape further, Luca's hand shot out, gripping her arm with a force that made her flinch. His touch was firm, possessive, as if he still held some claim on her. "Bree," he said, his voice low and urgent. "I will get you back. I won't give in."
She yanked her arm out of his grip, glaring at him. "Luca, you didn't want me when we were together. Why bother now?" Her words were heavy with the intensity of all the hurt he'd caused her.
His jaw tightened, his eyes darkening with a mix of anger and something else—something she couldn't quite place. "You're my wife. No one in my family has ever divorced. You've humiliated the family name," he said, his voice laced with entitlement and spite.
Bree took a breath, feeling her frustration surge. "I think you did that all on your own with your cheating, lying, and arrogance," she shot back, her voice

steady but filled with years of anger. She turned, walking quickly toward the cold food aisle, a rush of defiance and dread twisting in her stomach.

She couldn't take it any longer. Abandoning her trolley in the aisle, she bolted outside, her heart pounding. She rushed to the bench in the adjacent store, collapsing into it as she took long, deep breaths, trying to steady her pulse.

Luca kept appearing, his presence a constant shadow. At the bank. At the car wash. Outside her office and even near her home. Bree found herself altering her routine, her every movement calculated, but he still seemed to find her.

The torment, however, slowly faded as he realised his attempts to control her were fruitless. He didn't show up as often, and she finally breathed easier.

Then came the moment when he ignored the divorce papers. It wasn't until his lawyer told him Bree would pay all the fees if they could get the divorce finalised within a few months that he finally relented. He resigned himself to the inevitable, and Bree—ready for her fresh start—finally saw a glimmer of freedom.

Surrounded by friends, she let go of the fear that had gripped her for so long. She was ready to face whatever came next knowing that the worst was behind her.

62 | Petra

Back in London, Petra made plans for her move to Italy. The couple talked about the next steps. Petra would take over the vineyard tours, accommodations, and promotions, while Rico would continue running the distribution and delivery side of the company.

"It will mean I'll be away a lot; I have to travel all over the world, but you can come along sometimes, too," Rico said.

"Don't worry; as long as you come home to me, I'll be happy to wait for you. I've travelled enough; I'm more than content to stay put for a while," Petra said, pulling a fresh peach pie out of the oven and placing it on the side.

"Won't you miss your job in the travel agency?" he asked.

"No, they've already replaced me anyway," Petra grinned. "I'm meeting a wedding photographer today. Hopefully, I'll manage to book her. Can I borrow your car?"

"Sure, see you in a couple of days when I get back from Rome," Rico said. He handed over the keys, smiled, picked up his bag, and left the villa.

Petra felt the spring breeze tangle in her hair as she drove Rico's cabriolet along the winding Lake Valdo road. She couldn't quite believe the changes in her life since meeting him. It felt like a dream—a beautiful, improbable dream. She parked the car, checked her reflection in the mirror, and with a deep breath, stepped out to meet the wedding photographer at a bar in Rocca Pinta.

Bree was already there, waving from the corner with a warm, welcoming smile. As Petra approached, they shook hands, and the instant connection was undeniable.. After a round of introductions, they settled in and ordered lunch.

The conversation flowed effortlessly, the two of them chatting like old friends. By the time they finished, both of them felt something rare—a connection that could last beyond the meeting.

"So, tell me about your wedding," Bree asked, her tone light but genuine, bracing for the usual topics of menus, musicians, and shoes.

Petra's face softened with excitement. "Well, we're getting married in the vineyard of his villa. There will be antique white roses and lilies of the valley everywhere you look. I've been given the task of picking flowers, a photographer, and, of course, the dress. It's kind of a big deal. I have to get it right." She paused for a moment, then looked up as the waiter hovered by the table, ready to take their order. "He's handling everything else; I trust him completely. He threw the best engagement party I could've ever imagined."

"That sounds wonderful," Bree said, her voice full of admiration. "It must be hard to give up control of your wedding."

Petra smiled, her eyes distant for a moment, considering the question. "Not really. I mean, it's all coming together exactly how I'd imagined. And honestly, Bree, I'd love to have you as my photographer. Your photos are stunning, and you're English too, which helps a lot. I don't speak Italian yet, and with everything going on, I just feel like having someone who understands both languages would make a huge difference."

Bree's smile widened, a soft blush creeping onto her cheeks. "I'd be honoured to photograph your wedding. We just need to figure out what service you want, how many hours… you know, the usual."

"All day. I want the longest package you offer," Petra said, her tone full of excitement. She felt like this was a day she wanted to capture every single moment of. As they confirmed the details, a sudden shyness took over her. She pondered before asking quietly, "And, um, would you help me choose my wedding dress?"

Bree managed to hide her surprise as she replied, "Of course, I'd love to help you. I need a distraction right now."

"Is something going on with you?" Petra asked, picking at the crusty bread that had been delivered.

"Just the usual; I left my husband last month, an evil prick. I probably shouldn't tell you that, sorry. I photograph weddings yet, I don't believe in them."

"Surely you believe in love, though." Petra asked.

"I did, but I didn't love my husband; I just followed social expectations; I did it because it was expected, not because I wanted to, and now I have to pay for that decision."

"Well, I believe in love; I've waited a long time to find the right guy." Petra said, pulling out her phone, selecting an image of Rico, and pushing it towards Bree, boasting, "This is him."

"Ah, very handsome; I can see why you fell for him. I'm thrilled for you; not everyone finds love and manages to keep hold of it. The world is a lonely place without it," Bree said.

Smiling, Petra glanced at the picture and said, "Thanks."

"I found it once, and I let it go, or he let me go, whatever. It's in the past," Bree said, shrugging her shoulders.

"You never know when you will meet your past again." Petra said with a hopeful clink of a glass.

A few weeks later, the two new friends met in Carlotta's bridal store, the best in the north of Italy, drinking champagne. Petra knew Rico would expect something sexy, elegant, stylish, and expensive. She loved to watch his face fill with pride when her figure was on the show, so she decided to look at figure-hugging dresses. She chose a dress with a plunging neckline, illusion panel, tight bodice, luxurious embroidered lace, and a dramatic silhouette. Feeling like a bride, she grinned as she placed the veil in her hair and spun around in front of the mirror.

With a month left to go, Petra was ready to be a bride. "You're going to love him," she said proudly as they arranged that Bree would finally meet Rico at the villa for the weekend.

Rico was thrilled that Petra had a new friend. He'd found her too clingy recently, but with Bree to distract her, he had more free time. He sent the two girls away on a weekend trip to a spa hotel, leaving him with time to have fun at home. He bought the girls first-class plane tickets and given them some money to spend. He dutifully waved Petra off, waited for her to leave on a flight, and headed out to get up to his old tricks each weekend.

Bree accepted the invitation to spend a weekend in the villa and meet Rico. She was curious about this man who seemed to enjoy spending money on Petra, yet spent very little time with her.

"Bring a couple of nice outfits; he likes to spring things on me at the last minute," Petra warned.

"The nicest things I have are my new cycle shorts," she laughed. "Apart from my wedding uniform, we're a month too early for that."

"Don't worry, you can borrow some of my clothes; my wardrobe is a mini fashion show collection," she said proudly. "Rico keeps buying me clothes."

Bree understood what Petra saw in him—this tall man with a square jaw and straight mouth at the peak of his fitness. It was easy to tell that Petra loved the money and had been swept away by the romance of it all. Bree admired the beautiful life Petra would no doubt have with him, not to mention the villa and vineyards.

Yet Bree had been living in Italy for five years and could see through the Italian charm. The romantic gestures and the impressive clothes didn't blind her.

"It's nice to meet you finally, Bree," he said, studying her briefly.

"You, too; thank you so much for the fabulous trips away." She smiled and shook his hand firmly. She felt instantly unnerved by him; she wiped the skin on her arms, but the sensation of unease stayed with her. Everything about him projected a confidence that she immediately distrusted.

"You're most welcome," he said. Smiling, he spotted something in her eyes as he picked the phone out of his pocket and made an excuse to step aside.

"Come on, Bree; I'll show you around," Petra said, her smile warm with affection.

As Petra proudly walked around the property that would soon be her home, she saw the joy on her face. Bree sensed they were being watched from a distance. She turned and spotted Rico, watching her with an arrogant squint; their eyes locked for a second, and without a word, he receded into the shadows.

63 | Petra

"Girls, why don't you have a fun night out in the city, on me?" Rico said, thrusting five hundred euros into Petra's hand. "I've got work to do here."

Petra's fingers tightened around the money, her chest tightening as a brief flash of disappointment crossed her face. "If you're sure... Don't you want to come with us?" Her voice faltered slightly, betraying her regret.

Rico shook his head, a dismissive smile playing on his lips. "I've got things to take care of. You two enjoy yourselves."

He turned and walked away, leaving Petra standing there, her hand still clutching the cash, her eyes lingering on his retreating figure.

Bree, sensing the shift in mood, clapped her hands together and forced a bright smile. "Well, girl's night in the city for us, then." she said, her voice cheerfully upbeat, though there was a trace of relief beneath her tone at the idea of escaping Rico's presence.

The two women quickly dressed, their excitement building as they arranged for their driver.

When they arrived in the city centre, the streets seemed to pulse with life. Tourists and locals bustled around them, making the evening feel almost electric. Petra and Bree strolled through the crowd, their laughter rising above the noise, caught in the whirlwind of energy around them. A flock of pigeons took off from the ground as they passed, their wings fluttering in a chaotic blur.

They settled into a elegant bar in Piazza Bra, the cool evening breeze ruffling their hair as they took in the lively atmosphere. After opening a bottle of wine they quickly became absorbed in conversation, laughing and sharing stories. As they finished the bottle, they glanced around, noticing how the crowd around them had grown.

"Let's walk a bit," Bree suggested.

Petra, struggling a little in her heels, steadied herself with a grin. "Oh, here. I came here with Rico once," she said, her eyes lighting up as she pointed to a building that seemed as if it had been standing for centuries. "He owns this place."

Bree raised an eyebrow, taking in the building's towering stone façade. It looked weathered, almost forgotten, like a relic just shy of crumbling. Yet a single illuminated sign above the door hinted at something more. "Let's go in, then."

The waiter appeared almost immediately, his black jacket swishing behind him as he walked with purpose. "Table for two?" he asked smoothly.

"Yes, please," Petra replied, her voice carrying a note of quiet pride as she followed him, her footsteps echoing softly across the polished marble floors. The waiter moved with the confidence of someone accustomed to the finer things, leading them deeper into the heart of the restaurant.

The two friends waited as the servers pulled out their chairs for them.

Bree's view of the other room in the restaurant distracted her as a group of girls arrived, meeting up with some men who appeared to be businessmen. As she watched the girls greet the men, it was clear the younger, attractive, and stylish ladies were there on dates. The girls bore an uncanny physical resemblance to each other as they introduced themselves to the men. It looked like a selection process.

The men eyed the provocatively dressed girls before kissing them on the cheek and escorting them to the large table to join the others. There were sixteen people at the table, with a couple of empty seats. Occasionally, the girls stood up, usually escorted by another girl, went to the bathroom, and returned giggling. As the evening progressed, she concluded that they were call girls dressed to kill and would be paid handsomely for their services.

Bree was aware that she wasn't giving Petra enough attention, yet she found herself captivated by the group.

Bree held back a gasp when Rico strolled with authority into the room. Sharply dressed, he turned to the rest of the group, grinning. The men rose as he entered the room, and the ladies smiled flirtatiously. Obviously, the star attraction, Rico, drank in the adoration from the crowd as he talked with the group for a few minutes before moving to the side. He ordered a drink in a secluded corner, and the men went to see him one by one as if to pay their respects. Bree observed an exchange of something, possibly money or drugs.

Bree was relieved that Petra couldn't see this; it was a side of him that she was sure Petra wouldn't want to see. As Bree and Petra devoured their creamy meringue desserts, Bree fixated on the group of well-fed diners as they stood and fanned out of the room, assumingly to a hotel, suite, or maybe home. Bree took a final good look at the girls; she wanted to know more about them. She decided to revisit this place without Petra to see what she could find out, unless she could find something online.

The group dispersed, leaving Rico alone at the bar, accompanied by a tall, slim lady with blonde hair flowing down her back. Bree moved her chair to see him in a glass door reflection. Now that she had a clear view, she could see Rico's hand on the girl's back, sliding down and resting on her curvy bottom.

"What's wrong, Bree?" Petra noticed that Bree wasn't on her game.

She pivoted on her seat. "Nothing, just tired; I think I need some fresh air," she replied, offering to get the coats. She felt sickened as she kept Petra away from where she could see Rico; after all, he was supposed to be home.

With their coats in hand, Bree stopped in her tracks in the doorway, her mouth clamped open and her eyes fixated on him. Rico was with the leggy blonde, holding her hand and kissing her neck as he led her into the lift. Bree inwardly cursed, trying not to appear shaken as she linked Petra's arm and pulled her in the opposite direction.

RAW MISTAKES

Walking out onto the wide street through a bustling courtyard, Petra was waiting outside, enjoying the warm evening air. She turned to Bree with a look of delight on her face. "How lucky are we?"

Bree smiled in agreement and nodded as Petra chatted and laughed without a care in the world. Bree insisted they walk a while, taking in the city's beauty; maybe they could walk long enough for Rico to get home, his absence unnoticed by Petra.

64 | Bree

The cool morning air bit at her skin as she and Petra mounted freshly groomed and saddled horses. The trees whipped back and forth in the wind, their branches creaking and groaning, as they made their way out of the vineyard. Bree tried to focus on the rhythm of the ride, the steady clip-clop of the horses' hooves on the muddy tracks, but there was something nagging at the back of her mind. Something out of place.

She glanced over her shoulder.

Two figures on horseback were keeping a noticeable distance behind them. They weren't close enough to be considered a threat but were definitely too close for comfort.

Bree's pulse quickened as she noticed they had started to match their pace. Every turn she made, they mirrored it. They weren't exactly following—at least not in a direct way—but there was something deliberate in the way they moved. The men didn't look like locals; they didn't belong here. And that made her wonder even more. Was Rico having them followed? Or were they just two innocent riders who had taken a wrong turn and found themselves stuck in the maze of trails?

She kept her eyes on the path ahead, her stomach twisting. The horses trotted over a small ridge, and for a moment, she couldn't see them. But as they descended into the next valley, the figures reappeared, this time slightly closer.

"Bree, you seem distracted," Petra's voice cut through her thoughts.

"Yeah, I've just got some work problems," Bree replied, forcing a smile as she tried to shake off the feeling of being watched. "My wedding planner is incompetent. I need to replace her, but it's a hassle finding someone reliable."

"Yeah, I bet," Petra said sympathetically. "What about your ex? Is he still on the scene?"

Bree stiffened at the mention of Luca. She stole another glance over her shoulder, but the men had fallen back again, hanging just out of sight behind the trees. "Luca? God, no. I've changed my whole routine so he can't find me," Bree said, her voice low. "I'm throwing myself into work, going out... keeping myself busy."

It wasn't just Luca she was worried about now. The men behind them felt too deliberate, too persistent. It wasn't coincidence. She couldn't shake the sense that they were watching her, waiting for the right moment to make their move.

"It must be tough. I'm sorry you're going through all this mess," Petra said as they pulled the horses to the side and dismounted.

Bree's mind was still on the riders, even as she pretended to focus on the reins. The men hadn't made any attempt to approach, but their presence lingered in the air like a threat, subtle but undeniable.

Bree found it hard to concentrate as she drove home to Rocca Pinta later that day. She looked forward to getting into her comfy clothes, sitting on the sofa and watching anything that would take her mind off Rico.

The next morning, like every other workday, began with a quick cycle through the hills and a short ride to the office. Bree had made this routine part of her life, a way to shake off the fatigue from the day before. But today, something felt different. As she pedalled along the familiar route, she couldn't shake the unsettling sensation that someone was watching her.

At the bottom of the mountain, a man dressed in walking gear stood, taking selfies with a view of the landscape. It was a strange enough sight that it made Bree glance twice, but she shrugged it off. She continued on, pushing forward, her legs pumping the pedals with automatic precision. Yet, as she reached the other end of her route an hour later, there he was again. The same man, standing by the side of the road, his camera phone angled toward himself as he snapped another picture. His presence was impossible to ignore. He couldn't have walked that far in the time it took her to cycle.

Her stomach twisted. This can't be a coincidence. The thought that she might be followed flitted through her mind, but she pushed it away, telling herself she was overthinking. Still, her thoughts lingered on the people in the vineyards the previous day. The unease slowly spread through her chest, tightening. Was it possible? Could it be Rico?

Rocca Pinta was a small town. Everyone knew everyone, and an outsider stood out like a sore thumb. Bree was no exception. She worked alone in her small office, the usual bustle of the day feeling different, heavier. As the hours passed, she found herself staring at every figure that passed by the window, half-expecting to see the man with the camera appear again. Her mind kept returning to that nagging feeling, a whisper that wouldn't go away.

Then, as if on cue, he appeared. The selfie man. He walked into the same bar as her, casually sipping coffee and tapping away on his phone, as though they were just two strangers sharing the same space. But Bree could feel it. The unsettling familiarity of his presence gnawed at her. She tried to shake off the unease, forcing herself to concentrate on her work, but the sense of being watched remained, like a shadow that followed her every move.

Choosing to walk home from work seemed like the right decision, though the streets felt far too quiet, every footstep too loud against the pavement. She scanned her surroundings with a sharpness she hadn't used before, peering into the faces of those she passed. Her heartbeat quickened when she rounded a corner and saw him. The man from her cycle route, standing by the gate to her building. He didn't seem to notice her at first, but when he looked up and saw her, he quickly turned and fled up a narrow street.

Frustrated and unsettled, Bree pulled out her phone and called Erin. She needed to talk, to make sense of what was happening, but she had to be careful.

They agreed to meet at a quiet bar, one with a single room, one way in, and one way out—just in case.

As they walked through the car park, Bree filled Erin in on the strange encounters she'd been having—the man from the cycle ride, the unsettling figure in the vineyards, and the strange flashes of paranoia that had been creeping into her thoughts.

Her heart raced again when, just as they reached the entrance, she spotted them. Two shadowy figures standing off to the side, partially hidden in the dim light, watching. They were just outside the door, their bodies half-hidden by the wall, their eyes scanning the area. Bree's pulse quickened as they slipped through the door and made their way towards an empty table near her, taking a seat in her peripheral vision.

Bree kept her composure, trying not to let her unease show. But her instincts screamed that something was wrong.

Bree and Erin named these guys Tweedle Dum and Tweedle Dee; they weren't watching her but were there. Three times in one day couldn't be a coincidence. Bree chatted about inane topics, nail polish, hair, and work until Erin had to return to her hungry dog, waiting impatiently for his dinner.

Instead of leaving the bar, Bree ordered herself a glass of wine. She looked at Tweedle Dee, flashed him a friendly smile and raised her glass, asking, "Want to join me for a drink?"

He shook his head, signalling that he was there with someone. Tweedle Dum returned to the table, took a sip of his coffee, and whispered to Tweedle Dee.

Deciding enough was enough, Bree walked straight towards them, sat at their table, and joined them. "Would you like some wine, guys?" she asked. They refused politely; she didn't let the refusal beat her determination. "Can I ask why you two are everywhere I go today? Are you following me?" Bree watched as the thin line of his brow jumped in surprise.

They both glared at her. "No," one of the tweedles replied, shifting uncomfortably in his chair. "Probably just a coincidence."

"Well, if you're supposed to be skilled undercover cops, you have failed," Bree said.

One tweedle rose from his chair, grabbed his phone, and raced out without saying another word. Bree sipped her wine and stared at the guy who sat uncomfortably alone at the table. His eyes darted around the room, his face ringed with dark circles and a thin, dark moustache.

"Is Mr. fast-walking, selfie guy part of this operation, too?" she asked.

He flinched. "Sorry, who?"

"You know who I mean," Bree said firmly.

The first tweedle peered in through the window, glancing at her with clenched fists, furiously conferring with another smartly dressed man. The chatter grew more frantic as the taller man ran a hand through his black hair, closed his eyes, and pushed the door open. He took a moment to straighten his jacket, stretched his arm out and introduced himself as Captain Pellegrino from the Veneto police.

"We are sorry to have made you uncomfortable," the captain said, stumbling for an explanation.

Bree nodded, sipping her wine. She shot the agent a look and said, "Don't worry; I'm not driving."

"We aren't interested in whether you drink and drive or not; we are looking at much bigger things than that," he said. He glanced at his colleagues and then shot Bree a commanding glare. "We are interested in your seemingly new connection to Mr. Rico Marano. Do you think we can talk somewhere more private?"

Bree sat back, stunned, pausing before answering. Then suddenly she leant towards him. "Rico? Yes, it's a good idea to go somewhere else," she remarked. "You guys aren't blending in at all. Let's go to my office." She threw back the rest of her wine and headed outside. No one addressed a word to her as they walked past closed-up shops towards the office. The dark chill in the air perfectly matched the atmosphere surrounding them.

65 | Bree

Street lamps washed the window in a warm yellowy colour. Bree turned the key in the door as the policemen stood uncomfortably close. She walked to her desk and sat down, watching as the men dragged chairs over the grey-tiled floor.

"Ask away; ask me anything you like; I don't like the man," Bree said once they were all seated, her eyes anything but warm and inviting.

She watched them smile; their eyes blinked with incredulity. They asked her a stream of probing questions: how did she meet him, and when? How many times had she seen him? Were they involved romantically? They had barely begun when she let out an ironic laugh at the last one.

"I'm supposed to be his wedding photographer; I'm friends with his fiancé; there's no romantic connection there at all," Bree laughed.

The captain chuckled, and the tweedles stared at her. Something about the silence in the room made her want to carry on talking. "He's a creep and into some weird stuff, if you ask me," she said. "Look, I've seen some things I don't like; I don't want my friend to get hurt."

"What have you seen?" the captain asked.

Bree told him about the weekend, the girls, the unusual arrangements, and the introductions with the older gentlemen. Amused by their eyes jumping with excitement at her stories, the tweedles scribbled down notes. "I've only met him once, but my friend has told me quite a lot about his life and his business trips; what do you want to know?" Bree asked.

The captain began the next round of quick-fire questions. Bree responded with succinct answers, recounting the trips Rico had sent both her and Petra on, the mysterious deliveries, and the shadowy figures collecting them. The captain shuffled through a folder of dog-eared papers and photographs, pushing them slowly across the table towards her.

An hour later, Bree felt the burden of everything she had just voiced. Out loud, the details seemed even more suspicious, more convoluted than she had realised. The captain and his two colleagues—whom Bree had mentally dubbed the Tweedles—stood to leave, but not before one final exchange.

"We may need to speak with you again," the captain said, his tone oddly formal. "We'll need to pass this information on to those in charge." He paused for a moment, stacking his papers with deliberate slowness before placing his pen into his bag. "This is a lot of new information for us. Would it be possible to bring another detective in to speak with you?" His eyes gleamed with barely concealed hope.

Bree's response was almost immediate. "I've been happy to help, though I'm not entirely sure what it is you're doing. But this is my friend's life, her wedding. Can you try and speak to her?"

The captain gave a sharp exhale, his expression shifting slightly. "We already have a team following her. She just hasn't spotted them yet," he said, standing up and straightening his trousers before tugging his jacket down one last time. "We need to understand her involvement."

"Involvement?" Bree's voice tightened in disbelief. "You've got to be kidding. She hasn't a clue. She's just a simple girl, blindly in love with Rico," Bree said, her tone veering into frustration. "She thinks he's Mr. Perfect. She can't see through him."

The captain began running his fingers running through his greying hair as if trying to tame a thought that didn't sit well. "We'll be in touch soon," he muttered, handing her a business card with a measured courtesy. "Here's our number, just in case you have more information to share."

Bree nodded, distracted by the uneasy feeling that this conversation was far from over. "Sure," she muttered under her breath, already feeling the toll of the secrets they were keeping from her.

The captain's expression hardened as he hovered by the door, his voice dropping to a lower, more serious tone. "This matter must remain confidential. We're dealing with a complex, international operation. Any leaks, any talk, and it will all come crashing down. If you speak out, you'll be held for interfering with an ongoing investigation."

The trio left the room with efficient precision. Bree stood still, the silence in their wake settling heavily around her. Her mind churned with questions. At least she had done her civic duty, or so she told herself. But as she turned to leave, another thought struck her: Had she just ruined Petra's future without even knowing it?

66 | Bree

Bree woke at the crack of dawn, which, frankly, felt a bit melodramatic. She was sitting at the head of her dining room table, staring at the divorce papers as if they might suddenly sprout wings and fly off on their own. With a sigh, she hovered the pen over the dotted line. "Well, here goes my commitment to emotional unavailability," she muttered to herself, wondering if her decision to swear off relationships would result in her eventually adopting a dozen cats and talking to her plants.

Once she'd signed the papers, she placed the pen down with an exaggerated flourish, like a judge pronouncing a death sentence. She slipped the documents into the envelope, then reached for her phone.

"Erin, fancy lunch?" Bree asked, trying to sound casual, though she knew deep down it was a major life event. "I'm officially divorced. "

"Oh my god, of course, I'll be there at the usual place," Erin replied, her voice already bubbling with enthusiasm.

A few minutes later, Erin appeared, walking toward Bree holding a bottle of champagne like it was a trophy. "For later," she said with dramatic flair, clearly intending to make Bree feel better.

Bree pointed to a nearby table with a bottle of wine. "It's already been a very long morning," she said with a wink.

The two of them settled in, and without missing a beat, they began trading stories about their exes as though they were competing for the "Worst Partner Ever" trophy.

"Here's to the time he told me his car broke down, but actually, he was with his mistress at a petrol station," Bree said with a raised glass.

"Cheers," Erin chimed in, clinking her glass with Bree's. "And here's to when he told me he 'forgot' our anniversary because he was 'working late'... turns out he was at a strip club. Working on his ego."

Bree snorted with laughter. "To the time he said he was 'just friends' with the blonde, busty woman in the car, but I definitely did not see the word 'mum' written anywhere on her chest."

"Cheers to that," Erin laughed, raising her glass.

The other diners couldn't help but watch, intrigued by the spectacle of two women clearly enjoying their moment of freedom.

Just then, Erin stood up, her face full of mischief. "All together now, everyone," she said, her voice carrying through the restaurant. "She's just signed the divorce papers. Cheers."

The diners around them erupted into applause, their support louder than the clinking of glasses. A few whoops rang out, and someone even hollered, "Freedom." as if Bree had just been freed from a lifetime sentence.

Bree and Erin settled back into their seats, laughing and wiping away tears as the noise died down. They began discussing their plans for a weekend away—somewhere far from men and their terrible excuses—when a well-dressed couple slid into the corner table. The woman glanced over at Bree, her eyes widening in what could only be described as embarrassment while Erin raised an eyebrow.

The man, his back to them, looked over and locked eyes with Erin. His face was vaguely familiar, but something was off—his hair was shorter, his face somehow less charismatic. Erin's brain whirred for a moment before recognition hit her like a ton of bricks. She burst out laughing, her voice loud enough to turn heads.

"And here he is," she said, walking straight over to him, a mischievous twinkle in her eye. "The man of the hour—my friend's cheating husband. And look, he's already onto the next victim."

She raised her glass high, her grin practically sparkling with satisfaction. "Cheers," she said, as the man's face drained of colour.

He stood there, mouth agape. Erin's laughter rang out, the perfect punctuation to a moment of pure, unadulterated triumph.

67 | Bree

A few days passed with no news from the police. Bree and her planner started the last-minute touches on a few weddings. Finding a bilingual planner wasn't easy in Rocca Pinta, a task she knew she needed to undertake but wasn't quite ready to do.

On her first wedding day of the season, the captain reached out to her. Recognising his number, she replied immediately. "I've only got a minute; I'm off to a wedding," Bree said, reaching for her camera bag.

"I need you to come to Verona today," he said.

"Nope, sorry, I have a wedding; I'm a photographer, so I can't come," she replied, her face hardening in annoyance.

He groaned in protest. "Okay, we'll send someone to you; they will be there in an hour."

Bree sighed in frustration and said, "I finish at six you can come then; I can't be there earlier." She waited to hear his reply; instead, there was silence. "6 p.m. or not at all,"

The captain let a long pause hang on the line before he replied, "Okay, see you at your office at 6 p.m."

Bree had managed not to think about it for most of the day—burying herself in the frenzy of the first wedding of the summer like it was the most important thing in the world. She threw herself into every detail as if it were her very first event. By the time the day was over, her body ached from exhaustion, and her mind was spinning with the usual refrain: Could I have done something better?

She was on autopilot as she packed up her things and made her way back to her office, desperate for a quiet moment of reflection. But the moment she spotted the police outside her door, her heart sank.

With a sigh, she placed her bags down with a thud, then glanced up at the small army of officers standing in her office. "Six of you to talk to little old me?" she quipped, raising an eyebrow. "I'm flattered."

"Miss Morgan, we need your help," said the older cop, looking at her in the eye. He looked like an older version of Super Mario; he tapped his fingers nervously on his bag, his eyes fixated on hers.

"What can I do for you?" she asked, shifting in her chair as she downloaded memory cards to her computer.

"Firstly, I remind you that these conversations are confidential and will be recorded. Do you agree to these terms?"

Bree confirmed with a simple nod; with her eyes on her screen, she smiled at the images and said, "No problem."

He cleared his throat and said, "We have been involved in a task force for over two years now; we are investigating an international drug and prostitution ring." He left a long, irritating pause before he continued. "International police forces have already invested countless hours in this case."

"How am I involved?" Bree asked.

"Do you understand, or would you prefer to do this in English? His brows wrinkled as he used a condescending tone with her.

"Well, English will be much better for me, to be honest."

Super Mario nodded to a tall, broad-shouldered man with an earnest face and jet-black hair who introduced himself.

"Hello, Ms. Morgan; my name is Sergeant Dexter Garrod. I'm part of an international task force investigating, among others, Mr. Rico Marano," he said as he straightened a crease in his shirt.

Bree giggled; the name Dexter gave her flashbacks to one of her favourite television series. "Sorry, this is a serious matter; thank you for letting me do this in English; it'll be much easier. What can I do for you?" Bree asked.

"Thank you, Bree. Is it ok if I call you that?" Dexter asked, sitting down quietly.

"Of course," she replied with a smile. She liked this man already. Although she couldn't place his accent, she thought it might be from the Netherlands.

"Firstly, I have listened to the transcriptions of your previous conversations, but I have a few more questions. Then, we'd like you to help us and be our eyes on a mission," he said.

Bree scowled at them and said, "I want to help you, honestly, but I don't want to be involved in any missions. Let's start with the questions," she suggested, clutching her arms to her chest.

In the thirty minutes that followed, Bree told the same stories she had told the previous evening to the tweedles and the captain, this time in a lot more detail—timings, names, locations, and grilling her about the wedding in a couple of months.

"Can we check your phone?" Dexter asked.

"Feel free, but mainly it's wedding screenshots, a couple of pictures of my friends, not much," she said, sliding her phone over the desk. They flipped through pictures on her phone, seeing nothing of interest. She watched the disappointment flicker over Dexter's face.

"Do you have another trip planned away with Petra?" Dexter asked. He bit his tongue, refraining from asking for more details right away.

"No, Rico offered us a trip to Dubai for the weekend, but I'm fully booked with weddings until October," Bree replied.

"We think Petra is asked to take gifts filled with cocaine; we need to intercept them before they are handed over," said Dexter.

"What? No way," Bree interrupted him, her expression suddenly very serious.

"We need to find out what the gifts look like—the weight, the size, the wrapping." Dexter paused for a moment, pulling his shoulders back and rolling his arms. "When is Petra given the gifts?"

"I'm not sure; she has them when I meet her at the airport. Look, I know she doesn't know what's going on; she has nothing to do with this," Bree said.

"I know. We know Petra isn't involved in anything; we've checked her out. Do you think you can get her to talk to us?" Dexter asked.

"Me? Oh no, I'm not getting involved in this; look, she's my friend, and I want to help her, but I'm not going to ruin her life," Bree said, wagging her finger from side to side.

"All we need is an introduction; we can do the rest, but we need to know that we can trust her and you. If Rico finds out about this, two years' work is blown, and the investigation is dead."

"Let me think about it, please," Bree said. "This is big; I need a minute." She stood up and walked to the printer to escape his sight line.

"Of course." Dexter turned to her and asked, "How long do you need?"

"I don't know, so, to be clear, you want an introduction to Petra; after that, you'll do the rest?" asked Bree for clarification. "Will you be there, Dexter? Petra doesn't speak very good Italian and will find this all very intimidating. It will be totally out of the blue for her; she thinks the call girls are his friends."

"Yes, just an introduction, and yes, I'll speak to her," Dexter said firmly.

"Okay, I'll do it," Bree said, wanting the whole matter to be over as soon as possible. "When?"

"The sooner, the better. We will need Petra's help, but first, we need to see what she's like. We need to get a feel for her, her loyalties, and her situation. I suggest you invite her here or somewhere for the weekend, and I'll be there as your friend. We will make up a cover story. I could be your brother or your boyfriend, and we can discuss the details."

Bree took a deep breath and let out a long sigh and reluctantly said, "Okay."

"I'm staying in Verona; here's my card. I have all your details already; I'll be in touch. Most importantly, you need to contact Petra and arrange something as soon as possible."

"Is now okay?" Bree asked. "Can I have my phone back?" She picked it up and left a voice message, saying, "Hey girl, how are you doing? So, I've just had my first wedding of the season; it was beautiful. It's not long until yours. Do you fancy meeting up? I'm free tomorrow."

"Good, that was nice and casual," Dexter said.

As expected, Petra replied, "Hey Bree, yeah, I was wondering how your wedding went. Cool, meeting up will be great, but when? Rico is away this weekend, so I'm free as a bird. Do you want to come down?"

Dexter stopped Bree from sending the next message, saying, "We need to find the best location; somewhere I can be there too. Would it be strange if you took me there? Of course, it would. Why not get her to come here? Then I can be around," he said.

Bree wondered if he was thinking out loud or talking to her, but following his suggestions, she sent another message. "Hey girl, things are crazy here. Do you want to come up here? Maybe stay over. I've got someone I want you to meet," Bree said enthusiastically.

"Oh, exciting, fantastic, Okay, just let me know when I can come up in the morning if you like," Petra replied.

The girls planned to meet the following morning, spend the day walking, and go up the cable car. Dexter asked to be kept in the loop. They'd introduce him as a video man, possibly suitable for Petra's wedding, but also as someone Bree had a crush on.

Bree rolled her eyes and said, "A crush, how old am I? Petra knows I don't crush on people; they grow on me. Plus, you aren't my type; I'm more into casual and sporty guys. You're the new video man; much simpler."

Dexter grabbed his notes and rose; the other officers followed in silence, offering a nod as they left the room.

The following morning, with windswept hair and sun-kissed skin from her drive, Petra parked at Bree's house, curious about the person Bree wanted her to meet.

Bree had played it down, telling her he was a video man, the perfect one for her wedding; however, Petra sensed something in her voice that this was more than that. As the girls sat down for lunch, she noticed that Bree kept an eye on her watch. The warm spring breeze caressed their skin as they chatted. Bree's eyes flicked nervously around the terrace towards the entrance. She took a deep, nervous breath when she saw Dexter standing in the doorway.

He looked different in long khaki trousers and a grey polo shirt; he flashed her his most charming grin as he put his phone in his pocket, crossed the wooden deck and greeted them with a smile. He joined them at the table, and, after the introductions, they chatted about Petra's wedding. Dexter had done his prep. He had video clips on his iPad of weddings on the pretext of talking about putting himself forward as a candidate.

Bree's phone rang. Her finger pondered the accept button for a second, then pressed it and listened to the voice that said, "It's Captain Pellegrino. Please leave Petra and Dexter alone to talk. Make an excuse and return to the office."

"Petra, I've got to nip to the office; I've got an Amazon delivery," Bree said as she grabbed her bag and left with a smile and a wave. Four officers she recognised from the day before waited at the office.

"There's no point lying to Petra; the longer we lie, the more she'll distrust us. By now, Dexter will have told her everything. They will be heading back to the office soon.

68 | Bree

Bree scrolled through wedding photos on her computer while the officers waited silently, pacing around the office. She stretched her tense neck and poured a glass of water for herself as her friend walked in. Petra didn't say anything, shooting a bewildered look at Bree.

The police sat Petra down; after the formalities, they bombarded her with questions. Petra answered any way she could; she was helpful but vague, fearful of saying the wrong thing, Bree was aware that every answer Petra provided put Rico into more trouble.

Bree excused herself and left the office, stepping out for a brief moment of clarity. After grabbing a coffee and picking up boxed sandwiches, she returned. "Lunch," she announced, setting the boxes down on a nearby desk. "Energy food."

Her tone was firm, bordering on impatient, as she threw the bags onto the table. She couldn't afford any emotional turmoil right now—there was already enough of it swirling around her. "Everyone, stop it," she said, her voice taking on a sharp edge. "This is my friend. This is already hard enough for her. You don't need to make her cry. Don't you think this is devastating for her? Her whole world has been turned upside down. Be kind. Be respectful."

Bree reached for Petra's hand, giving it a reassuring squeeze, trying to calm her in the storm.

Petra's eyes glazed over as she withdrew her hand from Bree's. "I need a break. I want to talk to Bree," she muttered, voice unsteady. She grabbed Bree's arm and practically dragged her out the door.

Once they were far enough away from the office, the silence hit them both. Petra's breathing was shallow, her pulse pounding in her ears. She turned to Bree, her voice shaking. "What the hell, Bree? What is going on?" Her words hung in the air, desperate and raw. "You should have told me what you thought before all of this happened." Her face crumpled as she added, "I can't believe you let it go this far."

Bree's heart twisted. She hadn't meant to cause Petra more pain, but she knew she couldn't lie anymore. She exhaled deeply before answering. "Yes, I know. I should have said something earlier, but I wasn't allowed to. At that restaurant in Verona—" Bree paused, struggling with the impact of the truth. "I saw things that didn't sit right with me. I saw Rico with those women, and I suspected they were call girls. There were... circumstances. The way they treated him like he was in charge. I didn't want to just assume, so I kept quiet. I tried to investigate more, but then the police turned up, and... I was sworn to secrecy." She looked at Petra, hoping she could understand the position she'd been put in.

Petra blinked, her expression shifting from confusion to horror as she tried to process the words. "Okay. That makes sense. But I need to know what you knew before all of this, Bree. What else was going on?" Her voice was small now, barely above a whisper, as though the truth had begun to crush her.

Bree tensed. Telling the truth felt she was stabbing a cold, sharp knife in her friend's chest. "At the restaurant. I had to go grab our coats and I think I saw Rico waiting for the lift with a girl. I'm not sure, but it looked... wrong." She added the last part cautiously, hoping to soften the blow, but it was clear it hadn't worked.

Petra's face paled, and her fists clenched at her sides. "So, let me get this straight," shesaid, her voice hollow with disbelief. "Rico is running some kind of prostitution ring, involved in illegal gambling, and cheating on me with god knows who?"

Bree's nod confirmed the horrible truth, but she wasn't finished yet. After a pause, she added, "And the police... they think you're helping him smuggle drugs in the gifts he sends overseas."

Petra's face drained of colour. Her jaw went slack, and her breath caught in her throat. "What? No—no, I didn't know about that. How could they think that?" Her hands flew to her chest, as if she could stop her heart from breaking into a thousand pieces. "Oh, God... He dragged me into this mess too. What do I do, Bree? What do I do now?"

Bree's voice softened, but there was still strength behind it. "You tell the truth, Petra. That's the only way you'll clear yourself. You have to tell them everything you know. I'll help you, but you have to be honest."

Petra swallowed hard, her gaze locking onto Bree's. After a long, weighted silence, she nodded. "Okay. Let's do this," she said, her voice low and strained. "Let's just get it over with."

Returning to Bree's desk, Petra looked at Dexter and said, "Okay, I've learnt a few home truths from Bree; I'll need more proof before I give you more information. How do I know this is all real?"

The captain fumbled with his bag, pulled out a tablet, and flicked through hundreds of pictures. He pushed the images slowly towards her. Holding her breath, she swiped through images of Rico with women, kissing, exchanging money, and swapping parcels. Rico in casinos with businessmen Rico with mountains of cash.

"We have someone undercover, but we need someone close to him. We need you," Dexter said. "You're the only one who can push this investigation over the edge." He tried his best to phrase it delicately, but his tone was strained.

Petra glared at him. Inhaling a deep breath, she cocked her head and asked, "Me?"

"Rico has been great at covering his tracks; it's hard to pin anything on him; we know the names of most of his associates. We need the names of the others." He turned back to the other man handing him the tablet and said, "We need to know his travel plans and access to his computer."

"Okay, so you don't need much, then?" Petra growled, glancing over at Bree. "I can't help you with all that stuff. Okay, a few names maybe, and travel plans, although he usually springs his business trips on me very last minute."

"We need you to let us into the villa when he goes away; we will do the rest. You need to let us in, and then your job is done," Dexter said calmly, running a hand through his dark hair.

Petra took a deep breath, hesitating for a split second. "I'm done now. I've had it with you all." She waved her hand dismissively. She felt her face crumble, and hot tears sprang into her eyes.

Fear flashed over Dexter's face as he shifted in his seat. "I've saved my number in your phone under 'David Smith;' text me or call me when you have thought about it." Turning to face Bree, he forced himself to take a deep breath and said, "We are trusting you, both of you. It isn't going to be easy; we know that." His voice issued a warning. "You can call me anytime, though,"

69 | Petra

Escorting the officers out of the office, Bree let out a long, slow sigh. The stress of the day pressed heavily on her shoulders. As she reached Petra, she opened her arms, and Petra collapsed into her embrace, tears immediately flooding her eyes. Bree held her tight, her fingers gently stroking the back of Petra's head.

"Can we go to your house? Maybe just sit by the pool?" Petra's voice was thick with emotion as they walked to the car. She didn't want to be alone; she just wanted space to breathe, to think, to escape for a while.

Once at the house, Petra slipped into the cool pool, letting the water embrace her, a temporary relief from the mess in her mind. Bree watched quietly, letting Petra take the time she needed. As Petra emerged from the water, water droplets glistening in her hair, she grabbed a towel and began drying off. Her gaze drifted far off, lost in thought.

"I can't go back there," Petra said, her voice shaky but firm. "I can't lie to him. What will I even say to him? God, and those other women. What if he touches me?" Her voice cracked as the raw fear crept back in, making her chest tighten.

Bree walked over and gently touched her arm. "It won't be easy," she said softly, her voice steady, offering Petra the comfort of her presence.

Petra wiped a tear away. "I didn't believe any of it... not until I saw those pictures of him with that woman. I've seen her before—always with a different man. I just thought she was popular, you know? Not... not what they're saying she is."

"You've had to take in a lot today," Bree said, her tone a blend of sympathy and strength. "You've been so brave. You're stronger than you think."

Petra's expression faltered, a ghost of doubt crossing her face. "I still don't believe the drug stuff. That... that has to be made up. He wouldn't do that to me. I'm sure of it." She sounded unconvinced, her voice tense, the frustration clear in her eyes.

Bree rested against the side of the pool, her arms folded across her chest. "Were you sure he wouldn't cheat? Were you sure he wasn't running a prostitution ring?" The question hung heavy in the air, as if Bree was pushing Petra to face the deeper truth.

Petra looked away, the truth sinking in. "Well... yeah, I suppose I was sure. Or I wanted to be sure." Her shoulders slumped as she applied more sunscreen, her movements mechanical. "God, Bree... what do I do now?"

Bree crouched down beside her, her voice gentle yet resolute. "Stay here for a few days. Just tell him you're in the UK or that you're sick, and you're looking after me. Keep the distance. Go back the day before you're supposed to leave for the UK. Be kind to him, but if you need to, fake a headache. Just give yourself time to think."

Petra took a deep breath, staring at the water's surface. "Yeah, I'll have to. It's just one day, twenty-four hours of being with him and keeping my mouth shut. But I can't keep doing this. It's too much." She clenched her hands into fists, feeling the anger build.

The hours passed, and Petra slowly began to relax into a light snooze. But even in sleep, her mind raced. She called Rico that evening, her heart thudding in her chest as she explained her absence. There was a calmness in his voice that hadn't been there before, an understanding that Petra found unsettling. It was like the veil had lifted, and she saw his manipulation for what it was. His intentions were clearer now, and with that clarity came a wave of dread.

Her heart began to pound in her chest as the truth sank deeper. "This is too much," Petra whispered, her throat tight as she choked back tears. "I want out. Whatever happens... I can't marry him."

A few days later, Petra returned to the villa, her heart still heavy with everything she had learned. Rico greeted her with a warm embrace, but there was a coldness in her that he couldn't see. His smile was genuine, but Petra's eyes were distant, her mind elsewhere.

"Are you all right, darling?" Rico asked as they sat down for dinner, his tone smooth and reassuring, like he was trying to pull her back into his world. "You seem distant."

Petra looked up at him, her mind still swirling with the impact of her decision and situation. She forced a smile. "Yes, I'm just worried about Bree," she said, her voice almost mechanical as she kept her emotions locked away.

Rico didn't come up to the room until she was fast asleep. In the morning, he kissed her on the cheek and left the villa quietly. Hearing his car tyres skid in the gravel, she peered out of the corner of a window until his car was no more than a dot on the horizon.

Following Dexter's instructions, Petra methodically checked the villa for any hidden cameras or bugs. After a thorough sweep, she declared the house clear and sent Dexter a text to confirm.

Moments later, a convoy of cars pulled up outside. The door swung open, and a flood of officers, both in uniform and plainclothes, poured into the house. The air became thick with the sound of rubber gloves snapping and the occasional rustling of papers. Officers scattered in all directions, turning the house upside down with swift efficiency.

A small team of tech specialists gathered around Rico's computer, their quiet whispers punctuated by the clicking of keyboards, as they attached various devices. Petra stood off to the side, watching the controlled mess unfold around her. Dexter paced the room like a lion in a cage, his restless energy verging on annoyance. Amidst the flurry of activity, Petra felt isolated. She sank into the sofa, her eyes staring blankly out of the window, exposed and humiliated.

Petra tried to maintain her composure, but it was becoming increasingly difficult. The house, once a sanctuary, felt like a prison. She fought to keep the panic at bay as the officers rifled through every drawer, every folder, every corner. Yet, when she glanced around, everything appeared undisturbed, each item in its rightful place, but she couldn't shake the feeling of violation.

"So, did you find anything?" Petra's voice was strained as she addressed Dexter, who had just passed her on his way to confer with the team. All she needed was something—anything—that would bring an end to this nightmare.

Dexter flashed her a half-smile, but there was no warmth behind it. "Too soon to tell," he said, his voice low but firm. "We need to go through everything we've copied off his computer before we can make any moves."

Petra's frustration flared. "I can't come back here and pretend anymore. You have to find something." Her words were sharper than she intended, but the pressure was unbearable. Her focus flickered back to the officers, still working diligently, and her stomach churned.

"If we find something, we'll pick him up at the airport," Dexter replied, his tone more sympathetic, but it didn't quite make it to his eyes. "If we don't, you'll need to stay here... for as long as it takes." His words lingered in the air, heavy with implication.

Petra clenched her fists, her chest tightening with anger. "Well, I hope to God you're good at your jobs because..." She stood up, gesturing around the room. "I'm not coming back here. Not for you. Not for the police. Not for anyone." The words felt like a vow, but they came with a quiet resignation, as if the reality of her situation had fully set in.

She cursed under her breath as Dexter gave a nonchalant shrug, offering no further words of reassurance. The officers continued their search, oblivious to the storm brewing inside Petra.

Once they were finally done and the house fell into an eerie quiet, Petra closed the door behind her with a deliberate finality. She turned the key in the lock and stepped outside. The world felt so small as she got into the car, her foot pressing firmly on the gas as she drove toward Lake Valdo. The road stretched before her, but her mind was elsewhere—torn between the desire to escape and the pull of what she was leaving behind.

Petra felt the gnawing ache in her heart. She wanted to call Rico, to hear his voice, to convince herself that this was all just a misunderstanding—that life was still normal and their future together was intact. But then, in the blink of an eye, the mood shifted. She would want to call him and shout, unleash all the hurt and frustration she had kept bottled up. She wanted him to understand, to take responsibility, to feel her pain.

The conflicting emotions twisted inside her. If this was a colossal mistake, she would marry this man. But if it wasn't... She didn't know how to even begin to untangle her life from the mess he had entangled her in. She stared at her phone, willing it to ring. She would check it compulsively, waking in the night just to make sure there were no missed messages.

The hours dragged, and the silence between them grew. She toggled between wanting a message from Rico, needing his reassurance, and waiting for the call from Dexter that could end all this—either by bringing closure or pulling her further into the storm.

Two days passed, and then, the long-awaited phone call finally came.

It wasn't from Rico.

It was Dexter.

His voice was calm, almost unnervingly so, as he delivered the news. "Petra," he began, "we need you to complete one more task. Hopefully, it'll be the final one."

Petra's stomach sank. She had been expecting this moment for days, but now that it was here, she wasn't sure if she was ready for what was to come.

70 | Petra

"We need you to do one more thing for us. We need you to stay with him until he asks you to go on your next trip with one of those parcels." Dexter explained. "We will intercept the parcel and arrest you. You won't be under suspicion; then, of course, we will set you free; it's just a false arrest."

Petra listened in silence as he continued to explain it all. He told her that it would be over soon and that she'd be free to carry on with her life.

"So, I have to go stay there?" She lifted a glass of water to her lips; her mouth was too dry to speak too much.

"You have to act as normal as you can. He can't be suspicious of anything; he has to think you're still unaware of anything. Be yourself with him; be loving and friendly," Dexter explained insistently.

"He had asked me to go to Dubai, but I said no as Bree is working, and I didn't want to go alone," Petra told him.

"Why not with another friend? We have an English undercover officer who could act as your friend."

"Okay," Petra said hesitantly, rubbing her fingers over her mouth.

"You can take her to meet Rico; let's see if he trusts her enough to go with you. Maybe you can introduce her as a friend of Bree's," Dexter suggested.

The offer of a trip to Dubai had come unexpectedly, but Petra, eager to please Rico and escape her growing suspicions. A few days later, the hotels were booked, and Petra waited with an anxious energy, hoping that the package she was about to take was nothing out of the ordinary—a simple, innocent gesture between businessmen. But a nagging feeling gnawed at her, a sensation that the air around her was thick with hidden dangers she couldn't yet name.

On the morning of her departure, she was packing in her dressing room when she felt Rico's presence before she even saw him. The sound of his footsteps echoed in the doorway, and instinctively, she placed a pair of new tailored shorts in her suitcase, trying to focus on the mundane task in front of her to steady her nerves.

"Baby, will you take this over to Dubai?" Rico's voice was warm, but there was an edge of something Petra couldn't place. He handed her a beautifully wrapped parcel tied with a ribbon bearing his company logo. The logo, which had once seemed like a symbol of success, now felt like a chain.

Petra froze. Her breath caught in her throat. She couldn't bring herself to look him in the eye. She stared at the paper in her hands, her fingers trembling as she clutched it. "Of course, not a problem," she managed to say, though her voice sounded foreign, as if someone else had spoken the words for her. She forced a smile, the kind that never quite reached her eyes. "Will someone come and collect it as usual?"

Rico smiled back, too confident, too sure. "Yes, a client will meet you as usual in the arrivals hall at the airport," he said. His words were simple, yet Petra felt them pressing down on her.

She nodded, the smile on her lips stiff and fake. "Okay, no problem," she muttered, reaching out to grip his hand. His touch, usually warm and reassuring, now felt like an anchor dragging her deeper into uncertainty.

"I'm going to miss you," he said, and then, with a tenderness that almost felt too intimate for the moment, he kissed her. He handed her an envelope, thick with cash. "For you two," he said. "Treat yourselves. Have some fun on me."

As she slid the parcel into her hand luggage, the sickening thought crossed her mind: Is this how it starts?

Quickly, she fumbled for her phone, her hands unsteady as she texted Dexter: 'Got it.'

The reply came almost instantly: 'Okay.' Short. To the point. They'd gone over the plan countless times. The plan was simple: She was to act surprised, innocent, deny everything. She was to be arrested leaving Verona airport. Everything hinged on this moment, and Petra's heart began to pound harder, a steady drumbeat of fear in her chest.

Rico said his goodbyes, kissing her one last time before he climbed into the car, his driver pulling away from the villa. Petra stood in the doorway, her mind a whirlwind of confusion and doubt. She sighed, exhaling a breath she hadn't realised she'd been holding. As the car sped toward the airport, she refused to look back at the villa. She couldn't risk seeing him—not yet—but the sky, so vast and blue above her, gave her a fleeting sense of freedom, even if it was only temporary.

At the airport, Heather greeted her with a warm hug, the two of them exchanging the final pleasantries before the plan began in earnest. They looked every bit the part: two good friends, excited for a weekend in Dubai, their smiles bright, but Petra felt the walls closing in around her. As she smiled at the check-in agent, sweat began to bead under her armpits, her stomach twisting in knots. This isn't a holiday, she thought. This is a nightmare waiting to unfold.

She glanced around, scanning for any signs of sniffer dogs. Her heart raced, the thought of carrying the parcel through security filled her with dread. If I get caught... The idea that she could be detained in Dubai, dragged into a foreign prison, was enough to make her skin crawl.

The line moved slowly. They passed through security, no incidents, no sniffs from the dogs. But as Petra browsed the perfume selection in the duty-free store, she turned to Heather, her voice barely a whisper. "When?"

"At the gate," Heather replied, her tone low and urgent. "The dogs will be there." Her eyes darted to the side as Petra's stomach dropped even further. The gate. The final hurdle.

They left the shops empty-handed, the noises of the terminal around them suddenly too loud, too oppressive. They made their way to the gate, the heavy bag and parcel weighing down on Petra with every step. She tried to steady her breath, but it was no use. Her heart was hammering, and her skin felt slick with cold sweat. She sat down, the floor under her feet seeming to shift. She opened a book and placed it in her lap, her foot tapping restlessly, though her mind was miles away.

Heather nodded discreetly at someone in the departure area. He appeared to be just another passenger, but Petra could tell from Heather's glance that he was part of the operation. "He's one of ours," Heather whispered, barely audible.

Just keep talking to me, Heather's voice sounded in her mind, though her lips didn't move. "Don't look over."

But Petra couldn't help it. Her eyes flickered toward the approaching security officers, and her breath caught in her throat. Two large sniffer dogs rounded the corner, their handlers close behind. The dogs' eyes scanned the area, their noses twitching. The sound of their paws on the floor was the only noise that seemed to matter now. Her body went cold as the dogs moved toward the gate. They sniffed the air, moved on, and then—one of them turned back.

Her heart skipped a beat. The dog's nostrils flared, its body taut with focus. It turned away and then came back again, its leash pulled tight as it zeroed in on her bag. The handler's steps slowed, eyes narrowing as the dog sat firmly in front of her luggage.

Petra's chest constricted, and she fought to breathe as the pressure of what was happening settled in like a clamp around her ribs. She felt the ground tilt beneath her. For a split second, everything stood still, and in that terrifying silence, the realization hit her like a freight train: Rico had used her. She was a pawn, a mule, just another piece in his twisted game.

The hairs on her body stood on end, a wave of cold panic rushing over her. Her head fell into her hands, a momentary surrender to the overwhelming dread.

A stern voice broke through her thoughts. "Does this bag belong to you?" the handler asked, his gaze locking with Petra's.

71 | Nina

Nina had ticked most places off her bucket list of places to travel to over the years. She always felt at ease while travelling. Since meeting Manuel, who'd become her travel partner, she couldn't imagine travelling without him.

Enjoying his easy banter and acceptance of her need for adventure, she found him a pleasant and easygoing person to travel with. Manuel had mentioned Venezuela on his bucket list; it had been his dream since childhood, and the main reason they'd even travelled to Venezuela was to visit Angel Falls.

They had spent most of their budget on the falls, river trip, and internal flight, more than the other twenty-eight days combined.

"We should come back here again," Nina suggested after a few days on holiday.

"Let's see, ok? I'm not sure what I think of it yet," he replied. "A bit too much white sand and boredom for me." He shrugged after spending two weeks on the sleepy islands of Los Roques. "Not even the fish like me," he said a few days later, putting his gear back in a box. "When have I ever gone fishing and not caught anything?" he complained with a sour face. "Yesterday, I was out on that water for eight hours without even a bite."

"Don't worry. We're going travelling tomorrow, and we'll have lots of things to do," she replied.

A few days later, back on the mainland, they found themselves stepping off a creaking bus into the oppressive heat of a humid, sticky evening. Wrestling their rucksacks free from the rusty roof rack, they looked around the drowsy, sun-bleached town for anything resembling a hotel. Their eyes landed on a blue, faded building with a battered sign swinging precariously from a single hook, the word HOTEL missing its first letter. Above the main door, the remaining letters were barely legible, eroded by time and neglect. The door squeaked behind them and slammed shut; upon entering, the smell of stale body odour greeted them.

A man sauntered behind a plastic blind made of colourful stones and beads. Long black hairs poked out of his grey, stained vest as he ambled out of the room. He rubbed his eyes and looked at the clock. He glared inquisitively at them, not touching the cigarette drooping from his mouth. Reaching the reception desk, ash fell on Nina's hands.

She blew it off with a giggle and asked, "Do you have a room for tonight?"

He rubbed his stubbly chin as if deciding if these two tourists were worthy of his establishment. He grunted, looking at a board on which a row of keys hung on rusty nails. He handed them a key and said, "Ten dollars for the room."

Nina smiled and turned to Manuel, whose wide, incredulous eyes were fixed on the clerk. Stifling laughter, they grabbed their bags, darted up the creaky stairs, and shut the door of their room behind them. Manuel surveyed the grimy floor, his face a mix of horror and disbelief. "So, are the cockroaches included in the price, or do we pay extra?" he muttered, struggling to mask his disgust.

Nina perched gingerly on the edge of the sagging bed, the mattress sinking beneath her with a puff of dust that hung in the air like an accusation. She ran her fingers over the worn sheets, pausing abruptly when they caught on a hole. Trying not to react, she shuffled to obscure a dark brown stain encircling it. "I guess I'm sleeping fully clothed tonight," Manuel quipped.

"For five dollars each, what can we expect? Come on; it's only for one night." Nina stroked his arm as he shook his head in disgust.

She rested a wooden chair against the door handle before she slid her fully clothed body into the sheets. After hearing the patter of tiny animals through the night, Nina put a finger to her lips, and with quiet steps and whispers, they cast the key aside on the desk and walked to the bus station. Turning back to look at the exteriors, Nina burst into a fit of giggles.

Irritated by the heat and sweating in shorts and sandals, they waited impatiently at the bus stop. "Never any timetables are there?" Manuel moaned as the sun burned against his skin and beads of sweat rolled down his face.

"What would be the point? No one is in a rush here; we're lucky there is a bus at all." Nina said as she tried to sound upbeat.

A small, hand-painted bus screeched to a halt, and the driver gave a cheerful wave, beckoning them aboard. The vehicle jolted and bounced its way along the dusty, winding roads from Caracas to Chirimena, its passengers gripping seats or handrails for dear life. They chose spots well away from the blaring speakers that pumped out Caribbean rhythms at full blast.

Manuel watched Nina, his focus lingering on her animated face. She seemed exhilarated, as if the thrill of exploring a strange and unpredictable country far outweighed any fear. Her ability to laugh and smile, even in the most unsettling circumstances, both amazed and unnerved him. He couldn't help but grin as he saw her playfully interact with a young boy in the seat ahead of her, unbothered by the streaks his dusty finger marks left on her shorts. When the bus swerved sharply, she burst out laughing, her joy infectious despite the moment of fear.

Manuel clung desperately to a handrail, a sharp turn pitching him forward. Instinctively, he grabbed Nina's arm to steady himself. "Marry me," he blurted, his voice rising above the pounding music. The words shocked him the moment they escaped his lips.

As the bus braked suddenly, Nina's elbow jabbed him hard in the ribs. She turned to him, momentarily stunned, and burst out, "Are you crazy? Let's survive this bus ride first. Ask me again if we do."

Her words left him speechless. He winced with every jolt of the road, convinced she'd cracked one of his ribs. The impromptu proposal and her reaction churned uneasily in his mind, even as the landscape unfurled in lush, untamed beauty around them.

Hours later, the crisscross imprints from the sticky leather seats still marked their legs as they wandered through town, searching for their tour guide. A cheerful young man with an easy smile approached them, introducing himself as Faisal. "Sorry about the wait. It's impossible to guess when these buses arrive." He hoisted Nina's bag onto his shoulder and led them up the wooden steps to a stilted cabin.

"This place is beautiful," Nina remarked, admiring the surroundings.

"Tomorrow, we'll visit Angel Falls," Faisal explained, "but this afternoon, we'll meet the local community. If you're hungry, there's a food stall right over there." He pointed to a makeshift stand where vegetables were stacked into colourful pyramids, flanked by two circular hot plates.

At the stall, a tall man swayed to the music while kneading balls of dough. "Cornbread," Faisal said, motioning to bowls of beans, onions, and tomatoes. "You can fill them with whatever you like."

"Like Subway, but rustic," Nina joked as she selected her fillings. A local man rushed past, grabbing a long, finger-shaped treat. Curious, Nina followed suit, biting into a fresh, warm cornbread. "It's like a doughnut." she said, her eyes lighting up as she offered Manuel a taste.

Manuel grinned and ordered more, washing them down with a tangy yellow juice Faisal called passion fruit. Despite its name, it had the sweet, sharp taste of pineapple. As they ate, Manuel finally began to relax.

Later, aboard a handmade wooden canoe, they glided through a maze of waterways winding through the jungle. Manuel swatted at persistent flies, laughing as his hat was swept off his head and floated away, much to the amusement of Faisal and Nina.

That evening, seated on a bench under the stars and sharing street food, Manuel asked her again—this time without the chaos of the bus or a ring. "Yes, of course, I'd love to marry you," Nina replied, her voice soft, her laughter lingering in the warm night air.

Manuel smiled, but unease crept in as he wondered if this would change everything. Would she become one of those brides obsessed with wedding plans? Shaking off the thoughts, he resolved not to overthink it. As the trip continued, they rarely mentioned the engagement again, letting their adventure unfold as if the moment had been just another fleeting thrill in a journey full of surprises.

After weeks of longing for home comforts, they settled down for a family dinner. Gianni and Fabio welcomed them with hugs and a steaming plate of lasagna. Nina excitedly shared the proposal news, which received a muted reaction.

"When?" her father asked with a glare.

"Not for a while; don't worry, it won't be an expensive, flashy affair," she said as she offered him a reassuring smile.

"We have a bit more travelling to do before we get married. We're both still young so maybe in a couple of years." The full force of what had happened hit Manuel as he watched Nina chattering excitedly with her family about wedding venues.

RAW MISTAKES

A few days later, Nina searched in her bag for her car keys. Upon hearing her name, Nina turned around and smiled at her dad, who was leaning on his car in their garage. He finished polishing his glasses, and with just one look, Nina could see something was wrong. Wearing a deeply worried expression, he reached for Nina's hand and said, "Look, I want you to be happy. I want you to be married, of course, and give me lots of grandkids, but there is something about him I don't like; I don't trust him," her father said.

For a moment, Nina clammed up, rubbed her eyes, and leant out of the window towards him. "Dad, don't worry; he's great and looks after me. I'm your only daughter, and you worry, and I love you for that," she said as she slapped him on the arm in jest.

"I want to be wrong, but I get a strange sensation from him; something is off," he said as he supported himself on the door. Adjusting his glasses, Nina saw his brows tense.

"I hope you're wrong too, Dad, but come on, he can't be after my money; I don't have any." She almost chuckled at the thought, brushing off any of her father's concerns. "Thank you for your opinion, but right now, I have to get to work," Nina said, wrapping up the conversation.

"Okay, that will be my last word on the matter, I promise," her dad said as he watched her carefully reverse out of the door. Realising that his daughter was a grown woman, he forced himself to remain positive.

As she drove to the shop, Nina pondered his words. After some thought, she dismissed the idea that something was wrong. She pushed the worries to the back of her mind but promised herself to watch out for signals that something was amiss.

72 | Petra

Petra replied quickly, "Yes, it's my bag. Is there something wrong?" She tugged her jacket tightly, trying to hide the tremble in her hand.

"Please come with me. Are you travelling together?" the officer asked, gesturing toward Heather.

"Yes," Petra said firmly. "Please tell me what's wrong. Our flight is boarding now," she added, her voice quavering as she tried to sound distressed.

The officer, now joined by airport security, repeated his request more forcefully, adding, "I need your passports." Petra and Heather exchanged uneasy glances before handing them over.

Grabbing their other bags, they followed the uniformed men through a maze of doors marked 'Staff Only' and 'No Entry.' They were ushered into a sterile white room furnished only with a table and four chairs. A machine in the corner emitted occasional pings and hisses, adding to the tension.

"Our detection dogs alerted us to the possibility of narcotics in this bag," one officer announced, snapping on thin blue gloves. "Please observe as we open it."

Petra fought to stay composed, her high-necked shirt feeling suffocating. "No, there must be a mistake," she murmured, her voice tight.

Her mind raced. She suddenly remembered the large amount of cash in her bag and prayed it wouldn't raise any questions. The officer discovered the money but set it aside without comment. Methodically, he unpacked the bag, inspecting each item, swabbing surfaces, and testing for drugs. Every scan came back clean.

Petra let out a shaky breath, but her relief was short-lived. The sniffer dog was brought into the room, its handler flanked by two additional officers who introduced themselves as Dexter and the Captain. After flashing their credentials, they dismissed the other officers, leaving only the handler behind.

Petra's chest tightened when she caught Dexter's fleeting glance of recognition. His subtle nod steadied her nerves—but only slightly.

The dog zeroed in on a wrapped gift, scratching at it decisively. Its handler confirmed the signal before exiting the room with the dog. Dexter and the Captain wasted no time, filming and photographing every step as they dismantled the package. Petra's heart thudded as they carefully unwrapped what appeared to be an innocuous box of business gifts: engraved wine stoppers, a wooden caddy, and a branded wine cooler sleeve.

At first glance, it looked harmless, even elegant. But as they continued to examine each item, they uncovered sixteen small bags of white powder concealed within the objects. Dexter's expression remained grim, even as the

Captain's face lit up with satisfaction.

"Looks like you've missed your flight," the Captain said, his tone almost gleeful.

Petra slumped back in her chair, her palms clammy. Heather gave her arm a reassuring squeeze, but it did little to calm her.

Dexter finally spoke. "You've done a fantastic job, Petra. But we have to make this look real." He paused, his tone careful. "We'll leave here in handcuffs and take you to headquarters before releasing you. Standard procedure. We can't risk exposing you."

Petra swallowed hard. "Okay. I've never been arrested before," she said with a weak laugh. "This is... exciting, I guess. As long as I'm not really in trouble."

"You're not," Dexter reassured her. "But we need to decide what happens next."

Cold metal cuffs clicked shut around Petra's wrists as they were led out of the room. The stares of curious travellers burned into her as she was marched to a waiting car.

At headquarters, they removed the cuffs and left her and Heather in a drab grey room. Petra sank onto a worn sofa, exhaustion overtaking her. As her eyes fluttered shut, the day's events whirled through her mind.

She woke to the sound of the door creaking open. Dexter stood before her, shifting on his feet, and Heather entered behind him, now dressed in a smart black trouser suit.

Petra rubbed her eyes, her heart pounding. "Any news?" she asked, her voice hoarse.

Heather handed her a sandwich and a bottle of water. "We texted Rico from your phone, saying you'd been arrested."

Petra's stomach twisted. "And?"

"He read the message but hasn't replied," Dexter said, checking his watch. "It's only been twenty minutes."

The mention of Rico's name sent her mind spinning. She couldn't ignore the pang of longing she felt for him—a man who had put her future in jeopardy with his reckless choices.

73 | Petra

A knock on the door shocked her; a petite, fragile lady entered, set food for her, and stepped back. Petra unpeeled the sandwich, picked at the bread, and started eating in small bites. They asked her to provide a statement and respond to more questions.

In the early evening, Dexter informed her that they were sending her to a hotel for the night, not in Verona but in a different city. "We're hiding you, so you'll be sheltered from the backlash that will follow," Dexter said.

Petra shrugged as she looked around the hotel, its simple decorations and facilities a stark contrast to the luxury she was accustomed to. The noise of passing cars interrupted her sleep, preventing her mind from resting.

First thing in the morning, Dexter appeared at the door to her room and said, "We can't let you have your phone back yet, but if you need to contact anyone, you can do it now. Do you need to call your family? Friends? Let them know you're okay. We don't want anyone worrying about you," he said.

"Well, maybe Bree, I suppose. Can I tell her what is going on?" Petra asked.

"No, you can't tell her anything yet, but she has sent a few messages; maybe you could just reply so she doesn't worry."

Petra took the phone and scrolled through the messages. Bree sent a couple of messages asking how she was and if there were any updates. After replying to the messages, she placed the phone back in Dexter's hand.

"It has been a crazy twenty-four hours since you were found with the drugs." Dexter paused for a moment, then said, "We needed to link a few more parts together before we could move. There were a lot of different agencies involved; these things take time. You were amazing yesterday; I'm sorry we had to keep you here."

"Any news on Rico?" Petra asked.

"Our men were watching him when he got the text," Dexter said.

"Has he texted me back?" Petra asked, wondering if Rico even cared.

"No, nothing at all. We think he'll leave the country; our officers watched him pack a bag and leave within two minutes of you texting him."

"Are you going to stop him?" Petra asked.

"Not yet; we're following him and seeing what happens if and when he leaves the country. We will take you to the villa and vineyard when he has gone far enough to be safe. Now that we know what we are looking for, we hope to find drugs in the villa."

"I don't want to go back there," Petra said, her muscles tightening, ready to run.

"You can grab all of your belongings while you let us in. So, be ready to go as soon as we tell you. Where do you need to go? We will book your flights back to the UK if you like." Petra shrugged her shoulders and shook her head.

"I don't know yet; this is all so sudden. Can I go to Bree's?" she asked softly, her tired eyes apprehensive.

"Of course, we will drive you up there; I'll call Bree now and let her know," he said.

Dexter left Petra alone with her mixed emotions from the last two days. She was grateful that this, her next visit to the villa, would be her last.

74 | Petra

It was early in the morning when Petra arrived trembling at the villa. Letting the officers in, she shuffled upstairs to her room. If all went according to plan, that day would be her last visit to the villa.

Petra rushed into the bedroom, bolting the door behind her. She pulled out her suitcases, her hands trembling as she began stuffing them with clothes and belongings. Her gaze lingered on the dresses hanging neatly in the wardrobe. She yanked them off the rail, tossing them haphazardly into another bag.

Pausing by her jewellery box, she ran her fingers over the shimmering trinkets and Rico's extravagant gifts. The sight of them tightened a knot in her chest. With deliberate care, she carried the box downstairs, setting it beside the growing pile of luggage.

Her eyes fell on framed photographs of her and Rico. The smiles they once shared now felt distant, almost taunting. She picked up one frame, studied it briefly, then set it face-down. A bundle of printed emails caught her attention. They were love emails, filled with promises of a better life together. She flipped through them, but each line she read brought fresh tears.

Petra sat at the bedside table, pen in hand, struggling to compose a farewell note. Her thoughts swirled in frustration. Every attempt ended with the paper crumpled in her fist and tossed into the bin.

A knock at the door startled her. She turned the key and came face-to-face with the captain and three officers. Wordlessly, she stepped aside, gesturing for them to enter. Behind her, the click of a camera shutter punctuated her quiet exit as she retreated to the kitchen.

Unlocking the heavy wooden door, she moved into Rico's prized kitchen. The officers began their search, overturning cushions, dismantling furniture, and rifling through drawers. Their authority, bolstered by a search warrant, rendered Petra's protests useless.

Dexter approached her with a request. "We need access to the vineyards and the cellar."

Petra nodded, grabbing her keys. She left her bags by the door and joined the officers in their car. The vehicle jolted along the winding gravel paths, leading to the estate's main building. At the entrance, she punched in the access code and stepped aside, allowing them to proceed.

Her eyes fell on neatly stacked boxes of Rico's finest red wine—her favourite. With a shrug, she grabbed four of them and carried them to the car.

A uniformed officer watched her silently. Petra smirked. "If I'd married him, it would have been mine anyway. I think he owes me this much."

The officer chuckled, helping her load the boxes into the car. Leaning against a weathered stone wall, he lit a cigarette, the lighter's flicker catching her attention.

She took a moment before accepting the packet he offered and took one out. The familiar burn of smoke filled her lungs as she slouched on the wall, her eyes scanning the rolling hills.

With a sigh, she stubbed out the cigarette, grinding it into the gravel. Returning inside, she froze at the sound of commotion. Her pulse quickened, a sudden dread gripping her at the thought of Rico returning to find her here.

The room buzzed with activity, officers moving with determined purpose. The excited murmur of their conversation felt out of place in the otherwise sombre setting. From the shadows, Petra watched a cluster of uniformed men emerge from the underground cellar, their expressions grim and triumphant.

Petra closed her eyes and tried to picture the basement as it was before they turned it upside down. Remembering the two large oak wine casks there, she eyed Dexter and the Captain, smiling as their heads emerged from the cellar. "Got it," he said, turning back to the other agent. We got him." A ripple of applause from the surrounding officers followed.

However, the sight of Petra watching swiftly erased their smiles.

"Got what?" Petra asked.

Dexter dusted off his hands on his trousers and approached Petra. "We got it—his stash, his cellar full of his merchandise, some ready to go, some ready to prepare—but we got it, and that means we got him. Do you understand?".

"Yes," Petra replied, nodding slowly. She stared blankly at the door leading down to the cellar. Petra dropped to her knees and clasped her hands together. She erupted into tears and let out a wide grin. "It means I'm free."

"This means we can arrest him now; it ends here," Dexter said, twisting his hands as he spoke.

Dexter decided to keep the stash of money a secret from Petra. He estimated it amounted to two or three million euros—far more than she could have imagined. Taking her gently by the arm, he led her outside and signalled for a driver. "We'll have you taken to the villa to wait," he reassured her, his tone calm but distant. "It shouldn't take more than half an hour before you can leave."

Petra walked into the villa that had once been her dream home, now just a shell of bittersweet memories. She paused in the kitchen, opening the fridge to retrieve a bottle of water. Her eyes drifted to an apple in the decorative bowl on the counter; she took it absentmindedly.

Moving toward the main entrance, she settled onto the ornate iron bench she'd installed only months earlier. The cool metal pressed against her as she sat among her neatly packed belongings, a quiet sense of loss settling in her chest.

The crunch of gravel under tyres broke her train of thought. She straightened, watching as police cars returned to the villa. Officers emerged, loading her bags into the waiting vehicle with clinical efficiency.

Just as the car doors slammed shut, a sudden thought struck her. She jumped to her feet. "My phone?" she called out.

One of the officers turned to her. "We've placed a new phone in your bag," he explained. "It has a new number; I've written it on the box. Your contacts have been transferred over. We need your old phone for evidence."

Petra stared at him, torn between relief and unease. Starting over with a new phone and number felt oddly symbolic—a tangible marker of yet another forced reset in a life spinning out of control. She nodded faintly, gripping the apple in her hand though her appetite had long since vanished.

"Goodbye, Petra. Thank you," Dexter said softly, his tone carrying a mix of finality and regret.

Petra said nothing in return. Instead, she climbed into the waiting car, fastening her seatbelt with a quiet click. As the vehicle sped northward, her thoughts raced. She could only hope they had warned Bree she was coming.

Not long into the drive, the driver handed her a phone. Petra finally smiled when she saw Bree's name in a message. "It's Bree. I'm at home. See you in a bit."

Petra hated the idea of imposing on her friend without asking. The car pulled up at Bree's house soon after, and the driver began unloading Petra's bags and boxes onto the porch.

Inside, the house was silent and heavy with tension. Petra was the first to break it. "I'm so sorry, Bree. I had nowhere else to go," she said, her voice quiet and trembling.

Bree's expression softened, and she smiled gently. "You don't have to apologise. I'm happy you're here," she replied. Her smile faltered as she added, "But it's been a rough day. My wedding planner quit, and the wedding is tomorrow. I'm drowning in work as it is, and now this."

Petra studied her friend's hunched shoulders and weary eyes. With a confident smile that belied her own turmoil, she said, "I'll do it. It'll take my mind off all this mess."

Bree blinked in surprise. "Really?"

"Really. Just tell me what needs to be done, and I'll do it," Petra replied trying to lighten the mood. "I was almost a bride so I know most of the planning process."

For the first time that evening, a flicker of hope lit Bree's face. "You'd be saving me, Petra. Thank you."

75 | Nina

Nina and Manuel had decided to settle in Rocca Pinta to find a job for Nina, somewhere that would allow her to have her winter seasons free to travel.

"Just find a job, any job. I did; it was easy," he said too often.

"I don't want any job; I'm sick of being a waitress or serving burgers. I want something that will tax me a bit more, something a bit more interesting." She reminded him constantly, trying to find different ways to say no.

Nina was unsure of her decision to marry in Rocca Pinta Castle. Seeing so many foreign weddings there, she wasn't sure if it was for her, but being a local, she could get it and all the wedding services at discount prices.

Julia, Nina's cousin, now the proud owner of a lakeside hotel in Rocca Pinta, had offered them the use of the terrace for the reception; Nina had accepted as she ticked one more item off her to-do list.

Not long after Nina had moved to Rocca Pinta, Julia's family followed suit; only Nina's mother stayed behind in Monza. For a while, Julia had been unable to put the event that upended her life behind her—closing everyone out of her life—and she lost herself. A few years ago, she had found her way back to Rocca Pinta and a new career.

The only thing missing from Nina's wedding checklist was a photographer. For years, she had admired Bree's photography, but she wasn't sure she could afford it. Deciding to try her luck, she strolled towards Bree's office. Peering through the windows, she caught sight of Bree pacing about, juggling a phone call while tearing open Amazon parcels. Taking a deep breath, Nina pushed the door open.

Inside, the office was a controlled disorder of equipment, papers, and half-opened boxes. Bree, who rarely smiled, glanced up briefly before pointing to a chair.

Nina sat down hesitantly, swivelling slightly as her eyes wandered to the striking photographs adorning the walls.

"Sorry about the mess," Bree said, finally ending her call. She took a deep breath and offered a quick smile. "I'm Bree. How can I help?"

Nina returned the smile tentatively. "Hi, I'm Nina. I'm sorry to bother you; I was just... well, I'm getting married and wondered about photography."

Bree's brow tightened as she studied Nina. "I know you," she said, her eyes narrowing as she tried to place her.

Nina shifted uncomfortably, her shoulders drooping slightly. She braced herself for the usual comments.

"You used to work at Benatrip Travel Agency, didn't you?" Bree asked suddenly.

Nina blinked, surprised. "Yes, I did."

"I remember you from the end-of-season party your Benatrip had. I was the photographer," Bree said.

"Oh... sorry, I don't remember," Nina admitted, her cheeks colouring.

"Well, I don't remember you either," Bree said with a laugh. "There were far too many people. I only remember you from the images—your face was on my screen for days while I was editing."

Nina managed a small laugh as Bree's phone rang again. With a quick apology, Bree handed her a photo book. Nina flipped through the pages, admiring the crisp, vivid shots, while Bree dealt with her call.

Once the phone was back on the desk, Bree shifted forward, her tone warm and professional. "Right, let's talk. First, we'll check if I'm available." She pulled up a digital calendar.

"The fifteenth of March. At two in the afternoon," Nina said nervously. "I know it's last minute."

"That just means you're not a bridezilla," Bree said with a grin.

She handed Nina a price list. Nina's face fell slightly as she scanned the figures.

"Tell you what," Bree said. "Since you're local and the wedding's so soon, I'll give you a fifty percent discount. How does that sound?"

Nina's eyes widened. "Really? You don't even know me."

Bree laughed. "I'm not the ogre people think I am. Besides, anyone who survived working at Benatrip deserves a break. I did a stint there before photography, and it was miserable."

"My fiancé wants me to go back to a job like that, but I can't face it."

"Do you speak English?" Bree asked, tilting her head.

"Yes," Nina replied, sounding more confident now.

"And you're looking for work?"

Nina nodded. "Yes, but I'm picky about what I do."

Bree's eyes sparkled with an idea. "Have you ever thought about becoming a wedding planner? I did this huge marketing campaign with a friend who wanted to try something out, and I have too many weddings. I have one weddding planner but I need another one, maybe even two."

Nina's jaw dropped. "A wedding planner? Seriously?"

"You don't need experience—I can train you. The job's seasonal, from April to mid-October," Bree explained.

"That's perfect," Nina said, her grin widening.

For the next thirty minutes, the two discussed the role in detail. Bree's enthusiasm was infectious, and Nina felt a nervous excitement building within her. As they wrapped up, Nina shook Bree's hand, barely able to contain her joy. Bree didn't seem remotely concerned that she'd never done the job before.

Stepping outside into the brisk spring air, Nina took a deep breath. She couldn't believe she had almost talked herself out of visiting Bree's office.

76 | Carla

Carla hurried through the bustling streets of downtown, eager to meet a friend from university. A passing bus rattled the windows of the restaurant as Paul listened intently to her recounting her recent life events and her desire to start anew.

"Look, I'm not making any promises," Paul said as he poured coffee into her tiny cup, "but I have an English friend who lives by Lake Valdo. The last time I spoke to her, she mentioned she was looking for a wedding planner. I haven't spoken to her for a few weeks, so she might've found someone already, but I can ask," Paul added.

"Wedding planner? Really?" Carla's face brightened as she processed the information. "And she's English?"

"Yeah, she's great. It'll be a lot of work, but apart from her occasional mood swings, she's cool," Paul said with an eager smile.

Carla shifted in her chair, sipping the last of her coffee. "I like the sound of her being English. But I'm not sure I'm ready to be around love and weddings just yet," she admitted.

"Well, Bree's nothing like your typical wedding planner," Paul reassured her. "She doesn't believe in love or romance. To her, it's just a job. But she loves it. She lives for it."

Carla paused, thinking about the offer. "I get that. But my bank balance is telling me it's time for a real job. Waitressing isn't going to take me far. The insurance money's come through, but I'm saving that for a rainy day."

"Alright, I'll give her a call," Paul said, pulling his phone from his pocket.

After the pleasantries, Bree launched straight into a rant. "I can't believe how hard it is to find a decent wedding planner. It's not rocket science. You wouldn't believe the applicants I've had. They don't speak English, want to work just four hours a day, and one even asked for the whole of August off. I've found one, but I still need another."

"I might have someone for you," Paul said, hoping to be of help to both of his friends. "She's English, looking for a fresh start. Her husband passed away a couple of years ago. She lives in Milan but wants a change."

"I'm listening," Bree said, her voice lightened by interest. "You had me at 'she's English.' Will she be able to pick up Italian overnight?"

"She speaks Italian," Paul assured her. "She studied in Milan, and now she's back, doing some waitressing. I'm having lunch with her now."

"Sounds promising," Bree replied, her tone brightening. "When can she start?"

"If you'd like, I could come over to Rocca Pinta, bring her with me, and we could all grab lunch or dinner together," Paul suggested.

"When?" Bree asked, her impatience showing as they worked out the details.

Driving to Rocca Pinta two days later, Paul told Carla about life working in what Bree called the 'Wedding World.' Carla's eyes rested on the scenery—the deep blue colours of the water, the white pebbles distorted beneath the gentle waves. Resting her head on the glass, she imagined what it would be like to swim to the centre or to live somewhere so beautiful.

Bree instantly took a liking to Carla; there was something about her—determined, strong-willed, yet quietly charming—that made an immediate impression. They spoke briefly about the job and what it entailed, and before the coffee even arrived, Bree offered Carla a position.

Carla spent the night on Paul's sofa, the two of them enjoying a quiet evening in with takeaway pizza. They chatted easily, and although the evening was low-key, Carla felt a sense of calm she hadn't experienced in ages.

The next morning, Carla set off on her first walk down to the water. The pace of the city life seemed to fade with every step she took, the constant buzz of Milan dissolving into the peace and quiet of her surroundings. By the time she reached the lake, she felt lighter. Inhaling deeply, she savoured the scent of fresh paint in the air and ran her fingers along the wooden bench before settling onto it.

She unscrewed the top of her water bottle, feeling the coolness of the water as it ran down her throat, and for the first time in what felt like forever, she exhaled slowly, her body relaxing. The ducks bobbed gently on the water, and the sun, warm and inviting, bathed her shoulders, coaxing her to shed her denim jacket.

A broad smile crossed her face as she looked out at the breathtaking view—lush green hills and the dramatic grey mountains that rose in the distance. She recognised the Dolomites from the photos Paul had shown her, and for a moment, the beauty of the scene took her breath away. The sky above was a brilliant blue, with wisps of white clouds drifting lazily across it.

Carla glanced at her watch. She had two hours before meeting Paul for the return trip to Milan. She decided to wander by the lake, taking photos with her camera to send back home. There was no way to adequately describe the peace she felt in that moment—her pictures would have to do the talking. As she walked, occasionally glancing back at the village, her eyes landed on the imposing castle of Rocca Pinta, standing proudly at the top of the hill.

As she let the warm sunlight wash over her, she felt a sense of gratitude for this new chapter. With a soft laugh, she called out to the frogs by the water, telling them her news. To her surprise, her parents joined in from the background, offering their own strange kind of support from miles away.

"I've found a real job in Italy; I start next month," she told them excitedly. She was expecting a stream of objections and roadblocks. However, to her surprise, it was the opposite; her father spoke first.

"That's good news, darling; we are all thrilled for you. You need to stop waitressing and start fresh. Then, when you're ready, you can come back home and see where your life takes you," her father said.

Carla had no intention of spoiling this by telling them she wasn't planning on ever leaving. "Yeah, you're right, Dad; I just need to get my life together first."

Catching her breath, looking down at the steep steps she'd just climbed, her glance stopped on a purple sign: 'Rocca Pinta Weddings.' She saw a light shining through the window. She knocked on the door and heard a voice shouting for her to come in.

Bree smiled as she saw Carla. "Look, I've just done your sign for the desk," she said, proudly showing her the laminated white sign with the logo of Rocca Pinta Castle and her name in bold black letters.

"Oh my god, it's real, then," Carla smiled. She took the sign back, carefully placed it on the desk and said, "I can't wait; I'm so excited to do this."

77 | Carla

"This is your desk; try it out if you like." Bree suggested, pulling out her chair. Carla smiled and swirled around like a small child, "There's another new planner, Nina, starting a few weeks after you; I'll add another desk there for her."

"Have you got time for a coffee?" Carla asked.

As they closed the heavy glass door behind them and strolled through the village, passersby interrupted them with a stream of 'hellos' and 'ciaos'. They sat and talked like old friends; they shared stories of Paul and his English errors, the time he asked for a Jockey with cheese on top instead of a Jacket potato, and wondered why on earth he kept saying fly down instead of chill out. The sun umbrellas provided shelter as they chilled their hands on their iced teas.

"You'll get used to it; everyone knows each other here, and they are all somehow related to each other. I still haven't worked out who's who yet, to be honest," Bree said.

They hugged as Carla left; she would be starting just in time for the rush of weddings in a couple of weeks. A relieved Bree returned to her office, smiling.

Bree had managed to find Carla a little flat in the town centre; there would be a parking issue, but Carla didn't have a car yet; at least she had somewhere to live for now. Located on the second floor of an old, jaded building with a metal entrance gate and a dusty corridor, the silent, bright hall housed six wooden doors before arriving at hers, number seven.

Two weeks later, Carla pushed the door open and gasped in surprise. She stood there for a moment, taking in the simplicity of the modern decor. The kitchen was white, sleek, and minimalist, while the grey sofa looked inviting against the neutral tones of the room. She ran her fingers over the flat-screen TV, quickly turning it on. The bathroom smelled faintly of fresh paint, and the large wooden window overlooking the lake offered a breathtaking view. She walked onto the balcony, her mouth dropping open at the sight before her. The castle loomed large, right there in front of her. She couldn't believe her eyes.

Turning back inside, she opened the final door and stepped into the light and airy bedroom. The soft, natural light streaming in through the window made everything feel calm, peaceful. Carla fell back onto the bed, her arms spread out, a smile of disbelief tugging at the corners of her lips.

Unpacking the last of her belongings, she took stock of what she still needed to buy to make the place her own. She unwrapped a carefully packaged frame, revealing photos of her and Johnny. A soft pang of sorrow mixed with pride—

she knew he would be proud of her now. She was starting over in Italy, the place they had dreamed of living one day.

Carla poured herself a glass of wine, then settled into a chair on the balcony, gazing out at the view. She couldn't suppress the grin that spread across her face. For the first time in a long while, she felt a sense of peace.

Feeling lightheaded from the wine, Carla threw on a pair of sandals and decided to explore. She walked confidently toward the restaurant she had spotted from her balcony. The entrance led through a charming tunnel, and at the other end was a quaint courtyard with twenty wooden tables, each surrounded by creaky wooden chairs. The space was filled with the warm buzz of conversation, mostly from tourists.

She smiled at the waiter, taking a seat and listening in on a nearby table of English tourists discussing their upcoming wedding. The excitement on their faces was unmistakable, and as Carla sipped her wine, she tried to remain unnoticed as she listened to every word.

But then the realisation hit her: she would be planning weddings. The thought sent a mild panic through her chest. She'd only ever attended one wedding—her own. Was she really ready for this? Had she bitten off more than she could chew? She slouched in her seat, muttering quietly into her glass, "Shit, what have I done?"

78 | Nina

Nina and Manuel's wedding had taken place on a cold, wet day, the sky overcast and heavy with clouds. The rain had poured relentlessly, turning the streets into puddles and making everyone scramble for umbrellas. Shoes were soaked, dresses clung to legs, and hair became an unruly mess, but through it all, Bree had managed to capture the day's beauty. Despite the last-minute transport change and the relentless assault, pouring rain, Nina was amazed at how Bree's photographs seemed to turn the day into something magical.

Now, two weeks after the wedding, Nina was preparing to start her new role working for Bree. An overwhelming sense of anxiety had gripped her ever since she'd accepted the position. She was about to take on the responsibility of organising one of the most important days in a person's life. Every mistake would carry consequences. Nina had never been in a job with such weight, and the thought of it made her uneasy.

She'd always been in awe of Bree—the way she had built such an empire in a small Italian community where outsiders were often looked at with suspicion. Nina had never seen Bree do anything but work. Whether it was dashing around with cameras or showing clients around, Bree was always on the move, never stopping. Nina had never once seen her out for a drink or taking a break.

As she walked the short distance to her office, Nina reflected on her old commute in London. Now, in Rocca Pinta, not only had she found her dream job, but it was practically on her doorstep.

Nina steadied her hand as she placed it on the door handle and pushed it down. Inching the door slowly inward, she felt the warm air hit her face. Glancing around the office, she spotted a neat sign, 'Nina' on a stand. Next to her computer stood a glass of pens, a stack of Post-it notes, and a tin box full of paper clips, staples, and other office essentials.

Nina's eyes turned to Bree, who lifted her head from her computer keyboard upon hearing her enter the room and greeted her with a warm smile.

"Buongiorno, good morning," Bree said as she lifted her slim body off her chair and approached Nina. She collected a thick, heavy folder from the top of a nearby cabinet and handed it to Nina.

"Welcome to your first day with us," Bree said softly. "This is your desk; feel free to move things around as you like. Petra and Carla will show you the ropes when they get in, but please read this before you do anything. It will tell you everything you need to know."

"What is it?" Nina asked, her face instantly turning red as she glanced down at the front cover, which read, 'Wedding Planners' Bible: A Step-by-Step Guide to Rocca Pinta Wedding World.'

"Sorry, I just read the title," Nina said.

"Start your day by reading this; it will make much sense and answer most of your questions, mainly the new English vocabulary you'll have to learn."

"Ask if you have any questions; the girls will be able to help you when they get here," Bree said, already heading back to her desk with her arms crossed and her eyes already focused on the emails that needed a reply.

Nina pulled out her chair, rested her bag on the filing cabinet, placed the file on her desk, and sat down. The feeling of anxiety was slowly passing, her breathing returning to normal as she turned the pages. Nina nervously raised her hand and lowered it once more. She didn't want to ask Bree if she could highlight bits that were important to her. Bree, staring at the bright screen and tapping rapidly on the keys, didn't indicate that she wanted to be disturbed.

The only sounds in the office were those of clicking keys and turning pages. Nina shifted in her chair, causing Bree to look over and give her a blank look.

Petra's arrival shattered the silence. The door swung open, the cold air filling the room. "Buongiorno, ladies," she said with a smile. She rubbed her hands together as she removed her scarf from her neck. She pulled off her coat, hanging it on the coat rack behind the door.

"Hi, Nina, Nice to meet you; I'm Petra," she said with a warm handshake and a smile. "Let me show you around the office, although this is pretty much it." She pointed out the bathroom, the printers, stationery storage, fridge, small storeroom, and filing cabinets.

The door swung open, and Carla strode towards her, shaking Nina's hand and introducing herself.

"That silent, scary monster in the corner, is Bree," Petra said, laughing. Bree glanced to the side in Petra's direction, a hint of a smile in her eyes. "Don't let her scare you; she's the best." Petra continued, "See that look in her eye? The look that says, If you bother me, I'll bite? You'll grow accustomed to it; I refer to it as her 'Dexter' look, or occasionally the 'Maira Hindley' stare, depending on the day," Petra said as she let out a loud laugh.

"Oh, okay," Nina replied.

"Just carry on; do your own thing. Bree is an expert at blanking us out; she can pretend we aren't here and carry on." Petra explained.

Finally, Bree said, "I try to do all the work I need to concentrate on before nine; that way, I don't have to give you a scary look." Sometimes, like today, I don't manage. Just give me a few minutes, and I'll be much more chilled out."

Nina dutifully nodded as Petra pulled up a chair at Nina's desk. She looked at the folder she was reading and said, "I wrote that; it's my only literary achievement in this office."

"Can I highlight it?" she asked, her hands stroking the front cover like a beloved dog.

"It's only a copy; you can burn it if you like; you won't escape it, though; I'll put another copy on your desk."

Nina enjoyed Petra's lighthearted manner after Bree's silence in the corner. "You can take it home if you like; read it at your leisure. I think today we can look through a wedding file; what do you think?"

"Great," said Nina, pushing the papers to one side of her desk. A couple walked into the office and quickly left with Carla.

"They are marrying tomorrow; you'll go to that wedding and have a look," Petra explained.

Petra wheeled her chair over to Nina's desk and said, "Before we get to that, here is your password for your computer. Apart from the password, you don't need to remember anything else today; we will look at it when you need it. The server stores our files in this folder, and the database is located here." Petra moved her mouse around the screen, pointing out where Nina could find everything. "And this is a list of Bree's mood swing cycles and remedies," she said, throwing Bree a cheeky grin.

She listened intently as Petra explained her duties. Nina felt the knot in her stomach ease; she liked the office banter and hoped one day she would have the courage to speak to Bree in such blunt terms.

Part 2

79 | The Girls

The four women had forged a deep bond over the two years since they'd met. On a dazzling white spring afternoon, they basked in the warm, soothing waters of the natural spa lake on the shores of Lake Valdo, Italy. It was a day to celebrate the long-awaited—yet unofficial—hen do. They laughed and chatted eagerly, swimming past the sparkling water fountain towards the wooden hot tubs in the centre of the lake, their plastic champagne flutes raised high in the air.

Finally, after all the turmoil, one of them was getting married. The four friends, who had been through relationship together, had watched the bride navigate heartbreak, joy, tears, and resilience in the name of love. The bride herself, however, wasn't quite ready to talk about her big day. She avoided the topic at every opportunity, perhaps because working in the wedding planning industry had stripped away the usual excitement and anticipation that other brides experienced. The only thing she was certain of was her joy in marrying the love of her life.

"Today, no talk of my wedding," the bride declared, laughing. "We haven't had a proper catch-up in ages, so why not reminisce about last summer instead?"

Bree, Petra, Carla, and Nina had become like family since they'd met. They shared the happiest, most stressful, and most rewarding experiences of their lives in their demanding but fulfilling work environment.

"Spill the gossip, girls. Any scandals we don't know about?" Nina asked.

"How many do you want?" Petra asked.

Bree was the first to reply. "Well, at my last wedding of the summer season, the bride and groom fought and left the reception early." Bree explained. "It was about six when the restaurant manager noticed they had gone; their bags had disappeared. He thought they were coming back, but his waiter said they were fighting in the bathroom, that the groom slapped her, she stormed off, he followed her, and they weren't seen again."

"Another one for the 'D' list," Carla said. The girls liked to put couples on two kinds of imaginary lists: 'D' for divorce and 'F' for forever together. Carla, the best storyteller, loved a chance to tell her wedding stories. "Do you all remember that balloon garland Josie wanted?" The others shook their heads as Carla continued with her story, saying, "Well, Josie ordered this gigantic balloon ring with hundreds of balloons tied around it." Water splashed from her fingers as she tried to show the size. "It looked terrific until they started popping in the heat during the speeches."

"No, that must have been loud," Nina said.

"There were probably over four hundred balloons in it. But it was in the sun, and they must have overheated, and one by one, 'boom.' I was standing next to it, and everyone stared at me as if I were popping them myself, ruining their speeches."

"Which were no doubt boring anyway." Nina piped up.

"I got as far away from that thing as possible. They carried on with the dad's speech, and they just kept popping. By the end, there were only about thirty balloons, just dangling there, shrinking," Carla explained.

Petra laughed and, with a wide smile, said, "How lucky are we? We have the world's best job in the most beautiful country on the planet. Look where we are now; this is amazing." She looked around her in admiration at the bubbling water. The steaming water blurred their vision. "I can't believe so much has happened since that day you rescued me. Bree, it's been four years since you changed my life." Petra continued, overcome with sentimental nostalgia.

Relieved that the steam covered her blushing cheeks, Bree replied, "No, you saved yourself, put in the work, and got yourself here."

In unison, Nina and Carla raised their glasses and said, "To Bree, the glue that holds us all together."

"Right, enough girls," Bree said, desperately wanting to change the conversation. "What happened at your first wedding? Can you remember that far back?" Bree looked at Petra with a teasing look on her face.

"Oh, God, it was so long ago, I can't remember," said Petra, throwing Bree a look of warning.

"I think it's about time that your story is out in the world," Bree said mischievously.

"Wasn't it the drunken wedding? When they lost the groom?" asked Carla.

"No." Bree chirped in a playful voice, "That was her second wedding; the first was when Petra fainted during the ceremony." Bree punched her arm playfully.

"What?" Both Nina and Carla asked, "You fainted?"

"Do we have to tell this story?" Petra asked, glancing over at Bree in a rash, last-pitch attempt to keep the story quiet.

"The time has come. Do you want to tell it, or shall I?" Bree nodded. Petra's shoulders dropped in acceptance as she stared up into the sky, letting out a nervous sigh.

Bree took a deep breath, grinned, and started to talk. Carla and Nina listened intently. "Okay, so, as you know, it was Petra's first wedding. Petra's Italian language skills were pretty bad back then, so I taught her line-by-line what the registrar would say so she knew what she needed to translate."

"As we all did," Nina said impatiently.

"We'd practised the ceremony, but we only had one evening to get Petra ready. We planned for every variation; we thought we had it covered."

"I can't believe this is happening." Petra said before she dove under the steaming hot water jets, blocking out the words.

"Then the new registrar arrived, and I knew we were in trouble. He introduced himself and told us it was his first wedding and that he had been told to follow the wedding planner's lead; he was relying on Petra to point him in the right direction."

Carla pulled her hands up to her mouth and said with a cackle of laughter, "Not a good start."

"That's when I realised it was the blind leading the blind. I knew I would have to stand as close as I could to the ceremony table and try and help out, but I also had to get the pictures, too." Bree continued with a broad smile, flashing an apologetic smile at Petra. "It was a boiling hot day; the humidity was unbearable, and I could see Petra getting hotter and her face getting redder."

"Oh, Petra," Nina said, her hand hovering over her mouth.

Bree stopped laughing and, catching her breath, she continued, "It was going well; the bride arrived, sat down, and Petra managed the main part of the ceremony without any problems."

Petra threw both hands in the air before popping back under the water as Bree continued,

"She was doing well; she didn't look too flustered. She lost the plot when the registrar started talking about the bridesmaids' dresses being the same colours as Rocca Pinta's football team, and that day was his twenty-fifth wedding anniversary."

Fiddling with her hair, Petra tied it into a ponytail as she looked over at Bree, who squinted her eyes and nose in embarrassment and pleaded, "Bree, please, don't tell the rest of the story."

"I felt like I was watching it all happen in slow motion; I watched Petra stare at him, then at me, then back at him, then she grabbed the ceremony table and started to wobble."

"I didn't have a clue what he was saying." Petra said, placing both hands on her lower neck and slowly looking at the others, "He went totally off script."

"We all know Petra can talk herself out of anything, but not this; she just stared at me. I was at the back of the ceremony, and I could see she was panicking, but I couldn't do anything," Bree said, holding back the giggles.

Nina and Carla looked at Bree and said, "And?"

"I darted towards the front, pretending to take photos. I whispered to the registrar to stop talking, and right then, he turned to look at me and then at Petra, who had turned white."

"Bree, stop it; we don't need to tell this story." Petra pleaded.

Bree, unflinching, continued, "Then the registrar shouted at me, 'She's going to faint; help her,' but Petra was still talking a whole lot of nonsense. "What were your last words?" Bree asked.

Petra covered her face in embarrassment and said, "I think my final words were: 'The registrar says something. I don't know what,' and then I collapsed onto the floor."

"Luckily, the registrar was a male nurse. He dealt with Petra, and I took over. I climbed over Petra, who was lying on the floor with her arms spread-eagled." Bree explained.

"Bree carried on as if nothing had happened; she just handed out the certificates, and told the couple to walk down the aisle," Petra said.

"I left the registrar with Petra for a few minutes; by the time I got back up, she was fine, and we agreed to tell the guests that she'd just found out she was pregnant. They spent the afternoon congratulating her, asking if she was okay."

"Oh my god, Petra," said Nina. "How did we not know that story?"

Petra said laughingly, "I hoped it would never get out." She spun around and high-fived her friends.

"Well, come on, it wasn't that bad," Nina said, trying to reassure Petra. "Do you remember one of my first weddings when I got my words wrong?"

"Oh, yeah, I was there for that," Bree said, smirking knowingly.

"You remember how they used to hand out those gifts at the end of the ceremony?" Nina continued, and the others nodded. "Well, one year, instead of the book they give now, it was a calendar with photos of Rocca Pinta and a DVD of the lake."

"Sounds nice."

"Sure, except I announced to everyone they'd be receiving a colander instead of a calendar and a DVD player instead of a DVD. And to top it off, I told a hundred people that we'd have an evening of 'DJ and sex' instead of 'DJ and sax'." Nina finished, burying her face in her hands as the others burst into laughter.

"Oh, Bree, tell them about the 'boob wedding,'" Carla interjected, her grin mischievous.

Bree's eyes lit up. "Oh, yes, one of Carla's last weddings of the season. The bride—how do I put this—was... well-endowed."

Carla moved closer, clearly revelling in the story. "Bree, stop being polite. The woman was stacked, and she knew it. The neckline of her dress was so low it was practically an optical illusion."

Bree chuckled. "And let's not forget how she strutted down the aisle, flaunting every bounce like she was on a catwalk."

"Flaunting is one way to put it," Carla said, rolling her eyes. "As she turned the corner for the final stretch down the aisle, bam. Out pops a nipple. Just like that." Carla mimed the dramatic reveal, sending everyone into fits of laughter.

"The musicians were the best part," Carla continued. "One violin screeched so hard I thought they were playing the Psycho soundtrack."

"I didn't know what to do," Bree said, barely able to contain her laughter. "So I walked up to her, whispered discreetly, and she just popped it back in like it was no big deal."

Carla grinned, raising her glass. "The registrar spent the entire ceremony staring at her chest willing the other one to make an appearance."

The women clinked glasses, their laughter echoing as they swapped more stories—funny mishaps, disastrous weddings, heartwarming moments, love stories, betrayals, and outright chaos. For them, it was all in a day's work.

80 | Nina

In their brief marriage, Nina and Manuel had experienced an emotional roller coaster. Desperately trying to conceive, they'd naively assumed it would be straightforward—marry, get pregnant, live happily ever after. But the universe had other plans.

At first, they brushed it off, telling themselves it would take time. However, as the months ticked by, they began to realise it wasn't happening naturally or quickly. Two gruelling rounds of IVF followed, each one a cycle of hope, anxiety, and crushing disappointment. The treatments drained not only their finances but their emotional reserves.

As the strain mounted, their once-strong bond began to fray. Initially, they had faced the challenges as a united front, their love a balm against the struggles. But the cracks widened with each setback. Their conversations grew fewer and further apart until they stopped discussing it altogether. Then they stopped discussing much of anything.

Manuel, once her rock, had started vanishing for evenings at a time. His overnight fishing trips became a regular occurrence, as did late nights at work and his newfound habit of keeping his phone unusually close.

Sitting alone at the dining table, Nina glanced at the carefully arranged dinner she'd prepared—the flowers, the folded napkins, the perfectly lined glasses. She checked her watch for the umpteenth time and sighed. Rage simmered beneath her calm façade. Unable to wait any longer, she picked up her fork and stabbed at the ravioli.

When Manuel finally arrived, it was nearly midnight. He shrugged off his coat, hung it carelessly on the rack, and sauntered into the kitchen. Taking in the meal on the table, he let out a dismissive snort before heading to the fridge and retrieving a bag of salad.

Nina jiggled her foot under the table, anger bubbling to the surface. Rising to her feet, she paced the room, her voice clipped but steady. "So, where were you all evening?"

"I was with Stefano. We went night fishing," Manuel replied, dumping salad onto his plate without looking at her.

Stefano. The name had become a constant and annoying name in their recent conversations. Manuel had developed a renewed passion for fishing, supposedly thanks to his new work colleague. Yet, no fish ever found their way to the fridge, the house remained suspiciously free of the usual bait-box stench, and his breath reeked of alcohol more often than not.

Occasionally, Nina would see photos of the two men on social media—

always just the two of them, no suspicious female companions lurking in the background.

"I'd like to meet Stefano," she said, wiping her hands on a towel as she studied Manuel's reaction.

"Why?" he shot back, his tone defensive. He avoided looking at her, hurriedly refilling his glass.

"Well, you spend so much time with him. You know all my friends, but I don't know a thing about yours. Is he married? Does he have kids?" she pressed, her tone deceptively light as she tidied the placemats.

"No, and no," Manuel muttered, shoving his plate aside and grabbing the remote. His answers were clipped, the air between them thick with tension.

Before she could respond, Manuel pushed back his chair and stormed away.

Nina reached out as he passed, a friendly gesture, but he flicked her hand away dismissively. Her heart sank as she watched him retreat down the hall. Moments later, she heard the bathroom door slam, followed by the unmistakable sound of him banging around angrily in the dark.

Then, the front door flew open, letting in a blast of cold night air, and slammed shut behind him. Rushing to the window, Nina peered out. She watched as Manuel stumbled down the street, missing the curb and tumbling onto the pavement. He looked up, his face a mask of fury, and their eyes met for a brief moment before she hastily closed the curtains.

Through the gap, she glimpsed him staggering aimlessly, stepping first in one direction, then another, before finally disappearing into the shadowy streets.

Physically and emotionally drained, Nina wiped away a tear, fumbled for her phone, and called Bree.

"What's up?" Bree's voice came through, steady and familiar.

"I'm not sure what to do anymore," Nina said, her voice trembling. "I can't turn a blind eye to this."

"Turn a blind eye to what?" Bree asked, the clink of a glass audible in the background.

"Manuel. I think... I think he's having an affair." Nina paused, her breath hitching. "I've been burying my head in the sand for months."

The faint pop of a wine cork echoed through the call. "No, not Manuel," Bree said, sounding genuinely surprised.

"He's never home on time," Nina continued, her words tumbling out in a rush. "When he does come home, it's straight into the shower. Half the time, I tell myself he's just made a new friend, but then my mind flips, and I think Stefano is just a cover for... someone else. I can't take it anymore, Bree. I need proof. I need to know." She sniffled, swiping at the tears streaming down her face.

"Is he there now? Shall I come over?" Bree asked.

"No, he's out again. I don't even know when he'll be back. He was drunk, but it was fun watching him fall over." Nina said with a giggle.

"Right, I'm on my way," Bree said firmly, already grabbing her keys.

Minutes later, Nina was pacing the flat when the doorbell rang. She opened it to find Bree, who strode in, tossing her coat onto the sofa and without even asking, she opened a bottle of wine and handed Nina a glass of wine.

"Okay," Bree said, sitting down and fixing Nina with a steady gaze. "Start from the beginning. Tell me everything."

"The more I convince myself that Manuel's cheating, the more I start noticing things that seem to prove otherwise," Nina confessed, sinking into the chair opposite. "Sometimes I can forget it all while I'm at work. But then I come home, and something sets me off. A comment, a smell, a feeling... and I spiral into jealousy."

Bree spoke, carefully considering her words. "Nina, call it female intuition or whatever you like, but you have to trust your gut. It doesn't lie. I don't know Manuel very well—only you do. Only you know what's really going on in your marriage."

81| Nina

Nina started to spend more time at work; it was the only place she could be where no one would ask any questions. It was a great distraction from her home life, fraught with tension. Studying the horizon, lost in thoughts, Nina took deep breaths as she walked to the office, deliberately slowing her pace and recalling conversations with her Italian friends.

Nina had watched her friends go through the turmoil of cheating husbands and boyfriends. She'd listened as they talked about their suspicions; she couldn't bear the thought that she would be another on the list of wives being taken for fools.

Arriving in the office, Nina found Carla wiping her desk with a desk cleaner. "Any idea where Bree is?" Nina asked. Carla shook her head. "Do you have time for a talk?" Nina asked. Taking a seat across from Carla, she told her everything that had happened recently, from the fights to the absences.

"Can I do anything to help you?" Carla asked.

"I need a favour; I know you're on Tinder. Will you keep an eye out for Manuel?" Her eyes were filled with water as she continued, "I don't know what is going on. I can't even pinpoint when it started, but I think Tinder may be the answer." By saying the words out loud, her suspicions were magnified.

"Of course, I'll let you know, but I've not seen him yet," Carla said. "Do you really think he's stupid enough to go on a dating app?"

"Yes," Nina blurted out.

Two days after Manuel had stormed out of the home again, Nina woke to a noise in the corridor. Taking a moment to adjust to the darkness, she called out, "Manuel?"

"I need my gym bag," he shouted along the corridor.

Nina lay still in bed, propping herself on her pillows, before slowly getting to her feet. She threw a t-shirt over her and strutted into the kitchen. The crackling of plastic startled her as she spotted Manuel throwing the croissant wrapper into the bin. She watched as he pushed a croissant into his mouth and swigged juice from the bottle.

Sitting heavily in an armchair, Nina stared at him, unable to speak for fear of irritating him.

Laying his hands flat on the table, he glared at Nina and said, "What? What are you looking at?"

She gripped the arm of the chair, carefully choosing her words, saying, "I was just wondering where you've been and how long you're staying this time." Her voice trailed off nervously as his expression changed.

Drumming his fingers on the table, he scowled. "I've been out with Stefano and at work. I'm having breakfast and leaving. Do you have any more stupid questions?"

He placed a cup on the table and filled it quickly with coffee. Nina watched him with a puzzled expression as he grabbed a bag and filled it with as many possessions as possible. Returning to the kitchen, he gulped his coffee, put down his cup with a bang, and picked up his bag.

"Well, seeing as you don't seem to live here anymore, that will be five euros for breakfast, please," she fumed in annoyance. She spat out the words, wanting a reaction.

Manuel slammed his outspread hand on the table, glared at Nina for a moment, then turned away. He pulled open the front door and pushed the bag through before turning again to look at her, leaving with no further words or discussion.

His wide eyes scowled as he slammed the heavy door behind him. Nina turned away and shakingly buried her head in her hands before heading to the window. Peering down, she recognised the face from Stefano's profile: his chiselled cheekbones and stubby nose, his face rough with stubble. He smiled to greet Manuel, then glanced up, eyeing Nina curiously.

Nina watched dismissively as Manuel popped open the boot of the waiting car and placed his bags inside. As the car sped off, tears pricked in Nina's eyes as she perched herself awkwardly on the chair.

82 | Petra

Rico's arrest came three years after the police stormed the villa, marking the day Petra had left her life, dreams, and hope behind. While Rico managed to evade capture for years, whispers of his whereabouts circulated. Sightings were reported worldwide—some plausible, most far-fetched. Finally, he was caught in Naples, southern Italy.

The news showed Dexter, triumphant and smug, handcuffing Rico and parading him through the streets, revelling in the long-awaited victory.

Petra paled as she sat glued to the TV, clutching the edge of the sofa. Her picture loomed on the screen beside Rico's, a stark reminder of her entanglement in his downfall. She barely registered the knock at her door until it came again, sharper this time. Relieved, she opened it to see Bree standing there, concern etched on her face and a bottle of wine in hand.

"I thought you might need some company," Bree said gently, stepping inside.

Petra nodded, leading the way to the kitchen. Shrugging off her denim jacket, Bree set the wine down as Petra grabbed two glasses from a cabinet.

"I can't believe this," Petra muttered, her eyes flicking back to the screen. "Just because I'm British, I've become the face of the case in the UK."

"It's a massive scandal, Petra. You're bound to get dragged into it," Bree said, pouring the wine.

"And that photo of me they keep showing—it's awful. Couldn't they have picked a better one? I've never been so humiliated." Petra groaned, gripping the counter for support. "Every time his face pops up, I feel sick."

"Then stop watching," Bree said firmly. "You're not going to learn anything new. It's just the same loop every fifteen minutes."

Petra sighed, accepting the glass Bree handed her. "It's not just the TV, though. The journalists are relentless. I can't even log onto social media anymore without being hounded by messages from the press."

"At least they haven't connected you to the airport incident," Bree said with a conspiratorial smile.

"Thank God for that. Dexter promised it would stay buried. But you should see the hate messages I've been getting—accusations of trafficking, money laundering, you name it." Petra shook her head.

"It'll blow over eventually," Bree assured her. "These things always do. The press will move on to the next big scandal soon enough."

Petra sipped her wine, a bitter laugh escaping her lips. "Seems like everyone wants to talk to me—except Rico."

"Well, he's in prison now," Bree said, raising an eyebrow. "It's not like he can call without the guards listening in."

"He had plenty of chances to say something before all this," Petra shot back. "But he vanished. No explanation, no goodbye, nothing. Who does that? After everything, it's like I never existed to him."

Petra had done everything she could to disappear—dyed her hair a dark red, cut it shorter, swapped her glasses for contacts, and avoided any place that might connect her to her old life. It was never enough to escape the knowing and disapproving glances of people who believed they knew her, who thought they understood her story.

"Maybe I should just go public," Petra mused aloud. "Face the press, tell my side of the story, and be done with it. But Dexter told me to keep my head down."

"Do you regret it?" Bree asked softly. "Turning him in?"

Petra's expression hardened. "No. I had to do the right thing. But I hate knowing he used me—for my passport, my connections. I just... I wish I knew if any of it was real."

Bree reached across the table, resting a reassuring hand on Petra's arm. "It's not about him anymore. It's about you and moving forward. Don't let him take anything else from you."

As predicted, public interest in Petra gradually waned, allowing her to bury herself in her work with weddings. For a time, she managed to leave her problems behind, immersing herself in the blissful hours at the office or the memories she helped create. Work had become her sanctuary, a refuge where she could momentarily forget the loneliness and disappointments.

But recently, Petra found it harder to set aside her envy. Her body tensed as she watched wedding couples walk down the aisle, their faces beaming with joy as they exchanged a lingering first kiss. What had once filled her with excitement now left her fist-clenching and resentful. The romantic first dances, which used to inspire a warm jolt of happiness, now only served as a bitter reminder of what she lacked.

Petra couldn't shake the growing anger and jealousy within her. She longed to be in their place. More than anything, she wanted to be a bride, to experience the joy she witnessed day in and day out. Yet, instead of inspiration, these moments felt like a cruel taunt. Alone in the darkness of her apartment, she nursed her wounds, convincing herself that her time would come—that she just had to wait a little longer.

The exhilaration Bree often described after a successful wedding no longer resonated with her. The adrenaline rush her colleagues celebrated felt alien to Petra, replaced by a heavy, gnawing dissatisfaction. She tried to mask her discontent, not just from the couples she worked with but also from Bree. After all, she owed Bree everything; without this job, she'd be drowning in debt and possibly homeless.

Petra barely recognised herself anymore. Gone was the hopeful, adventurous woman who had left the UK to chase love in Italy. Now, she felt consumed by bitterness, her isolation gnawing away at her sense of self. The distance between her and Bree was widening, and she noticed how often Bree and Carla spent time together without her. It stung, feeling like an outsider in her own circle.

The fear of being left out burned more than she cared to admit. Her frustrations, which she had worked so hard to suppress, began bubbling to the surface. She started making snide remarks during conversations, unable to muster genuine joy for her colleagues' successes or happiness. Whenever Bree or Carla shared good news—a fruitful day at work, a pleasant date, or a piece of exciting news—Petra found herself unable to resist the urge to comment bitterly.

"Well, of course, that would happen to you, not to me," she muttered repeatedly, her words laced with envy and frustration.

The final blow came when she saw pictures of Bree and Carla on social media, smiling brightly, drinks in hand, surrounded by friends. Her jaw tightened as a burn of resentment churned in her stomach. The sense of being left out, of being overlooked, stoked the flames of her bitterness, leaving her more alone than ever.

83 | Petra

Petra had not been having the best of luck with weddings. Bree seemed content with her work. However, Petra began to think she brought bad luck to the happy couples.

On that particular day, it was a big event. It had been a late booking, and planning such a complex day had been a challenge. Bree, the photographer for the day, and Petra set off for the one-hour drive along the lakeside to a beautiful, bustling town at the south of Lake Valdo. Leaving plenty of time to spare, they chatted about the day and the events that had been planned. They loaded the car with flowers, ribbons, and cake stands.

As Bree drove, her phone started to beep and ring incessantly.

"Will you see who it is?" Bree asked, concentrating on the slow-moving traffic and numerous pedestrian crossings.

"A whole lot of voice messages and missed calls," Petra said as she tapped into Bree's unlock code and began to listen. When Petra listened to the first message, her mouth dropped wide open.

"Hi, this is Sarah. I've screwed up. I mean, really, I don't know what to do. Call me back. I don't think he wants to marry me today." she cried.

Bree cursed under her breath as she searched for somewhere to pull over.

Petra listened to the second message from Nicholas, the groom: "So, I've just discovered I'm marrying a manipulative, lying bitch. There is no way I'm marrying her, not after what she did. The wedding is off."

Still driving, Bree shook her head in dismay. "You really are a bad luck charm, aren't you?" she laughed. "Any more messages?"

"Yep, another two," Petra said as she hit play on the third message. "This is to let you know there will be no wedding today. Thank you. Bye, oh yes, this is the groom's mum, by the way."

"Shit, what's happened?" Bree asked, finally pulling over to a car park.

The fourth message was from Sarah again. Screaming, "Help me, this can't be happening." Her desperation was unmistakable. There wasn't much of a message, just an upset bride letting it all out to an unbiased party.

They pulled out the colour-coded wedding file from Petra's bag and looked at all the beautiful wedding services that had been arranged.

"What a waste. I was looking forward to the harpist and the jazz band this evening," Petra said.

"Oh god, all the other suppliers will be driving down soon. We need to get this sorted out quickly. Before we cancel anything, we need it in writing from them, and we need to see either the bride or groom in person," Bree said. She took Petra's phone and said, "Hi, Sarah. It's Bree. What's going on?"

"Oh god, help me. I didn't think he'd find out. What do I do?" Sarah cried.

"If I'm going to help you, you'll need to tell me what has happened." Bree insisted.

"Please, you have to talk to him. Tell him I love him, and I'm sorry." Sarah continued, "I know he will forgive me, just not in the next four hours. He needs to forgive me now."

"I will see what I can do. I'll be there in about twenty minutes."

Silence greeted Bree on the line. She heard only sniffling as she ended the call.

Arriving at the hotel, she slowly pulled up and headed to the reception.

"Hi, I'm the photographer for today's wedding. I need to see the bride or the groom, please. Room number one hundred and twenty-seven," Bree said with a smile.

"Everyone is going crazy; there are a lot of tears, and people are threatening the bride." The receptionist said in almost a whisper, "Other clients are complaining about the banging and screaming. You have to make it stop."

Bree nodded as she turned away, spotting Nicholas with his family, sitting on a large, soft sofa. Petra eyed the glasses dotted around the table, surrounded by empty bottles of whisky.

"Hi, Nicholas. We heard your message, but we were already nearly here, so we came to see you and see if we could help you," Bree said softly.

Nicholas stared at his phone for a while, despondent, until his mother nudged him: "Nicholas, these ladies are talking to you."

Nicholas finally looked up from his phone and said, 'Thanks for coming. You didn't need to. There isn't going to be a wedding."

"Is there anywhere we can talk in private?" Bree asked.

He nodded, wrapping his fingers around the bottleneck. He moved to another sofa. Bree and Petra followed him as he said, "Sorry, I'm staying here for now. My wedding clothes are all upstairs, and I don't want to look at them."

Bree touched his arm gently. "Nicholas, I know this is hard, but is there anything you can tell me to help us understand what is going on?"

He looked at them, gulped down the last drink, and started talking. "You should speak to my mum; she is the one who told me everything," he said. He gestured for the delivery of another bottle.

"Let's start by hearing your side of things," Bree said.

"Last night, we had the hen do. The ladies all went out drinking. My mum texted me about eight and said it was all going well; everyone was drinking shots, but it was fun," he said. "After that, I didn't really look at my phone. I was with the guys, and we had a really chilled evening—beers and shots—quite a lot of shots, but it was one of the calmest stag dos I've ever seen." Nicholas said proudly.

He took a deep breath, sipped his drink, held it in front of his face, and said, "Hair of the dog." Finally, he mustered up a smile. "Mum, will you tell the wedding planners what happened? I can't face it," he said, reaching for his electronic cigarette.

Mum sat down and introduced herself: "Hi, I'm Jacqui, the mother of the guy who isn't getting married today."

"Okay, so we don't want to intrude, but the hotel has asked us to go up and speak to Sarah. First, we want to find out what has happened."

"Alright, it's a bit long-winded. I'll try and keep it short."

"We're in no rush; take your time," Bree said.

"Last night, during the hen do, I went to the bathroom; I didn't feel great, so I just sat down in a toilet stall for a few minutes." Jacqui paused, and Bree offered her an understanding nod. "Then Sarah and her maid of honour came in; they were in a fight, so I sat still and tried to hide. Sarah was talking about a man called Carl and how she loved him and was using Nicholas so that Carl would leave his wife. I had my phone in my hand, so I clicked on voice memos and started to record it all."

"Okay," Bree said, unsure what else she could say to that.

"Do you want to hear it?" She didn't wait for Bree to reply: "So, before I could press start, Jessica asked if Sarah had heard from Carl." Jacqui pressed play and held her head by the phone. They gathered around and listened to the recording. Sarah's voice was the first one they heard.

"Yes, he called me yesterday; he told me that he loves me, but he can't marry me, and that I'm not the girl for him. I told him that I was going to marry Nicholas even though I don't love him, but he said he doesn't care." Crying, she continued, "What am I supposed to do? I love Carl, but he treats me like a doormat. He uses me for sex when he wants, but he's the only man I think about."

Petra covered her mouth to stop herself from gasping; with wide eyes, she glanced at Bree as the bridesmaid replied.

"You know Carl is married. He uses the word 'love' to keep you happy. He is playing you. He is a prick. Someone who loves you wouldn't do this. They wouldn't let you marry another man. He is married and cheating on his wife. He doesn't love his wife, and he doesn't love you."

"Shut up, you don't understand it." Sarah snorted.

'You have a wonderful man in Nicholas, but you shouldn't be doing this to him. He deserves better. He deserves to have you to himself, not like this. I'm sick of having this conversation with you, and you can't do this to him. Pull yourself together. Doing this is not going to make Carl love you. You aren't happy. You haven't been yourself in three years with Carl."

Sarah interrupted Jessica's monologue, "He loves me. I know he does, or he wouldn't tell me that. You can't see it. You aren't in this thing." Sarah cried; the shots had slurred her words, but there was no doubt at all about what she was saying: "I don't want to marry Nicholas, but it will make Carl jealous, so I'm doing it. Honestly, once I'm married, I'll find an excuse to avoid having sex with Nicholas anyway. Carl is my first thought in the morning, the last at night, and when I'm in bed with Nicholas, I have to pretend he's Carl, even to get excited."

There was silence. Bree and Petra hoped this taped conversation was over.

Sarah continued, "I've decided what I'm going to do. I want to get pregnant with Nicholas' baby, and I'll tell Carl it's his. That way, he will have to leave his wife for me."

"Sarah, you're my friend; I love you, but I don't want to have any part in this anymore. You need to tell Nick you aren't marrying him; you need to do it yourself; otherwise, maybe I will. I'm no longer your matron of honour. You're on your own tomorrow," Jessica said.

They heard a door open and close once and again, and then the recording stopped. "That is such a horrible story, so sad. I'm sorry you have had to go through that," Bree said. "We'll cancel everything for you; don't worry about anything at all."

'What about the guests?' Nicholas asked. I don't want to share this information in a group message.

"Don't worry," Bree replied. "We will go to the venue at the right time and make sure everyone knows. News like this has a habit of travelling very fast. I'm sure everyone will know before the wedding starts. We'll start on everything now. Once again, I'm sorry for this happening to you," Bree said calmly.

Bree and Petra went up to Sarah's suite. Alone with empty champagne bottles around her and an empty ice bucket sitting by her feet, Bree explained that they'd heard the recording.

"Oh shit, sorry. I heard about that. Is it bad?" Sarah asked with wide, pleading eyes.

"Yep, very bad," Petra said. The girls retreated and left the room, waving goodbye to everyone. They sat in the car and began to make cancellation phone calls.

"Excuse me, wedding planners," a female voice called. Petra and Bree looked out of the window as a woman approached, saying, "Sorry, I don't know your names. I'm Jessica, the maid of honour."

"Oh, yes, I recognise your voice," Bree said.

"Yeah, sorry about that. I saw Jacqui go into the bathroom. I knew it was a now-or-never moment. I didn't think she would record it all, but I knew she would have heard it and that she would have done something in time," Jessica said.

"That was a brave but wise thing to do," Bree said.

As the engine started and Bree reversed out of the car park, Petra spoke up, "What the hell is happening with my weddings?"

"I don't know Petra, but it can only get better, and, as we have been paid for a whole day's work, pizza is on me this evening," Bree said with a wide grin.

84 | Petra

Petra wasn't wasting any time searching for meaningful connections, her heart still yearning for love despite the bruises left by Rico and a string of other disappointments. Though the pain of loss had left her shattered, she bounced back quickly, diving into the world of dating with a fierce determination.

Most of her dates came from Tinder, a platform that had given her equal parts excitement and exasperation. Tonight, Petra felt a flutter of hope as she dressed for her latest outing. Straightening her hair and slipping into a flowing silk top paired with a long skirt, she winced at her reflection.

For once, she was pleasantly surprised to find her date matched his profile picture—a rarity in her experience. Her excitement faltered within moments of their meeting. Though he arrived impeccably dressed in a suit, the conversation quickly veered into unexpected territory. As he sipped his water and loosened his tie, he began waxing lyrical about the two great loves of his life—his mother and his grandmother.

Petra stirred her coffee, smiling politely, even as her mind rebelled. She listened as he recounted endless anecdotes: his mother laddering her tights, his grandmother's doctor's appointments, and their insistence on feeding him lavish meals twice a day. The initial charm of his family devotion gave way to monotony, and Petra found herself stifling yawns as the sun bore down on her chair.

Her phone buzzed faintly in her lap—a lifeline. Bree had promised to be on standby, ready to rescue her at a moment's notice. Petra was reluctant to use the clichéd "I have an emergency" excuse, but her patience dwindled with every passing minute. Finally, she could take no more. Gripping her phone under the table, she quickly typed, Help. Now.

Feigning an apologetic smile, Petra stood abruptly. "I'm so sorry—I have to go. My friend needs me." Without waiting for a response, she turned and walked away, relief flooding her as she escaped. Her heels clicked against the pavement, but her mind buzzed with frustration, her fury barely concealed beneath her composed exterior.

Back home, Petra forced herself to push the disappointment aside. She poured a glass of wine, opened Tinder, and scrolled through the swarming faces of potential matches. Letting out a small sigh, she allowed herself to imagine the possibilities of the next adventure.

85 | Carla

As time passed, when Carla thought of Johnny, it was no longer with tears of sadness. Time had diminished the sense of loss. Still, she imagined him opening a restaurant here, somewhere by the lake, a nice Sicilian restaurant, in memory of his grandparents. Carla had started to hatch a new plan, a pipe dream: one day, when she had enough money, she'd open a restaurant in his honour, manage it, and throw herself into it just like he would have done. But, for now, she would carry on doing weddings.

In wedding world, Carla found her happy place; her outgoing and exuberant personality shone. Struggling often to keep it under wraps, she was prone to being sarcastic, and her frequent eye-rolling in disapproval had gotten her into many sticky situations, relying on her smile to get her out of those same binds.

Carla entertained her friends for hours with the stories of the weddings she had arranged—the fun, tragic, and unbelievable stories that made them smile. Bree and Carla had become steadfast friends; their sense of humour and similar backgrounds connected them, causing envy from Petra, who wasn't shy about letting her feelings be known.

The two girls were famously hopeless in the kitchen, often finding themselves knee-deep in burnt pans and regret before resorting to their trusty fallback—takeaways. One day, feeling unusually ambitious, Carla invited Bree over for what she promised would be a culinary triumph: pan-fried potatoes with garlic, spices, and chicken.

Carla rummaged through her sparse kitchen arsenal, pulling out a flimsy wok that had definitely seen better days. Tossing everything in with what she thought was oil, she busied herself tidying up as chaos brewed on the stove.

"Bree, come look at this," Carla called, tilting the wok toward her friend.

"Looks nice, smells... decent," Bree said diplomatically as she grabbed the cutlery to set the table.

"It's frothy," Carla said, her nose wrinkling in confusion.

Bree wandered over, peered into the pan, and winced at the bubbling foam that resembled a science experiment gone wrong. "Uh, yeah, that's probably just the starch. Add more oil; it'll be fine."

Carla poured another generous glug of "oil" into the pan, only for the foam to rise even higher, threatening to spill over the edges. "Bree, I think I've created a monster," she said, laughing nervously.

Bree grabbed a spoon, determined to investigate. She scooped up some of the suspicious froth, blew on it dramatically, and popped it into her mouth. Her face contorted instantly. "What is this?" she sputtered, rushing to the sink and spitting it out. "It tastes like a bubble bath."

Carla took a hesitant taste herself, only to recoil in horror. "Right. Pizza it is," she said, already reaching for her phone.

"Again?" Bree snorted. Carla ignored her, still staring at the pan in disbelief. "What is that taste, though? What did you put in here? Show me the oil," Bree demanded.

Carla handed over a sleek glass bottle. Bree held it up, squinting at the suspicious contents. "This is an interesting colour for oil."

With a dramatic flair, Bree poured a drop into the sink and rubbed it between her fingers. Her eyes widened. "Carla, you've been frying your potatoes in dishwashing liquid," she shrieked, dissolving into uncontrollable laughter.

"No way," Carla gasped, snatching the bottle.

"Yes way. What's with these fancy unlabelled bottles, anyway?" Bree asked, still wheezing.

"I hate clutter. Labels are messy. I pour anything I buy into these matching ones so they all match." Carla declared, as though this were the most logical statement in the world.

"Carla, you've fed me suds. I could blow bubbles with this meal."

Carla doubled over laughing, clutching the dishwashing liquid like a trophy. "Well, at least the pan's getting a good clean."

Closing the door behind them, they walked to the nearby restaurant. Carla was desperate to tell Bree about her latest date.

"Why use those awful sites if you don't want to meet anyone?" Bree asked her.

"I honestly don't know. The guys there are usually creepy or married, and it's just a way to meet new people and make new friends. I've been here for a while and don't know anyone outside wedding world."

"Yeah, I understand. I mean, I pretty much live in the wedding world too."

"I suppose I like meeting these people; I think I'm ready to feel something again—anything, just something. I joke that I'm not ready, but I could be, but he will have to be pretty special. But right now, all I feel when I meet them is the urge to laugh.

"Well, you have had a few crazy dates and entertaining stories to tell. But it's nice that you're open to the idea now; who knows what may happen in the future?" Bree said she was proud of her friend, who was much braver than her.

"When I go on these dates, it makes me appreciate what I had with Johnny; it seems real, but when I see the weddings with these couples that are so in love, I doubt my marriage. We never had that undying love, the romance, or the connection they have. So I wonder if I've made Johnny out to be a hero when really, he was just my first love." Carla spoke, holding her glass mid-air, lost in her memories.

"Don't doubt that. Come on, you had a marriage that lasted with a man who loved you. You can't start questioning it; you should enjoy those memories and stop comparing everyone to him," Bree said.

"Yeah, I know you're right; at least I had that love. In the meantime, I'm meeting some people I may not be clicking with, but some are just normal guys; maybe we can be friends; I need that right now."

As they sipped wine, waiting for their food to arrive, Carla suddenly froze, her face betraying a moment of panic. "Oh, crap, we're out for dinner, and we didn't invite Petra. If she finds out, she'll kill us," she said, rolling her eyes dramatically and resting her hands on her knees.

"I know exactly what you mean. Do you feel like you're constantly tiptoeing around her, or is it just me?" Bree asked, leaning in conspiratorially.

"No, it's not just you. It's maddening," Carla replied, exhaling sharply. "Last week, she told me about a date she had with a Virgo. She said she wouldn't date one ever again. So, naturally, I pointed out that I'm a Virgo and asked what was so wrong with us. You know what she said? 'Exactly, look at you.'"

Bree's jaw dropped. "What is wrong with her?"

"Remember that day at the wedding last week when it rained all evening? I asked her for a lift home, and she said she would think about it and then left without me. I texted her, asking if she was coming back, and she said to ask you for a lift; we both knew you were at another wedding, so I walked home in the rain," Carla explained, her voice exasperated. "So, guess who got to walk home in the rain?"

Bree groaned. "She's been acting so off lately. I wasn't going to say anything, but she's different—always moody, always bitter. And jealous of everything and everyone."

"Jealous of what, though? We are just as unlucky in love as her." Carla asked, brushing some curls from her face.

"Maybe the fact that we're always eating out together," Bree suggested. "But when we do invite her, she's either on a date or she refuses to eat whatever we cook. Instead, she says we should invite her when we go out—except we never plan to go out. We only end up at restaurants because our cooking is a disaster."

Carla sighed, shaking her head. "I know. I feel sorry for her, though. She keeps getting her heart broken. She dives into every date like she's planning a wedding with some guy she's just met. I think she believes settling down will magically solve all her problems."

"She's been like that ever since the whole Rico fiasco," Bree said. "Bitter and jealous. She doesn't realise that nobody's life is perfect—she only sees what she's missing."

"She was in full-on victim mode a few weeks ago," Carla said. "At that wedding, she was staring at the bride with eyes so green, I thought she'd turn into the Hulk. I asked if she was okay, and she just walked off."

"I hate talking about her like this, but she's becoming unbearable," Bree confessed.

"She's on those dating apps too," Carla said. "But while I attract weirdos who won't leave me alone, she attracts guys who vanish into thin air. She takes it as rejection, instead of realising we all have to kiss a few frogs first."

"So, how was your date today?" Bree asked, eager to lighten the mood.

"It wasn't a date—it was coffee. And a disaster, obviously," Carla said, slicing into her crispy chicken. "I've nicknamed this one 'Helmet Head.' He was already there when I arrived, waving at me. We sat down, ordered drinks, and I noticed he still had his helmet on."

Bree laughed. "What? Why?"

"I asked him if he wanted to take it off, and he said, 'No thanks, I prefer to keep it on. It's safer.'" Carla mimicked his tone with a smirk.

"Safer than what?" Bree asked, giggling.

"Exactly what I asked," he said, 'No thanks, I like my helmet. It's new.' So, I finished my coffee, paid for it, and got out of there. Haven't heard from him since, thank God," Carla said, rolling her eyes.

"Well, at least you tried," Bree said, chuckling.

"I think I'm dating because it's expected. A woman of my age and, let's face it, my beauty," Carla said with a playful grin, flicking her curls over her shoulder. "But all I really want is someone to share dinner with, maybe catch a movie. Until then, I guess I'll just collect these ridiculous stories."

Laughing, they signalled for the bill and headed home, brainstorming ways to help Petra break out of her vicious cycle of heartbreak.

86 | Nina

Nina returned from work late five days later and glanced around her. The smell of roast chicken wafted around the kitchen. Manuel stood with Nina's apron tied around his waist and an oven glove in one hand.

"Is chicken okay?" he asked with a wide smile.

"Eh, yeah, I guess," she replied with curious eyes. Manuel held out the white roses, but she didn't move to touch them.

"Sorry about that; I'm going through some stuff at work." He walked towards her and hugged her, kissing her cheek. "Forgive me?" he asked.

"You've been gone for days; that's all you can say," Nina replied, wondering exactly what he wanted to be forgiven for; she had such a long list.

Manuel smiled as he passed her a piece of chicken to taste. "Tastes good, right?" Nina didn't reply; she accepted the tender chicken, nodded, and walked to the table.

The following mornings and weeks, Nina often woke to an empty bed. Nina felt foolish for believing that a plate of chicken and a smile meant things had changed. She knew the signs; she knew the lies. She was waiting to see how many he could make up. She hoped he would be original, at least; she deserved some excellent excuses. Instead, she was met with silence, no explanations, and just an absent husband.

When he did return, Nina had trouble keeping up with his mood swings. If her attitude didn't match his at that moment, it always led to a fight. She preferred silence.

One cool evening at the end of the summer, having finished a beautiful, stress-free wedding, Nina sipped a glass of wine, laughing at a Friends' re-run. Suddenly, she jerked her hand to her chest as pain shot through her. Struggling to catch her breath, she tried to calm herself, grabbed the arm of the chair and attempted to push herself up. Reaching for her phone, she clutched her chest and fell to the floor in agony, wheezing for breath.

87 | Nina

With perfect timing, Manuel entered the house with anger on his face. Glancing over at Nina, writhing in pain on the floor, he threw his bag on the floor and knelt in front of her. "What's wrong?" he asked in concern.

Nina shook her head in reply, pointing to her chest. For the first time in months, she recognised an emotion other than anger in his eyes.

"Nina, why didn't you call me?" he asked, "We're going to the hospital now."

Manuel grabbed her bag, shoes, and phone before scooping Nina into his arms. Carrying her to the car, he carefully laid her in the back seat, ensuring her head rested gently. Slamming the door, he rushed to the front, turned the key, and pressed his foot heavily on the accelerator. The headlights carved a path through the dark streets, their beams blurring in Nina's fading vision as she slowly slipped into unconsciousness.

Bursting into the emergency room, Manuel shouted for help, his voice cracking with panic. He cradled Nina's limp body as staff rushed forward, their calmness stark against his rising hysteria.

Within seconds, they whisked her away through swinging doors, leaving Manuel frozen in place. He shook himself and began pacing the sterile, brightly lit corridor, his mind racing back over the last few months—the arguments, the mistakes, the hurt he had caused her.

For what felt like hours, the hallway remained eerily silent. Finally, a doctor emerged, his expression unreadable as he approached.

"Mr. Genta?"

"Yes," Manuel said, his voice barely audible.

The doctor's tone was firm but measured. "Your wife has a collapsed lung."

Manuel frowned, his hand rubbing his temples. "What does that mean?"

"The left lung isn't functioning. We'll insert a tube to help it reinflate, and she'll be attached to a breathing machine until it can work on its own. It's a routine procedure, but it will take a few hours. We'll keep you updated."

Manuel sank into a chair as the doctor's words settled over him. Nodding numbly, he whispered, "Thank you," though his mind was already elsewhere—on Nina, on her pain, on how helpless he felt.

The waiting room clock ticked relentlessly, each second stretching into eternity. Manuel typed and retyped messages to Nina's parents, only to delete them in frustration. His phone felt heavy in his pocket as dawn approached.

At 5 a.m., a different doctor appeared, his presence commanding Manuel's attention.

"Family of Nina Ruggero?"

Manuel leapt to his feet. "I'm her husband."

The doctor gave a small nod. "The surgery went well; she's out of danger. However, we'll need to transfer her to a specialised lung ward at Arco Hospital for further care. You can accompany her in the ambulance or follow by car."

Relief and exhaustion warred within Manuel as his knees threatened to give out. "Can I see her?" he asked, his voice trembling.

"She's still sedated, but we expect her to wake soon. Follow me," the doctor replied, leading him through the maze of hallways.

Manuel's jaw dropped open as he watched her pale face, so peaceful yet marked by the toll of her ordeal.

The days turned into weeks. Nina's recovery was slow, marked by pain and patience.

"How much longer?" she asked every morning.

The doctor's response never wavered. "We must wait until your lung reaches full capacity. It could take weeks or months. The machine is your lifeline for now."

Manuel visited her daily, determined to be the husband she deserved. He brought her home-cooked meals, sneaking roast chicken and potatoes past the nurses, much to Nina's delight. They shared quiet moments over wine disguised in juice bottles, her cheeky grin lifting his spirits.

Every few days, they braced for the results of her X-rays. Nina's hopeful expression gave way to resignation as the doctor shook his head, saying, "Not yet, Nina, sorry."

Six long weeks later, Nina finally stepped back into their home. She paused in the doorway, taking a deep, careful breath, before sinking onto the sofa with a contented smile.

88 | Nina

Manuel was caught in a dilemma. Before Nina's lung collapsed, he had booked a holiday to Mexico with Stefano. It had seemed like the perfect getaway at the time, but now everything had changed. For weeks, he'd stayed quietly by Nina's side, promising to be a better husband, pushing the trip from his mind. But Stefano had already left—and now he was waiting for him.

Photos from the trip pinged to his phone: sunlit beaches, cocktails, a life unfolding without him. Each one tugged at him with growing intensity. He felt robbed of the break he had planned, uncertain whether staying meant loyalty or simply guilt.

He knew it was time to say something.

That morning, he laid out a tray with fresh fruit and warm croissants, balancing it carefully as he entered the room. Smiling gently, he took Nina's hand and drew a deep breath.

"Nina, before you went into hospital, I did something stupid." He stirred her tea slowly, avoiding her gaze. "I booked a trip to Mexico with Stefano."

Nina's brow tensed as she stared at him. "What? When?"

"I was going to tell you that night, but then everything happened and... I didn't know how to bring it up." He pushed a slice of mango towards her, the silence that followed almost suffocating..

Nina waited, clearly expecting more. But nothing came.

"And?" she prompted, offering a faint, unsure smile.

"Stefano's already there. What do you think I should do?"

There was a quiet firmness in his tone, a resolve Nina didn't miss. He shook his head slightly, already frustrated that she hadn't immediately agreed. In his mind, he'd laid it out clearly—now he needed her to understand.

"No, you have done enough; you have been amazing; you deserve a break," she said calmly. She nodded, doing her best to hide her hurt.

He blinked in astonishment as she smiled and spoke in hushed tones. "Really?" He asked.

"I'm home now; I'm fine; my dad and brother are here, and they enjoy spoiling me." She reached over, touching his hand gently. "The girls will be here all the time, I guess. I think you should go; enjoy your holiday."

A wide smile grew on his face as he squeezed her hand tightly. "You're the best; thank you so much," he said, his voice cracking just a little as he smiled.

Four days later, Nina lay in bed listening as he crammed clothes into a large gym bag and snuck quietly out of the door.

89 | Petra

Petra wouldn't give in; she would keep trying until she met the right guy. The thought of being alone caused her to stand motionless, her body filled with anger, until the moment faded, and she regained movement. Meeting guy after guy both in person and online, she did everything for them, making them feel special, bending over backwards to please them, and morphing into a female version of them.

Petra prepared for the next date with her usual care, her hair slightly curled at the ends, her make-up perfect, and her favourite jeans with a silk shirt that, in the sunlight, would show her slender figure.

Ivo greeted her with a sweet smile as he walked towards her. He kissed her on both cheeks before he invited her to sit down. The summer sun remained a brilliant, blinding white for their mid-morning coffee and continued to shine as they chatted and laughed comfortably over lunch. The clear blue sky darkened when they finally thought about saying goodbye.

Petra felt relaxed, telling jokes and laughing freely; her skin tingled as he gently held her hand as they walked through the cobbled streets to her car.

"I would love to meet you again; what do you think?" he asked confidently.

"Me too," she said; her skin turned crimson before he edged forward and kissed her.

Her vibrating phone and continual beeping sent her heart skipping over the next few days as they planned the next date a few days later.

As he greeted her, to her delight, he kissed her gently, placing his arm around her back as they strolled along the beach. The slight breeze was not enough to stop the freshly ironed white shirt from plastering against his chest. The shade of the trees on the bench was a refreshing treat from the heat as they watched grandparents push buggies along the lake. Petra grasped his hand tightly, already imagining her doing the very same with Ivo many years later.

By the time the third date arrived, Petra was bubbling with excitement; her voice had a sing-song quality as she greeted him. The pair giggled uncontrollably as they dined in a beautiful restaurant overlooking the lake and watched the shimmering blue waters. His large, dark brown eyes, set evenly in his rounded face, and his floppy, messy brown hair were not her usual type. She poured herself into the novelty of his interest, choosing her words carefully, aware that one wrong word might change everything.

For the fourth date, Petra invited Ivo up to Rocca Pinta to stay for the weekend. She planned a quick trip to the castle, carefully planning the restaurants. She spent a day cleaning her house and plucking and pumping her body. She had finally done her nails, her hair looked great, and the vegetarian lasagna and salad were ready for his arrival.

The morning he was due to arrive passed without any signs of Ivo. Four hours later, startled, she answered the phone on the first ring.

"Sorry, I had a crazy morning. I'm leaving home now; see you in an hour," he said.

Let down and disconcerted, Petra waited patiently. Opening the door, he greeted her with a smile; she gestured to the lunch on the table.

"Oh, sorry, I ate on the way here," he said, snubbing her food.

"So, what happened this morning?" she asked, hiding her annoyance.

"Oh, nothing really, just a couple of errands. So, how about a dip in your pool?" he said.

Petra took a forkful of lasagna and walked him out to the pool. Despite the heat of the day, they relaxed under the shade of the pool, chatting while the sun slowly moved behind the mountain.

As they moved the date to the bedroom, Petra's cheeks turned a deep shade of pink, her breath catching as Ivo's fingers brushed against her arm, their touch featherlight yet charged with an unmistakable longing. His gaze, steady and adoring, held hers as though she were the only thing that mattered in his world.

Hours later, as the stillness of the room wrapped around them, her eyes traced the delicate contours of his pale face, memorising every line and shadow. The warmth of his touch still echoed on her skin, a silent testament to his desire and the unspoken connection they had shared.

Petra gently reminded him with a soft voice that they had a dinner booking. "We can cancel if you like; we can stay here, but if we are going to go, we need to make a move."

"Just give me time to get in the shower, and I'll be out."

After patiently waiting for her turn in the bathroom, Petra sang softly in the shower, her heart light with thoughts of the future. She pictured the wedding dress she would choose, imagining the way it would flow as she walked down the aisle towards Ivo. Wrapping herself in a towel, her smile was so wide it nearly hid her eyes as she stepped into the steam-filled hallway.

She stopped in her track when she saw him by the front door. His hand was already on the handle, his bag slung over his shoulder. His face was tight with something she couldn't yet name. "Petra, I'm so sorry," he began, the words tumbling from his lips like an avalanche. "My dad called; he's not feeling well. I have to get to him."

Confusion flashed across her face. Her voice trembled as she asked, "Were you about to leave without saying goodbye?"

The question hung in the air, met only by the tense silence between them. Ivo's grip on the handle tightened as he avoided looking in her direction. A bead of sweat formed on his temple. "No," he said finally, his voice low. "I was waiting for you. I wanted to tell you." His tone shifted, hurried and pleading. "I'll call you when I get home. We can talk tonight, okay?"

Before Petra could respond, the door was already closing, his words trailing behind him like an afterthought. She heard the sound of his car speeding off into the night, leaving her frozen in place, staring at the door.

Forced to cancel their weekend reservations, Petra waited in vain for the call later that evening. Her text remained unanswered, and Ivo did not call her. Feeling even more isolated, she closed the blinds, looked at the dirty plates in the sink, picked them up, and, one by one, threw them angrily at the door; her painful screams filled the room.

As sleep played tricks on her, she huddled under the covers and gripped the sheets as the warm wind brushed past the curtain; she lay alone with her thoughts.

90 | Petra

A few days later, Petra packed her work bag and shared her excitement with the others. "It's just the bride and groom today, with you guys as witnesses. It should be simple."

"No, Petra, you can't say that; come on, it's bad luck," Nina interjected with a sharp shake of her head.

"You've just jinxed the wedding," Carla chimed in, wagging a finger playfully.

Petra rolled her eyes with a small laugh. "Relax, nothing's going to go wrong."

Emily and Tom had chosen to leave behind the chaos of planning a large wedding in the States, opting instead for an intimate ceremony—just the two of them. They'd spent the morning apart, Emily preparing for the day while Tom made his way to the wedding terrace.

Tom decided to stop at the castle's ice cream shop on his way. With a bright grin, he waved at Petra, who stood waiting at the top of the castle steps, holding a strawberry cone. "Thanks, Petra," he said cheerfully, taking it from her hand.

As he climbed the terrace steps, distracted by the melting ice cream dripping onto his fingers, his foot caught an uneven edge. His balance faltered. Time seemed to slow as he plummeted forward, his hands instinctively reaching out to break the fall. A sickening snap rang out as his palms slammed against the stone, and he cried out in pain.

Petra whipped around at the sound of his scream, her heart leaping into her throat. Sprinting down the stone steps, she found Tom hunched over, his face pale and slick with sweat. He was cradling his arms awkwardly, trying to pull himself into a seated position.

"What happened? Are you okay?" Petra knelt in front of him, scanning him for injuries.

Tom grimaced, his voice strained. "I'll be fine, but I think... I think I broke my arms."

Her eyes widened in alarm. "We need to call an ambulance. You can't stay like this."

"No way," he replied firmly, though his voice wavered with pain. "I'm getting married first. Then I'll go to the hospital."

Petra blinked, stunned by his determination. "Tom, you're in pain. You can't go through with this—you can barely move."

He managed a weak smile, his lips trembling. "I used to play rugby. I've done worse than this. Trust me, I can handle it. I just need to get through the ceremony. After that, I promise, I'll go to the hospital."

Her lips pressed into a thin line as she wrestled with his stubbornness. "Are you sure? Emily will notice something's wrong."

"Please," he said, his voice softening. "Don't tell her. She'll only worry and try to call it off. This is our day, and I'm not letting anything ruin it."

Reluctantly, Petra nodded, though unease prickled at her. She glanced at his swollen hands, the skin already beginning to bruise. "Alright. But if you can't stand or walk properly, I'm stepping in."

Tom chuckled faintly, the sound laced with pain. "Deal."

As Petra stood, helping him to his feet, she felt an unexpected wave of sadness crash over her. Watching Tom's determination to marry Emily despite his obvious pain struck a chord deep within her. A storm of emotions swirled in her chest—envy, hopelessness, and a gnawing ache she couldn't suppress. Tears stung her eyes, but she blinked them away, focusing instead on supporting him up the steps.

"Let's get you married," she said quietly, her voice steady despite the turmoil within.

Emily navigated her way through a crowd of schoolchildren alongside Bree, taking in the piercing blue skies as they walked up the steps to the wedding terrace towards Tom. The breeze moved her hair gently around her shoulders, and the sun brightened her heart-shaped face. Emily's eyes lit up as she set her eyes on Tom. Planting a kiss on his cheek, she spotted a pained expression flicker across his face. Sitting with his jacket placed over his hands, she relaxed as she reached for his hand. Feeling pain shoot through him, he smiled fleetingly at Petra, then at the registrar, and then back at Emily.

"I need to tell you something. I didn't want to, but it's only a matter of time until you find out." Taking a good, long look at his bride, he felt his vision go blurry.

Petra watched a wave of distrust wash over Emily as Petra reached forward and lifted his jacket from his shoulders. "I fell over, eating ice cream."

Emily stole a glance at him, paling. She studied his arms and hands, her brows wrinkled.

"You fool; we need to get you to the hospital now. What on earth were you thinking?"

"I was thinking that I wanted to marry you today. If we go to the hospital, we'll have to cancel the wedding, and I don't want to cancel. I can get through this if you just put your own ring on." He let out a painful laugh.

"I love you, you clumsy idiot." Emily let out a deep sigh, turning to the registrar. "Give us the quick version, please."

She placed her own ring on her finger, kissed his, and slipped it into his jacket pocket.

The relief on Tom's face as they were pronounced husband and wife was nothing to the anguish and jealousy Petra felt herself drowning in.

"You can go to the town hall and sign the register once you have been to the hospital." The registrar said sympathetically, "Don't worry; you're legally married."

As the couple walked away with Bree for photographs, Nina let out a giggle. "See, you jinxed it."

Petra, unable to manage even a forced smile, threw her belongings in her oversized work bag, flung it over her shoulder and turned away without another word. Feeling increasingly isolated, her face streaked with tears as she clung to the railing and shrank away into the distance.

91 | Bree

Carla and Bree lingered by the window during their morning coffee break, watching the rain streak down the glass in uneven trails.

"There's something fundamentally wrong with me," Bree said suddenly. "I'm either unlovable or the backup plan—the one guys leave when they find their real true love."

Carla turned to her, frowning. "Bree, don't say that. You're amazing, and any guy would be lucky to have you."

Bree gave a soft laugh, shaking her head. "It's fine; I've come to terms with it. It's my destiny to be a single cat lady—except without the cats, because, let's face it, I don't even have time for them."

Carla smirked, trying to lighten the mood. "Well, don't give up hope. You know you can always go on a dating app and find someone right away."

Bree wrinkled her nose. "No, honestly, Carla, that's not for me. Dating apps are exhausting. I'm not looking for anything right now anyway. I'm just having one of those nostalgic days, you know?" She paused at she looked out at the rain. "That said... there is this one guy I've noticed. But I'm not doing anything about it. If it's meant to be, fate will step in."

Carla's grin widened, her curiosity high. "Sometimes, you have to give fate a little shove. Who is he? Tell me everything."

Bree sipped her coffee, a secretive smile playing on her lips. "I'll tell you if something happens. Until then, I'm keeping it to myself."

"That's so unfair," Carla protested.

Bree just shrugged. "Patience, Carla. You'll know when I know."

Bree thought about the tall restaurant manager who'd caught her attention recently. Their chemistry was undeniable; their secret glances and discreet touching as they passed at work brought a smile to her face each morning.

Robby was a year younger than Bree. His thick black hair was starting to turn grey, and his narrow face and jokey smile made him look younger than his years. Within a couple of weeks of working together at a wedding venue, taking his sweet time, Robby asked her out. His interest flattered her, sparking something inside her. Bree accepted.

On a sleepy Sunday night, when he picked her up in his old, beaten-up Ford Fiesta, she faced him, talking slowly and clearly, "I'm not looking for anything serious, just so you know."

"Me neither," he replied with a smile.

Robby shared a flat with his elder brother, Enzo, a short man with shaggy brown hair and smiling black eyes. Enzo ate only fried chicken and chips, washing it all down with chilled beer no matter the time of the day.

At first, Bree enjoyed the light-hearted relationship with Robby; there seemed to be no demands or expectations. She also enjoyed spending evenings with Enzo; his quick wit entertained her, and their laughter carried through the house in the evenings.

Despite their promises to keep it light and carefree, the fights started early on. Robby's compulsion to cancel plans at the last minute, leaving Bree dressed up with nowhere to go, was always the main reason for the arguments.

"If you want to go out, I don't care what you do; that isn't the issue here. Don't leave me sitting, waiting for you to turn up all evening when we've made plans." Bree complained one evening after she sat alone in a bar waiting for Robby to arrive.

"What are you talking about? I'm always with you," he said, brushing away her concerns. The tone of hostility was unmistakable, despite Bree's calm manner.

"Look, I'm not complaining that you're going out. I'm happy for you to do your own thing. If you want an out, I'm giving you an out. Why don't we just split? This isn't fun anymore." Bree said as she considered whether to turn and walk away herself, leaving this relationship behind her. She loved her time alone, feeling that Robby and his drinking eat into it whenever he demanded her time and left her standing.

"Are you crazy? Come on. Just because Juventus are doing well and I want to watch the match, you want to break up?"

Bree, in no mood for this, shrugged it off. Before she could protest, he leapt forward and headed for the shower. She tried to brush off the behaviour, enjoying her work, her friends, and her time with Enzo too much to let it spoil her summer season.

92 | Carla

Carla often wondered if she was given the crazy weddings on purpose, or if Bree allocated them, knowing she could cope with anything.

"Maybe it's you; maybe you bring it out in them," Nina said one morning as Carla huffed and frowned in the office. "I'm tired of boring weddings; nothing ever happens at my weddings." Nina looked disappointed. "I honestly think it's your big personality that rubs off on them."

"Today is going to be a nightmare," Carla groaned, pacing the office. "Jade and Aaron ignored all our advice. We suggested staying in Rocca Pinta, but no—they booked a place all the way up north at Lake Valdo. We advised a lunchtime wedding, and they've gone for 5 p.m. On Ferragosto of all days. Traffic is going to be hell."

"Yep, Ferragosto—the day every Italian heads to the beach. It'll be gridlock," Nina chimed in, shaking her head.

"And since the wedding's so late, they have to be on time, or we're screwed," Carla admitted, running a hand through her hair.

"I'm free today if you need an extra hand," Nina offered.

"Bree is with me, so I should be fine, but thanks," Carla replied. She checked her phone, frowning. "The bride should already be at the hairdressers, but no one's shown up yet."

Dialling Jade, Carla glanced at the clock, her scowl deepening as the bride's complaints filled her ear. "Leave the bridesmaids; it's your day, not theirs. You need to be ready on time, Jade, or this whole thing falls apart." Despite her best effort to stay calm, Carla's frustration bled into her tone.

Ending the call, she turned to Nina with a groan. "Called it, didn't I? I knew timing would be an issue."

"Where are they?" Nina asked.

"Still at the hotel. Something about bridesmaids fighting over prosecco and a ripped dress," Carla explained, exasperated. "They're already forty minutes late for hair and makeup. I'm heading to the salon now. Maybe the hairdresser can sort me out while we wait." She tugged at her tangled hair with a half-hearted laugh.

An hour later, a frazzled Jade burst into the salon. The beauty team sprang into action, working quickly to transform the bride. Jade's shoulders relaxed as she smiled at her reflection in the mirror, lightly patting her styled hair.

Meanwhile, the bridesmaids lounged noisily, popping prosecco bottles and criticising the hairdresser's work. Jade shot Carla a desperate look.

"Ladies," Carla snapped, her patience finally wearing thin. "Your time is up. The hairdresser has other clients. No more changes—accept the styles you have and leave. Your taxi is waiting."

The bridesmaids groaned in frustration, flashing Carla venomous looks, but begrudgingly allowed the beauty team to finish their work. Jade's expression softened with gratitude as Carla shepherded the group out.

Back at the hotel, Jade barely managed to slip into her dress and sandals despite the chaos. Her bag was packed, and she was ready, but the bridesmaids were still in various stages of undress, wandering aimlessly as music blared in the background.

"Bridesmaids, you have five minutes, or I'm leaving without you," Jade called, her voice trembling. It came out barely above a whisper. Frustrated, she took a deep breath and shouted louder, "Five minutes. I mean it."

Her maid of honour shot her a glare, snatching a lipstick from Jade's hand. "You'll have to wait. We'll be ready when we're ready. Stop rushing us."

Jade surveyed the scene in disbelief. Only one bridesmaid was dressed; the rest fussed over jewellery and makeup. Noticing the pile of carefully chosen bridesmaids' gifts on the table, Jade swept them into a box and shoved it out of sight with an angry shrug.

A sharp knock at the door cut through the din. Her father's voice boomed, "Jade, are you ready? The car's waiting."

Jade's anger bubbled to the surface. "Girls, this is my day, and I'm ready. How you're still in your underwear is beyond me. I'm leaving. Get your own taxi."

Grabbing her silver clutch, she marched to the door, pulling her stunned father along. The bridesmaids stared after her for a long moment before bursting into laughter, as though it were all a joke.

Her father cast them a look of disdain before ushering his daughter to the door, into the lift, and towards the hotel exit.

"We're ready. Let's get this party rolling," Dad said, his attempt at humour falling flat as Jade climbed into the eight-seater taxi, now an absurdly large space for just the two of them. Jade barely heard him; the sweet father-daughter moment she'd once envisioned was now clouded by frustration as she struggled to suppress her simmering anger.

"Are you sure about leaving your bridesmaids behind?" he asked cautiously. "It seemed like an ugly power struggle in there." His voice was measured, but the tension in his expression betrayed him. His stepdaughter was the maid of honour, and he could already picture her fury—and his wife's—when they found out. He let out a long, loud sigh, caught in the crossfire of family drama.

"Positive," Jade replied curtly. "I've had enough stress this morning. If I go back, they'll know they've won, and it'll only get worse."

Her father glanced at her, weary from the morning's chaos, before turning to stare out the window. The sluggish traffic mocked them, the dashboard clock ticking ominously as Jade stared at it with a scowl. Despite the air conditioning, she couldn't cool down.

Over an hour late, they finally arrived in Rocca Pinta. The bells of a nearby tower chimed as the taxi pulled to a stop. Jade felt a pang of relief as she spotted Bree perched on a low stone wall, fidgeting with the cameras hanging around her neck.

"You made it. We've been trying to call you," Bree said, looking both relieved and uneasy. "Your bridesmaids called—they said you left without them."

Jade's voice cracked. "I don't think I had any signal in the tunnels," she said, her frustration spilling over.

"Well, they're still at the hotel, so I guess this is happening without them." Bree gave a small shrug, her unease melting into pragmatism.

Jade's voice turned desperate. "So... we can still get married, right? I'm not too late?"

"The registrar left an hour ago, but he's waiting in a bar just below the castle. Once he knows you're here, he'll come back," Bree reassured her. "Although leaving him in a bar might not have been the best idea. Who knows how sober he'll be." she added with a laugh.

"I honestly don't care if he's drunk, as long as he's there," Jade replied, a fragile smile breaking through her stress.

Relief swept over Jade, but her body betrayed her under the stress. A sudden rush of dizziness clouded her vision, and a suffocating wave of heat coursed through her chest, leaving her breathless and weak. Her legs wobbled uncontrollably, her balance faltering as though the ground beneath her had shifted. With no strength left to resist, her knees buckled, sending her crumpling to the cobblestone street. Her wedding dress billowed out as she collapsed, its once elegant lines now tangled around her legs, a poignant reflection of her unraveling day.

"Jade," Bree gasped, waving down a passer-by to redirect traffic. She propped Jade's legs up on her heavy camera bag and instructed Jade's father to run to the chemist next door.

Moments later, the chemist's doctor rushed out, kneeling beside Jade. He checked her pulse and breathing, speaking calmly. "She'll be fine; she just fainted. But her dress is far too tight. It's restricting her breathing—we'll need to loosen it."

Jade came to, disorientated. "What... what happened?" she mumbled, cradling her head in her hands.

The doctor smiled reassuringly. "You fainted. I'm afraid your dress is too tight. You'll need to loosen it—or we may have to cut it open."

"No. The dress is perfect." Jade protested, her voice trembling.

"Let's try unzipping it a little," Bree suggested gently, carefully pulling the zipper down a few inches.

"Okay, let's see if you can stand," the doctor said.

With her father's help, Jade got to her feet, wobbling slightly. "I can breathe now," she admitted, "but the back of my dress is wide open. I can't walk down the aisle like this."

"I've got it," Bree said decisively. "I'll borrow a veil from the hairdresser to cover the back. You can return it tomorrow."

Minutes later, they stood at the hairdresser's door. As if on cue, the stylist emerged, veil in hand, and quickly pinned it in place, hiding the gaping back of the dress.

Jade hugged Bree and the hairdresser in gratitude. With her father's arm steadying her, she tottered towards the castle, wobbling in her heels but determined to make it down the aisle.

Carla handed the bouquet to a flustered Jade as the music began to play. The registrar, slightly unsteady on his feet, hurried past, while Bree busied herself fluffing out Jade's dress. Jade steadied her nerves, forcing a bright smile as she stepped forward. She looked at as many guests as she could, mouthing "Sorry" repeatedly.

Her eyes finally found Aaron's. He stood waiting at the end of the aisle, a soft smile on his face. She mouthed "Sorry" once more, feeling the stress of her chaotic morning lift slightly as he nodded in understanding.

Before the registrar could begin, Jade turned to address the seated guests. "I'm so sorry," she said, her voice trembling slightly but earnest. "Thank you all for being here—and for your patience."

Her words were met with warm smiles and murmured reassurances, the tension in the room dissipating.

The ceremony proceeded seamlessly. Rings were exchanged, the register signed, and the vows sealed with a tender kiss. The crowd erupted in applause as Jade and Aaron walked back down the aisle, sparkling with happiness.

As the newlyweds disappeared into the crowd of well-wishers, Carla caught sight of Jade's stepmother in the audience, her expression dark with barely concealed anger.

"You shouldn't have let this happen without my daughter," she hissed, leaning in close to Carla. "She's the maid of honour."

Carla bit back a sharp reply, forcing a professional smile. "I didn't have any say in the matter. But if Jade had been any later, the wedding wouldn't have happened at all. It's a good thing she made the call she did." Without waiting for a response, Carla turned on her heel and walked away, her smile fading as she pulled out the thick wedding planner file she carried everywhere.

The day was far from over. Carla spent the next several hours rearranging schedules, coordinating transportation, and managing late-night mishaps. By the time she finally sank onto her sofa at two in the morning, her head was pounding. She stared at the ceiling, the question she'd been avoiding all day now unavoidable:

How much longer can I keep doing this?

93 | Bree

Bree and Robby sat on the couch, laptops open, scrolling through holiday options. Bree's excitement was palpable, while Robby seemed more subdued.

"I'm in," he said finally, "but maybe we should hold off booking until the end of summer—give ourselves some time to sort everything out."

Bree raised an eyebrow. "Fair enough, but if you're not serious about it, just say so. I'd rather know now so I can make plans with my friends instead. That's all I'm asking."

Robby nodded vaguely, his focus drifting elsewhere.

As the season wound down, Bree brought it up again, her patience wearing thin. "So, where are we going? And when? Any thoughts?"

Robby winced, scratching the back of his neck. "Oh... I meant to tell you. I'm actually heading to Lanzarote with the boys—old friends from home. We just booked it."

Bree stared at him, her jaw tightening. "You meant to tell me? Right. I don't know why I even bother." She stood abruptly, grabbing her phone from the coffee table.

"Bree, come on, don't be like that—"

"Don't be like that?" she cut him off, spinning to face him. "You don't even tell me you're booking another holiday? What am I to you, some kind of backup plan?" She didn't wait for a response, storming out and slamming the door behind her.

Robby, his own frustration simmering, muttered under his breath and snapped off the car stereo as he got out. Without a word, he slammed the metal gate shut behind him and strode off towards work.

By the time the sun set, Bree had made up her mind. Sitting with her friends, a glass of wine in hand, she finalised the booking for a trip to California. With a decisive click, the confirmation sealed more than just her travel plans—it marked the moment she let go of Robby's indecision and disregard. California felt like liberation. She hadn't said the words aloud, nor had Robby, but in her heart, Bree knew it was over. There was no going back.

94 | Bree

Two weeks later, the dark, damp night seemed to seep into Bree's bones as she heard the knock at her door. She glanced at the clock, hesitant. Inching the door open, she was met with Robby's disheveled figure. His eyes were bloodshot, his face pale and worn, and his breath carried the sharp tang of cigarettes and stale beer.

Without waiting for an invitation, he brushed past her and slumped into the soft armchair, his shoulders hunched as though he carried the weight of the world. "It's Enzo," he said hoarsely, his voice barely audible over the sound of his uneven breathing. "He died this afternoon."

Bree froze, her heart sinking. "Your brother? Oh my god, Robby, how?"

Robby buried his face in his hands, his words tumbling out like stones. "I found him in bed. Called an ambulance, but... they said it was sudden. A brain aneurysm." His voice cracked as he spoke, the pain in his words slicing through the air.

Bree moved closer, her instinct to comfort overwhelming her shock. "I'm so sorry. I can't even imagine—"

Robby cut her off, pulling off his jacket and flinging it to the floor. Bree hesitated, then fetched a beer from the fridge. When she handed it to him, he glared at the unopened bottle, his frustration clear. She silently passed him the bottle opener, watching as he cracked it open with trembling hands.

"Talk to me," Bree urged gently, her voice soft but steady.

"I've just had some devastating news," he snapped, his tone sharp as a blade. "Leave me alone."

Robby rose abruptly, swaying slightly, and turned on the television. The blue light flickered across his face, but his eyes remained vacant. Bree swallowed her frustration, her own emotions clawing at her throat. She knelt by his side, her hand resting on his knee in a silent offering of support.

Minutes passed in heavy silence before Robby's trembling hand reached out, tapping Bree's shoulder. She turned, meeting his tormented gaze. He tried to speak, but the dam finally broke. He let out a ragged sob, his face crumpling. Bree's tears fell freely as she held his hand, letting him unravel without a word.

Later, Robby retreated to the patio with another beer in hand. He lit a cigarette, the bright ember a faint light against the black night. His eyes lingered on a photo on his phone of himself, Enzo, and their sister, taken in happier times. Smoke curled around him, mingling with the cold air as he stared into

RAW MISTAKES

the void. Finally, he flicked the cigarette into the darkness and headed back inside.

"Can I stay here?" he asked quietly, his voice raw. "I can't go home. Elena's coming tomorrow. After that... I'll figure something out."

"Of course," Bree replied, her voice soft and reassuring. "Stay as long as you need."

Robby nodded, the unspoken gratitude clear in his eyes. Without another word, he disappeared into the bedroom.

Bree stayed up long into the night, listening to his restless movements and the occasional sound of muffled sobs. She felt the grief as though it were her own, and when the phone rang at dawn, the sound jolted her from a light sleep.

Elena's voice came through, frantic. "I'm in Rocca Pinta. I can't find my brother. Is he with you?"

"Yes, he's here," Bree replied softly. "Come over; he's asleep."

Minutes later, Bree watched from the window as Elena's car pulled into the driveway. When Elena stepped out, her tear-streaked face crumpled further at the sight of Bree. "Thank you," she said, her voice thick with emotion. "He called me last night. I knew he'd been drinking."

Bree nodded, leading her inside. "He's not said much. Just the basics, then he shut down."

"That's Robby," Elena said with a sad smile. "He bottles everything up until it bursts. And then he drinks too much. Give him a chance to clear his head," Elena suggested

Bree offered her coffee, the warm gesture an unspoken comfort. As they sat in the quiet kitchen, Bree realised that, in this moment, all she could do was be there—for Robby, for Elena, and for the memory of Enzo that now loomed over them all.

Smelling the coffee, Robby practically jumped out of bed, moving quickly towards the kitchen. Scowling, he grabbed one of Bree's shop bought jam-filled croissants, breaking off a piece with a bite that seemed to suggest some small pleasure in the moment.

Bree, however, noticed the tension in the air and excused herself with the excuse of a shower, giving Robby and his sister the space to talk.

When she returned, Robby's face was serious, his eyes heavy with something unspoken. He glanced at Elena briefly before turning to Bree with a raw urgency in his voice.

"I need you with me at the funeral. Please... come with me."

Bree froze for a moment, uncertainty flooding her as she looked to Elena for guidance. Elena nodded gently, her expression soft. Robby's plea echoed in the quiet space between them, and Bree knew there was no way to refuse.

"Me?" she asked, her voice barely above a whisper.

"Yes, I need you," Robby repeated, his voice shaking with the thought of what he was asking.

After a long pause, Bree finally nodded, her heart heavy with a mix of emotions. "Okay," she whispered, the word tasting heavy on her tongue.

Three days later, Bree, Petra, Carla, and Nina piled into Bree's white Nissan Qashqai. The snow had begun to fall heavily, blanketing everything in a quiet, sombre white as they made their way towards the Swiss border, Robby's home town. The drive felt endless, each mile weighing on Bree's chest as the fear of the day ahead pressed on her.

When they arrived, Bree's heart clenched at the sight of Robby standing with his parents and sister. Their faces were etched with grief, their bodies slumped as if carrying an invisible weight. Robby's eyes caught hers across the crowd, and without a word, he reached out, his hand trembling slightly. He pulled her toward him with an urgency that made her chest tighten. She could see the cracks in him now, the rawness of his sorrow spilling out in the simplest gesture.

Bree followed him, her legs heavy with the weight of the moment, every step feeling like a mile. Inside the church, mourners filed out slowly, their faces swollen from tears. The air was thick with the heaviness of loss.

As the crowd began to thin, Robby stepped away from his family, his hand finding Bree's again. He led her down a narrow, snow-covered path, the trees around them silent witnesses to his pain.

Surrounded by the stillness of the winter forest, Robby finally spoke, his voice cracking through the quiet. "I need to talk. Really talk."

Bree nodded silently. As they walked, the crunch of snow beneath their feet seemed to echo in the cold, the distance between them and the rest of the world growing with every step. Bree couldn't shake the feeling that this was the moment when everything would come to light — when Robby's walls would finally crumble, and she would see the truth of what had been hiding behind those red-rimmed eyes.

"Thanks for being here," Robby said, his voice thick with emotion. "It means a lot."

"Anything," Bree replied softly. "You know how much I cared about Enzo. He was a good friend."

Robby inhaled sharply, as if speaking was almost too much. "I know," he whispered. "I don't know what I'll do without him."

As the words hung in the cold air, a fresh wave of grief crashed over him. Robby stumbled to a stop, grabbing hold of a nearby tree for support, his body shaking. In a moment of raw vulnerability, he collapsed to his knees, his sobs breaking through the stillness.

Bree stood there, her heart aching as she watched him. She could feel the depth of his pain—how much he was carrying alone.

When they returned to the family home later, Robby clung to her, unwilling to let her go. She could feel his grief pressing against her, but there was something else too, a need that wasn't just about Enzo. He fed off her presence, clinging to her as though she were the only thing keeping him tethered to the world.

In the days that followed, Robby retreated into himself, distancing himself from his family. He returned to Rocca Pinta after the funeral, his retreat an attempt to drown out his grief in a haze of denial. He moved into Bree's house for the winter, but instead of finding peace, he found drink. Living in the grip of anxiety and turmoil, he turned to the only comfort he knew: alcohol.

Each evening, he arrived home red-faced and furious, his words slurred as he ranted about work and everything else that seemed to be falling apart. He staggered through the rooms of Bree's house, searching for another bottle, only to collapse onto the sofa, oblivious to the toll his behaviour was taking on her.

Robby began to twist the truth about everything, including his drinking, and Bree could feel the tension building between them. He blamed her for every wrong turn in his life—his job loss, his spiralling out of control—but none of it was her fault.

Bree soon realised that Robby's days were spent stumbling from one pub to the next, his lies growing thicker with each passing day. She could no longer ignore the cracks in his story, the way he tried to hide the truth from her. As much as she wanted to help, she began to wonder if there was any part of him left that still wanted to be helped.

95 | Bree

Four months after the funeral, Bree walked through the door of her home, her good mood quickly evaporating. As she entered the kitchen, the thick smell of marijuana hit her like a wall. She squinted, taking in the mess of her surroundings, and then flung the windows open, letting the cool air rush in.

She could feel the tension rising in her chest, her patience stretched thin. "If you want to do drugs, fine, but not in my house," she scolded him sharply, as though she were reprimanding a child who refused to learn.

Robby, sitting at the kitchen table, looked at her with wide eyes, an almost childlike innocence mixed with the haze of smoke clouding his thoughts. He let out a long, smoky exhale and threw his head back in laughter, as if her words were just an amusing interruption

Bree felt a pang of loss as she looked at him. She missed the carefree relationship they once shared, the easy laughter and connection. But now, all she could see was a man slowly falling apart in front of her, and the helplessness that filled her heart was becoming unbearable. She longed to support him, but each day it felt like his struggles were sinking her too.

A long, grueling week at the office had left her exhausted, and now, waiting for Robby to return, her nerves were frayed. When he finally burst into the room, the force of his entrance knocked her bag from the chair, its contents spilling onto the warm wooden floor.

Bree bent down, hastily collecting her belongings, her anger bubbling to the surface. As she pushed everything back inside, her eyes flared with frustration. "That's enough," she said, her voice tight with emotion. "I can't do this anymore. You need to sort yourself out or leave my house. I can only imagine the hell you're going through, and I'll always be here for you, but not like this." Her tone was firm, her expression set.

Robby looked at her, his face softening for a moment. "No, I promise I can do better. I'm so sorry," he said, his voice sounding calm and sincere, though Bree could see the underlying uncertainty in his eyes.

She shook her head, her heart heavy. "You're draining me, Robby. And by the looks of it, you are draining all the bars, too," she snapped, her frustration spilling over.

Without another word, Robby stormed out into the cold night air, his footsteps crunching in the silence. Bree watched him go, knowing he wasn't ready to face what was really happening. She stayed still, staring at the door long after it had closed behind him.

Hours later, after a night full of restlessness and cold sweats, Robby quietly returned, slipping into bed beside her. His body was warm next to hers, but the silence between them felt colder than ever.

The next day, Bree watched in silence as Robby packed his things. It was a slow, painful process. She knew that only he could change, but first he needed to accept that. It would only happen if he was willing to face the truth about himself.

Bree struggled to sit up the following morning. Her head throbbed with fever, her body weak and shivering beneath the blankets. As she placed the back of her hand to her hot face, the sound of a key turning in the door startled her.

"Hello?" she called out, her voice barely above a whisper, hoping it was her cleaner arriving early.

But it wasn't. Robby's voice came softly from the doorway, "It's me; I've come for the last of my things."

Bree could barely summon the energy to lift her head. She was so exhausted, her body betraying her in every way. Her breath was shallow, and her pulse was slow and weak. She dropped back onto the pillow, barely able to keep her eyes open, and weakly listed her symptoms.

"Bree, you're sick," Robby said, his voice thick with worry. He moved quickly, his usual recklessness replaced by a tenderness that caught her off guard. He dampened a cloth with cold water and gently placed it on her forehead, the coolness soothing her fevered skin. Then he brought her water and carefully set down a row of medicines on the cabinet next to her.

Sitting on the floor beside her, Robby helped her hold the water bottle, his touch gentle but firm. He rose to his knees, fluffing her pillows and adjusting the covers, his actions tender and full of care. For the first time in what felt like forever, Bree felt her anger melt away, replaced by the warmth of his kindness. She closed her eyes, overwhelmed by the unexpected tenderness.

As the fever finally broke in the early morning hours, Bree opened her eyes and spotted Robby sitting in the chair by the bed. A blanket was draped around him, and his eyes were closed, exhaustion pulling at his features. The sight made her heart ache, and for the first time in weeks, she felt a glimmer of the man she once knew.

Over the next couple of days, Robby stayed by her side, helping her shower and dress, feeding her soup, and making sure she rested. His actions were soft and patient, as if trying to make up for everything he had put her through. When she pushed the soup away, he stroked her forehead gently, his voice full of quiet affection.

"You had me worried," he said, his fingers lingering on her skin.

Bree blinked up at him, overwhelmed by the genuine concern in his eyes. "Thank you," she whispered, touched by his presence.

A few days later, as she felt herself getting stronger, Robby gathered his things again, ready to leave. But this time, something had changed between them. There was a shift in the air, a promise unspoken. "Bree," he said softly, "I'm sorry for what I put you through. I was a mess. I promise, I'm on a fresh, new path now. I'll prove it to you."

She nodded at him, her heart swelling with pride and a bittersweet hope. As he walked out the door, the finality of his departure lingered in the air. Yet, for the first time in a long while, Bree believed in the possibility of change.

96 | Bree

Having managed to move out and found accommodation with his friends, Robby seemed to be on a new path. His behaviour had changed; he had a new job and appeared to have turned a new leaf.

Bree found it overwhelming to be in a serious relationship with someone she never really wanted to be with. Aware that breaking up with Robby wasn't an option, his reliance on her had become apparent.

As time passed, he turned to drink once more. Bree struggled to balance her desire to help him with her desire to distance herself from the semblance of the man she had once known. His behaviour changed as he drank more as the season progressed. The relationship between them deteriorated considerably. Spending time with him without getting into a fight had become impossible.

Awaking most mornings with a throbbing headache, Robby managed to filter out the conversations around him, grunting when spoken to. His new colleagues, a group of twenty-year-old waitstaff, would regularly leave him at Bree's house, stumbling and mumbling incomprehensibly.

Bree hardly recognised him anymore. The carefree man he once was had vanished; he was still physically there, but grief had consumed him.

Whenever Bree tried to break things off, he wouldn't let her go, turning on the charm and showering her with attention. On the occasions they broke up, he kept his distance, waiting for Bree to find happiness or move on; only then would he return, chasing her once more.

As the season drew to a close, Bree knew it was time to end it once and for all. This was never meant to be a love story. In the two years they had been together, they'd never once said, "I love you."

As the first autumn leaves began to fall, Robby invited Bree to dinner. Looking nervous, he asked, "My sister's doing the London Marathon in October. Will you come with me? You know she loves you and would love to have you there."

Bree waited for a moment, realising how bad an idea this was, but found herself agreeing. "I guess I can; I'd love to go back to London and stock up on some things. Maybe I can see my family while I'm there."

Bree booked flights and hotels, putting the breakup on hold for the last few weeks of the season.

97 | Nina

Glancing around the crowded airport, filled with anxious passengers, Manuel fanned himself with his ticket, each movement more mechanical than the last. He boarded his flight to Mexico, buckling himself into his seat. Nina was a world away, her presence fading with the miles, as his thoughts turned to his future—and to his new love.

Back home, Nina began to find comfort in her father's cooking, the warm, comforting meals helping her regain her strength. As she lay on the sofa, catching up on Netflix with Fabio, she could almost forget the storm raging within her. Her father's care, the three healthy meals he prepared each morning, and the quiet rhythm of life in their home provided a fragile sense of normality. But even as she sought distractions, her heart remained tethered to Mexico, stricken with worry as news of the hurricane's devastation poured in. Thousands were reported dead, and Nina couldn't shake the image of Manuel caught in the disaster.

Days passed with no word from him. She had too much time to stew in her own thoughts, each one darker than the last. Eventually, unable to bear it any longer, Nina invited the girls over. Three days had gone by since Manuel left, and she was still living in a limbo of uncertainty, holding on to the faint hope that he'd return with the clarity she so desperately needed.

When the doorbell rang, Nina greeted the girls in her pyjamas, her clothes hanging loosely on her frame. Bree, Carla, and Petra settled onto the sofa, cups of tea in hand. Nina tried to explain, her voice wobbling but she skirted the deeper fears that gnawed at her.
"So, he booked it before I got sick," Nina explained, her voice distant. "I didn't want him to go, but I let him call my bluff. And it backfired."
"Why?" Carla asked gently.
"I don't know," Nina replied, unfocused. "Lately, things haven't been great. I didn't mind being alone, but I feel awful for dumping all my health care on my dad and brother. They're doing everything for me."
"We're here, Nina. You don't have to do this alone," Carla said, her voice steady. "Although, I promise you don't want us to cook for you."
"If he really wanted to be here, he would be. He left and I haven't heard from him since. Not even a message to say he's arrived." Nina's voice cracked, her smile barely masking the pain. She blinked back tears, feeling the ache of

abandonment.

"Maybe some time apart will help," Bree suggested, her tone soft but firm.

"Yeah," Nina said, lost in thought. "All the baby talk... it was too much. Maybe this will be the fresh start we both need." Her heart leapt as she saw the caller ID. "It's Manuel," she said, looking at the phone, then glancing up at the girls. Without waiting for a response, she answered.

Manuel's voice was tight with regret. "Nina, I'm so sorry I came to Mexico. I shouldn't have. It was selfish and thoughtless of me."

Nina's breath caught in her throat. "You did what you thought was right," she said, her voice a little stronger. "I'll be waiting for you when you get back."

"Yes," Manuel continued, his words urgent, "we can start again. Being away has made everything so clear to me. I was stupid. The baby talk... it just overwhelmed me."

"It's okay," Nina reassured him, though her chest felt tight.

"I'm taking a bus to Mexico City. The flights are better from there. I'll get a flight as soon as I can. At the latest, I'll be home Monday on my original flight," he promised.

Nina's breath hitched, and a sob caught in her throat. She ended the call and gently caressed the phone, trying to steady herself. Her heart raced, a surge of emotion flooding her chest as she shared the news with her friends.

"You see?" Carla said, her voice calm. "He just needed some time away to gain perspective."

A few days later, the day of Manuel's original flight arrived. Nina threw on some clothes, the denim feeling unfamiliar against her skin, and buttoned her jacket up to the neck. She gripped the bannister and descended the stairs, her steps lighter than they had been in a long time.

Bree was waiting outside in the car. "Let's do this," she said as she pulled away from the driveway, her voice steady.

As they drove toward the airport, Nina gazed out of the window, the world unfolding before her. But her mouth felt as dry as sand, her stomach knotted with the uncertainty of what awaited her at the airport. "I just wish he'd let me know whether he was coming in today or not," Nina said, clearly frustrated.

When they arrived at Verona airport, they strolled across to the arrivals hall. Two seats were available, and they sat down, watching the flight arrival board in silence. Each passing minute felt like an eternity, Nina's thoughts swirling with so many words she couldn't voice.

"It lands in ten minutes; if we wait here, we should see him coming out," Bree said, helping Nina settle into a seat.

Both women exchanged nervous glances, each of them caught up in the emotional whirlwind of the moment. Around them, emotional reunions unfolded as passengers spilled out of the sliding doors, eager to embrace their loved ones.

Nina's stared at the tired, worn-out faces of the travellers, searching for Manuel. The excitement bubbled inside her, a sharp contrast to the anxiety she could hardly contain. This was a moment for a fresh start—for both of them.

Bree began scanning the luggage tags of the arriving passengers. She confirmed the flight was right; at last, the hall began to fill with passengers from Mexico. But as the flow of people slowed to a trickle, and then stopped altogether, Nina's joy began to morph into something else—something she couldn't quite name. No sign of Manuel. Her heart sank.

She looked at Bree, her expression flickering between hope and uncertainty. Bree shrugged, her face creased with confusion. "Wait here," she said, her tone soft as she approached a uniformed security guard.

The minutes stretched into what felt like hours as Bree stood by, waiting for answers. She returned a moment later, her face pale. "No, there's only that flight, and the luggage hall is empty, sorry," the guard had said, dismissing her with a wave.

"No one left at all?" Bree asked, her voice tight with frustration.

"No, sorry," the security guard said curtly, turning away. Bree stared after him, muttering under her breath before she turned back to Nina.

"Let's go," Bree said, her voice calm but insistent. "There's no one else coming through." She saw the flash of confusion on Nina's face, the faint disbelief in her eyes.

Gently, Bree gripped her by the elbow and guided her toward the exit, trying to keep her own emotions in check for Nina's sake.

Nina's steps faltered as they walked to the car. Once inside, she collapsed into the passenger seat, her head falling into her hands. The sobs came without warning, overwhelming her as the confusion and pain threatened to swallow her whole. "Where is he?" she whispered to herself, her voice raw with anguish. Why hadn't he come? What was happening?

Bree sat beside her, doing her best to stay composed. "Maybe he just missed it, as simple as that," she suggested gently. The alternatives—those darker possibilities—were too much to even consider.

Nina cleared her throat, noticing the doubt in Bree's eyes, and sighed. She slid back in her seat, her mind a whirlpool of questions. "He's not coming back," she murmured bitterly, the words tasting of resignation.

Once inside the apartment, Nina sank into the sofa, flushed with the intensity of her mixed emotions. As Bree opened the door to Fabio, Nina was still rambling, the words tumbling out nonsensically as tears streaked down her face. Fabio, looking shocked and deeply moved, cut her off mid-sentence. He took her hand, pulling her into a tight hug, and she clung to him for support, her body shaking with the force of her distress.

Bree placed a steaming cup of coffee in front of Nina, and Fabio turned to her, his expression fierce. "I'll kill him for what he's doing to her," he muttered, his voice trembling with rage. He began pacing, his anger visible in every step.

"The flight landed, but Manuel wasn't on it," Nina said, her voice strained. "He didn't even call to say he missed it. What happened to him?" Her question hung heavy in the room, unanswered and filled with desperation.

"I guess we just need to play the waiting game," Fabio said, trying to offer some form of hope. "Maybe he'll be on the next flight."

Nina felt the long, stressful days dragging on. She agreed reluctantly to contact Manuel's parents. "They haven't spoken in years," she explained quietly, but the feeling of dread settled in her stomach as she dialled the number. She braced herself for whatever might come.

When they answered, the conversation was cold, distant. Nina carefully explained the situation, her words measured. She could almost hear the disgust in their voices as they asked how he could leave his sick wife behind. The indifference in their tone only deepened Nina's confusion. "Well, that's just how he is," they said. "He disappears when things get tough." No further explanation was offered, just an unsettling silence on the other end of the line.

Nina ended the call with a heavy heart, more lost than ever. Fabio stepped in, his resolve firm. "We'll figure this out," he said.

Over the next few days, Nina contacted the Mexican consulate, hoping for answers, but was met with indifference. "Maybe he found himself a prostitute and is having some fun," they suggested dismissively. The suggestion stung, but it only added to her growing frustration. The uncertainty gnawed at her, the lack of answers pushing her further into a pit of anxiety.

As the days stretched on, Nina's stress grew. She wasn't sure whether she'd ever get any answers, but one thing was certain: her world had been turned upside down, and she didn't know how to navigate the endless questions Manuel had left behind.

98 | Carla

Carla stepped into the office; she had been a wedding planner for Bree for two years, yet this was the one that had caused her more stress than any other. The word 'bridezilla' didn't adequately explain the magnitude of her demands.

Carla eyed the clock as she flapped her water-logged umbrella and placed it on the stand. "Today, of all days, it has to rain? Really? What did I do in my past life to deserve this?" Although she spoke in jest, she was seriously concerned about her bride. "And, of course, they have their own photographer, so you aren't there."

Bree shrugged her shoulders with a wide smile. "Oh, don't worry; I have my own bridezilla today, three hours after yours."

"Yeah, when the rain is due to stop," Carla said.

"It's only rain." Bree giggled, "You won't melt," pausing for just a second as she stirred her coffee. "Although I believe bridezillas melt into little puddles of wax when exposed to water," she teased, trying to push up her reading glasses that were no longer on her nose.

"In the bathroom. Bree, your glasses are in the bathroom; honestly, you mustn't need glasses if you can never find them. You have been at the computer all morning and only just realised you don't have them." Petra said.

"So, this morning, I have been to the florist, counting petals; the bride won't accept a rose, not even one rose with less than sixty petals in it." Carla wiped the raindrops from her leather bag and placed it by her side.

As much as Carla loved her job, she didn't find it taxing anymore. It was fun. She loved the people she met, but she needed more to keep her brain active. She had been thinking for a while about what else she could do. Carla didn't want to leave her job; she had money in her bank from Johnny's life insurance policy; she had ignored it since it arrived; it was just sitting there earning no interest.

Over the weeks and months, she had been thinking more and more about opening a restaurant; it had become a constant thought in her mind. There were rumours that the restaurant they often used for wedding receptions was closing. Maybe this was her chance; she could open a restaurant—a wedding reception venue to beat all the others.

The restaurant she had found had been closed for four years since the previous owner died in a sailing accident. She had asked around and asked anyone she knew why it was closed and why someone else had not opened it up again.

"No one used to go there; I guess the drink-driving laws made the police stop at the end of the road," Fabio had told her one morning while she threw it into a casual conversation.

Carla knew it was a risk, a considerable investment that could go wrong. Managing to set up an appointment with the previous owner's brother, she laid out her ideas.

The owner pulled his exhausted body up the steps. He had a Santa Claus vibe about him, with a round, lined face, grey hair, and a bushy white beard.

"Why do you want to open a restaurant?" he asked her. "To be honest, I'm not sure if I'm going to rent it out; I'm thinking of knocking it down and making it into an apartment for my niece and nephew."

Carla explained her idea for the restaurant, a perfect wedding venue. "The guests will arrive by boat, and at the end of the evening, they will leave by taxi."

The owner nodded his approval. He felt a sense of trust in this young lady; with little or no restaurant experience, he felt she could make it work. She told him about her husband, the insurance money, and his dream of owning a restaurant. Santa smiled, raising his thick eyebrows as she talked.

"If you want it, it's yours," he said.

Carla gasped for a quick breath of air as shock washed over her face. "Okay, I just need to speak to my boss, Bree, first. If I do this, it will mean my job changes too," she told him. Wobbling with nerves, she rose to her feet, shook her hand, and wondered what she had gotten herself into.

99 | Carla

The autumn evenings were drawing in earlier, and throwing her bag on the floor, she watched Bree fall into her chair in exhaustion. Carla waited until she heard Bree let out her signature end-of-work sigh.

"So, how was the wedding?" Carla asked Bree.

"Strange," Bree replied.

"What does that mean?"

"Do you remember, Monica? When she was in here a couple of days ago, she was boasting that she and high heels are best friends and that she wouldn't have a problem on the cobbles." Bree giggled as she spoke.

"Oh yeah, I think I rolled my eyes at that comment," Carla asked.

"Well, the cobbles got the better of her. She was wearing platform heels; she couldn't walk two steps without falling over."

"So, how did she get to the top? On her hands and knees?" Carla asked.

"Oh no, I jokingly suggested she find four strapping men to carry her around like Cleopatra," Bree said, watching Carla pull her hands over her eyes and shake her head.

"And did she?" Carla asked.

"Yeah, the best men and ushers carried her up the steps and down the aisle; they plonked her down by the groom."

"Now, I wish I had seen that."

"I have photographic evidence; don't worry," Bree giggled.

"I suggested getting some flip-flops from the shop outside, but she refused; she liked being carried around; they even carried her through the streets and onto the boat. Luckily, they took it the right way, but honestly, sometimes I had to stop myself from shaking my head in disbelief."

"Oh, you have your poker face down to perfection, Bree. Don't worry."

"Tell me about your day; how was the petal counting bride?" Bree asked.

"Shall I tell you over drinks? Wine?" Carla asked, feeling a knot grow in her stomach.

"Stupid question; you know I never say no to that after a wedding," said Bree, grabbing her bag and keys and taking one last look over her desk before locking up. "You need to tell me all about today." Bree reminded Carla, who rolled her eyes in desperation.

"Not today; I'm not ready to re-live it yet." Carla laughed.

The two girls linked arms, strolled to their favourite bar by the office, ordered wine, and talked about Petra's latest love adventure.

"Bree, I need to talk to you," said Carla just as the drinks arrived.

Bree looked up at her, her eyes full of fear. "Oh no, that is never good; please don't tell me you're leaving."

"No, of course not," said Carla; she then continued to explain her ideas about the restaurant, Johnny's money, and her plans. Her hands trembled with excitement as she spoke. "I'll hire a manager. I can't do both the restaurant and weddings; I know that. I'll hire a someone to do it." As Carla finally finished her well-practised speech, she felt her shoulders relax. Bree looked at her with a blank look on her face.

"Well, what do you think?" Carla asked, concerned, holding her breath, nervous about Bree's reaction.

"I think it's a wonderful tribute to Johnny. I think it will keep you busy, and you should go for it." She took time to continue. "It's going to be hard work, and without a manager, you won't be able to do both, but if it works out how you just explained it all, I think it could work," Bree said.

"Do I have your blessing then? I mean, I haven't made a final decision yet, but if I do, what would you say?" Carla asked, her eyes wide and shining with a childlike wonder as she waited for Bree's reply.

"Of course you do, and we need more wine to celebrate." Bree flashed her a broad smile, signalling the barman to bring another round of drinks.

"Shall we go and visit it? I'm sure Santa won't mind; I'll ask him for the key."

"Why do you call him Santa?" Bree asked.

"Wait until you meet him; you'll see. He is the spitting image of Santa," Carla giggled.

The next morning, Bree and Carla buzzed with excitement as they drove toward the restaurant. Bree chatted animatedly, her words filling the car, while Carla remained quieter, her thoughts focused on what lay ahead. As they pulled up to the building, Carla's heart sank slightly. The restaurant's bore the marks of time and neglect—chunks of plaster were missing from the once-bright white walls, exposing weathered brick beneath. Wooden beams, warped and rotten, lay in disarray on the ground, a grim reminder of the work that awaited them.

Carla clutched a ring of keys, her fingers trembling slightly as she fumbled to find the right one. After several tries, the heavy wrought iron gate creaked open, and the metallic click echoed behind them as it locked into place.

Bree followed close behind, her gaze sweeping across the courtyard. She brushed a stray cobweb off her face, flinching at the sticky threads clinging to her fingers. Each step up the stone staircase was accompanied by the sound of broken tiles crunching underfoot. A large palm tree, untrimmed for four years, cast a large shadow over the cracked, dark red tile restaurant floor. Lifeless plants filled the garden, their twisted brown branches splitting over the years of the relentless wind.

Carla looked over her shoulder at her friend. "So, what do you think?" she asked excitedly. Adrenaline coursed through her body as she looked around.

"This place has potential," Bree said, her voice carrying an optimistic lilt as she squinted at the dusty windows. "It's going to be a lot of work; you know that, don't you?"

Struck with satisfaction, Carla started to describe her vision, saying, "Dancing up there." She pointed to a raised platform with dust-covered wooden panels and a bamboo roof.

"Oh, open air, that will be nice," Bree said. One old wooden chair with a missing back slat rested on the wood in the corner.

"Drinks and cake over here. There will be fairy lights on the trees here, or maybe lanterns." Carla exploded into a nervous laugh. "The dining area would be here," she said, pointing at the large covered terrace. Pulling at some plastic blinds, she said, "They are perfect for the rain and sun." Turning to the lake, she spotted a jetty. "Over there, that's where the boat can dock; the weddings can arrive there."

"You've thought it out," Bree said.

"So, what do you think? Please, be honest." Carla pleaded with a straight face, worried that her friend wasn't caught up in the romance of it all.

Bree stopped and looked around, scanning the horizon. She smiled at the birds fluttering about above their heads. "I think it's going to be expensive and time-consuming," Bree said, rubbing her hand over her mouth and chin and saying, "I think it'll be an elegant restaurant if you put your mind to it," she said.

"So, shall I do it?" Carla asked. Bree could hear the need for approval in Carla's voice.

"If you think you can afford it, why not?" Bree said, looking around once more at the work to be done. "This work is going to cost a lot. Just think of plumbing and electricity problems; it has been closed for a long time." Bree gently touched Carla's arm, reassuring her.

Carla froze for a moment; she felt deflated. She thought she had considered everything, but she had concentrated on the aesthetics, the chairs, tables, and decorations; she had not thought of the costs of bringing it back to life.

"Not really; I have some savings from working here, and Johnny's life insurance will cover the rent for this summer, but after that, no, I can't afford it, so I can't fail."

Carla sat back on a wooden beam, the lake now behind her, looking at the property that would soon be hers. Suddenly, Bree heard an unusual cracking sound as Carla let out a terrified scream. The sun-faded wooden beam gave way beneath her. Turning quickly, Bree reached out and firmly grabbed Carla's arm. Using her whole-body strength, she pulled Carla back to safety. They peered down the road below; the beam shattered and splintered on the floor.

"I guess they need fixing too," Carla said, as her mouth split into a booming laugh. Lying a hand against her chest, she spoke in a quiet, trembling voice, "I'm going to do it; I'll call the owner now and let him know. What have I got to lose?"

100 | Carla

Rushing from the contract signing, Carla relaxed into her office chair. She loved office days every now and then; it was a great time to catch up with her emails and get ready for the next few weddings.

Carla scrolled through her emails, her eyes skimming over subject lines until a name caught her attention: Suzanne and Billy. A smile tugged at her lips as she recalled the couple from Scotland who had tied the knot in Verona the year before. The city of love had been their backdrop, and she expected the email to contain joyful news—perhaps an announcement of a baby or plans for a return visit.

Clicking on the email, she began to read, her initial grin fading with each line. The email began: "Hi Carla, you may not remember me; I married Billy last year.Unfortunately, the marriage didn't go well; he has moved in with another woman."

Carla froze, her mind racing to recall the couple more vividly. Were they the same bright-eyed bride and groom she had worked so closely with? She pushed the thought aside and continued reading:

"I've been told that he's planning to travel to Verona to have the marriage annulled. I'm tracking his credit card payments, and he's in Verona. If they contact you for help, could you let me know?"

Carla pulled her keyboard closer, typing an email full of empathy and understanding. 'Of course, we will let you know if they get in touch with us; please leave us your number.'

Expecting to hear nothing else, Carla listened in surprise the following morning as a colleague in Verona Town Hall explained she needed Carla's help.

"Hi, Carla, we have a couple here; they want to annul their marriage; they married last year." She gave their names and asked, "Can I pass them on to you? I have tried to tell them it isn't possible, but they won't leave." Carla waited for the call to be passed to her; instead, the lady from the town hall returned on the line. "Carla, I'm not sure what has happened, but they have just left; as soon as I told them you were on the phone, they bolted."

Carla forwarded the email that the bride Suzanne had sent, translated into Italian; the lady called her straight back, her voice filled with confusion and concern. "So, I don't understand; that wasn't the bride who came in?"

"No, that must have been the mistress." Carla explained. "Wow, so they were faking it. Just when I think this job can't surprise me, it does."

Meeting for celebratory drinks with Bree several hours later, Carla looked pale and said, "I've signed the restaurant contract. What if I'm making a mistake?" Bree could hear the panic in Carla's voice.

"You're going through buyer's remorse; you're doing the right thing," Bree said, trying to reassure her friend. As they returned to the small bar by the office and ordered some sandwiches to take away, they cheerfully discussed names for the restaurants and looked over some manager candidates from the people they knew in Rocca Pinta.

"I'd like to tell Nina, but then I have to tell Petra too, and you know what she will be like; I can see the questioning look on her face. Can we leave it just between us until I get the keys in the New Year?" asked Carla.

"Of course, our little secret, but you know this is Rocca Pinta; word will spread like wildfire; it won't be a secret for long," Bree said.

"I know, but I just want to enjoy it for a while first," Carla said quietly.

As the summer season for weddings drew to a close, Carla and Bree sipped chilled juice, waiting for their last big wedding to end.

"So, what are we going to do until I get the keys?" Carla asked, "I fancy a holiday; what about you?"

"We could go away for a few days." Bree agreed, packing her cameras into her bag and smiling at the groom as he stumbled past.

"I'll go anywhere but Greece; any other suggestions are welcomed." Bree chirped, smirking.

"One day, you will have to tell me why you have it in for Greece; last time I asked, you said the same thing." said Carla.

Bree let out a long sigh. "Haven't I ever told you about when I lived in Greece?" Bree asked. Carla shook her head in reply.

"Well, it's a long story. Do you want to hear it?" Bree asked. Carla nodded, grabbing their glasses and moving to the comfy chairs.

Bree stretched her legs out under the table and started to talk. Bree reminisced about her first day in Greece, her walk down the gorge in Nik's shoes, their first date, and their first kiss without omitting any details. Bree's eyes sparkled as she talked passionately about Nik and her life in Greece. The happiness dripped from Bree's eyes until, suddenly, her lips started to tremble.

Bree wiped her eyes with her sleeve, transported back to the day she parted ways with Nik. Warm tears spilt down her face; her breath caught in her throat as she described her winter season in Italy and her dreams of getting back to him. Tears dripped from her eyes, talking of that fateful Sunday afternoon when he broke the news that he would marry. Bree felt herself once again aching in pain as the bittersweet memories came flooding back. The setting sun shone through the trees as Bree finished talking. She closed her eyes and breathed a sigh of relief.

Carla opened her mouth to reassure her, but no words came out. Her eyes were narrow as she looked up at the swaying tree. She tucked her hair behind her ears before whispering. "I'm so sorry, Bree," Carla said.

Bree caught her breath; slowly, she rose to her feet as her expression changed into a smile. "I want to treasure those memories as if they are high-definition photographs, not carry this hate inside me anymore," Bree said, tipping her head back to the sky. She rubbed the bottom of her nose with her finger, trying to hold back the tears. It had been a long time since she had thought about Nik and her life there with him. She was content with her life, but stirring up the memories of when she was completely happy had woken some dormant feelings.

"Thank you for telling me all of that; you sounded so happy back then." They clinked their glasses, and Carla said, "Nik did what he had to do; it's family, after all. They were sick and they needed him; I doubt he had much choice." Carla paused as she thought back to her own situation and said, "I was happy with my husband, Johnny, but we never had that kind of all-consuming love; we fought a lot, and we had fun making up; we planned for the future, but we never really had that romantic love that you had." She waited for a moment, trying to find the right words and said, "I guess we had a love we knew would last, but we had to work at it all the time."

Bree nodded as she listened. "I thought I'd never breathe again once we split up; I've never loved since then, not even had a real crush that lasted more than a few weeks. And, well, Robby. That's just weird."

Observing Bree's difficulty in discussing Nik, Carla smiled excitedly and shifted the conversation, saying, "Okay, let's get back to where we're going on holiday."

"You know what? I don't care; if you want Greece, we can go there, but not Crete. Spain or the south of Italy sounds nice; if we are out of here, I'll be happy. I've just got to go to London with Robby to see his sister in the marathon next weekend; then I'm free for the whole winter."

Carla reached for her computer and typed 'European holidays.' Now Greece was no longer on the blacklist; her eyes lit up as images of blue waters appeared on her screen. "I've always wanted to go to Greece; how about Thessaloniki? Is that a safe zone?"

"Yep, I need to get over it. Honestly, Thessaloniki is fine with me," Bree said, smiling, covering her discomfort at the thought of returning to Greece.

Carla noticed a car park across the road. "The taxi is here." Grabbing their belongings, they disappeared discreetly into the darkening skies. Sitting in the taxi, Bree stared at the ground silently for a few moments before turning to Carla, a tide of emotions flowing out of her.

"Talking to you about Nik has made me realise how awful things are with Robby; I mean, I don't even like him anymore. We used to have fun, but now it's a whole different story. I'm going to break up with him after London. I can't do it before then; it wouldn't be fair; it's all booked and organised."

Carla flashed a surprised look. "I like him; he's lovely, but not for you." She paused, trying to find the right words to help her friend. "You'll never meet anyone while you're with him, and from what you say, he isn't happy either, so I agree. It may be best, but only you can decide that."

"It will hardly be a surprise; he'll probably be happy if he stays sober enough to remember me breaking up with him." Bree paused as she stepped out of the taxi. "I think I deserve better, either better alone or better with someone else, but not with him."

Although she gave her a sceptical look, Carla had no choice but to agree.

101 | Petra

Petra's longing for love was stronger than anything else; she felt happiness slipping away with each failed date, each unreturned message or call. She missed her friendship with Bree, and her resentment towards Carla proliferated with her inability to accept Bree's choice not to spend as much time with her.

Petra shivered as the uncomfortable prickling sensation shot up her spine when she glanced at couples. Everywhere she turned, she spotted happy couples. Blinded, she was incapable of noticing the sad, bored expressions. She kept her ears open for break-ups in the village, quickly devising a plan to catch the newly single guy's attention before someone else got to him.

Petra thought about her friends with envy; Carla always complained that the men she met would not leave her alone. Nina was going through something; she didn't know what and had no intention of finding out, but at least she had a husband, even though he was a bit of an idiot. Bree seemed to be in a toxic relationship with Robby that Petra envied. Petra wished the three girls would stop complaining, she would be happy with someone like Robby. She could change him and make him love her. She would just have to become the perfect girl for him. She would love to be in Carla's position and have men falling at her feet.

Petra decided that enough was enough; she took the advice that she had been given over and over again by the girls. It was time to start over. She was bored, lonely and discouraged. She took in her reflection in the mirror, her eyes red, her features disturbed from the weeping,

Petra felt delicate; her past insecurities ate away at her, and her heart was bruised black and blue. It wasn't strong enough to face another bashing. Deciding to try Carla's way, she'd try to enjoy being alone. Carla's words rang silently through Petra's ears: "Find yourself, be happy alone, then when you're happy alone, you can look for someone, you watch. Once you're happy in yourself, it will happen automatically, love will appear."

Feeling suddenly good about herself, she jumped off her garden chair, grabbed her computer from her coffee table and sank into her sofa with her laptop on her legs.

Petra typed into Google 'How to be alone' and laughed at the answers, with suggestions such as:
1. Find God & join a church (not her thing)
2. Discover what you truly desire (a man)
3. Take up a new sport (already done)

4. Take up new hobbies (she had been doing that for the last year)
5. Learn the perks of being alone (she couldn't think of any)
6. Spend time in nature (Yawn, yawn)
7. Go on a date alone (where is the fun in that?)
8. Stay away from social media and TV. (Once again, boring)

Petra pushed the computer away, uninspired by the frustrating dead ends, letting her head rest against the cushion. Returning later to the screen, her eyes moved around the screen, trawling the endless Google searches and lists of useless ideas, discarding them one by one.

Petra looked through articles on hypnotherapy, meditation, and soul-searching. Only one caught her interest: a month-long spiritual retreat in Africa. She typed the link into her browser, shifting on her sofa to fit nicely into the cushions. Her eyes brightened as she was intrigued by the words. Yoga, chanting, organic food, meditation, creative art, chakra balancing, ancient rituals, and ceremonial dances. She read slowly, taking in each word.

The attendees would be involved in planting and growing the food they would prepare and eat. There would be counselling suited to each person; she was spellbound. Petra compared many different sites; some were religious retreats, and she skipped over those quickly until her eyes landed on a beautiful retreat in the heart of the Maasai territory in Zanzibar, Tanzania, Africa. She scanned the website, fascinated by the photos. She stared open-mouthed at the prices.

Petra checked the dates; the next retreat started in two weeks. Without thinking and with nothing left to lose, she emailed the contact on the website, held her breath, and then sent the request. She sat back on her sofa, putting the brightly lit laptop aside. She moved excitedly into her kitchen, rummaging through the pantry for fresh food. She picked up the remnants of snack wrappers from the house and smiled. It was strange to feel excitement move through her body for something other than a man or dating.

After a night of interrupted sleep, Petra leapt out of bed and eagerly reached for her computer. A grin formed on her lips as she spotted an email, reading the subject 'Wishing Tree Tranquilly Retreat.' She opened it with a surge of hope, pouring over the pages in front of her, filled with images of colourful but simple bedrooms and smiling participants.

Pouring all morning over the information, pictures showed attendees dressed in light and airy summer clothes, smiling for photos as they tended the vegetable and spice garden. She looked at the small print. She was almost convinced until her excitement was dampened as she read the 'important information' section.

'We suggest you use this time to remove yourselves from the use of electronics. While the retreat understands the need to travel with such items, they will be put in a safe until the end of the experience.' She read in stunned silence, calmly and thoughtfully placing her computer to the side for a few moments before feeling adrenaline surge within. She looked at flights.

Finding plenty of availability, she felt her heart thud as she pondered her return date. Reading the information once more, she saw there were safaris, beach holidays, tours, and adventures. Spoilt for choice and not ready to make a decision, she booked a flight for a month after the end of the retreat and would take each day as it came.

Buzzing with excitement, Petra sank back onto her sofa and felt relief run through her that she was finally doing something for herself that didn't involve a man.

102 | Petra

Petra slid on her running kit, locked the door behind her and ran along the beach, changing direction after five kilometres, heading towards the office. Hardly sweating, she pushed the office door to find Bree hunkered down at her desk.

She noticed how happy Petra looked; she moved her hand away from the keyboard and sank back in her chair. "Petra, it's nice to see you running again," said Bree. "What, or should I say, who has put that smile on your face?"

Petra raced to Bree's desk with rising excitement, moving some stationery to make space for her elbows, and talked enthusiastically. Her eyes sparkled as she told Bree what she had decided to do. Bree took it all in, word by word. She was elated to see Petra so high-spirited; she hadn't seen that in her since they met and were planning Petra's wedding.

Bree couldn't believe what she was hearing; she smiled and said, "I think that is a great way to spend your three months off. I went on my honeymoon to Zanzibar."

"Please tell me it's nice." Petra begged; her eyebrows curled together as she hoped Bree would not shatter her joyous moment.

"It's beautiful and stunning; however, just make sure you take lots of stomach pills; I had a dodgy stomach from the prawns, I think." Bree told her.

"Oh, it's a vegan, organic retreat, so I should be fine, but thanks, I'll pack some," she said, tapping her fingers on the desk.

"I have a friend there, Markus; he is actually from Rocca Pinta. He's a chef over there for the Rock restaurant," said Bree. Petra looked at her blankly; she had no idea what that was.

"It's one of the world's most photographed restaurants, on a rock in the ocean; at high tide, you have to get a boat, and at low tide, you can walk." Bree took a breath, smiling as she said, "You should see the colours there; the ocean is turquoise, blue, and green; it changes colour all the time. You can walk on the ocean floor at low tide, watch the crabs, and see starfish."

"Really?" Despite what Bree was describing, she had problems imagining it. "Oh my God, Bree. I'm even more excited now."

Bree told Petra everything she could remember about this magical island in the Indian Ocean: the friendly people and the sounds of the upbeat music. "Do you want a lift to the airport? I'm going to London the same morning," Bree offered, and Petra happily accepted.

103 | Nina

Bree had so much to say to Nina but knew it was her job as a friend to keep her mouth shut for now. Some things she had recently heard in Rocca Pinta fell into place and made her question Manuel's story. Over a week had passed since Manuel hadn't arrived on the flight. Bree busied herself in the kitchen, whipping up a sandwich and heating up a shop-bought soup.

Nina stared at a printout of an email from the consulate. On hearing an impatient ring on the doorbell, Nina rose to her feet and peered out of the window. Letting out a squeal of joy, the paper fell from her hand and drifted to the floor. Her eyes rest on a tanned, smiling Manuel.

Pulling herself together, she looked deeply into his eyes, listening to his unmistakable deep voice as he shouted to her.

"Hi, babe, I'm back. Will you buzz me up?" he asked.

Nina nodded, dashing over to the buzzer. She turned to Bree. "He's here; he's alive." Her voice jumped with excitement; laying a hand against her breastbone, she opened the front door. Listening to the sound of worn feet dragging on the stairs, she let out a cry of joy.

Nina welcomed the weary traveller with a warm embrace. Manuel looked around the dining room and said, "Oh, it's great to be home."

Bree threw on her jumper and picked up her bag. "I'll see you then; I'll leave you two guys to catch up."

"No, Bree. Stay," Manuel insisted.

Reluctantly, Bree dropped her bag onto the chair and sat down. Silence filled the room, but Bree's angry stare never left him. It was painfully obvious—if Manuel had managed to make it back from Mexico, he could have called. At the airport. From Italy. Anywhere. But he hadn't.

"So, what's going on here then?" Manuel finally asked, as if he were the guest of honour in a well-rehearsed charade. He tasted the soup and reached for the salt.

Bree's hand shot out, snatching the shaker from him. "Surely you ate on the plane. This is for your wife, who needs to build up her strength." Her glare was icy, cutting through Manuel's nonchalance.

He blinked, stunned by her abruptness.

"So, tell me about your journey," Bree continued, her voice razor-sharp. "Nina has been worried sick about you."

Manuel avoided her eyes, deflecting instead. "Nina, how are you feeling now? Did your family help you?" He neared with a faint smile, brushing his fingers over Nina's hand like nothing had happened.

But Bree wasn't about to let him wriggle away. "Manuel, how did you get from the airport?" she demanded, her tone as cold as a glacier.

He tensed, fumbling with the glass in front of Nina. "Uh, a friend on the same flight gave me a lift."

"And why didn't you call Nina? At the airport? In Mexico? Or even Italy?" Bree pressed. "If planes were taking off, I'm pretty sure phones were working."

The sweat on Manuel's brow betrayed him. He lowered his head, his silence an admission.

Bree leant forward, her arms folded tightly across her chest, shaking her head in disbelief. When she finally steadied herself enough to speak, her voice came out in a sharp hiss. "You've had an entire flight to come up with something convincing," she said, her tone dripping with disdain. "Or did you really think Nina would just welcome you back without demanding an explanation?"

Manuel's face darkened as he shot to his feet, pacing like a caged animal. "This is between my wife and me," he growled, turning to glare at Bree. "Stay out of it."

Bree stood, unfazed. "Oh, I'd love to stay out of it," she snapped. "But when you left your wife after six weeks in the hospital, when you disappeared for two weeks during a hurricane, and now you show up without so much as an explanation, it stopped being just between you two. You made it everyone's problem."

Manuel flinched, but Bree pressed on.

"Who does that? Who abandons their wife when she needs them the most? Oh, wait, that's right—you do. You disrespectful, selfish prick."

Nina shot to her feet, tears streaming down her face, and bolted from the room. Bree and Manuel both froze as they heard the bedroom door slam and the key turn in the lock.

For a moment, Bree stared at Manuel, her fury replaced by cold contempt. She shook her head. "Unbelievable," she muttered, before walking to the bedroom door.

She knocked softly, her voice gentle now. "I'm sorry, Nina. I was out of line," she said.

The door cracked open, revealing Nina's tear-streaked face. "No, Bree," Nina whispered. "You weren't. You asked the questions I was too scared to ask."

"Do you want me to stay or go?" Bree asked softly.

"I... I don't know. Maybe it's best if you go. I'll try to get answers out of him."

Bree nodded, hugging Nina tightly before stepping back. "You know where I am if you need me," she said.

Back in the kitchen, she grabbed her bag, taking one last withering glance at Manuel. He opened his mouth as if to protest, but her sharp glare silenced him.

"Man up. Tell her the truth," Her words lingered, heavy in the suffocating silence. "Grow a pair of balls. I hear that you like them."

"What?" Manuel muttered.

"You know what I mean." Bree hissed, slamming the door behind her.

The following morning, Nina sloped into the office. Heading for her desk, she sat back in her chair.

"So, what did he say?" Bree asked.

Tossing a pen around in her hands, Nina shook her head. Bree wheeled her chair over to Nina's desk and grasped her hands. "You don't need to talk, but if you do, I'm here."

"Coffee?" Nina suggested. Locking the door, the girls walked quietly to their local bar, now quiet; the end of the season had left many workers sleeping in.

Holding the hot cup to her lips, Nina finally spoke, saying, "I don't believe a word he said, but I have no proof to the contrary, so I guess I have to."

Bree shifted inward and asked, "What did he tell you?"

Nina stared at her cup, her expression hard and emotionless and replied, "Oh god, well, to sum it all up, he told me that he missed his first flight as he couldn't get to the airport because of the hurricane. Then he said that he was forced to camp down in a survival tent provided by the government and managed to get a flight a week later."

"And what don't you believe about it?" Bree asked, with the suspicion that it was all a lie.

Nina looked vague and unsure. "Not sure. I guess if I hadn't seen his first flight land without him, I might have believed it, but knowing that his flight left and that tourists with suntans and sombreros stepped off of his plane, it can't have been as terrible as he described."

"How did you leave it?" Bree asked, concerned for her friend; Manuel seemed to have done an excellent brainwashing number on her.

"He thinks that I believe him," Nina said, letting out a long sigh. "Anyway, he's gone to work, so at least that is something."

Bree took her hand and looked down, processing the news, deciding that she had already said too much.

104 | Bree

Bree always felt restless before a big wedding. The wedding event was to be attended by over a hundred guests. She walked down the stairwell from the roof to the hotel reception. The President Hotel, a stunning four-star venue on the shores of Lake Valdo, was one of Bree's favourites for photos. Surrounded by stunning, perfectly maintained, ornate gardens, Bree took a deep breath as she took the bridal bouquet out of the basket. She greeted the florist with a smile and discussed the play for the day.

Bree arrived twenty minutes early. The receptionist cheerily told Bree the bride and bridesmaids were not yet back from the beauty salon. Spotting a smartly dressed man sitting alone at the bar, she approached, pulling out the buttonhole for the father of the groom. Glancing at her wedding checklist, she checked the name of the father, Alan.

Bree introduced herself and pinned the purple rose buttonhole to his jacket. He offered her a drink. She declined the brandy and accepted a coffee. She watched as he swirled brandy around his glass.

Alan's tongue, loosened by the brandy, flapped quickly, dripping family secrets into the conversation like candy. "I can't believe my daughter, my beautiful Laila, is marrying that commoner, that idiot." Convinced this stranger would understand, he rested his feet on a stool and started to talk once more. "He isn't worthy of my daughter." The disapproval in his voice was clear as he said, "I tried to get her to cancel this farce of a wedding. She's doing it to annoy me; she's always been a rebel. This is just one more on a list of disappointing decisions she has made."

Bree sat back in silence as Alan carried on talking. "I tried to bribe her. I told her I'd buy her a shop for her candles and scents if she didn't marry him, but she ripped up the cheque. Then I told her I would buy her an around-the-world plane ticket, but she said she would accept two halfway around-the-world tickets, one for her and one for him."

"Oh, dear," Bree said, stuck for words.

"For a while, I tried to leave them alone, tried to accept it, but I can see through his muscles. Oh, yes, he likes to go everywhere with his shirt off; it's his one selling point." He paused while a fresh drink was placed in front of him, then scowled. "I even hired a private investigator; there must be some dirt on him; he just wants her money."

Bree nearly spat her coffee out on the table. "Yes, but they do seem very much in love."

Ignoring Bree's comment, he continued, "The P.I. didn't find much, then

Laila found out what I was up to, and I had to stop. I had to let it be or risk losing my daughter, so here we are." Alan stared at Bree, expecting a reply.

"I don't know them, really; it's hard for me to comment," Bree said.

"The wedding of the century, and of course, I have had to pay for him to be here, his holiday, his wedding, his friends, a whole lot of money for nothing."

Bree took in the gold Rolex and expensive suit, nodding and sipping her coffee and said, "We see a lot of couples in this line of work, and in just two days of working with Laila and Steve, I've noticed they do seem very happy together. I suppose you just must be hopeful and embrace love."

Alan shook his head; his face darkened at the suggestion of love. He stared at his drink before drinking it in one long gulp. "You'll see today. His side of the wedding isn't exactly the most savoury bunch, and I can't imagine spending Christmas lunch with them. I can hardly take them to the country club, either."

Bree pulled her camera straps onto her shoulder as Laila walked into the hotel reception. She felt a small measure of relief as she edged away.

Happiness gushed from Laila, looking stunning even in jeans; she gestured for Bree to follow them up to the room. The room looked shabby in comparison to the elegant lobby and immaculate gardens. Bree sunk herself into her job, trying to look at everyone discreetly. There was something unusual about the bridesmaids; four of them, with grace, charm, and beauty, fussed and clucked around Laila. One of them hung back; her dress sat awkwardly on her frumpy figure, and tattoos of a male face peeked out from the blue satin. "I'm Steve's sister," she said as Bree held back a knowing nod.

A roar of applause met the first kiss at the stunning ceremony in Rocca Pinta. Bree watched as Laila's parents scowled; her mother rested her head on Alan's shoulder as salty tears dropped from her eyes.

A few hours later, taking a few minutes to catch up over dinner while the wedding party indulged in their five-course meal, Nina and Bree swapped stories of the day. "There is something weird about today. I heard Steve say something inappropriate after the ceremony," Nina said. "Steve said, 'I hooked the rich bitch;' he high-fived his friends at the same time."

Bree felt herself turn pale, pulled her chair in close, and whispered, "Brace yourself for what the father of the bride said this morning."

"Oh, this isn't good," Nina said.

"Well, I guess we've done our job; we can't get involved with family dynamics and politics," Bree said.

As the band began playing the first few bars of the first dance, Bree took her final pictures. The girls said goodbye to the wedding party and stopped for a drink at the bar before walking along the moonlit lakeside.

"Look at those two; they are getting into it over there," Nina said, spotting a couple in a passionate embrace on the lakeside, almost hidden in the shadows.

"Hey, maybe we should give them a business card," Bree giggled.

Engrossed in each other, they didn't notice Bree and Nina pass. Bree stopped first; her jaw dropped open as she nudged Nina, dragging her under the shadow of a tree and said, "Look. Look who it is."

"Steve?" Nina said.

"That isn't Laila," Bree said.

"What shall we do?" Nina asked.

"Well, our job is done, but this isn't fair on Alan and Laila. We have to let them see this." Bree turned away, fishing in her bag for her camera. She discreetly zoomed her lens and snapped a series of images. "I can't leave without saying anything, not after seeing how upset Alan was this morning," Bree said, heading back to the hotel.

"I'll stay here and keep an eye on them," Nina replied.

Bree approached Alan and muttered with a flat, quiet voice, "I think you may like to go for a walk along the beach. You may like what you see, or maybe you won't." Although Alan appeared perplexed, he showed no signs of moving, so she carried on talking, saying, "This is not my concern, but, building on our conversation this morning, I believe you and your wife might enjoy a walk along the lake and perhaps you should film what you see."

Alan looked at her and paled, sitting back in his chair. Sensing his hesitation, Bree whispered, "This could be the answer to your problems."

He pushed back his seat and rose to his feet. Loosening his tie, he grinned and took a last sip of his wine. Realising that this could be an important moment, Alan helped his wife up off the chair.

"Over there," Bree said, pointing to the beach.

Laila's mum, Patricia, saw it first. She pinched her eyes shut in disbelief and then opened them wide. The image hit her with a blinding force. Alan saw it, too. He muttered to himself and grabbed his phone from his pocket. Pressing record, he handed the phone to Patricia and said, "Keep filming."

Alan turned back to Bree, his heart racing. He stood stiffly, both hands in his hair. Feeling the blood return to his face, he shook his head. Feeling annoyed, he walked confidently towards the rocks and the couple and called out. "Excuse me, I don't think you should be doing that, not when you have just married my daughter," he said, jabbing a finger into Steve's chest as he turned.

Alan glanced at the lady and asked, "Who are you?" The girl put her head to the ground and took a few strides back; her brown hair stuck to her sweaty neck.

"No one, just a friend," she replied shyly.

Steve moved his shifty black eyes towards his father-in-law. "You're not going to tell Laila, are you? She won't believe you anyway. Not after everything you've already done to separate us." He felt his face go hot as sweat covered his body. His mind spun, and his chest felt tight.

"You're damn well right. I'm not going to tell Laila. You are. It's all on film, so yes, she will have to believe it," he barked at Steve. "This marriage will be annulled; there won't be a divorce for my girl." Alan turned away once more, shaking with anger. He didn't want to hear what Steve had to say; it made no difference.

"You will tell her; you owe her that. All that matters is that you admit this, and we can annul this false marriage." He looked over to the girl, who stood alone, broken, and crying.

Steve moved to the rock, pushing the girl away from him.

RAW MISTAKES

Nina and Bree watched in silence as Steve walked towards the hotel, his shoulders drooping and his jacket dragging on the floor behind him.

Picking up her camera bag, Bree turned to leave, saying nothing more. She felt a tap on her shoulder.

"Thank you very much. That was a sweet moment to end all of the suffering," Alan said as he left, showing her a look of gratitude.

105 | Nina

Since Manuel had returned from Mexico, his behaviour had become that of a perfect husband, although he still avoided any advances. He was attentive to Nina's every need, the perfect host when her friends visited, and he shopped and cooked.

Nina wanted to keep this version of her husband and put the rest behind her. Stefano seemed to be a thing of the past; the late nights at work had stopped, his phone was left in sight, and it felt like their marriage was back on track.

On a cold winter morning, looking for any way to avoid heading out into the snow, Nina started to plan Manuel's birthday present. Since IVF, they'd been careful with money and agreed on just a couple of small gifts for birthdays. Although the cold, snowy days had put a curb on his fishing and rock climbing, Nina decided to make him a personalised T-shirt with a logo Bree had crafted in Photoshop, incorporating a fly-fishing reel and a rock in one carefully crafted image. The image was just missing some text, so Bree suggested she find the name of his fishing rod, and she would wrap that around the logo. Unable to find his rod, she looked for something else.

Revelling in a rare moment alone, Nina pulled out boxes stored at the back of his wardrobe. Immediately, she stumbled across and found love letters in a shoe box, clipped to a photo. Feeling uneasy, her eyes stopped on the photos of the petite young woman in the picture. There were no envelopes, just letters. Feeling her heart plummet to her stomach, she perched on the edge of her bed, her eyes scanning over the childish writing on the first letter. A smile of relief washed over her face; these letters were ancient, she guessed from a teenage crush. She finished reading the first one out of curiosity. It was cute; it was signed, 'Love, Selena'. Manuel had mentioned Selena to her years earlier; they were thirteen years old, and the letter was full of innocent love quotes. Nina decided to leave the rest; she wasn't there to pry.

She flipped through boxes and papers, her hands trembling slightly, until she stumbled upon an envelope filled with photographs. It felt different from the rest—its edges crisp, its contents somehow newer. Her curiosity piqued, she peeled open the back and peeked inside, letting her fingers brush against the stack of images.

Most were faded, grainy family photos: Manuel and his brother as children, playing on small bicycles in what looked like a dusty courtyard. But among these worn memories, a handful of shiny, glossy prints caught her attention. Their bright colours and smooth texture stood out.

RAW MISTAKES

Carefully pulling them out, her heart began to race. At first, she stared in disbelief at the first image: Manuel and Stefano, seated at a tropical bar, laughing over bright, fruity cocktails. Their body language was intimate, their expressions warm. But her stomach tightened when her eyes moved to the next photo.

There they were, faces close, eyes locked as they kissed—selfie-style, with one of them holding the camera. It was undeniable, raw, and completely unexpected. Her breath hitched, and her hand shook as she placed the photo aside, her gaze falling to the third image.

Stefano lay sprawled across a bed, barely covered by a crumpled white sheet, his cheeky, boyish smile directed at the camera.

The photograph slipped from her trembling fingers. Nina felt her pulse pound in her ears as she jumped to her feet and rushed to the bathroom. The acidic taste in her throat burned as she gripped the cool porcelain of the toilet basin. Her stomach twisted violently, and she heaved, retching as waves of nausea overtook her.

106 | Nina

Nina slumped to the bathroom floor, her head resting against the cold tiles of the wall. Her breathing was shallow, her chest tight as she struggled to process the images that had just shattered her reality. The words tumbled out of her lips in a trembling whisper.

"My husband is gay."

She stared blankly ahead, the words echoing in the hollow silence of the room. It sounded foreign, impossible, a cruel punchline to a joke she wasn't in on. Yet, she repeated it again, and again, the syllables sticking in her throat like shards of glass. Each repetition brought a new wave of nausea, and she lurched forward, retching into the toilet until her body felt hollow and weak.

The numbness in her legs began to fade, replaced by a trembling ache. She gripped the counter and the doorframe, using whatever she could find to pull herself upright. Her body swayed as she shuffled back to the bedroom. The sight of the photos still lying there made her stomach churn anew, but she forced herself to look at them again.

Her fingers trembled as she picked up her phone, snapping pictures of the incriminating images. The cold logic of self-preservation kicked in, and she carefully placed the photos back exactly where she had found them, ensuring no trace of her discovery remained.

Collapsing onto the sofa, Nina blinked back hot tears that threatened to spill. Her mind raced with questions, each one cutting deeper than the last. What had she missed? How long had this been going on? What did this mean for her, for them? She wasn't ready for the answers. Not yet.

She checked her watch. Manuel would be home soon. The thought of facing him in this state was unbearable. Her pulse quickened, and she knew she had to get out, to think, to breathe. Grabbing her bag and slipping into her shoes, she pulled her coat from the hook by the door and stepped outside.

The bitter winter air hit her face, sharp and biting, but it brought clarity, however fleeting. She winced as a shooting pain gripped her stomach, the physical manifestation of her turmoil. Sneaking around the back of the house, she walked as fast as her shaky legs would carry her, needing to put as much distance as possible between herself and the suffocating walls of her home.

Once she was far enough away, she fumbled for her phone and typed a message to Manuel, her hands shaking as she tried to keep her tone casual.

"Hey, Bree needs me to help her in the office; I'll probably have drinks later with the girls. See you later."

She hit send and waited. The reply came quickly.

"Okay, no problem. I'll be home in a few minutes. Take your time. It will be fun for you to get out finally."

The casual ease of his message sent a fresh wave of bitterness through her. She shoved the phone into her pocket, her jaw tightening. She needed a lifeline. Someone to help her navigate this storm.

Pulling the phone back out, she typed a quick message to Bree.

"Hi, I've told Manuel I'm with you. If he asks, please cover for me; I don't want to see him."

The reply came almost instantly.

"No problem."

Nina exhaled shakily, grateful for the support of her friend. But even with Bree's reassurance, she felt the unanswered questions pressing down on her. Alone, and now far from home, she kept walking, desperate to outrun the ache in her chest and the storm in her mind.

107 | Nina

Heading into the office, Nina walked straight to her desk. Her first move was to stalk Stefano online. She strummed her fingers on the desk while waiting for her computer to jump to life. She grabbed a pen and paper. She opened his Facebook page and looked through it with different eyes, this time not looking to see if he existed but to see if he was married, had a girlfriend, a boyfriend, or anything. There were an abundance of pictures of a man called Federico. He looked like a friendly guy, out and about a lot; his status said single, and there were no pictures of him draped over or around women.

Nina clicked on his name, Federico, found his page, and started scrolling through all the images he had posted over the years. As she scrolled back, she saw what she assumed was an ex-boyfriend; they looked close in the many photos they had posted. He wasn't hiding anything at all; he was out of the closet. There were hundreds of pictures of a handsome, tanned guy, and there was no doubt they were a couple.

Nina wrote down the names and put question marks beside them. She marked Stefano and Federico with a tick. She returned to Manuel's page and went through all of his friends, writing their names and working out whether they were married, engaged, single, straight, or gay.

Nina lost track of time. She hadn't eaten all day; craving a glass of wine, she scanned around the shelves. Her eyes stopped on a stash of bottles they had been given as gifts by couples they had married. Digging around in Bree's drawer, Nina pulled out a corkscrew, opened a bottle of full-bodied red wine, poured herself a large glass and looked at her phone for the first time since she started searching for leads. She had been there for three hours; it was dinner time, and she still wasn't ready to go home. She decided to send a text to Bree.

"Are you free for dinner? I need you; everything is a mess."

Bree was online and quickly replied, "Sorry, I can be back in an hour."

"No problem," Nina said, placing the phone to her side. She leant back in her chair and closed her eyes. Disturbed by the beep of her phone, she smiled and opened a message from Carla.

"Hey, Nina, Bree says you need company. Do you want to come here? I'll cook." Before she could reply, Carla sent another text message, saying, 'Found two frozen pizzas; you're safe to come around.'

Nina sent a quick okay message and headed to Carla's house, grabbing a couple of bottles of gifted wine from the office before closing the door and heading out.

Placing her woollen hat over her hair, she dashed, looking around her and straining her ears for any sounds. As she moved, she wondered what she would tell Carla. She knew Carla could keep a secret but wasn't sure if she was ready to say the words out loud to anyone else. Repeating those four words to herself was difficult enough.

Carla opened some wine in preparation for Nina's arrival. Nina entered Carla's house breathless, panting to a welcoming smile and a glass of red wine in Carla's outstretched hand. She waved the two bottles she had taken from the office, sat them on the table and took a large gulp. Carrying the already almost empty glass of wine, she followed Carla into the kitchen.

'You look terrible, the worst I've ever seen you," Carla said, always honest, never decorating shit as she liked to say.

"I've had a hell of a day." Nina finished her wine, poured herself another glass and started to talk. The words she thought she would not be able to say rolled off her tongue with ease. She told Carla everything she had seen and learnt in the last few hours.

Carla placed her glass down and embraced a shaking, traumatised Nina. Carla listened as Nina sobbed; they drank and picked the edible bits off the burnt pizzas.

An hour later, Bree arrived, rushing through the door. "What's happened?" she pointed at Nina in the spare room, fully clothed, spread-eagled on the bed.

"Well, I wasn't expecting that; I thought things had sorted themselves out," Bree said. Bree told Carla about her evening. "Robby, oh my god, what a mess. He was shaking so badly that I took him to the hospital. He had to have his stomach pumped; he'd been on a seven-day bender," Bree said.

"Not long until London, then you can get rid of him," Carla said. "How do you feel about that decision?"

"I can't wait; I need him out of my life," Bree explained. "I keep thinking about Nik, and I don't want to accept anything less than that. Is that wrong?"

"No, I think you're looking for Nik 2.0. and I'm looking for Johnny 2.0. Maybe we'll be alone forever; who knows?" Carla chuckled as they turned on the television and sank into the cushions.

Awakened by the clattering sounds of the bin collection outside, Nina sat up, cradling her head in her hands. A wave of dizziness washed over her, and she groaned softly as she stood, making her way to the fridge. She poured herself a tall glass of water and downed it in one go, the cool liquid soothing her parched throat.

Glancing around, she noticed Carla lounging on the sofa, one leg crossed over the other, her slipper dangling precariously from her foot. Carla gave her a knowing smile.

"How's the head?" Carla asked, her tone light but laced with concern.

Nina let out a weary sigh and slumped onto the sofa beside her. "Did I blow it all out of proportion?" she asked, her voice barely above a whisper as she turned to face Carla.

Carla paused for a moment, tilting her head as she considered the question.

"I don't know," she admitted carefully. "I don't think so. But... as much as I despise him for the whole Mexico thing, this isn't just a straightforward case of a husband cheating."

Nina's eyes dropped to her feet, her shoulders sagging.

"He's going through some serious stuff," she murmured, her voice cracking slightly. "This sucks for him, too."

Nina slumped forward, resting her elbows on her knees. "Yeah, I know," she said softly. "But still—I wish he were cheating with a woman. It would be so much easier." She reached for a croissant from the packet on the coffee table, tearing off a piece and popping it into her mouth.

Carla paused before speaking, her voice gentle. "Bree came around last night while you were asleep. I told her everything. I hope that's okay."

Nina nodded, her expression softening. "Of course. Bree knows everything anyway." She sighed deeply and reclined back against the sofa. "I think I'm going to go home now. He'll be at work, and I can look around. Maybe I can find more—something concrete."

Carla studied her for a moment, her brow furrowing in concern. "Do you want me to come with you?" she asked, her tone cautious yet supportive.

Nina shook her head, a faint smile playing on her lips. "Thanks, Carla, but I need to do this alone."

Carla nodded, understanding in her eyes. "Okay. But call me if you need anything, yeah?"

Nina reached over, giving her friend's hand a grateful squeeze. "I will. Thanks."

108 | Nina

Manuel stayed home the following day, forcing Nina to pause her search for the truth. She tried to distract herself by binge-watching Netflix, convincing herself she might be overthinking everything. But no amount of escapism could silence the unease gnawing at her.

That night, unable to sleep, she stared at the three incriminating photos on her phone, the images burning into her memory. The hours dragged on, and by Monday morning, she was counting the minutes until Manuel left for work. Once he was gone, Nina wasted no time. Armed with a cup of coffee, she slipped into the closet where she'd stored the box she'd found before. She pulled it out, placing it carefully on her lap, and began her search again.

Inside the box were more photos—snapshots of Manuel and Stefano in Mexico. Most were innocent images of their holiday: candid beach moments, restaurant dinners, and touristy smiles. She found no further proof, just keepsakes like Manuel's boarding pass, itinerary, and a few napkins from restaurants they had presumably visited.

As she put the items back, something caught her eye. The itinerary. She picked it up absentmindedly, but as her eyes fell on the dates, her breath hitched. She flipped through the document, scanning every line with growing clarity.

The details were unmistakable. Manuel's return ticket was for a fourteen-night holiday—not the seven nights he had told her. The truth landed like a punch to the gut. Memories of that dreadful week flooded back: sitting at the airport, watching passengers disembark with no sign of him, the tears she cried driving home, and the gnawing fear that something terrible had happened. Yet all along, he had stayed behind intentionally.

Her heart raced as she realised time was running out. Manuel would be home soon. She stuffed the itinerary into her purse, threw on her camel coat, and bolted out of the house.

At the office, Nina pushed open the door, fumbling with her keys to lock it behind her. She let the heavy glass hold her as she caught her breath, the consequence of her discovery pressing on her. The ringing of her phone jolted her from her thoughts.

"Hey, where are you? How did it go yesterday?" Carla's curious voice asked.

"I'm at the office. It went from bad to worse," Nina replied, her voice trembling.

"Wait there. I'll be there in five minutes," Carla said, hanging up after a quick farewell.

Carla arrived minutes later, using her key to unlock the door. She stepped inside, shaking the rain off her coat as she watched Nina frantically gather papers from the photocopier.

"What's all this?" Carla asked, gesturing toward the stack of copies.

"Evidence," Nina said tersely, holding up the newly printed pages.

Carla waited for the photocopier to stop whirring before approaching. "Okay, sit down and tell me everything," she said, gently guiding Nina to a chair.

Nina collapsed into the seat, her frustration spilling out. "He lied about everything. And I mean everything." She grabbed a highlighter and began marking sections of the documents, her anger palpable.

Before Carla could respond, they both turned toward the sound of a key turning in the lock. The door creaked open, and Bree walked in, her expression puzzled.

"Girls, what are you doing here?" Bree asked, taking in the scene.

"Nina needed to copy some evidence," Carla explained, shooting a concerned glance at Nina. "This is her safe place."

Nina nodded silently, her grip tightening on the papers.

"Right," Bree said decisively. "We're going to my house. You need a break from this." She grabbed Nina by the arm, urging her to stand.

"See you there. I'll drive over after locking up," Carla said, switching off the office lights.

109 | Nina

As the car sped towards Bree's house, Nina regained her composure and adjusted her posture. They waited in silence for Carla to arrive. Pondering her words, Nina looked at Carla and Bree and started to let it all out. "He lied about everything—the Mexico thing, his flights, his return date."

"Okay, start from the beginning," Carla said.

Nina pulled out copies of the flight tickets, boarding pass, and itinerary and placed them on the table. "Do the maths?" she said, exasperated.

Carla looked confused, feeling that she had missed a step. She rested her urgent gaze on Bree, who ran her fingers down the papers. Stopping and gasping a deep breath, Bree turned to Carla.

"What date did he arrive home?" Bree asked.

"The seventh," Nina replied, her voice shaky.

"But he arrived on the fifth in Italy; where was he for two days?" Bree asked.

"Oh, that isn't everything. It's merely the beginning."

Bree counted days on her hands, and then she looked at Nina, her mouth wide open, stunned to reply for a few moments, "What the hell? Do you think he ever intended to come home after a week?" She paused and studied the itinerary, saying, "The lying bastard."

"No, the itinerary and the ticket clearly show he was booked on a fourteen-night holiday. When he told me he was going away for a week, it was a blatant lie."

"What's that"? Bree asked, looking at the small piece of card in Nina's hand.

"This is the boarding pass. He boarded the plane on the fourth."

Bree's face froze, and her mouth opened. "Shit." She focused on the pass. Everyone looked stunned; silence filled the room.

"I don't know what to do. If I confront him, I'll have to open a whole can of gay worms; I'm not ready yet," she said.

"Oh god, Nina, shit," Carla said, blinking quickly, still shocked; she rested her hand gently on Nina's arm. "I don't know what to say about any of it. What a lying git; I get why you're so mad, and yes, if you mention it, it will all come out unless we can find another way to bring it all up."

"Any ideas? I thought I was going clinically insane, but he was just lying," Nina said to her two friends.

"Nope, none at all. Let's think about it and figure out what to do. First, you must calm down." Carla said.

"You can't think straight like this. I understand you don't want to calm down; I get it, but you need to see through all the emotions and work out what you want to do. It's time to be pragmatic," Bree said.

"Let's separate the two issues." Carla suggested, "Whatever has happened, you're finally getting closer to the truth." With a deep sigh, she watched as Nina sat down on her chair and said, "The first one is that your husband is gay; the second one is that he lied to you, again."

"Let's try to think about one at a time. First, him and Stefano." "Let's try and think about what Manuel's life must have been like, like living a lie and trying to figure out who he was, all while hiding it from you and everyone," Carla said as she watched her friend wince at the sound of his name.

"Now, the lies about the flight and holiday," Carla continued. "What's going through your mind about that?"

"I feel gullible, taken for a ride; I've been too unsuspecting; despite all of the facts and the feeble excuses, I chose to believe him like a stupid child." Her breath came in short gasps between tears. "I don't know who I am anymore. I've let him run rings around me, manipulate me, and take the flack for his ever-changing moods." She thought for a few moments and said, "I'm going to order the T-shirt, give it to him, and tell him what I found. That will give me a few days to get my head around it."

110 | Nina

For the next few days, Nina lived in the heart of a perfect storm, surrounded by emotional waves, thrown up high and dropping suddenly down. She tried to pretend that life was normal and planned her days around when Manuel was at work.

The day the t-shirt arrived, Nina kneaded flour with yeast, making Manuel's favourite pizza from scratch. She placed expensive wine carefully on the table with two large wine glasses.

He arrived home looking worn out and threw his gym bag on the floor. Nina sliced the pizzas and poured him a large beer along with the carefully wrapped gift. "This was going to be for your birthday, but I wanted to give it to you early," she said with a smile.

Squishing it to guess what was in the parcel, he pulled out the soft material; his eyes glistened as he took in the personalised design.

"Nina, it's wonderful. Thank you so much," he said, holding it up against his body. Taking off his sweaty gym shirt and quickly trying on the T-shirt, he slid his hands down his toned body and said, "It fits perfectly; thank you." He leant in towards her and kissed her on the cheek.

Taking a deep breath, she spoke calmly to him while she placed the steaming pizza slices on the plate. "When I was looking through your things for ideas on the design, I saw some things that confused me a bit." Unable to look at him, she busied herself, tossing a salad.

His eyes darted around the room, and his face flashed with panic. With squinting eyes, he tried to picture where she could have looked for the logo. Pulling a slice of pizza away, he bit into it, licking cheese from his lips. "Where did you look?" he asked shyly, his face washed with trepidation and dread. A shiver ran down his spine as he wondered what to say next.

Nina continued, "I found your travel itinerary for Mexico." She paused, waiting for a reaction. She forced a tired and measured smile. The room suddenly grew tense.

"Oh," he said, glancing around and scratching his head. That wasn't what he expected from this conversation. He didn't even know he kept it. He took a deep breath of relief until panic washed over his face out of nowhere.

"I looked at it over and over again; nothing made sense. Now I need you to explain why you lied to me about it. When you were due to arrive home and why you were in Italy for two days before you even bothered to come home."

He stared into his salad, cursing under his breath. Manuel glared at her, holding words inside him. Whatever he said would be a lie; he had told so many lies that the truth and lies were all now in one melting pot. He bristled at the direct questions. "Okay, I have some stuff I need to tell you, I guess," he said, reaching out to place a hand on hers.

To Manuel's horror, Nina's voice grew shrill with rage. Nina shook him off, flashing a glaring look of warning. "The truth, please."

Manuel stood up abruptly, turning his back to her and staring at the wall. His shoulders were tense, his words slow and deliberate. "Yes, I booked the trip for two weeks. That was a lie," he admitted, glancing at her briefly over his shoulder. "But I realised I'd made a mistake, so I tried to change my flight and come back early. That's when I called you."

He turned around, leaning heavily on the tall back of a dining chair. His eyes fell to the pizza sitting untouched on the table.

"Okay, carry on," Nina said, her voice steady despite the storm brewing inside her.

"I couldn't get an earlier flight," he continued, his tone rising defensively. "So, I stayed. Then the flight I was already booked on got delayed by two days. I had no choice but to wait at a hotel near the airport." His words echoed loudly in the quiet room, but Nina's expression remained unchanged.

She locked her eyes on him, her voice soft but sharp. "No phone in the hotel, then?"

"Honestly, that's what happened." he muttered, his voice pleading now. "I'm not lying," He turned away, dismissing her question as if it held no weight.

Nina tilted her head, her expression hardening. "You forgot the boarding pass," she said, her voice cutting through the tension like a blade. She reached under the cushion and pulled out the incriminating papers. "You boarded your flight on the scheduled day. You chose not to call me. You chose not to come home. You lied the entire time you were away. You lied when you came back. You lied to my face."

Her voice wavered as she poured herself a large glass of wine. The truth had taken hold of her, its weight impossible to bear.

Manuel flinched, visibly grappling with his response. "You don't know what you're talking about," he said, his voice uneven. "I do. I was there." But the words rang hollow, and an oppressive silence fell over them.

Nina stared at him, her disbelief turning to cold disdain. "You're not the man I fell in love with. Not the man I married. I can't do this anymore," she said, her tone final. Her fierce scowl lingered on him, and she noticed the way his temple throbbed under her unrelenting scrutiny.

Manuel flinched as she picked up her wine glass, now full to the brim. "I want you out of the house," she said firmly. "I'll stay away tonight, but by the morning, you need to be gone."

He looked shaken, his voice breaking as he shouted, "You don't mean that. You're not thinking straight." He ran his hands through his hair in frustration, his movements frantic.

Nina's voice was steely. "You've lied to me over and over again. You've disrespected me, manipulated me, gaslighted me. You've made me feel like I was losing my mind. I've had enough."

She hurled the wine glass at him. The liquid splashed across his face, soaking his shirt. Manuel stepped back, stunned, and wiped his face with trembling hands. In a sudden fit of rage, he ripped his t-shirt off and threw it to the floor, his breathing ragged and heavy.

Nina moved through the house like a whirlwind, her hands shaking as she grabbed essentials for an overnight stay at Bree's. She shoved toiletries, cosmetics, and a change of clothes into her bag before stopping in front of him.

"Do you have anything else to add?" she asked, her voice cracking like a whip.

Manuel let out a small cough, buying time. His words came out haltingly. "You don't understand. I wasn't lying."

She shook her head, her tone laced with disgust. "You don't know when to stop, do you? The game is up."

She walked toward the door but turned back to deliver one final blow. "Next time we meet, I'm going to need an explanation for the photos I found. You and Stefano kissing in bed."

Her words landed like a thunderclap. Manuel froze, his expression shifting from shock to fury in an instant. "What?" he hissed, his voice low and dangerous.

Nina's lips curled into a grim smile. "That should give you enough time to come up with another lie."

Her words hung in the air as she stepped out of the room, slamming the door behind her. Outside, a wave of desperation washed over her, threatening to pull her under. But she didn't look back.

111 | Nina

Manuel diverted his glare, and they looked at each other in disdain with narrow eyes.

Nina shut the door behind her, the cold winter air biting her cheeks. She took a deep breath, letting the sharp chill steady her, then hurried into the night. The streets were quiet, her hurried footsteps echoing faintly against the buildings as she made her way to Bree's house.

By the time she arrived, her breath came in ragged gasps. She knocked once before the door opened, Bree's concerned face greeting her.

"I'm so sorry," Nina began, the words tumbling out. "I know you've got so much going on right now—"

Bree waved off the apology. "Don't worry about that. I'll always be here for you." She stepped aside to let Nina in, closing the door softly behind them.

Bree guided her to the sofa, handing her a glass and a bottle of wine. "Here, this is all yours. I've got my own bottle, don't worry," she said with a small smile.

Nina poured herself a generous glass and took a long sip. "I don't think this will be enough for what I'm feeling, but it's a good start." She glanced at her phone, the screen blinking with unread messages.

Just then, Carla arrived, giving Nina a reassuring hug before sitting down. Nina exhaled sharply and looked between her friends. "Where do I even start?" she muttered.

"Start at the beginning," Bree said.

Nina recounted everything—Manuel's lies about the flight, the confrontation, the wine thrown in his face, and finally, the bombshell about Stefano. Her voice cracked as she relayed each detail, mimicking his gestures and tone with bitter precision.

Bree listened intently, her expression a mixture of disbelief and anger. "I can't believe he lied again," she said, handing Nina some popcorn. "He really thought he could keep playing you."

Nina scoffed. "He refuses to admit the game is up. He just... keeps denying everything."

The conversation faded as Nina broke into tears, the sobs wracking her body until she had no more left to cry. Eventually, she fell into a restless sleep on Bree's sofa, waking suddenly at intervals throughout the night.

By morning, she was up before dawn, throwing on her coat and tying her hair back. She slipped out of Bree's house into the predawn streets, wandering aimlessly as her mind replayed the events of the previous night.

Passing her own house, she saw Manuel's car still parked in the driveway.

She froze, her feet tapping anxiously against the pavement. For a moment, she stared at the door, unsure whether to go in. But doubt won out, and she turned away, the cold wind tugging at her scarf as she made her way to a nearby bench. Sitting there, she felt paralysed, helpless against the torrent of thoughts and emotions swirling within her.

When the bakery opened, Nina bought croissants and takeaway coffee, returning to Bree's house. She placed her phone on charge and absently scrolled through social media, the glossy images of carefree lives only deepening her sense of isolation.

Bree appeared not long after, wrapped in her dressing gown and smiling sleepily. They sat together, eating breakfast in comfortable silence, chatting about Nina's Instagram feed. But Nina's appetite was nonexistent, and she only picked at the edges of her croissant.

Finally, she turned to Bree, her voice hesitant. "I need another favour."

"Anything," Bree said without hesitation.

"I need to go through the messages. I don't want to read them, but I need to know what he said."

Bree nodded, a flicker of understanding crossing her face. She picked up Nina's phone, scrolling to the top of the message thread. Occasionally, she glanced up at Nina, her coffee in hand.

"I need to reread these," Bree said after a moment. She started again from the top, her voice measured. "He starts with a bunch of sorry messages. Then it's, 'We need to talk,' followed by more apologies." Bree paused, taking another sip of her coffee before continuing.

"Next, he says, 'Sorry, I lied. I didn't want to hurt you.' Then he switches to, 'I'm going through a tough time.'" Bree scrolled further. "Oh, here we go—'I promise not to lie anymore.' And the last one, I'm guessing before he went to bed, is: 'I need you. I can't do this without you.'"

Nina listened silently, her face a mix of anger and heartbreak. She reached for her coffee, taking a shaky sip as Bree gently placed the phone back on the table. "So, no mention of the main issue? There was no mention of the pictures?" Nina asked.

"No, nothing," Bree said. "Do you want to read them?"

Bree followed Nina's instructions, picked up her phone, and called Manuel. His first words asked how Nina was doing, but she ignored him. "Nina just needs to know if you have left the house or not," she said.

"Yes, I've just got to go back and get the car; I didn't want to drive. I hit the vodka after the fight; you can tell her she's free to go home," Manuel said.

"Good, unless you've decided to tell her the truth and finally be honest with her, then please, just leave her alone until she's ready to talk."

"Okay, just tell her I'm staying with my brother."

Bree agreed, ending the conversation. Bree walked home with Nina, settled her in, and left her to her day. Nina wanted to be alone, and she respected that.

112 | Bree

Bree was excited about the winter; instead of being bored and going to the office for the sake of it, she offered to help Carla set up the restaurant in the New Year. They agreed that after Bree's quick jaunt to London, she and Carla would take a trip to Thessaloniki and then start planning the opening of the restaurant.

The day Bree and Petra left Rocca Pinta, Petra was full of excitement, and Bree was filled with dread. Bree watched Petra repeatedly flip through her shoulder bag, checking for her passport and tickets every few minutes.

"You seem so much brighter; I think this trip will do you good," Bree said.

"I feel so much better; I haven't felt this positive and so relaxed since the day Dexter walked into our lives." Petra laughed and scowled at the same time. "I wanted to pack a couple of bottles of gin for the retreat, but I guess that is sort of defeating the point," she giggled.

"So, are you excited to go home?" Petra asked Bree.

"Well, it's going to be a strange weekend. I'm planning on ending things with Robby," Bree said, keeping her eye on traffic.

"Oh, god, why?" Petra asked.

"Well, I guess I've realised how awful things are with him; I don't even like him anymore. He's only been gone a week since the end of the summer season, and I love being at home again; my house is my happy place without him turning up drunk at my door," Bree said.

"Oh my god, I didn't know; I thought you and he would just be toxic forever," Petra laughed.

"I thought about breaking up with him when he left last week, but we have this marathon shenanigan. His sister is running, and I love her; I want to be there for her," Bree said.

"Yeah, she's so nice; I can't believe she is going to be running a marathon," Petra replied.

"I know, it's amazing. Robby wouldn't have gone without me; he avoids cities because they frighten him. So, I'm just getting this out of the way before I end things," Bree said. "I've known it was toxic for a long time, but I told Carla about Nik recently, and it brought up a lot of emotions. I hadn't thought about him in a long time. I know with Nik it was young love, and I can't expect to find that again, but I'm not angry anymore, and I want something more like that again, not this mess I have with Robby," Bree said with nostalgia.

"I guess I can't understand. I think I would be happier with someone like Robby than living alone," Petra said.

"He's all yours; feel free to take him," Bree laughed. Walking from the car park to the airport, Bree helped Petra with her bags.

"So, here we are at the same airport, on different emotional journeys." Petra said with a grin, "Good luck." Feeling the weight of her passport in her bag, Petra waved to Bree and strode towards the gate.

Bree looked around for Robby, and they greeted each other with a friendly smile and kissed on the cheek. Bree noticed the dark circles around his eyes, his blotchy skin, and his stale breath. She looked into his bloodshot eyes, disinterested in asking him about his previous night out; she asked no questions. Placing her headphones in her ears, she closed her eyes, thinking of the words she would use to break up with him in just two days.

Buckling his seatbelt, Robby closed his eyes; his loud, vibrating snore caused stares from the other passengers. He jolted himself awake as the plane touched down on the rainy runway.

The feeling of the damp, cold British air sent a smile across Bree's face. She was ecstatic to be back in London after such a long time. Once they dumped their bags in the hotel, Bree strolled around Covent Garden, across Leicester Square, and Piccadilly Circus, feeling the excitement all around her, with Robby lurking behind, annoyed to be sightseeing. A sense of magic permeated the air as the marathon, set to take place the next day, drew groups of chatty, nervous runners and spectators as they took in the sights before the big day.

The cold rainwater seeped into her shoes, penetrating her jacket, and her shoulders dripped with the English weather. Nostalgia swept over her as she peered into shop windows, smelling the stale beer as a pub door opened and closed. Youngsters stumble out, holding the door open with their bodies for someone else to come out.

Bree's mouth watered as they passed the bustling pubs and restaurants, the scent of spices, roasting meats, and baked goods wafting through the crisp evening air. London's food scene was a playground, and Bree was ready to explore every corner.

"Pizza," Robby suggested, with a hopeful grin.

Bree stopped in her tracks, glaring at him. "You're in London, Robby, and you want to eat Italian?" She crossed her arms. "Why not be adventurous for once? Try something new."

He gave her his best puppy-dog eyes. "Come on, Bree. British food is terrible—boiled cabbage and stew? Please, have a heart."

Bree rolled her eyes and pulled out her phone. "Fine. There's an Italian place eight minutes from here." She tilted her screen toward him. "Enjoy."

His face lit up. "Oh, thank—"

"But," Bree interrupted, stepping over a large puddle, "I'm not coming with you. I'll see you back at the hotel later. I have real food to find."

"Wait—you're leaving me alone? In London?" His voice rose an octave. "I could get stabbed. Mugged. Or worse—forced to eat something weird."

Bree shrugged, adjusting her scarf. "Sounds like a you problem. Good luck."

She strode off, smiling to herself as she spotted the glowing sign of a Chinese restaurant up ahead.

Moments later, a tap on her shoulder made her turn, her smile vanishing. Robby stood there, drenched from the rain and looking like a sad, wet dog.

"You can't leave me," he whined. "I'll die out here."

"Not my problem," Bree muttered, stepping forward. But Robby followed, his boots splashing in every puddle along the way.

Inside the restaurant, the warm dazzle of lanterns and the enticing aroma of soy, garlic, and ginger welcomed them. A cheerful waitress led them to a table, and Bree noticed Robby looking increasingly miserable as he took in the scene.

"I could be eating pizza right now," he muttered, slumping into his chair.

Bree ignored him, scanning the menu. "This is going to be amazing."

Robby, meanwhile, stared at the menu like it was written in hieroglyphics. "You know what I like," he grumbled, sliding it across the table. "Just order for me."

Bree smirked. "Gladly." She carefully selected the spiciest dishes she could find, adding a few surprises for good measure.

When the food arrived, Robby's expression shifted from disdain to sheer horror. He poked at the plate of noodles like they might bite him.

"It's just spaghetti," Bree teased, twirling a generous forkful and popping it into her mouth. "Try it."

He muttered something under his breath and finally took a bite, his face twisting as the unfamiliar flavours hit his tongue. "Why is it sweet and spicy? What's wrong with normal food?"

Bree laughed, sipping her wine. "You mean bland food? This is what flavour tastes like."

Robby scowled, attacking the breadbasket instead. He gnawed on a piece like it was a lifeline, while Bree savoured every bite of the meal.

By the time they left, Robby was grumpier than ever. A passing car splashed a puddle over his shoes, and he let out an exasperated groan. "Taxi. Now."

"Nope," Bree said cheerfully. "We're taking the tube."

"Why?"

"It's cheaper," she replied with a sweet smile, knowing full well the idea of saving money would win him over.

Robby reluctantly followed her into the maze of tunnels. Bree navigated the station with ease, delighting in his obvious discomfort as he stumbled through the crowds and up the escalators.

On the train, Robby flopped into a seat, glaring at his phone. "No signal. This city is the worst."

Bree, standing nearby, held onto the overhead strap with one hand and her takeaway box of leftovers in the other. She smiled to herself, watching him sulk.

"Don't worry," she said, her tone dripping with mock sympathy. "Maybe tomorrow we can try sushi."

Robby groaned, sinking deeper into his chair.

Bree shook her head in silence, her thoughts swirling as she watched a group of chattering, laughing people board the train, filling the space near the doors with energy and noise. They were young, energetic, and their matching jackets and rucksacks hinted at a group event—runners, perhaps. Her chest warmed unexpectedly as she caught the soft lilt of Greek in their conversation.

The familiar tones of the language stirred something deep within her, pulling her into a distant memory. Bree strained to recall the Greek she'd once known, her mind working to piece together fragments of words. Her lips twitched into a small, wistful smile as she read the embroidered logo on one of their rucksacks, translating each letter with care.

Their sudden roar of laughter jolted her back to the present. Bree's breath caught in her throat as a man among them spoke, his voice rising above the din. It wasn't just familiar—it was painfully, intimately familiar.

Her heart clenched. That laugh. That voice.

She looked up sharply, her eyes darting toward the source. The back of a man's head came into view—dark, slightly tousled hair, broad shoulders wrapped in a navy jacket. The train lurched to a halt, sending a ripple through the standing passengers. Bree steadied herself instinctively, but her focus remained locked on him.

The man turned.

Bree gasped audibly, her hand flying to her mouth. Time seemed to stop, her pulse thundering in her ears. The train, the crowd, even Robby's oblivious scrolling—all of it faded into the background.

It was him.

The piercing grey eyes. The unforgettable smile. The subtle tilt of his head that used to drive her wild. The years had added a goatee and perhaps a touch of weariness, but the essence of him was unchanged.

She felt heat flood her face, her body immobilised as if cemented in place. Her heart raced, torn between elation and dread. She watched as he strode to the open doors, his movements easy and confident, the same as they had been when he walked out of her life.

Nik.

113 | Bree

Bree scrambled to her feet, pushing through the jostling crowd to reach the window. Her trembling hands pressed against the cold glass, fingers splayed as if she could bridge the space between them. For the first time in years, she saw him fully—his rich, coppery skin radiant even under the harsh fluorescent light, his broad shoulders moving with that effortless grace she'd once memorised. He hadn't changed, and yet, he had.

He turned, laughing over his shoulder, a light-hearted comment tossed at a friend. Her stomach churned, a storm of emotions surging. He was here, within arm's reach, yet somehow as untouchable as a dream.

And then his eyes found hers.

The noise of the train evaporated. The world fell silent, leaving only the roar of her heart in her ears. For one agonising second, their gazes locked, and, for Bree, the years apart melted away. The man's jaw slackened, the corners of his smile faltered, and a smile flickered across his face. Or was she imagining it, desperate for some sign he remembered what they once had?

The train doors hissed shut.

"No," she whispered, her voice cracking as she pressed harder against the glass. Panic gripped her as if the closing doors were sealing away something irreplaceable.

The man left a hesitant glance lingering in her direction, just before the tube shuddered into motion. The fleeting connection dissolved, leaving only the ache of its absence.

Bree sank back into her seat, her hands trembling. Her breath was shallow, her chest tight, as if the air had been sucked out of the carriage. The phantom warmth of his gaze lingered on her skin, an unbearable reminder of what could never be.

"Nik," she murmured under her breath, a fragile sound tangled in wonder and despair.

Robby glanced up from his phone, frowning. "What?"

She didn't answer. Her thoughts were consumed by the image of Nik's face, by the questions she had buried long ago but now threatened to overwhelm her. Was this chance, fate, or something crueler? The possibilities surged through her, each one more intoxicating—and terrifying—than the last.

114 | Petra

Petra stared out the tiny airplane window as they descended. White sandy beaches and blue coral reefs appeared through the clouds. Landing, she was the most scared she had ever been. Fear filled her as she doubted her decision to travel to Africa alone. She eyed the shed-like arrival hall sitting at the side of the runway. Petra filled in her visa application and arrival forms and followed the other weary travellers through the system.

This was certainly not a climate suited for her clothing. In hopes of crossing, sweating passengers squeezed past each other. She wrapped her jumper around the handle of her case; her t-shirt had stuck to her skin, and her jeans were damp with sweat and hindered her every move. Frustration filled her body as she tried to fill in immigration forms; humidity had puffed up the pages, the paper ripping as she pressed too hard with her pen.

Petra scoured the room, looking for anything resembling an air conditioner. Instead, she spotted one broken fan dangling precariously from the ceiling. After a painful twenty minutes of waiting, she loaded her bag onto one of the few remaining trolleys as soon as it came into sight on the carousel and followed the 'Exit' sign.

Shielding her eyes from the bright glare of the sun, Petra let a smile widen across her face. She walked out into the burning air, strolling the steep pathway towards the waiting drivers. A sea of faces with nameboards tried to catch her eye. She glanced nervously around, feeling panic rising inside as she approached the last of the drivers. She knew she was looking for Mustafa; finally, she saw it: 'Petra-The Wishing Tree.'

She appeared weary as she approached. "Mustafa?" she asked shyly.

His wrinkled and stained trousers hung on his boney hips. He had a scruffy, unloved air about him. His ripped and dirty T-shirt was too big for his thin shape. Although held up with a piece of rope, his long trousers looked new; he jaunted barefoot through the puddles.

Petra was surprised when she inhaled the smell of damp tarmac. "Has it been raining?" she asked, pointing at the puddles on the ground.

"It always rains at Zanzibar airport," he said, pulling his trousers up with his hands as he walked. They pulled out of the airport, and a bump in the road sent her slender body to the roof. Her hand quickly jumped to her head as she screamed in pain.

"Sorry. Welcome to Zanzibar," he said, his dark brown eyes laughing.

Petra didn't appear to be listening as Mustafa talked, pointing out the sights in front of her. It was a far cry from the luxurious holidays and travel she had experienced. She knew that a limo would not make what she was looking at more pleasant—row upon row of buildings, stone or brick walls with tin roofs. Rubbish and unfinished buildings littered the dusty, dirty roads, stretching as far as the eye could see.

Her soul brimmed with joy as she drove further from the airport, surrounded by the striking colours of Africa. Girls and women in flowing dresses—an array of oranges, reds, purples, and greens—were flurrying across the road, seemingly unaware of the oncoming traffic. Searching for a breeze, she opened the car window; the smell of fried fish filled the air.

"No, Close the window." Mustafa shouted just as a truck carrying sand rushed by, pushing a cloud of dusty grains into the car.

Petra looked at her reflection in the window, her hair now white and dusty. Leaning forward, she patted the dust out of her hair.

Mustafa laughed again. "Zanzibar," he said, as if that explained everything.

Petra didn't open the window again; she suffered the heat with as much dignity as possible, wiping sweat from her neck with her sticky wrist. Mustafa pointed out the sights of the city. Private schools and newly painted university buildings stood out prominently among the poverty-stricken structures they surrounded.

The sun glistened on the tops of the slow-moving cars as Mustafa dodged mopeds coming at him from either side. Petra's eyes stopped on the market, where people of all ages were handing over money and receiving brown bags filled with items of their choice from the large mats on the dusty floor in return.

She pressed her face close to the window as they drove slowly past a locked-up, neglected, fun park. The rusty teacup ride and a large wheel with missing seats appeared to be remnants from Europe that Zanzibar had retrieved from the rubbish.

Mustafa found a spot to pull over, pulled out a bottle of water and poured it over the windscreen. He walked back to his seat, resumed his position behind the wheel, and said, "You can open it now," pointing at the window.

The warm breeze drifted onto her face as the air entered, and the light scent of lemongrass and cinnamon wafted into the car. They bumped and dodged down a wide street flanked by mango trees, the sun filtering through lush green leaves on either side of the road. The landscape ahead was rich, luscious, and tropical green; young children were playing by the side of the road. They waved and smiled at the taxi as it quickly passed, scattering a trail of dust in its wake. The stalls by the roadside were smaller, selling bananas and what looked like grilled corn on the cob. Petra's eyes widened in disbelief as an open truck stopped at the side of the road, only to be filled with people before soon setting off again.

Mustafa laughed as he swerved potholes in the cement road. Petra clung hopefully to the thought that this was a small island; surely, the treacherous drive would be over soon. Occasionally, they passed a stray goat, cow, or camel, but apart from that, the road had now cleared.

Finally, the taxi turned off the road without slowing, speeding down a sand track until Mustafa found the brakes, making the last half-mile too long. The coral-and-sand driveway crunched under the wheels. As Mustafa drove cautiously through the gates, Petra realised there was no turning back.

115 | Petra

Petra pulled her bag over her shoulder and stepped onto the ground, looking around her. Weeds surged between the stones, and a cracked window and swinging door creaked in the wind from a wooden hut that didn't entice Petra to want to enter. A boy appeared out of nowhere, collected her bags, and quickly disappeared.

Georgie, the host, walked Petra to the lounge and handed her sweet nectar, passion fruit juice, and mango fruit juice from their land. She spoke with a slight Scottish accent as she welcomed her to the retreat. "You must be tired. I'll show you to your room. Come on," she said, grabbing a bottle of water from the fridge. Petra's mood was a stark contrast to the chilled vibe of the retreat. "You're the first to arrive today; another eleven people are arriving throughout the day. You can do anything you like. The beach is about fifteen minutes away, and we can arrange a taxi to take you there. There are some lovely restaurants you could try; they all have Wi-Fi," Georgie told her.

"Oh, I thought we weren't allowed out of here, and I read we can't use our devices either," Petra said, slightly confused.

Slipping a strand of mousy brown curly hair behind her ear, Georgie let out a little giggle. "This isn't a prison; you're free to leave whenever you like; we know this is a holiday for you, and today is your first day. Tomorrow we'll start with the retreat, and then we suggest you stay away from your devices, but we aren't monsters."

Taking a moment to process the news, Petra spoke in mock relief, "Phew."

"This is about finding yourselves inner happiness and tranquillity, not about being locked in here for a month. If you find inner peace in Netflix, that's your choice." Georgie paused, taking the empty glass from Petra's hand. Petra wasn't sure if she was relieved or disappointed.

Despite her weariness, she wandered the retreat, stopping at the garden and vegetables.

Entering her private room, decorated in a simple African style, she noticed that there were no home comforts apart from mosquito nets around the bed and on the windows. Taking only a few minutes to unpack, she retreated to the welcome shade of the balcony, sinking into the softly cushioned chair with a book. Throughout the day, she heard footsteps and chattering as others, including Georgie, walked past, all of them looking as tired as Petra.

Around seven, Georgie called her from around the corner of the stone wall. Dinner was served. Relieved to finally be able to feed the rumbles coming from her stomach, Petra jumped to her feet and rushed off her balcony.

Petra looked around the table at the twelve strangers. They had no common ground; they ate their food quietly; just the occasional comment about the heat penetrated the silence. Petra squirmed uncomfortably in her seat. She felt an unexpected hush fall over the group. The warm lights that filled the room was dimmed; it was finally time to be able to throw her aching body onto her bed.

Petra woke up feeling refreshed as the sun rose. The ventilator swirled the still, warm air around the room. Beautiful splashes of red turned her white curtains a soft orange. She parted the curtains to admire the rich colours of the landscape that surrounded the building. Surpassing all of her expectations, the sheer magnificence of the place took her breath away. Baobab trees stood as tall as the eyes could see, and a red dirt road weaved its way up to the window.

She dressed quickly in a pair of loose blue shorts and a floaty blue and white top that reached almost her knees and headed to the main house or clubhouse.

Georgie greeted them individually, waiting for the entire group before introducing the staff, the instructors, specialists, and teachers. "We will divide you into four groups for the first week; the plans will change every morning; you can view the daily plan on this notice board." Georgie pointed to a wooden framed corkboard and said, "You have all been matched with a listener; they are psychologists on their year out from studies who you can talk to; you will see here who you're with."

Slapping a mosquito from her arm, Petra studied the intricate Makuti roof, the pastel décor, and the wooden shelves. Colourful orange and blue cushions sat plump and inviting on a stone sofa.

"Each day will start with yoga at 5.30 a.m. Please sign up the evening before if you wish to join."

"This is Tara," Georgie said, placing her hand on the back of a petite, olive-skinned lady from Turkey, "She is the group leader for the daily discussions and group therapy."

Tara introduced the resort staff: "We'll be eating lunch with the staff daily; it helps open your minds to new and other life situations." Silence fell upon the room. "Now it's your turn to introduce yourselves; one by one, tell us about your journey that brought you here."

Listening to her peers, Petra couldn't help feeling chilled and moved by their words. Feeling more nervous, she worried about what she would say. Should she start with, "Hello, my name is Petra, and I'm a man-o-holic?" She listened to tragic stories of loss and survival from others. Feeling shallow and like an alien spirit among them, she decided to tell a different story. She quickly forced the muscles in her face to maintain a smile, travelled back in time a few years, and recounted the story of Rico and the police and how it transformed her life. She hadn't talked about what had happened back then for a long time, preferring to bury it as a terrible experience.

When story time was over, Petra felt her muscles relax and her smile return. She hoped she didn't sound too pathetic and was relieved to see the others listening to her with interest and flashing their understanding looks.

Petra's first morning was spent in the garden; they planted vegetables, peppers, and tomatoes. She collected some broccoli and carrots that a previous group had grown. She felt her pale skin burning and was glad for the sun hat they had provided; a wide-brimmed straw hat with a purple ribbon kept the burning sun off her face.

Before lunch, Petra and her group were taken to the kitchen and given tasks to carry out to prepare food for everyone. There were twelve participants to feed, plus ten staff. Petra noticed that most of the staff she met had simple, almost English names that were easy to remember. She was paired with a local girl, Serena, who taught her how they prepared food in Zanzibar as she went along.

She spoke enough English for her job, explaining the use of the different spices in the broth they were preparing today.

"Do you all have English-sounding names?" Petra asked.

"No, my real name is Awoka, but we chose names that are easy to remember if we work in tourism."

The late afternoon was for meditation and contemplation. Having never meditated, she forced herself to gaze across the dense forest, holding in the embarrassed giggles. Feeling powerless to give in to her thoughts, there was a moment of silence before she burst out laughing. By the end of the day, Petra was mentally exhausted.

The group chatted for a while before turning in early that evening. While lying in bed, Petra heard the rhythmic pounding of feet in the distance, along with some quiet musical sounds that seemed mystically to be coming from the other direction.

116 | Bree

Bree fell back in her seat, her head resting on the glass, her heart racing. Robby's voice shattered her thoughts; she turned around and stared at him with a cold, unwelcoming smile. Had she just seen Nik?

With sweating hands, she gripped the handrail as the tube reached their station. A few minutes later, she tried to memorise the writing in Greek and English from the rucksack.

As they emerged from the tube station, Bree paused, her focus fixed on the towering buildings around her. The neon lights flickered like restless fireflies, and the bass-heavy thrum of music seeped into her senses. For a moment, the city overwhelmed her, its relentless energy clashing with her exhaustion. She rubbed her temples, trying to focus, but the memory of those piercing grey eyes lingered like a ghost.

Fatigue pressing down on her, Bree skipped any pretense of unwinding and went straight to bed. She scribbled scattered notes into her journal, each word an attempt to tether herself to reality. The letters she'd once read replayed in her mind, disjointed fragments stirring unease. Sleep remained elusive. She stared at the cracked ceiling, tracing its uneven lines over and over, her thoughts a tangled web of doubt. Had it really been Nik she'd seen? Or was her mind cruelly conjuring images of the man who had once been her world?

By the time the first pale light of morning crept through the window, Bree realised the night had slipped away entirely. The city was waking, its noise gradually building outside. As Robby stirred, she pushed herself out of bed, flipping open the Venetian blinds to let the morning in. She pulled on her jeans and sweatshirt in hurried motions, tossed a raincoat and umbrella into her bag, and headed for the door.

"I've got to call Carla; I'll see you downstairs," she called over her shoulder as she left.

The crisp morning air hit her like a balm. Bree inhaled deeply, her breath visible in the cool dawn. Her fingers trembled slightly as she dialled Carla's number.

"Carla, oh my god, I think I saw Nik on the tube," she blurted, her voice breathless with excitement and disbelief.

"What? Are you sure?" Carla's confusion mingled with concern.

"I think so. I mean, it looked and sounded like him," Bree replied, her words tumbling over each other. "But it was only for a second. Then the tube pulled away."

"Did he see you? Did he recognise you?" Carla's voice sharpened with curiosity.

Bree pondered for a moment. "I think he smiled at me, but he could've been smiling at his reflection. It was dark. He could still be vain—or just amused by some random stranger on the tube."

"What are you going to do?" Carla asked, her tone urgent.

"I don't know... Look for him, maybe. Oh, shit, Robby's here. I have to go," Bree said abruptly, glancing at her approaching companion.

"Good luck. Let me know what happens," Carla pleaded before the call ended.

Bree slid her phone into her pocket as Robby joined her. Together, they stepped out into the bustling streets, the city already alive with movement. Bree watched him as they walked. His disinterest in her mirrored her own feelings toward him—a quiet, unspoken indifference that neither seemed inclined to address.

They'd planned their morning carefully, setting off early to avoid the crowds. Their steps were brisk, purposeful, pausing only for a quick stop at Starbucks where a muffin and cappuccino served as a quick breakfast. The air carried the buzz of something exciting as they approached Blackfriars station, weaving through the throng of runners and spectators.

At the twenty-four-mile marker, Robby's friends were already waiting. Perched on a low wall overlooking the course, they waved as Bree and Robby approached. The streets around them buzzed with energy, a kaleidoscope of colours and movement. Bree's thoughts, however, remained elsewhere—on piercing grey eyes, fleeting smiles, and the haunting possibility that Nik was not a phantom of her imagination but a part of her reality once again.

Bree scoffed as Robby rummaged through their food supplies, crumbs spilling from the bread roll he chewed with unapologetic gusto. He slurped loudly from a beer can, oblivious to her growing irritation. Turning her focus to the crowd, Bree scanned the sea of faces and colourful outfits, her eyes darting with one purpose only. She searched for the orange and blue logo of the Thessaloniki running club, hoping their marathon tops matched the team colours she had seen online. The odds were slim, but she had resolved to spend the day watching for any sign of them.

Robby and his friends were immersed in casual conversation, passing time as they awaited the arrival of the first runners. Bree's mind, however, wandered down paths of uncertainty. What if Nik wasn't running at all? Perhaps he was here only to support his team—possibly with his wife at his side. The thought hit her like a gut punch. Fear and jealousy mingled, twisting her stomach. But last night, there had been no women in sight, just his male companions. Regret flashed through her as she wished she'd had the presence of mind to check his ring finger in that fleeting moment.

The electrifying atmosphere of the marathon rose around her, with cheers erupting as runners began to pass. Bree stared into the endless stream of faces. With forty thousand participants and countless spectators, how would she ever find him?

She felt detached from the scene, her fixation on Nik eclipsing the event. Robby didn't notice her growing withdrawal, nor did he seem to care. Bree felt ridiculous—caught between the desperation of a love-sick teenager and the self-awareness of a woman who feared she might seem unhinged.

She sat back against the cushion, a wave of loss washing over her as exhaustion took hold. Six hours of waiting had brought her nothing but disappointment. Her eyes ached from scanning the crowd, but still, she searched for blue and orange.

And then, there they were—a cluster of tops in the colours she'd been seeking. Her pulse quickened. She couldn't make out the logos clearly, but she was sure it was the team. Her heart leapt as she thought she saw Nik among them, but in the daylight, he looked different. Uncertainty crept in, and within seconds, he was gone.

A sinking feeling settled over her. How foolish had she been to believe she'd find him at the London Marathon—or even on a tube?

Disheartened, she tried to rejoin the conversation around her, cheering and clapping for the runners. When Robby's sister finally passed, she feigned enthusiasm, though her energy was waning.

The relentless noise and crowd wore her down. Excusing herself, she promised to reconnect with the group later and began weaving through the throng, her eyes still darting, scanning.

And then she froze. Her heart skipped a beat. There he was. This time, she was certain—it was Nik. His face was flushed, glistening with sweat, his movements laboured but determined. He ran with a small group, his focus locked ahead. Bree tried to call his name, but her voice drowned in the bellowing cheers of the crowd. Before she could push forward, he disappeared again, swallowed by the sea of runners.

Her stomach flipped, the exhaustion that had gripped her now replaced with adrenaline. She stood rooted to the spot, her breath shallow, until the tide of the crowd jostled her into motion. Disorientated, she looked for a quieter street, leaning against a wall to steady herself. Her mind whirled with fragmented thoughts as she pulled out her phone, using Google Maps to guide her back to the hotel.

As she walked, Bree caught sight of a row of empty shuttle buses. One stood out—its sides emblazoned with the colours she'd been seeking. The sign on the front read: Shuttle Bus—Running Groups. Heart pounding, she approached, squinting to make out the list of running groups painted on the side. Her breath hitched. One of the names matched the logo from his rucksack. Snapping a photo, she caught the bus's destination: Shawcross Hotel.

Fire ignited in her chest. Dizzy and overwhelmed, she rushed back to her hotel. There, she indulged in the soothing rituals of a hot shower, clean clothes, and much-needed nourishment.

Now, perched on the edge of the bed with a towel wrapped around her still-damp body, Bree wrestled with her next move. Should she go to Shawcross

Hotel and look for Nik? Or should she leave it to fate? If he had seen her, wouldn't he look for her?

Her mind spun with possibilities, each more tantalising—and terrifying—than the last.

Perhaps Nik had forgotten her. Maybe she had been just one of many women who'd crossed his path over the years. The thought gnawed at Bree as she picked up her charging phone, her fingers hesitating before opening Facebook. She typed his name into the search bar but came up empty. Frustrated, she tossed the phone aside and tried to refocus. Bree dressed quickly, applying a touch of makeup and brushing out her still-damp hair. She slipped into her skinny jeans and the one nice top she'd planned to wear to dinner that evening with Robby's sister.

Restless, she Googled the hotel where Nik was supposedly staying. It wasn't far. Sitting still felt impossible, so she set off, the voice on her navigation app guiding her through the bustling streets of London.

With every step, a sense of foreboding crept over her. What would she say to him? After all these years, what did they even have to talk about?

Twenty minutes later, Bree stood outside the hotel, its tall, white walls gleaming in the afternoon sunlight. The reflection from the building opposite almost blinded her as she dithered at the entrance. Her stomach churned, but before she could overthink it, she forced herself to step inside.

To her right, a sleek hotel bar caught her eye, its black marble floors and dark wooden counters polished to perfection. Platters of sandwiches and snacks sat neatly arranged on the bar. Bree approached the reception desk, her nerves tangling as she waited for the receptionist.

"Hello," she began, her voice steadier than she expected. "I'm supposed to meet a friend—he's running the marathon. Can I check if I'm in the right place? His name is Nik Daskalakis, and he's with the Thessaloniki Runners."

The receptionist typed swiftly before glancing up. "Yes, you're in the right place. However, they aren't here now."

"That's no problem," Bree replied, forcing a polite smile. "I'll grab a coffee. I just wanted to make sure I had the right hotel." She turned away, her heart racing.

Settling into a seat with a clear view of the reception area, Bree ordered a juice and a bite-sized sandwich. She perched nervously on the edge of her chair, her mind a whirlwind of second-guessing. What was she doing here? Picking up her phone, she answered Carla's call with a heavy sigh.

"So? Any updates?" Carla's impatience was palpable.

"No. Well... I'm pretty sure I saw Nik again at the marathon. And now—well, I'm at his hotel waiting to see if it really is him." Bree's words tumbled out in a rush.

"What? Oh, my god. Bree."

Bree explained how she'd found the hotel, then added, "But I think I'm going to leave. I feel like a love-struck teenager. What am I even doing here? He might not even remember me."

"If what you've told me about your time together is true," Carla countered, "he hasn't forgotten you. Stay. You'll regret it if you don't."

"But he lives in Thessaloniki," Bree reasoned. "Maybe I can wait until we go there. I could find him then."

"Oh, Bree," Carla teased, "you're a regular detective, aren't you?"

"Carla, I don't know what to do. I feel paralysed—like I can't make a rational, adult decision."

"You're there now," Carla urged. "Your only other option is to leave a note at reception with your number. But if this guy really is the love of your life, do you want to risk him never getting that message?"

Bree sighed heavily. "No, I guess not."

"Go outside. Get some fresh air, but don't leave that hotel. Stay there," Carla insisted.

Pushing her chair back, Bree grabbed her bag and headed for the exit. She stood for a moment, watching the bustle of the street, when a shuttle bus pulled up. Her breath caught as a wave of blue and orange tops spilled out of the bus, runners chattering and laughing.

"Carla, I've got to go," Bree stammered into the phone. "I think Nik is in front of me."

Ending the call, Bree froze. She spotted him immediately, his figure unmistakable. Nik tugged a rucksack onto his shoulder, his face leaner than she remembered, his goatee a surprising addition. His damp hair clung to his forehead, and he moved with the weary pace of someone who had given everything to the race.

The group of runners climbed the hotel steps, their voices lively as they exchanged words of congratulations. "See you later," Nik said to his friends, his voice carrying through the air. "Well done, guys. I'm taking the first shower."

As he used the last bit of energy he had to climb the steps, his eyes drifted upward—and locked onto Bree's. Recognition sparked on his face as he muttered, "Breezy?"

117 | Bree

Nik's forehead wrinkled in surprise; his jaws slackened as he stopped moving. Regaining his composure, he raced towards her with a smile filled with recognition and warmth. Taking a moment to drink her in, he flung open his arms in greeting.

Bree stepped into his embrace, leaning into his body and melting in his arms. The warm breath on her neck sent shivers up and down her spine.

Slowly, he pulled back, grabbing her hand; he guided her inside. Running a finger over her cheek, he finally spoke.

"Breezy, my Breezy, what are you doing here?" He stepped away from the group, taking her hand, feeling a surge of confidence rip through him. He pulled her close to him and kissed her on the lips.

"Sorry, I'm not sure if you wanted me to do that," he said quietly.

Bree smiled and leant in to kiss him, tingling more with every touch.

"Breezy, I can hardly stand. Let's sit down," he said. Keeping a firm grip on her hand, he led her to a soft, black leather sofa. "I knew it was you on the tube; I didn't sleep thinking about how I would find you."

"What about your wife? Is she here?" She asked, a feeling of dread coursing through her veins as she waited for his reply. She didn't want to ruin the moment, but she had to know.

He leant forward; his eyes narrowed in confusion. "My wife? I'm divorced. I wasn't married for long."

Bree smiled and touched his arm as he placed his hand on her knee. "Me too," she said, her eyes drinking into his beautiful face.

"When I saw you on the tube, I knew it was you. I tried to find you on Facebook last night, but you weren't there. You used to be there." Nik swallowed as his eyes admired her face. "I watched you a lot over the years, and then you disappeared. I told my friends that I would be scouring the streets of London today and tomorrow looking for you. They think I'm bonkers."

Bree explained how she had found him and said, "I wasn't sure if I should come or just leave the past alone."

"I had none of those doubts. I have thought about you all the time—eight years of thinking about you—and when I saw you, I knew we had to meet again," Nik said.

Bree held his face in her hands, placing a soft, gentle kiss on his parted lips. Her phone beeped, and the smile disappeared from her face. She'd forgotten about Robby; she wanted to ignore him but knew she had to reply, so she said, "I'm sorry, I have to read this message," she told Nik. The message read, 'Found sis, going to have food. Call me when you wake up, and we can meet; if not, see you at the hotel tonight.' Bree responded with a thumbs up, and that was it. Her attention turned back to Nik.

"Boyfriend?" he asked, barely audible; his face dropped suddenly.

"Yes, boyfriend, but a long, complicated, and almost over story," she said as his heart sank. Bree watched the flicker in his eye quickly fade and a sad look grew across his face.

"Of course, you have a boyfriend; why wouldn't you have one?"

"Nik. You don't have to worry about him; I'm going to break up with him as soon as we get back to Italy. It was already a done deal."

Far too slowly, his panic subsided. "I don't have a girlfriend; I prefer running." He paused, scared of her answer to his next question and asked, "Do you need to leave? Is he waiting for you?"

"No, don't worry about him. I'll go to the hotel later; he's with his sister now; he doesn't care where I am," she said, wanting to change the subject as quickly as possible.

"Bree, I need a shower; I smell so bad. Can you wait here while I take a shower? I'm sharing a room with friends, so you best wait down here."

"Sure," Bree replied.

Nik held her face in his hands and said, "Please don't leave."

Bree nodded. "I'll be over there." She pointed to a stone fire pit.

Nik reluctantly slid out of the room. Bree felt her heartbeat return to normal as she sat alone, nursing a cup of hot coffee.

A tall black man with a broad smile and a curious glint strode confidently across the room and stopped at her chair. "Hey, are you Bree by any chance?" he asked. His soft voice surprised her, his accent impossible to place, and his eyes soulful and full of life.

Placing her cup down, she smiled at him and said, "Yes, guilty."

"I'm Zac; Nik asked me to keep you company until he returns. I hope that's okay with you. I think he's scared that you'll leave."

Bree blew the steam away from the coffee as the muscled stranger slumped into his chair across from her, signalling for the waiter to bring him a drink. "Zac? Oh my God, I can't believe I finally get to meet you. All of Nik's favourite stories were always about you." Bree tried to make small talk about the marathon as Zac interrupted her with questions about herself.

"I've been hearing about you for years; you've got to give me something to report back." He rubbed his shoulder muscles before leaning forward, placing both hands on the table.

Bree threw her head back in laughter. "Okay, ask away," she said, laughing once more at his cheeky expression. "No wedding ring; that's good. Kids?"

"No. No kids," she confirmed.

"Job?" he asked with a curious twinkle.

"I have a copy of my C.V. on my phone if you want it." She crossed her ankles in front of her, leaning forward, resting her elbows on the table.

"No, I don't need the C.V., but thanks," he said, nodding at the waiter and placing his juice in his hands.

"Where do you live?"

"Italy," she replied.

Bree leant closer to him, amusing him with a chuckle of good humour. "Is this a two-way interview? Am I allowed to ask questions?"

"Sure, but Nik already knows about me. I'm under strict orders to find out as much as I can about you before he gets back." he smirked.

"Ah, that makes sense," Bree said, unable to contain her smile. "I have lots of things I want to know about him, too. Are you allowed to defect and come over to my side?"

"With that smile? I'd have problems resisting."

"Does he have a girlfriend? He says he doesn't, but somehow I doubt that."

"Nothing he can't sort out with one phone call; nothing serious." Zac laughed as Nik bounded into the room.

"See, she didn't leave," Zac said, turning to Nik as he strode across the bar, making his way to them.

"Thank God," he replied, placing a gentle hand on Bree's shoulder.

"I didn't find out much; she is a tough cookie," Zac said.

Nik pulled up a leather armchair, placed it close to Bree, reached out for her hand, and knitted his fingers around hers. As the three of them chatted easily, Bree heard the sound of footsteps near them. Nik nodded a distracted greeting as Bree turned around. A group of freshly showered runners hovered around them.

"Come on, we're hungry," one said.

"Okay, we are all here; let's go," Zac said.

Nik glanced at the clock and leant into Bree, whispering slowly, "Breezy, please, I want them to meet you, and I have to go with them; we have been planning this for so long; please, come with me."

"I don't know, Nik; maybe you should go without me." Placing her hands on her lap, she focused on the group heading towards the door. She wanted more than anything to be with him, but not like this. Not in a crowd.

"I would rather be here with you alone, but we can leave as soon as we have eaten," he whispered.

Understanding he wouldn't take no for an answer, Bree nodded as she felt his hand slip into hers as he pulled her to her feet. They followed behind, lost in their own company, as the others enthusiastically talked about their day and fantasised about food.

As they entered the nearby restaurant, Nik made arrangements to add another seat to the long table. Nervously sitting between Nik and Zac, she remembered almost nothing of her basic Greek. She did, however, remember how Nik made her feel safe, loved, and special. At the table, she fiddled nervously as the others eyed her suspiciously. She shifted in her chair, noticing their curious looks; she wanted to stand up and shout, "It's okay, I know him; I'm not just a girl he picked up; we were in love. We were supposed to marry." Instead, she sat quietly, feeling Nik's eyes on hers. He placed his comforting hand on her knee and stroked her thigh.

Once the food was ordered, Bree turned as she heard a thudding noise around her. Nik rose to his feet, pushed his chair back and looked at the group, ready to step into the spotlight. Bree looked at him; his posture was straight, and he was bold and assertive.

"No, you still do your speeches?" she asked, the others laughing.

"Yes," one of the men said. "It isn't considered a real evening if he doesn't say something to us all."

"Shut up, all of you," Nik said, smiling. "First of all, well done to every one of you, especially you, Desi; you beat us all." Although he spoke in English, they all understood him.

"Now, the main event of the evening: this beautiful creature by my side. I'm sorry for not introducing you all to her, but well, I didn't want you stealing her from me, especially you, Desi." His voice was scornful. The group laughed as Desi waved his hands in the air.

Desi, a tall, lean man with a shaved head and a wide, cheeky grin, lapped up the attention. "Oh, you've slept with the whole of Greece, and now you're working your way through London? God, Nik, give it a break." Desi teased.

"You collect women like I collect fridge magnets," another person called out.

Nik flashed Desi a threatening look in jest and said, "This is Bree." The sound of her name on his tongue made his eyes smile.

"The one that got away." shouted Zac as the group exchanged glances. The room began to grow quiet.

Nik let the silence hang. "Yes, that one. The only girl I have ever loved; the only girl I ever wanted to marry," he said with unshakable conviction. He paused for effect. "Yes, we all know I was married, but well, you know how that went."

They all cheered as Nik beamed with joy and waited for them to calm down. "Go, Nik." Desi shouted.

"As you know, I thought I spotted her on the tube last night, and well, I did; here she is. Bree Morgan, although, who knows, you may know her one day as Bree Daskalakis; she almost was a few years ago," he said cheekily, looking at Bree and leaning in to kiss her. He gripped her hand tightly. Bree's face turned crimson. She looked down at the floor, shaking her head and laughing at their bemused yet amused faces.

"Too difficult to pronounce. Have any of you got an easier name?" Bree laughed, feeling comfortable in this group.

Dasi raised his hand in jest and said, "I'll change my name to whatever you want if you marry me."

"Well, from what little I've seen so far, I'll need to speak to at least three of your ex-girlfriends and check your references before I'll even contemplate going on a date with you," she teased Desi with a smile.

Waiting for the group to calm down, Nik sipped his drink, and Bree smiled serenely. "Bree, some of you know about her; some of you I've only met recently don't. This girl is the one who ruined me for all the others," he said, holding his hands out wide.

"Are you the naked, white-shirt one?" Desi asked, "The one who flashed the mum?"

"Don't forget I flashed the Aunty too," she said, grinning, mimicking the opening of a shirt on her chest. "Let's say I was hardly ready for a formal introduction."

The group laughed. "So, please be kind, speak English, and, Desi, hands off." A mischievous grin spread across Nik's face and he took his seat.

Zac stood up and said, "Everyone, well done; you did it. You survived the London Marathon. Bree, welcome; it's nice to meet you finally."

The group raised their glasses, and the sound of clinking filled the room. Zac set down his glass and wiped his forehead. They chatted excitedly, cheering and applauding throughout the evening. In their black shirts and white ties, the servers scurried around them, filling their plates with pasta and topping their glasses with wine. Feeling Nik beside her once more, her built-up anger and resentment washed away. By the end of the evening, she knew she never wanted this weekend to end or to leave his side.

Tipping generously and waving to others, they walked out into the chilly London air. Feeling excitement streaming through his veins, Nik wrapped his arms around her waist, guiding her in the vague direction of her hotel. The pale moon broke through the trees as they stopped around the corner from the restaurant. Finding a bench, they sat.

"I hope that wasn't too much for you," he said, stroking her face gently.

"No, they are all lovely; I used to love that about you—your love for your friends," Bree said. Bree extended her legs and placed them over his knees, her arms wrapping around his shoulders. She kissed him gently on the cheek.

"And I loved how much you fitted in with them all, just like tonight," he said. As they walked towards Bree's hotel, they chatted and laughed about old times, catching up on each other's lives.

"I hate the thought that you have to go back to him, what's his name, Bobby," Nik said, looking at the hotel entrance, his voice slightly shaking.

"Robby. Don't worry, I'll stay away from him; he is probably drunk or asleep already." She pointed up at her window on the second floor. "The light is off; look."

"So, tomorrow, 7 a.m." Nik asked for confirmation of their plans.

"Yes, I'll be there, outside your hotel." She pulled out her phone, they swapped numbers, exchanging one final longing kiss.

"See you tomorrow, then."

118 | Bree

That night, sleep washed over Bree easily. She heard Robby staggering in the corridor, fumbling for his key. She turned over and closed her eyes once more. At the first glimmer of daylight, Bree selected some items from her case, slipping a black woollen jumper over her head and pulling up her dark blue figure-hugging jeans. Glancing at Robby sprawled on the bed, she eyed him dismissively and closed the door slowly behind her. She walked down an empty hallway, peered around the corner, and exited the hotel.

The grey morning sun cast a strange light over the streets as Bree retraced her steps briskly to Nik's hotel. Wandering, alone with her thoughts and concentrating on the morning ahead, she greeted passersby, each with a warm smile and a friendly 'Good morning.'

Nik's chest expanded as he saw her approach, marvelling at the changes in her. She had left him a girl; now, a confident, strong woman walked towards him. He studied her face; her complexion was still perfect, her hair shorter, but she smelled the same. The same vanilla scent he loved so much hung in her hair. She'd acquired some fine lines around her mouth and eyes, but the same dancing, joyful eyes had remained unchanged.

He lifted his body from the cold, stone steps and wrapped his arms around her. Their kiss, a lingering, meaningful meeting of souls, blackened out the environment. Her lips felt only his; his hand gently embraced her cheek as the pair looked into each other's eyes and smiled.

"Oh my god. Your goatee, you shaved it off," she said, stroking his chin fondly.

"Yeah, I never liked it, and I remember you hated it last time I grew one." He smiled as he rubbed his chin. "There is a coffee shop down the road," he said, leading her away. She felt the warm air on her neck as they entered the brightly lit cafe, and she felt the comfort of Nik's hand on her back.

"Okay, let's talk," Nik said.

"The idea of never kissing or holding you was too much, so I tried to move on; it just took me a long time." Every few seconds, he paused to look at her or to kiss her. "The day you phoned saying you may be returning to Greece should have been a great day, but I messed it up. I shouldn't have told you my parents had found me a girlfriend; I didn't intend to marry her," he said, watching Bree's eyes fill with tears.

"But you did," she said, unsure where the conversation was going.

"I should have just laughed it off; I made you think it was a sure thing."

"Wasn't it?" she asked.

"Well, no. I intended to tell them I wouldn't go through with it, but when you hung up, I was so angry with you," he said, gripping Bree's hand.

"Sorry," she muttered, her eyes dropping to the floor.

"So, I agreed to marry her. Then, as my anger subsided, I saw what I had done and vowed to make it right again one day. Marrying her was a mistake," Nik said. He took both of her hands and continued speaking. "The day that ring arrived, I had a breakdown. I realised what I had done—that I'd ruined it forever. Bree, I'm so sorry. I wrote to you for almost a year."

"I moved," she replied with a shaky voice. "I did get a few letters, but I was too angry to read them, and then I moved to another area, and I didn't get any others."

He sounded happy even though he was talking about sad events: "My father died shortly after the wedding, and my mother three months later. The children Thea wanted never arrived, then the fights started, and the marriage fell apart."

"Oh, Nik, I'm so sorry," Bree said.

"Thea, my wife, well, ex-wife, knew I didn't love her as I should; you always were a threat to her; she always tried to compete, then one day she met someone else," he smiled. "That was the day I was set free from that horrible marriage, and I vowed never to marry again," he explained as he moved along the sofa to make room for another customer who needed a seat.

Bree grabbed her cup, taking a large gulp. She realised it was her time to speak. "I saw on Facebook that you got married; it was the day my ex-husband proposed that I checked you out. I didn't want to marry him, but then I saw your wedding photo; perhaps I did it out of spite or because I was so hurt that you moved on so quickly, and I just went with the flow," she said.

"What a mess we made of all of this," he said, wincing as the patron sitting beside him on the sofa elbowed him in the back. "I moved to Thessaloniki; Anna got me a job at the agency; I went there because I knew that was the place you had mentioned, but I couldn't find you," Nik explained.

"I didn't go; I didn't want to be in Greece without you. There were too many memories," she said. "Although I'm due to go there on holiday with a friend in a few weeks, who knows, maybe we would have met there," she said with a smile.

"Maybe it means it's our time once again; you know, fate has a way of working its magic." He bought his face closer to kiss her again. "I sold my dad's land and the house. Now Zac and I have a tour agency; we bought out Anna's company when she was sick, so I'm just a male version of Anna now, buried in an office all day and running way too much."

Bree exhaled a breath of relief and took a bite out of her muffin. She then filled him in on her life, including the weddings, photography, business, and Robby.

"What now?" Nik asked, his face serious. The question carried a weight that stilled the air between them. He glanced at his watch—9:45 a.m. Time felt like sand slipping through his fingers, each grain emphasizing how little they had left. A sense of urgency laced their small talk, his gaze fixed on her unreadable eyes.

"I don't know. What do you want to happen?" Bree asked, her voice trembling despite her effort to appear composed. The thought of this being just a fleeting reunion, a quick coffee with an old flame who would soon disappear from her life, made her chest tighten.

"I want to be with you," he said firmly, his words cutting through the din of her uncertainty. His dark eyes softened as they searched hers. "That is for sure. And you?"

Relief washed over her like a warm wave, and her lips curved into an uncontrollable smile. She hadn't expected him to say it, not so plainly, not so soon. "I know I want to be with you, too," she admitted, her voice light with disbelief. Then, more resolutely, she added, "So, if that's what you want, we'll work something out."

Nik's face lit up with a rare, boyish grin. "I'm free now until March. I could come to you in Italy, or you could come to me in Greece," he offered.

Bree's heart thudded at the possibilities. "I'm free now, too. I have to go to the office most days, but I don't have any weddings until March," she said, hesitating slightly. She knew there was much more to explain about her life in Italy, but now didn't feel like the time.

Nik let his voice drop to a whisper and said, "We'll figure it out. I just needed to know you want to see me again. I can't say goodbye today thinking it's the end." He rested his forehead gently against hers, the warmth of the gesture melting away her lingering doubts.

"I feel the same," Bree murmured, her voice catching with emotion. "Nik, I've missed you so much."

The moment hung between them, delicate and unspoken promises forming in the space they shared.

Finally, Bree broke the spell with a reluctant, "Shall we go?" Glancing at her watch, she sighed, and together they rose and walked toward the door.

"This isn't goodbye," Bree said firmly, wrapping her scarf around her neck. Her voice carried a mixture of determination and fragility.

"No, it's a 'see you soon,'" Nik replied. He pulled her into a final embrace before letting her go. "I'll walk you back."

Hand in hand, they stepped into the bustling streets, oblivious to the buzz of the city around them. They slowed as they reached her hotel, her saddened gaze lingering on its facade.

"Text me from the airport," Nik said, his voice thick with reluctance as he released her hand.

"You too," she replied. "You'll land in Greece as I leave here. Whoever lands first texts, okay?"

"Okay." Nik nodded, and for a moment, they stood there, unwilling to part. Bree wrapped her arms around his neck, her breath warm against his ear as she whispered, "See you soon," before kissing him softly.

Nik smiled, but then pulled back with a teasing glint in his eye. "Bree, not in broad daylight. Robby might see."

She laughed, her voice light and carefree for the first time that morning. "I'm breaking up with him in six hours. I really don't care."

RAW MISTAKES

He watched her run into the hotel, his chest tight with a mix of elation and longing. Bree entered her room with a pang of guilt, only to find Robby still snoring, tangled in the sheets. Relief mingled with frustration—had she been robbed of precious minutes she could have spent with Nik?

As the shower ran, she sat silently, scrolling through the photos she and Nik had taken earlier. Each one was a snapshot of joy and possibility, giving her some hope of what might come next.

119 | Bree

The chilly winter morning passed quickly; Robby's sister entertained the small group with her plans for the next marathon. Bree's eyes darted around her, hoping to catch one more glimpse of Nik in the city or airport. She checked the flight board, and dismay crossed her face as she noticed Nik's flight had left on time, so there was no way they would bump into each other and have a few final moments together.

With relief that this was the last time she would have to spend time with Robby, Bree grinned as the plane lifted away from the runway. She'd left Robby to sit with his sister on the plane, and she took her seat alone towards the front. Leaning on the window, she listened to music and closed her eyes, smiling. Not even the journey with Robby and the impending breakup could spoil her good mood.

It was time to break something that was already broken. After saying goodbye to Elena, Bree grasped her only moment; standing tall with her hands in her pockets, she aired her thoughts. "Robby, look, I think we need some space from each other."

He looked at her, shocked but unbothered. "Okay, that's a good idea, if that's what you want," he said, his face void of emotion.

"Yep, we aren't good together anymore," Bree said confidently.

"We could be better," he said, then shrugged. He knew it was over; he didn't even want to get into a discussion. "I was going to break up with you by text sometime."

"Okay, then we both agree." Bree said. They stared at each other for a moment, then they kissed goodbye quickly on the cheeks.

"See you in the summer then," he said. They both turned and walked to their cars, like two friends with no history, and neither looked back.

Bree took a deep breath of fresh air, letting it out slowly as she laughed at how easy the breakup had gone. Once again, pulling her collar up, she tightened her scarf, shoved her hands deep into her pockets and turned her face away from the biting wind.

She sat in her cold car as the engine warmed. Unwrapping her scarf, she looked around. One of Robby's jackets was on the backseat, a can of Red Bull sticking out of his pocket; she threw Petra's empty water bottles on the back seat, connected her iPhone to the car stereo and let out a loud sigh of relief as a cheeky grin appeared.

Grabbing her phone, Bree smiled as she texted. 'Landed in Italy, two-hour drive home now; I told Robby it's over; I'll text you when I get home," She before sending it, resisting the urge to write 'Love you,' at the end of the message.

As she turned to the rearview mirror, she glanced at her reflection, unable to hide her smile. She jumped as her phone beeped with a message from Nik: 'Wonderful, Text me when you get there. I love you.' She shivered in delight at his words and turned onto the main road. Bree drove home feeling free, remembering the weekend events, the warmth of his embrace, and the hope in his eyes.

Occasionally, Bree flushed with fear. The last time she'd felt this happy with Nik—this open to his love, this hopeful—he'd found a wife just a few months later. She didn't want to fall into the same trap again. Bree decided to keep her feet firmly on the ground. Her pride would not let her do it again; she would rather brave loneliness than survive heartbreak with Nik.

120 | Bree

Bree hadn't told Nina about the events of the weekend, but she was excited to get it all off her chest. She had meant to text Carla; she had not texted her since she set eyes on Nik in the hotel.

She waited impatiently for Carla and Nina to arrive for drinks. Nina arrived first with a defeated expression on her face. "Nina, how are things with you?" Bree asked.

"Well, I haven't seen Manuel since I told him to leave. Nina said, "He's vanished; I don't know where he is, likely with Stefano."

Bree was hesitant to share her story; she tried to play down the magnitude of the event in London and waited for Carla to arrive before she did so, starting with, "Nina, I'm so sorry; I know you probably don't need to hear all of this."

"Oh, Bree, don't be silly; the good news is what we need right now; carry on."

Bree beamed as she told them the whole story, from the beginning, the first time she laid eyes on him in the tube: "I want to go and see him, but I'm scared he will say no, and then I'll be heartbroken all over again."

The girls seemed amused; Bree had left Italy with a loser of a boyfriend and come back with the love of her life. "If you don't ask, then you will never know," Carla said. Do it; ask him. You have no weddings; we'll do the emails."

"Okay, if it all goes tits up, it's on you two," she said, wagging her finger at the two friends as she stood up. Picking up her phone, Bree walked outside. After a couple of minutes, Bree pushed the door open, bursting with excitement and taking a deep breath.

"Okay, so I asked him about going over there, and he said no." She said with a blank expression before letting a smile wipe over her face and saying, "Because he is going to come here instead. He has already looked at flights; he wants to see where I live and where I work. He wants to see my world."

"When?" asked Nina as her hand flew up to her mouth in disbelief.

"He's going to book flights now, but he wants to come on Friday, which is in three days; oh my god, in three days."

"For how long?" Nina asked, taken aback by the speed at which this was all moving.

"He'll book one way, for now, and go back when he feels like it," Bree replied, shifting excitedly in her seat.

"How do you feel about that? I mean, about not knowing when he will be returning and having him here all the time; you aren't used to that," Carla said.

"I hope he never leaves, so I don't mind him coming indefinitely, and if he loves me, he will love my life and will fit in here, so I'm feeling good—great in fact; I can't wait to see him." She paused, looking at the calendar, marking a red N on the empty white box.

"And without the Robby curve ball, too," Carla said.

"Yes, exactly. And you, my fabulous friends, my two annoying, stubborn, ball-breaking rocks, will be the first to meet him. Be kind, be gentle on him," she said, looking at them with a playful scowl.

"Yeah, we meet him first." Carla high-fived Nina with a grin.

"Do not give him the inquisition when he arrives, ok? Don't tell him about my bad luck with men, please; leave me with some dignity," she laughed.

121 | Nina

Nina lived in shock for a few days before finally agreeing to talk to Manuel again. She hadn't been able to forget the words her father had said before they married; he'd known something was up, and she'd ignored him.

"Want to talk?" she texted Manuel.

"Yes, when?' he asked.

"Now, I'm at home," replied Nina. She made her way to the mirror. She looked at herself; she looked lousy, not that he would notice.

Once he'd taken off his jacket and taken a seat, Nina found the courage to talk. "Okay, what do you have to say?" she asked. "I don't care about your lies about the ticket, the flight, or whatever; the only thing I care about is you, well, you and Stefano, and what the hell that's all about."

Manuel nodded. "First of all, I'm sorry; I'm sorry I lied the other night, and well, when the whole Mexico thing happened." His hands tightened into fits as he spoke. "I was only trying to hide the other stuff, the Stefano mess." Manuel, fighting to find his voice, looked down.

"Well, you don't need to hide it. Tell me everything," Nina said.

"I think I always knew I was gay or attracted to guys, at least, but I tried to suppress it for so many years." His throat tightened as he considered his next words: "It's hardly something I can talk to anyone about, not my friends or you." He paused, trying to judge Nina's reaction. He knew he was shattering her world.

"Okay, that makes sense," Nina replied with a calm smile.

"I felt ambushed the other night," he said apologetically with a rumpled and anxious face as he reached out and touched her shoulder—a gesture that once would have made her smile now made her wince.

Nina rested her hands on her knees, slowly nodding. "What now?"

Ignoring her question, he carried on talking: "I was ashamed; you know how it is here; everyone talks, and gossip is an art." He crossed his legs and shifted uncomfortably on the sofa. "You know my family is Catholic; you know my family values. I had no one to talk to, apart from Stefano, and well, it all just happened, I guess, out of the blue." His face dropped to the floor.

"Just him? Stefano," she asked.

Manuel nodded. "I'm sorry, Nina." Feeling his honesty for the first time, she reached for his hand. He kneaded his shoulder as he spoke, expressing his emotions and no longer trying to justify his feelings.

Nina felt something for Manuel she had not felt in a long time, a connection. She tried to appreciate how hard it must be for him, trying to muddle his way through this and hide it from everyone.

The conversation went long into the night before they both fell asleep in the marital bed. They hadn't concluded anything, and they had made no decisions about how to proceed, but she felt they were finally reading from the same book; they just needed to get onto the same page, which could take a while.

The following morning, they were both drained but managed one small, final conversation.

"I'm not ready to be the talk of the town yet," he said. "Can we carry on like this until we can work out what to do?"

Nina frowned at him. "So, lie?" she asked calmly, hoping to avoid one of his explosions.

"Well, if you want to call it lying, then ok," he agreed. Manuel stood up as if the conversation were over and strutted away before she could continue.

"Excuse me." Nina piped up, "I haven't finished talking yet." Manuel turned, strolling back to her. She tried to calm herself. "On a primal level, it feels wrong to lie, and for what reason?" She glared at him, waiting for an answer. "To protect you?" What about me?" she asked, her voice irritated by his silence.

"What about you?" Spit shot from his mouth as he spoke, "You aren't the one who has to face the world with a life-altering secret." He looked at her with fury in his eyes.

"No, I'm the one who has to give up her dream of a happy marriage, children, and a future with her husband," she said. Her eyes glossed over as she threw her arms down in frustration.

"Look, the end justifies the means, so why not lie? Just a couple of months while I get my head around it, then we'll talk again." Manuel snarled at her as he pushed past her, storming out of the house.

When he returned, Nina noticed that Manuel was different; he was smiling again. A weight had been lifted off his shoulders. They ate their breakfast each morning as if nothing had happened. They talked about their days before heading off to work and off to their lives, acting out as a happy couple to all concerned. Now in separate bedrooms, Nina went along with Manuel's plan to pretend that nothing had happened.

122 | Nina

Nik returned to Thessaloniki a changed man, his usual brooding demeanour replaced with a lightness his colleagues noticed immediately.

"Nik. What happened over there? Did you meet an English girl or something?" one of them teased, leaning against the desk.

Nik's colleagues had long given up on trying to set him up. Despite his charm, quick wit, and undeniable good looks—qualities that left no shortage of admirers—he was infamously unattached. His self-imposed three-date rule was well known and often mocked, but now, something in his expression hinted that the rules might have changed.

"I found Bree," he said simply, his lips curving into a smile that made his colleagues lean in closer.

"Bree? As in the cheese?" someone asked, earning groans from the group.

"No," Nik chuckled, shaking his head. "Bree, as in the woman I thought I'd never see again."

"Wait, how? Where? Do you have a picture?"

Before he could answer, another voice chimed in. "Did she even recognise you? I mean, you're practically ancient now," a colleague joked, earning laughter all around.

Nik reached into his pocket and pulled out his phone. The photo of Bree and him in London marathon was already his screensaver. The group gathered around, letting out murmurs of admiration.

"Wow, she's stunning," someone said, breaking the silence.

"Is this serious?" another asked.

Nik was pensive for a moment and then said, "That's the big question. We haven't worked out the details yet," he admitted, though the grin on his face suggested he was ready to move mountains.

As the group pressed for details, Nik recounted the story. His voice grew animated as he described the marathon, his decision to find her hotel, and that fateful moment in the reception area.

"I saw her standing there, and I just froze. I mean, I couldn't speak, couldn't move—just stared like an idiot," he admitted, laughing at himself.

"Well, don't you always?" Desi called out as he walked into the room, his words laced with playful sarcasm.

"I've searched for her on Facebook so many times over the years," Nik continued, his tone softer now. "She was there once, but then her profile disappeared. I started to think... maybe something had happened to her. Maybe she..." He trailed off, shaking his head as if to dismiss the dark thought. "But she's real. I've seen her, held her, spoken to her. And I'm not letting her slip away again."

In the back of the group, Daisa quietly stepped away, her heart sinking. The photo of Bree, radiant and smiling up at Nik, was seared into her mind. She could see it clearly even without looking again—the way Bree gazed at him, the love in her eyes, mirrored in his. It was a connection she'd never share with him. Daisa's throat tightened, but she forced herself to stay silent, retreating to the edge of the conversation.

Nik's phone buzzed, pulling him out of his thoughts. The room fell silent as he glanced at the message, his grin widening. "She's arrived in Italy. And..." He paused for dramatic effect. "She dumped her boyfriend." He pumped his fist in the air, his uncontainable joy spreading to the group. "I'm not letting her slip through my fingers this time," he declared, already typing a reply.

"So, let me get this straight," one colleague teased. "You met her once, and now she's ditched her boyfriend for you? That's some kind of magic."

"What can I say?" Nik replied, throwing his head back in laughter. "I must have superpowers."

"What about all your admirers?" Desi asked.

"It's time to pass on the little black book," Nik said confidently, looking directly at her with a grin. "You can have it, Desi. I won't be needing it anymore."

123 | Bree

Friday morning, Bree rushed to the airport after somehow managing to oversleep. She had pictured herself in a new dress, with perfectly curled hair and bright red nails; instead, she threw on her fitted black trousers, sweating under her black leather jacket; she pulled her hair back in a sleek ponytail and placed her foot heavily on the accelerator.

Bree's heart thumped, and her eyes darted around the arrival hall as she checked her phone for messages. Sipping a takeaway coffee, she spotted Nik strolling out with a spring in his step. His eyes were alight with joy as she threw herself into his arms.

"Welcome to Italy." She smiled as she grabbed his hand and turned to the exit. Dark clouds sped across the chilly morning sky, a cool wind whipped around him, and he took his jacket from his bag and slipped his arms in. Happiness sparked in him like a long-forgotten memory as he wrapped his arm tightly around Bree's waist.

Bree clicked the remote, unlocking and popping the boot open. Nik threw his bags in and stepped into the car. Adjusting his seat, he sat back and looked at the vehicles blurring past.

Bree talked excitedly, distracted by his hand on her knee. A low mist hung over the lake as the car followed the windy road. A few minutes later, he blinked, reaching for his sunglasses, as the fog cleared suddenly and he saw the calm waters for the first time.

Pulling up into Bree's car park, Nik looked at the garden and pool. Smiling, he glanced around her house with a child-like wonder, the place felt like home. It was gleaming and white, with colourfully plumped cushions on the sofa. The light shone through the patio doors, reflecting and bouncing off the white kitchen around the flat.

"Just so you know, Magic Marigold came this morning; she cleaned the place; I've not improved over the years," she said, laughing.

"Who?" he asked quickly.

"My cleaner; I call her Magic Marigold. I'd be lost without her. Surely you haven't forgotten how messy I was, and still am," Bree said.

"And I'm still always late wherever I go." Nik shrugged his shoulders as he dropped his bags to the floor.

"Yeah," she agreed. "Routines are hardwired; we're old now, I guess." She teased with a wide smile. His eyes danced as he pulled her close. Out of the corner of his eye, he spotted a framed photograph of them in London.

Wrapping a towel around him as the steam from the shower trailed behind him, he opened the bathroom door and let out a wild laugh. His eyes scanned Bree, naked, covered by only a white, unbuttoned shirt.

"Okay," she said, "I think this is where we left off." Slipping it off her shoulders, she led him into the bedroom.

As the October day was drawing to a close, they sat together, swapping their life stories.

"Hungry?" Nik asked as he peeled himself away from Bree. Rummaging through her shelves, he looked around in confusion. "How do you survive?" he asked.

"Frozen food selection at Lidl," she replied cheekily.

"We're going shopping."

"What, leave here? I like it here," she pleaded as she slowly eased herself off the sofa and into her jeans. She grabbed the moped keys. "Let's go," she said. "Two wheels this time."

"No way, we are doing a real shop, not a little one; car keys, please." He held out his hand and said, "I expected to find a sink filled with dirty dishes from what I remembered of you and clothes on the floor, but no food; that amazes me."

124 | Bree

Tall, vaulted ceilings greeted them, and the scent of spit roast meat filled Bree's favourite restaurant as they entered a few days later. Bree looked at her watch and shook her head as she spotted that Carla and Nina were already waiting. Nik greeted them like old friends. "It's nice to meet you," he said.

Carla gave Bree an approving smile. When he turned around to take his seat, Carla mouthed 'Wow, he's hot.' at Bree.

The four bonded instantly; they talked about how they met and shared stories of their time in Greece. Nik charmed them and won their approval; importantly, they loved how he looked at Bree, held her hand, and kept her glass topped up.

Towards the end of dinner, Bree went to the bathroom. Nik looked at Carla and then at Nina; He seemed impatient and worried. "I love her, you know," he said. "I want to marry her; I need your help, though." He paused, then reached into his jacket pocket. "Can you hide this for me?" he asked, handing Nina a box.

"Oh, my god." Nina blurted.

"It's a ring. The last time I proposed to her, it was in front of our friends. This time, I want it to be personal; I need help finding the perfect spot."

"Wow. Do you have a single, younger brother, just like you, for me?" Carla laughed.

"Of course, we'll help you," said Nina. They quickly exchanged numbers. The girls held back excited giggles, noticing his impatient demeanour had gone. He slumped into his chair with a mischievous grin.

Knowing how much Bree loved cycling, no matter the weather, hot or cold, he decided on a proposal during a cycle ride. Nik planned to buy a bike, but Bree was impatient to show him the area on two wheels, so he borrowed one.

"I need your help again, girls," he said as they met up discreetly on a trip to the supermarket. "So, I'm proposing we cycle up to the turquoise lake on Saturday, and I'll do it there. Can you bring a picnic in the car and set it up, maybe with some alcohol-free champagne? I don't want her cycling drunk; oh, can you put the ring in the basket, too?"

125 | Bree

Nik texted that they were leaving; it was about ninety minutes of hard uphill cycling. Bree, bubbling with enthusiasm, prepared small rucksacks for both of them: water and cereal bars, a camera, and rain gear, just in case.

Nik was more of a speed cyclist than an uphill one. As the mountain tops neared, despite the cold mountain air, he felt the sweat pouring down his back. Bree looked fresh, as if the hill climb were just a stroll through a daisy field. He persevered, knowing what was waiting for him; he knew the girls would be there by now, set up and ready. He saw messages arriving on his watch; they were from the group they'd created. Nina and Carla were going overboard that day. Nik was worried Bree would wonder who the messages were from, but it wouldn't be long now until he could tell her everything.

The mountains loomed above, and Nik wondered how much further. He wanted to stop; he needed a rest, but Bree was way ahead of him.

"We're here, slow coach; I thought you were a cyclist," she said, smiling.

"You know we don't have all these mountains back home, but at least we get to go downhill on the way back; I'll beat you then," he said, wiping the sweat from his brow with his sleeve.

They locked the bikes to the metal railing and strolled through an abandoned car park. The lake appeared as if by magic as they reached the ridge. It was turquoise blue and shaped like a diamond. Silence echoed from the mountains; the willow trees lining the water's edge stood perfectly still, reflecting on the water like a mirror. The only sounds were the murmurs of two fishermen in the distance.

"Don't be surprised if Nina and Carla are here; they love it here, and I'm sure they drove past us at the bottom of the mountain."

"I didn't notice," Nik said. "I was just watching that mountain loom over us, wondering if we'd ever make it."

He took her hand as he led her down the stone path to the lake. The girls texted him, telling him to go right to the bottom of the track. Feeling his breath tighten and his hands clamp up, he squeezed her hand tighter.

"I love that reflection over there," he said, leading her in that direction rather than the one she was going in. As they headed towards the water, he tried to remember the instructions from the girls. They had said to get to the island and stop by a large, grey rock; the picnic would be laid behind it. He saw the rock, and he felt his breath tighten. His hands clamped up as he continued to walk, unable to look her in the eye.

Bree saw the picnic first; a large blue blanket lay on the pebble beach, and a beige wicker picnic basket was sitting in the middle, with two large cushions beside it. She turned to walk around it. Nik pulled her back and pointed at the blanket.

"This is for us," he said. "I wanted a special moment with you; the girls arranged it. Bree looked at him, confused. She loved how he called them the girls, as if they were their kids.

"Oh my god, really," she said, as warmth flooded through her.

Bree turned to the picnic blanket, saw the cushions, and moved to sit down. As she peered into the basket, Nik saw his opportunity; he knelt one knee on the rounded cobbles, worn away by age. He reached into the basket, pulling out the ring, still in its box. She turned around, about to ask him when they had arranged all of this and saw him kneeling, still red in the face, with a line around his face from the helmet. Her heart skipped a few beats, then doubled in speed.

"That's my ring, the one I posted back," she said, staring at the ring.

"Yes, I kept it for you; I knew I would marry you one day." His lips produced a small smile as he held the ring out with both hands.

"Breezy, I have waited, searched for you, and pictured your face in my dreams for eight years." He paused, trying to judge her emotions; she was staring at him with a vacant look of surprise, and his heart was hammering in his chest. "I can't imagine not spending every day with you, not waking up next to you, not seeing your beautiful smile each night." His delivery was faultless, and after a short pause, he continued, "Bree, will you marry me? Will you be my wife?" he asked. He was sweating, but he didn't care; this was his moment, the moment he had waited for all those years. She stood unblinking; her brow jumped in surprise, and tears began to spill over her smile.

A slight tingling of guilt tugged in her stomach; she could see his nerves and fear of rejection; she wanted to wash it away. Had she not made him feel loved enough that he still had doubts? Instead, Bree, with her hands cupped over her mouth, failed to hide her shock.

Nik's heart bounced as he watched Bree's expression shift from surprise to pure joy. Her eyes sparkled, her smile widening until it seemed to light up her entire face. In that moment, time seemed to stretch and bend, the world around them fading into a blur. He could hardly believe this was happening, that this woman—who had once been a fleeting thought in the back of his mind—was now standing here, ready to change everything.

Her gaze flickered down to the ring, then back up to him, and without another word, she dropped her hands from her face, her fingers twitching eagerly. Nik's breath caught as she wiggled her fingers at him, a playful twinkle in her eyes.

A grin tugged at his lips. "Is that a yes, then?" he asked, his voice light, but his heart was anything but.

Before he could even finish the question, Bree's voice broke the silence. "No. It's a hell, yes," she shouted, her words tumbling out without hesitation, full of excitement and a joy.

The moment her words echoed in the air, Nik slid the ring onto her finger, the weight of it suddenly feeling real. But it wasn't the ring that mattered—it was the promise in her voice, the certainty in her eyes.

He reached for her, pulling her closer, his hands trembling slightly as he cupped her face, feeling the warmth of her skin beneath his fingertips. She was his now, in a way that went beyond just the proposal; this was a moment, a turning point, and everything felt like it was falling perfectly into place.

Bree's hands rose to meet his chest, and without thinking, she pulled him into a kiss—sweet, urgent, full of the love that had been building between them for so long. It wasn't just a kiss; it was a surrender, a promise, a declaration of everything they had and everything they would become.

Nik responded with equal fervor, his lips capturing hers with a hunger that spoke of how deeply he had fallen for her, of the years they'd spent apart and the moments that led them back to this. His hands tangled in her hair, pulling her even closer, as if he could moor himself her to him and never let go.

For that brief moment, the world was theirs—no distractions, no doubts, just the certainty that they had found something rare and precious. When they finally pulled away, their foreheads resting against one another, their breaths mingling in the space between them, the words were unnecessary. Everything they needed to say was in that kiss, in the way their hearts beat together, in the shared knowledge that this was the beginning of something beautiful.

And as Nik smiled at her, his heart swelling with emotion, he whispered, "I love you, Breezy."

She smiled back, her eyes glistening with tears. "I love you too, Nik. So much."

He pulled her hand gently to the ground and sat her on a blanket as he saw a message from the girls on his watch.

"Can we come out now?" they asked. Nik waved his arms for them to come. They arrived, running from behind the tree-covered island, screaming with joy and laughter.

Bree hugged them, thanked them, and showed them the ring. "It's my ring, the one he gave me the first time he proposed."

"Nice. I repeat, do you have a single brother for me?" Carla joked.

"Will you join us for lunch?" Bree asked.

"If you don't mind us gate-crashing," Nina laughed.

126 | Nik

An hour later, they said their goodbyes to the girls and set off; their sweet chatter could be heard from afar, interrupted by birds chirping under the bright blue sky.

"See you at the bottom of the mountain." Nik smiled as he placed his feet on his pedals and pushed off just seconds before her. Happiness and relief rushed through him. On a high and feeling invincible, he leant into the hairpin bends of the road, keeping his hands far from the brakes.

The scent of the white flowers along the road delighted Bree, who moved at a slower pace. Replaying the proposal in her mind, her mind flew quicker than her wheels, off into their future, trailing happiness behind her for anyone to collect. Bree was well aware of her boundaries and kept within them; speed scared her. As her wheels carried her effortlessly down the twisty road, Bree reflected on how strange life was. Two weeks earlier, she was unhappy, an orphan of love with Robby, yet now she was engaged to the guy who had once shattered her life.

Nik finally admitted to himself that he was in trouble when his front wheel struck an unseen stone in the road. The impact threw him off balance just as a bus came speeding around the corner. He barely had time to react before his knees slammed into the bus's front windscreen, and the jarring force of the crash cracked his back. His body flew over the roof, and with a final scream, he tumbled onto the tarmac below. He didn't feel the ground strike him, nor did he hear the screech of the bus's brakes or see the terror in the driver's eyes. All he could feel was the cold air as his helmet rolled into the grass beside him.

The driver's heart raced, blood pounding in his ears as panic set in. His hands shook uncontrollably as he called out for help, shouting for a doctor and for anyone nearby to warn oncoming traffic. The bus had blocked the road in both directions, adding to the havoc.

Meanwhile, Bree was descending the mountain, enjoying the breeze when two men flagged her down urgently. "Accident. Slow down, be careful." one of them shouted, his voice frantic. Bree dismounted her bike and began to walk, spotting a footpath ahead that could get her around the scene.

She assumed Nik had already passed through, but as she neared the commotion, something caught her eye—a rucksack, the very one she had packed with care that morning. Her pulse quickened as she approached, fingers trembling as she ran them over the fabric. The realization struck her like a bullet—it was his. A wave of weakness washed over her, her body unsteady as she scanned the crowd. Nik's mangled bike lay by the rear of the bus, but it was the trail of blood that pulled her forward. Shaking uncontrollably, Bree pushed past the onlookers, hearing voices of despair, following the path to where Nik lay.

"Nik, no. Nik." Her cry barely escaped her, but it was enough for the crowd to part, letting her pass. The sight before her made her stomach drop—his lifeless face was pale and unmoving, and for a moment, everything else faded into the background. All she could focus on was the cold breath she thought she could still feel on her skin, watching his life slip away.

127 | Petra

As each day passed, Petra felt more at home in the retreat, becoming more united with her old, relaxed self. They were encouraged to talk about their feelings at the end of each day and what they had learnt about themselves. Petra found it easy to talk to Penny, her therapist, in her daily therapy sessions; sitting on cushions under the shade of a tree was her favourite part of the day. It felt like she was talking to a friend without having to be polite, let the others speak, and wait for her turn.

Two small minibuses took the group out of the retreat on day three. A guide escorted them around the spice farm, explaining and quizzing them on spices.

Leafy green trees surrounded the Spice Farm; muddy paths were trodden through weeds and shrubs. The guide, a tall man in a brown uniform with a palm leaf hat, identified himself as John Mayor. He guided them to each plant, explained how it was cultivated, collected a sample, and allowed them to smell or taste it.

The tour ended with fresh fruit tasting, juicy pineapples, fresh, chilled coconut water, green bananas, hot and spicy ginger tea, and the chance to buy little bags of colourful and overpriced spices.

Returning to the retreat, Petra spotted a teenager, Charlie, hovering around the clubhouse. Georgie's fifteen-year-old daughter speaking with an American accent was a welcome breath of fresh air.

"My mum pays me twenty dollars to help out at the weekend. I call it child labour." Charlie said, laughing. The eye-rolling, scantily dressed teenager wasn't trying to find herself, at least not in the way the others were; she wasn't trying to find inner peace. Charlie was trying to get through two days, earn some money, and survive the weekend.

"I'd much rather be at the beach with my friends, but my dad is working too, so I'm stuck here," Charlie said, eager to talk to someone other than her mother.

"What are you doing here?" asked Charlie. "What are your issues? You look normal, apart from that hat. I'm not supposed to talk to the guests; my mum disapproves, but you seem normal enough."

"Thanks," Petra said.

"You aren't from Italy, are you?" Petra nodded her answer.

"Well, Mum says the normal one of the group this month is a lady from Italy," Charlie explained.

"Yep, I'm the only one from Italy, and I'm honoured to have made the normal list," Petra laughed, folding towels as she talked.

"Oh yeah, my mum gives me the rundown; normal, usually only one or two per group; weirdos, most of them. She can predict who will be there first, wanting their phone, who will leave early, who will have a breakdown, which two will hook up within a week, who will leave in the middle of the night, and who will be rummaging around looking for the stash of booze." Charlie let out a shy laugh, covering her mouth with her hands. "I shouldn't have told you that she'd kill me."

"Don't worry, I won't say anything." Petra paused, reaching into the washing machine for more towels. "Now, about that phone and the stash of wine," she said, smiling, hoping Charlie would get that it was more than a joke.

"Oh, you're the normal one, then. My mum says that a normal person would need a drink and gossip with a friend after a few days of this." Charlie said, shoving her hands in her short pockets.

"I like your mum more and more, but seriously, does she have some wine?" Petra urged.

"My mum is the queen of wine. Come with me," Charlie said.

Georgie, nursing a cup of tea, looked up as she saw Charlie and Petra approach. "Sorry, I thought you were all out meditating; I'll put the computer away," she said.

"I don't care, honestly. Look, I wanted to ask you something," Petra said.

Charlie said, "Mum, I didn't corrupt her, I promise. Oh god, but she's cool, and she has that 'I want out of here' look on her face." Petra looked at Charlie, surprised at her honesty, and nodded in agreement.

"Mother dearest. Wine. This lady needs some of your wine," Charlie said sarcastically.

Georgie laughed. "See, Charlie, I told you she was the normal one. Would you like it in a mug, like me?" she asked, bringing out her yellow mug that concealed a large dose of chilled wine. Or straight from the bottle?"

Petra laughed. "A mug will do nicely, thanks."

She sat on the chair, sipped the wine slowly, and then gulped it down. "Okay, now I can survive another three weeks of this." Petra said, moving her eyes around the area, showing that she meant the retreat.

"Come on, you have another three weeks; you'll need a few more glasses."

She ran her fingers down the bottle, stopping on the label. The image showed a large rock surrounded by water, with the logo 'The Rock' restaurant. Petra recalled Bree's friend working there and said, "Oh, 'The Rock,' there is a guy I need to look up. I think he is called Markus; my friend knows him. He's from Rocca Pinta, the same town that I'm from." explained Petra.

"Markus? Yes, I know him well; he is a good friend of mine. My husband manages 'The Rock' restaurant, and Markus is the chef; yeah, he is a fantastic guy."

"Well, I'll book a hotel in that area on the website after my stint here is over, and I'll stop by and say 'hi' to him," Petra explained.

"Which hotel?" asked Georgie.

Petra gave her the name, "It was one of the suggestions on your website."

"No, I can't believe it. That is where I work when I'm not here. I only come here three months a year when the other manager returns to the UK. At the end of the month, I'll be returning to the hotel for the next nine months." Georgie smiled, reaching into the fridge for another bottle.

Laughter shattered the silence in the retreat as the two girls sipped their mugs of wine. Knowing she had a new friend, an ally in the retreat, Petra felt the burden of loneliness leave her side. She had a friend on the outside. With hurried whispers and excited giggles, they planned that the three girls would dine at 'The Rock' restaurant on their first night out in the real world.

Water spilt into the sink as Georgie hid evidence of the wine mugs. "Same time tomorrow then; I know a quiet little place we can go."

"And the next day, too," laughed Petra, holding her hands to her side as she wobbled through the retreat, tip-toeing past the darkened rooms around her.

128 | Petra

After a week, another area of the retreat opened up to them. The perfectly tended garden was full of palm trees and colourful, string-woven hammocks hanging from the trees. Double mattresses lying on concrete slabs, some in the sun and some in the shade of the trees, were laid out for relaxation. Bamboo poles, tied together and held up with large wooden sticks, created stripey shadows and shade over the top, and upturned white cement vases were placed carefully by each set of chairs to be used as book stands. Each member of the group accepted an empty journal and agreed to fill at least a page each day with their musings, thoughts, emotions, and challenges.

One hot, sticky morning, Godfrey took the group to the tiny village of KizKuliza to see how the locals lived. They walked from the retreat for about five minutes through the overgrown bush. A small, trodden path showed them the way as they followed the unfamiliar sounds of children playing and laughing in the distance.

Petra was relieved they had all been asked to cover their legs, shoulders, and stomachs. The protruding twigs and branches caused havoc as they caught on her long, baggy trousers. They marvelled at the quiet as they meandered through the crumbling stone buildings—forgotten debris scattered amongst the weeds and bushes. The blue and white walls rimmed the outside of the school, a rectangle with just one room filled with kids of all ages who screamed in delight at the visitors. The carefully hand-painted alphabet sat on the wall with English words next to each object's drawing.

"Jambo," they shouted as they waved at them. "Jambo," the group shouted back.

A is for apple, B is for banana—sang a girl in a blue uniform with a yellow headscarf; the children hung out of the stone windows, high-fiving the group for attention.

Petra heard the splashing of water before she spotted a woman kneeling on the floor, scrubbing clothes with a simple bar of soap and water from buckets. Sun-bleached clothes blew in the breeze, hanging over tree branches.

Godfrey, proudly stretching out his arms, introduced his mother to them. "This is my mom." He paused for people to say hello. "She has a good life here, enriched because I work in tourism; I bring money home for eleven months of the year, a good wage that can only be earned with tourists." She nodded and smiled even though she didn't seem to understand what he was saying: "I'm happy that now that she is older, she doesn't have to work in the fields farming the spices; she just collects them for sale." Godfrey said, walking the group around the corner.

His mother muttered a greeting in Kiswahili, smiling with a shy wave.

"This is where she cooks." He walked them to an open-air cooking space on a patch of hardened sand. Rocks surrounded a small fire, and a cauldron-style pot heated a slimy yellow substance. "This is Ugali; it's like mashed potatoes, but without the potatoes and with corn." The group peered in with blank faces and said, "We eat this most days, with beans and rice."

"Can we try it?" an English group participant asked.

"We will be serving it tonight at the retreat; once cooked, we serve it in banana leaves."

Petra smiled at the ladies around her. They looked content, unaware of the horror going through the minds of those watching them. The group toured the village through narrow sand paths and gravel walkways; they were just in time for the water truck delivery. The brakes of the large red truck squeaked as it pulled up, and the driver cut the engine, wiping sweat from his brow with his sleeve.

Women, men, and children appeared out of nowhere with large buckets or containers. They lined up by the side of the truck, and the driver, a tired-looking man covered in a veil of dust, stepped out, unhooked his water pipe, and water started to flow out of the hose into the water containers. One by one, the people walked away carrying their heavy buckets, placed them on the ground, and returned to join the queue to fill the next one.

"The retreat and another nearby tourist resort donate this water; they each send a water truck a week," Godfrey explained. "We live off the land here, from the spices you have already seen; we work as a village; we all work on the land. Once a week, we go to the market and sell our crops. The money is shared among the villagers to buy rice and beans. We don't need a lot; if we had washing machines and ovens, where would the ladies get together? For them, it's time to gossip. Yes, the ladies here gossip too, just like you all do," he laughed.

Petra watched the women move swiftly around the village in colourful, long dresses. The children played happily in the sand; they squealed and laughed, rolling a rubber bicycle tyre in the dirt, wearing mostly Western clothes. Petra recognised the names of football teams printed on the boys' and men's clothes.

"Where do they get the clothes from?" One of the groups asked, "Not Amazon." Godfrey laughed. "Mainly, these clothes are left by people such as yourselves; when they go home after a holiday, especially the ones in the large resorts, they leave clothing." He paused as the water truck drove past, throwing a trail of sand in the air.

In her long floral-printed trousers and plain white t-shirt, Petra wiped her eyes from the dusty sand as Godfrey folded his arms and got straight back to business. "The women here prefer traditional clothes; they are more practical and cooler for the hard work they have to do." He turned and gestured to a group of men. "The men working in the fields or on the land find Western clothes much more useful. They also sell shorts and T-shirts in the city and nearest town, but they are too expensive for a villager like this to afford," he explained.

"This is our television. We have just this one in the village, which the retreat donated," he said proudly, pointing to a Baobab tree. "Come, look—the Tree of Life. We can eat the leaves and the fruit. We will never be hungry with these trees here." He gestured for the group to come closer. "Here is the TV." The villagers had fixed the television with ropes, part resting and part hanging, so they could watch it. "On Saturday, we watch a film, and when the football is on, all the men and boys watch the Champions League matches. I support Liverpool," he said, pointing out a footballer's name on his top.

With a thankful and overloaded mind, Petra followed the group back; she looked stricken, feeling ashamed, thinking about how much she had and didn't need. She felt a surge of envy; tears stung in her eyes. If these people could be happy with so little, why was she so incredibly unhappy with so much? She refocused her mind on her silk gown on the bed, a luxurious item she didn't need and chose to concentrate on the birds and trees instead of her frivolous spending habits.

129 | Petra

That evening, over dinner, the group discussed things they could leave behind for the villagers, items of clothing and shoes. Petra regretted travelling so light; she didn't think the locals would be interested in receiving a few skimpy bikinis, the only thing she had packed too many of in her small bag. She knew that next week, a trip to the city of Stonetown, the island's capital, was on the itinerary; she decided she would shop there for clothes and fabrics to give the villagers. She had watched in awe as some ladies in the village accepted deliveries of beautifully patterned and colourful material from a small truck.

They had touched the materials slowly and gently against their skin. Before taking enough for whatever they were planning to do, she recognised the same excited sparkle in their eyes that Petra had when her Amazon deliveries arrived.

The work around the retreat was simple; the outings to the village, the spice farm, and the Maasai village had all been educational, but more than that, they made Petra appreciate her own life and rethink all of her values. Her outlook had already changed after just two weeks. She enjoyed her time alone and wrote about it in her journal each evening.

On the weekends, she looked forward to Charlie's upbeat and lively company; the relationship between Charlie and her mum was similar to the one portrayed in The Gilmore Girls. They were friends first and family second. Although Charlie, with crossed arms and frequent eye-rolling, forced a downward smile around her mum, Petra could see that she was happy to spend time with her.

Petra craved some real food'. The rice, beans, spices, couscous, and vegetables were highly flavorful, and she could feel the difference in herself, her skin, and her sleep. Nonetheless, she was haunted by images of bacon, something she had not had in ten years.

Georgie's wide smile greeted her in the garden. Petra was swinging on a hammock, trying unsuccessfully to write at the same time. Georgie giggled as Petra dropped the pen onto the ground, reached over for it, leaning too far, and rolled clumsily out of the hammock straight onto the dusty floor. Georgie laughed out loud, watching her dust herself off, look at the hammock, curse at it, and get back in.

Georgie waited for her to get comfortable in the hammock again before approaching her from behind.

"Hi, Petra." Georgie said, not mentioning the events she had just watched unfold. Petra turned quickly to see her friend losing her balance again and wobbling, rolling, and cascading to the floor.

"I keep doing that." Petra said, embarrassed, "Aren't these supposed to be relaxing? They are just a joke." She got to her feet, wiped herself off, and walked away from the hammock, choosing to stretch out on a large mattress under the shade of softly blowing branches.

They swapped stories excitedly about their days; Georgie told Petra of her life in the shamba. She noticed that Petra looked so much more at peace now; she guessed she was getting what she wanted out of this retreat.

The first two weeks at the retreat had been about self-exploration, self-expression, shedding the guilt and negative emotions connected to past events, and finding who they were and their place in this world. It wasn't about forgetting the past but accepting it.

Acknowledging that their choices had brought them to this point, the lives they were living were a consequence of their decisions until that point. Now, they had the power to change their futures. It was all up to them; from now on, they would learn about the tools they already had within them to take the following steps.

From now on, it was all about negativity and positivity, removing negativity from their lives, predominantly negative human influences. Georgie knew this was when people would often crack, see the negativity surrounding them, and finish the day wide-eyed, open-mouthed, with the realisation of a possible change ahead.

Petra winced as she heard the bell ringing; it was time for their group session. The bell was an unwelcome sound in the first two weeks, but now she started feeling excited about the day's schedule. She knew that each day, bit by bit, she was healing from the traumas of the past. Petra had realised, more importantly than anything, that what happened with her and Rico was why she was there; that whole event made her the unhappy, bitter, envious person she had become.

Petra listened in wide-eyed disbelief as the life coach described various personality traits, urging them to recognise such behaviours in the people around them and within themselves. The idea of identifying patterns and disorders seemed simple enough, but as Petra took notes, she quickly realised the unsettling truth. As she read through the descriptions, she saw Rico and her recent flings, but when she came across the term 'Avoidant Personality Disorder,' her heart skipped a beat. She blinked in disbelief; she'd never heard of it before, but the symptoms seemed to match her exactly.

Her mind went blank, and her chest tightened. She felt panic rise in her throat as she stared at the page. Her body seemed to react involuntarily: her shoulders slumped, her palms grew clammy, and dizziness crept in. Desperately, she gripped the edge of her cushion, scooting it closer to the chair as if it could hold her together. She wanted to flee, but at the same time, didn't want to miss anything.

Her cheeks flushed, and she quickly turned her face away, trying to mask the rush of heat. She wiped away a few stray tears, but her composure broke as her chest hollowed out. She lurched forward, her head sinking into her hands, the weight of the revelation too much to bear. The life coach paused, sensing her distress, and announced a break. But Petra barely registered the words, her mind spinning as if she were floating above the room, detached from everything below.

Penny, noticing Petra's discomfort, quickly approached and took her hand, leading her to the shaded loungers. They sat in silence for a moment before Penny spoke gently. "What's going on, Petra? What's happening with you?" Her voice was soft, comforting, and Petra felt a wave of gratitude for her presence.

"I... I don't know where to start," Petra replied, her voice thick with emotion. "It's all too much to take in."

"Did you recognise someone in the descriptions? Maybe someone who hurt you or someone you've hurt?" Penny asked, her tone still warm and patient.

Petra closed her eyes for a moment, struggling to put her thoughts into words. "Yes... I saw myself," she whispered, her voice almost breaking. She glanced down at her notepad, her hands shaking. "I saw myself in the description. I have an 'Avoidant Personality Disorder.'" She paused, staring at the words as if they were foreign, as if they weren't really her. "I never knew," she added softly.

Penny squeezed her hand gently. "If that's true, Petra, then you're already on the right path," she said with a reassuring smile. "It's not something you were born with—it's shaped by your experiences. We can work through it together. Recognising it is a big breakthrough. You're already tearing down that emotional wall."

Petra let the silence stretch out for a moment as she absorbed Penny's words. Slowly, she moved forward, feeling more grounded. "I don't want to be like this anymore," she murmured, her voice shaking with emotion. "I hate myself. I don't want to be this person. I just want to be free of her... of me."

Penny's grip on her hand tightened, offering silent support. "We'll do this together," she promised.

In the distance, Petra could hear the life coach continuing the session, but it felt like a muffled echo in her ears. Her mind was still reeling from the revelation, but Penny's presence was a comfort.

"I guess..." Petra trailed off, her forehead creased as she tried to gather her thoughts. "It's the things I heard. I've always had this intense fear of disapproval, of criticism. I think it's because I grew up in a big family, being the eldest. I didn't get the attention I wanted... and when I did, it was always negative—being told off, told I wasn't good enough. I always feared being shamed, ridiculed for doing something wrong."

Penny listened attentively, her voice soothing. "Let it out, Petra. You're here for a reason. You're doing the right thing."

Petra nodded slowly, her chest tightening again. "I think I grew up feeling inferior to everyone else. The worst at school, the ugliest in the group..." She paused, her expression shifting as she struggled with the vulnerability of it all. "It's not just my family. My friends don't really include me in anything. Well, they invite me sometimes, but I always feel left out. They're always talking about their problems, and I just don't want to hear it. It's all the same... they all have their perfect lives, and I don't fit in anywhere."

Penny sat back for a moment, taking in Petra's words. "Tell me more about that. You say they invite you, but you don't want to go... Why? What do you suggest they do, and why do you feel left out?"

Petra took a deep breath as she collected her thoughts. "I've asked them to come rock climbing with me, and, well, I guess that is it; they are always off at each other's houses, chatting about their perfect lives, and I just sit at home, alone, and go on bad dates."

"Listen to your words. Do they go rock climbing without you?"

"No, they hate it; they tried once and hated every second," she said, scowling.

"So, you want them to do something they have tried and don't enjoy?" she asked, scrunching her eyebrows towards her nose.

"Well, no, I want them to like it; I do," she said with a hint of anger in her voice.

"You can't make people do what you want them to do. Have you thought about finding something else you can all do together? Something that you will all enjoy? They invite you to their house, but you say that you don't like that and that they talk too much about themselves."

"Exactly."

"That's what friends do; they talk about themselves, their problems, and their lives. You say they talk about their perfect lives but also about their problems; that means their lives aren't perfect either," Penny said. Her calm manner and self-assurance comforted a still-shaky Petra.

"Well, I guess," Petra said.

"Do you think that they have perfect lives? I believe that no one has a perfect life." Penny said, trying to look Petra in the eye.

Petra stared at the floor, unable to meet Penny's gaze. "No, they are all going through stuff; I just don't know what?" she said, with a child-like realisation that life was not as simple as it looked.

"So, I think this is something you need to think about; you have friends with problems, but you don't know what they are. You have problems, but you think they don't listen. I understand you feel three against one; however, remove that thought and think about them individually. Do you think you're a good friend?" Penny asked, hoping she managed to cover the disbelief in her voice, "Don't reply now; think about it."

"I can't think about anything else right now, Penny; I can't do it," she said sharply.

"Okay, let's leave this for now. Go and have a walk, lie down, and take some time. I'll find you before dinner, ok?"

Petra nodded, muttering a quiet, humble 'okay' before pushing herself up, grabbing onto a table for extra strength. With her head down, she took quick strides back to her room, hoping not to see anyone. In her room, she turned on the fan, feeling the humid air move around her. Petra lay flat, hugging a pillow close to her chest, her knees bent up to her belly as she felt her eyes close.

Throwing the pillow behind her, she propped up her aching body, crossed her legs, and shook her head.

Petra's skin tingled under the cold shower. Wrapping up in a large soft towel, she grabbed both sides of the sink and stared at her reflection. Her puffy eyes and blotchy face stared cruelly back at her. Time, or maybe just that day, had moulded her face into someone she barely recognised. A gentle knock at the door startled her; the unbroken price tag caught around her neck as she pulled a flowery dress over her shoulders.

The visitor knocked again. Petra appeared nervously and looked through a crack in the door at a serious-looking Penny. "Are you okay? Did you miss dinner?" Penny asked.

"I think I'm also a narcissist; I've got some of those traits, too," Petra said, shutting the flimsy door behind her and gesturing for Penny to sit on the balcony. "I seem to enjoy making people unhappy. I'm never happy for them; I get mad and jealous when I see people getting what they want." Petra turned pensive as her mind flickered between memories and flashbacks of her reactions to others' news.

Penny sat in silence, stroking Petra's trembling hands; there was nothing to say. Petra was fighting demons and devils in her brain, and she could not start the healing process until she had reached rock bottom.

Night had fallen upon them, thunder rumbled in the distance, and the unfamiliar smell of rain drifted in the gusts of wind. Penny said nothing apart from the odd reassuring word. This was a significant emotional breakthrough for Petra; she had begun to rip through the veil of denial she had been hiding behind. She'd written the narrative, making herself the victim; this was the first time she'd realised she had played a significant part in her choices.

Slowly and calmly, Penny reassured Petra that this reaction was a natural course of events here at the retreat and that anyone here who didn't have a similar moment of clarity wasn't being true themselves.

"You say you think you're a narcissist. Can you explain why?" Penny asked.

"I guess, oh, I don't know; I think a lot of the character traits describe me too." She spoke in a series of starts and stops: "I try to manipulate people to get them to like me; I pretend I'm something I'm not, hoping they will want to be with me. I change depending on who I'm with, especially with guys. I become what I think they want to be; I'm not me. I'm a fake version of me."

Feeling warm raindrops on her feet, Penny pulled her chair away from the edge of the balcony. "I think we all have personality traits we don't like; I think sometimes we have all been a little bit narcissistic too. Having a few traits doesn't make you a narcissist. It will be best if you figure out why you behave that way. Why do you react like that? Why do you think they won't like you? Why do you need to change who you are? Why don't you think you aren't good enough?" Pausing as if for dramatic effect, she looked Petra in the eye and said, "These are all questions to find answers to; only you can do that; only you know; it's all inside you; you need to dig deep." Penny said, taking a long breath and pulling out a pen and paper.

"I don't know why. Can't you tell me the answers?" she asked.

"I can tell you what I see, but that is my evaluation of you; I can't tell you what you need to know. You're going to do that on your own. I need you to do something. You need to answer some important questions, think about them, and write down your feelings and emotions. Then, tomorrow, we will talk. Come and see me instead of doing yoga. We'll go over them and see how you feel."

Petra wrote the questions in her journal—the same ones Penny had already asked her in their conversations.

Penny paused by the door for a second before leaving. Glancing back over her shoulder, she whispered, "You did well; you can do this. Tomorrow is another day," she said with a reassuring smile.

130 | Bree

"Why isn't it raining?" Bree murmured in disbelief. "Things like this... shouldn't happen on a sunny day." The world around her felt surreal, as though the weather itself should mirror the devastation unfolding before her. She could hear the frantic voice of the bus driver, speaking to emergency services, following their instructions with a robotic calmness. Bree gasped, her hand trembling as she pressed it over her mouth, eyes wide in horror. She watched as the driver gave CPR while another passenger desperately tried to staunch the bleeding, their movements quick but futile.

Bree knelt by Nik's side, her knees scraping the cold tarmac, her fingers squeezing his hand so tightly, as if her life depended on it. She wasn't sure if he was still alive, the way his body lay so still, but she couldn't leave him. Not now. Not like this. Her voice was a raw scream, a pleading demand: "Nik, you have to fight. Please, fight for me." She begged, praying for some sign that he could hear her.

The world blurred around her—cars honked in the distance, an endless line of traffic backed up. A man raced up the winding road, shouting in a calm but urgent tone, "I'm a doctor. Let me through." His cracked leather bag hit the ground with a thud, and without wasting a second, he took over from the weakening driver, his hands steady as he checked for vital signs and ordered another volunteer to take over CPR. "Keep talking to him," the doctor instructed Bree, his voice cold but filled with the intensity of a life-or-death urgency. "If he's alive, he can hear you."

Minutes dragged on like hours, and Bree stayed with Nik, her voice hoarse from shouting, until the police arrived. They cleared the scene, but Bree barely registered them. Her focus was solely on the ambulance's wailing sirens as it neared, her heart sinking further. Nik was carefully placed on a stretcher, his body limp and fragile. "There's one seat in the back," the paramedic said flatly.

"I'll take it," the doctor replied, his face unreadable as he climbed into the ambulance. He threw Bree a quick glance—hope, or perhaps just the faintest flicker of it. Without thinking, Bree grabbed Nik's rucksack and tossed it into the vehicle with him.

"We'll take his bike to the station. Do you want to come with us?" a policeman asked.

Bree shook her head, her voice strained as she looked at the traffic jam. "I'll ride. It'll be faster." She couldn't stand waiting any longer, not when time felt like it was slipping away.

Minutes later, Bree arrived at the hospital, her legs like jelly beneath her as she stumbled through the doors just as the ambulance pulled in. She followed the stretcher as far as she could before being stopped, the sterile smell of the hospital air thick in her lungs. Her hands gripped the edge of the wall as she tried to keep herself together. A silent scream echoed in her chest when she saw Nik being rushed past her, the sight of him like a knife to her soul. Her eyes stayed on him, locked in terror, unable to tear away from the image of his broken body.

She called Nina and Carla, her voice cracked and full of pain. When they arrived, their eyes were red from crying, their faces drawn in shock. Hours stretched on in a blur of waiting, and then two doctors finally appeared, their faces blank, unreadable. They didn't need to say anything more than, "Are you family of Nikos Daskalakis?"

Bree nodded, her heart pounding in her throat. "Yes."

Without further explanation, they guided her to a seat, the heaviness of their silence pressing down on her chest. "Nikos is still alive," one of them finally said, his voice clinical and distant. "He lost a lot of blood, and he's in critical condition. The surgery was successful, but he needs to be monitored for the next few hours."

Bree's eyes widened, her breath catching. "He made it?" she whispered, as though she couldn't quite believe the words.

The doctor nodded, his expression softening slightly. "So far, yes."

Nina and Carla, sensing her unsteady legs, wrapped their arms around Bree, steadying her as the world felt like it might collapse beneath her. "Can I see him?" she asked, her voice barely audible.

"He's in a medically induced coma," the doctor replied, his tone still clinical. "You can see him for a minute, but... he's not out of the woods yet."

Bree nodded, her heart sinking as they led her to the room. Nik lay motionless, covered by a sheet except for his face. His arms were in casts, his legs unnaturally swollen beneath the covers. The doctor explained in a detached manner about the bleeding on his brain, how the damage to his spine couldn't be fully assessed yet due to the swelling. Bree's eyes burned as she stared at him—his face almost unrecognisable, swollen and bruised, his head shaved with a row of stitches marking the raw wound.

"Nik," Bree whispered, her voice trembling. "It's me. I'm here. You have to keep fighting. For me. For us. I love you so much." Her voice broke on the last words, the pain threatening to crush her chest. "Please... just keep fighting."

The doctor returned, gently but firmly insisting that she leave. "Please," he said, "let us do our work. You need rest—and change your clothes."

Bree glanced down at herself. Her cycling shirt was stiff with dried blood, flakes of it falling like powder as her fingers brushed the fabric. With a soft, broken sob, she kissed Nik on the lips before standing up. "We'll take care of him," the doctor said quietly as she reluctantly stepped away.

As Bree walked out of the room, the doctor's words hung in the air: "He's in a coma. There's nothing we can do right now. You should go home. Nothing will change immediately."

She nodded, her mind numb. Nina and Carla drove her home in silence, the sound of the engine humming in the background as Bree stared out of the window, unable to erase the image of Nik lying in that hospital bed from her mind.

"What does a man in a coma need?" Bree asked, her voice hoarse from worry, glancing over at the girls.

"You," Nina replied softly, a sympathetic smile forming on her lips.

Bree quickly packed the essentials—cosmetics, her phone, chargers, and her computer. She took a fast shower, the hot water offering her a brief, fleeting sense of normality, before she rushed back to the hospital, her movements almost robotic. Being in her car again, with the hum of the engine beneath her, gave her a sense of control that she hadn't felt in hours. For the first time in a long while, she wasn't relying on anyone else, except the doctors.

When Bree arrived at the hospital, she found herself once again in the same sterile corridor where the hours had stretched endlessly before. She hoped Nik hadn't been moved yet. A nurse appeared, and Bree immediately asked about him. "He's still here. He's alive," the nurse confirmed. "But he's not out of the woods. All you can do now is wait."

Bree's stomach churned. She sat on the cold chair, her mind racing as she stared at the sterile walls, the air thick with silence. But then, just as the first light of day began to creep into the room, a tap on her shoulder startled her. She turned to see the doctor standing behind her, his expression a mixture of fatigue and something else—hope, perhaps.

"Mrs. Daskalakis," he said, his tone gentle but firm. "We've moved your husband to a private room. He's a fighter. He survived the night. You can see him now."

Bree exhaled a breath and a long, trembling sigh of relief. She nodded, not trusting herself to speak. The doctor walked her to the new room, speaking quickly about Nik's condition as they moved down the sterile hallways.

When they entered the room, Bree's eyes scanned the space—a small water jug sat on a table beside a lounge chair, and a soft cushion lay on the seat of a plastic chair. The beeping of the machines filled the room, a sound that had become strangely reassuring.

Bree sat, her heart thudding in her chest, glancing out the window at the town below. From up here, everything seemed so ordinary—people walking through the streets, oblivious to the torment unfolding above them.

The doctor's voice broke through her thoughts. "He's still in critical condition, but surviving the night was the first hurdle. You can stay as long as you like, though you may have to leave during rounds."

Bree nodded, too numb to speak. When the doctor left, she pulled the chair closer to Nik's bed and stroked his limp, bruised hand. His skin felt cold and colourless beneath her touch. She wrapped her fingers around his, whispering softly, "Nik, I'm here. You have to fight. For me. For us."

Suddenly, the shrill ring of a phone pierced the silence, cutting through her fragile composure. She glanced over at Nik's rucksack, now sitting forgotten in the dark corner of the room. Reaching inside, she fumbled for the phone and answered, her voice trembling.

"Hello?"

"Hey, it's Zac. Is that Bree? Does he have you answering his phone already?" Zac's voice light, filled him humour.

Bree wiped away the tears that had begun to sting her eyes, her voice cracking. "Hey, Zac. Nik had an accident... He's in the hospital, in a coma." Her words barely made sense, even to herself. "It happened yesterday. He survived the night, but... he's still...."

"What? Oh my God..." Zac's shock was clear even down the phone. Bree heard his breath catch in his throat.

She explained as best she could, detailing everything that had happened, her voice breaking with each word. After the call ended, she sank back into the chair beside Nik, the phone slipping from her hand and into her pocket, her shoulders slumping in defeat.

The hours stretched on, the stench of the hospital now a part of her, the annoying fluorescent lights above her a constant, dull presence. She hadn't eaten in over twenty hours, but hunger had long since abandoned her; all she could feel was an aching weariness, a bone-deep exhaustion that no amount of rest could soothe.

Nurses came and went, their footsteps quick and purposeful, but always disappearing before Bree could muster the energy to speak.

She quickly learned which nurses would answer her questions and which would ignore her, brushing her off as if she were just another part of the room. But none of that mattered. All that mattered was Nik.

The hours felt endless, but eventually, she felt the presence of someone behind her. She turned to find Zac standing there, pale, his face lined with exhaustion.

"Bree, sorry it took so long," he said, his voice thick with emotion. "I had to fly to Milan. Commerical flight, you know."

Without another word, Zac pulled her into a brief hug, then slowly made his way to the foot of Nik's bed. He stood there for a long moment, his face tight with grief and disbelief. His hands hovered near his mouth, then dropped as he turned away, his face contorting in pain.

Bree filled him in on the updates she had received, her voice low but steady. Zac listened in silence, nodding gravely. He lowered himself onto the bed, his eyes fixed on his best friend, lost in a world of helplessness. "He's a fighter," Zac finally said, his voice rough. "He's going to pull through."

But even his words didn't seem enough to chase away the fear in the room. The night stretched on, the beeping of the machines a constant reminder of how fragile life really was.

"Hello, I'm the brother," Zac said, his voice steady but low, as he glanced at the doctors beginning their rounds. They exchanged brief looks but asked no questions, letting him stay.

Bree's face crumpled as the tears she'd been holding back finally spilled over. Her chest tightened, and her breaths came shallow and quick. "I'm so sorry," she managed, her voice breaking. "It's all my fault."

Zac shook his head firmly, stepping closer. "No, Bree. This isn't your fault. If he was on that bike, it's because he chose to be. You know Nik—no one makes him do anything he doesn't want to do."

Bree looked at him through blurry eyes, guilt clawing at her. "I hardly know him," she whispered. "We wasted so much time."

Zac gestured for her to sit down. His calm presence was a balm against the storm raging inside her. For the first time in hours, she felt a flicker of relief. As she watched him rub his eyes and stifle a yawn, her concern shifted.

"Bree, go home," Zac urged gently. "Take a shower, get some sleep, and come back later. Or tomorrow. I'll stay here, and I'll call you if anything changes."

She reflected for a moment, but finally nodded, exhaustion overtaking her resistance. Her movements were heavy as she left the hospital, the sterile corridors blurring into a haze.

At home, the hot shower did little to wash away the dread clinging to her. She set an alarm for an hour and collapsed into bed. When it blared, reality jolted her awake. Damp sheets tangled around her legs as she fumbled into jeans and headed back to the hospital, feeling like a ghost of herself.

131 | Petra

Petra stroked her rumbling stomach. Dinner would have been cleared away by now; there would be no food until breakfast. She knew that wine and Netflix would be the perfect medicine to get away from her problems. For the first time, Petra fully understood why they were supposed to stay away from their devices; they needed to concentrate, not escape.

Leaning on her terrace wall, she pondered the questions she had to answer. She had no answers—just more questions; she wrote these down, too. Once again, her night of self-pity was interrupted by a quiet knock at the door.

Expecting Penny and her round, deeply tanned face, she smiled at the sight of Georgie, and what seemed to be a goody bag.

"I have a surprise for you; I told my husband about you and your overload with curried vegetables, so he gave me this." Georgie handed over a plastic container; the steam seeped out of the corners of the lid, and a strong scent of vanilla flew out. "It's from 'The Rock' Restaurant, homemade gnocchi with prawns and vanilla. This will rock your taste buds for sure." Fumbling around in a bag, she handed her a glass and said, "A real, live glass, not a mug, and wait for it, a bottle of wine."

Petra feigned surprise and then let out a wicked laugh. "You're my saviour," she said, lifting the cover of the Tupperware and wafting the smell towards her nose.

"Oh my god, this is fantastic—the best thing I've tried, ever," Petra said, her fork already going for the next Gnocchi.

"I know. Pretty bloody fantastic, isn't it?"

"Georgie, I've had the worst day, and this is just what I needed. Thank you so much."

"Yeah, I saw you with Penny today; I guessed it was a tough one. If you want to talk, I'm here; I've finished for the day." Georgie said.

"Thanks; you're so sweet, and this, pointing to the food and wine, is my perfect cure," she said, easing her way through the tasty food in front of her.

As much as she didn't want to talk anymore, she found herself telling Georgie about the list of questions and her inability to answer them. "I need to speak to my friends at home; I need to clear some things up."

"Sleep on it, then tomorrow, if you still want to, I'll give you your phone, and we can get it all set up. Is that okay?" Georgie said.

"Yeah, thanks. It's just something I need to do." Petra explained.

RAW MISTAKES

"Look, I don't know much about all this type of thing; I know that you won't get the answers by staring at a piece of paper. Why don't you go for a walk around the grounds? I know it's dark, but you're safe inside. Put that pen and paper down and think about you and your life." Georgie said.

"Yeah, I guess. It's better than drawing this stuff," she said, pointing at the doodles on the paper.

Petra finished her wine and Gnocchi and hugged Georgie, grabbed the torch from the wall, and headed outside. The retreat at night had a different feel; she could make out the dark clouds covering the moon as she walked around the perimeter. Petra paused mid-step when she heard a sudden crackling sound behind her, the noise breaking the otherwise silent night. Her heart pounded, thudded even, and a cold wave of fear washed over her. She clenched her torch tightly, its faint beam flickering as she spun around, searching for the source of the noise.

"Hello?" she called out hesitantly, her voice trembling slightly as she pointed the torchlight into the darkness.

From the shadows, another light appeared—an iPhone torch, its beam aimed in her direction. A figure began to emerge from the dark. Petra froze, her mind racing. The figure was tall, thin, and dressed in red and black, carrying what looked like a staff. The shimmering knife at his belt caught her eye, and her breath hitched.

"Okay, Poa, Freshi," the figure said in a calm, accented voice, stepping closer. The words sounded strange, foreign, and only added to her unease.

"What... what do you want?" Petra asked, her voice barely above a whisper, taking an involuntary step back. She tightened her grip on the torch, her mind flicking through every alarming scenario.

"I'm your Maasai. I watch you safe home," the man said, gesturing to the retreat's centre.

His words made no sense to her in her state of heightened panic. He pointed towards the nearby buildings, urging her to move. "Go inside, please. Safe inside," he added, his voice steady and calm.

Petra's torchlight revealed more details of the figure—the striking traditional red and black shuka draped over his body, the staff he carried, the simple rubber shoes on his feet, and the knife at his belt. Her pulse was still racing, but there was something about the way he held himself that wasn't threatening.

She paused, her panic giving way to a cautious curiosity. As her fear subsided, realisation dawned—this must be the Maasai warrior she'd heard about, the one tasked with watching over the retreat grounds at night.

Her shoulders dropped, and she exhaled deeply. "Oh... you're here to... protect us?" she asked hesitantly, her voice regaining a touch of steadiness.

The man nodded, finally easing her nerves. "Yes. Safe home. Go inside now."

Feeling a flush of embarrassment, Petra nodded, her torchlight now steady as she turned and headed towards the retreat, glancing back once to see the Maasai warrior standing quietly, his watchful presence no longer a source of fear but of reassurance.

132 | Petra

Bree looked exhausted, usually stunning, but not that day; Petra noticed the dark rings around her eyes. Petra couldn't work out where she was; she wasn't in the office or at her house. Could it be a hospital? Bree looked like she had the weight of the world on her shoulders. Once the first pleasantries were out of the way, Petra spoke first. Bree had been secretly dreading the video call since it had been arranged. She had no clue what was going on, but seeing Petra in person made her smile; she had missed her friend, and even with her oddities and negativity, she still worried about her.

"Bree, thanks for being here," Petra began. Bree got the impression this was a well-rehearsed speech; it sounded very formal. "Before I say anything else, I must explain what is happening. I have been at this retreat, and it's more than anything I could have ever imagined. I have been on an emotional rollercoaster and am now confronting my past mistakes and trying to correct my wrongs. Is that okay?"

Bree muttered a quiet, tired "yes."

"I want to talk to you; I'm not sure where to start, so I'll start with an apology. I'm sorry for everything: for being a bitch, always having a catty comment ready, not being happy for you, and never being there for you. You helped me more than anyone ever before, and I have been ungrateful, and I have never supported you. You've gone through a divorce, and I wasn't there. You have had a shitty relationship with Robby, and I wasn't there. I have been jealous of your success, thinking I deserved it more than you. I'm so sorry for everything. My jealousy ruled my emotions; my envy controlled my every move."

As Petra stopped talking, there was silence. Bree didn't know what to say; she had not expected this. Hearing these words, she became unexpectedly emotional.

"I accept your apology; I know you've been through a lot, and I appreciate your words and sincerity," Bree replied, flicking her blonde hair behind her ears.

"I want you to stop making excuses for me; you said I have been through a lot; that is not an excuse to be a cruel and unpleasant person. You have been to hell and back recently, and you're still kind to everyone. In the future, I will need you to help me and call me out if you see I'm behaving unkindly. Can you do that?" Petra asked.

"Of course, I will, as long as you're sure," Bree said with a questioning voice.

"Yes, I need that; I will ask the others too." She took a sip of her drink and said, "I want to do this in person, but I need to get this off my chest now. Can you not tell the girls? I want to be able to speak to them both myself." Bree agreed.

"I'm so sorry that you have had to go through all of this; it must be tough," Bree said, always thinking about other people. "I'm glad you've reached this place, though; you look much more at peace with yourself, and the tan suits you too," she laughed.

"It would be lovely to speak more with you when you're home, but right now, I'm having a hell of a day. I shouldn't be using my phone here; I'm hiding around a corner so I don't get spotted, but I need to get back."

"Where are you?" Petra asked.

"I'm in the hospital; a, ehrmm, friend of mine had a bike accident when we were cycling. It's serious; I need to get back," said Bree, in a hurry now.

Petra heard someone call Bree's name; it sounded like Carla. "I appreciate your words, and we can carry this on another time; I'm so sorry I have to leave you right now. I'm proud of you, Petra; don't forget that." The final words drifted into the phone as Bree handed it over to Carla, who said a quick hello and goodbye before ending the call.

133 | Petra

Petra's body ached from the lack of sleep, and her mind weary from the haunting thoughts that had kept her company through the long, sticky night. She'd found herself thrown back in time to her family, mainly her siblings, and the distance between them and how it had become like that. She imagined her father's voice hovering above her bed: 'Determination and hard work will lead to happiness.' Petra couldn't remember how she imagined her life would turn out as a child, but she was pretty sure it was nothing like how her life was now.

As the morning sunrise replaced the velvety darkness, Petra moved slowly to the end of her bed, crippled emotionally by the thoughts that had weakened her whole body. She threw on some clothes, grabbed the notes she scribbled during the never-ending night, and walked towards a waiting Penny. Her eyes looked puffy, and her shoulders slumped.

"Didn't you sleep last night? You look shot," Penny said.

"Oh god, I must look like a mess; I didn't sleep at all, and I didn't get much written down either," Petra said.

"May I look at these?"

"They don't make much sense. But you can look if you like," Petra said, easing her body gently into a wooden garden chair.

Penny read through the notes, making no sense of what she was reading. The writing appeared smaller at the end of each page, as if turning a page would have been too much of a distraction from her thoughts. "Maybe you can explain some of this to me if you feel comfortable doing so," Penny said.

Petra nodded and moved her chair closer to Penny. She started to explain some of the words, sentences, and squiggles. She talked about being the eldest of five siblings, the one who was supposed to be a grownup and help around the house even when she was just a child. Her parents expected her to be perfect—not to cause trouble, not to mess up, and because of her constant fear of not meeting their expectations. She never felt loved by her parents; she only lived for their approval.

Penny gave Petra a reassuring nod and said, "This is a good start for you."

Petra entered the empty breakfast room; a smile crossed her face as she realised she was alone. After quickly eating a pancake and some fresh fruits, she decided to take a break and drag her heavy body back to bed. She awoke almost two hours later, feeling lighter and more carefree. She stepped onto her terrace and winced at the bright light. Reaching for her sunglasses, she sank into the soft, cushioned chair. Sucking and biting the end of her pen, she looked at the unanswered questions on her list. This time, her thoughts were not scary; they were real. She just had a challenge ahead of her.

Three hours passed by the time she finally moved to the lunch table. The group returned, chatting about the experience. She realised the old Petra would have been scared of missing out and would hate hearing them talk about something she had missed. The new Petra was happy to listen to them talk, realising that on this occasion, she had decided not to go on the trip.

She had missed a lot of the session the day before, so there were some things she needed help understanding. Instead of keeping quiet, afraid of making a fool of herself, she decided to speak up and ask for help. Some of what was said hit home, but she managed to hold it together.

"You're all here for different reasons, but many of you, with your actions or words, have hurt yourselves or your loved ones in the past," the life coach said, ensuring he looked everyone in the eyes. "Your actions can change someone's life or your own; you should act differently. Who is going to give me an example?" he asked.

Silence fell over the room; Petra looked around her; most people were looking down, avoiding eye contact, dreading being called upon to talk.

Petra's quiet voice broke the silence. She had not spoken in the group until now, thinking herself different from the others and considering her situation insignificant.

"I've done lots of things I'm not proud of," she said, suddenly sitting up with a straight back. "A few years ago, my friend had a boyfriend; he was cute and sweet and I hated watching them together. I was jealous that he was taking my friend away, and even more so because she had something I desired more than anything: a boyfriend." She paused feeling the eyes of the group on her.

"Go on," Tara said.

"They were in those obsessive days of early love; I felt sick watching them together. I told her I had seen him with another girl and that he was kissing her in the park. It was all a lie. I wasn't ashamed; I was pleased that I had put some doubt in her mind. He denied it, so I started rumours with other friends that spread within the group; hearing the gossip from others, not just me, she broke up with him. I had no proof, no reason to do it, except for pure and bitter envy."

Petra shook her head as she talked, looking at the room rather than the staring gazes of those listening to her. She was surprised to see a deep look of sympathy, not hatred, from them.

"Today is the first time I've talked about it; I've never told anyone."

"How do you feel talking about it?" Tara asked.

"Well, guilty; I've never thought about what I did until now."

By the end of the evening, a couple more of the group were talking to listeners; as she wandered through the retreat, she watched as tears were shed and anger was released. She saw Penny in the distance talking to another participant; Petra gave her a smile and a thumbs up, letting Penny know she was good.

134 | Petra

The following day, Petra scanned the notice board, excited to see a trip to the ocean had been planned, followed by a trip to visit a seaweed farm. Petra racked her brain for a reason not to go, but unable to find one, she added her name to the sign-up sheet.

She glanced in surprise at Matt, who chose to sit beside her. He had short, wavy hair and wore a pair of thick-framed glasses. His skin rubbed against hers as the minibus bumped them around. The stubble gathered around his chin; a bulge in his stomach suggested too much fast food and alcohol in his life before entering the retreat.

Petra had heard Matt in the introductions talking about his journey here. He had entered the retreat after losing his business through thoughtless, rash, and stupid decisions. Petra tensed up unexpectedly as Matt touched her hand and said, "Petra, I want to thank you for your story yesterday; that was brave of you. I've done a lot of stupid things that I'm embarrassed about; I bet we all have, but you found the courage to share them."

Taking in his words, Petra smiled and leant back in relief. She rested her head on the glass in silence, trying to remember the rest of his story. He had become obsessed with money and the glitz of the highlife, having lost track of what he had started the business for to create an amazing life and give his employees a happy working environment. His obsession with being right, not listening to others, and being obnoxious had sent his business down the drain. He'd refused to listen to people telling him times were changing; he thought he knew best. He'd mistreated his staff and made their lives at work miserable. He found himself at the Wishing Tree retreat in Zanzibar, ready to change and start a new life with a new mindset.

Petra looked around her, counting just five others on board. Climbing off the bus, she inhaled the salty scent of the Indian Ocean. Her eyes narrowed, focusing on the calm waves. She reached for her sunglasses, and Petra gazed at the clear blue water in front of her, drinking in the colours that Bree had described. Feeling the burning hot, fine, white sand under her feet, she threw her flip-flops back on and wandered towards the water's edge. The water below lapped over the sand and around her ankles. She inched deeper in until she could feel herself cooling down.

Realising she was alone, she glanced around her and walked over to the rest of her group, spinning her flip-flops in her hands. Godfrey called her over to observe a group of local ladies dressed in long, colourful dresses, kneeling, sitting, and standing in the water, tending to the poles in the sand that held the seaweed. The guide elucidated the process of cultivating seaweed in the ocean and its various uses.

Returning to shallow water, Petra quickly turned her head around to see who was splashing her. "Matt." she screamed as she kicked her feet back towards him.

Petra and Matt walked together along the beach, lagging behind the others. She told him about her wine evenings with Georgie. Her eyes lit up as she described the mouth-watering food she gave her.

"Georgie is a bootlegger?" he asked with a surprised look, "I wouldn't have thought it of her."

"As far as I'm concerned, I'm on holiday, and if I use my own money, then why not? I'm sure you can join us if you like." She chewed her lip nervously as she finished, unsure if she wanted him to crash their private parties.

Noticing the others in their group had disappeared, Matt nudged her and pointed at a restaurant on the beach; she smiled as they turned and sank onto a large, ocean-facing sofa.

Petra rolled up the arms on her t-shirt; her slender arms were already turning brown where the sun had managed to reach. Petra inhaled the beautiful scent of the crispy samosa before biting into it; the fiery flavours sparked the tastebuds on her tongue.

Matt let out a sigh of enjoyment, his eyes wide open as he tasted fluffy coconut bread with a spicy coconut sauce, licking his lips after each bite. Petra giggled as the condensation on the bottles of the ice-cold beer in Matt's hand dripped onto his shorts.

The waitress returned, weighed down by her plates, fries, sweet prawn, fish curry, and spicy squid in breadcrumbs.

"Petra, we can't go back to that place; I want to stay here forever." He laughed as his fork hovered over the dishes, not knowing which to dig into first. They moaned in delight as they bit into each dish, oblivious to the curious looks from other diners.

"Oh, my god." Petra giggled. "This is heavenly," she said as the sweet flavours of the curry hit her lips. Petra sat back on the cushions, her hands rubbing her stomach. "Take away?" she asked the waitress as she pushed the plate away.

"You know something strange. I was worried, you know, about spending another month here after getting used to the safety of the retreat, but now, I'm so excited," Petra said, carefully picking up the takeaway boxes and placing them in her bag. Reaching for her flip-flops and beach towels, they stood up to leave.

"I think I'll love it here on the beach—well, not here; I'll be a few miles from here, but you know what I mean," Petra said.

"Me too; I'm going up to the north of the island, to Nungwi, but I have to say, this place looks nice enough." Looking at his watch, Matt urged Petra to hurry up as he paid the bill.

"Oh my god, twenty dollars for all of that—that's so cheap." he said, putting his wallet back in his rucksack. As they neared the bus, they saw the concern on Godfrey's face quickly replaced by frustration.

"Where were you? We were worried," he scowled.

"We went to the restaurant," Matt said, pointing in the direction they had just come.

He shot them a disapproving glance. "No, we were over there," he said, pointing to a small restaurant on the beach. "Organic Maasai cooking, including delicious seaweed dishes."

Petra and Matt glanced at each other and let out a spontaneous laugh. "Sorry," Matt said, looking down like a scolded child.

Mustafa smiled at them as they waited to board the bus; the new blue shirt that Matt had given him hung off his slight figure.

"We are going to a local shop now. We will buy food for the next few days: rice, sugar, some potatoes, eggs. You can see how we do things here," Godfrey explained.

Matt looked at Petra, flashing an unimpressed glance. "Can we pay Mustafa to come and collect us later?" Matt shouted over Godfrey, who shot a look of disapproval.

Mustafa stepped forward. "Yes, no problem," he quipped.

Godfrey reluctantly agreed as they arranged to pay Mustafa five dollars to return in three hours.

As Matt and Petra strolled away from the bus, Matt let out a fist pump into the air and said, "We're free; what shall we do?" He stood with his back to the ocean, facing the car park. Petra placed her hands on his shoulders and turned him around.

"Swim?" Petra suggested, nodding towards the water. They returned to the restaurant that had made them feel alive just a few minutes earlier, asked to leave their bags and clothes and ran to the water's edge over white, fluffy sand. As the tide retreated, they bathed in the blue ocean waters.

As the afternoon passed, Petra realised she had misjudged Matt; his contagious smile and ability to laugh at himself amused her greatly. His round face concealed a squared jaw, a stark contrast to the arrogant, smug Matt she had encountered during the group introductions on day one. They chatted freely about their life mistakes and all the things they had done that they were embarrassed about; they shared their worst moments and memories. In the safety of each other's company and the privacy of that sandbank, they were not being judged; they were being forgiven.

Drying themselves off and throwing on some clothes, they waved to Mustafa and approached the minibus.

"Okay, where do we go now?" he asked eagerly. "Retreat or somewhere else?"

"Any suggestions?" Petra asked, reluctant to end the day so soon.

"I will take you to Paje, a big town with shops and bars. Okay?" Mustafa suggested, smiling as his only two passengers spread out in the seats. Mustafa scanned his phone and said, "African beats." He smiled as the music covered the roar of the engine.

Petra watched with wide eyes as they passed small groups of ladies effortlessly walking with boxes on their heads, an older man on a push bike small enough for a child struggling up the slight incline. They passed large billboards with pictures of deluxe hotels, promising relaxing holidays by the sandy beach.

As promised, Paje offered a sign of normality—not quite European life, but stall after stall of fresh produce—with tourists wandering around flimsily dressed. They heard the wheels crunch on the gravel as Mustafa pulled into a car park, slowing to a stop.

"There's a big supermarket there, and there's a smoothie bar there." They sprinted enthusiastically up the uneven pink stairs. Feeling a shiver as they opened the door to a rush of air conditioning, they exchanged a knowing smile.

135 | Petra

Picking up a red basket, Petra browsed the shelves with glistening eyes as she recognised the shapes and colours of the bottles, tins and boxes on each dusty shelf. She carelessly threw boxes in her bag: chocolate chip cookies, Pringles, pizza-flavoured crisps, salted crackers, shortbread, and coke. Reaching the final aisle, she looked around. "That's it?" she said to Matt, who nodded.

"It's tiny," he laughed, tracing his steps back through the shop, ensuring she had not missed any items.

With a heavy basket, she handed over the items, flipping through the red notes in her purse, hoping she had enough cash. The wad of money had no meaning, and the numbers the teller showed her on the calculator were of no value.

Matt followed behind her, handing over money himself for his purchases. The darkened, heavy glass door opened, letting in a burst of humid, hot air and bright light.

Mustafa took their bags as they walked past the smoothie bar with its green grass and garden furniture. Happy-looking tourists meandered around the town, browsing shops for souvenirs. Matt pointed laughingly at the signs above the shops: 'Harrods, Ikea, Home Bargains, Zara.' The handwritten signs differentiated the shops only by name, displaying the same: sun-faded clothes, wicker baskets, and hand-carved wooden animals in each shop.

"Hello, Ciao," said the shopkeepers in smiley voices. Come look," they suggested as the pair smiled. They continued quickly through the town, passing a makeshift roundabout constructed from old car tyres cut in half and placed in the sand.

"Here," Mustafa announced. He stopped outside a doorless shop with battered white walls lined with wooden shelves stocked to the brim with gleaming bottles of wine, vodka, gin, amarula, and konyagi.

"Yes, this is my kind of shop," Matt said, jumping quickly up the steep steps and smiling at the man at the desk. He browsed as Petra bought wine for her and Georgie, enough to last the remainder of their stay. Matt grabbed a couple of bottles, handing them to the shopkeeper, who followed them around the small store with a basket. Once again, handing over the musty-smelling pink notes, they walk out of the shop with satisfied grins. Mustafa rushed ahead, guiding them down a tiny, dark gap between two houses to his waiting minibus.

"Retreat now," he said, placing the key in the ignition.

"Yeah, I guess," Matt said, clinging to his precious bottles. "These won't survive on that road if I don't look after them," he said to Petra, who reached quickly for her bottles, nursing them on her lap as the minibus jolted them around. Matt handed Mustafa a generous tip; his gesture said it was nothing, but his eyes glistened at the crumpled notes in his hand.

Back at the retreat, Georgie stored their takeaway food and bottles in her fridge, just keeping one out each for the evening ahead. Refreshed after the afternoon by the beach as promised, Matt arrived on her balcony, proudly waving the bottle of Vodka above his head like a prized possession.

136 | Bree

The days turned into weeks. Bree's friends stopped by each morning, shuttling Zac between the hospital and her home in shifts. Together, they endured thirty-six long, grinding days before the doctors finally suggested lightening Nik's coma. The holidays came and went unnoticed. Bree and Zac ate vending machine dinners and shared a silent glass of beer by the bedside on New Year's Eve. There were no celebrations, only gratitude that Nik was still alive.

The room was still except for the beeping of the monitors, each sound a lifeline tethering Nik to the world. Bree and Zac stood just beyond the glass, their hands tightly clasped.

Inside, the doctors watched Nik's vitals carefully as the medication holding him in the coma ebbed away. His chest continued to rise and fall, shallow but steady. A couple of hours passed before Nik started to stir. Zac paced the room, his loud footsteps caused Bree to wince.

Bree's breath caught, and she straightened, eyes wide. "Did you see that?" she whispered, her voice trembling.

Zac nodded, his grip on her hand tightening. The doctors exchanged glances, their movements suddenly more deliberate as they monitored the subtle signs of awakening. Nik's head shifted slightly, his brows knitting together as though caught in a vivid dream. Another twitch, this time in his arm.

"Come on, buddy," Zac murmured, his voice barely audible.

The beeping of the monitor grew erratic for a moment, then evened out. Nik's eyelids fluttered, and Bree's heart leapt into her throat. His lips parted as if to speak, but no sound came out, only a faint, laboured breath. Slowly, his eyes opened, unfocused and hazy, as though he were staring through a fog.

"Nik," she said softly, her voice shaking. "It's me. It's Bree."

He blinked, his gaze wandering around the room, then settling on the window, where the sunlight poured in. His lips moved again, forming no words, but the effort was unmistakable.

"Nik," she repeated, her voice stronger now.

His eyes finally found hers, a faint glimmer of recognition passed over his face.

Zac followed, standing at the foot of the bed. "You scared us, man," he said with a broken laugh. "Don't ever do that again."

137 | Bree

"Where am I?" he asked, looking around him and speaking in Greek. His eyes were glazed with agitation. Slowly and with effort, he moved his head.

Zac neared the bed and touched his friend's arm. "It's ok; you're safe, you're alive, I'm here, we are here," he said, pulling Bree closer.

"Breezy? Is that you? What are you doing here?" He looked at her through lazy eyes before quickly shutting them; the simple task of speaking had worn him out.

While he slept, the doctors visited. "It's customary to wake in a state of confusion," they said, noticing the concern and fear on Bree's face, who held back tears in front of them.

When Nik woke, there was more life in his eyes. He looked at Zac, Bree, and Zac again. Thoughts passed slowly and painfully across his eyes, and then the searching froze. "I remember seeing you on the tube; I remember doing the marathon; then, it's blank," he said in English, gazing unbelievably at Bree, reaching out to her. All reason was lost to the tingle of his skin against hers as she felt her eyes well up.

"Bree, do you mind?" Zac asked.

Bree moved aside to make room as Zac spoke in Nik's native tongue, explaining what had happened, where he was, and how much time had passed.

Nik visibly relaxed and lay in silence for a few moments. The information arrived faster than he could take. He opened his eyes and moved his fingers in the direction of Bree; she quickly moved towards him.

"You're here. Thank you. Can I hold your hand?" he asked.

"Well, it's your engagement ring she's wearing, so I think you need to hold her hand." Zac said, a loud laugh filling the quiet room.

"That's your ring, the one I gave you in Crete; how did you get it?" he asked, struggling to assemble the puzzle pieces.

"You gave it to me; you don't remember?" she asked, a tear dripping off her cheek onto his hand.

"Of course, but you sent it back. Bree, you're so goddam beautiful; I never stopped loving you; you need to know that," he said.

Bree sat on the edge of his bed, placing her hand on his face, and kissed him on the cheek. "I know, you told me that when you gave me a ring on the day of the accident," she said slowly, whispering the words, afraid to scare him. His memory tricked him, remembering things from long ago but refusing to bring up the events of the last few weeks before the accident.

"So, we are engaged. You agreed to marry me after all this time? You still love me?" His eyes were heavy and unfocused.

"Yes, of course," she said.

Leaning back and closing his eyes, he fell into a restful sleep. Awaking with a stir to his legs, he looked around the room as if seeing it for the first time. He studied the machines that had kept him alive for so long, quickly turning away, trying to tune out the distractions.

"Breezy, I'm sorry," he said. "When you came to my hotel in London, I vowed I'd marry you; then, when I moved to Italy, I bought the ring with me. I remember the lake, the ring, and the picnic. I remember the thrill of your yes carrying me down that mountain. I remember it, all of it." He paused, holding her hand tightly. "Bree, even though I'm an idiot, do you still want to marry me?" His voice was husky and quiet.

"Well, that is the third time you have proposed, and this is the third time I have said yes. Do I get another ring or just this one?" She wiggled her slim fingers to show the ring.

Zac and Bree stood over the bed; Nik was alive and mentally alert. The doctors asked them to leave while they did some tests. Finally, able to leave the room together, they walked past the coffee machine that had become a save haven to them, heading to the coffee shop.

"Zac, I can never thank you enough for being here, for coming to Italy for this, for your friend. I would have been lost without you."

Zac held both of her hands and replied, "Bree, thank you for letting me be here and for being here for him; he needed you, and you were there. I can see why he spent all those years waiting for you." The pair both took deep sighs, picked up their cups and took long, slow sips.

"Okay, enough of all this emotional stuff; come on, let's go back," Bree said, carrying their coffees and walking the familiar, soulless corridors back to the ward.

When they returned to the room, the doctors were finishing up. The taller of the two doctors spoke first, looking at Bree. "Your husband is a miracle; he'll recover in time. He'll need to work on his mobility, but he'll be good as new in a couple of months."

Nik smiled at Bree; he mouthed the word 'husband' to her with a questioning smile.

"When can we take him home?" asked Zac.

"Not yet; we still have tests to do, and we still want to monitor him for another week, but after that, he can go home."

Zac took Bree's hand and squeezed it tight. Bree fussed and clucked around Nik, ensuring he had everything he needed, until he finally insisted they leave. "I'm fine here; you have lives to get on with; get on with them; don't worry about me; just come and see me when you have done all your other things," he said.

Bree finally slept for almost six hours, clutching Nik's shirt close to her chest and inhaling his faint scent. Her sleep was no longer haunted by nightmares, and she now awoke with a smile, not a frown.

Once Nik was stable again, talking, and set to go home, Zac left for his journey back to Greece. "See you soon; I'm coming over as soon as I can move properly. I've got to pack up my house," Nik said as he tried to hug his friend goodbye, restricted by his injuries.

Bree watched as Zac clambered behind the wheel of his rental car and drove away for one last time.

138 | Bree

A few days later, the hospital doors hissed open as Nik left for the last time.
Bree had been to the hospital so often now that she felt like a member of an exclusive club, no longer lost in the maze of identical white corridors. She pushed the wheelchair towards the car and helped him in. Nik smiled as he felt the sun on his face.

"I'm free," he said, opening the car window. Struggling to get to his feet, he hobbled into Bree's house. He made a beeline for the fridge.

"Food, decent food. Bree, please tell me you went shopping," he said with a hopeful grin.

"Yep, all your favourites are in here." She opened the fridge and said, "Everything a sick man needs to get better."

"But who is going to cook it? Not you, I hope," he laughed.

"No, look, I've got you a stool with wheels; you can move around the kitchen as much as you like," Bree said proudly.

He moved to the sofa, gesturing for Bree to join him.

She placed her hands on his legs, leaning in for a kiss. "I can't believe you're here," she said as they closed their eyes in relief.

While Nik pottered around on his mobile stool, Bree, finally feeling ready to face Petra, slouched onto her sofa. Taking a deep breath, she waited for the video call to connect. Her fingers toyed nervously with the edge of a cushion as the screen flickered to life.

"What's going on over there? I get the feeling you aren't telling me something," Petra said, her voice tinged with curiosity and concern.

"Okay, well, it's a long story." Bree took a moment, swallowing hard. "It's Nik. Do you remember him?"

Petra's brows knitted as her eyes drifted to the side, searching her memory. Slowly, a smile spread across her face. "The guy from Greece?" she asked.

"Yeah, the love of my life. The one I never forgot," Bree admitted, her voice softer. She exhaled and continued, her words tumbling out quickly. "We met up in London. He came here, and... he had an accident."

Petra's face dropped into a frown. "Oh my God."

Bree watched her closely, half-expecting to catch a flicker of envy, but there was none—only concern. She pressed on. "He was in a coma for a long time. He's out now, but things have been... a bit crazy."

Petra nodded, her expression resolute. "Okay. Well, I'll be there soon. Let me know how I can help, okay?"

RAW MISTAKES

Relief flooded Bree's face. "Okay," she agreed, ending the video call. As the screen went dark, she sank back into the cushions, her chest rising and falling with a long, satisfied breath. Into the quiet room, she whispered, "Welcome back, Petra. I've missed you."

139 | Bree

Bree invited Carla and Nina to the office, where they made a beeline for the coffee machine. With steaming mugs in hand, they settled into chairs and filled Bree in on the latest updates.

"Now, we need to arrange your wedding," Nina announced with a grin, her tone playful but determined.

Bree laughed, shaking her head. "No, not yet. Come on, give us some time to adjust to having him back home."

"Fine," Carla said with mock exasperation, "but when you're ready, can we plan it for you? A surprise, maybe? You must be sick of organizing weddings. This way, you'll actually get to enjoy the excitement for once."

Bree raised an eyebrow but smiled. "Okay, I guess. But Nik gets to decide everything. After what he's been through, he deserves his dream day."

"And Petra will be back soon," Carla added, "so she can help, too."

Bree nodded thoughtfully. "Alright, but I have some conditions: no flash mobs, no wild parties, and definitely no massive guest list. Just the important people. And there's no rush—it can be next month or next year, whenever Nik feels up to it."

The three shared a laugh and clinked their coffee mugs in agreement. Once Bree became preoccupied with work, Carla and Nina snuck off to see Nik.

They found him in the kitchen, moving carefully a sheen of sweat on his back from the unseasonably hot weather. He paused to wipe his brow and smiled when he saw them.

"We've spoken to Bree about the wedding," Carla began, a teasing smile on her lips. "She's given us the green light to organise it—as long as you agree to everything."

Nik slouched against the counter, intrigued. "Really? And when does she want to do it?"

"She says that's up to you," Nina replied. "Next month, next year—whatever feels right."

Nik's face lit up with excitement. "Next year? No way. The doctors said I'd be fine in a month or so. Let's aim for a couple of months. I need something to look forward to."

Carla and Nina exchanged grins. "Alright, it's settled," Carla said. "Let's get planning."

The three huddled around the table, excitement buzzing in the air as they started brainstorming. For Nik, it was the spark of joy he hadn't realised he needed.

140 | Bree

Bree hurried around the flat; scanning the room, she nodded. Nik had all the remote controls beside him, and the water and snacks were on the table. He kissed her on the cheek as she delivered his morning coffee. She placed a glossy magazine behind him and kissed him goodbye.

"I'm going to the office; I'll be back as soon as possible," she said. Nik looked at her harshly and gestured for her to sit down.

"You can look after me when we are old, okay? I've just spent almost two months in the hospital; I need to do things for myself now and for you, if you will let me," he pleaded.

He felt a decade older. Squinting in horror at his reflection in the mirror, he felt a wave of irritation wash over him at his inability to even dress without falling.

"I love you for protecting me, but I'll never get better if you do everything for me. Please, give me some space to try and do things," he pleaded nervously.

"Okay, what can I do? But I won't be happy until you can run ten kilometres," Bree said.

"Firstly, let me struggle around the kitchen; let me try and do my thing. It will be slow, but I want to try," he said. Bree nodded in acceptance of his terms. "And after you finish work, I want to go outside for a walk on the lake. I won't get far, but I need to start somewhere," he said, determined.

"Okay, but only if I come with you the first few times," she said.

"I want you to come with me; that's the idea," he replied.

That afternoon, he struggled to keep up the pace after insisting that Bree didn't slow down just for him. They walked further each afternoon until, one day, he outpaced her. As he ate regular meals, his strength grew. With physiotherapy, his muscles strengthened, and the dark shadows that had formed around his eyes disappeared. Once again, without vanity, Bree noticed him stopping to inspect his image on any reflective surface, adjusting his hair. The more he talked, the wider his gestures became, and the more his old self returned, the stronger he became. Her hands clasped over her mouth the morning he awoke, finally strong enough to hold her in his arms and make love to her, as he had dreamed of doing for weeks. He moved slowly, barely aware of his movements, as Bree shivered in enjoyment at his touch.

The following day, they woke slowly, enjoying the warmth of the bed and the soft touch of love on their skin.

"I know you want me all to yourself, but we have forever together; you're not keeping me hidden in here anymore, Bree; show me around your world," he said, wondering if she had something to hide.

"Okay, but be prepared for stares and curious glances." She flashed him a knowing look.

They stepped outside; the air was filled with soft, constant rain that hardly seemed to fall. They walked the streets of Rocca Pinta, past the closed shutters of the shops and boarded-up restaurants. Umbrellas hid the faces of the passersby, although they seemed not to notice people walking quickly around them, removed from the world, engrossed in each other's company.

"Coffee?" Bree asked, feeling the cold rainwater dripping through her coat.

"Definitely," he replied.

"Ready for this?" she asked as they entered the bar she frequently visited with Carla and Nina.

As the flimsy door closed behind them, all eyes were initially on Bree. She watched as everyone glared at Nik, confused. Nik relaxed as he felt the easy, reassuring touch of Bree's hand on his arm as she guided him through the staring faces.

Unsure where to look, she pointed to an empty table. Brushing off the rain, she removed her coat, and he followed suit. Sitting uncomfortably, she looked around her; people quickly glanced away, not wanting to catch her eye. She knew the people of the village well enough to know that this stranger would be the gossip of the town for the next few days.

141 | Bree

They must have all heard about Nik, his accident, and his recovery. They were just too rude to ask, just rude enough to stare. As the waiter came over, he smiled, and she introduced Nik to him, knowing that was enough; within seconds, they would all know everything they wanted to know.

"This is Nik; I'm sure you heard about the accident; well, here he is. He lives here now with me; we're getting married once the weather warms up," she said, rubbing his thigh in a gesture of support.

The waiter cast him a glance, not knowing how to react. Out of respect for Bree, he shook Nik's hand. "Nice to meet you," he said in English. His eyes widened in surprise as Nik introduced himself in fluent Italian.

"Nice to meet you too. Can you make my coffee strong, please?" he asked the server. His mouth dropped; no one had told him that this outsider from Greece could speak Italian, which changed everything.

He turned back to the bar, whispers quickly turned into loud chatter, and customers stopped staring.

She stretched out her leg to give a nice kick under the table. "Kiss me," Bree said.

He closed the gap and kissed her; the glances again turned to them, and then, satisfied by this new relationship status, they returned to their conversations.

"Thank you. Now, that is what I was dreading—the stares—but we've done it now; we are officially, in their eyes, a couple. People don't kiss in public around here; that is way too much emotion for them."

They drank their coffee, paid, and left. Bree waved a generic goodbye to everyone before retreating.

"What was that all about?" he asked, showing an unimpressed expression.

"That was the Rocca Pinta welcome, otherwise known as a grilling or a roasting. Give them a few days, and they will get used to you; we'll go in tomorrow with the girls and then another couple of locals, and they'll get accustomed to you. Don't worry."

"Are you sure you want to live here?" he asked. "Thessaloniki is much friendlier."

"They are here, too; it just takes a while, but you watch, find common ground, and you will be fine. Come here on football night with one of my friends' husbands or boyfriends, and they'll love you."

"Are you sure?" Nik asked.

"Don't worry; they need to get used to you and us. They are used to me being alone here, with the girls or friends; you're the first guy I've been here with."

"Oh, so an honour then," he said, grabbing her hand and hurrying her along. Avoiding the large grey puddles and splashes from the passing cars, they made it back home.

Within a few weeks, Nik was strong enough to face a trip back to Greece. He needed to close his house up, set up his business for smart working, and get his belongings. Not wanting to spend even a day without her, he insisted Bree go along; she didn't take much convincing.

142 | Bree

A short Ryanair flight brought them to Thessaloniki, where Zac was waiting with open arms. He embraced Nik, his eyes misting as he noticed the changes in his friend. Nik grinned, his delight growing as the sights of home unfolded before him.

Bree rolled down the car window, letting the warm air carry in the unmistakable scent of Greece.

Nik wasted no time introducing Bree to everyone he knew. He hugged his friends and colleagues with infectious warmth, his smile lighting up the room.

Bree finally got a glimpse into his daily world—his workplace, his morning routines, and, most importantly, his friends. Many of them were part of his running club, and she recognised a few faces. However, she couldn't help but notice the subtle glares from a few women in the group, their irritation thinly veiled. Bree was unfazed, though; Nik's attention was solely on her. Oblivious to the effect his rugged jawline and piercing blue eyes had on others, his smile was reserved for Bree alone.

"Party tomorrow evening, same time and place," Nik announced, clapping his hands. "Spread the word."

Preparations for the party were a team effort. Zac managed the logistics, Nik handled the cooking, and Bree took charge of decorations. By dusk, guests began to arrive, their arms laden with drinks, snacks, and dishes of all kinds.

"Alright, everyone, it's time," Nik said, standing tall as he adjusted his shirt. Speaking in Greek, his voice boomed across the room. Zac quickly moved to Bree's side, whispering the translation into her ear.

After expressing his gratitude to the crowd, Nik switched to English, gesturing for Bree and Zac to join him. "These two saved me. Without them, I don't know where I'd be right now."

Zac chuckled. "Pretty sure it was the doctors who saved you, not us."

Nik shook his head, his voice steady with emotion. "The doctors saved my life; you two brought me back to life." He draped an arm around each of them.

Then he turned to Bree, his eyes softening. "And you're all invited to a wedding in Italy. My best man here will give you the details when we set the date. But for now, for anyone who hasn't met Bree—here she is."

The crowd erupted in cheers, and Bree's cheeks flushed crimson.

Accustomed to being in the background, she quietly slipped away as Nik continued mingling with his friends. In the kitchen, Bree washed glasses, grateful for a moment to herself. Nik found her there, a flicker of concern in his eyes. "Are you okay?" he asked gently.

"Yeah, I'm great," she said, smirking as she playfully wiped soap suds on his face. "Go back out there and enjoy your evening. Your friends have missed you, and we both know how much you love being the centre of attention."

Nik hesitated then smiled. "If you're sure. I just don't want you to feel left out."

He lingered a moment before slipping back to the party. Soon after, Zac entered the kitchen carrying a heavy bowl of bottled beers. "He sent you, didn't he?" Bree teased.

Zac grinned. "Come on." He plucked the dishcloth from her hands and tossed it into the sink. Grabbing two large cushions, he led her out onto the balcony and motioned for her to sit.

"Look at the stars," he said, pointing upward. "See that one? I like to call it Kebab. Don't you think it looks like one?"

Bree burst into laughter, her tension melting away. They sat together under the starlit sky, naming constellations with ridiculous names, their laughter blending with the distant music of the party.

"I'm going to miss him, you know," Zac said quietly. "I'd love to visit."

Bree smiled warmly. "We'll call the spare room yours, okay? You're part of my family now. I'm lucky to have you as a friend."

143 | Bree

Bree wandered Nik's house searching for her keys and glasses. His house was an Aladin's cave of sports gear, the boxes neatly stacked in the corner, marked with Greek letters that she could not make out.

Everything seemed to have a place apart from the desk covered in papers and notes. She slid her hand over the wooden desk, not wanting to move anything. Her eyes stopped, focusing only on one thing: a pile of dusty letters all addressed to Bree in the mountains in Calenda Alto. She flicked through them, inhaling the scent of the faded envelopes, before quickly returning them to where she found them.

With a couple of cups hanging on a rack and everything neatly hidden behind cupboard doors, the kitchen was spacious and silent. She moved to the balcony, overlooking the city lined with parks. The chirping of birds filled the chilly air, and the occasional honk of cars below reminded Bree she wasn't alone.

Nik wasn't strong enough to do all the heavy lifting; he arrived with Zac. The room was filled with noise as they loaded boxes onto a trailer, preparing it for the road trip to Italy. Nik would rent his house as an Airbnb, keeping it for his holidays and visits. Zac didn't need much convincing to go with him.

As they drove Bree to the airport, Nik looked at her and reached out his hand. "I wrote these to you a few years ago, but they all came back unread." Nik handed her a pile of envelopes and said, "I would like you to have them—something to read on the plane." She looked at the envelopes she had seen in his room. She nodded and kissed him goodbye.

Bree hurried through security and down to the boarding gate. Showing her ticket, she made her way through the door to the plane and her seat. Holding the letters close to her chest, she slouched low in her chair and studied the dates on them. They had been stored in chronological order, from first to last. Her palms itched, wanting to open them. With a trembling hand, she read the note, a handwritten scribble he thrust into her pocket as he kissed her goodbye and said, "I love you now, more than ever; see you in seventeen hours." She smiled and opened the first letter, dated a week after the phone call.

At first, the letters were stilted; she touched the paper, running her finger across the words. Her heart skipped a few beats as she read, 'I won't marry her; just answer me, and I will leave my family. I can't do this anymore; I need to be with you.' The raw emotion in his words was palpable, and tears slid down her face as she carefully placed the letter in the envelope and opened the next.

The words on the page became fluid as the days went by, perfectly capturing every emotion he felt, with the exception of one letter that sounded almost desperate. There were just six words on the page, nothing else. 'I'm not marrying her, hear me?'

She flipped through the dates on the envelopes again; he'd written every day for six weeks, then a couple a month for a while. As the wheels hit the tarmac with a thud, she realised where she was. Looking around her, she put the letters in her bag; she had over twenty more to read. She dried her eyes with her scarf, thinking of the last note: 'My father is very sick; there is very little chance he will survive. I will marry the girl to make him happy in his final days. I'm sorry.'

She caught a glimpse of herself in the mirror. She wiped the mascara from her eyes with her scarf and quickly drove home to read the rest. Hugging a cup of hot tea, she wrapped a blanket over her, her legs folded under her on the couch, and opened letter after letter.

'Today is my wedding day; I'm marrying a girl I don't love. I'm thinking of a girl I love. You.' Bree's eyes welled up once more, and she took in more of his emotionally charged words. 'I'm doing this for my family, but you are who I want to see at the end of the aisle,'

Now, opening a letter from a few months later: 'My parents have both died now. My wife has left me. I may be heartless, but I'm glad she's gone; I'm free. Please tell me where you are, and I will come to you. I love you.' This was the last letter for a month, then the last one, that read: 'Breezy, my Breezy. I know you don't get these; they have started to come back to me. This is the last letter. It's time for me to move on. I'm going to Thessaloniki to create a new life. I hope that you are there. That is where you said you were offered a job. I will work with Anna for now. I will look for you. I love you.'

She held the letter to her heart before carefully placing it in its envelope and wiping her tears again. She awoke early and began pottering around the house. Her domestic bliss was interrupted by banging on the door, standing up with a jolt, looking at the time, and brushing her hair down with her hands. She opened the door with a smile. Nik and Zac stood with tired faces, both heading straight to the sofa.

"You read them?" Nik asked, spotting the letters on the table.

"Twice," she said.

I'm sorry I put you through that," she said with wide eyes.

"We can talk about it later," he said. He pulled her hand away and led her into the privacy of the bedroom. "Just tell me, did you see them and send them back?" he asked, his eyes searching for hers.

"No, I promise; the first time I saw them was on your desk last week," she said.

144 | Bree

A couple of weeks later, Nik let out a frustrated sigh as he heard footsteps approaching outside the door. Rising from the sofa, he set the kettle on, anticipating Bree's return from the office.

"Hey, honey," Bree said warmly as she stepped inside, wrapping her arms around his waist. She immediately noticed the tension in his expression. Placing her hands on his face, she gently turned his head to meet her gaze. "What's wrong?"

Nik avoided her eyes, his shoulders slumping. "I guess I'm just... bored. Being here alone, without my friends, it's starting to get to me."

Bree's concern deepened as she watched him sink into the corner of the sofa. "I know it must be hard. I'll try to spend less time at work. Maybe I can take a few days off, and we can go somewhere nice, just the two of us."

Nik shook his head, his voice heavy with resignation. "It won't change much. I'll still feel the same when we come back. I think... I think I'm just missing home."

Bree's heart clenched. The fear of what that might mean rippled through her as she felt her smile fade. "Do you want to move back to Greece?"

Nik glanced at her, catching the flicker of worry in her eyes. He wanted to reassure her but found no words. "I don't know," he finally admitted, his voice subdued.

Despite the turmoil inside, Bree remained composed. "If you need to leave, I understand," she said gently. "Maybe I can look into moving there too. Starting fresh. I can't expect you to make all the sacrifices. And it's not like I'm unfamiliar with life in Greece—I love it there."

Nik's tense expression softened slightly, though uncertainty lingered in his voice. "No, it's not just that. I think I just need... something. A purpose. A reason to get up in the morning. I've got savings, and the remote work helps, but I need more than staring at a screen all day. I need meaning."

Bree nodded, her tone encouraging. "In Italy, things can take time to fall into place. It's often about who you know. I'm sure it'll work itself out soon."

"I hope you're right," Nik said, leaning back. "But I don't feel like I can stay here indefinitely without something to do. Zac needs me at home, and I can't just... play house with you, as much as I love being here. Coming to Italy might have been too impulsive. Maybe I wasn't ready to give up my life in Greece."

Bree reached for his hand, her touch steady and reassuring. "Nik. It's normal to question things now, to rethink your options. I just hope I'm part of whatever plans you make."

Nik looked at her, his eyes softening. "Bree, you always understand me so well. I'm just feeling a little lost, that's all."

"Then let's figure it out," she said with a small smile. "It's unpaid, but how about helping Carla and me at the restaurant? I know you're still building your strength, but we can find plenty of small ways for you to stay busy."

Nik's lips curved into a grin, a glimmer of relief in his expression. "Yeah, I'd like that. I'll come with you tomorrow. Thank you, Bree. Maybe it'll help me clear my head for a bit."

145 | Bree

Carla felt her heart thud as she turned the keys to the interior section restaurant the day they started work. The doors were shut and uninviting.

This abandoned restaurant, with a faded and broken wooden facade, was slowly rotting around the cracked windows. Carla felt goosebumps crawl up her arm as she put her hand on the faded brass door handle. The heavy door creaked open and banged back. A splinter of wood fell to the ground from the impact. The wooden roof of the terrace was covered in splinters, and ragged iron nails protruded from the pillars. Small, stagnant puddles of water lay on the moss-covered cobbles, reflecting the white clouds floating across the sky.

Looking back at Bree, Carla shouted instructions: "Bree, you start the list of things to do," she said, handing her a piece of paper and a pen. "First, fix the entrance door, paint the entrance gate, call the gardener, and buy paint." As they walked around, her voice echoed through the space, listing every crack and creak that needed attention.

"The kitchen looks new," Nik pointed out, pulling off white sheets carefully draped over the oven and hobs. "We'll need to get someone to check it, but it looks solid."

Nik unboxed the phone and inserted the new SIM card. His face lit up. "We're online," he called out. The tall bar stool towered over the desk, but he perched on it, balancing the computer on his lap. Within minutes, he was typing and scribbling notes. "I've found a gardener. He'll be here tomorrow morning," he announced with pride.

Carrying a set of car keys, Nik returned later with four plastic wicker chairs and a garden table. "Our office," he declared, setting them up in the garden. Bree laughed, watching him arrange them with exaggerated precision.

By lunchtime, Nik had spreadsheets tracking expenses, a typed-up to-do list, and appointments arranged with plumbers, electricians, and handymen. Carla slumped into a chair, burying her face in her hands.

"What have I done?" she whispered, her voice breaking. Her eyes darted from the peeling paint on the walls to the scuffed tiles underfoot. Her decision pressed down, a tangible thing she couldn't shake off.

Nik crouched beside her, his voice steady. "You've taken the first step. It's crazy now, but give it time. You'll see."

The plumber arrived shortly after, his face lined with scepticism as he inspected the brown water gushing from the pipes. "This place is a mess," he said bluntly, shaking his head. "You'll need to re-plumb the entire system."

Carla flinched at his words but nodded. Before she could spiral further into doubt, two young men approached, their faces bright with enthusiasm. "Our uncle did the original plumbing here," one said. "He's retired now, but he'd love to help out. We'll get you a good price."

By the end of the week the pieces started falling into place. Nik had ordered wines, drafted bar menus, and worked tirelessly alongside Bree and Carla. The garden transformed as the gardener trimmed the palms, letting sunlight flood the terrace. Dead plants were replaced with kumquat trees, cobblestones were weeded, and illuminated vases brimmed with colourful flowers.

Two days later, Zac pulled up to the restaurant He stepped out into the warm afternoon sun, greeted by the overwhelming scent of fresh paint that hung in the air like a promise of new beginnings. As he approached the front gate his eyes scanned the exterior—once so uninviting, now slightly less dreary but still a long way from its potential. The faded sign above the door seemed almost embarrassed by the shabby state of the place. The paint that had been slapped on it didn't quite mask the cracks and chipped edges, and the windows, while clean now, still carried the ghosts of years of neglect.

But despite the tiredness of the place, something about the air felt different. It felt like a space that had started to wake up.

His eyes twinkled as they landed on Bree. She was standing near the kitchen door, her clothes covered in streaks of white paint, her hair pulled back into a messy bun. There was something endearing about the sight of her, a woman who had no problem diving into the mess of it all.

She looked up, her lips curling into a grin. "Welcome back, Bro," she said, her voice a little breathless, as if she'd been working non-stop all day.

Zac chuckled, shaking his head as he scanned the room. "You're... a sight for sore eyes." He let out a booming laugh, shaking his head in mock disbelief. "And this place—wow. It's... a lot."

Bree, noticing his scrutiny, tried to brush some of the paint off her leggings. "Yeah, we've got a long way to go. But it's... it's getting there."

He stepped closer, his eyes lingering on her for a moment longer than necessary. "You've got a vision, though. I can see it. You're not just slapping some paint on the walls and calling it a day. There's life here—just needs some work."

Before Bree could respond, he glanced around the room again, taking in the peeling wallpaper, the mismatched chairs stacked in the corner, and the half-finished bar area. "I think you're gonna need more than fresh paint and a few good ideas. This place needs a lot of love... and a good menu. But, hey, that's what I'm here for, right?"

Bree raised an eyebrow, a playful challenge in her voice. "And what exactly do you mean by that?"

Zac's smile was easy and teasing. "I've got some ideas already. I'm just waiting for the right moment to swoop in and wow you with them all."

Her smile widened. "We'll make sure you have all the time you need to swoop."

Nik appeared, holding a bottle of turps. "Nice look," Zac teased Nic, letting out a booming laugh.

"I've been following her with this. She leaves paint everywhere." He gestured at the shiny new computer and a trail of tiny white drips across the tiles.

Bree rolled her eyes but grinned. "You're lucky I didn't paint you, too."

The tension lifted as laughter filled the space. Slowly but surely, the restaurant began to feel like a place full of promise instead of problems.

146 | Carla

They had been there a month before the restaurant started to look like the perfect wedding venue. Glossy white tiles had replaced the broken red ones. White, soft drapes hid the cobweb-covered wooden ceiling. The white, tall-backed chairs were washed and stacked in the morning sun.

Bree's prints of Rocca Pinta's castle had arrived and been hung on the freshly painted white walls. The scent of spices filled the air once more as Zac tested menus in the kitchen. As he tried his hand at some Italian dishes, they were delighted with the flavours he created. The bold flavours of Italy combined with the richness of Greece were perfectly cooked and seasoned.

"Why can't you come and work here?" Carla asked.

"Well, I would; I'd love to, but you know my business partner," he said, flashing a broad-eyed glare at Nik. "He's run off to Italy to be with an English girl, so I'm stuck in Greece for now, anyway," he replied, biting into some freshly made focaccia. "I'm here until you get a chef sorted out." His voice carried a hint of frustration, a longing to be somewhere else: in Rocca Pinta.

Bree left Carla and Zac talking. She looked for Nik. She smiled as she saw feet sticking out from under a cupboard and cables pulled inside. Suddenly, music blared out all around them.

"We did it." Nik said with a fist pump, brushing off the dirt from his work clothes, then teased Bree with his dusty hands.

"You two make me want to stop being single, and I love being single. " Zac laughed, his voice tinged with a hint of an emotion Nik couldn't quite place. "Well, not so much now that my wingman has left me," he said, slapping Nik on the back with playfulness in his tone.

Carla moved away from the distractions of the group and studied the list of things she still had to do: Find a manager. Find a chef. Go to Ikea. Sleep.

The first three haunted her sleep and distracted her days. She checked the job announcements hourly, but there were no replies. Did no one want to manage a restaurant or be their chef? It was the manager's position that put a frown on her freckled face. Carla wasn't fooling herself that she could do this without some help—in fact, a lot of help. The manager would need to speak at least three languages, cope with drunken wedding guests, have the patience to deal with bridezillas and be tactful and discreet when wedding scandals happened.

Outside, Carla was enthusiastic, but inside, she was terrified. The bills were coming in, and they were much higher than she expected. She lost hope of having enough money to cover one summer season. She had enough to pay the rent for three months, and the contract was for three years. She was starting to regret this rash decision. Living with this secret, a terrible fear caught her heart.

147 | Petra

The three days in the retreat flew by. Petra and Matt were their own lonely little group; they considered themselves the damaged screw-ups. They felt they were both to blame for being there—no one else. They also had a very different plan of attack for their lives than the others, with very different issues. They both felt like different people from those who entered the retreat and looked forward to meeting up after therapy to talk about what they had learned. They planned how they would behave in the big, evil world once they were set free.

The last outing, away from the retreat, was a trip to the city of Stone Town, the island's capital. From what Petra had seen on her way from the airport, it wasn't a place that would hold her interest. However, a curious Matt teased and pleaded until she relented. Without the tiredness that accompanied her on her previous drive-through, she was surprised to find herself appreciating the charm of the journey. As the sun rose, the world seemed to be returning to life. The long, straight road entering the city was flanked by storefronts offering one product per shop; the empty ones were closed up with large, rusty padlocks. One sold armchairs, sitting in the morning sun, with frayed and ripped armrests. Intricate carvings on wooden bed heads lined up along a white wall show a man sitting on a pile of bags of cement, concentrating and carving his next work.

Petra's eyes opened wide as traffic came to a standstill for six skinny cows to cross the road. A camel walked past them quicker than the slow-moving traffic.

A man selling bunches of bananas held them up to the window, trying to tempt them to buy one, but everyone turned away without acknowledging him. Petra wiped her brow; she couldn't do anything about the sweat dripping down her whole body.

Petra pulled her body in tight as the roads, congested with vehicles, merged into one, making it impossible to work out which side of the road was right or wrong. Mustafa beeped his horn angrily for no apparent reason other than to instill fear in the group.

Turning off the main road onto a more minor, equally dusty highway, the landscape changed before their eyes. The dilapidated, rusting, and neglected old cars with bald tyres, missing mirrors, and smashed lights replaced the new, white minibuses filled with smiling tourists. Petra stared, wondering if she was looking at a poorly defined car park or a scrap yard.

Dressed for the city, Petra made sure her knees and shoulders remained hidden. She had ripped the tag off her flowy, blue dress earlier. She briefly enjoyed the familiarity of wearing long clothing before the warmth and dryness of the sun turned her smile into drops of glistening sweat, which fell with a frustrating tenacity to her ankles.

"Welcome to Stone Town, my city." Godfrey told them as he jumped off the minibus, "Please be careful of your bags, phones, and money when you're in the city," he said as the group quickly grabbed their bags and held them close. "While Zanzibarians are honest, many outsiders are not, so be careful. Follow me."

The group, wide-eyed and open-mouthed, followed him; Petra and Matt lagged behind like mischievous schoolchildren, resenting having to follow a leader.

They traipsed through the dusty streets; a man sitting on stacks of wood watched them approach. "One dollar, please," he begged.

Turning the corner of a derelict ruin, presumably once a home, men sat on a crooked tree trunk, now used as a makeshift bench. Above them, the buildings were now taller, with layers of closed shutters leading up to the sky. Godfrey stopped and rested on an intricately carved door while the group caught up.

"You've already met my mother; now you'll meet my aunt and possibly my cousins. Come in, everyone. Welcome." Godfrey said as he pushed open the heavy wooden door leading into a silent, dim stairwell. As they climbed the three flights of stairs, their footsteps pounded into the silence.

"Fernanda," shouted Godfrey as the plain brown door squeaked open.

Seeming too young to be an aunt, a smiling lady appeared, offering a warm, sweet smile before crossing her arms over her body and saying, "Welcome, please come in."

The house groaned with the sheer weight of time; it felt heavy as if sinking lower into its foundations with every passing day. Aunty F's kitchen smelt homely of fresh bread and spices. The white walls reflected a haze of dusty sunlight from the one cobwebbed stone window.

Godfrey handed them a cup of tamarind juice. "From the garden downstairs," he said as they sipped the sweet nectar. Petra felt her face quickly pull in disgust as she turned away, leaving the juice on the faded wooden stand.

The dining room felt lighter. Light spilt in through two more oversized windows, casting a spotlight on the brown plaid sofa with heavy oak arms and the fraying braided rug. Peeling paint fell from the walls, and one lonely floor lamp with a dented shade stood by the door, lighting the kitchen and living room together.

Leaving the house and stomping back downstairs, a weather-ravaged door hung askew.

"This is our garden. We feed our family well from this land, and we also sell the food to neighbours for some extra pennies." Weeds growing around the door made the 'Keep Out' signs unnecessary.

Waving a friendly goodbye, Godfrey placed some pink notes in his aunt's hand before calling the group to follow him. The skies turned a shade of dark grey as he guided them through the quickly narrowing alleyways of the city.

"What are we doing now?" Matt called loudly to Godfrey.

"We are going to visit the house of wonders, the baths, the fort, the Forodhani gardens, then a simple, home-cooked lunch." Matt noticed one of the Canadian brothers roll his eyes at the thought of another home-cooked, organic lunch.

"Okay, tell us what time to meet and where, and we are going off on our own," he said abruptly, resenting being dragged around a city when he was more than capable of using his own eyes and a guidebook.

Godrey flashed Matt a harsh stare. "Okay, Forodhani Gardens at four. Mustafa will be there, or lunch at one."

Matt interrupted him. "We will be there at four. Is anyone else coming? I know of a restaurant that does anything from club sandwiches, pizza, sushi, burgers, samosas, and local food," he said. Petra watched the Canadians exchange glances before quickly striking their hands in the air.

"Us, please, yes," the older brother replied with a smile.

Godfrey shot Matt a disapproving glance before ushering the small group away. Matt raised his hand. "My group, follow me," he said, mimicking Godfrey's voice and hand gestures.

He followed the map Georgie had provided and quickly found the gardens and the hand-carved sign for the 'Cape Town Fish Market', a deceiving name for a restaurant as elegantly simple as this one. They sat over the water on a wooden terrace, rows of sailing Dow boats and more modern speed boats bobbing on the water. As they cheered together, cocktails and food started to arrive.

"Thanks, Matt, and Petra, of course. We've had it with organic food; I needed this," Pete said, eagerly slicing his salami and mozzarella pizza.

"Before we go, we can order some to take away food and heat it in Georgie's microwave; that's what we have been doing for the last week," Matt said.

They chatted easily over lunch and, before paying, ordered takeaway food to last at least four meals each. They hid as much in their bags as possible so as not to create an unpleasant situation with Godfrey and the others.

They arrived before Godfrey and the group, handing their food to Mustafa to hide in the luggage compartment as they waited under the shade of the garden trees. Godfrey forced a smile upon his return; his grimace quickly returned once he realised the five rebellious strays had found a restaurant happy to sell alcohol to the lively group.

148 | Petra

The day they were due to leave the safety and comfort of the retreat had finally arrived. Minibuses collected people all morning as they went off on other trips and safaris, and some headed off home. They were reunited with their phones, iPads, and computers; they swapped contacts and promised to stay in touch. Petra was sure she would keep in touch with Georgie, Matt, Penny, and a couple of the workers, too, but she wanted to leave the old version of herself behind. These people had seen her at her worst; she wasn't proud of the person she was before she entered the retreat. She needed to make a new, kinder, more caring, and more empathetic version of herself. She needed to be a person she would be proud to call a friend.

Georgie had talked Matt out of heading to the north of the island: "Too many hotels, tacky restaurants, and too many beach boys selling souvenirs on the beach; it's like Blackpool, just hotter."

Matt was also sold on the quiet, unspoilt beaches of Michamvi, the area of Zanzibar where Petra was heading. Avoiding any emotional farewells, he had booked into the hotel where Georgie worked. Impatient to leave, they called Mustafa to pick them up. Mustafa had changed his shirt this time, but the same rope held up his ripped trousers. Petra glanced back at the stunning retreat, mouthing 'Thank you' as she took one final look.

"Aren't you worried?" asked Petra, her words filled with nervous humour.

"What about?" Matt asked confidently, "Life on the outside? We aren't alcoholics; that isn't AA; it's a mind reset; we got this."

They arrived at the hotel, Shango, a basic but clean African-style hotel, much simpler than the retreat. The rooms weren't ready, so they dumped their bags in the freshly painted white reception area and headed straight into the ocean. The low tide meant they could float in a water pool, catch some rays, and relax.

Soaking in the warm water, they devised a game plan: they would take turns calling people to whom they felt they needed to apologise. They would do it now while they still had each other to rely on if it all went pear-shaped. They would talk as much as possible, just like in therapy, and they promised to stay friends—no flirting, nothing more than friends.

Petra had surprised herself since she had met Matt; she had not even considered him a potential partner. Penny's words filled her head: "You can't be happy with anyone else until you can be alone. Before you can love anyone else, you must first love yourself.

On the other hand, Matt had had his fair share of women and sex in the last two years; he had been one type of men that Petra had dated. He had become a man whore and had decided, too, that he needed a hiatus.

She could see how he had managed to be sexually active; he was attractive. His brown eyes were perfectly symmetrical. Two little dimples on either side accentuated his thin lips, making even the slightest smile appear much larger. His dark brown hair was always perfectly styled; even in the retreat, he spent time with his gels and creams, ensuring it stood up at just the right angle. Now that he'd lost some weight in the retreat, he looked a very different man from the one who entered.

This new agreement was working for both of them; their unusual friendship was easy; they were each other's rock out in the world, and now, after just three days of freedom, they were already feeling normal again. The warm ocean breeze, the cold beers, and the hot and spicy dishes were their new normal.

As promised, Georgie, Charlie, and Petra booked into 'The Rock.' They took the small rowing boat to the small wooden stairway leading up to the restaurant. A maasai warrior welcomed them to 'The Rock.' Antonio, the restaurant manager, Georgie's husband, greeted them. His eyes lit up as he saw his beautiful wife walk into the room.

He reserved one of the best tables on the small terrace to the side of the restaurant. As they dined, the waves gently splashed the wooden slats under their feet—the dark wooden napkin holders and menus perfectly contrasted with the white tablecloths on the tables.

Antonio presented them with the menus and a list of beautiful fusion dishes. Seeing Petra's indecision, he suggested a sample menu—a selection of the most popular dishes. The girls agreed and enjoyed plate after plate of mouthwatering delicacies. Finally, Georgie and Charlie told their stories about how they got there: a Scottish girl with an Italian husband and an American-sounding daughter.

Petra was fascinated, feeling admiration for them, giving up their life in Milan on a whim and making this new adventure a success. She felt the familiar pangs of jealousy, raw envy creeping up, and the unwanted burning rage bubbling inside her. She recognised what was about to happen and knowing that she could quickly spoil the peaceful moment between new friends, she excused herself to go to the bathroom.

149 | Petra

Petra stood still, staring at her reflection, thinking about what she had learnt at the retreat.

"We are where and who we are because of our choices. Don't be envious of other people's lives; they have made sacrifices and choices to get there." Petra continued to gaze at her reflected image, touching her soft, tanned face, and said out loud, "They made those choices; nothing is stopping me from making the same choices." She repeated the words several times, then, after one last glance in the mirror and a long, deep breath, she said, "Choices, it's all about choices." The bubbling rage sank away; she felt much calmer already. She made her way back to the table and joined her friends.

Georgie and Charlie talked about school, work, their friends, the sacrifices they had to make to be there, the struggles they had initially, and how they thought Italy was a world away and wouldn't go back. This was home now.

As they took the boat over the choppy waters, arriving at the beach, they said quick goodbyes. Petra hurried to the hotel to meet a waiting Matt. She had missed him during the evening, on many occasions thinking she wished he had been there. She described her mixed feelings about Georgie's life stories, her jealousy, and how removing herself from the situation and taking a moment alone had calmed her down. She told him the words she had repeated, 'Choices,' and her change in attitude.

"Well done; see, you can do this. You recognised you had an issue, saw it happening, and talked yourself off the shelf. You got through it with your head held high. I'm proud of you." His words sounded like Penny's; she had to avoid poking his eyes out.

He bent forward towards her, hovering with his lips by hers. As she relaxed into the kiss, he pulled away. Petra's heartbeat started to quicken; they had vowed not to do this. He pulled back quickly, screwing his face as if in an internal struggle.

"I'm sorry. I don't know what came over me."

"I think that bottle of wine came over you." Petra said, laughing it off.

"I'm honoured that you thought about it, but I'm proud that you pulled away from me; both of us have had a 'Next Step' breakthrough tonight," Petra said.

Putting the moment behind them, the following day, they hired a moped, and the pair explored the island's white sand beaches, avoiding tiny villages; they had seen enough of those. They chose the tasty fusion food offered on the beaches rather than the rice and beans on the roadside stand. Taking turns in driving, they photographed the fishermen as they mended nets by the side of the road, dust-covered leaves and palm trees along the sandy tracks, and children happily playing with skipping ropes and old, ripped water tanks.

They spent many evenings with Georgie and Charlie as the tradition of chilled wine, accompanied by salamis and cheeses from Italy, continued. They had called people they had hurt in the past; they cried together, laughed together, and slept apart, enjoying the platonic friendship that had formed between them.

Once Matt left, Petra's mind regularly turned to him, his smile, his laugh, and his searching eyes. Matt was busy sending applications for various jobs, having decided not to be a boss for a while. He worked nine to five, collected the money, and worked on himself before throwing himself back into the shark-ridden world of business, of which previously he had been one of the king sharks.

The more time Petra spent with Georgie, the more she loved her life. She had very little in Zanzibar but wanted for nothing. Petra felt envy over Georgie's ability to be content with so little. Although her house was beautiful, they had solar power water pumps that never worked, a simple rust-covered oven, two hobs, and a washing machine, also rust-covered, that shook the house when it reached spin. Georgie didn't complain or even notice; she was content with her family, having left the stresses of Milan behind. Lying in bed at night, Petra looked around her with a smile, wondering if she could start a life over there.

150 | Petra

Now alone and with her thoughts skipping between Matt and her home in Italy, she video chatted to the girls.

Her final morning in Zanzibar arrived; she had booked Mustafa for her transfer. She had gotten very used to his erratic driving, feeling once again the warmth of the retreat when she saw him. She hugged him close as she said goodbye.

The tiny airport lounge had more people than chairs. On the screen where flight information should have been displayed, an error message was flashing with a handwritten note with curly sticky tape attached saying 'Broken.' Two men in crisp white police uniforms showed uncomfortably hot waiting passengers a handwritten list with details of the gates, of which there were only three.

The door from the gate led straight onto the glistening and hot tarmac. Passengers pushed and shoved to the steps of the plane, gasping and cusping, feeling the burning handrail under their skin.

As she sank into her business-class bed, the guilt of her luxurious life took over. Thoughts of the remote villages and joyful faces filled her memories. Her mind was trapped in a place she had already left.

Petra stepped back with a wince as the bitter wind of Milan hit her tanned skin. She threw her thick black jumper over her travel clothes and jumped onto the bus back to the train station for her onward journey.

As the train quietly took her across the north of Italy, she admired the freshness of the exteriors, the largeness of the pavements, and the brightness of the landscape at night, despite the cloud covering the stars and moon.

Petra dropped her bags onto the floor with a thump, taking in her fresh, clean surroundings. Clasping her hands together, she smiled. Her shiny kitchen and perfectly plumped cushions welcomed her home. As she unpacked, memories washed over her of Zanzibar, Matt, and Georgie. Shaking her white shorts to put in the wash, stained with the red soil from the days on the moped, sand fell onto her polished wooden floors.

Exhausted, she sank into her sofa, her weary body aching from her travels, unsure how this cold, crowded country with unhappy faces fit into her life anymore.

151 | Carla

The spring days were warming up the ever-lengthening hours of sunlight. Bree managed the wedding bookings. She'd always believed that things happened for a reason; she believed in fate, especially recently, but having Carla open the new restaurant was perfect timing. The restaurant they had been using for weddings until recently had closed, leaving many couples stranded. Carla's restaurant was much more suitable than the previous one, so they swapped their weddings over.

The Rocca Pinta grapevine had sent the news that Robby was now without a job. "What do you think, Bree? He's a good manager," Carla said.

"Yeah, that was before he started drinking, though. It's totally up to you. But I don't think Robby is a fantastic idea right now."

"Of course, I understand. He will try and get you back; he always does once he sees you've moved on," Carla said.

"Exactly, and the restaurant he was managing went out of business—not a great sign," Bree said.

"Okay, I'll keep looking. I wish Zac could stay," Carla said to Bree as they watched the two men fix coat hooks down the corridor. "I go all girly and stupid when I see him," she said, looking at Bree for a hint of approval.

"Well, he is fantastic, I agree, but he is the eternal single type. I can't see him settling down, plus he lives in Greece," Bree said, her smile turning downwards into a frown.

"I know; I guess it's just my little fantasy; maybe the fact that he's in Greece works well for me. He's the one I can't have. You managed to tame Nik; maybe I can tame Zac." Carla laughed.

"Go for it; good luck," Bree said, unsure what to make of the conversation that sprung up out of nowhere.

The restaurant opening looked like it would be ahead of schedule, three weeks earlier than expected.

"News, guys." Carla announced excitedly, "We have a last-minute booking for a wedding." She screwed her face as if delivering terrible news: "Two weeks from tomorrow, a wedding for forty Italians." Before pausing for a second, she asked, "Can we do it?"

The group looked around, and Bree spoke first: "We will have to do it; you need to do it."

"What about the restaurant license? The chairs, they still aren't here." Zac said, cocking one eyebrow high in Nik's direction.

"I'll get on to it; they should all be ready this week," Nik said confidently. "We need to sort the terrace out," he said, looking towards the dirty floors.

Zac had found a sweet little Brazilian chef, Sully. "I'm sure he won't be all smiles and laughter once we get busy; you know that chefs have a reputation for being fiery and arrogant." Zac warned, "But for now, it's him or no one. We have no choice but to give him a go."

"He seems nice enough, so I don't see why not," Carla said.

"Why don't you open up a few days before the wedding and give him a chance to prove himself? I won't be here; I've got to return to Greece." Zac said.

They decided to open a few days before the first wedding, hoping for some passing foot traffic to test the waters. The first night was a pleasant surprise. Twelve diners wandered in—just random tourists who'd spotted the lights and decided to stop for dinner.

The next morning, they woke to three glowing five-star reviews. It was a sign of things to come. That evening, after work, they celebrated together—popping open a bottle of champagne, nibbling on the leftover food, and standing back to admire the small triumph.

The following night, they opened again. To their delight, eight of the twelve from the previous night returned, clearly having spread the word. By the end of the evening, they'd served twenty-four clients. The restaurant was buzzing with energy, and Carla felt the momentum building. She felt ready for the wedding—almost prepared. Bree and Nina weren't worried at all; between the three of them, they had organised and run countless weddings. They could do this in their sleep.

But in a quieter moment, Carla couldn't help but wonder if it was all going to come crashing down. She knew better than most that first weddings often didn't go as planned. There was always a chance it could be a disaster.

They dressed in black trousers and white shirts, looking sharp, though their nerves were palpable. From the outside, no one would have known the collective anxiety building behind their polished appearances. As the last swimmers trickled off the beach, they stood at the door, watching the boat approach. The sound of excited chatter from the wedding guests echoed in the air, and the restaurant buzzed with nervous energy.

Carla turned on the soft background music and signaled for the team to bring out the carefully prepared finger food. Platters of delicate canapés and mixed dips were placed on the buffet table, ready to greet the arriving guests.

The bride and groom were the first to arrive. Their eyes swept the venue, their expressions lighting up. The place looked immaculate. There was a soft, almost Spanish feel to the space—whitewashed walls, olive trees, and brightly coloured flowers in the terracotta pots.

A last-minute addition, the herb garden at the entrance, proved a hit. The scent of rosemary and thyme greeted the guests like a warm embrace. Nik, always the gracious host, handed the bride and groom glasses of champagne and led them to the buffet table. The wedding guests followed eagerly, diving into platters of Sicilian Arancini, crispy cured ham, creamy local cheeses, fresh fruit, and steaming, golden pizza. The smells were intoxicating.

As the music shifted to something more romantic, the couple walked hand in hand to the dining terrace, their eyes filled with wonder. The tables had been set exactly as they had requested, with white drapes hanging gently from the ceiling, and crisp white linens draping the tables. The space had a serene elegance to it—refined, but not overly formal. The wildflowers from the hills above Rocca Pinta, a mix of delicate purple and white blooms, broke up the otherwise clinical white decor, adding just the right amount of colour and life.

For a moment, as they surveyed the room, everything seemed perfect. The work, the sweat, the long hours—they all melted away in this quiet, almost magical moment. It was all worth it.

152 | Carla

Nik had taken on a supervisory role; his legs weren't strong enough to walk for seven hours straight around a restaurant. He visited the tables and checked that the guests had enough wine, water, and bread, leaving the girls to carry the plates. Nik charged phones, arranged taxis for people leaving early, handed out entertainment packs for the children, ensured that the pregnant ladies didn't get any food they shouldn't be eating, and checked that the guests with allergies had the correct meals. There was so much to think about, but Nik was in his element; he thrived on the adrenaline rush.

At the end of the meal, the wedding party moved to the well-tended garden for the wedding cake. The branches of the olive and magnolia trees were now lit with fairy lights, and waves lapped on the pebble beach where kids were skimming stones. The DJ played soft music, then, upon Nik's signal, he swiftly moved into the couple's first dance song, and the evening's festivities began.

By midnight, the guests were almost gone; just a few stragglers were left. They waited for the last taxi to take those drunken few home. Carla poured them all the drinks of their choice, the chef heated some food for them, and they sat down. Six weary but fulfilled workers basked in the glory of what they had just pulled off.

"To Johnny," said Bree.

"To Johnny," the others joined in, clinking glasses high.

"To Carla and the journey she took to get here," the others cheered.

As the group finished the last jobs they had to do before going home, Carla pulled Bree to one side. "I think I have found my new manager, but I wanted to check with you first."

Bree looked surprised but didn't interrupt as Carla continued, "I think Nik would be perfect; we couldn't have done it without him this evening; he's a star. He's so professional, but I don't want to offer it to him without asking you."

"Yes," she shouted without thinking. "Although you shouldn't be asking me, thank you for doing so. You need to ask him; he makes his own decisions. I agree he would be perfect for the job, but I can't answer for him," Bree replied excitedly.

Bree grabbed the last few glasses off the table and headed inside. Nik walked out of the kitchen, holding some bread, picking pieces off, and throwing them into his mouth.

He touched her arm, leant in, and whispered, "Thank you." Bree looked at him, surprised. "Me? What have I done?" she asked.

He opened his arms, pointing to the whole restaurant. "Look what we have done, all of us, but you gave me a chance; I've not loved doing anything this much since I was guiding; I feel alive tonight; I have a purpose and feel useful." He raked his fingers through his hair and said, "I haven't had that feeling from a job in so many years," he babbled in joy.

"Please go and tell Carla what you just told me," Bree told him, suppressing a smirk.

Minutes later, Bree watched Nik hug Carla; over his shoulder, Carla gave her the thumbs up and a wide grin.

Nik rushed over to Bree, gleaming with joy. He clasped his hand around hers, pulled her in close, kissed her on the forehead, and whispered, "Thank you." He took a step back and smiled at her. "I can't be seen playing favourites with the staff; off to work," he said, laughing as he patted her on the bum.

Nik was a happy man. He had the woman of his dreams, whom he had waited all these years for. He was living in a beautiful place and was about to start a new adventure, far from his dreary life back home. He had met some wonderful, funny people who had welcomed him with open arms. He had a job that he would never have thought of but one that had found him. Now, he had it all, and he would marry Bree Morgan in two weeks.

153 | Bree

Bree had been so consumed with the restaurant and the start of the wedding season that she hadn't given her own wedding much thought lately. The dress was safely stored at Carla's house, waiting for the big day. The guests had been invited; she knew her parents were coming, along with her sister and her family, plus a couple of close friends from back home. Nik was excited to see his friends again, too—some of his cousins were travelling over, along with a few old colleagues. But mostly, it was going to be friends on his side.

Now, as the day drew closer, Bree felt a sudden surge of excitement at the thought of seeing her family. She hadn't realised how much she'd missed them until now. The sound of a knock at the door broke her from her thoughts. She uncrossed her legs, placed her juice on the table, and jumped up from the sofa. As she swung open the door, she was greeted by her sister, Amber, with a warm, welcoming hug.

Amber stepped inside, and Bree introduced her to Carla, who had just arrived in a figure-hugging red dress with high heels and her hair perfectly straightened.

"Wow, Carla, you look fabulous," Bree said with a grin, taking in the sight of her friend's polished appearance.

Carla twirled playfully, a coy smile on her lips. "Thanks. Well, Zac's around, and, you know... I want to make a good impression."

Bree's eyebrows shot up in surprise, but she couldn't resist teasing, "You'll definitely make a sexy impression dressed like that."

Carla chuckled softly, but inside, she was still adjusting to the emotions that had surfaced unexpectedly at the mention of Zac's name. Since he'd left, she found herself aching to see him again, her mind constantly drifting back to the moments they'd shared. She had been stealing glances over her shoulder all day, hoping to catch a glimpse of him hovering near Nik. But so far, he had remained elusive.

Carla wasn't sure if Zac was even aware of the effect he had on her. But when he smiled, when those gentle dark eyes locked onto hers, and when his infectious energy filled the room, it was impossible not to feel drawn to him. There was something about him—something she couldn't resist.

"Do you know what's happening at the wedding?" Bree asked Amber, pushing formalities aside, eager to hear more.

Amber shrugged, taking off her glasses and pinching the bridge of her nose in mock frustration. "Yes, of course, but I'm not telling you anything. You wanted a surprise, remember? Deal with it." She burst into laughter.

"I didn't want a surprise," Bree giggled. "I just didn't want to have to plan it."

"You'll love it—all of it," Amber reassured her, giving her a playful shove toward the bedroom. "Now get ready, because in an hour we're heading out for dinner with the wedding party."

As she dug through her suitcase, Amber called over her shoulder, "Mum and Dad will be there too, so let's get sloshed now and behave ourselves in front of them." She grinned as she turned toward the kitchen to pour them both a large glass of wine.

Bree picked out a deep blue dress and small, simple black kitten heels. "Any good?" she called out to Amber, her voice rising above the music that was now blaring through the house.

Amber nodded approvingly. "Perfect. Let's go."

By the time they climbed into the waiting taxi, Bree's green eyes were twinkling with excitement, and also wine. She clung to her plastic glass as the taxi bumped along the cobbled streets. When they arrived at the venue, she immediately spotted her family. A wide smile spread across her face as she made her way toward the bar, past the bottles neatly laid out, and into a sea of familiar, smiling faces.

Her father stood up, clearing his throat to address the group. "I'm doing my speech now, here, with you guys. I'm not doing it in Italian and Greek too," he said with a grin. Bree's cheeks flushed pink as he began to recount some of her childhood antics—embarrassing stories of her teenage escapades that left her cringing.

Once it was over and the room filled with chatter, the sound of the door opening caught her attention. Bree looked up, and her tipsy eyes widened when she saw Nik and Zac walking in.

Bree's voice rang out, louder than she intended, "Welcome back, Bro," her tone carrying a warmth that bordered on love. She grinned at the sight of him, his larger than life presence filling the room.

"Everyone, this is Nik and his best friend, Zac," she announced, her voice booming. She quickly glanced at her sister, her face turning sheepish. "Whoops."

Amber's voice rang out from the other side of the room. "Too much wine, maybe?"

Bree laughed, looking at Zac and shaking her head. "I didn't mean to shout," she muttered under her breath, but the warmth of the moment made her care less about the slip-up.

"So, are you ready to take this leap of faith, Nik?" Bree's dad asked, his voice gruff as he shook Nik's hand.

Nik's eyes softened as he met Bree's father's gaze. "I've never wanted anything more in my life," he said, his voice filled with sincerity. He turned to Bree, his eyes glistening as he spoke again. "I wanted to come and say 'hello' first. I didn't see how we could make this dinner work with all the different languages flying around," he added with a laugh. He gently placed his hand on the small of Bree's back. "Now I'm going to take her quickly to meet my group. I'll have her back in ten minutes."

RAW MISTAKES

Zac gave Carla a light touch on the arm. "Come on, I need some moral support."

Carla's heart skipped a beat at his touch. She turned her face away, feeling the warmth of a blush creeping up her neck. She suppressed a smile, but when she looked up, Zac's warm grin had her feeling like she'd just stepped into a whirlwind. He pulled her away from the group, and together, they walked into the cool winter evening.

After a few minutes, they arrived at Nik's favourite restaurant, where the scent of cigar smoke and whisky greeted them at the door. Bree and Carla were introduced to the boisterous group of friends and family, each of them offering warm embraces and hearty welcomes.

As they settled into the party, Carla glanced over her shoulder, catching Bree's eye. "We have to go back to the other party," Bree called, a mischievous smile on her face. "Don't worry, you can ogle Zac tomorrow," she teased, her voice light and playful.

With that, Bree and Carla stumbled back into the party with a cheer. They raised their glasses high and, in unison, proclaimed, "To the wedding tomorrow."

154 | Carla

As the party ended, breathing in the cool, misty air, Carla stepped out into the night to walk the short distance to her house. She slowed as she heard footsteps quicken behind her. She tried to walk as calmly as possible, but her legs were trembling. She looked over her shoulder and saw a tall man striding towards her.

"Carla?" he asked with a questioning voice.

"Zac." She let out a sigh of relief as he approached her, a small smile creeping onto her lips. "You scared me."

"Me? With this innocent smile?" he teased, his eyes glinting mischievously. "To be honest, I'm lost in the maze of these streets. They all look the same at night."

Carla rolled her eyes, the corner of her lips curling into a playful grin. "Yeah, one cobbled street looks the same as another, I guess."

"I should've turned left at the shoe shop opposite the handbag shop," Zac said, his voice almost exasperated. "But now that they're all closed, I can't tell them apart. I have no idea where my Airbnb is."

Carla tilted her head back and let out a soft laugh. It was a genuine, carefree sound, and she linked her arm with his. "I know where you're staying," she said with a sly grin. "Bree told me. I'll take you there. You're almost there, anyway."

"Thanks," Zac said with a dramatic sigh, "Otherwise, I'd be roaming the streets all night like a lost puppy."

"Well, I've had too much wine. You need to help me walk," Carla teased, pointing at her high heels. "These shoes were a terrible idea."

As they walked together, the streets stretched out in front of them, quiet except for the occasional murmur of late-night pedestrians. The only sound was the rhythm of their footsteps.

Carla stopped at a large brown door, sliding her hands over its rough surface. "This is you," she said.

Zac chuckled. "Now I'm going to have to walk you home, and then you'll have to walk me back. It's a vicious circle we have here."

Carla smiled, the warmth of the moment melting away any lingering tension. "Don't worry, I'm just around the corner."

She stood too close to him, her heart racing as she felt the heat of his breath on her hair. The world seemed to shrink, and in that moment, all that mattered was the space between them.

"Night, then," Zac said, his voice a little softer than before.

Carla turned away reluctantly, feeling the disappointment settling in her chest.

"Unless I can offer you a coffee?" Zac's voice stopped her in her tracks.

Carla slowly turned back towards him. Her heart fluttered, and she glanced at the door behind him before nodding. "Sure, why not?" she said, her voice barely above a whisper.

She slipped off her high heels, her bare feet cool against the floor as she followed him inside. Zac closed the door behind them, filling the kettle with water. He gestured to the small table where they could sit, but Carla was distracted by the casual jumble surrounding his suitcase in the corner.

"Be careful, it's hot," Zac warned, handing her a steaming cup.

Before Carla could stop herself, the words slipped out. "Like you," she muttered under her breath, feeling the heat rise in her cheeks.

She quickly turned away, her hands trembling as she took a step back. Zac's arm gently touched her shoulder, and he turned her around. His eyes locked with hers for a brief, charged moment before he set his cup down on the table, his fingers lingering on hers as he removed her cup from her hand.

The air between them thickened. He pulled her close, and Carla couldn't suppress the small gasp that escaped her lips as she felt the heat of his lips on hers. The kiss was tentative at first, but soon, it deepened, his hand finding the small of her back, pulling her in closer.

Her heart raced as she responded, her arms wrapping around him, drawing him closer. The kiss slowed, the soft, lingering touch of their lips leaving them both breathless. When they finally pulled apart, their foreheads rested against one another, and they shared a quiet, shared gasp.

Zac pushed a curl from her face, his thumb brushing her cheek. He kissed her again, more softly this time, before pulling back, his hands slowly dropping to his sides. "Unexpected," he said, a lazy smile curling on his lips.

Carla couldn't help but grin. "Good, unexpected, or bad?" she asked, her voice full of playful challenge. She watched as he grabbed his coffee, lifting it to his lips before responding.

"Definitely the good unexpected," he said. "And you?"

"Long-awaited," Carla giggled, keeping her eyes on the steam rising from her cup. "I've sort of wanted that since I met you in the hospital."

Zac turned away, the revelation hanging between them like a heavy secret. He placed his coffee in the sink, his movements deliberate, almost hesitant. "Well, you hid it well," he said, his voice quieter now. "We have an early morning tomorrow, so I suppose we should call it a night."

Carla pasted a smile on her face, her heart sinking slightly. "Yes, of course. See you tomorrow, then," she said, walking toward the door. She reached for her shoes, the moment still echoing in her mind.

Her hand hovered on the door handle for a second before she pushed it down. She was about to leave when she heard his voice.

"Carla, one more thing," Zac said, his tone more serious than before. He stared at her, and for a moment, the world outside seemed to disappear.

"Look at me," he said softly, his voice tender yet insistent.

She turned back, her eyes lowering to the floor. Zac let out a quiet laugh. "You're drunk. I'm very drunk," he said, trying to lighten the mood. "Let's see how we feel about this in the morning."

Carla nodded, her breath catching in her throat. She picked up her bag, her eyes meeting his one last time. As she turned towards him, her body brushed against his chest. He placed his hands gently on her face, lifting her chin with a softness that took her by surprise.

"Good night," he said, his voice barely above a whisper.

He let his lips brushing against hers in a soft, lingering kiss. Carla melted into the moment, her body tingling with the sensation of him. When they finally pulled apart, the distance between them felt unbearable.

"Night," she whispered, her voice so quiet that Zac barely heard her.

She walked barefoot down the narrow steps, her mind a whirlwind of emotions. As she dashed through the streets, her heart bounced in her chest. She had never felt more alive, more desirable, than she did in that moment.

155 | BREE

The following morning, Bree's father searched for a clear spot to sit but instead found himself staring into a whirlwind of bridal havoc. The once-tidy flat was now strewn with ladies' underwear, make-up, hair curlers, and an impressive collection of handbags. Shoes and perfumes cluttered every inch of the white dining table. The flurry of underwear-clad women made him avert his gaze to the floor, focusing instead on his feet as the bridal party hurried past him.

"Girls, my dad's here—cover up," Bree giggled, clutching her soft grey towel tightly around her chest.

"Can I look up now?" he asked, keeping his eyes firmly on the floor.

Bree glanced around and nodded. "Yes, all clear." She smiled, holding up a white dress and pinning it at the waist, causing the bodice to sag. "Hopefully, it looks better on me." Her words lingered as she disappeared into a chorus of giggles behind a closed bedroom door.

Minutes later, his jaw dropped, and his eyes welled up as Bree emerged, gliding towards him in a vintage lace and satin wedding dress that ended just below her knees. Her ash-blonde hair, styled in sleek retro curls tucked elegantly behind her ears, perfectly complemented the simple but striking look.

Bree twirled, sending the knee-length fabric swirling, then smoothed it back into place with a graceful touch.

The girls took one last admiring glance at Bree before grabbing their bags. "Right, we need to go, or we'll be late," Carla announced. They hugged Bree quickly and dashed out of the room.

Bree kicked off her slippers, stepping into her white heels, which made her taller than her father. "Do you even know what's happening today?" she asked, a hint of impatience in her voice.

"Of course, but if I told you, I'd have to kill you," he teased with a laugh. "All I'm allowed to say is that we're leaving in fifteen minutes. Oh, and there's a gift for you from Nik in the cupboard behind the cleaning products. He said he knew you'd never look there." He stretched out his hand, groping for the box as described, and handed her a sleek black package. He adjusted his trousers and sat back down.

Bree's eyes widened as she untied the ribbon and lifted the lid. Her breath caught as she revealed a white gold necklace with a delicate hexagon of diamonds hanging from it. She stroked the pendant with her fingertip, marvelling at its beauty.

"May I?" her father asked. Putting on his glasses and fumbling slightly with the clasp, he secured the necklace around her neck. "There's also this," he added, handing her a letter. Bree froze at the sight of the handwriting. The envelope bore no postmark, and as she carefully unfolded the handwritten note inside, her breath hitched. It was dated two years earlier.

She held the letter but struggled to read it as tears began to trickle down her cheeks. "He's so good with words; I can't read this now," she laughed through her tears. Pressing the letter to her heart, she felt her father's reassuring hand on her back. "I'll kill him for ruining my make-up," she joked.

"Bree," her father began softly, "I know how much he loves you. I know it's been a long, and well, bumpy journey to get here, but I'm so proud of the caring, loving woman you've become. I'm thrilled you're marrying Nik today."

"Stop it, Dad, please," she begged, blinking rapidly. "This make-up won't survive if I keep crying." She rested her forehead against his.

"Time to go," he murmured, brushing a tear from his own cheek with his finger.

156 | BREE

Bree nervously opened the iron gate and stepped cheerfully into the waiting tuk-tuk. The engine chugged to life as the three-wheeled white vehicle set off, met with applause and shouts from passers-by. Blushing, she waved at the smiling strangers lining the streets, only to frown slightly when the little car didn't veer towards the castle.

"So, not the castle then?" she asked, glancing at her father, who silently drew two fingers across his lips in a zipping motion.

The tuk-tuk bounced over cobblestones, swaying with every turn. A warm breeze brushed the back of her neck, sending a shiver of nerves through her before her father's reassuring touch calmed her nerves.

"Here? How? I thought it was closed," she murmured as she stepped out, staring up at the large, hand-carved door of the Captain's Palace.

"The town hall made an exception for you," her father whispered, offering his hand to help her down. "They thought the romance of the surprise was worth it."

The soft strains of a string quartet playing Stand by Me echoed through the narrow, dim stairway leading up to the ceremony room. In the ceremony room, sunlight streamed through the tall windows, creating a warm glow. Bree took a deep breath and smiled up at her father.

As the music paused, every head turned to face her. Her father linked his arm with hers and nudged her forward. The quartet resumed, their melody carrying the pair into a sea of beaming faces. Bree tried to absorb it all, but her gaze locked on Nik's, and the world around her faded.

In a perfectly tailored black suit, Nik stood at the front of the room, his fingers adjusting his tie with a mixture of excitement and nerves. The fabric felt tight against his collar, a reminder of the enormity of the moment. Pride radiated from his freshly shaven face, the slight glisten of moisture in his eyes betraying his struggle to hold back tears. He swallowed hard, his chest rising and falling with deep breaths as the soft strains of the quartet swirled around him.

When their eyes finally met across the room, everything else seemed to blur into the background. Bree's radiant smile was a beacon, and Nik's lips curved into an involuntary smile of his own. He mouthed the words, "I missed you," his expression softening into a look of pure adoration. The corners of his eyes crinkled as she began to glide towards him, her every step making the distance between them feel like an eternity.

When she reached him, Nik opened his arms, drawing her in with a tenderness that spoke of both relief and devotion. He kissed her hair, the subtle scent of jasmine filling his senses. "You look stunning," he whispered, his voice a low murmur, thick with awe and emotion. He cupped her face gently, his thumbs brushing her cheeks as if to anchor himself in the reality of the moment.

The registrar began to speak, the formal words floating somewhere in the periphery of their consciousness. Bree and Nik, however, were caught in their own universe, their hands tightly clasped. His thumb traced slow, deliberate circles over her knuckles, a silent assurance of his presence. Their eyes locked, unspoken promises passing between them with every glance.

From her seat, Carla tried to concentrate on the vows, but her attention was elsewhere. She was still sparkling from the excitement of the previous evening, though her thoughts kept drifting to the best man standing a few paces away. He was striking in his own right, his sharp black suit perfectly tailored to his tall frame. He held the delicate ring dish with a reverence that contrasted with the flicker of nervousness in his movements. His fingers twitched, and his eyes darted briefly to Carla's, igniting a spark that made her stomach flutter.

When Ginny, the ceremony translator, stepped forward to prompt them, Nik and Bree finally broke their gaze, their focus shifting momentarily to the delicate bands resting on the heart-shaped ring dish. As Bree slid the cool metal onto Nik's finger, her hands trembled slightly, and a breathless laugh escaped her lips. Nik took her hand in his own, steadying it, and together they completed the ritual, their smiles growing wider with every second.

When Nik slid the ring onto Bree's finger, her green eyes shimmered with excitement, catching the light like emeralds. The room erupted in a collective sigh of admiration.

"You may kiss the bride," the registrar finally announced.

Nik didn't hesitate. He cupped Bree's face, tilting it upwards before leaning in, his lips meeting hers in a kiss that was long, passionate, and filled with the promise of forever. Bree melted into him, her arms winding around his neck as the room erupted in cheers and applause. When they finally pulled apart, Nik turned to the crowd, raising their clasped hands in triumph before throwing his fist into the air with a grin that lit up the entire room.

They both beamed with uncontainable excitement, their smiles radiant as they linked arms, stepping in perfect rhythm down the aisle.

157 | BREE

Downstairs, the waves lapped gently against the palace's grey stone walls as a cork popped, sending champagne fizzing into the crowd. Bree and Nik emerged into the gardens, squinting against the sunlight with identical smiles of joy. Confetti and rice rained down, accompanied by delighted cheers and laughter. As Nik reached for his sunglasses, he let go of Bree's hand, just in time for Nina to press two glasses of champagne into their hands.

The wedding toast unfolded as a garden party beneath a cloudless blue sky and rising heat. Among the flowers, wooden tables draped with crisp white tablecloths were laden with perfectly plated canapés, chilled drinks, and fresh floral arrangements.

"Oh my God," Bree gasped, reaching for a glass of water. "You did all this?"

Footsteps crunched on the gravel behind them, and they turned to greet their colourfully dressed family and friends. Handing her champagne flute to a passing server, Bree moved to embrace each guest in turn, her face glowing with happiness.

Occasionally, her eyes drifted to Nik, who radiated warmth as he greeted his friends with high-fives and easy laughter. He kissed the Italians twice on the cheeks, the Greeks three times, and shook hands with the British guests, seamlessly adapting to each custom.

When Bree had finished hugging the last of her family, she waved at Nina, Carla, and Petra, who were busily arranging flowers nearby. Then, she spotted some familiar faces in the crowd and let out a delighted squeal.

Dropping her hand from her mouth, she darted through the throng and opened her arms wide. "You guys. What are you doing here?" she cried, tears of joy sparkling in her eyes as she pulled Anna, Elka, and Alenka into a group hug. "I don't care how you got here; I'm just so glad you came."

"Nik emailed us an invite, so here we are," Anna said warmly.

Nik joined them, slipping his arm around Bree's waist. "I had to invite them. They looked after you that night with the 'crazy monster,' remember?" he said with a laugh, relieved by Bree's reaction.

"So, you married the cheese," Anna teased, her tone affectionate. "About time."

"Well, life happened," Nik replied, grinning as Bree sighed theatrically beside him. "But we got there in the end."

"You two were always meant to be together," Anna said. "You've no idea how relieved I was when he called to say he'd found you in London."

"Excuse me," Bree protested, raising her eyebrows. "I found him, thank you very much. He wasn't wandering the streets of London like a lost puppy." She gave Nik a playful nudge. "That was all me."

Behind them, the lake shimmered in the sunlight, and the quartet struck up a livelier tune. Nik whisked Bree away with a smile, leaving Nina, Carla, and Petra linking arms and exchanging gleeful high-fives.

"We did it," Petra said with a satisfied grin. "This is all us. To the best couple we know."

"To the best couple," Nina and Carla echoed, raising an invisible toast before clinking their imaginary glasses.

"Girls, I need to talk to you," Carla said suddenly, pulling them towards the shade of the palace turret. Its cool shadow offered a brief reprieve from the heat.

"So, last night, I might have been a bit drunk," Carla began, her face scrunching in a mix of embarrassment and amusement. "And I kissed Zac."

Nina's jaw dropped. "Oh my God, Carla. Out of nowhere?"

"Well," Carla admitted, glancing at her feet. "I've had a crush on him since I met him. And last night, I told him."

"Watch out," Petra said suddenly, her voice low. "He's heading this way. Look casual. Fake laugh on three. One, two, three."

The trio burst into muffled, awkward laughter just as Zac appeared behind Carla. She felt his gentle touch on her back and turned, meeting his gaze with a warm smile.

"Love's in the air today," Zac said with a soft chuckle. "It's contagious."

"Dangerous, though," Carla replied, her tone playful as she caught the glint of mischief in his dark eyes.

They exchanged a few words, the conversation light but charged, until someone called Carla's name from across the garden.

"Bridesmaids' duties," she said with a grin, stepping away. Zac watched her retreat, a flicker of longing in his eyes that he didn't seem to realise was so plainly visible.

158 | BREE

A sleek, white two-seater boat glided towards the palace walls, the sunlight bouncing off its polished surface. Bree's eyes widened with admiration.

"Let's go," Nik said, "Where are we going?" Bree asked, her tone light with curiosity, though entirely unconcerned. The sheer joy of the moment left her perfectly content to let Nik take the lead. His eager smile was contagious as he offered her his hand and guided her onto the shiny white leather seats. The boat jolted gently as it pulled away, their guests clustering at the water's edge, waving and cheering as petals floated through the air.

Settling back into her seat, Bree nestled into Nik's arms, her gaze drifting upwards to the lazy clouds dotting the bright sky. The boat skimmed across the water, its wake glittering behind them.

"What's next? And what about the guests?" she asked, tilting her head to meet his eyes, her expression a mix of excitement and curiosity.

Nik chuckled, pulling her closer. "They're off on their own boat trip. As for what's next, I'm keeping it a surprise," he teased, his eyes gleaming mischievously.

The boat veered gently, passing the castle and the palace. The soft sound of the engine blended harmoniously with the sound of waves lapping against the hull.

Nik reached into an ice bucket, retrieving a bottle of champagne, which he poured into crystal flutes. They clinked glasses, sharing a moment of serene silence.

"Are we going to Carla's restaurant?" Bree asked suddenly, her excitement unmistakable. "Please tell me we are."

Nik's grin widened. "You guessed it."

Bree's eyebrows shot up. "But how did you arrange it all so quickly? It only opened last week."

Nik shrugged modestly. "We decided as soon as Carla started working on it. The girls kept you busy while I sorted everything behind the scenes. I didn't want you to see it until today."

Bree laughed, shaking her head. "So, I've designed my own venue without even realising it. Not bad—I couldn't have done it better." She paused, narrowing her eyes playfully. "You aren't working tonight, are you?"

Nik raised his hands in mock surrender. "Not a chance. Ginny's got everything under control."

"Good," Bree said with a satisfied smile, leaning in to kiss him. "Then you're all mine."

An hour later, their boat docked at a long wooden jetty leading to Carla's restaurant. Their guests waved from the shore, cheering as Ginny stepped forward with more champagne flutes. Hand in hand, Bree and Nik walked through an archway of white roses.

The setting was enchanting—trees arched overhead, their branches framing the blue sky, while golden lanterns dangled like stars.

Picking up a menu, Bree ran her fingers over the embossed initials N & B. She looked up at Nik, who was watching her intently.

"Carla suggested merging our names," he said, chuckling. "But we vetoed that when we realised we'd end up as 'Brick' or 'Nee.' So, initials it is."

"We could have done, ehm, DaskaMorgan," Bree said with a giggle. "Although, that actually sounds too much like Dexta Morgan. We definitely don't want any of that on our wedding day."

With everyone settled at their tables, Bree laughed, glowing with happiness as servers brought out her favourite dishes. She savoured every bite, from the creamy mushroom risotto to the Dijon-crusted lamb cutlets. When dessert arrived—a towering tiramisu with edible flowers—she pushed her plate away with a laugh.

"If I keep eating, I'll need a new dress," she said, giggling.

The laughter quieted as Ginny approached, her smile tight. "Bree, can I borrow you for a second?" she asked gently.

Bree frowned but stood, brushing crumbs from her lap. "Do I need shoes?" she joked, wiggling her bare toes.

"I'll bring her right back," Ginny mouthed to Nik before leading Bree away into the staff area.

Inside, Ginny lowered her voice. "Robby's here. I tried to ask him to leave, but he won't. He's... not in great shape."

Bree's stomach sank as she glanced outside. Robby sat slumped in a chair, his legs stretched out, eyes red-rimmed, and his hand waving vaguely at a server for another drink.

"Thanks, Ginny. I'll handle it," Bree murmured. She grabbed a glass of wine from the bar, taking a steadying sip before stepping outside.

Robby's head turned as she approached, his expression blank, his lips moving as though mid-conversation. Bree perched carefully on the arm of a chair, setting her glass down with a faint clink.

"Robby," she said softly, her voice steady despite the tension tightening in her chest.

159 | BREE

Bree's stomach churned as she faced Robby's curt question. "You got married?" he demanded, his tone sharp and accusatory.

"Yes," Bree replied, her voice steady despite the knot tightening in her chest. "Sorry, I should have told you, but it's been a crazy couple of months."

Robby's jaw clenched, and his voice rose in anger. "I came here, back to Rocca Pinta, hoping to get back with you, only to find out you got married today, the same day I arrived."

Bree's body tensed, but she maintained her composure. "You didn't want to get back with me, Robby," she replied, her tone firm but calm. "If you did, you would have been in touch these past few months. You can't expect me to sit and wait for you and your whims to change direction."

"Bree, I miss you," Robby said, his words slurring together.

Bree took a deep breath, her voice quiet but resolute. "Whether I'm married or not doesn't matter." She watched as his head sagged to one side, his eyelids drooping. "You're drunk, Robby. You need to leave."

His eyes snapped open, and he stumbled to his feet, wrenching his hands together as he spoke. "I love you."

Bree's voice sharpened. "You don't know what love is. I'm not a possession you can claim just because you suddenly want me."

Robby's movements grew erratic as he staggered forward, grabbing her around the waist and pulling her close. "Get off me." she screamed, thrusting her arm out and shoving him back into his chair. Bree's hand trembled as she slammed her wine glass onto the table, the Chardonnay spilling across the polished surface.

Carla and Zac, seated at the top table, exchanged a quick glance before rising. Zac strode over, his presence solid and commanding, placing a steadying hand on Bree's back.

"Is that him?" Robby snarled, his eyes darting to Zac. Before Bree could answer, Robby shot out of his chair and lunged at Zac, spewing a torrent of racial slurs. Zac's expression darkened, and with a swift defensive move, he sent Robby sprawling onto the floor.

"Get out of here," Zac said, his voice cold. "I don't know who you think you are, but you're not welcome."

Robby clambered to his knees, his voice shaking as he spat out, "I'm the one you stole her from."

Zac's lips curled into a sardonic smile. "Oh, I've heard about you. You're the one who let this incredible woman slip away." He jabbed a finger into Robby's chest. "And she's married to my best friend now. Leave her alone."

Robby's face twisted with fury as he stumbled to his feet, grabbing Bree's wine glass and downing it in a single gulp. Without another word, he stormed out of the restaurant, the gate slamming shut behind him. Bree peered over the wall into the night, watching him stagger and sway as he disappeared into the distance.

"Thank you," Bree said, her voice trembling slightly as she turned to Zac. She placed a hand on Zac's arm. "It means a lot that you stepped in."

Zac's expression softened, and he gave her a reassuring smile. "Bree, I'll always be here for you. We're family now, and family means everything to me." He paused, then let out a booming laugh. "Besides, Nik told me to come over and make sure you were okay. He didn't want to ruin his suit."

Bree chuckled, the tension in her chest beginning to ease. "I heard that," Nik called from as he neared his tone teasing. "Cheeky git. You told me not to come. You said you'd handle it."

"Yeah, well, I like being the hero," Zac said with a smirk, linking Bree's arm and leading her back to the table.

Nik's eyes lingered on Bree, his expression pensive. He dug his fork into a decadent chocolate dessert and said, "So, Robby's back, is he?"

Bree shook her head, a wry smile tugging at her lips. "Drunk as usual."

Nik's mouth quirked into a small grin. "I'd forgotten all about him."

"Yep," Bree said, leaning into Nik's shoulder. "Me too."

160 | BREE

On the horizon, the lake faded into the hills as night replaced the sparkling, orange sun. As the party livened up, Greek and English music played even louder. "Please, no, we don't have to do a fist dance, do we?" Bree asked with a scowl as Nik pulled her towards the DJ.

"Yes, we do; come on," he urged her, leading her by the hand to the wooden dancing terrace. With a fabulous, easy swish of the dress, Bree reluctantly stepped up to the dance floor. Cameras flashed as they stumbled around under the fairy-lit trees. Bree waved her arms, urging her guests to join in again.

"Why is dancing the only thing we do badly together?" she asked with a grin.

Nik shrugged his reply: "We are good at everything else, so who cares? Breezy, come with me." Taking Bree's hand, he led her down to the lakeside.

The moonlight shimmered on the still lake, and a gentle evening breeze tousled her hair as she battled with the metal steps to the beach. Nik reached into his jacket pocket and pulled out a photo of her from their Samarian Gorge walk. "I've carried this with me since we took it. I thought I could never love again, but I did, with you."

"Nik," she whispered, gazing at the photo in her hands. They sat on a nearby rock, the soft melody of distant music drifting towards them.

"You made me the happiest man then, and you make me the happiest man now," he continued, his voice filled with emotion. "Thank you for marrying me today. I promise to make you smile every day, to be there when you cry, to laugh with you when you're happy, and to support you in everything you do. I'll help you become the best version of yourself, and I'll give you all of me, every single day. You will never be alone again."

Bringing her hand to her lips, she tilted her head to the side and looked into his loving, dark eyes. "I wanted to say those things in my vows, but I decided to say them just to you. So here I am, telling you how much I love you." His voice softened as he pressed his lips to hers.

"Nik," she whispered, her breath slow and shallow. "How did I get so lucky?" she asked, placing a hand over her heart. "I love you more than words can say. I feel complete with you. I didn't realise I was broken until you put me back together." Tears welled in her eyes, and she swallowed the lump in her throat.

She felt his hand gently on her elbow as she continued, "You make me smile when I wake up, and happy when I go to bed." Reaching for his hand, she placed it on her cheek and whispered, "I never want to be without you again."

Nik's hand grabbed hers as he led her back inside. The music had quietened, and Bree said her goodbyes to the last departing guests, promising to meet them tomorrow. Her parents were the last to leave, exhausted but content.

Nik appeared around a corner, waving for her to join him. She walked towards him, stepping out of the restaurant and into the gardens of the hotel next door. Her breath caught as she looked around. Candles floated on the surface of the pool, and fairy lights hung from the olive trees. Beach towels were laid out on the grass, and the soft glow of glasses on tables flickered in the dim light.

"An after-party?" she asked, eyes wide.

"Only the crème de la crème left," he replied, gesturing to the select group of guests remaining: her sister Erin, Ginny, Anna, Alenka, Elka, and his closest friends. Nik guided Bree to sit on one of the towels. The others gathered around her, also sitting on towels. Ginny passed out glasses, ice, and opened a bottle. As she poured, Bree recognised the scent.

"Ouzo. I haven't had this since we were in Rethymnon," Bree said, excited as a waiter set down two iced drinks in front of her.

"I know," Nik said, "Carla told me the smell makes you think of me, and that it brings back memories of how things went wrong." Bree nodded, her hand resting over her heart. "Well," he continued, "we can't let you live with those memories, especially not with your favourite magic potion." He handed her a glass with a smile.

Bree inhaled the scent, letting out a contented hum. "Oh, my best friend, welcome back."

Nik chuckled, "As I remember, your 'magic juice,' as you called it. So, from today, I dedicate the wonderful, beautiful, strong scent of guaranteed hangovers to you, my beautiful wife." The group burst into laughter, raising their glasses before drinking.

Nik still had things to say. "Everyone, I would like to welcome you all to our first date," he said, smiling at Bree and opening his arms out wide, gesturing to the pool and gardens. "Our first date as a couple, we went to sea. I had a picnic prepared; there were stars in the sky, lights in the trees, and we drank too much ouzo. We swam, we drank some more, and we ate my homemade meatballs and spicy rice," he said, pointing to the cool boxes. "Help yourselves, everyone."

"To my husband and my friends, both old and new," Bree said as she raised a glass, looking at each person individually. "As you know, or maybe you will learn one day for those who just met him, Nik loves to do his speeches." She paused as she pushed herself off the ground. "Now, for the first time, it's my turn."

"Zac, you're the best possible best friend-in-law I could have imagined, and all of you guys," she said, looking at his friends. "You're all welcome over here whenever you like. Girls, my fabulous sister, you know you are my everything, my life support system; I love you all," she cried. "Okay, so I'm not good at these speeches, but to you three." She turned to Anna, Alenka, and Elka. "You were there at the start; you were there for our first fight; you got me through."

She pulled Nik towards the pool, looked at the floating lights, and turned towards him. "Where is your phone?" she asked, and he pointed to the table.

"Good', she replied, "Now jump." He looked at her, remembering that on their first date, they ended up in the ocean. "One, two, three," she said slowly, grabbing his hand and taking another deep breath. She pulled him into the pool. Emerging breathless, Bree was the first to say, "I don't recommend that; the water is freezing."

161 | BREE

As Nik and Bree disappeared from sight, Carla lagged behind to close the restaurant, "I'll help." Zac said as the stragglers carried glasses and blankets back to the restaurant. He followed her so closely that she could smell his cologne. Taking the last taxi home, Carla felt her hand sliding over to touch Zac's leg. He turned to her, leaning in, and kissed her lips with a smile.

Zac reached out his hand to Carla, helping her out of the taxi and wrapping his fingers around hers once more. Carla nodded in agreement, her breath quickening as she fumbled in her bag for her keys.
"What gentleman would I be if I didn't help you home?" he asked with a wide grin, laughing but not turning around. He glanced down at her feet, noticing her freshly painted nails.
"I think it's you who needs help—you drink ouzo like I drink water," Carla teased, giggling.
"Well, here we are," Carla said as they reached her door. She balanced against the metal frame and slipped off her shoes. The conversation paused as she noticed the weary look on Zac's face. "Help me up the steps, please," she said, her voice soft.
Flinging the door open, Carla glanced around her tidy house, focusing on the unwashed cups. She closed the door behind them, exhaling as she threw her bag onto the floor. Feeling suddenly shy, she moved to the sink, soaking her hands under the warm water as she rinsed the cups. Reaching for a towel, she leant back against the kitchen counter.
Zac walked toward her, wrapping his arms around her waist and kissing her slowly. "I haven't stopped thinking about last night," he murmured.
"I don't think we're any less drunk than we were last night," Carla said, gently pushing him back.
"I know, probably worse," Zac replied, unwinding himself from her arms. "Probably best to leave this. It's not a good idea, not this drunk."
"Yeah, I agree." She exhaled, feeling secretly relieved. "I'd like to remember it."
"So, let's have another drink," he said, "Give us a good reason not to do what we both want to do." He pulled out a bottle of wine, pouring two glasses. "And we've got to be up in four hours. Well, I do," he added, unable to stop pulling her closer.
"Cheers to us being all grown up and sensible," Carla said, clinking her glass with his. Turning on the music, they settled on the sofa, curling up under a

blanket. Soft melodies filled the room as they relaxed, and drifted off to sleep.

Carla woke with a jolt, rubbing her eyes as she stood. "Good morning, Carla," he said, his frown quickly turning into a grin. "Your kettle doesn't work."

Carla stumbled towards him, jiggling the cable with a smile. "There." Standing far too close for a second too long, Zac bent forward and kissed her neck. She felt her hand tremble as she reached for his face and pulled it to her lips.

Pulling apart, she turned her attention to the kettle, splashing coffee into her cup, throwing in some sugar, and stirring vigorously. Feeling lightheaded and dizzy, she perched on the arm of the sofa. "What are your plans for today?" she asked.

"I'm meeting Nik and Bree in thirty minutes. We're showing our group around Rocca Pinta and then having lunch somewhere. Do you want to join us?" he asked.

"For lunch, maybe. I'll speak to Bree," she said, rubbing her hand gently on his back as he sat on the sofa beside her.

Placing his coffee down, Zac stood and threw his jacket over his shoulder. "See you later then," he said, kissing her gently before walking away. He stole one last glance over his shoulder as he closed the door behind him.

Later that day, Bree and Carla finally sat down to enjoy their coffee. They nestled into the comfortable corner of the bar, a quiet spot near the window where the sunlight filtered through the glass. Carla wrapped her hands around her mug, savoring the heat that spread through her palms.

"So, Bree, I have something to tell you." Carla paused, reading Bree's face, before continuing, "I kissed someone. I'm not sure if you'll be mad."

Interest sparked in Bree's eyes as she placed her cup on the saucer. "Spill the beans," she said with a wide grin.

"Zac and I kissed a few times," Carla confessed, excitement bubbling inside her.

"Carla, oh my god," Bree gasped, her mouth falling open. "When?"

"The night of the rehearsal dinner, then last night, and this morning too," Carla giggled, excitement pouring from her words.

"Repeat: oh my god." Bree smiled, her disbelief evident.

"It was so nice. He stayed on my sofa. I think we both wanted it to go further, but we had drunk way too much," Carla explained.

"Oh my god, sorry, I don't know what to say. What now?" Bree asked, looking at her with concern.

"We didn't get that far. He had to leave to see you guys this morning, and I haven't heard from him since."

"Well, we can arrange drinks tonight before dinner if you like," Bree suggested. "You know we've got the pizza place booked for seven; he'll be there for sure."

"Yeah, that sounds nice."

"Okay, so come round to ours at six," Bree said, flashing a cheeky grin. "I'll invite him too. Finally, it's my turn to be a matchmaker."

A few hours later, Carla stood nervously in Bree's house as Nik strutted around.

"This one?" Nik asked Bree, changing his shirt for the fourth time.

"This is why we're always late," Bree laughed as she walked out of her room, ready in a simple woollen dress, her hair tied back in a tight ponytail, slipping her shoes on.

"Is Zac coming?" Carla asked quietly.

"He should've been here already. He drove some of the Greeks back to the airport, but he's on his way back," Bree explained, smiling as she watched Nik slowly eye himself in the mirror.

Hearing a knock on the door, Carla called out, "I'll get it." She turned for the door and was suddenly tongue-tied as she saw Zac standing still in all black, his face breaking into a smile.

"Am I allowed in?" he asked, and Carla flung the door open, stepping aside to let him pass.

Carla beckoned him indoors, watching as he hung his jacket on the chair. Zac turned to Nik, who was holding ties in the air, and said, "Come on, dude, get away from the mirror."

Zac and Carla exchanged fleeting glances across the room, their eyes locking for a moment

"Mate, do you think this tie works, or should I go with the black one?" Nik called out, holding up two ties with exaggerated uncertainty, his attention absorbed by his reflection in the mirror.

Zac shrugged off his jacket, hanging it carefully on the back of the chair as he glanced over at Nik,

"I think you're overthinking it, Nik," Carla said, trying to keep the mood light. She didn't want to admit how much she was aware of Zac's presence, how his proximity made her heart beat just a little faster.

It was nice to be just the four of them after so many days filled with family, friends, and wedding festivities. The whirlwind of events, the constant bustle of others, and the family expectations had finally given way to this simple, peaceful moment.

Bree sank back in her chair, a soft smile on her lips as she sipped her wine. There was a certain calmness to the evening, one that felt like a welcome break from the chaos.

Carla caught Zac's eye once more, and this time, the glance lingered just a little longer. There was something about the quiet in the room that made everything feel more intense, more personal. They didn't need words to communicate; it was all in the small gestures, the way his gaze softened when it met hers, the way she felt her heart beat a little faster each time.

Nik and Bree were absorbed in their own banter, the ease between them

It felt, for the first time in days, like they were allowed to just be—no roles to play, no expectations to meet, just four people sharing a drink and the comfort of each other's company.

"Well, I'm sorry to say. The last night of family and friends awaits. Let's move our butts," Carla said with a playful grin, gulping down the last of her drink. The warmth of the wine still lingered in her chest, but she couldn't avoid the impending need to return to the whirlwind of wedding festivities.

"Can't we just stay here? I'm sick of having to always be the best man." Zac joked, stretching his legs out and leaning back in his chair.

Nik smirked, eyeing him over the rim of his glass. "You were best man for one day, Zac. One day," He let out a dramatic sigh, his face twisting into a mock serious expression. "I will always be the best," he teased, giving Zac a playful nudge.

Zac rolled his eyes with a grin, shaking his head as he pushed himself to his feet. "We'll see about that," he said, looking between the two of them. "But tonight, I'll let you have the title. One night only."

Carla laughed, a sense of warmth settling over her as she watched them. "Alright, alright, best men," she said with a wink. "But seriously, we better get moving. There's no escaping this last hurrah."

162 | Carla

As the evening with their remaining friends and family drew to a close, Nik and Bree said their farewells, gently closing the heavy glass door behind them. Nik pulled his woollen coat tightly around him and turned to Zac. "Drinks back at ours?" he asked.

Zac glanced at Carla, who gave him a small nod. They walked along the lakeside in the quiet of the night, the only sounds being their footsteps on the gravel and the distant rustling of the trees. Zac stayed close to her, and occasionally Carla felt his hand slip around her back for a fleeting moment. Each time, she trembled at his touch, a warm feeling spreading through her despite the chill in the air. She smiled to herself, wondering if he could feel the same.

Once inside, they sat on the sofa. Bree and Carla exchanged silent glances, each woman lost in her own thoughts.

"So?" Bree whispered, breaking the silence.

"Nothing, I guess," Carla whispered back.

"Girls, come outside," Nik called from the door. "I've got blankets."

Nik flung blankets over everyone, then poured drinks before turning to Zac. "Bro. What's going on with you back home?"

"The same, I guess. Working every day," Zac replied, his voice a little distant.

"Playing every night? Still keeping up with the single life?" Nik teased, his eyebrows raised in playful accusation.

"No, not really," Zac answered, his tone faltering slightly.

"What about that girl you invited? Why didn't she come to the wedding with you?" Nik pressed, leaning forward with curiosity.

"Oh, I don't know. She wanted to, but I thought it'd be nicer without her here," Zac muttered, his face paling slightly.

Carla watched in silence, noticing the sudden discomfort in Zac's expression. She took a long sip from her drink, poured another glass, and sank back into her seat.

"Any other ladies on the scene? Come on, give us some gossip," Nik urged, nudging Zac playfully. Bree kicked his shin under the blanket, sending him a sharp look. He blinked in confusion and pulled the blanket tighter around him, a little flustered.

The sharp ring of a phone sliced through the stillness of the moment. Zac glanced at his screen, pressed the accept button, and stood up. Carla watched as he walked into the room, his voice lifting in laughter, his smile widening with each passing second.

"Who knows which one of these girls will still be around next month, never mind next week?" Nik commented, blissfully unaware of the seriousness in Carla's expression. "Looks like he's taken over my role as the single stud at home."

Zac caught Carla's eye from across the room. For a moment, their eyes locked, and she quickly masked her thoughts with a forced smile, turning her attention back to Nik.

"So, does he have a girlfriend?" Carla asked, trying to sound casual, though the question weighed heavily on her.

"Well, not one in particular. A few, I guess. We were both womanisers back home—until Bree, of course," Nik grinned, throwing a mischievous glance toward Bree, who shot him a glare. "He'll settle down when he meets the right one. Until then, he'll have his fun."

Carla's heart skipped a beat. She forced herself to focus, knowing the conversation wasn't about her, but she couldn't help the knot forming in her stomach. "You mentioned a girl he invited to the wedding?" she asked, her voice quiet, careful not to press too hard but unable to ignore the curiosity gnawing at her.

"Not sure, really," Nik said with a shrug. "She's one of our colleagues, works in the office. He was really into her until she became interested, now who knows?" His tone was flippant, but it left Carla feeling unsettled.

"Ah, okay," Carla murmured, quickly changing the subject as Zac stepped back onto the balcony. Lost in thought, she turned to face him, then glanced at Bree. "I'm going home now. I'm shattered," she said, offering everyone a tired smile as she rose to her feet.

"I'll walk you home," Zac offered, his voice soft but insistent.

Carla straightened up, her tone firm. "No, it's okay. My bike's been here since the morning of the wedding," she said, trying to dismiss the offer with a casual wave. She masked her emotions as best as she could. Bree stood up with her, walking her to the door.

"Are you okay?" Bree asked softly, her concern evident. "Nik doesn't know what's happened with you two; he's just messing around."

"Yeah, I guess," Carla sighed, her shoulders slumping slightly. "I think it's time I stop living in fantasy. He's enjoying his single life. We don't have the bond you two have, and I don't want a one-sided relationship—or these complicated feelings I've got right now."

Bree nodded gently. "I get it," she said, her voice understanding. "But you know, Zac's a great guy. I don't think he'd mess you around."

Carla gave a small, wistful smile. She appreciated Bree's words but wasn't entirely sure she believed them.

Carla nodded. Calmness washed over her as she considered turning back for one final look at Zac. Instead, she called out a farewell and closed the door behind her.

She unlocked her bike, but before she could ride off, Zac appeared from behind her. "Have I done something wrong?" he asked, reaching for her hand.

"No, but you're leaving tomorrow. Who knows when you'll be back, if ever?"

she said, trying to hold back the flood of emotion building up inside her.

"I'll be back soon enough; don't worry about that, Carla," he replied, his voice low. "I like you."

"Me too. Let's just see what happens in the meantime," she said.

"Okay, if that's what you want," Zac said, a hint of surprise in his tone.

He brushed his lips gently against her cheek, before pulling away. "See you then."

The next morning, Carla woke slowly, turning the pages of a book before she was interrupted by an impatient knock at the door. She threw on a silk kimono and poked her head out the window.

Zac stood below, his back arched as he looked up at her, his eyes catching hers. "Do you want to come up?" she asked, surprised at how the mere sight of him could brighten her morning.

"I can't; I'm leaving now," Zac said, gesturing to his car, which was parked illegally in the narrow street. "Couldn't decide between flowers or a plant, so I got you both."

"For me?" Carla gasped, her hand cupping her mouth to hide her surprise. "I'll be down in a second."

She rushed down the stairs, eyes landing on a row of yellow flowers. Zac handed her both the plant and the bouquet.

"Thank you," she whispered, drawing closer to him.

Zac held her waist gently and kissed her cheek. "I have to go," he said, his voice regretful. "Don't want to miss my flight." With a heavy sigh, he pulled away.

"Thanks so much for these," Carla smiled again, her heart a little lighter. Zac unbuttoned his jacket and turned away, heading towards his car.

He gave Carla a quick wave, climbed in, and drove off, the sound of his engine fading into the distance.

163 | Nina

Nina had taken to studying other people and their behaviour, wondering how many of her friends were pretending to be happy when their worlds were shattered to pieces. She felt increasingly isolated and robbed of her future, and she found herself shedding tears unexpectedly. She was uninterested in getting to know new people or watching Netflix all weekend alone while she waited for Manuel to decide it was time to come clean.

Now, with Bree's wedding done and dusted and Carla's restaurant up and running, Nina decided it was time to take up a new hobby. Remembering her aptitude for music as a child, she pondered her options, choosing online courses to keep herself busy without facing anyone in person. Manuel hardly came home anymore, and when he did, he acted like she didn't exist.

Apart from a triangle and recorder in school, Nina had never even touched a musical instrument. Searching for distractions from the lie she was living with Manuel, she looked for his guitar. Feeling a sense of worry, she rummaged through his belongings, pulling out the oversized case and avoiding smaller boxes and envelopes. Grabbing the guitar, she took it out of its brown leather case and sat down on her sofa, placing it to the side.

Nina opened Google and typed the words "guitar for beginners". She scrolled down until she found a YouTube link, clicked on it, and waited. The first link was an American man with bushy eyebrows telling viewers not to try and learn to play the guitar on YouTube. She clicked the next link and then the next until she found an Australian lady who seemed to be able to provide her with what she needed.

Nina had decided she would be the next Eric Clapton, playing on stage for millions. Maybe she would be discovered on a show like 'X Factor'. She would be the lady who turned up looking like she had no chance of playing a note and would stun the judges and crowd with her skills. Nina had kept her perfect singing notes hidden from her friends; she hadn't sung in public since she was eleven, and now, singing over her guitar, she enjoyed the sound of her voice.

The guitar was a different ball game; she couldn't hit the cords. She played all morning, had a break, and tried again. Her mind was filled with clefs, keys, and notes swirling around her. As the weeks turned into months, Nina found it easier to sing the notes on the screen than strum them on the guitar. Her knowledge of music was basic, but her fond memories of singing to her family as a child came rushing back; they were happy times.

Nina pulled her cover tight around her shoulders, immersing herself in YouTube videos while reading music and practicing her guitar chords. Each day, she felt herself improve slowly; she could play the F, A, C, and E chords, sounding not like a cat in pain. Learning more and more, she decided to try and put together her newly discovered chords and start to play 'Stay with Me' by Sam Smith. The simple chord repetition and chorus were straightforward to understand, and soon, she sang the songs and words from a YouTube video scrolling across her screen. She beamed with pride as the melody and words created by her voice and fingers filled the empty house.

Waking up early every morning, she gave herself time to put the guitar back in its case and pack her music sheets away before he entered the house. Resting her hand on Manuel's guitar, she pushed it back to the wall of the overfilled cupboard. She snapped open her computer, looked at the Google page and typed guitars. Creating a shortlist of guitars, she gasped at the prices. Her jaw dropped as she pulled up the list from lowest to highest. There was no way she could afford any of these, although, with the amount of money Manuel was going through on his secret weekends away, she thought she deserved a treat.

Choosing a guitar she couldn't afford, she input her card details. She shook her head in confusion as the card was declined. Trying another card, her eyes were wide and desperate as the same thing happened. She rubbed her temple, placing the computer to the side. She searched through Manuel's desk, looking for passwords for online banking. Frowning, she took the notepad out of his drawer and opened the banking app to check the funds on their joint account. Nina scanned through the outgoing payments. She looked at the balance, twenty-seven euros. Raising the palm of her hands on her forehead, unable to believe her eyes, she let out a sigh of frustration. Tapping a pen on the notepad, what she saw left her startled.

"Money, where are you?" She asked the screen as she felt herself collapsing inward and a shiver ran through her.

164 | Petra

Since returning from Zanzibar, Petra made a concerted effort to be a better friend, looking for areas to improve herself and staying single. Knowing that Nik worked evenings, Petra started inviting Bree to dinner more regularly. She accepted invites from the girls to go out. Now Nina was also free; they enjoyed mystery box challenges, cooking with ingredients each person brought. When it was Bree's turn, she brought food from the restaurant. That night, it was just Bree and Petra. Bree sank into the sofa of Petra's house, opening a glass of wine as Petra washed away pots and pans.

"So, how is it? Married life? Is it as you imagined?" Petra asked.

"Are you sure you want me to talk about this? I don't want to make you sad again," Bree said.

"No, this is the new Petra; I'm putting all of that behind me."

"Good for you; I'm pleased," Bree said, "Well, married life is strange, but not because of the marriage bit, just because he works every evening; I work all day, so we don't get much time together."

"That must suck," Petra said.

"I'm not complaining; I'm just so happy that I get to wake up next to him. He tries to get home for lunch when I don't have weddings, so we just need to adjust a bit. When he first got here, it was all new. Then he had the accident, and we were busy getting the restaurant up and running. Now, I guess, this is real life," Bree said.

"But you'll have all winter together once wedding season is over, just the two of you," Petra said.

"Yeah, we are going to Greece, maybe doing some travelling, maybe even moving into a bigger house; we have lots of plans," Bree said excitedly. We're planning a honeymoon in Australia. "What about you and Matt? Are you going over to see him?"

"I've got a quiet week in July, so I might go over," Petra said with a weak smile. "Although we're close friends, and I enjoy spending time with him, I don't see him as a potential boyfriend."

"That's good; friends are important. Look at Zac, Fabio, and the musicians from the weddings—we all love them, but they're just friends," Bree replied.

"Any news on Zac and Carla? She hasn't mentioned anything to me," Petra asked.

"No, they haven't spoken. I think she's annoyed at him," Bree said with a sigh. "Nik was going on at Carla about Zac's womanising ways. Carla doesn't trust herself not to get hurt, so she's pushed him away."

"I'm surprised; I thought they'd work well together," Petra said, her tone subdued.

"Me too," Bree admitted.

"I'm thinking of going back to Zanzibar as soon as the season ends," Petra said, changing the subject. "Maybe I'll try to buy some land or a house. I might even write."

"Write? About what?" Bree asked with interest.

"Maybe a book—who knows? Perhaps about weddings or us. We've got a pretty crazy life," Petra said with a small laugh.

"That would be fun. I can just imagine you sitting on the beach, typing away," Bree said warmly.

"It's just a dream for now," Petra said. "But I've got a whole lot of bad dating experiences to start with—and, of course, the wedding stories. You and Nik—now that's a story in itself," she teased. "To think of all those years you two wasted, and yet you still managed your happy ending against all the odds."

"Yeah, I'm lucky," Bree said softly. "I mean, we lost a lot of time, but we found each other again. I suppose you never know when things are going to work out. Sometimes, I wonder what would've happened if I'd taken a taxi that night instead of the tube," she said, her voice filled with nostalgia.

Petra muttered a quiet "Yeah," retreating into her thoughts.

Bree noticed the sadness on Petra's face. "Sorry, did I say too much?" she asked gently.

"No, you're fine. I'm working on my anger issues and jealousy, but I suppose I just get lonely," Petra admitted. Her eyes glistened, and her voice was soft.

"Well, I'm here whenever you need me. You know that," Bree said with a reassuring smile.

"Yeah, and now that you're not going to bed when the sun's still up, we could even go out for dinner sometime," Petra joked, lightening the mood.

"I'm only up because I wait for Nik," Bree said with a laugh. "Sometimes he doesn't finish until really late, so I'm constantly shattered."

"I can imagine," Petra replied sympathetically.

"It's tough sometimes," Bree continued. "He comes home and wants to talk about all his work problems, which I get—I want to listen. But the problems are about couples whose weddings I've arranged. It's strange, knowing what happens afterwards that I never knew before."

"What kind of stuff? Scandals?" Petra asked.

"Sometimes," Bree said, grimacing. "He tells me about the fights, the drunken guests, the vomiting... and other things. The other evening, he found a pair of black lace knickers in the men's bathroom. Dirty ones."

"Ugh, gross," Petra said, pulling a face. "How do we not know about this?"

"I guess we're already gone by then," Bree said with a shrug. "Last week, at Samantha's wedding, a guest tried to pole dance on one of those decorative pillars—you know, the ones with the flower arrangements on top?"

"Yeah," Petra said, intrigued.

"Well, the pillar toppled over, the glass vases fell onto her, smashed into her face, and she ended up in hospital for stitches," Bree recounted.

"Oh my god," Petra exclaimed, bursting into laughter.

"And a couple of weeks ago, the best man decided to dance on one of those glass tables by the DJ booth," Bree added.

"Oh no. The glass tables?" Petra gasped.

"Yep. He went straight through it, of course. Hospital trip for him too," Bree said, shaking her head.

"What does Nik think of it all?" Petra asked.

"He loves it," Bree said with a wry smile. "But I hate hearing about it because the next day, I have to meet the couples and pretend I don't know a thing."

"Well, all good material for my book," Petra said happily, her spirits lifting.

165 | Nina

Focusing as much as she could, Nina felt the blood rush to her head as she stared at the bank account once again. Her eyes darted across the screen, tension mounting with each transaction she clicked.

Seated hunched over her computer, her expression was stony as she confronted the growing mountain of debts: rock climbing gear, expensive fishing rods, and overnight stays at luxurious hotels in Venice, Rome, and God knows where else.

Her unease deepened when a single transaction caught her attention. One large withdrawal stood out—the account had been almost emptied the day before her lung surgery the previous year. Her breath caught. Why had he withdrawn over twenty thousand euros?

Straightening in her chair, Nina inhaled deeply, trying to steady herself. Her wide, incredulous eyes returned to the glaring screen. Grabbing a pen and paper, she began jotting down notes. The withdrawal coincided with the day she'd been admitted to the hospital. Her heart raced as she turned to the list of upcoming credit card transactions; it seemed never-ending. Scratching her head in frustration, she flipped through her notepad, searching for access codes, her fear tightening its grip.

Nina checked her personal savings—thankfully untouched. She moved to his account; nothing seemed unusual there. What was he doing? Her pulse quickened as she navigated to the page for blocking credit cards. Without giving it a second though, she froze both cards linked to their joint account. Her hands trembled as she searched for the contact details of the bank manager.

When the call connected, she blurted out, "Please explain to me what's going on with my account. I don't know if it's been hacked."

"Let me take a look," the manager replied. Nina could hear the rapid tapping of his keyboard and the occasional click of his mouse as he muttered quietly.

"There are quite a few unusual transactions on your credit cards," he said after a moment. "However, on the fifteenth of March, our credit card department contacted your husband, who confirmed all the transactions as his own."

Nina's stomach churned. "You didn't think to call me, too?" Her voice was tight with anger.

A pause. "We only require one cardholder to verify unusual transactions," the manager said evenly.

"But it's my money too," Nina shot back, her voice trembling. "I don't understand why I wasn't informed." She took a shaky breath, her grip tightening on the phone. "He's withdrawn most of our money and racked up twelve thousand euros on the credit cards. I need the entire account blocked. Now."

"I'm sorry," the manager replied, his tone placating. "We can't do that without authorization from both account holders."

Nina's eyes narrowed. "What can you do?" she demanded, her voice rising.

"I see you've already blocked the credit cards," he said calmly. "I can limit outgoing transactions to two hundred euros per day."

Her heart sank. She opened her mouth to protest but paused, her mind spinning. "So, he can still spend my money?" she scoffed bitterly. "This has to be a joke."

A growl escaped her throat as helplessness pressed down on her. She slumped against the wall, clutching the phone. The silence on the other end felt like a taunt.

"Please come in tomorrow morning at 8:30 a.m.," the manager finally said. "We'll see what we can do."

As the call ended, Nina stared at her phone, her hands trembling. Bewildered and defeated, she struggled to piece together what to do next.

166 | Nina

As she waited for sleep to come, Nina convinced herself she was worrying over nothing. Yet, when her alarm wrenched her from sleep, her eyes immediately landed on the empty side of the bed where Manuel should have been. Pulling back the duvet, she dragged her feet to the floor and began her day.

Pacing outside the glass-fronted bank, she could feel the rain seeping into her shoes, each cold droplet adding to her growing annoyance. The minutes dragged painfully until the doors finally slid open with a hiss.

Striding into the manager's office, she tossed her raincoat onto the empty chair beside her. The room was sterile and void of personality—no smiling family photos, no colourful artwork on the walls. It was as bland as the man who greeted her. The manager smiled mechanically as he vigorously shook her hand and introduced himself as David.

Nina cut through his pleasantries, her tone sharp as she took a seat. "What can you do to help me?" she demanded, her glare unyielding. Her voice carried the simmering anger she had been holding in.

David straightened, leafing through a stack of papers. "Thank you for bringing this to my attention. Yesterday afternoon, I reviewed the accounts in question—your joint accounts, your private account, and your husband's private account." He adjusted his glasses, picking up several sheets.

Irritated by his self-importance, Nina narrowed her eyes and let out a huff.

David continued, unfazed. "Let's start with the joint accounts." He pushed two thick bundles of papers towards her, each bound with a clip.

Nina's brows knitted together. "What do you mean, joint accounts? We only have one."

David looked up briefly. "No, you have two," he replied, pushing his glasses further up his nose.

Nina opened her mouth to protest, but confusion stopped her short. She shook her head, rubbing her temples, before reaching for the papers.

"This second account was opened on September 3rd," David explained. "Your husband opened it, and you completed and signed the paperwork here." He pointed to a scribble at the bottom of the page. "A few weeks later, he transferred the funds from the original account to this one."

Nina slid the document closer, squinting at the signature. "Who signed this? It wasn't me." Her voice was steady but icy. Reaching for a blank sheet of paper and a pen, she scribbled her signature several times. "This is my signature," she said, tapping the page in front of her. "That is not my signature." She jabbed her finger at the offending scribble.

David pulled the two signatures together, his gaze flicking between them. Although there were similarities, the differences were clear. Saying nothing, he turned to his computer, clicking rapidly through the system. The printer in the corner buzzed to life, spitting out a page. Sliding his chair over, David grabbed the report. He compared the new printout with the documents in front of him.

"Let's confirm," he muttered, calling for his assistant. A man with fair hair, steel-rimmed glasses, and a snub nose entered, still clutching a coffee cup. David thrust the papers towards him.

"Are these the same? Look closely," David instructed.

The assistant studied the signatures. "No," he replied confidently. "At first glance, they look similar. But this one lacks the tails on the G's, the N is too straight, and the R isn't rounded." He glanced at David. "We can run them through the signature recognition software to be sure."

David nodded. "Good idea." Turning to Nina, he said, "Please sign here." He handed her a stylus and tablet.

Steadying her hand, Nina signed her name. Her new signature appeared on the computer screen, alongside the original one from their records. "These two are a match," the assistant confirmed, taking a screenshot. He scanned the contested signature next and quickly ran it through the system.

"These two are not a match," he declared, his tone triumphant.

David exhaled and shifted forward, placing the papers in front of Nina. "Mrs. Ruggero," he said gravely, "it appears we have a situation. Someone has forged your signature. We'll need to investigate further."

Her initial relief quickly gave way to frustration. "Yes, I can see that; what next?" she asked, her voice trembling as her lips quivered.

The manager faltered, searching for the right words "We will need to block both of the joint accounts temporarily and follow guidance from our head office," he said, attempting a stern tone but faltering under her glare.

Nina's eyes widened with disbelief. "I asked you yesterday to block them, and you told me you couldn't." she snapped, resisting the growing urge to stand up and slap the man.

"Yes, well, given the latest developments, I can act now," he replied uncomfortably, avoiding her gaze.

Nina's forced smile vanished. "I need printouts of the transactions," she demanded, her voice edged with icy control. "I need them to investigate further."

The manager shook his head apologetically. "I'm sorry, but once the accounts are blocked, you'll no longer have access to them."

Nina's anger boiled over. "How am I supposed to confront my husband without evidence? I need proof." Her voice cracked as she buried her face in her hands, trying to steady her emotions.

The manager sighed, stood up, and placed a hand on her back, subtly guiding her towards the door. He ushered her out, closing it firmly behind her.

The warm air from the bank followed her as she stepped outside into the cold drizzle. She glanced around and noticed the staff lingering near the water coolers, throwing awkward glances her way. Pulling her raincoat collar higher, she lowered her head and walked away, feeling their eyes burning into her back.

As the bank's sliding doors hissed open again, a petite figure approached her. Nina stepped aside to let her pass, but the woman stopped beside her.

"You left your bag, Mrs. Ruggero," came the soft whisper.

Nina glanced at the bag, puzzled. "It isn't mine," she replied, her brow furrowing.

"Just take it," the voice urged. Before Nina could respond, the woman turned and re-entered the bank, her pink silk shirt a blur in the corner of Nina's vision.

Hesitant and uneasy, Nina picked up the bag and hugged it tightly against her chest. Her heart thudded as she rushed to her car. Settling into the driver's seat, she unhooked the leather clasps with trembling hands, her pulse quickening. She reached inside and pulled out a bundle of papers, setting them aside before driving out of the car park.

The clock on the dashboard ticked steadily as Nina turned towards Bree's house. Bree, her ever-patient friend, would help her make sense of this mess.

Stepping into puddles, Nina smiled faintly at the gate security, wiped her shoes on the well-worn rug, and rang the bell.

167 | Nina

Bree put down her book and opened the door. Seeing Nina's stern, exhausted face, she pulled her friend inside and led her to the dining table.

"What has he done now?" Bree asked. She couldn't imagine anything, or anyone else leaving Nina in such a state.

Nina dropped the bag onto the floor and slumped forward, her face buried in her hands. "I think he stole my money," she muttered.

Bree's eyes widened. "That's a serious accusation. Where is he? Are you sure? Have you told the police?" Bree asked, her voice rising with concern. She knew what Manuel was capable of. "If he knows you've found out... it doesn't bear thinking about."

"I hate him," Nina spat furiously. "I never want to see him again."

"You need to explain everything to me," Bree said softly, touching Nina's damp shoulder. "Start from the beginning."

Nina nodded and took a deep breath. "Okay, so..." She paused, collecting her thoughts before recounting everything—both accounts, the overdrafts, the credit cards, every unsettling detail.

Bree listened intently, shock on her face. "What's in the bag?" she asked suddenly.

"I don't know," Nina admitted. "Just papers, as far as I can tell. It's over there by the door."

"Let's take a look," Bree suggested, her voice calm but firm.

"Can you help me go through it?" Nina pleaded, her wide eyes shimmering with desperation.

"Of course," Bree replied, squeezing Nina's hand before retrieving the bag.

Bree reached for the bag and emptied its contents onto the coffee table. The corridor echoed with the sound of barefoot footsteps.

"Nik, Nina is here; put some clothes on," she called, smiling.

The footsteps receded, followed by the sound of drawers and doors banging as they vibrated through the walls. Moments later, the steps approached again.

Nik appeared, his hair tousled and eyes heavy with sleep. He looked down at Bree and grinned before leaning in to kiss her gently. "Hi, Nina, good morning," he said, smiling.

Nina winced as her gaze drifted to his bare chest. When Nik turned, a long scar running down his back caught her attention.

"You look busy, ladies; I'll leave you to it," he said quickly, retreating toward the bathroom.

Bree scurried to the kitchen. She spread out the papers, slid her glasses onto her nose, and pulled up a chair for Nina. With a sigh that betrayed the enormity of the task, Bree began sorting the documents into piles. She reached for a stack of Post-it notes and a couple of pens.

"What are we looking at?" Nina asked.

Bree paused, her gaze lingering on the papers. "These are the documents you signed when you opened the first account after marrying Manuel," she said, scribbling on a Post-it note before sticking it to a stack of papers. "These are for the new account. These cover the withdrawals, and these are the signatures. And here," she added, placing more notes, "are the credit card documents—two for the old joint account, three for the new one."

"Is he using credit cards on the new joint account, the one he faked my signature on?" Nina's voice trembled as she tried to process it all.

"Yes, he's spent quite a lot on those cards, by the looks of it."

"God, this is a mess." Nina's eyes took on a haunted look as anger began to rise in her chest. Panic crept down her spine as she stared at the table, overwhelmed by the papers strewn across it.

Nik called sweetly for Bree, who stood and joined him in the corridor. In the reflection of a shiny glass cabinet, Nina caught sight of Nik pulling Bree into his arms. His hand rested on the curve of her back as he kissed her passionately. Even in the dim reflection, the intensity of their connection was unmistakable.

Bree returned to the table just as Nik grabbed his top and headed for the door. "I'm going for a run, ladies; I'll bring breakfast," he said, flashing them a quick smile before leaving.

The two women turned their attention back to the papers. Bree ran her polished finger down each line of text, pausing to highlight key points. Nina struggled to focus; her vacant gaze betrayed her rising frustration.

"Things will make sense soon enough," Bree reassured her. "Just give me time." Her hands moved swiftly as she jotted down notes.

Nina's eyes wandered, seeking distraction. She noticed how much the house had changed since Nik's arrival. Once soulless, it was now lined with framed photos and carefully tended plants. The never used treadmill had been replaced by a floor-to-ceiling bookshelf filled with neatly stacked books. Squinting, she read the bold author's name on several covers: Nik Daskalakis.

"He's a writer?" she asked, picking up a book and skimming the first paragraph.

"Oh, yes, but they're in Greek, so I have no idea if they're any good," Bree replied with a smile. She pulled a hardback book from the shelf. "This one's called Bree. He says I won't know what's in it until I learn Greek," she laughed, clutching the book to her chest. "But I'll convince him to read it to me one day."

She set the book down and refocused on the task at hand. "Right, back to business. I see a disturbing picture of a man trying to steal all your money," Bree said, shooting Nina a serious look. "On the twenty-third of September, Manuel withdrew all the funds from your joint account and transferred them into a new joint account. He also tried to apply for a loan to buy a new house. Since he

RAW MISTAKES

needed your income to qualify, he opened the joint account to fake your involvement."

"Why didn't he just do a bank transfer?" Nina asked, her voice shaking.

Bree shared a knowing glance with her. "He probably didn't want it to be traced. He must have assumed you wouldn't find out about the account."

Bree gestured to a scanned document, her finger pointing to the words with a withering scowl. "Here it is, in his own handwriting—'Leaving my wife'—as the reason for the withdrawal."

Nina stared at the papers, her disbelief palpable. "None of this makes sense," she said slowly. "Shouldn't this have raised a red flag? How does someone open a joint account without the other person co-signing? And why would a bank approve it?"

She stooped forward, her tone growing sharper. "Look at the name on the documents. Someone named Marco Lomba authorised all of this." She shook her head, disbelief etched on her face.

168 | Nina

"None of the guys I met this morning were called Marco," Nina said, her tone uncertain, unsure whether to feel relieved or alarmed.

"Why would he let him do this?" Bree asked, her gaze fixed on Nina. The revelation that Manuel had been planning to leave while she was hospitalised still hadn't fully sunk in.

"Why?" Nina echoed Bree's question, her mind spinning with disbelief. Bree glanced at her notes, fiddling with her pen as though it could somehow offer answers.

"Let's pull up your new joint account," Bree suggested, reaching for her laptop and logging in to access the account details.

The figures on the screen made Bree lean forward, scribbling notes in her notebook while listing transactions.

Nina sank back into the sofa clearly baffled and unable to concentrate, her expression dazed and distant.

"Well, here's some good news," Bree announced, her voice rising in excitement. "The money he took out is here. I can see the date and the cash deposit," she said, pointing at the screen.

"Can I access it?" Nina asked impatiently, leaning forward.

"His salary is also going into this account," Bree added, a hint of amusement in her voice. "Wow, security guards earn a lot of money. I should consider a career change." She immediately regretted the joke, realising it wasn't the time.

"It's all the overtime." Nina explained.

"There's way more money in this account than the debts he racked up in your original joint account," she said, her voice sharp with disbelief. Over fifty thousand euros sat untouched—far more than enough to cover the debts.

"What?" Nina blinked, as if snapping out of a trance. "Sorry, I'm just so confused right now."

"We need to act fast. You need to get this account unblocked and recover your money. I can only see what's here; I can't do anything else yet. I can't even access the transactions panel," Bree said, her tone growing frustrated.

Bree refreshed the screen, then gasped as the transaction panel lit up. "Oh my god, it's not blocked yet. We can do this." Her voice quickened, and she barked orders. "Grab a pen and paper, and give me that code generator from the bank." She slid the laptop off her lap and moved to the dining room table.

This sudden shift in energy snapped Nina out of her stupor. Her eyes now alert, she joined Bree. "Okay, what do we do?"

"First, we check if he's getting notifications for any transactions. He can't know about this until it's done." Bree navigated through various screens, frowning as she discovered his phone number linked to the account. She swiftly replaced it with Nina's number. "Okay, done. Let's hope he doesn't notice that change," she said, glancing at her watch.

"He starts work in an hour and can't use his phone during his shift. We have a window until seven," Nina said, her voice steadying.

"We need to be quick. We can't transfer the money to your other account—he still has access to that."

"Then where do we send it?" Nina asked.

"To me," she suggested after a pause. "It's safer that way. What do you think?"

Bree hesitated, her heart racing with adrenaline. "You have a transfer limit of fifteen thousand euros per day; we need to change that first."

"Can we do that?" Nina asked, sceptical.

"We don't want to steal—it could backfire if this goes to court. We'll only recover what he took. That way, you're on the right side of the law," Bree said, her voice firm despite the rush of nerves.

"Let's do it," Nina said, meeting Bree's gaze with a determined smirk.

"First, we need copies of all these documents before I write any more notes on them," Bree said. She picked up the phone and dialled Carla. "We need you. Can you get to my house now?" she asked urgently.

Carla's voice crackled with concern. "What's happened—?"

"Just get here, please," Bree cut her off, then hung up.

Minutes later, Carla arrived, dripping wet. "I came on my bike. My car's at the restaurant," she explained, catching her breath.

"Take my car. Photocopy these papers and bring them back. Don't tell anyone where we are, especially Manuel," Bree instructed, handing over a pile of documents.

Carla raced to the office, dodging rain puddles in the car park, and quickly copied the documents. She stapled and organised them neatly into a folder, then returned to Bree's house. On her way, she spotted Nik outside the bakery.

Rolling down her window, she called out, "I'm running errands for Bree. What's going on at your house?"

"No clue," Nik replied, holding up a bag of croissants and takeaway coffees. "I went for a run but didn't make it far, bloody rain."

Carla gestured for him to get in. They returned together, and Nik let them in with his key.

Bree greeted Carla with a relieved smile as she handed over the documents. "I made copies and kept the originals intact. I hope that's okay."

"Perfect. Put the originals over there, and let's get started," Bree said, her voice steady but urgent.

169 | Nina

"Bree, call Fabio; I need to speak to him," Nina ordered, slipping off her cardigan and draping it over a chair.

Bree dialed the number and placed the phone on speaker.

"Fabio, hi, I need you to change the locks on my house. Can you do it now?"

"Well, I'm just—" Fabio began, but Nina cut him off.

"Please, Fabio. I can't have Manuel in my house."

"I've got my key. I'll use that," Fabio replied firmly.

Meanwhile, Bree scanned the figures Nina was scribbling down and did a quick calculation.

"We're up to thirty-six thousand euros," Bree said. "I've managed to move twenty thousand so far, but I'm blocked now. I don't know if I can do more today."

Nina's heart pounded against her ribcage. Her hand shook as she gripped the pen. The tension in the room was fierce, there was a mission to complete.

Nina's phone rang, breaking the tension. "Fabio," she answered, putting him on speaker.

"Hey, so Manuel pulled up just as I was arriving," Fabio said. "I told him you are staying at Bree's place and that you needed me to grab some stuff for you. He looked like he'd been out all night and said he was coming home to get changed. What's going on?"

"Wait until he leaves, then go back and change those locks," Nina instructed.

Fabio found a seat by the window of a nearby coffee shop, keeping a discreet eye on the street. He sipped his coffee as he watched Manuel—now in his uniform—drive off in his black Nissan Duke, heading towards the main road out of Rocca Pinta.

Once he was sure Manuel was gone, Fabio acted fast. His hands trembled slightly as he replaced the lock, anxiety washing over him despite his experience. Tightening the final screws and checking the key, he grabbed his toolkit and drove to Bree's house. The retreating clouds cast a faint light over the driveway as he knocked on the door. Nik opened it, his expression one of mild confusion.

"I have another job for you," Bree said, cutting to the point. "Go to the Unicredit bank on the main road. Look for a petite woman with mousy brown hair in a ponytail wearing a pink shirt. You need to get her to call me. Tell her you're Nina's brother and keep it discreet." Her tone brooked no argument.

Bree quickly stood up and rummaged around a drawer, pulling out a yellow leather purse. Running her fingers over the inside pockets, she removed some high-value notes and credit cards. "Take this; tell anyone who asks that you're returning the purse she left in the bar this morning and you are just returning it."" She scribbled a message: "Call N.R. with Bree's number." Nik was surprised; he had never seen Bree so assertive, demanding, and overprotective of her friend.

"I'll come with you," Nik he said, stepping outside with Fabio.

As they drove to the bank, Nik asked, "Do you have any idea what's going on?"

Fabio shook his head. "Not really. It's all very cloak-and-dagger. I guess they'll tell us when we need to know, but Nina is scary as hell."

"Bree's not messing around either," Nik replied as they parked.

Inside the bank, they scanned the room for a pink shirt and high ponytail. Nik approached the desk, his charm on full display.

"I found this purse at Dodo Bar this morning," he said with a smile, his Greek accent thickened for effect. "The waiter said the owner works here. She's wearing a pink shirt."

The teller's eyes lit up. "That's Paula," she said, picking up her phone. After a brief call, a petite, anxious woman emerged from the back. Her wary eyes darted around as she approached the desk.

Nik held out the purse. "I saw you leave this at the bar," he said, flashing her a meaningful look. "Do you know my friend? His sister was here earlier."

Paula's cheeks flushed as she realised what was going on. "Oh, I didn't realise I'd left it. Thank you so much," she stammered, clutching the purse. Her voice was barely audible as the two men left.

Returning, Nik and Fabio silently entered the room. Bree outstretched her hand to Nik, squeezing it tightly for a moment.

"Forty-three thousand euros," Carla announced, pushing her calculator aside. She underlined the figure and boxed it dramatically.

"That thieving bastard," she muttered through clenched teeth. That means twenty-three thousand to go. Bree sat straight, rolling her neck in circles. She smiled at Nik, pulled him towards her and kissed him quickly. "Sorry, Nik," she whispered, mouthing, "I love you." He smiled back and placed his hands on her shoulders as if to start a massage.

"We gave her the purse; we think she understood," Fabio said.

"Now we have to wait for her to call us," said Bree. "We are stuck until she does; if she doesn't, we wait until tomorrow morning until we can go back."

Nina looked around the room. Taking a long, deep breath, she spoke, "I'll tell you everything, but it's a very long story, but for now, I'll tell you that Manuel has stolen forty-three thousand euros from me, and we are trying to get it back." Her expressionless face turned back to the papers in front of her.

Fabio gave a look of confused pity. Feeling betrayed and hopeless, Nina sat back in her chair, shut her eyes, and let out a deep sigh. Bree grabbed Nina's hand as everyone else looked at each other in shock. Questions echoed around the room, interrupted abruptly by a vibration on the table.

"That has to be her," Bree said, picking up the phone and putting the call on speaker.

"Hello, this is Paula from the bank." Bree thanked her for calling and introduced herself and the people with her. Nina started to talk; she thanked her for the papers they had gone through, copied, and understood.

"We have worked out that he has taken forty-three thousand, two hundred euros from me so far, including the credit card payments; I'm trying to get that money back. Luckily, the account hasn't been blocked yet," Nina said.

"Yes, that's my job, but the papers haven't reached my desk yet." Nina could hear the cheeky tone in her voice: "I have until the end of the day to find the papers and set up the blocks on all your accounts."

"We've managed to get twenty thousand back, but I've reached my daily limit on the account. Can you change it?"

"No, I can't." She paused, thinking for a moment: "You can still withdraw money from the account in cash." The group could hear her inhaling her cigarette; the sound was disturbed by the blowing gale outside. "If you can be ready to come within a moment's notice, I can let you know when the manager leaves; normally, he goes out before lunch to meet a customer. Give me your email address. I'll email the withdrawal slips for you to fill out. Fill them in by hand, sign them, and have them ready; it will be quicker."

"Okay," replied Nina.

"I'm risking my job here, but what they're doing is wrong," Paula said. "Come in with someone else; let them do the talking. Try and look different from this morning; change your clothes, hair, anything."

With that the call ended.

In a hopeless attempt to look different, Nina and Bree rummaged around her wardrobe. Walking back towards the group, the room filled with giggles as Nina's disguise, a long black woollen coat, leather boots, and blue woolly hat with a bobble on top. "I look like an oversized spy," she said with reluctance in her eyes. The leather boots left too much room at the toes. Rolling up her arm sleeves, she said, "I'm ready; who is coming with me?" Nina asked.

"Alright, so they know me." Bree said, "They have seen Fabio and Nik already today; Carla, you have an account there too, don't you? So, they know you. What about Petra?"

Bree quickly called their last member. This time, she had time for a greeting before getting to the point.

"Are you in Rocca Pinta?" Bree asked, "We need a favour. Can you get to my house in the next few minutes? Hurry, it's important. Keep your phone by you in case something changes."

When Petra arrived she felt the electricity in the room. "Oh, everyone is here. We even have Inspector Gadget over there." She chuckled, eyeing Nina's outfit. Only Nik laughed, more to break the awkward silence than a genuine reaction to the joke.

Petra noticed Bree looked different; dark shadows surrounded her eyes, and her hair looked unkempt. Bree ran her fingers through her hair, scratching her scalp.

Nina paced the small kitchen area, strutting around the Ikea dining table, to the sofa, over to the fridge and back again. Nik slotted Nespresso capsules into the machine one at a time for the group. A nervous silence filled the room, all fixated on the phone on the table. The sounds of ringing broke the silence.

"This is it." Fabio said, pressing the 'accept call' button on the phone.

"The manager has left, the assistant too; come now, and I'll make sure I'm in front of the house," Paula said.

"Okay, coming," said Nina.

"Petra, let's go," she said, looking at her bewildered friend. "Hurry."

"I'm the getaway driver," said Fabio as he grabbed Bree's car keys.

Fabio instructed Petra to hand over the papers, collect the money, and leave. "You both need to look confident; look for Paula in a pink shirt, and hand her these papers." Fabio said

Following instructions, Nina quickly spotted the lady in pink and headed to her desk. "How may I help you?" she asked, looking up, her eyes narrowing, playing the part perfectly.

Nina handed over the signed papers and clicked on some keys on her computer. Paula's eyes darted around her, checking the front entrance and looking behind her.

Within two minutes, the girls were handed the four piles of euros. Nina was surprised at how small it looked; it didn't look like twenty-three thousand euros.

"Would you like me to block your account now?" she asked.

Nina nodded in reply. "Have a good day, ladies." Paula said, looking at Nina, her eyes glossy and blank.

"Got it," Nina said excitedly to Fabio as he quickly left his spot outside the bank and headed back to Bree's house.

Nina waved her bag around to the others; her smile was now genuine. "We got it all." A cheer filled the room: "We did it. You did it; I couldn't have done it without you, all of you," Nina said before running into the bedroom to strip off all the layers of disguise.

170 | Nina

Inside, the friends all took a seat. As the last forkful of pasta with pesto sauce that Nik had whipped up was devoured, Nina moved to the sofa and started to talk. Pausing occasionally for a sip of coffee, she told the story of her suspicions of Manuel's affair last summer, Manuel's friendship with Stefano, the discovery of the ticket and boarding pass, and the incriminating photos. Her eyes welled up as she recounted the lies, the fights, and the denials.

"We exist in a 'don't ask, don't tell' household." She finished talking with a sour look on her face. Silence surrounded them before the questions started.

"What's next?" Nik asked.

"No idea; I need to not be at home when he gets home, although I don't know when that will be. I need to put this money in an account; I need to start over, just me and my guitar."

They discussed how to tell Manuel. Should she call or text? Should she collect his things and take them to Stefano's house? Nina didn't want him bashing the door down while she was there alone.

"He needs to know before he gets home, which is usually around seven, if he bothers coming home at all."

"Let's go there now," Fabio suggested, "Let's all go, pack up his things, and take everything to Stefano's house." The group looked at Nina for confirmation, who nodded.

"You're staying with me for a few days," Fabio announced, wrapping his arms around her. "Until all of this blows over."

With a quick glance at his watch, Nik waited for a natural pause in the conversation before speaking. "Well, my friends, I must take my leave. I've got a wedding to host tonight. Now, which one of you lovely ladies is the planner?" he asked, his gaze briefly drifting to the sink filled with dirty dishes.

"That would be me," Petra replied, raising her hand with a small smile. She checked her own watch and added, "I should get going too. Thankfully, it's a 5 p.m. wedding, and the sun's shining again."

With that, the pair headed out together, while the others made their way to the car park.

Travelling in two cars, the group arrived at Nina's house, quickly gathering whatever belongings of Manuel's they could fit into suitcases or bags. With barely a word exchanged, they tossed the packed items into the cars. Nina watched, a surge of exhilaration coursing through her, as the last of his possessions were loaded. Leaning her back against the wall, she exhaled deeply, observing the car splutter and lurch down the street, carrying away the remnants of his presence.

Once they were gone, Nina moved through the house like a whirlwind. Her gaze flitted between her phone, the blank space where Manuel's oversized wall clock had once hung, and the door. The beep of a new message broke her rhythm. She read it, her expression darkening as she rubbed her temples, struggling to absorb the unwelcome news.

The sharp glare of sunlight greeted her as she dashed out of the house, running towards Bree's building at full speed. Breathless but resolute, she paused outside, basking momentarily in the warmth of the sun on her face. Her reprieve was short-lived as the two cars, now unburdened of their heavy loads, pulled into view, disrupting the quiet moment.

171 | Petra

Petra rushed to the office, relieved to have had a morning of distraction. She was nervous about the day's wedding. She'd met the couple yesterday. Jolene, the bride, had told her all about her religious family, from whom she had rebelled and distanced herself over the years.

"They're a nightmare; everything is about the church. You have no idea the stress I have gone through because I'm having a civil ceremony, not a church wedding."

"Yes, your father has emailed us asking to do a reading," Petra said.

"Oh no, what did you say?"

"We told him we would check with you, and it must be short due to the time constraints in the castle—no more than fifteen minutes."

"Okay, well, I suppose if it keeps him happy, that is fine with me, as long as it's short," Jolene said, wishing to keep the peace at all costs.

"Yes, we will make sure he knows it's no more than fifteen minutes."

"We came overseas to do the wedding our way. We didn't want or need the stress from my family. It's hard to explain. Our family was cultish and as a child, my whole life revolved around the church; every day there was something—a bible study, a prayer group—we couldn't escape it," Jolene explained with nervous laughter.

The groom, James, sat quietly, nodding. He didn't even really mind her father and his overbearing ways. They didn't live close, so they didn't see each other often. James didn't dare suggest to Jolene that she should compromise more and let her father have some involvement; he kept his opinions to himself.

"I've been having nightmares about him ruining the day. I've managed to keep him out of the loop, saying that you're doing it all, and I have to turn up and say, "I do"."

Finally, James spoke, "We even insisted on paying for it ourselves to keep them out of it. If they were paying, they would expect to be involved."

Running through the finer details, they discussed the music for the ceremony. "Nice choices," Petra said, looking at the list of Motown songs. "The musicians have rehearsed, and they sound great; I heard them yesterday."

"Who is your photographer?" Petra asked.

"Some guy from church. My dad needs to make sure there are no poses he deems inappropriate or provocative."

"Yeah, that's the only thing they are paying for; I wanted Bree. I love her photos, but he said there is too much passion in them."

Petra laughed as she asked for the photographer's name and handed over a timing sheet for him. "What does your dad think of your dress?" Petra asked.

"Ah, well, I showed him one in a magazine that I thought he would approve of, but I didn't buy that one. By the time he sees it, it will be too late," Jolene said as she let out a cheeky giggle. "I'm sure he's packed my mother's high-necked, loose, full-sleeved wedding dress just in case, to make sure no skin is on view."

Reading her notes before the wedding, Petra took a long, deep breath, snapped her file shut and headed up to the castle. Jolene, arriving at the castle, stopped in her tracks and glared at her brother. "This is Dad's church music. Where is my music?"

Petra ran down to greet her with a pale face and said, "Your father has provided the music for the string quartet; he won't let them play anything else. He's standing over them, making them play his choice of music."

"It's your day, but if you want peace and quiet, just give him this," her brother said reluctantly. "He's already going to freak out when he sees that dress." Her dress was an ivory mermaid dress, strapless, and designed to accentuate all of her curves.

"No, I won't. I've already compromised with the photos. Honestly, that guy should be a monk; he's doing everything he can to make me look frumpy." She paused for a moment. "Do you think I can book Bree for tomorrow for a re-shoot?" she asked.

"I'll check. What about the music?" Petra asked.

"Look, I don't want to be a bitch or a bridezilla, but I want the music I chose. Can you please tell James to sort it out?"

A few moments later, Jolene walked down the aisle with her brother to the music of her choice. Wiping away beads of sweat from her hair, she felt her father's eyes on her. Petra watched his frown deepen as he looked his daughter up and down with a scowl.

Once they were pronounced husband and wife, Jolene's father was invited to the front. "There will now be a short reading by John, the father of the bride," Petra said, stepping back from the ceremony table.

John, a smart but stern-looking man, strolled to the front, bible in hand. He asked the wedding party to hold hands as he read the Lord's Prayer. Jolene shook her head and looked down, cringing inside as the prayer started. "Amen," he said, finishing his prayer.

Petra neared the table once more, lifting her folder to her chest, ready to guide the couple out to the champagne toast on a lower terrace. Instead, John placed the Bible on the table and continued a speech about family values, the church community, and the importance of prayer.

Jolene could see Petra out of the corner of her eye; she was trying to get Jolene's attention. They somehow managed to understand each other without words, just with a few glances. Jolene had no idea how long this had been going on, but she was guessing over forty-five minutes. Her guests started to stand, seeking out shade; others burned up under the sun. Jolene nodded, giving the signal to Petra to try and get this to stop.

Petra wracked her brain about what to do. She calmly walked to the back of the wedding terrace and whispered to the musicians to be ready to play at her next nod. She walked back to the front of the wedding terrace, hovering just in view of the musicians and waited impatiently for the next gap in the sermon. As soon as Jolene's dad took a deep breath, Petra nodded to the musicians. The music started playing, and an upbeat version of 'It Takes Two' filled the air.

Petra gave the signal to the wedding couple to walk down the aisle. Taking the moment, they walked to the applause of their eighty hot and thirsty guests.

John looked around him, confused and irate. He was only halfway through his sermon. The string quartet quickly set up downstairs, and cheers echoed as champagne bottles opened. Just as everyone had gotten a drink, it was time to go.

Jolene knew that there had been an hour allocated to the champagne reception in the castle, which should have been more than enough in the Italian summer heat. She tried to hold on to her frustration.

"We paid a lot for this toast; surely we can stay longer," John said.

"We can't stay longer," she said. "We have a boat trip booked. When we booked it, they told us that we had to be on time. If we're late, it will be cancelled as they have another trip after ours. I had all this planned for two years, every single moment. You ruined it all with your never-ending religious waffle. You were told to speak for no more than five minutes, and you couldn't give me that."

"And you promised me a respectable dress; you look like a whore." The way he looked at her made Jolene shiver. "Well, seeing as you always acuse me of being one, I thought I'd dress like one." With that she turned her back to him, grabbed her husband's arm and walked away.

The couple sped off in the three-wheeler Tuk Tuk, pulling up at the beautiful wooden sailboat. Decorated with white and pink peonies, an acoustic guitar was waiting to serenade them as they sailed away from the village. Jolene finally felt herself calming down. The wedding party enjoyed the welcome breeze on the water, taking in the scenery before docking in front of the lakeside restaurant for the wedding breakfast.

Pulling Petra aside as they entered the restaurant, John spoke loudly, "I'm not sure what happened; the quartet started to play, and I hadn't even finished my reading. I think I'll try and finish the whole thing before my speech."

Petra asked him to sit down, and she decided it was time to tell him, in her own words, politely, of course, to butt out. She pulled out the timings of the day and inched them towards him; the timings were printed in black and white. She showed him the detailed itinerary, listing all that had been missed at the champagne toast and how late things were running.

"The chefs have been told the speeches will be approximately twenty minutes in total, as per the information from your daughter. They will have the food ready at five-thirty on the dot. If you do continue your speech, the food will be ruined."

"That isn't my problem," he protested loudly.

"No, it's your daughter's problem, and from the little I know, she wants her day to run exactly like this." Petra tapped on the printout. "The live band will be starting at seven; the cake is going to be served at ten, then after-dinner pizza at eleven thirty."

"You have to be joking. Who are you to tell me I can't do what I want at my daughter's wedding?" John launched into her. "You don't know who you are dealing with. You watch me; I'll talk as long as I want, and I'll say what I want; this isn't your wedding."

Petra leant over to grab some water. "This is the day that your daughter has chosen; this is her dream wedding, and it's my job to make sure it all runs exactly the way she wants. I'm sorry that you don't want your daughter to be happy today. My only concern right now is that I do what she has asked and paid me to do." She paused as John's face looked like it was about to explode. "Now, please, let me do my job, and after fifteen minutes of your speech, you will be asked to finish. There will be another two speeches after yours."

Petra, shaking inside, felt her stomach churn. She smiled and walked away. She turned to see John leaving the venue, hands in his pockets, his own arrogance following him like a black cloud. As she turned back to the wedding party, she wasn't sure if she had done the right thing or not.

Jolene approached her, smiling, "Thank you; that took a lot of balls; you were great. Now, let's hope he doesn't come back."

John didn't return for his speech. The constant calls from the bride's brother made him return, which he later regretted.

"Why did you ask him to come back? He's going to ruin the evening too. At least Mum is sitting down, pretending to enjoy herself. Dad can't do that." Jolene expressed her frustration at her brother's foolishness.

Jolene had ignored her father's demand for a dry wedding—no wine, no beers, just soft drinks. He had permitted only a glass of champagne to toast the couple. Jolene ignored his request to create a different playlist for the reception.

Once the live band arrived, Jolene and James asked Petra to help them with the translation. "We have had enough with Dad; he isn't going to ruin this, too. Please, the band and our playlist are non-negotiable. We have chosen our songs, and we want only those."

The band agreed as they started to play the first dance. As expected, about five songs in, the soft start-off music, such as Dancing in the Moonlight and Love Is in the Air, had been played, and more upbeat songs were put on. Single ladies came on, and all the ladies rushed to the dance floor, hitching up their skirts and kicking off their shoes.

John strutted over to the musicians. He appeared red in the face as he leant over the musician's console. "I demand that you stop this music; this is inappropriate for a wedding." They showed him the email from Jolene choosing her songs, shrugged their shoulders, and carried on. John continued to talk to them, signalling frantically for them to take their earplugs out.

The singer glanced at him, pointing to his earpiece, gesturing that they could not hear him, and continued singing.

Once again, John, red-faced with anger, edged towards Petra. There was an intake of breath around the room, his eyes wide with rage. He frowned for a moment, taking a step back.

"Please, I kindly ask you to respect your daughter's wishes and not change her music choice," Petra said, forcing herself to keep her voice soft and calm.

"You get out of my way," he said. For a brief moment, everyone stared, and a chill filled the air. The crowd parted for him to leave. A loud round of applause roared out as he jumped into a taxi.

Petra arrived home, exhausted; her mind went back to Nina and her problems, so she sent a quick text and crawled into bed.

172 | Nina

"Manuel and Stefano aren't together anymore?" Nina asked her brother in a desperate whisper, seeking confirmation.

"Yep," Fabio replied with a nod. "We took everything to his brother's house instead."

"Then where's he going all the time?" Nina pressed, her voice trembling.

Fabio hesitated, taking a deep breath before meeting her gaze. "That's the thing. Stefano said Manuel is with someone else now—someone who works at your bank. That's all he could tell me."

Nina felt her legs weaken beneath her. Reaching for the wall, she pressed against it, her mind racing. "I guess it all makes sense now. They must have been in on this together," she murmured, her words barely audible. Her friends quickly ushered her inside, helping her into a chair as her motionless body sank into it.

"What now?" Bree asked, her concerned eyes fixed on Nina's pale face.

With trembling hands, Nina fumbled through her bag and pulled out her phone. She opened her last message to Manuel and began composing a new one: I know what you did. I want a divorce. Everything you own is at your brother's house. Don't come home. Her eyes darkened with determination as she pressed the send button and shoved the phone away, a look of disgust twisting her features.

"I've told him I want a divorce," she declared to the room.

Fabio handed her a cup of coffee, his touch gentle as he stroked her back.

Several minutes later, Manuel read the message, his face tightening with anxiety as panic gripped him. He read it again, his hand trembling, before tossing the phone onto the bed. Turning to Marco, he held out the device, his expression twisted in disbelief.

Marco's eyes widened in horror as he read the message. Manuel leapt to his feet, his movements frantic.

"Where are you going?" Marco asked, watching him step into his trousers and tighten his black leather belt.

"To sort this mess out," Manuel snapped, pulling on his shirt. His voice was raw, edged with desperation. "I don't know what she means by I know what you did, but this whole divorce thing? It's not happening." His tone hardened, his fear twisting into anger. "I'm not going to be the talk of every dinner table in the village for the next month," he spat, snatching his car keys.

Marco grabbed his shoulder, gripping firmly. "Don't do this. Lie low for a while. Let it blow over. You know how to handle her." Manuel shoved him aside, barging past. "Where are you even going?" Marco called after him.

"Home," Manuel growled. "She told me not to go there, so that's where she'll be."

Without another word, he stormed out, slamming the door behind him.

Manuel drove recklessly, his foot heavy on the gas as he weaved through traffic with sharp turns and abrupt stops. Arriving at the house, he stepped out of the car, sighing heavily as he kicked at the gravel. He approached the door, fumbling with his key, but the lock wouldn't budge. Staring at the key in disbelief, he tried again, only to feel a fresh wave of dread wash over him.

Realisation dawned, and frustration boiled over. He pounded his fist against the door, each hit growing more frantic. "Bitch. You changed the locks," he bellowed.

Seething, he turned and kicked the door before storming back to his car. Slamming the door shut, he revved the engine, pressed his foot to the gas, and sped off into the distance.

173 | Nina

Sitting at Bree's coffee table, Nina sipped her coffee, her expression determined despite the slight tremor in her hands. "I won't be bullied anymore," she whispered, her voice barely audible, as though speaking to herself.

Fabio cast her a compassionate glance while the others huddled around a computer, whispering and jotting down notes as they searched for a good divorce lawyer.

The loud banging on the door made Nina check her watch with a groan. "Did anyone tell security not to let Manuel in?" she asked, looking around.

The group exchanged uneasy glances. "No, I don't think so," Bree replied as the room fell silent.

The banging resumed, followed by Manuel's muffled voice. "Please, we need to talk," he pleaded through the door.

Nina glanced at Bree, who shrugged. "It's your call," Bree said evenly.

Nina nodded to Nik, who waited for a moment before turning the knob and opening the door.

Manuel stood frozen for a moment, staring at the scene before him. Four hard-faced people met his gaze with unflinching stares. His expression darkened as he spotted Nina. Brushing past Bree, he stormed toward her.

Towering over Nina, he ran his hands roughly through his hair, his voice sharp and venomous. "Nina, you bitch, you changed the locks."

She shifted uncomfortably, but before Manuel could move closer, Fabio stepped between them, his presence firm and protective.

Nina met Manuel's furious glare with a newfound strenght. Her voice steadied, surprising even herself. "I told you not to go back. Your stuff is at your brother's. The house is mine—you know that." She let out a bitter laugh, her anger bubbling to the surface. "All those years of living rent-free, and you still had to steal my money."

Manuel's face contorted with disbelief as he squeezed his eyes shut, then opened them wide. Taking a step closer, he shoved his glasses into his pocket. "Steal your money? What are you talking about?" he demanded, scanning the room as though searching for an answer. His voice rose, filled with rage. "You're all plotting against me, brainwashing my wife."

Nina's trembling gave way to fury. "They don't need to brainwash me," she snapped. "These are my friends. They love me, care for me, and protect me from an animal like you." Her voice shook with anger, but she pressed on. "And just so you know, I got all the money back."

Manuel's eyes darted around the room, his rage turning to paranoia. Pointing a finger, he snarled, "You all need to stop sticking your noses where they don't belong. Stay out of our lives."

His gaze flickered to Fabio, then back to Nina, his face pale and his movements stiff.

When Nina stepped forward, her voice cut through the air like a blade. "So, you, your banking boyfriend, your life full of lies—leave me alone once and for all." Her words spilled out before she could stop them. "I won't be silenced anymore. And you can't hide behind this farce of a marriage any longer. You're gay, Manuel. So what? Nobody cares. Be proud of who you are. Own it." Her voice rose as she stood her ground.

Manuel recoiled as though struck, his expression a fury and humiliation. Without another word, he turned and stalked toward the door.

Nina followed him, her voice calm but cold. "You'll be getting the divorce papers soon. I don't want to hear from you again. Stay away from me, my friends, and my family."

Manuel paused at the door, his face flushed with anger. He twisted the knob and stepped out into the dark corridor, his shoulders slumping in defeat.

As the door closed behind him, Nina extended her middle finger toward it, then turned back to the room, stunned. The silence broke as her friends cheered, their voices lifting the weight that had settled on her chest.

Excitement coursed through her as she darted toward the kitchen. "What have you got that's strong? And I mean strong," she demanded, her tone firm but breathless.

Bree handed her a bottle of ouzo with a grin. "Magic potion," she said with a laugh, pulling out shot glasses.

Pouring drinks for everyone, they gathered around the table. Nik raised his glass. "Here's to Nina—we're proud of you, girl."

Nina pushed her hair behind her ears and downed the shot in one swift motion, a faint smile breaking through her exhaustion. She collapsed onto the sofa, drained but alive.

"I could've walked away so many times, but I never did," she admitted, handing her glass to Bree for a refill. Raising her refilled glass, she toasted, "To freedom."

Her grin spread wide, her tears flowing freely. And for the first time in a long while, she felt truly free.

174 | Carla

Nik took a deep breath as he walked into work. Pushing the door open with a feeling of dread, he forced a smile on his face and entered the kitchen. Sully glanced over and grunted in Nik's direction, pouring tomatoes into a large pan and looking away.

As Zac had warned, Sully, the chef, had become a different person from the one Carla employed five months earlier. His friendly, kind eyes were now filled with fury at the smallest conflict or complaint. His calm and friendly nature had been replaced with arrogance and contempt. Nik saw Sully's expression harden with a request for fries instead of potatoes. His patience was wearing thin, and he chose to avoid any conversations other than those necessary.

Sully, not using the same tactic, enjoyed provoking Nik as a part of his daily routine.

As Carla stepped into the restaurant on a sunny Tuesday morning, she stopped suddenly in her tracks, closing the door slowly and quietly behind her. Hearing screams from the kitchen, she stood in the shadows, listening to the tense voices. Sully's figure loomed into view, blocking out the sun and banging his fist on the gleaming work surface.

"You don't get it," Sully shouted to Nik. "You don't understand; I can't keep making food for Bree without tomatoes; it isn't my fault she is allergic," he screamed, casting an icy stare.

"She is my wife. She sends us all the weddings," said Nik, forcing himself to smile. "Therefore, she is our biggest customer, and if she can't eat tomatoes, then the least you can do is keep the goddam tomatoes away from her food. Do you want her to die?" Nik asked, his eyes full of fury.

"Honestly, I don't care; she is nobody to me. You're all nobodies to me." He paused, waving a knife in his hand towards his second chef, who was cowering in the corner.

"What's your problem?" Nik screamed. "You're a chef; you cook, that's it. Carla is the boss, yet you can't seem to respect that." Nik turned in haste, noticing Carla in the corner. He stormed out of the gate with rage following him.

She followed him to the car park, his eyes filled with piercing anger and his fists tightly clenched.

"Honestly, Carla, we need to get rid of him; he is so obnoxious," Nik complained, kicking the green recycling bin against the stone wall. He winced in pain.

"But he has a contract. We can't fire him, so what can we do? His food is good, the reviews are good, and the kitchen is spotless."

"I know, sorry, I shouldn't be putting all of this on you. You pay me so that you're not involved in all of this," Nik said apologetically.

"Can't you put up with him until the end of the season?" she pleaded, looking steely and determined, knowing she was asking the impossible.

"I know, sorry; I just can't deal with his issues anymore. Since his wife left him, which I can see why she did, he's turned into a monster," Nik said, tilting his head back.

"I don't know what to suggest." Carla complained, "I know it's hard, but we can't afford to fire him with full pay and get another chef in. Plus, who will we find?"

"I know, sorry, Zac warned me that chefs were like this; I should have listened and kept a closer reign on him," he said, scratching his head and reaching for his jacket.

Carla stuffed her hands in her pockets and walked away, feeling Nik's eyes on her. She wanted to get rid of Sully; she hated that this job was the cause of the pain in Nik's face. Turning back to Nik, she said, "I promise we'll get someone else next year, okay?" The thought of the restaurant without Nik, should he leave, sent panic down her spine.

175 | Carla

A few days later, Carla reached for her ringing phone, "Hey, Nik," she replied calmly.

"You need to get down here now. The shit has hit the fan," he instructed, saying no more.

"What? Tell me," she insisted with urgency.

"No. Just get here." Nik ended the call.

Grabbing her bag, she revved the engine of her car, the warm air doing little to calm her growing concerns. Parking quickly, she ran up the steps, her heart racing.

Nik paced the gardens, his hands running through his hair in frustration. From behind, Filip, the Brazilian kitchen hand, appeared. He edged towards Carla, pointing his finger close to her face, his hand trembling. "Me or him. Get that chef out of my life," he demanded, his voice strained and thick with emotion.

Carla stepped back, her brow furrowing. "Where's Sully?" she asked, her tone sharp.

Filip's voice shook as he replied, "He's gone—after attacking me with a knife and trying to kill me." His words, muffled slightly by his accent, hung heavily in the air.

Carla turned to Nik, her eyes searching his face for answers. Nik shrugged, visibly uneasy. "I wasn't here. I just got the call to come, and this is what I walked into," he explained.

Carla glanced around. The second chef sat in the corner on the sun-scorched grass, his head bowed under the shade of a palm tree. Two waiters lingered nearby, their faces tense.

Filip stepped closer to Carla, his rage boiling over. "I told him I didn't want the fish for lunch—it smelled off, old. I asked for something else. I didn't want to be sick." He paused, waving his fingers near his nose. "That's when he grabbed the knife. He held it to my throat and put his arm around my waist so I couldn't move. The knife was here." He pointed two fingers at his neck, his expression raw with fear.

Carla kept her voice steady. "Then what happened?"

Filip took a deep breath, his anger laced with disbelief. "Then he hit me in the face with a saucepan and ran out." He gestured towards the door, his hands still shaking.

"Can everyone come here?" Carla called, motioning for the staff to gather around. She addressed them firmly. "Did anyone see what happened? Someone? Anyone?"

The group remained silent, exchanging uneasy glances.

Filip pointed to Luigi, one of the waiters. "He saw it all. He took the knife from Sully and threw it in the sink."

Carla followed Filip's gaze to the sink, where a black-handled knife lay against the metal basin.

Luigi shook his head, staring at the ground. "No, I didn't see anything," he mumbled, his voice barely audible.

Nik stepped forward, his tone probing yet calm. "Luigi, are you sure? Why would Filip lie about something like this?"

Luigi's eyes darted around the terrace, avoiding both Nik and Carla.

Carla shifted her focus to the second chef. "What about you? What did you see?"

Luigi didn't lift his head as he answered. "The fish was off, that's true. But I didn't see anything. I told Sully we couldn't serve it, and he kicked me out of the kitchen. I was upstairs in the flat when it happened." His voice trembled, but there was a hint of insecurity in his words. Rising to his feet, he added, "I wasn't there."

Carla and Nik moved to the side, their voices low. "What the hell happened?" Carla whispered, shaking her head.

Nik exhaled heavily, his frustration palpable. "I don't know. I just got home. I left early—Bree's off today, and I wanted to surprise her." He ran his fingers through his hair again, searching for clarity. "I want to believe Filip. I don't see why he'd make this up. But the others—" He trailed off, glancing at Carla.

"I'm so confused," Carla muttered, clearly frustrated.

Nik turned back to the group, his tone firm. "Filip, take the night off. The rest of you, back at your normal time tomorrow, all right?"

The staff began to disperse, but Filip remained rooted to the spot.

"I'm not working here anymore," he said, his voice rising with anger. "Not with that man. He's crazy—he wants to kill me." He lit a cigarette with shaky hands, glaring at the ground.

Carla nodded, her tone firm but measured. "If that's your decision, fine. But we'll consult our legal advisors tomorrow and take it from there."

Filip grabbed his bag, storming down the steps. The metal gate clanged shut behind him, echoing through the gardens.

176 | Carla

"What the hell?" said Carla. She sat slowly down on the garden chair next to Nik, the afternoon sun beating down on them, "What do we do?"

"Let me go and talk to them without Filip," Nik said as he jumped to his feet and moved upstairs and knocked on the staff apartment door.

Carla watched as he emerged a few minutes later, shaking his head. "They're sticking to their stories; they say they saw nothing at all." He let out a deep breath and huffed. "I'm not sure whether I should believe them; they couldn't look me in the eyes."

"Nothing to add at all, none of them?" Carla asked.

"Nope, they looked down at the floor the whole time, talking to that disgusting dirty carpet; I know they were in a state of shock, but I still told them to get the place cleaned up; they are living like animals up there," he said.

"Well, the only thing we can do is talk to Sully and see what he says," Carla said. "I guess we will meet here again at five when he starts work."

Later, Carla wrapped her denim jacket around her shoulders as she waited with Nik for Sully to start his shift that evening. They were unsure he would be there at all; if he'd done what he was accused of, they were sure he wouldn't dare to show his face.

Instead, he arrived with a spring in his step, a charming smile, and a friendly greeting: "Both of you here, what an honour?" Sully said, looking at Carla. The menacing stare had gone; his eyes were now warm and compassionate.

"We need to talk to you about earlier. Can you tell us what happened?" Carla asked. They'd agreed that Carla would talk, seeing as Nik and Sully seemed to exist only in conflict.

"When?" he asked, showing no recognition of any issue that would require discussion. He sat down, kicking his feet up on the table.

"A knife? Something about fish and a saucepan?" Carla explained, avoiding an accusative tone in her voice.

Sully squinted, cracked his knuckles, and stared at Carla. "No idea. Anything else?" he asked before heading inside, unwinding the blinds from the kitchen windows.

Carla and Nik stared at each other in disbelief. "Really, he has no idea what we are talking about?" Nik asked, "Okay, so we can't do anything until the legal guys advise us, so, Carla, go home; I'll let you know if anything happens," Nik said.

Carla placed her phone on her sofa, expecting it to ring with another disaster. She checked it every ten minutes or so until, finally, once the restaurant closed, she felt a heavy sensation wash over her as she dropped off to sleep.

177 | Carla

Carla's stomach flipped when Filip returned to work the following morning, accompanied by the police. Two uniformed men stepped confidently into the restaurant, their eyes darted around as they took in the surroundings. Filip pointed out Nik and Carla.

"Carla Carpenter?" They looked at her. "Nikos Daskalakis," they said, turning their faces to Nik. "We're here to talk to you about the events of yesterday involving Mr. Sully Morras," they said, "and to provide security for Mr. Filip while he collects his belongings from the staff quarters."

"Is Mr. Sully Morras here?" the other officer asked.

"No, he arrives at ten," Nik said as he watched the policemen check their watches in unison.

"We need to speak to you all individually about the events of yesterday; you first." Looking at Carla, she ushered them to a table and told them what she knew. Nik followed suit once she had finished.

"So, none of the management was here?" The policeman's tone was condescending; his eyes flashed a glare of mistrust.

"The restaurant was closed. We eat lunch after the shift, but I wanted to eat at home with my wife, so I left after the last customer." Nik explained.

The policeman nodded in approval. "That seems fair."

Luigi, the waiter, and the second chef arrived; Carla noticed the worrying exchange of glances between them before being called over by one policeman. They nervously gave their statements and returned to work looking beaten and scared.

Sully strutted into the restaurant with his usual arrogance, one hand firmly in his pocket, stumping out a cigarette in the first ashtray on his way in. His face turned five shades paler before he smiled at the stern-faced policeman. Sully's glance moved over to Nik, looking for an explanation. The policeman gestured for Sully to sit down.

"I'll stand." Sully said arrogantly.

"No, you'll sit," the policeman ordered as Sully pulled out the chair and perched on the edge.

"Please excuse us," they said, looking at Carla and Nik, who quickly retreated.

Leaning on the white wall inside, they peeked through the glass for any clues as to what was happening, watching the animated gestures of the three men.

After half an hour, the two policemen stood up, gesturing to Carla and Nik to come out.

"Well, someone is lying. This story is more complicated than it seems." They looked sharply at Carla, who made a half smile as if someone had told a joke. "We will investigate further; in the meantime, Filip will be demanding full pay, although he will not be returning to work. You can take it up with your legal advisors."

When they finally had some alone time, Carla rubbed her fingers around the corner of her mouth, looked at Nik and said, "Okay, tomorrow we are closed, but we still need a chef; we have a wedding in three days."

"I'll go into the kitchen," Nik said reluctantly. "I'll get Bree to come and do front-of-house management. Don't worry, Carla; we'll sort it out."

"We've already underestimated him once. If any of this is true. We need to be prepared for this evening," Carla said.

178 | Carla

The policemen shot a hardened look as they walked past Carla and Nik towards their car. Carla felt Sully's smile on her face as she heard his whistles over the radio in the kitchen. Ignoring it, she sat with Nik in silence in the garden until Sully was out of earshot. "What now?" Carla asked, sweeping her hair back into a ponytail.

Nik's forehead creased as he waited for a reply from anywhere other than Carla, who sat open-mouthed across from him. "Legal advisor, I guess? I'll call them," Nik said. He dialled the number and left the phone on speaker, placing it on the table.

As Carla took notes, Nik asked questions. They finished the call with only one thing clearer than before. If they found the kitchen hand another job with the same conditions, he would have to accept it, which would relieve them of the obligation to pay his wages.

Carla felt immediately lighter; she knew her restaurant colleagues were always looking for staff, and that was a problem they could solve immediately. After a few phone calls, they arranged it, and Filip immediately agreed to switch jobs to a nearby hotel.

They all received set times to visit the police station for official statements the following day. Carla and Nik weren't present at the time, so they only spent a few minutes sharing their version of the events, followed by an hour of questions about their behaviour and experiences with the chef.

It became clear that the police didn't care for his attitude and believed him guilty. The idea had only just entered her mind that he could be guilty when the police enticed her to sign papers to say just that. Carla shook her head, pushing the papers away. "I wasn't there; I didn't see it. I don't like the chef. I think he is arrogant and very obnoxious, and I can't wait for him to be out of my kitchen for good at the end of the season, but I can't sign to say he did this without any proof," Carla said.

"Okay, but why employ him?" the policeman asked, shaking his head in disbelief.

Carla crossed her ankles in front of her and swallowed hard. "I can't fire him because he has a contract," Carla said. "If my staff who were present say he didn't do it, then I have to believe them." Her voice filled with agony and apprehension as she collapsed back into her chair.

Shaking her head as she left the police station, Carla splayed out on the bench outside, waiting for Nik. Bree joined her, placing her shopping bag by her side. She squeezed Carla's hand tightly. "It will be all right; you know that, don't you?"

"Huh," Carla muttered in reply.

"He did it; I know it. That bastard, but we have no proof." Nik paced in front of Carla's bowed head, feeling anger begin to swell in him. "Of course, I couldn't say that," he said.

"I can't face him anymore. Can we close tonight?" Carla pleaded.

"It's your restaurant. You can do whatever you like, but we do have reservations," Nik said. "We need to open, but you don't need to be there; that's my job," he said. "I've already failed you by allowing all of this to happen. Just go home; actually, go to my house and get drunk with Bree, please," he said, looking at Bree with a smile. "She is finding this all very stressful. You two need a night of girly drinks."

179 | Carla

Nina waited impatiently for the three-wheeled tuk tuk to arrive with the bride, hoping to catch a glimpse of the driver. As she heard the chug of the engine near the narrow streets, her heart skipped a beat.

A new driver, tall, always smiling, friendly, and smartly dressed, arrived. Nina didn't think the attraction was mutual, but she was enjoying that finally, after years in an unhappy marriage, she felt excited to see someone else. Now that the news was out that Manuel was no longer living with her, she felt free to enjoy exciting new emotions.

Nina decided to keep the real reason for the breakup to herself; Manuel's sexuality was of no one's business but his own. The police had become involved in the money theft, and the lawyers were dealing with the divorce. Nina hadn't had any contact with Manuel for months. She tried to put the whole mess behind her.

Petra tried to convince her to join Tinder to get herself out there, but Nina wasn't ready yet. Her friends felt that she should be dating already. Instead, she, with her new guitar, had started to play once a week at a bar in a nearby town. Keeping her musical interests secret from anyone but her work colleagues, she felt she had control over her life once more.

As she waited for the driver, Simon, she felt a long-forgotten spark of interest and desire. She had thrown into a conversation that they could meet for coffee, but so far, he had not taken the bait. She flapped her long, boho skirt around her legs, looking for a breeze. She felt herself redden as he neared.

"Hi, Nina," he waved through the windscreen. "I thought it was Petra today," he said.

"I'm just helping out, as it's a big wedding," she said as he turned his attention to the bride and opened the door for her to step out of the car.

"Hi. I'm Nina, Petra's colleague. I'm here to walk you up to the terrace," Nina said. Simon's eyes rested on her as she talked, and she waved goodbye.

Bree appeared at her side. She snapped photos as the bride started her climb up the castle steps.

"You're here to walk her up the steps? Nina, come on, you know that's what I do," Bree said. "Oh my god, you like him. I get it; he's cute." Bree murmured in Italian, keeping the gossip hidden from the bride.

Nina turned away, embarrassed, before muttering something Bree couldn't understand.

"We'll talk later; you aren't getting away from today without spilling the gossip," Bree said as they reached the top of the steps. Nina spread out the train as the bride headed off up the steps, and she stepped back. She ran back down quickly, hoping to catch a glimpse of Simon once more.

Leaning on his tuk-tuk, licking melting ice cream from the cone, he smiled at her. "So, how about that coffee, then?" he asked. Nina nodded and smiled.

"Hop in, and I'll give you a lift," Simon said, reaching for the small metal latch. The door flung open, and Nina slid inside.

As Simon beeped his horn, the crowd roared, excited to see a wedding pass. As they saw Nina alone without flowers, the applause became muted. "Where's the groom?" a man shouted from the street.

"He didn't show up," Nina laughed as the ripple of applause grew louder. Nina turned her face towards Simon. "This is fun," she said. He continued to beep the horn as Nina shrugged her shoulders at anyone who smiled. "He jilted me at the altar," she shouted with a smile.

As Simon let his foot off the pedal, Nina shuffled out of the tuk tuk with a jaunty spring in her step; her skirt picked up dirt as it dragged on the floor. Simon linked Nina's arm and said, "I'm the groom," he laughed as they saw passersby eyeing them curiously.

"It was a nice surprise to see you today; I thought I wouldn't see you until Saturday, which is when your next wedding is, isn't it?"

"How do you know that?" she asked curiously.

"I checked the list. I asked Bree to put the names of the wedding planners on there so I could call if there were any problems, and I always check to see when you're on duty. Do you want to go out to dinner with me tonight?" he asked.

Nina felt her cheeks redden as there was a long pause. "I'd love to, but I'm already busy tonight; I'm singing at a bar," she said shyly.

"You sing?" he asked. "So do I. Where are you performing?"

The words slipped out of her mouth as she told him, "Well, I may just have to pop along and see you."

"Please don't tell anyone. Only Bree and the girls know about it," Nina said.

Simone put his finger to his lips, saying, "Our secret."

180 | Carla

Wearing a dress chosen especially for her singing gigs, Nina perched gracefully on the stool. She adjusted her guitar strap and glanced at the lyrics glowing on her tablet. After a quick mic tap, she took a steadying breath and launched into an intricate solo, her voice cutting through the warm, dust-filled breeze of the open-air terrace. The audience responded with enthusiastic applause after each song, their energy boosting her confidence.

About thirty minutes into her set, her eyes lit up as she spotted Simon slipping into a seat a few rows back. He raised his glass in silent admiration, a relaxed smile playing on his lips. The terrace began to fill with workers unwinding after a long day, their conversations mingling with the occasional dry gust of wind that swirled the dust around them.

Despite herself, Nina kept stealing glances at Simon. His gaze was fixed on her, his attention a welcome distraction. Every time she finished a song, he nodded appreciatively, rising to applaud with the crowd.

At the end of her first set, Simon gestured for her to join him.

"My god, your voice is amazing," he said as she approached, his voice filled with genuine admiration.

Nina offered a small, bashful smile. "It didn't feel that way. The dust in the wind—it was drying me out."

"You'd never know. You were brilliant," he assured her, his words like a balm to her self-doubt.

Nina took a long drink of water before heading back to the platform. As she approached the mic, the chatter dimmed to an expectant silence. But as she began to sing, something shifted.

 Simon noticed her pale slightly, her voice trembling as she stumbled over a line. Her eyes flicked toward him, filled with an expression he couldn't decipher. She shook her head, and the guitar in her hands quivered slightly. Concerned, Simon stood and made his way to the platform, pulling up a stool beside her. He waited for her to finish the song, her struggle visible to the crowd. When the last note hung in the air, he gently took the guitar from her hands.

"I'll play; you sing," he said softly, his voice calm and steady.

Nina shifted closer to him. "My ex-husband is out there. With his boyfriend," she muttered under her breath, the words laced with tension.

Simon's smile was reassuring. "We've got this. Don't worry." He adjusted his shirt collar and began strumming a warm, familiar melody. Nina inhaled deeply, willing her heartbeat to slow. When she sang again, her voice was directed at Simon, her gaze locked on him as though he were the only person in the room.

Gradually, her confidence returned. The warmth of Simon's support grounded her, and she dared to glance out into the audience. Her eyes landed on Manuel. He was nursing a drink, his face tight with discomfort.

As their eyes briefly met, he rolled his eyes and abruptly walked away, leaving Nina with a churn of emotions. She pressed on, finishing the song with her eyes closed, beads of sweat tracing down her back. The crowd erupted in applause, their enthusiasm lifting the moment's weight.

"Thank you so much; I owe you one," Nina said, her voice soft as she carefully placed her guitar in its case.

"They loved us. That was so much fun," Simon replied, his excitement infectious as he pushed his stool back and ordered drinks for them both.

"Do you want to talk about it?" he asked gently.

Nina started to shake her head but found herself opening up instead. The words spilled out, untangling the burden she'd carried silently for too long. Simon listened intently, his expression thoughtful.

"Well, everyone in Rocca Pinta knows," he said when she finished. "It's no secret. People have seen how much time he spends with Marco—and everyone knows Marco is gay."

Nina's eyes widened. "Really? Everyone knows?"

Simon nodded. "Absolutely. His secret's out. You don't need to worry anymore. And after our performance tonight, he probably thinks we're a couple, so... you won this one."

A light laugh escaped her, and for the first time that night, she felt a weight lift from her shoulders. Tilting her head back, she gazed at the starry sky. A moment later, she neared him and pressed a gentle kiss to his cheek.

181 | Carla

Sully proclaimed his innocence as he worked with a smug air of confidence from that day onwards. The police presence became intrusive. They arrived each day, striding confidently into the restaurant, looking around, and watching the young office workers that filled the tables shift uncomfortably in their seats. The staff worked with their heads down, trying to impress the police with their skills.

The curse of not knowing the truth kept Carla awake at night. She wanted her bed to swallow her up and spit her out in October once it was all over.

Two weeks later, Carla walked into the restaurant to pay the wages. Outside, Luigi and the second chef lingered near the entrance, their expressions uneasy. Spotting Nik nearby, they motioned for him to join them.

"We need to talk," Luigi said, his voice tight, avoiding eye contact.

"What's happened now?" she asked sharply, her tone edged with annoyance.

The two young men exchanged a glance, hesitation hanging in the air like a storm about to break. Finally, Luigi nodded, steeling himself. "We lied," he admitted, his voice barely above a whisper.

The air between them seemed to thicken, the silence deafening. Carla's jaw tightened as her patience began to wear thin. "Go on," she urged, her voice colder now.

Luigi crossed his arms, as if bracing himself against his own words. He let out a deep breath. "Filip was right. It happened exactly the way he said it did." He hesitated, his gaze flicking nervously to Nik before continuing, "I took the knife out of Sully's hands and threw it in the sink."

Carla's eyes widened, her stare snapping to the second chef. She arched an accusatory brow, her body rigid. "And you? What's your part in this?"

The second chef shoved his hands deep into his pockets. His voice was low, almost detached. "I took the saucepan from him. Grabbed him by the wrist to stop him. Then he turned on me, tried to hit me. I ran into the storeroom to get away."

Carla's stomach clenched, her anger igniting. Her glare burned into him like a blade. Nik stood frozen, his glare darting between the two men. For a moment, he couldn't find words, his mind struggling to process what he'd just heard.

Then, with a sharp exhale, he exploded.

"Why?" Nik's voice rose, his hand rubbing his forehead in frustration. "Why the hell did you lie to us?"

Luigi flinched but pressed on, his fingers nervously twisting the hem of his rolled-up shirt sleeve. "Because Sully went mad—he completely lost it. He grabbed the saucepan off the shelf and smashed it into Filip's face. Then he said if we told anyone, he'd use the knife on us next. And that it'd be a boiling pan next time," Luigi said, his voice shaking, the fear still fresh in his mind.

Nik clenched his jaw, his fists tightening at his sides. "And now? Why come clean now?" His voice was edged with both anger and disbelief.

Luigi shifted uncomfortably, stepping out of the harsh sunlight that caught the sweat glistening on his brow. "We couldn't take it anymore," he said, his words tumbling out. "The guilt—it's been eating us alive. We lied to you both, and it's...it's not right."

Carla's chest heaved as she struggled to contain her rage. Her mind raced, torn between fury at the betrayal and the sinking realisation of what had transpired under her watch. Nik stood beside her, his glare fixed on Luigi, searching for some sign of sincerity.

"Well, we need to have a talk now," he said, looking at Carla. She stood with her hands over her mouth, staring in disbelief at the two men. "Get to work; say nothing to Sully for now," he instructed as they walked up the steps to the entrance, exchanging glances.

Carla leant against the window frame, staring at the horizon. She shook her head, swallowing hard, before speaking, "What the hell?" She closed her eyes, feeling anger rising from within her like a monster.

"We need to get rid of him; that is the only solution," Nik said, raising his eyebrows as he spoke. "We are going to have to rely on his good nature that he will go. We can't tell the police why we're firing him; the guys would get in trouble with the police," he said, watching Carla twitch her mouth from side to side.

"But if we tell him we know what happened, then he'll know that the guys have told us, and then they'll be in danger," she said, taking a deep breath and feeling her eyes well up in despair.

"I know, exactly. We need to fire him without telling him why and somehow find a new chef all at the same time. What a mess."

"I don't suppose that Zac can come over?" she asked hopefully.

"No, he is up to his eyes in it over there; now I'm so busy here; I've already put too much work on him, and I doubt he can leave," he replied, watching Carla's face drop in disappointment.

"Let's get today out of the way, sleep on it, then, in the morning, meet for coffee and make a decision." Carla agreed as they made their way indoors. Sully brushed past her, placing receipts on the till and fumbling inside to draw the petty cash. She shivered at Sully's cold, arrogant face. Looking at her, he shifted closer, hovering with his face too close to hers.

The following morning, Carla put down her croissant as Nik and Bree strutted into the coffee bar. Stirring her cappuccino, she looked at Nik and asked, "Any ideas?"

"We are closed tomorrow anyway for the day, so tonight after the shift ends, we sit him down, fire him, get his keys, and watch him leave," he said.

"Do you think it will be that easy?" Carla asked as she took a long sip of her cappuccino. "I don't think he's going to walk out. It's going to end up in conflict."

"I know, but we'll both be there; we'll deal with it together," Nik assured her. "He's not going to take his stunning fall from grace without a fight."

182 | Carla

A cool wind slipped through the cracks in the wooden doors as Carla took a deep breath and walked into the kitchen. She felt Sully's eyes on her but ignored him as she nodded at Nik. As she waited, a heavy knot formed in her stomach.

"Sully, once you have finished, can we talk to you, please?" Nik said, adopting a serious expression.

He finished folding a tea towel, set it aside, and said, "I'm already finished."

Nik sat at the wooden, sturdy staff table, the silence broken only by the windows rattling in their frames as the gusts seeped through the gaps.

"I'm sorry, Sully, but this isn't working out." Nik ran his fingers through his hair before he continued, "We will have to let you go. We will pay you for the whole of next month, so you have time to get a new job sorted out. However, we can't continue working together like this," he said calmly.

The atmosphere froze over as Sully glared at them both, stunned by the words. "You're firing me? After everything I have done for this place, without me, you would have closed down months ago." Sully pushed out his chair and, without a word, stretched out his arms and slammed his fists on the table. "Why? Why now? Who are you going to replace me with?" His voice filled with rage as he locked eyes with Carla. He took a deep breath and let out a curse, snarling animosity.

"No one. We haven't hired anyone yet to replace you. We've just made this decision, and we haven't thought that far yet." As Carla spoke, she realised how stupid her words sounded and how unprepared they were for what would happen next to the restaurant without a chef.

"Why?" he shouted, his hands grabbing the table, his knuckles turning white, and his breath steaming in Carla's face.

Nik, who was still sitting, entered the conversation and stated, "We just aren't happy with your work."

"You aren't satisfied with my work? As simple as that? No other explanation?" Sully started to raise his voice even more. As Carla tried to speak, he silenced her with the palms of his hands. "You can't get rid of me that easily. I have a contract with you. Another two months; pay me for two months, or I stay."

Nik looked at Carla. He saw the fear in her eyes; she let the table take the stress of her stress as she rested on it. her hands crossed over, lost for words. Nik raised his eyebrows in agreement. "Sully, sit back down, now," he shouted, feeling the anger rise in his throat. For a second, they locked eyes as Sully pushed the chair away and moved backwards from the table.

Sully's hand moved behind him, fingers curling around the neck of a wine bottle from the display shelf. Without warning, he hurled it with trembling hands. Nik barely ducked in time as the bottle sailed past him, shattering against the wall with a deafening crash. The room fell into stunned silence, the faint clink of broken glass punctuating the stillness.

Nik straightened slowly, his eyes locking onto Sully. "You want to play it that way?" he said, his voice low but razor-sharp. He swallowed, steadying himself. "Fine. Consider this your first warning. By tomorrow, I'll have two more, and you'll be out of here."

Sully's lip curled as he stepped back, his gaze flicking between Nik and Carla with cold fury. "You'll never get rid of me," he spat, his voice dripping venom. "Without me, you're nothing."

Before Nik could respond, another bottle came flying. This time, the glass exploded against the white wall, dark red wine streaking down like blood. Nik's jaw tightened as he gestured toward the spreading stain. "That's two," he said calmly, though his voice carried a dangerous edge. "Carla, type up two warnings."

"Sully, calm down." Carla's voice wavered as she stepped forward, her tone both pleading and firm.

But Sully was far past reason. His face twisted with rage as he fixated on Carla. "Get out of my restaurant" he roared, his voice echoing off the walls. His eyes were wild, unhinged.

Carla froze, her shock quickly giving way to anger. "Your restaurant?" she shot back, her voice rising. She took a step closer, trembling with fury. "This is my restaurant. All mine. Not yours."

Her words seemed to snap something inside Sully. His hands shot out suddenly, wrapping around her throat.

Carla's scream was cut off as he slammed her against the wine-streaked wall, his grip tightening. Her hands clawed at his, desperate for air, her face reddening as her breaths grew shallow.

"Let her go." Nik shouted, lunging forward. He drove his knee into the back of Sully's legs with brutal force. Sully buckled, his hands releasing Carla as he collapsed onto the floor. She slid down the wall, clutching her throat and gasping for air.

Nik didn't hesitate. He hauled Sully up by the shoulders, spinning him around. "That's three," he snarled, his voice reverberating with fury. "You're done. Get out. And don't you dare come back."

Nik shoved Sully toward the front door, throwing it open with a sharp yank. Sully stumbled onto the terrace but turned abruptly, his eyes blazing with defiance. He lunged toward Carla, his hand outstretched.

"No way," Nik roared, driving his fist into Sully's stomach with a sickening thud. Sully staggered backward, winded, but Nik didn't relent. He grabbed Sully's arm and twisted him toward the exit. "Get. Out. Now," he barked, shoving him through the door with a final push.

Sully stood outside, panting, his face flushed with rage. He pressed himself against the glass, his glare burning with unfiltered contempt. "You'll regret this," he shouted, his voice muffled by the pane. After a tense moment, he turned on his heel and stormed away.

Inside, the room was still. Carla plonked herself down on the nearest seat, her breaths shallow. Nik remained by the door, his fists clenched, his chest heaving as he stared after Sully.

Carla finally looked up at Nik, her voice hoarse but resolute. "Thank you," she whispered. Her words were small, but the sincerity behind them was immense.

Nik shouted towards him, "And we filmed all of that, so don't think you can deny this, too." Nik bluffed. He locked the door behind him, keeping his eyes firmly on Sully's slow-moving figure. Nik stood frozen, watching Sully disappear around the corner as he walked, his shaking head bowed to the ground.

Nik heard a car door slam in the distance. Once the headlights of Sully's car passed, he turned to Carla and took her in his arms. She pounded her fists on his chest, shaking with fear and disbelief as salty tears streamed down her face.

"You're coming home with me tonight," he said. "I'll look after you, or do you need to go to the hospital?" His eyes glittered with rage as he spoke.

Carla shook her head. Nik grabbed their belongings, turned off the lights and led Carla by the arm. She stumbled to the door, looking shell-shocked.

Bree smiled and jumped off the sofa at the sound of the key in the door, wrapping her dressing gown closed around her naked body as she looked at Carla. Her eyes were red, and her hands were shaking as she clung to Nik.

Bree looked at Nik and then at her friend rushing to help her to the sofa, where she remained silent, hugging her knees with closed eyes. Nik took Bree's hand and led her to the bedroom.

"We need to look after her. I hope that's okay," he asked, not waiting for her reply. Sitting slowly on the bed, he told her about the events of the evening. Bree listened quietly before throwing on a long t-shirt and returning to her friend.

"He thinks he's Superman, above everyone else." Carla cried, her eyes quickly blinking as Bree took her a cup of tea. "I can't believe how quickly he formulated a plan to keep them all quiet." She placed the cup on the table. Carla pointed to the wine bottle with a half-smile.

"It's over now. He's gone, and it's behind you; he can't touch you now," Bree said, sincerely hoping her words were true. "Tomorrow, we'll get the locks changed at the restaurant, file the three warning letters, and report it to the police," Bree said as she poured wine for Carla.

It was a long time before they went to sleep. Bree heard Carla's footsteps around the house during the long night. Before going to bed, she heard Carla shaking the door and the windows of her room, ensuring they were securely and tightly shut. Nik held Bree tight, squeezing her as his nightmares sent spasms and shudders through his body.

183 | Carla

The next morning, Bree stirred awake to find the bed beside her empty. Suppressing a smile, she reached for her phone to reply to the message that had just come through. Pulling on her soft white dressing gown, she padded into the kitchen, where Carla sat hunched over a steaming cup of tea. Her poached eggs sat untouched, pushed to the side of her plate.

"Morning," Bree said softly, leaning down to stroke Nik's head as he sat at the table, hands full of toast.

Nik glanced up with a faint smile. "Morning. Sleep well?"

"Better than expected," Bree replied, glancing at Carla before turning back to Nik. "What's the game plan?"

Nik swallowed the last of his toast and gestured toward the pan on the stove. "There's more eggs if you're hungry." He pushed his plate aside and continued, "I'm running to the restaurant now to make sure Sully hasn't done anything stupid. After that, I'll bring Carla's car back. Then we'll figure out our next move."

"We're closed today, right?" Bree asked, helping herself to tea.

"Yeah," Nik said. "Gives us a little breathing room."

As Nik approached the restaurant a short while later, he slowed to a jog. The street outside was eerily quiet, or was it just his imagination. A sudden noise behind him made him freeze. Footsteps.

He spun around, his pulse quickening. A dark figure emerged at the top of the steps, silhouetted against the rising sun.

"Sully?" Nik called out, his voice sharp.

A gruff laugh answered in Greek. "Relax, bro. It's me."

Zac stepped out of the shadows, a teasing grin on his face. Nik's tension melted into relief as he opened his arms and pulled Zac into a quick, firm hug.

"Man, am I glad to see you," Nik said, finally managing a real smile. "Have I got a story for you."

"Bree gave me a bit of the rundown last night," Zac replied, releasing him.

"There's more to it," Nik said, lowering his voice as he glanced around. "But not here."

Once Nik had walked through the restaurant he locked up. The two men walked to Nik's car, and as they drove, Nik filled Zac in. He spoke quickly, his words tumbling out like he'd been holding them back for hours. Zac sat quietly, one hand covering his mouth as he listened. By the time they reached the house, his wide eyes betrayed his disbelief.

"Wow," Zac said finally, exhaling sharply. "That's... a lot. So, let me guess—you need a chef?"

Nik nodded, his fingers releasing his grip the steering wheel as he turned the engine off. "Yeah. Can you? I mean, is it even possible for you to get away?"

Zac slouched back in his seat, a grin creeping across his face. "If you're okay with a few late nights on the computer, I can swing it. I'll manage a couple of weeks, no problem. But you'll have to help me with the office stuff."

"Office work?" Nik echoed, raising an eyebrow. "That's been a while."

Zac cackled. "Yeah, exactly. Remember spreadsheets? Databases? Good luck, mate."

Nik laughed for the first time in what felt like days. He clapped Zac on the shoulder, a swell of gratitude overtaking him. "You have no idea how much this means," he said, his voice thick with emotion.

Zac shrugged it off with a smile. "What are friends for?"

184 | Carla

Carla and Bree sat cross-legged on the sofa. Carla wiped a tear from her eye with her sleeve. "I wish I had never opened the restaurant; it's such a mess," Carla said.

"No, you did a great thing, and this is just a bump in the road. You can do this. The restaurant has been amazing; the wedding couples love it, and we'd be lost without it," Bree said.

"I know, I just feel torn right now and I feel awful for Nik; he's had a terrible time of it recently, and now, with no chef, I'm not sure what will happen. It isn't as if you and I can cook; come on," Carla said finally smiling a little.

"We could have potatoes and washing-up liquid on the menu. It could be popular," Bree laughed. "Carla, don't worry; I know for sure we will find a solution today—in fact, this morning."

"Why? What do you know?" Carla asked, feeling her friend was up to something.

"I asked around for a new chef, and I think we will have one by lunchtime," Bree said.

"Bree, tell me, please. Who is it? Why is he without work at the height of the summer season?" Carla asked.

Bree looked up from her coffee and frowned. "Shh, too many questions, Carla; it's still early in the morning. I haven't finished my first coffee yet."

The girls smiled towards the door as they heard Nik's key turn. Bree beamed at her husband as he burst through the door. He headed to the girls, kissing Bree on the forehead and saying, "Thank you."

After stepping back, he looked at Carla and said, "Guys, I have good news. I know how much we need it,". Bree raised an eyebrow, flashing Nik a knowing look.

Carla stared blankly as the door opened. Zac peered around the corner with a wide smile.

A murmur of relief filled the room as Bree jumped off her seat into his arms and said, "Welcome back."

Carla snapped out of her trance and wrapped her arms around Zac. "Welcome back." In the quiet warmth of his arms, she felt battered and flustered simultaneously. A blush ran up her neck at the touch of his skin on hers.

Zac slowly exhaled, and as he laughed hardily, he stared into her innocent and fearful eyes. "I should surprise you guys more often," he said as he closed the door behind him.

"Not only is Zac back, but he's our chef for the next few weeks," Nik said.

Carla's jaw dropped open, and she hugged him again, saying, "Thank you." The feeling of darkness that hovered over her suddenly lifted.

"Carla, just so you know, as Zac is here, I'm going to have to help him out with some office work for the agency, smart working. We can't both be here and not work there. Okay?"

"I can help; just let me know what I can do, either in the restaurant or for the agency. My season is slowing down now, so I'm all yours," Bree said.

Zac slid his jacket off his body and turned to Nik. "That sounds great to me. Between the three of us, we can do it."

"That's not all, Carla. Zac has offered to stay with you for a few days, so you have someone to watch over you and the house. He'll make sure Sully isn't around to bother you. What do you think?" He looked at Zac, who nodded in agreement. "Is that ok?"

Carla's eyes gleamed as she heard the news. Her smile sparkled as she looked at everyone. "Sure, that will be great. Thank you so much," she replied as Bree flashed her a knowing smile.

"Right, we are off to the police station," Nik announced.

Carla let out a huff, grabbed her bag, and said, "See you later, if we survive."

Hours passed, and back at home, Zac guided Bree through the agency's online booking and accounts systems. Bree hunched over the laptop, her concentration unbreakable as Zac explained shortcuts and best practices.

Carla and Nik walked in, their exhaustion evident in their slouched postures and weary faces.

"She's a natural," Zac said, giving Bree's shoulder a light squeeze as he looked up at Nik. "This is going to work; I can feel it."

Nik smiled, his pride unmistakable. "Bree can do anything she puts her mind to."

"Except cooking and dancing," Bree quipped with a laugh, shooting Zac a mock glare.

Carla groaned, cutting into their banter. "I'm starving. That police interrogation was brutal." She opened the fridge with a yank, rummaging for something to eat. "We had to spill everything—every last detail—and they brought the staff back in for a proper grilling. Luckily, the police believed them when they said they lied out of fear, so they're off the hook for now."

Nik exhaled deeply. "At least that's behind us now."

"Let's hope so," Zac said, closing his laptop and stretching his legs. "Carla, if you drive me to your place, I can drop my bags off and then we'll hit the supermarket. I'll cook us all something for lunch."

"Deal," Carla replied, grabbing her keys and her bag.

The short drive was quiet at first, the purr of the engine filling the silence. Zac was the first to break it. "I'm sorry you're dealing with all this right now," he said, one hand resting lightly on the wheel.

Carla glanced at him, her gaze softening. "Thanks. But having you here really helps—a lot. For the restaurant, I mean."

Zac smirked, his tone playful. "Oh, just for the restaurant? Not quite the reply I was hoping for."

She chuckled. "I was surprised you didn't get in touch this summer."

"You didn't, either," he countered. "We can talk about it later, but... truthfully, I wasn't in a good place. I had some things to sort out."

Her voice softened. "Did you sort them out?"

"Mostly," Zac said, his tone lighter. "Since Nik left, I've sort of been filling in as the town stud. Let's just say I found myself in a couple of... sticky situations. I couldn't drag you into all that."

Carla raised an eyebrow, her confusion evident. "Well... okay. Glad you worked it out," she said carefully.

Zac's grin widened, sensing her unease. "Don't worry—I'm a reformed man now."

Carla pushed open the door to her house, letting Zac step inside. He dropped his bags onto the guest room bed, turning back to her with a impish twinkle in his eye.

"So, what about you, Carla? Any sticky situations I should know about?" he asked, his tone playful.

She flashed him a cheeky smile. "Nope. I've been steering clear of glue lately—completely glue-free."

Zac laughed, leaning against the doorframe. "Good. I'd hate to see you stuck."

185 | Petra

The following evening, Bree rounded up the girls for a pizza night with Nik, Fabio, and Zac. Seven friends, one crowded table, and enough drama to fuel a soap opera. Nik launched into his updates on the recent chaos. It didn't take long before the jaws around the table began to drop.

"Wait, wait," Petra said, holding up a hand. "You're telling me there were flying wine bottles *and* saucepan beatings?"

Nik nodded solemnly. "And an attempted strangling. Don't forget that part. Police interrogation wasn't exactly a picnic either."

The group sat in stunned silence, broken only by Fabio's slow clap. "I feel like I've been living the wrong life," he said, shaking his head. "Life in a hardware shop is so boring compared to all of this business."

"I'd swap with you," Carla said. "I know it sounds funny the way Nik tells it, but honestly, it has been horrible."

"Oh, I'm sorry Carla. Nik uses humour to cover what's going on in that heart of his," Bree said.

"Carla. I'm sorry. I didn't mean to be insensitive. I was just…"

Carla interrupted, "It's okay. I know what you were trying to do. Can we just change the conversation?"

Bree cleared her throat. "Right. So, for a while, Zac's staying with us. But to make that work, I'll be doing some computer work for them each morning. A few hours of digital drudgery."

She turned to Petra and Nina with a pleading look. "Do you think you two can cover the emails more while I do this? Pretty please?"

"Of course," they replied in unison, nodding with exaggerated seriousness.

Petra's face lit up with a mischievous yet excited grin. "I know we were supposed to change the subject, but all of this—everything you just said—*has* to go in my book."

Nina raised an eyebrow. "Your book?"

"Yeah, I've been toying with the idea since the retreat," Petra said, practically vibrating with delight. "I started writing journals back then, and honestly, our lives are so ridiculous, it'd be a crime not to share it with the world."

"Ridiculous is putting it mildly," Bree deadpanned. "We're a walking reality show."

Petra leaned forward, her eyes sparkling with enthusiasm. "Do you all mind if I write about you? I can change your names if you want. Although, let's be real, you're all too iconic for fake names."

"Anyone who minds, speak now or forever hold your peace," she added, with a mock-serious tone, raising an imaginary gavel.

Silence fell, followed by a ripple of laughter.

"Okay, then," Petra said triumphantly. "It's on. I'm doing this."

"Here's to the book," Nik said, lifting his glass. "We've all made enough mistakes to fill at least a trilogy. And hey, I've published a few books—happy to point you towards some good publishers."

"I have a feeling there's plenty more to come," Carla added, her tone a mix of amusement and foreboding. "Our story's far from over."

"Far from over?" Fabio smirked. "It's barely intermission."

They all raised their glasses, laughing, as the pizza arrived—because if they were going to be the stars of Petra's future bestseller, they might as well celebrate in style.

186 | Petra

The girls gathered for a low-key birthday celebration at Carla's house two days later. Carla had deliberately kept it simple, avoiding any fuss that Nik and Zac might stir up if she had celebrated at the restaurant. The thought of waiters singing 'Happy Birthday' while marching around with a cake and thirty-plus candles made her shudder.

After unwrapping gifts, they dipped sticks into the cheese fondue set. Petra switched on the music, grinning. "African beats," she announced, swaying her hips in rhythm while wrapping her long cardigan tightly around her.

Later, as they dragged furniture around Carla's terrace for movie night, Nina broke the unspoken tension. "So, what about Zac? What's going on there?" she asked, casually sipping her wine.

"Nothing," Carla replied, a little too quickly. "Absolutely nothing."

"And how do you feel about that?" Nina pressed.

Carla took a sip of her drink and said, "I'm not sure. I hoped something might have happened by now—he's been here a month. The first day, we talked about what went wrong last time, and I thought we were moving forward. But since then... nothing."

"That's odd," Nina said, her brow furrowing.

Carla noticed Bree's silence but continued. "He's been distant, he's always at work."

"Is he seeing someone?" Petra asked.

"I don't think so. He gave me the impression he wasn't. We live in the same house and work together, and I've seen no signs of a girlfriend. Honestly, I've been too busy to think about it much until now."

"That's probably a good thing," Petra replied.

Carla nodded. "Yeah. He even gave me rent last week—out of the blue. I didn't ask for it and didn't accept it."

"Well, it's a big change for both of you," Nina said thoughtfully. "Before, you were just friends. Now you're living and working together."

"Maybe it's for the best," Nina added after a pause. "You're technically his boss."

"Not really," Carla corrected. "He's not working for me, just helping out."

"Are you paying him?" Nina asked.

"I think so—I told Nik to sort it out," Carla said, shrugging. "But I haven't checked."

"Then you are his boss," Nina teased.

"Oh great, so I'd be hitting on an employee. That sounds like a lawsuit waiting to happen," Carla replied with a grin.

"Not if you're not sure you're paying him," Petra joked, earning a laugh from the group.

Nina spoke with a wicked flicker in her eye. "Or don't pay him at all. Problem solved. Then you can jump his bones."

The laughter died down as popcorn and fresh wine appeared. Nina restarted the conversation. "But seriously, Carla. Are you interested in him?"

"I don't know," Carla admitted. "I've stopped ogling him, if that's what you mean. He's just Zac now. The hot guy saving our bacon at the restaurant. Although, I won't lie—he does look amazing in nothing but a towel."

"Maybe he feels the same—for now," Nina offered. "But don't forget, you're his boss, and you're Nik's boss. His wife is your boss. It's a lot for him to deal with."

Bree glanced at Petra and Nina, who had moved to the kitchen to refill glasses and prepare more snacks. Lowering her voice, Bree finally said her piece. "Carla, can I tell you something? Zac's exhausted. The job is draining him. On top of that, in the two hours he has off, he's doing accounts with Nik or me at our house. He's working his ass off."

"Okay," Carla replied.

"He's an anxious type, always worried about something," Bree began. "Nik couldn't be happier with Zac's work ethic and they are finally working together again. You're not going to like what I'm about to say: you're both where you need to be right now. Trying to make it more than that would probably do more harm than good."

Carla sighed. "Yeah, I hear you."

"I feel like I'm betraying Nik's trust here," Bree admitted, glancing away. "But I know Zac is into you—really into you. The thing is, he got into a mess at work last year with someone, and he's determined not to let it happen again. That's why he's keeping his distance—it's not personal. He's just focused on fixing things, especially after what happened with Sully. He feels awful about hiring him in the first place."

Bree's words made Carla sit up straighter. "That... actually makes sense. I respect him for that. Although, hiring Sully wasn't his fault, and I need to tell him that."

"No, Carla. You can't say anything. That was a private conversation between me and Nik."

"Okay, don't worry," Carla promised.

Bree continued, her tone softening. "He's struggling to juggle the pressure of two jobs, but the season's almost over. You close soon, and I don't think he's in any rush to head back to Greece."

Carla hesitated, then asked the question she'd been holding back. "Is he seeing anyone?"

"No. And I know he'd like to be with you, but not while all of this is going on."

A wild rush of excitement flared within Carla. "Thanks, Bree. I promise I won't let anything happen. I owe Nik and the restaurant too much."

"Shhh," Bree whispered as Nina and Petra returned with snacks. Pulling a blanket over their legs, the group snuggled together for the movie.

An hour later, the door opened. Zac and Nik stepped in carefully, carrying a chocolate cake with a single large candle flickering in the centre.

"Happy birthday, Carla," they said in unison.

Bree leapt up, throwing her arms around Nik and kissing him passionately. "Alright, who gave my wife way too much wine?" Nik teased, guiding Bree back to her seat.

"We all did, and we drank our own fair share too." Nina laughed, gesturing to the empty bottles lining the door.

Nina swirled her skirt dramatically and grabbed two glasses. "Can you stay and join the party?"

"It would be rude not to," Nik replied, taking a glass and plonking himself down next to Bree.

Petra turned the music up, swaying her hips and wrapping her arms around Zac.

He stiffened. "Petra, I don't dance."

"Oh, come on, just ease into it," she coaxed, pulling him along. Noticing Carla's tense expression, Petra smiled slyly and let go. "Carla, take my place?"

Caught off guard, Carla hesitated before stepping forward. Zac held out his hand, and she reluctantly took it, shooting Bree a worried glance.

Zac pulled her close, his touch light yet firm. She forced a polite smile but felt awkward under his gaze.

"Stroke of genius," Nina whispered to Petra as they settled back down.

Bree threw her head back in a mischievous laugh. "Just be yourself," she mouthed to Carla, who offered a weak smile in return.

"You smell like fried fish," Carla quipped nervously, trying to pull away and retreat to the girls.

"You look lovely tonight," Zac said, his tone sincere. "Purple suits you—it makes your eyes pop."

Startled, Carla glanced at him, her face heating. She turned towards Nik, catching Zac's smile out of the corner of her eye. Their gaze locked for a fleeting moment before she bowed her head and turned away.

As the row of empty wine bottles grew, the impromptu party wound down. Back at home, Zac and Carla lingered in silence by the door.

Carla felt him standing too close, his presence filling the quiet. Bree's words replayed in her mind, their weight both sobering and overwhelming. She took a deep breath, managed a distracted goodnight, and pushed her bedroom door open, closing it swiftly behind her.

RAW MISTAKES

187 | Nik

On an unseasonably warm morning at the end of the summer season, Nina bounced into the office enthusiastically. "Girls, the moment is here. Tomorrow, I'm going to sign my divorce papers." The girls chirped up with cheers, applause, and glee. "So, we will be celebrating tomorrow night. Who's with me?" Nina asked.

Petra and Bree agreed readily. Carla thought for a moment before saying, "Tomorrow is the last night of the season. We close until Easter. If you want, you can all come to the restaurant. We can get Zac to whip something up for us; we have to finish all the food, and of course, we have a fully stocked wine cellar."

"That sounds perfect," Nina said as they quickly made plans.

The following evening, as the dark night was closing in, Bree and Nik pulled over at a roundabout and waited for Carla and Zac to step into the car.

"Thanks for coming early, Carla; I wanted to decorate the place a bit and make a bit of a big thing out of the divorce," Bree said. "As a divorcee myself, I get it. It's a huge deal."

"No problem at all; pleased to help."

Parking the car in the small, weed-covered car park along the road from the restaurant, the group stepped out. "You go ahead, guys; we are going to put balloons in the car park and on the railings here," Carla shouted.

Nik crouched down to pick up a few chairs scattered by the wind as he moved towards the main building. As he straightened, his eyes fell on the door. The lock was mangled, its mechanism twisted unnaturally. He pulled out his key instinctively but stopped short, staring at the damage.

"Someone's been here," he muttered to Zac, worry creeping into his voice.

He pushed the door open cautiously. It groaned on its hinges, an eerie sound that echoed in the empty space. Zac stepped in behind him, chatter spilling from his lips, but Nik's attention was elsewhere.

The usual, homely scent of the kitchen was gone. Instead, the air carried a strange, almost chemical heaviness. Nik inhaled deeply, his instincts prickling.

"Wait," he said sharply, grabbing Zac's arm to stop him mid-sentence. His voice dropped to a whisper. "Do you smell that?"

Zac blinked at him, confused. Then his eyes widened. "Gas," he whispered, panic flaring in his tone. "Nik, we need to get out. Now."

But Nik shook his head, his expression grim. "We can't leave it like this. If there's a leak—"

"Are you crazy?" Zac's voice rose.

Nik ignored him, stepping further inside. A faint hissing sound reached his ears, guiding him toward the source. He moved quickly, his breathing shallow, his senses on high alert. Rounding a counter, he spotted the main valve. The knob was slightly askew, a screw rattling loose.

"I've got it," Nik shouted, his voice muffled as he pulled his shirt up over his nose. He tightened the knob with steady hands and staggered back, the hiss dying away. Relief flickered in his expression as he stumbled toward the hallway.

Zac wasn't far behind, but his attention snagged on something. His gaze locked on faint glimmers in the corridor ahead—pinpricks of light moving unnaturally in the darkness. A sick feeling bloomed in his chest as he stepped closer.

"What the—?" Zac murmured, his throat tightening. He froze. Three candles sat flickering under a wooden workbench, their flames dancing in the shadows. Horror rooted him in place. The heat of his own breath felt unbearable as realisation struck him like a punch to the gut.

Bree and Carla arrived moments later, laughing as they carried the last of the decorations. Bree dropped her bag on the floor, frowning at the distant shouting.

"What's going on?" she asked, squinting toward the sound of shouting.

Carla shrugged, but something in the frantic tones made Bree's stomach twist. She stopped just short of the entrance, panic on her face.

"Get out," Zac screamed. "There are candles—lit candles. We have to go, now." He pivoted, sprinting toward the back exit, the nearest one. His shoulder slammed into the door as he kicked it with all his strength, the wood splintering under the impact. "Get out. Get out." he bellowed again.

Nik's footsteps thundered behind him, but before he reached the door, a shadow flickered in the corner of his vision. Someone's hand—a pale blur in the dim light—grasped the main switch on the wall.

"Don't." Nik screamed, his voice raw.

Bree turned a corner towards Nik's voice. She opened her mouth to call out, but the words never came. A blinding flash consumed her vision, the air itself seeming to implode around her.

The world erupted.

The explosion tore through the restaurant, a deafening boom that shattered glass, wood, and steel in an instant. Nik felt the force rip past him, his body hurled backward. Shards of glass rained like a storm, cutting through the air with brutal precision. Heat roared around him, a monstrous wave swallowing him whole.

Then, darkness.

188 | Fabio

Fabio slammed on the brakes, the car skidding to a jarring halt. He flung his hands up to shield his eyes from the fiery glare ahead. For a moment, he sat frozen, the pulse of the explosion still vibrating in his ears. Then, as if propelled by instinct, he pushed open the car door.

The air hit him like a wall—thick with smoke, dust, and the acrid stench of burning. He yanked his arm over his face, coughing as he squinted into the darkness.

"Stay here," he barked at Nina and Petra, his tone brooking no argument.

Fabio advanced cautiously at first, his boots crunching against shards of broken glass and splintered wood. Each step brought the scene into sharper focus, and dread tightened in his chest. The restaurant—it wasn't a restaurant anymore. It was a ruin.

Wooden beams lay twisted and charred, tables shattered into unrecognisable heaps. A hanging sign, now detached, swung weakly from a single chain. Fabio's stomach churned as he caught sight of a figure slumped against a tree at the edge of the wreckage.

A man. Blood streaked down his face, pooling at his lips. His body was pinned beneath a warped railing, his chest rising and falling in shallow, desperate gasps. The sound of his strained sobs cut through the still-settling dust.

"Nina. Petra. Get over here." Fabio shouted, already pulling at the railing with trembling hands.

The two women scrambled out of the car, the devastation stealing the breath from their lungs as they approached. Together, they hauled the railing off the man, its twisted metal resisting with a creak.

The man tried to sit up, but his body betrayed him. "I... I work there," he rasped, his voice cracking under the pain of his injuries. "The staff... they went inside. I saw them."

Fabio's jaw clenched as he raked a hand through his thick, dark hair. His heart thudded like a drum in his ears. "How many?" he demanded, his voice rough.

The man's bloodied gaze drifted toward the ruins. For a moment, he seemed to lose himself in the horror before him. Then, with visible effort, he sucked in a trembling breath. "Nik... Zac... Carla... Bree... and two waiters," he managed, breaking into a fit of violent coughs.

"Six people," Petra murmured, her voice barely audible, as though saying it aloud made the number more real.

The scene around them was mind-blowing. Passers-by, thrown back by the force of the explosion, hovered at the edge. Some were crouched low, others craning their necks to take in the catastrophe.

Whispers of utter shock and fear rippled through the onlookers as their eyes darted from the shattered windows to the dust-shrouded mound of debris that had been the restaurant.

Thoughts of his friends played heavily on his mind as he imagined nothing but an abrupt and terrifying end.

Fabio stripped off his jumper, tossing it aside as he clawed at the wreckage with bare hands. "Start digging."

What happens next?

Find out in the second part of this series: Better Mistakes

ABOUT THE AUTHOR.

Gwen Courtman, originally from Manchester, UK, has called Italy home for most of her adult life. She moved to Italy following her heart, and today, she divides her time between the serene Italian lakes and the vibrant African island of Zanzibar. It is here, gazing out over the emerald waters of the Indian Ocean, that Gwen becomes fully immersed in the captivating lives of her fictional characters, breathing life into their stories.

When she's not writing, Gwen leads a busy life as a wedding planner and photographer in Italy. She also travels the globe, gathering inspiration for her next book.

Books in this series:

Raw Mistakes
Better Mistakes
Secret Mistakes
Inevitable Mistakes
Final Mistakes.

Also by Gwen Courtman:
Whispers of the Wild.
Murmurs of the Wild.
Secrets of the Wild.
Treasures of the Wild.

Stay up-to-date with new releases, behind-the-scenes glimpses, stories, Q&A, and videos from the locations that inspired the books.

Visit her blog at: www.gwencourtmanauthor.com

Printed by Amazon Italia Logistica S.r.l.
Torrazza Piemonte (TO), Italy